A SWORD FROM RED ICE

Unknown territory, that was what his life had become. Yet what choice did he have but to embrace it?

Rising, he made swift ⌐ ⌐ ⌐ . The dimness of the tent ⌐ ⌐ ⌐ clothes, boots and weapons ⌐ ⌐ ⌐ outside.

A piercing frost had crac ⌐ ⌐ ⌐ slept. No wind could live in s⌐ ⌐ ⌐ ⌐ was paralyzed. The cookfire in the center of the tent circle had shrunk to a dim, red glow. Frozen smoke accumulating around the base was slowly suffocating the last of the flames. The lamb brother on night watch was away from his post. Raif tracked his footsteps to the corral and spotted him calming the milk ewe.

The animals knew.

Raif crossed to the fire, closed his fist around the lamb brother's bone-and-copper spear and tugged it from the earth. "Here," he said, as the man approached him. "Take it."

A SWORD FROM RED ICE

Book Three of Sword of Shadows

J.V. Jones

www.orbitbooks.net

ORBIT

First published in the United States in 2007 by Tor,
Tom Doherty Associates, LLC
First published in Great Britain in 2008 by Orbit
This paperback edition published in 2008 by Orbit
Reprinted 2009 (twice)

A CIP catalogue record for this book
is available from the British Library.

ISBN 978-1-84149-184-4

Typeset in Electra by M Rules
Printed and bound in Great Britain by Clays Ltd, St Ives plc

Orbit
An imprint of
Little, Brown Book Group
100 Victoria Embankment
London EC4Y 0DY

An Hachette UK Company
www.hachette.co.uk

YA

For dear Fergus
for all his kindness

ACKNOWLEDGEMENTS

Thanks are due to Jim Frenkel and the good people
at Tor for making this a better book.

The Northern Territories

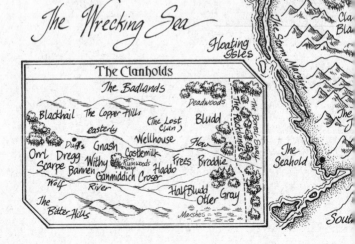

The Breaking

The Wrecking Sea

of G

The Storm Margin

Cla
Bla

Floating
Isles

The Clanholds

The Badlands

Deadwoods

Blackhail   The Copper Hills   (The Lost   Bludd
                                 Clan)
           easterly   Wellhouse

     Duff's Gnash   Flow
Orrl Dregg   Withy Castlemilk   Broddie
Scarpe   Bannen   Rumwoods   Frees
         Ganmiddich Croser Haddo
Wolf   River
                        HalfBludd Otter Gray
The
Bitter Hills   Marshes

The Deadwoods

Bludd

The Badlands

The Rocklands

The Boreal River

The J

The
Seahold

South

CONTENTS

SWORD OF SHADOWS:

The Story So Far

Raif Sevrance of Clan Blackhail was out shooting ice hares in the Badlands with his brother Drey when his father and chief were slain back at camp. Upon returning to their clanhold, Raif and Drey found that Mace Blackhail, the chief's foster son, had declared himself head of the clan. Mace had been present at the camp that day, and blamed the murders on Vaylo Bludd, chief of a rival clan. A week later, when word arrived that Vaylo Bludd had sacked the Dhoonehouse, events seemed to bear out Mace's story of Bludd aggression. Raif found himself isolated. He alone believed that Mace Blackhail was a liar and a chief-killer.

War against Clan Bludd followed, as Hailsmen sought to avenge their chief's death. When Mace received word that a caravan of Bluddsmen were on the road, heading west to occupy the Dhoonehouse, he ordered an attack. Raif rode with the ambush party, and was horrified to discover that the caravan contained women and children, not warriors. He refused to kill them. By disobeying an order on the field and deserting his fellow clansmen in battle, Raif made himself a traitor to his clan. Four days later, Raif left Blackhail in the company of his uncle Angus Lok. Raif's oath to protect Blackhail had now been broken. There was no going back.

The two men headed south. When they arrived at Duff's stovehouse, they discovered that the story of the massacre of innocents on the Bluddroad had preceded them. When challenged by a group of Bludd warriors, Raif admitted to being present during the slaughter. He did not tell them that he took no part in the massacre—loyalty to his clan prevented him from defending himself at their expense. With this admission, Raif forever damned himself in the eyes of Bluddsmen. He was the only Hailsmen they knew for a certainty who was present during the slayings.

Angus Lok and Raif made their way to Spire Vanis, the city at the foot of Mount Slain. Upon arrival, they rescued a young woman named Ash March who was being hunted down by the city's Protector General, Marafice Eye. Angus had a strong reaction when he saw the girl and immediately put himself in danger to save her. Raif's newly formed skills with the bow proved invaluable. He single-handedly rescued the girl by placing arrows through her pursuers' hearts.

Heart-killing, it was called: the surest and quickest way of ending another person's life. Raif Sevrance was slowly coming to understand that he was master of it.

Having escaped from the city, Raif, Ash and Angus turned north toward Ille Glaive. During the journey Raif learned that Ash was the Surlord of Spire Vanis' adopted daughter. She had run away because she feared that her father intended to imprison her in the Inverted Spire, which lay beneath the tower known as the Splinter. Heritas Cant, a friend of Angus Lok's, provided the reason for Ash's father's behavior. According to Cant, Ash was the first Reach to be born in a thousand years. She possessed the ability to unlock the Blind, the prison without a key that contained the destructive might of the Endlords. The Endlords' purpose was to annihilate the world, and every thousand years they rode forth to claim more men for their armies. Cant informed Ash that she must discharge her Reach-power or die. The only place to do so safely was the Cavern of Black Ice; anywhere else and she would tear open the Blind and free the Endlords.

Raif and Angus agreed to accompany Ash to the cavern in the far north. As soon as their small party reentered the clan-holds they were captured by Bluddsmen. The Dog Lord, Vaylo Bludd, ordered Raif's torture in the Ganmiddich tower. The Bludd chief had lost seventeen grandchildren during the slaying on the Bluddroad, and Raif Sevrance had to pay for those losses. After days of torture, Raif developed a fever and began to fail. Yet when Death came to take him she changed her mind. "Perhaps I won't take you yet," she told him. "You fight in my image and live in my shadow, and if I leave you where you are you'll provide much fresh meat for my children. Kill an army for me, Raif Sevrance, any less and I just might call you back." Raif feared the grim words would become his life.

The night before he was due to be killed by Vaylo Bludd, Raif was rescued by a group of Hailish warriors led by his brother Drey. "We part here. For always," Drey said as he let his younger brother, the traitor, slip away.

Later that day Raif met up with Ash. While Raif was being tortured, Ash had been handed over to Marafice Eye, who planned on returning her to her foster father in Spire Vanis. Vaylo Bludd had a debt to repay. Penthero Iss, the Surlord of Spire Vanis, had aided Vaylo's taking of the Dhoonehouse. Vaylo had come to regret Iss's sorcerous help, and sought to end all relations with the surlord. Ash March was payment in full.

Ash escaped Marafice's custody after his men attempted to rape her. Drawing forth her Reach-power, she blasted Marafice's party, killing everyone except Marafice himself and the Surlord's special spy, Sarga Veys.

Ash's and Raif's journey to the Cavern of Black Ice proved arduous. Ash's health quickly deteriorated. After crossing the mountains, she collapsed in the snow. Unable to help her, Raif drew a guide circle and called out to the Stone Gods. Two Sull Far Riders, Mal Naysayer and Ark Veinsplitter, heard this call, and rode to Ash's aid. Upon seeing her, they suspected that Ash was the Reach. They also suspected that Raif was *Mor Drakka*, Watcher of the Dead—the one predicted to destroy the Sull. Not surprisingly the Far Riders were cool with Raif as they tended Ash. After a few days, the Far Riders led Ash and Raif onto a frozen riverbed and pointed the way to the Cavern of Black Ice.

The cavern lay beneath the river. Ash discharged her power, but it was already too late. By blasting Marafice Eye's men in the Bitter Hills, she had caused a tear in the Blindwall. Back in her home city of Spire Vanis, a nameless sorcerer who had been enslaved by her foster father was already working to open the break. "Push and we will give you your name," the Endlords promised him. Bound by chains, broken and tortured, the sorcerer accepted the deal. "Baralis," the Endlords named the sorcerer as he broke open the wall.

As this was happening, the clanwars were spinning out of control. Blackhail waged war on Bludd in revenge for the killing of the Hail chief; Bludd fought Blackhail for the slaying of its women and children; and Dhoone, dispossessed of its roundhouse by Bludd, fought to regain its territory. The clanhold of Ganmiddich, which was traditionally war-sworn to Dhoone, was overtaken first by Bludd and then Blackhail. Mace Blackhail, now chief of Blackhail, forced an oath of loyalty from the Ganmiddich chief and then garrisoned Hailsmen in the Ganmiddich roundhouse to insure it was upheld.

Meanwhile, infighting amongst Dhoonesmen over the chiefship came to a head. Skinner Dhoone was the deceased chief's brother and first choice for the now-vacant chiefship, but the brash up-and-comer Robbie Dun Dhoone fancied the title for himself. The two factions split the clan down the middle. The deadlock ended when Robbie tricked Skinner into attacking Withy, the clan who made kings. Skinner's forces and Skinner himself were cut down by Bludd, freeing Robbie to take the chiefship of Dhoone. When infighting amongst Vaylo Bludd and his seven ungrateful sons resulted in the Dhoonehouse being held by a skeleton force, Robbie seized his chance and retook the Dhoonehold. The small occupying force of Bluddsmen were slain, and only Vaylo, his lady Nan, his two remaining grandchildren and a guardsman escaped.

Robbie wasted no time naming himself chief and king. His half-brother, Bram Cormac, was left to pay the price for this victory. For in order to secure sufficient numbers to retake Dhoone, Robbie had sold his brother to Castlemilk.

Back at Blackhail, the slain chief's widow, Raina Blackhail, struggled to come to terms with her new life. Like Raif, Raina suspected that Mace, her foster son, was responsible for her husband's murder. At first she had not supported Mace's campaign for chiefship, but Mace put a stop to her opposition by raping her. Silver-tongued, he claimed the union was consensual: a momentary weakness between two grieving adults. Aware that most people in the clan believed his story, Raina chose to keep her silence. Her place in the clan was at stake; tell the truth and she would be branded a liar. Clannish honor demanded that she and Mace marry, so Raina wed her foster son and became chief's wife again.

From this position, she watched the decline of her clan. Mace had been born at Clan Scarpe, and it wasn't long before his old loyalties started to show. When the Scarpehouse was burned down by a neighboring clan, Mace opened the doors of the Hailhouse to Scarpe. Scarpemen in their hundreds poured into Blackhail and set about consuming its resources. When Augus Lok, newly freed from captivity by the Dog Lord, visited Raina, he planted the seed of dissent. "I will be chief," Raina found herself saying after he had left. Her husband was a chief-killer who had ordered the slaying of innocent women and children on the Bluddroad, and plunged his clan into needless war. Surely she could be a better chief than that? The two people she informed of her intentions—the senior warrior Orwin Shank and the clan matron Anwyn Bird—agreed with her, and Raina set about looking for opportunities to claim power.

After departing Blackhail, Angus Lok returned to his home east of Ille Glaive. Upon arrival he found his worst nightmare had come to life: his house was empty and burned down. His three daughters and his wife were gone. Dead. Angus was a ranger, a member of the secret society known as the Phage. His work involved opposing the rise of the Endlords, and he blamed himself for leading evil to his door.

Leaving the Cavern of Black Ice, Ash and Raif headed north into Ice Trapper territory. Once there, they met up with Mal Naysayer and Ark Veinsplitter. Raif was drugged, and awakened to find Ash and the Far Riders gone. Sadaluk, Listener of the Ice Trappers, informed Raif that Ash had chosen to leave, and could not be followed. Raif reluctantly accepted this and decided to head east. Sadaluk gave him two parting gifts: a sword salvaged from the corpse of a Forsworn knight and a single arrow. "Grow wide shoulders, Clansman," Sadaluk told him. "You will need them for all of your burdens."

With a heavy heart, Raif departed. He had decided to join the Maimed Men, an outlaw clan who lived on the great cliffs above the Rift. During his journey he learned firsthand what the Endlords and their Unmade could do to men. In an ancient fastness on the edge of the Great Want, he found the smoking, disintegrating corpses of four Forsworn knights. They had been attacked by the Unmade—who were now escaping from the Blind—and as the knight's bodies smoked to nothing the Endlords claimed their souls. One knight remained alive but mortally wounded, and Raif learned that the only way to stop the man's body from becoming unmade was to kill him, thereby depriving the Endlords of his death. It was a chilling lesson, and Raif found himself embracing the name the Listener had given him, Watcher of the Dead.

No man who was whole could join the Maimed Men, and upon arrival at the Rift, the tip of Raif's finger was taken by a man named Stillborn. Traggis Mole, the leader of the Maimed Men, was suspicious of Raif's claims to be a crack bowman, and ordered a test of arrows. Raif won the test, claimed a prize of a rare Sull longbow and earned the name Twelve Kill. His opponent was killed and thrown into the Rift.

Meanwhile, Ash had become Sull. In a deep mountain cavern east of Ice Trapper territory, the Far Riders drained her human blood to make way for Sull blood. Ash learned the Sull were an ancient race whose numbers and influence were in decline. At one time they had occupied the entire Northern Territories; now they had been reduced to a region of land in the east. The Sull believed it was their destiny to fight the Endlords and the Unmade, and by becoming Sull Ash agreed to take on this fight. As they made their way south to the Heart of the Sull, they were pursued by the Unmade. Just north of the River Flow, they were attacked by unmade pack wolves. Ark was killed and Mal continued fighting as Ash floated to safety on an unhitched bridge. "Daughter" had been Ark's last word to her. The endearment almost broke Ash's heart.

Penthero Iss, the Surlord of Spire Vanis and Ash's foster father, had been planning to use Ash's Reach-power to seize control of the clanholds. With his daughter gone, he decided to send an army to attack the clanholds and chose Marafice Eye as its leader. While the army marched north, bent on attacking rich and vulnerable Ganmiddich, the surlord was left unguarded and vulnerable in Spire Vanis. Rival grangelords sharpened their knives. Yet it was not a rival for the surlordship that brought down Iss: it was Crope, the faithful servant of the sorcerer who was enslaved beneath the Splinter. Crope and his lord had been separated seventeen years earlier when Iss had captured Baralis. Crope himself had been seized by slavers and sent to work in the mines. It took him seventeen years to escape. As soon as he was free he traveled across a continent to save his lord. Crope had giant's blood in his veins and he brought down the Splinter, killed the surlord, and carried Baralis to safety.

Meanwhile, Effie Sevrance, Raif's eight-year-old sister, had been forced to leave her clan. Effie had been born to the stone lore and was able to tell when bad things were about to happen. She was present when Raina was raped by Mace, and Raina feared this knowledge made Effie vulnerable. Seeking to remove the girl from Mace's sights, Raina sent Effie to Clan Dregg. As she traveled south in the company of gold smugglers, Effie began to master her lifelong fear of being outside. When her wagon was attacked by Dhoonesmen she was able to hide until the danger passed. The smugglers were killed during the attack, and Effie was left to fend for herself. Finding a secluded clearing near the Wolf River, she settled down to catch fish and live alone for a while. However, she was soon spotted by a chance predator, who swooped in and kidnapped her.

The gold the smugglers had been transporting had come from a Blackhail mine, Black Hole. Traggis Mole, believing that Raif's loyalties still lay with his former clan, not the Maimed Men, ordered Raif to participate in a raid on the mine. The raid was a success. Quickly overcoming the miners' defenses, Raif's party entered the mine and seized the stockpile of gold. As he climbed to the surface, Raif encountered his childhood friend Bitty Shank. Bitty was now a sworn Blackhail warrior, and he refused to let Raif leave with the gold. Raif had little choice but to fight and heart-kill his old friend.

Bereft and believing he was damned, Raif headed out alone into the uncharted territory of the Great Want. He had learned from the Maimed Man Thomas Argola that a long-deserted fortress lay hidden in the depths of the Want. By finding it he hoped to stop the formation of a second crack in the weakened

Blindwall. The Great Want was filled with flaws, and a *Shatan Maer*, an unmade creature of terrible power, had found one such flaw and was pushing against it. The flaw lay beneath *Kahl Barranon*, the Fortress of Grey Ice. Using the arrow given to him by the Listener, Raif located the position of the fortress. Once there, he quickly found the flaw and waited for the *Shatan Maer* to emerge. The battle that followed was long and grim. The *Shatan Maer* possessed inhuman strength and quickness . . . but Raif Sevrance was Watcher of the Dead. He had deserted his clan and slain a fellow clansman. He was forever damned and had little to lose. And there was no other living man who could heart-kill as he could.

The *Shatan Maer* fell, the flaw in the Blindwall was sealed, and the North was freed from danger for a while . . .

PROLOGUE:

The Hail Wolf Returns

Inigar Stoop opened his eyes and blinked into the darkness of the guidehouse. The smoke fires had gone out while he slept, and it took him long moments to make sense of the unfamiliar shadows of deepest night. Something in his chest wasn't right. His heartbeat was the same as ever, but there was a vague soreness beneath his ribs, a sense that muscle had been working while he slept.

Indistinct forms loomed around him, their edges bleeding into the darkness like ink spilled on cloth. To calm himself Blackhail's clan guide named the forms in his head—the little stone font where he drew his water, the hog-backed coffer where he kept his ceremonial robes, the statue of Ione that had been carved from a riven fragment of the guidestone by the great warrior-guide Harlec Sewell—but the ache in his chest persisted. Raising a hand to knead his rib cage, Inigar became aware of the great stillness he disturbed. The guidehouse was as cold and quiet as a grave dug for a horse. The smell of damp earth had pushed through the sandstone walls, and Inigar could feel its coolness moving through his lungs. Fighting the desire to shiver, he swung his legs over the side of the pallet and rose to standing.

Something is wrong here.

Rock dust crunched beneath his bare feet as he crossed toward the firepit. He had not swept here in many days, and debris from the guidestone lay thick on the flagstone floor. The time for spring tilling was fast approaching and every farmer in the clanhold would soon demand a measure of this dust to scatter in his fields along with the grain. Night soils to fertilize the earth; stone soils to hallow it. Nothing shed from the Hailstone was wasted. Sometimes Inigar thought he was as much butcher as shaman—dividing the carcass of the monolith, grinding down its bones.

But a carcass meant death, and this guidestone *had* to be alive.

The gods stored part of their souls here.

Inigar brought his hand to his forehead, pressed fingers deep into his pulse points and almost succeeded in halting his thoughts. *Please Gods, do not withdraw from this clan.*

Yet hadn't the retreat already begun? Frost had been living in the Hailstone since the Eve of Breaking, when good clansmen had turned against their own, sending a hound to the fire and trying a child as a witch. It went back farther than that, though. Frost could not enter a shored-up house. Blackhail's house had been vulnerable for half a year, ever since its chief had been slaughtered in the Badlands by nameless raiders. Something evil had punched a hole through clan walls that day. Something immense and calculating, whose age was greater than the earth he stood upon and whose purpose Inigar feared to name.

I cannot dwell on it. A guide blunted by fear is no good for his clan. Sharp of mind and sharp of chisel: that is the way we must be.

Working from touch alone he slipped on braided leather sandals and pulled a polished pigskin cloak across his shoulders. Air was quickening. The short gray hairs at the base of Inigar's scalp rocked in their follicles like loose teeth. Once as a seven-year-old he had climbed down a wellshaft on a dare. The well had been known as Witch's Cunt, and a collapsed embankment upcountry had poisoned its water with tar. It was old beyond knowing, and so deep that as Inigar had descended, probing for toeholds in the dark, the very nature of the air had changed. Saturated with groundwater, it resisted exhalation. That sense of aliveness, the sudden revelation that air had a will of its own and there were some places in this world where it would rather not be, had haunted Inigar's dreams for fifty years. He had felt it two other times since then: the day on the great court when Raif Sevrance had sworn his oath to his clan; and here and now in the guidehouse at the hangman's hour before dawn.

The guide's swollen fingers sifted for a flint and striker along the workbench. Ice growing in the heart of the Hailstone made the guidehouse colder by the day. Fires could not warm it, and the dour and god-fearing masons of Blackhail had insured sunlight never entered this place. As Inigar knelt before the firepit and struck a light, he found himself wishing for a single window in the south wall so that he could throw back its shutters and let in the glow of the moon. The great bodies that circled the earth had powers to combat darkness that no man-struck flame could match.

Still. He felt some easing in his chest when the kindling finally took and the red glow of a smokepile seeded with iron filings lit the room. Yet even as he took his first deep breath since waking he became aware of the presence of the guidestone.

The great turning-wheel of its awareness, the sense of seeing and knowing, was gone. What was left was something forceless, an ember flickering after a fire. A year ago Inigar could not lay a hand upon the monolith without feeling a jolt of life. Now the stone would rip off his skin if he touched it without the protection of padded gloves. Ice had spread through the guidestone like cancer; cumulating crystal upon crystal, sparkling, sharp and irreversibly cold, gnawing away at the rock. Two weeks ago the guidestone might have sent out a flare, a feeble attempt at communion, a weak assertion of power. Touch it tonight and Inigar knew what he would feel: something dying beneath the surface.

Reaching for the bellows, Inigar returned his attention to the fire. The first thing he had been taught as an apprentice was how to tend a smokefire. The old clan guide Beardy Hail had been uncle to Dagro Blackhail, the chief. Beardy never explained things more than once and never gave praise for a job well done. Every morning when he took possession of the guidehouse he would inspect the smokefire for flames. A flame of any sort was not permitted. The smokepile had to *smolder*, not burn. Inigar had spent most of those early days attending the fire; chopping green wood, breaking coal, filing iron. Too much fuel and flames would ignite, too little and the fire would die.

For years Inigar had wondered why it mattered—smoke resulted either way—yet one day, when Beardy was laid up with the gout and unable to check the smokepile, Inigar had come to an understanding.

Any fool could build a fire; stack logs, lay kindling, strike a flint and blow. Once lit, the fire would burn hot and die out in its own time. But a *smoke* fire was never done. You could not walk away and leave it unattended. A smokefire had to be fueled and doused, stacked and banked, raked and poked and pumped. Most of all it must be watched.

It was, Inigar decided, the most important lesson Beardy had ever taught him. A clan guide must be vigilant. He could not afford to turn his back and let his clan burn or die. A smolder must be maintained. And the watch never cease.

Inigar's dry old lips cracked a smile. Beardy had been, without a doubt, the most foul-smelling clansman in Blackhail. He kept pigs for a reason Inigar had never fathomed and took a bath only once a year. The smile turned into a wheezing cough, and Inigar slapped a palm against the floor to steady himself. Fifty years of inhaling smoke did that to a man, addled the lungs. As he crouched by the glowing smokepile and waited for the hacking to stop, an impulse he didn't understand made him reach for more wood.

Tonight he wanted light, not smoke.

Aahoooooooooo.

The skin on Inigar's hands tightened so quickly with gooseflesh his fingers jumped. A wolf howl, close and to the north. Yet the wolves had long since abandoned the territory around the Hailhouse and its man-smelling forests and fields. What did it mean?

Inigar held his swollen hands over the flames, glad to feel the heat. The light in the guidehouse was increasing, but instead of calming it unsettled him. The flames flickered wildly, yet he could detect no draft. The shadows they created swung crazily around the room. He took his time turning his gaze to the guidestone. A wolf had howled in the Hailhold and he feared what he might see.

The monolith steamed. So vast it pulled motes of dust from the air as surely as the moon pulled waves onto the shore, it stood black and still and wounded. Deep fissures dissected it like forks of frozen lightning. Pores once brimming with shale oil were now filled with lenses of ice. The narrow cane-and-timber ladder that Inigar used to access the carving face was white with hoarfrost. Only yesterday he had stood on those rungs and chiseled out a heart for a fallen clansman. A young woman in this very house awaited delivery of the fist-sized chunk of granite. Widows without bones needed stone.

So much work to do in times of war, so many calls upon the stone. *I best get to it then. Stop fussing over a late-season cold snap and get down to the business of men's souls.*

As Inigar stood to fetch himself water, he caught sight of the northern face of the monolith. A crack as wide as his forearm and as tall as two men had opened up overnight.

Dear Gods, help us.

Could he have done more? Mace Blackhail was a strong leader, a fine warrior, and a fiercely ambitious chief. The Stone Gods demanded jaw, and Mace Blackhail had so much of it he could barely keep his teeth from springing apart. Jaw had landed him the chiefdom and driven him into war. Under Mace's leadership, Blackhail had seized control of Dhoone-spoke Ganmiddich and was now challenging old boundaries in the east. Mace had rallied Blackhail warriors and reclaimed the Hailish badge. He'd fired up the sworn clans with talk of glory, making weary and jaded allies eager to fight at his side. Bannen had been Hail-sworn for a thousand years but it had ever been a weak alliance. The clan that called itself "the Ironheads" did not follow others lightly. Somehow Mace had managed to do what other Blackhail chiefs could not: gain the respect of that proud and grudging clan. Now there was talk of Bannen and Blackhail riding out to meet swords with Dhoone.

Thanks to Mace, Blackhail warriors stationed across the clanholds this very night were filled with the passion and terror of war—and was that not what the Stone Gods loved best?

A thin film of ice had formed over the water jug and Inigar punched it with his finger and drank. The bald-eagle foot resting against the apple of his throat bobbed up and down as he swallowed.

Jaw was a tricky thing. It was courage in all its forms from bravery to recklessness. It was seizing the moment and acting without hesitation, and being brazenly sure you were right. Mostly it was sheer bloody-minded audacity: pulling off something no one else thought could be done.

It was not cunning or deceit. Inigar closed his fist around his eagle lore and weighed it. A bald eagle saw much and so did he. Mace Blackhail was not a perfect man, Inigar had known that all along. Yet a chief had been slain and a new one needed anointing, and Mace Blackhail had been the first to stake a claim. That was jaw and it counted for something. Now Inigar wondered if it counted for enough. Half a year later questions about the raid remained unanswered. Mace had returned from the Badlands, claiming he had barely escaped the hell-forged swords of Clan Bludd, yet Raif Sevrance had also been at the campground that day and swore he saw no evidence of Bludd.

And then there was Raina, Mace's stepmother and wife. Inigar claimed little knowledge of women—they did not fight and so mattered little to him—but he had been struck by the changes in Raina Blackhail. She hid them, as was fitting for a chief's wife, yet eagle lores could not hide from their own kind and Inigar observed things that others did not. She hated her husband, and shrank back whenever he touched her. It was a little thing, easily covered by other movements, yet Inigar had made a note of it. He'd seen such behavior before: in women who had been raped or beaten.

Imagining he had heard a sound, Inigar set down the water jug and listened. Nothing. Where was the dawn? Where was the kitchen boy with fresh bread and ewe's milk still warm from the teat? Aware he was becoming agitated and feeling the soreness shift strangely in his chest, Inigar tried to calm himself. The wolf had not cried out again. He was just hearing echoes in his head. Eagles had never been known for the ears.

The air was growing unstable. Flames began leaping free of the fire, and mist ceased rising from the monolith and began to cumulate around the base. The crack in its northern face suddenly looked to Inigar like a newly opened vein. Something vital was pumping out.

"What happened on the Eve of Breaking?" Inigar cried,

suddenly needing to hear the sound of his own voice. "Did Mace order the killing of the girl?"

Had it been enough, that order to murder Effie Sevrance? Or had the guidestone been keeping tally all along and judged it one misdeed too far? Inigar had heard the whispers: Mace had killed the swordsman Shor Gormalin, ordered the slaughter of innocent children on the Bluddroad, and arranged the murder of the Orrl chief Spynie Orrl.

There was that noise again. Inigar's head whipped around as he tried to hear. For a moment he thought he detected something, almost knew what it was, but then it was gone. Cold made his eyes slow to focus, and it took him a moment to realize that he could no longer see the Hailstone clearly. Mist folded in on itself, twisting and swirling, mushrooming outward in quiet lobes before being sucked back by the monolith.

Inigar pushed his fist against his rib cage. Thirty years he'd attended the stone, and not one day missed in all that time. He knew the lay of the stone; knew that its northern face was the hardest, and that its southeastern foot was deeply veined with silver and did not take well to the grindstone. He knew where the greatest concentrations of quartz could be found, and the best places to tap for sacred oil. He knew its cavities, its lines of cleavage, its rusts and lichens and flaws.

History was carved on its many faces like text in a book. The iron ring on its northwestern corner where the kingslayer Ayan Blackhail had been chained whilst awaiting judgment still stood, immovable now and swollen with rust. A series of blunted steps cut into the east face told of the time when the monolith had stood ten feet taller and had lain on the greatcourt, exposed to rain and frost. Clanwives had once climbed those steps and watched as their husbands returned from the War of Sheep. Every chief since Stanner Blackhail had left his mark upon the stone. Black Harald and Ewan the Bold, Mordrag, Gregor, Duncan, Albor and his son also named Albor, Theobad, Allister and more. The line of marks was long and uncannily telling. Black Harald had chosen crossed swords as his mark, but at some point during his chiefdom he must have ordered the clan guide to take up his chisel and change it. The points and hilts of the swords could still be seen, but the blades had been hewn away, replaced by a thickly carved dram cup: the sign of parley. Mordrag's mark was a deeply bored hole, fitting for the man who called himself the Mole chief; Ewan's was a half-closed fist, poised to crush the Bloody Blue Thistle of Dhoone; and Albor the Second had chosen a horseshoe, just like his da.

Dagro's mark was unfinished, the stag and swords he'd chosen mere tracelines in the stone.

Inigar's gaze lapsed upon the circling mist as his thoughts fell inward. *I know this stone like the back of my hand, but do I know this clan?*

Should he have looked further after Dagro's death? One event, two differing stories: had he dismissed Raif Sevrance's account too soon? The boy had called Mace a liar, said that Dagro had fallen by the rendering pit, not by the tent poles as Mace insisted. Even Raif's brother Drey, who was a staunch supporter of Mace, had agreed with his younger brother's version of events. Yet Raif Sevrance was just a boy, barely seventeen and without an oath. His father had been slain at the same time as Dagro, and he was simmering with rage and grief. The murderers had escaped, unchallenged and unpursued, and Inigar knew what kind of feelings that stirred in a man. Someone had to be made to suffer. Inigar had assumed that Raif's anger toward Mace was simple misdirection. A raw boy looking for someone to blame. Had he been wrong?

Ahooooooooooo.

The wolf. So close now the horses would be stirring in the stalls and the chickens pecking at the wire in the coop. Inigar knew how they felt: uneasy, restive, trapped.

Sucking in icy air, he listened for a response. Every summer since the Hundred Year Cull, bands of Hailsmen rode out along the far borders to hunt pack wolves that ranged too close to the hold. The slain animals were skinned, not butchered. For while no Hailsman ate wolfmeat, many enjoyed the pleasure of walking on wolf-pelt rugs. In recent times the cull had grown sparse as packs moved north and west, out of range of Hailish steel. Pack wolves were cautious. They had pups and yearlings to protect, and their collective wisdom gave them an advantage over solitary beasts.

The animal that howled this night was not part of such a pack though, for nothing but deathly silence returned its call.

A lone wolf.

Fear and understanding slowly began to coalesce in Inigar's thoughts. Something terrible was about to happen. Here, in the exact and sacred center of clan.

The Hail Wolf had returned home.

Inigar stood perfectly straight and still and decided what he would do. Mist from the guidestone glided across his face yet he did not shrink back or blink. Quite suddenly his greatest mistake was clear to him. It had not been misjudging Mace Blackhail or taking an oath from Raif Sevrance that he knew from the very beginning the boy was doomed to break. No. Grave though those errors were they did not match his failure to train an apprentice guide.

He had wanted Effie Sevrance so badly he'd refused to consider anyone else. She was so powerful, that was the thing, the augers that preceded her birth so potent. And she had been born to the stone. No one in any clan at any time Inigar could remember had been born to the guidestone. Yet that was the girl's lore, and he had coveted its power for his office and himself. Possessiveness had made him blind. Other candidates had been worthy—Jebb Onnacre, Nitty Hart, Will Sperling—yet he had rejected them out of hand.

Now who would guide Blackhail when he was gone?

A sound, pitched so low it was almost beyond hearing, pulsed through the guidehouse like an earth tremor. This time Inigar heard it clearly, instantly recognizing the source. The Hailstone. The vast chunk of black granite and blackened silver that had been cut from the great stone fields of Trance Vor seven centuries earlier and floated a thousand miles upstream along the Flow was returning the call of the Hail Wolf.

Ice mist switched violently, sending waves rippling out from the stone. Inigar could smell it now: cold and vast, like the sky on a clear winter night. It was the smell of gods. A part of his brain, made just for this moment, came to life solely to recognize the scent. Tears sprang to his eyes. Here was everything he had ever wanted: to exist in the presence of gods. To regard them and be regarded. To know and to be known.

AHOOOOOOOOOOOOOOO . . .

At his last moment what should a man do? Inigar thought of all he had been and all he had hoped to be . . . but he would not dwell on his failings. The time for that was done. He thought of clan; of the Shanks and Sevrances, the Blackhails, Murdocks, Ganlows and Lyes. Imperfect men and women, but the sum of the whole was good. He thought of Embeth Hare, the girl who would have wed him if he'd asked. "Inny," she had said to him on that perfect summer day as they lay out on the hay piles, soaking in the sun. "If you decide to become Beardy's apprentice you must never forget two things. It's not enough that we fear the gods. We must love them also." When he had asked her what the second thing was, she had pulled up her skirt and made love to him. His first and only time.

Embeth had always been smarter than him. Wind whipped against his face as ice mist started to rotate around the guidestone. Faster and faster it moved, round and round, blasting tools and smoking embers from its path. The gods were leaving Blackhail. And what sort of gods would it make them if they left quietly without a sound?

No longer able to stand in the hurricane, Inigar dropped to his knees. The air was full of debris now; strips of leather, shammies, ashes, woodchips, and dust. The oak workbench he'd sat at every day slid across the room, legs squealing. A powerful blast of air sent it smashing against the wall. Inigar felt little shards of oak pierce his shoulder. A moment later something punctured his hip. Looking down he saw his chisel poking from the pad of muscle at the top of his thigh. He took its handle in his fist and yanked it out.

An eye was forming above the center of the guidestone. It was beautiful and terrible, a calmness in the storm of spinning clouds. A noise, bass and so full of power it set the walls and floor vibrating, boomed out of the stone. Inigar's eyes and nose began to bleed. His pigskin cloak was snatched from his back and sucked into the tow. He was beyond feeling pain now, and barely registered the missiles slamming against his side. He was the guide of Clan Blackhail and he had his chisel in his hand, and witnessing the gods' power was not a bad way to die.

Suddenly everything stopped. Litter dropped from the air,

thudding and tinkling. Mist sank away like water down a drain. The guidestone stood still and silent, as old as the earth itself. Wonder and sadness filled Inigar's heart. Who would guide Blackhail when he was gone?

And then the Hailstone exploded into a million bits of shrapnel and the clan guide knew no more.

The man who had lost his soul approached the house. Timbers framing the doorway were black and shiny. Creosote deposited during the burning gave them the oily iridescence of ravens' wings. The door that had once been suspended between them had fallen on the front stoop. Its metal hinge pins had popped out of their casings like cooked sausage meat. Charred panels in the door crumbled as the man's weight came down on them. In a different life he had stained and waxed the panels, proofing them against the brutal winter storms that hit from the north.

Protecting this house from harm.

The man rocked backward, bringing force to bear on the heel of his left boot, crushing the brittle wood, stretching the moment before he entered the house.

When he was ready he stepped into the remains of his hallway. Fire had burned intensely here. The interior walls had been limestone-and-horsehair plaster skimmed onto wood lath. His mistake had been to paint them. Oil in the paint had accelerated the burn, working against the natural retardant of the lime. The smoke produced would have been black and toxic. It would have burned holes in a child's lungs.

The man did not pause. He could no longer trust himself that far. Walking through the center of the house he passed the stairs and the black skeleton of the stair rail. Snow had found its way in through the partially collapsed roof and open windows, and lay in thin drifts against the risers of each of the nine steps. The man knew snow; knew that what he looked at was dry with age, the granules loosely packed and rolled into pellets by the wind. Footsteps stamped into the drifts held no interest for him. Men had come later, after the house had cooled and the snow fallen. The curious and opportunistic. Young boys on dares; thieves in search of locked boxes, silverware, metal for scrapping; officials gathering information along with a fine story to tell their wives over supper. The man understood the pull of such places. Death and ruin dwelt here, and a person could come and view it and be glad it was not his family, his house, his life.

Ignoring the footsteps, the man headed down the central hall toward the kitchen. His mind was working; cataloguing details, noting absences, testing them against the theory coalescing in his head.

It was the only way to remain sane.

The devil was in the details. The damage to the doors and exterior walls was far greater than in the interior of the house. Here, in the kitchen, the stone fireplace was barely damaged. The fire irons had been stolen, not melted. The facing stones were black, yet the heat had been insufficient to crack the mortar between them. On the opposite wall, where the external door was located, the destruction was far worse. The two windows were black holes. Plaster surrounding them had warped and cracked. Varnish on the adjoining floorboards had blistered. Part of the wall above the eastern window had fallen in taking a chunk of the upper story along with it. The man looked up and saw sky. When he looked down he noticed that one of the house's exterior sandstone blocks had tumbled in. Its once dusty orange face had been smelted into glass.

Xhalia ex nihl. All becomes nothing: words he'd learned from the Sull. They spoke them in times of grief as a comfort . . . and in times of joy as a reminder. He'd thought them wise and fair.

He was wrong.

His wife and daughters were dead. His three girls and the woman he had loved for half his life were gone.

Murdered.

The moment he had turned the corner in the road and seen the burned house he knew. He had lived with risk for so long that the anticipation of disaster had become a reflex, a string held at tension waiting to snap. A muscle contracting in his gut had told him everything. The walk through the house had simply confirmed it. The blaze had burned from the outside in. Fires had been set at windows and doors. The occupants had been trapped inside and forced to fill their lungs with hot, lethal smoke.

The man pushed a fist against the charred plaster and took a breath. And then another. His wife and girls had trusted him with their safety. And he had failed them. He, who knew more than most about evil and the men and women who practiced it, and knew just how long they would wait for an opportunity to bring harm. He, who had dedicated his life to opposing the dark and unfathomable forces of destruction.

Those forces had come to bear on this house — he had led them here. How could he have been such a fool? How could he have imagined that it was possible to outwit them? They were beyond his comprehension; unbound by earthly forms. What had he been thinking when he'd made the decision to hide his most precious girls from them in plain sight?

Eighteen, five and one; those were their ages. Add them up and you'd get exactly the number of years he'd known his wife.

The man breathed. Inhaled. Exhaled. Pushed himself off from the wall.

The back door was there so he took it. Never again would he enter this house.

He had one job to do, and he did not care how it was done. Those who had planned and executed this would die. He had one cold and empty lifetime to take care of it.

Outside, the late-afternoon sun was shining. In the woods beyond the yard a woodpecker was drilling a softwood for lice. A brisk wind spun clouds to the south and drove the stale smell of char back in the house. The man's gaze swept over the remains of the kitchen garden. A row of unharvested winter kale was yellowing in a raised bed. Tarp still covered the woodpile. Three distinct earthen mounds beneath the shade oak caught his attention.

The ground had been too hard to bury them.

The man swayed. His first act of will was to steady himself, to force his knees to rigidity and suck air into his lungs. His second was to kill his lifelong instinct to call on the gods for comfort. The gods were dead, and he was no longer bound by their commands.

Moving forward, he cut a straight path to the graves. Only

three. The baby must have been buried with her mother. A different man would have taken comfort in that.

The man without a soul refused it.

All becomes nothing, he murmured as he knelt by the graves and began to dig.

ONE

Want

Ash.

Raif woke with a start, immediately sitting upright. His heart was pumping hard in his chest and there was a rawness in his throat as if he had been screaming. A quick glance at Bear showed the sturdy little hill pony's ears were twitching. Probably had been screaming then.

Ash's name.

Raif shook his head, hoping to drive away all thoughts of her. Nothing could be gained by them. Madness lay in wait here, in the vast and shifting landscape of the Great Want, and to worry about Ash March and crave her presence was a sure way to drive himself insane. She was gone. He could not have her. It was as simple and as unchangeable as that.

Rising to his feet, Raif forced himself to evaluate the landscape. Thirst made his tongue feel big in his mouth. He ignored it. Light was moving through the Want and the last of the bright stars were fading. In the direction that might have been east, the horizon was flushed with the first suggestion of sun. The landscape seemed familiar. Scale-covered rock formations rose from the buckled limestone floor like stalagmites, craggy and jagged, silently farming minerals as they grew. On the ground, a litter of lime fragments and calcified insect husks cracked beneath his boots like chicken bones. Bear was snuffling something that a while back might have been a plant. As Raif's gaze moved from the distant purple peaks floating above the mist, to the canyon lines that forked Want-north across the valley floor, he felt some measure of relief. It looked pretty much like the place he had set camp in last night.

Anchored, that was the word. The Want had not drifted while he slept.

Grateful for that, Raif crossed over to Bear and started rubbing down her coat. She head-butted him, sniffing for water, but it was too early for her morning ration so he pushed her head back gently and told her, "No."

The puncture wounds caused by the *Shatan Maer*'s claws had stiffened his left shoulder muscle, and as he worked on Bear's hooves he felt some pain. When he made a quick movement up her leg, a cold little tingle traveled toward his heart. Stopping for a moment, he put a hand on Bear's belly to steady himself. Something about the pain, a kind of liquid probing, had unsettled him, and he couldn't seem to get the *Shatan Maer* out of his head. He could smell its rankness, see its cunning dead eyes as it came for him.

Shivering, Raif stepped away from the pony. "Do I look mad to you?" he asked her as he massaged the aching muscle.

Bear flicked her tail lazily; a pony's equivalent of a shrug. The gesture was strangely reassuring. Sometimes that was all it took to drive away your fears: the indifference of another living thing. The pain was just the last remnants of an infection, nothing more.

Although he didn't much feel like it, Raif set about taking stock of his meager supplies. Fresh water had become a problem. The aurochs' bladder rested slack against a block of limestone, its contents nearly drained. The little that remained tasted of rawhide. Raif doubted whether it would last the day. There was food—sprouted millet for the pony, hard cheese and pemmican for himself—yet he knew enough not to be tempted by it. He wanted to be sure where his next drink was coming from before he ate. Yesterday he'd learned that it wasn't enough just to see water. In the Want you had to jump in it and watch your clothes get wet before you could be absolutely certain it was there. Yesterday he and Bear had tracked leagues out of their way to pursue a glassy shimmer in the valley between two hills. They stood in that valley today. It wasn't just dry, it was *bone* dry, and Raif had been left feeling like a fool. You'd think he would have learned by now.

Unable to help himself, he flicked the cap off the waterskin and squirted a small amount into his mouth. The fluid was gone before he had a chance to swallow it, sucked away by parched gums. He was tempted to take more, but resisted. His duty to his animal came first.

As he poured a careful measure into the pony's waxed snufflebag, Raif wondered what heading to take next. As best he could tell, five days had passed since he'd left the Fortress of Grey Ice. The first few days were lost to him, gone in a fever dream of blood poisoning and pain. He did not recall leaving the fortress or choosing a route to lead them out of the Want. He remembered waking one morning and looking at his left arm and not being sure that it belonged to him. The skin floated on top of the muscle as if separated by a layer of liquid. It leaked when he pressed it, clear fluid that seeped through a crack Raif supposed must be a wound. The strange thing was it hadn't hurt. Even stranger, he could not recall being concerned.

At some point he must have regained his mind, although there were times when he wasn't sure. The wounds on his neck were healing. He'd stitched the deepest one without use of a mirror, so gods only knew what he looked like. As for his arm, it certainly looked a lot better. And he was definitely sure it was his. His mind was a different story though, a little foggy around the edges and prone to fancies. The first day that he tried to ride his head had felt too light, and he'd convinced himself he was better off walking instead.

He hadn't been on Bear since then, and he'd spent the last three days stubbornly walking. Occasionally Bear looked at him quizzically, and had once gone as far as head-butting the small of his back to encourage him to ride. She had wanted to help, he knew that, and the one thing she had to offer was her ability to bear his weight.

Raif licked his lips. They were as dry as tree bark. Reaching inside the grain bag, he scooped up a handful of millet. Bear, whose thoughts were never far from food, trotted over to investigate. She ate from his hand, lipping hard to get at the grains that were jammed between his fingers. She didn't understand that in many ways she was the one who was caring for him. Her company alone was worth more than a month's worth of supplies. Bear's stoic acceptance of her situation lightened his heart. Caring for her needs—making sure she had enough food and water, tending to her coat, skin, and mouth, and keeping her shoes free of stone—kept him from focusing on himself.

And then there was her Want sense. The little hill pony borrowed from the Maimed Men had an instinct for moving through the Great Want. Instead of fighting the insubstantial nature of the landscape, she gave herself up to it, became a leaf floating downstream. As a clansman trained to navigate dense forests, follow the whisper-light trails left by ice hares and foxes, and hold his bearings on frozen tundra in a whiteout, Raif found traveling through the Want frustrating. The sun might rise in the morning, but then again it might not. Entire mountain ranges could sail on the horizon like ships. Clouds formed rings that hung in the sky, unaffected by prevailing winds, for days. At night a great wheel of stars would turn in the heavens, but you could never be sure what constellations it would contain. Sometimes the wheel reversed itself and moved counter to every wisdom concerning the stars that Raif had ever been taught. Orienting oneself in such an environment was close to impossible. As soon as you had established the direction of due north, decided on a course to lead you out, the Want began to slip through your fingers like snowmelt. Nothing was fixed here. Everything—the sky, the land, the sun and the moon—drifted to the movement of some unknowable tide.

The Great Want could not be mastered or explained. Ancient sorceries had scarred it, time had worn away its boundaries, and cataclysmic disasters had scoured it clean of life. The Want was no longer bound by physical laws. To attempt to traverse it was folly. The best you could hope for was rite of passage. Somehow Bear knew this, knew that relinquishing—not asserting—control would carry one farther in this place.

Every night since they had left the fortress the pony had stumbled upon a suitable place to set camp. She found islands elevated above the vast mist rivers that flowed across the Want at sunset, sniffed out caves sunk deep into cliff faces, and hollows protected from the harsh morning winds. She'd even located a riverbed where ancient bushes had been sucked so dry of life juice that they burned as smokeless as the purest fuel. The hill pony hadn't found drinkable water yet, but Raif knew that out of the two of them she had the best chance of discovering it.

That, and the way out.

Frowning, Raif scanned the horizon. A constant bitter wind blew against his face, scouring his cheeks with ice crystals and filling his nose with the smell of ozone and lead; the scent of faraway storms. Part of him was content simply to drift. As long as he was here, at the Want's mercy, he need make no decisions about the future. Questions about whether to return to the Maimed Men or head south in search of Ash had little meaning. In a way it was a kind of relief. The past three days were the most peace he had known since that morning in the Badlands when his da and Dagro Blackhail had died.

That sense of peace would not last for long. *Mor Drakka*, Watcher of the Dead, Oathbreaker, Twelve Kill: a man possessing such names could not expect to live a peaceful life.

Kneeling on his bedroll, Raif reached for the sword given to him by the Listener of the Ice Trappers. The once perfectly tempered blade was warped and blackened, its edges blunted and untrue. Plunged into shadowflesh up to its crossguard, the sword had been irrevocably changed. It would never be more than a knock-around now, the kind of blade a father let his son train with until the boy developed a proper degree of skill. Raif began to grind the blade regardless, using a soft shammy and a makeshift paste of limestone grit and horse lard. The rock crystal mounted on the pommel flashed brilliantly in the rising sun, and Raif found himself recalling what the Listener had said when he handed over the sword.

It should serve you well enough until you find a better one.

Strange how he hadn't given the words much thought until now. This sword had once been the weapon of a Forsworn knight, its blade forged from the purest steel, its edge honed by a master swordsmith. To most clansmen it would be a prize to be treasured; oiled lovingly every tenday, drawn with silent pride for the inspection of honored guests, passed through the generations from father to son. Yet the Listener had hinted that for Raif there would be more.

Abruptly Raif resheathed the sword. It was time to move on. Today was a good day in the Want. A sun rose, traveling at a constant speed and arc, and banks of low-lying clouds moved in the same direction as prevailing winds. Well, almost. Raif shrugged as he hiked along a limestone bluff. He'd take small discrepancies over big ones any day.

The bluff was rocky and hard going, riven with cracks and undermined with softer, lighter chalkstone that was crumbling to dust. Gray weeds poked through holes in the rock. They may have been alive; it was hard to tell. In the distance Raif could see a range of low-lying mountains, spinebacks, laid out in a course that fishtailed into the bluff. Realizing he was in for a steady climb, he reached for the waterskin.

Straightaway he knew it was a mistake. His mouth and stomach were anticipating water, his throat muscles were contracting in readiness to swallow, yet he could not take a drink. The waterskin was as good as empty. Nothing could be spared. Swallowing the saliva that had pooled under his tongue, he tucked the waterskin back into its place behind Bear's saddle. When his stomach sent out a single cramp of protest, he ignored it. He had to think.

Why am I going this way? Any other heading would lead him off the bluff and away from the mountains. No climb involved. So why accelerate his thirst? Why not simply head downhill and take the easy route? Chances were the Want would shift on him anyway. A day from now those mountains could have melted into the mist.

Raif squinted at the sun, thinking. It was a winter sun, pale and crisply outlined against the sky. When he looked away its after-image burned in front of his eyes. As it cleared he became aware that his breath was purling white. The temperature was dropping. The Want had two degrees of coldness: bitter and glacially raw. Since leaving the fortress Raif had counted himself lucky to have encountered only the first. Bitter he could live with. Bitter was the normal state of things for the clanholds in midwinter. It gave you chilblains and sometimes frostbite in your ears and toes. As long as you were bundled up and well fed you could live through it.

Raw was something else. Raw killed. It froze your breath the instant it left your mouth, coating every hair on your face with frost; it numbed the most thickly wrapped hands and feet and then when it had numbed them it turned them into ice; and it altered the working of your mind, made you think it was hot when it was deadly cold, that you just needed to rest awhile and everything would be all right.

Raif shivered. He decided to stay on course, but could not say why. At his side, Bear blew air at force through her nostrils, forming two white clouds. The little pony had been bred to live at high elevations in the far north. Her coat was thick and wiry and her leg hair formed shaggy skirts around her hoofs. She would probably fare better than him, but he wasn't taking any chances. He unrolled her blanket and threw it across her back. As he fastened the toggles beneath her belly he contemplated for the first time having to kill her. He would place his sword here, well below her rib cage, and thrust up through her first and second stomachs to her heart. It was the swiftest death he could give, the instant cessation of blood pumping from her heart to her brain.

Heart-kill, it was called. All hunters aspired to it: that perfectly placed, perfectly powered, blow that would stop all animals in their tracks.

Oh gods. Why am I even thinking of this? Straightening up, Raif slapped Bear's rump, encouraging her to walk on.

For a while after that he did not think, simply walked. They fell into a rhythm, Bear matching him exactly in speed and rate of climb. Occasionally she would nudge him. Sometimes he nudged her back. As he walked he savored the pleasure of working his body hard and forcing his lungs to expand against his chest wall. It could last only so long. They had no water, and he had no choice but to consider his responsibility to Bear. She was his animal. He owed her food, water, shelter and safety. In the event of injury or sickness he owed her a swift death. Tem, his father, would have stood for no less. *"You have an animal, Raif—I don't care whether it's a dog or a horse or a one-legged flying squirrel—it gets fed before you get fed, watered before you drink, and if it's sick you take care of it."* Even then as a boy of eight he had understood all that his father had meant by "taking care of it."

Raif held himself back a moment, let Bear walk ahead of him on the trail. He wished it were that simple. Wished that he hadn't felt a small thrill of anticipation as he contemplated running his sword through the hill pony's heart.

Kill an army for me, Raif Sevrance, Death had commanded him. *Any less and I just might call you back.*

Ice cracked down as they headed Want-west along the bluff. Clouds disappeared, abandoning a sky that had grown perfectly blue. The landscape clarified. Rocks, mountains, even the distant horizon became sharper and more easy to read. The wind had died some time back and the air was diamond clear. Raif could see for leagues in every direction, and spun round to take it all in. He saw a vast dead volcano rise from the valley floor, saw boulders as big as roundhouses strewn across a dry lake bed, spied thousands of gray stumps rising from the headland, a forest of petrified trees, and spotted a deep flaw in the landscape where a vast shield of rock had been pushed up by underground forces. None of it was familiar. And there was no telltale glint of water.

Raif licked his lips and winced in pain. He wondered if they'd turned black. It had to be midday by now and he hadn't had a drink since dawn. The day before he had allowed himself only a cup of water. Time was running out on him. He knew some of the dangers of dehydration from his time spent on longhunts. There was little freshwater to be had in the badlands of Blackhail. The majority of standing pools and lakes were brackish, thick with minerals percolated from the bedrock. Running water was little better, mostly sulfur springs, salt licks and leachfields. A man had to be sure where his next drink was coming from. Dehydration could make your eyesight deteriorate and your muscles cramp, and just like the cold it could play tricks with your mind and have you seeing things that weren't there. Raif smiled grimly. One way or other he would likely be insane by the end of the day.

Giving in to his thirst, he held the limp waterskin above his head and squeezed a few drops into his mouth. His tongue felt big and clumsy, barely able to register the wetness of the water. Bear, noticing the waterskin was in use, trotted over and butted his chest. He shook the skin. So little liquid was left that it didn't make a sound. Raif glanced at his sword.

Not yet.

Prying open Bear's jaw, he thrust the waterskin spout deep into her mouth and then collapsed the skin with force, ejecting the last of the water. He was taking no chances: Bear was a sloppy drinker.

His spirits lifted after that. Bear's wounded expression made him laugh. The sun was shining. He could even see where he was going—no small mercy in the Want. The bluff gradually broadened into headland and they began to make good time. Directly ahead the mountain ridge loomed closer, and Raif could now see that its lower slopes were mounded gravel. He tried not to let that bother him. Experience had taught him that climbing loose stone banks was hard work. Still, it would keep them warm.

And make them sweat. Raif blinked, and noticed for the first time that his eyes felt no relief. He was out of tears.

What are we going to do?

Three days back they'd passed a narrow canyon that had contained ice. The frozen liquid had been the color of sheep urine, and he just couldn't bring himself to pick it. Water hadn't seemed like much of a problem then. One thing the Want never seemed short of was ice. Now he would give anything to return to that canyon . . . but in the Want there was no going back.

Raif scratched Bear's ear. There was nothing to do but carry on.

As the day wore on the cold deepened. Hoarfrost glittered on every rock face and loose stone. Raif's fingers began to ache and the tip of his nose grew raw from constant rubbing—ice formed every time he took a breath. Bear's muzzle had to be removed. Metal was a lightning rod for frostbite and could not be left resting against skin. The hill pony seemed grateful enough to be free of the bit, but Raif could tell she was growing listless. Instead of walking abreast of him, she had fallen behind, and she was becoming less particular about her footing. Twice now she had stumbled when a front hoof had come down on loose scree.

It wasn't long before their pace began to slow. Raif lagged, allowing Bear to catch up with him. He leaned into her and she leaned into him, and they bumped against each other with each step. The corners of Bear's mouth were in a bad way—the edges crusted with little red sores—and her tongue had started to swell. Raif's throat was swollen. When he swallowed, saliva no longer filled his mouth. His teeth were so dry they felt like stones. The worst thing was the drifting. He caught himself doing it from time to time, allowing his thoughts to float away, light as air. He thought of his little sister, Effie, of her shy smiles and serious gaze. He and Drey had taught her to read, though neither of them had been scholars so they probably hadn't done a very good job. She'd probably overcome it. Effie Sevrance was smarter than both of them combined. How old would she be now? She had been eight when he left the roundhouse. It upset him when he couldn't decide whether she was still eight or had turned nine.

And then there was Drey. There was always Drey. An image of his older brother came to Raif immediately, the one that never went away, the one of Drey on the greatcourt that winter morning, stepping forward when no one else would. *I will stand second to his oath.* The words burned Raif even now. He had broken that oath and shamed his clan. Yet the worst was that he'd let down Drey.

Drey . . .

Raif's thoughts drifted into a dark place. Falling, he thought of the men he had killed: some named and many nameless. Bluddsmen, city men, the lone Forsworn knight in a redoubt filled with death. Thirst followed him down, gnawing, gnawing, like a rat at the back of his throat. His lips had shriveled to husks and when he smiled at something playing in the darkness they cracked and bled.

Pain brought him back. Blinking like a man shaken suddenly awake, Raif looked around. The Want had shifted. Something subtle had changed, a rotation of perspective or a shortening of distance: he could not decide which. The mountain ridge that they'd been heading toward all day was now upon them, looming dark and rugged and barren. Part of Raif had been hoping to find glaciers in the high valleys but from here he could tell that he'd badly misjudged the ridge's elevation. What he'd imagined were mountains were little more than spine-backed hills.

Without warning the wound in his right shoulder sent out a bolt of white-hot pain. Knee joints turning to jelly, he instantly dropped to the ground. The headland's limestone had given way to softer chalkstone, and Raif fell into a bed of pulverized chalk. Massaging his shoulder, he hacked up freezing dust.

Bear came over, anxiously prodding him with her head. The little hill pony had a frothy scum around her lips, and her tongue was now too big for her mouth. It lolled to the side, black and bloated. Raif thought about his sword.

If not now. Soon.

Flinging his left arm around her neck, he allowed her to pull him to his feet. A queer tingle of pain shot along his shoulder as he dusted chalk from his cloak. It was losing its capacity to worry him. He needed water. Bear needed water and shelter— her exposed tongue would be frozen meat within an hour. Worry about anything other than those two things was becoming beyond him. Ignoring the pain, he moved forward.

The point where the headland joined with the ridge was a quicksand of chalk and gravel. Walking on the chalk was similar to walking on dry, powdery snow. With every step Bear sank up to her hocks, sometimes further. Initially the heavier gravel was suspended across the chalk like lily pads over water, and both Raif and Bear learned caution. The gravel might hold, suspended beneath the surface by more gravel, or it could sink so fast it created suction. Every step was an ordeal. Every couple of steps one of them had to halt to pull out sunken feet or hooves.

When his right eyeball started to sting, Raif realized he was beginning to sweat. Baked dry by the sun and stiffened by the frost, his cornea seized up the moment salty fluid from his temple slid into his eye socket. His hands and face were now numb, so when he ran a fist across his forehead and his glove came back wet it was a shock.

He was losing too much water. Swallowing hard, he forced himself to stop and think. Ahead, the gravel bank darkened as the charcoal granite of the spineback hills began to peek through. Farther along an entire ridge emerged, rising from the sea of stones and broadening into a rock mass that fused with the first hill. *There*, Raif decided. *We'll go as far as the junction.*

The high vantage point would enable them to see what lay ahead.

If there's no water we're damned.

It was the last clear thought he had until nightfall. Bear began wheezing during the climb across the gravel banks, a sharp little piping noise that sounded as if it were coming from a broken flute. And she shied for the first time. When they reached a deep chute filled with younger, sharper scree she refused to cross it, digging in her back hooves and weakly tossing her head. Raif went on ahead awhile, but she wouldn't follow, even when he called her, and he was forced to go back. Light was beginning to fail, and more than anything else he did not want to lose sight of her. He feared the landscape might shift while he wasn't looking and the Want would cancel her out.

It was becoming hard to think. There should have been a way around the chute—he even saw it once, laid out like a treasure map before him—but he couldn't keep the facts in his head. Bear didn't want to walk through the jagged scree. The chute was narrow. Maybe they could double back . . .

He lost time. Standing on the hillside, thoughts stalled, he was aware only of the intense cold. Ice twinkled in his eyelashes when he blinked. Something—he couldn't say what—snapped him back. For an instant he wasn't glad; everything took too much effort here. It was easier to drift. Yet when he saw Bear he felt shamed. The little pony was standing where he had left her, shaking and making that little piping noise when she inhaled.

"Come on, girl," he coaxed, trudging toward her through shin-high gravel. "Not far now. We'll go down a bit and then around." He didn't know if they could make it that way, but it hardly seemed to matter anymore. Doing was better than thinking in this place.

Night fell in layers. The sun hung on the farthest edge of the horizon and smoldered. A dusk of long shadows made it difficult to see the way forward. Overhead the first of the big northern stars ignited in a sky turning deep-sea blue. Raif had taken to plowing the breath ice from his nose and chin and shoveling it into his mouth. The moisture it rendered wasn't sufficient to be called liquid, but the sensation of fizzy coolness

on his tongue was deeply pleasing. When he tried to perform
the same service for Bear, she shied away from him. Blood was
oozing from a cut on her back heel, and she'd started to carry
her head and tail low. She wouldn't go much farther, he realized.

He owed her a decent end. As he peered through the darkness toward the turn of the hill his spirits sank. They'd barely
made any progress since sunset, simply retraced their steps from
the chute. Glancing from his sword to Bear, he made a decision. One hour. No more.

He was gentle with her as they took their final climb.

Starlight lit the hillside, making the rocks glow blue. Raif
thought about how he'd first met Bear—she'd been a replacement for the horse he'd lost in canyon country west of the
Rift—and how she had carried him to the Fortress of Grey Ice.
She had kept him sane, he knew that now. After the raid on the
silver mine at Black Hole he was nearly lost. Bitty's death had
been too much to bear.

Raif girded himself for the memories. He would not fight
them off or deny them: Bitty Shank, son of Orwin and sworn
clansman of Blackhail, deserved better than that. He had not
deserved to die at the hands of a fellow clansman.

Oathbreaker, Raif named himself, his lips moving. That
morning on the greatcourt he had sworn to protect his clan . . .
and he had not protected them.

He had killed them.

Raif sucked in air, welcoming the cold into cavities close to
his heart. He was damned. And how should a damned man live
his life?

A crunching sounding to his left brought him back.
Swinging around, he saw that Bear had stumbled to her knees.
Oh gods. He scrambled over to her, not caring where he placed
his feet. Nightfall had sharpened the frost and walking through
the gravel was like wading through sea ice. Bear was shivering
intensely. Her eyes tracked him as he approached, and everything he saw in them told him he could not wait any longer.

"Little Bear," he said softy. "My best girl."

She was cool to the touch. Even now, she pushed her head
toward his hand as he stroked her cheek. Kneeling, he moved

his body alongside her, wanting to give her his heat. Her heart was beating out of time; he could feel it against his chest. Gently, he rubbed the ice from her nose. She was calm now; they both were.

"My best little Bear."

Raif kissed her eyes closed and drew his sword. No one in the Known World could deliver a death blow with such accuracy and force, and for the first time in his eighteen-year life Raif Sevrance was grateful for that fact.

It was a mercy for both of them.

Curling himself around her cooling body, he lay and rested for a while in the Want.

TWO

The Sundering

Raina Blackhail ordered the halved pig's carcass to be hauled from the dairy shed to the wetroom. Two days it had lain there, exposed to the warm and fragrant air, and the flies must have done their job by now. Besides, the smell was making her sick.

Jebb Onnacre, one of the stablehands and a Shank by marriage, was quick to nod. "Aye, lady. Couple of days in the wetroom and you'll have some fine maggots to spare."

Raina showed a brief smile. It was the best she could manage this cold midmorning. She liked Jebb, he was a good man and he bore his injuries stoically, but the night the Hailstone exploded, destroying the guidehouse, stable block, and east wall of the roundhouse, it seemed the weight of those structures had fallen upon her shoulders. And she had been bearing it now for a week.

"I'll rig up a platform. Give it a little air along with the damp." Jebb had lifted the carcass onto a sheet of oiled tarp in preparation for dragging it through the hay. Raina could tell from his hopeful expression that he wanted to please her, that by offering to do more than was necessary he was showing his support.

She was grateful for that. It gave her what she needed for a genuine smile. "Thank you, Jebb. I'd forgotten the maggots need good ventilation to grow."

Jebb cinched the end of the tarp in his wrist. "Aye, lady. Makes you wonder what else we've forgotten as a clan." With that, he jerked the carcass into motion and began dragging it toward the door.

Raina watched him go. His words had given her a little chill and she pulled her mohair shawl snug across her shoulders. The air in the shed was dusty with hay and the mites that fed on it made her throat itch. Gloomy gray light flooded the dimness as Jebb flung back the doors.

The stablehand's head was still wrapped in bandages. Jebb had been sleeping on a box pallet in one of the horse stalls when the Sundering happened, and had ended up with a chunk of granite embedded in his skull. He'd bled for two whole days. Only the gods knew why he wasn't dead. Laida Moon, the clan healer, had pronounced it to be a miracle of "the thick Onnacre head." Jebb had embraced this diagnosis with such enthusiasm that he'd started referring to himself as "Old Thickey."

Wearing one's injuries with pride had become a way of life in the Hailhouse. Gat Murdock had lost an arm. Lansa Tanner was still abed with injuries too numerous to mention; it was likely she would lose an eye. Quiet, big-boned Hatty Hare had suffered burns on the right side of her face and shoulders. Duggen Harris, the little hay boy, had been burned even worse. Noddie Drook, whom everyone called the Noddler, had been slammed so hard against the wall of the Dry Run that he'd smashed six ribs and punctured a lung. And so the list went on: Stanner Hawk, Jamie Perch, Arlan Perch . . . Raina shook her head gently. There were too many injured to name.

The dead, though, they had to be named. She could not call herself chief's wife if she did not catalogue the dead.

Bessie Flapp. Gone. The shock of the explosion had stopped her heart. The new luntman, Mornie Dabb, had been lighting torches in the tunnelway. His body was found three days later, blown all the way to the kaleyard. Mog Willey, Effie's childhood friend. He'd been on his way to the guidehouse to deliver Inigar's morning milk. His body was found in two pieces. Joshua Honeycut and Wilbur Peamouth, two stablehands like Jebb, only they were up and about that morning, preparing breakfast and scouring the workbenches for Jon Crickle, the stablemaster. Also dead. Craw Bannering's head had been severed. Vernon Murdock, brother to Gat, hung on for four days before succumbing to his injuries. And it was a mercy the little milkmaid, Elsa Doe, had just lived out the day.

Inigar's body had not been found, and Raina had an instinct that even when work crews cleared the rubble heap that had once been the guidehouse it would still be missing. Oh, he had died along with the Hailstone, she did not doubt it. But it would be just like Inigar to confound people in death. He had never been an easy man to get along with, and he was not going to be an easy corpse to find.

Stop it, Raina chided herself. *What am I doing, making light of the dead?*

Shamed, she continued to name the ones lost. It was a long list: thirty-nine clansmen and women as of this morning. Not counting the tied clansmen, those who farmed and worked their trades in the Hailhold but did not live in the roundhouse year-round and had not spoken oaths to defend it. Many of the tied clansmen who had died had been camped against the great fold's eastern wall. Part of the floor above had collapsed upon them. Poor souls. They had come to the roundhouse seeking protection during the war.

And then there were the Scarpemen. Raina's mouth tightened as she made her way toward the stable door. She was not going to count those. They had no business being here, had sworn oaths to a foreign clan. What was Mace thinking, to invite close to a thousand warriors and their families to stay indefinitely in the Hailhouse? True enough, Scarpe's own roundhouse had been destroyed by fire, but let them build a new one — and stay within the Scarpehold while they did it.

Scarpe losses during the Sundering had been high. Many had taken to camping in the old grain store that lay hard against the eastern wall. The bell-shaped structure had been letting in rainwater for years, and the mortar was black and rotted. When the guidestone exploded, the walls and ceiling had caved in. Children had died; and perhaps if she looked deep enough inside herself she could find some sympathy for them.

But today she wasn't going to try. Nodding her farewell to the new stablemaster, Cyril Blunt, she left the old dairy shed that was being used as a temporary stable. The cold of outside shocked her. Strange unseasonable winds were blowing stormclouds west. A wet snow had begun to fall and already the pines around the greatcourt were dusted white. People had begun to whisper that when the guidestone had exploded it had blasted away spring along with the roundhouse's eastern wall. Normally Raina had no patience with such superstitious nonsense. But it *had* been unseasonably cold this past week, and if the gods could split a guidestone into a million separate pieces then they could surely rob a clanhold of its spring.

Raina Blackhail, take ahold of yourself. There are already enough doomsayers in this roundhouse. We don't need one more.

Breaking into a run, she followed Jebb's draglines toward the hole in the eastern wall. The sound of work crews hammering and sawing assaulted her ears. Nothing was more frightening to a clansman than a breach in his roundhouse wall and the rebuild went on day and night. After sunset, huge oil-burning torches were lit and the night crews took over. The night crews wore pot helms with candles fixed above their visors with blobs of wax. It was a strange thing to see. Strange and good. Every able-bodied Hailsman and Hailwife in the roundhouse—either with an oath or without—worked toward the reconstruction in some way. Longhead, who for as long as Raina could remember had been head keep of the Hailhold, had come into his own. The man was a wonder. Even with an inch of flesh missing from his left leg.

He came toward her now, hobbling with the aid of a bent stick. Never a man to waste words on greeting he got straight to the point. "Raina. I need to know when I can start clearing the guidehouse. We can't seal the wall till it's done."

Raina took a breath to steady herself, then another to give herself more time. Dagro, her first husband, had taught her many things. *Think before you speak* was one of them. Seven days had passed since the Sundering. Seven days where the remains of the guidehouse had been left untouched. Raina could view the rubble from where she stood: a two-story heap of dust and jagged rock punctured by hunks of broken wall. Even though she'd seen it over a dozen times before, she still had to stop herself from reaching toward her measure of powdered guidestone for comfort. The Hailstone was dead.

As she looked on, the wind picked up, sending snow skirling and blowing plumes of dark gray powder from the rubble. Once men had treasured that powder; carried it into battle, borne it across continents, slipped it beneath their tongues as they spoke oaths, rubbed it on the bellies of their newborns, and sprinkled it over the closed eyes of their dead. It had been used as sparingly as gold. Now it was blowing in the wind.

Yet Longhead was right. Something had to be done about it. But what? And who was left to decide?

Raina studied Longhead's face carefully. He was a man who had grown into his name, developing in his later years a high forehead and a long chin. Never married and seldom courted, he spent most of his time working alone and in silence. Raina wasn't even sure if Longhead was his first name or last, or some nickname he'd picked up along the way. She wasn't sure about much to do with the head keep, she realized. Including where his allegiances lay.

Looking into his bloodshot eyes she wondered if she detected some disapproval of her husband, Mace Blackhail. Above all else Longhead was a man who liked to get things done, and Mace's failure to reach a decision about the remains of the guidestone was preventing Longhead from completing the most important task in the clanhold: rebuilding the eastern wall. Part of Raina couldn't even blame Mace. He was clan *chief*, not clan guide. He guarded men's bodies, not their souls.

Inigar Stoop was dead, and he had neither trained nor picked a successor. So who was left to save them?

It was a question that kept Raina awake at night, sweating and turning in her bed. The gods had abandoned Blackhail, and there was no clan guide to call them back.

Had Inigar realized the depth of his failure as the first splinters from the guidestone punctured his heart? Raina thought it likely that he had, and she felt some measure of pity for him. He had been a difficult man and she had not liked him, but during the last few years of their acquaintance she had found him worthy of respect.

Aware that Longhead was still awaiting her response, Raina made a decision. Gesturing toward the remains of the guidehouse, she said, "I will speak with my husband in due course."

She could tell from the slight shrinking of his pupils that this answer did not satisfy him. She had chosen caution and spoken as a good wife, and she could see now he had expected more from her. He must have watched her this past week, she realized. Seen how she had taken charge of caring for the wounded, setting up a surgery in the dim and yeasty-smelling warmth of the oasthouse, and arranging to have potions, wound dressings and medicinal herbs brought in from every farmhouse within ten leagues. She had been the one to decide that the stables should be housed in the old dairy shed and that the horses be buried in the Wedge. When Anwyn had asked where the dispossessed Scarpemen should be housed, Raina had not deferred the decision to her husband; she was making arrangements for their shelter even now. The same with the relocation of the hayloft and a dozen other things. She had made all decisions herself.

The question of what to do about the remains of the guide-stone was different. She had no expertise here. No one did. And although she recognized Longhead's query as an opportunity to claim power, she did not want to gain it at the clan's expense. There were matters here too important for that. The future would be set by the stone. Whatever became of its remains would be remembered by every man, woman and child in this clan. History would record it, rival clans would judge it, and scholars and holymen would mull over its significance for a thousand years. Nothing less than the pride and future of Blackhail was at stake.

So no. She would not decide the Hailstone's fate single-handed, and if that disappointed Longhead then so be it. "Talk to me tomorrow," Raina said to him, taking her leave. "I'll know more then." Stepping smartly around a cord of logs, she left him staring at the back of her head.

She felt a little breathless as she entered the smoky dimness of the roundhouse. It took some getting used to, this business of wielding power.

Two skunks and a handful of raccoons had been spotted in the roundhouse this past week, and Raina noticed the scent of animal musk as she made her way through the ruined east hall. It was cold too, and air switched back and forth as the wind moved through the wall. Oh, they had tarped and timbered it, but the outside still got in.

How could it not? Seven days ago the Hailstone had

exploded and blown open the entire roundhouse. According to Hatty Hare, who had been up early, intending to ride out from the roundhouse to set traps, a giant fireball had rolled through the guide corridor and out along the stables. Hatty had been knocked off her feet. When she was found, three hours later, she was buried beneath a foot of dust and char. Ballic the Red, who'd been riding back from Duff's stovehouse when it happened, told a story of seeing a flash of silver lightning split the northern sky. Raina herself had seen the great mushroom cloud of dust rising from the guidehouse, heard the whirr and snap of timbers as chunks of stone flooring collapsed. The hole punched in the eastern wall wasn't that big really—about fifteen feet by twenty—yet the wall was three-feet-thick sandstone and the floor underneath had been unable to cope with the weight.

The roundhouse was still finding its level. Just last night part of the ceiling in the chief's chamber had collapsed. Water was coming in from somewhere—Longhead pronounced it likely to be a broken well system—and the lower chambers were knee-deep in sludge. Countless cracks throughout the roundhouse were spilling dust, and some were growing longer. Crews of workmen and women were shoring holes, shoveling debris and bailing water.

Here, in the destroyed east hall, child-sized hunks of sandstone still lay strewn across the floor. Strange smelt lines radiated outward from the hole, and not for the first time Raina fought the desire to reach out and touch them. Gods did not leave quietly, without a trace. These were their footprints, she decided, these lines that sparkled like black ice and attracted metal so strongly that anyone who walked through this chamber bearing a sword could feel it pull away from his skin. Raina's own maiden's helper, worn in a squirrel-fur sheath at her waist, *jumped* toward the wall as she passed the greatest concentration of lines.

Holding the knife against her hip, she made her way toward the entrance hall. Approaching the main stair, she spotted Jebb Onnacre, pig carcass still in tow, talking to Merritt Ganlow by the greatdoor. The stablehand was explaining how maggots were farmed. How the carcass needed to be exposed to the air for at least two days to enable flies to lay their eggs beneath the skin. The pig's carcass was then stowed somewhere warm and damp to encourage the eggs to hatch and maggots develop. Done right, and within a week the carcass would be a mass of squirming yellow worms. Poor Merritt, gods love her, was doing her best to look interested whilst trying not to breathe in the stench. Raina decided to rescue her.

"Laida needs the maggots to clean out the wounds," Jebb was saying, oblivious of the greenish tint spreading over Merritt's face. "Eat the pus, they do. Leave the living flesh."

"Merritt," Raina called. "Have you a moment?"

"Raina!" Merritt exclaimed, her voice almost hysterical with relief. "Just the person I was looking for."

Raina had never seen Merritt move so fast, and might have laughed out loud if it hadn't been for the look of mild hurt showing in Jebb's brown eyes.

"Jebb," she said quickly to divert him. "Can you go and see Anwyn when you're done? There's some heavy lifting she needs a hand with."

"Aye, lady." Jebb nodded, all hurt over Merritt's desertion forgotten. "I'll be sure *not* to tell her who sent me."

Raina did laugh then. She and Jebb were becoming co-conspirators, united in their mission to lighten the clan matron's workload. No one worked harder than Anwyn Bird, no one was up earlier or went to bed later, or did as much good for the clan. Gods help you, though, if you even *suggested* that she might need a helping hand. Raina had taken so many scoldings over the matter that she now left Anwyn to herself. Well, almost. Anwyn Bird was her dearest, oldest friend and she could not stand by and watch her work herself to the bone.

Merritt wrinkled her nose as Jebb dragged away the carcass. "We've taken a vote," she said to Raina, wasting no time. "The widows have decided to give up their hearth—but only for use by Hailsmen, mind. We won't have no Scarpes near the wall."

And so it continues. Raina took a deep breath, orienting herself to deal with this newly delivered problem. Dagro had once told her that in cities they had halls of learning where men could study ancient histories, languages, astronomy, mathematics and other wondrous things. He said it could take a decade to master a discipline. Raina had thought it rather long at the time. Right now she'd like to go there, and take all ten years to learn to be a chief.

I will be chief. Two months ago she had spoken those words out loud in the gameroom, and even though only two people in the clan had heard them—Anwyn Bird and Orwin Shank—it did not lessen their meaning. She had spoken treason against her husband and chief, and when she thought of it now her skin flushed with fear. Yet she could not and would not take it back.

Mace Blackhail was Dagro's foster son, brought from Scarpe as an eleven-year-old boy. Dagro's first wife, Norala, had been barren and a chief was always anxious to have sons. Yelma Scarpe, the Weasel chief, had sent him one. Raina had never liked him. She saw flaws in her new foster son that her husband had been blind to. Mace was secretive, he arranged for others to take the blame for his misdemeanors, and he had never given up being a Scarpe. Dagro saw it differently. To him Mace could do no wrong. Mace was the best young swordsman, the most promising strategist and a faithful son. That blindness had killed Dagro in the end. Mace Blackhail had planned the murder of his father and chief. Even now Raina did not know what happened that day in the Badlands, but two things were certain. Mace had ridden home from the slaughter and lied about the outcome, and one month later named himself chief.

She would not think about the other wrongs he had done. Not here, with Merritt Ganlow's sharp green eyes inspecting her. Think too long about that day in the Oldwood and everything she had worked for might come undone.

Making an effort, Raina said, "When I spoke with Biddie about using the widows' hearth to house clansmen I recall no talk of barring Scarpes."

"Well you wouldn't, Raina," Merritt replied, cool as milk, "as it was my idea to bar them."

Of course it was. Raina had known Merritt Ganlow for twenty years. Her husband, Meth, had shared a tent with Dagro on that last fateful longhunt, and the two men had been friends since childhood. Merritt had a sharp mind to go with her green eyes, and a prickly way about her. She had taken to widowhood with both zeal and resentment, and had made no secret of the fact that she disapproved of Raina's hasty marriage to Mace.

"You have a habit of putting me in a difficult position, Merritt Ganlow," Raina said to her.

"You have a habit of *being* in a difficult position, Raina Blackhail. All I do is point it out."

She was right, of course. The damage to the roundhouse meant that both Hailish families and Scarpe ones needed new places to stay. The widows' hearth was, in Raina's opinion, the finest hall in the entire building. Housed at the pinnacle of the great dome, it had half a dozen windows that let in light. Someone had painted the walls with yellow distemper and someone else had thought to lay wooden boards across the floor. It was a pretty chamber, airy and full of sunlight. Unlike any other room in this dour, lamp-lit place.

Take a hold of yourself, Raina warned herself. It was too late to do anything about where she lived now. The Blackhail roundhouse had been built for defense, not beauty, and she had known that from the moment she first spied its hard, drum-shaped walls all those years ago when riding across the Wedge on the journey from Dregg. What she needed to concentrate on now was space. Families had taken to setting down their bedrolls in corridors and storage areas, and lighting cookfires and oil lamps wherever they pleased.

Raina glanced around the great half-moon of the entrance hall. A scrawny boy was chasing an even scrawnier chicken up the stairs, two Scarpewives dressed in black tunics and black leather aprons were fussing around a vat full of potash and lye, a handful of tied Hailsmen had claimed the space under the stair as a gaming room and were lounging in a circle, downing flat ale and throwing dice. On either side of the greatdoor, burlap sacks stuffed with bedclothes, pots and pans and other household items had been stacked ten feet high against the wall.

It would not do. Merritt and her sisterhood of widows knew that too, and when Raina had approached them about giving up their hearth they had expressed willingness to do so. Only now, two days later, Merritt Ganlow had tied some strings to the deal.

"You like the thought of Scarpes in the widows' hearth as much as I do," Merritt said, her voice creeping higher. "The widows' wall used to mean something in this clan. You needed a bracelet of scarred flesh to stand there." Yanking up the sleeve of her work dress, Merritt thrust out her left wrist toward Raina. The widows' weals were plain to see. Ugly purple scars that would not be allowed to heal for a year. Every woman who lost a husband in Blackhail cut herself, scoring a circle around each wrist with a ritual knife known as a grieveblade. Raina had always thought it a barbaric practice, hailing back to the Time of the First Clans, yet when Dagro had died she had begun to understand it. The pain of cutting her flesh had been nothing—*nothing*—compared with losing Dagro. Strangely, it had helped. When the blood pumped from her veins and rolled around her wrists she had felt some measure of relief.

To Merritt she said, "You cannot blame Scarpe widows for not practicing the same rituals as we do. Their pain is still the same."

Merritt was contemptuous. "They *tattoo* the weals—dainty little lines inked in red. And they heal within a week. Then what? They're like bitches in heat. Run off and remarry so fast it's as if they never gave a damn for their first husbands all along. And I tell you another thing—"

"Hold your tongue," Raina hissed. She was shaking, frightened by how close she had come to slapping Merritt Ganlow. *He raped me!* she wanted to scream. *That's why I remarried so fast. Mace Blackhail took me by force and told everyone I agreed to it. They believed him. And if I hadn't married him I would have forsaken my reputation and my place in this clan.*

Merritt glanced around nervously. Too late she realized her raised voice had drawn unwanted attention her way. The men under the stairs had halted their gaming and were looking with some interest at the head widow and the chief's wife. The two Scarpewives, pale women with dyed-black hair and lips stained red with mercury, stared at Merritt and Raina with unconcealed dislike.

"Open up! Warriors returning."

Three hard, deep raps against the greatdoor followed the shouted command, and all attention shifted from Raina and Merritt to the half-ton of force-hardened rootwood that barred the Hailhold's primary entrance. Straightaway, things started happening. Mull Shank appeared out of nowhere and together he and one of the young Tanner boys began lifting the iron bars from their cradles. The cry "Warriors returning!" was relayed through the entrance hall and up the stairs toward the great-hearth. Anwyn Bird, who had the ears of a deer and the uncanny ability to know exactly when her strong beer was needed, emerged from the kitchen cellar, hoisting a two-gallon keg on her shoulder.

As the door was pushed back on its greased track, Raina turned to Merritt Ganlow. "So you're set on opening the widows' hearth solely to Hailsmen?"

Merritt's face had slackened somewhat during all the excite-ment, and for a moment Raina hoped that it might stay that way. It wasn't to be. Merritt's mouth tightened and her chin came up. "I'm sorry, Raina, but I won't change my mind. This is the *Hail*hold, not the Scarpehold, and if someone doesn't make a stand against it we'll all be wearing the weasel pelts before we're through." With that, the clan widow stalked away, staring down the two Scarpewives as she passed them.

She was bold and she was right. Raina raised a hand and rubbed her temples. Her head was beginning to hurt. Of course she agreed with Merritt. How could she not? As she stood here waiting to see who would come through the door, she could smell the foreign cookery, see the weasel-pelted Scarpe war-riors gathering to discover who had returned and why, and feel the oily smoke from their pine-resin cook stoves passing through the membranes in her lungs. Now was not the time to take action against them, though. Why couldn't Merritt see that? The Hailstone had exploded, taking the heart of the clan with it. The Hailhouse was no longer secure. There was no clan guide. Blackhail was at war with Bludd and Dhoone, and right now, like it or not, most warriors were loyal to their chief.

Realizing she was pressing her head when she should have been rubbing, Raina flung her arm up and out. If Dagro had taught her one thing it was caution, and caution told her to wait for a better time to show her hand. It was all very well for Merritt to play at making a stand. In reality she wouldn't have the nerve to repeat to Mace what she just said. No, she was banking on Raina Blackhail doing the dirty work for her, deliv-ering a nasty little message to the chief.

Well I won't do it, dammit. Raina stamped her foot, crunching debris from the Sundering beneath the heel of her boot. Now all she had to do was come up with a plan. Surely the tenth one she'd needed this week.

Raina's mind slid from her problems as she saw who walked through the doorway. Arlec Byce and Cleg Trotter, two of the original Ganmiddich eleven who had held the Crab Gate for over a week whilst the Crab chief returned from Croser, entered the roundhouse. Saddle-bowed and weary, the two men shied back when the smoke from the cookfires reached them. Arlec's twin brother had been dead for many months, killed by the Bludd chief himself on Bannen Field, and Raina still wasn't used to seeing him alone. He was wearing his betrothed's token around his throat: a gray wool scarf, knitted lovingly if rather hastily, by Biddie Byce. When Arlec noticed Raina's gaze upon him, he bowed his head wearily and said, "Lady."

Raina smiled gently at him, knowing better than to inquire at his return. Whatever news he held must be first revealed to his chief. Ullic Scarpe and Wracker Fox, two of the Scarpe warriors crowding around the door, knew no such discretion and began blasting the pair with questions. Big Cleg Trotter, son to gentle-mannered Paille and the first-ever warrior in his family, had no experience with interrogation and after frowning several times and trying unsuccessfully to ignore the Scarpes, he blurted it all out.

"Drey sent us with word. He needs reinforcements. Ganmiddich's under attack—by city men!"

An excited murmur passed through and then beyond the room. Within exactly a minute, Raina reckoned, everyone in the entire roundhouse would know the news. Ganmiddich under attack by city men. Would the ill tidings never stop?

"Arlec. Cleg."

Gooseflesh erupted on Raina's arms and shoulders at the sound of her husband's voice. Mace Blackhail, the Hail Wolf, had emerged from his parley in the greathearth. Dressed in a Scarpe-dyed suede tunic embossed with wolf fangs, he took the stone stairs swiftly, without sound. Already aware that the chance for secrecy had been lost, he fired off his first question.

"Which city?"

Cleg swallowed nervously. Arlec spoke. "Spire Vanis."

A murmur of fear darkened the room. This was not the answer any had expected. It was no secret that Ille Glaive, the City on the Lake, had long had its eye on the wealthy border clans, but Spire Vanis? What were the Spire King and his army doing so far north?

If Mace was surprised he did not show it. Nodding once he said, "And their numbers?"

Cleg swallowed again. His lore was the red-footed goose and he wore what might have been one of their desiccated feet, hooked through a ring in his ear. "We counted eleven thousand before we left."

This time Mace raised a pale hand, halting the murmur before it started. He was wearing the Clansword, Raina realized, the weapon forged from the crown of the Dhoone kings. Someone had made him a scabbard for it; a finely glazed strip of silverized leather with a she-wolf tail trailing from its tip. "We have five hundred warriors there. Ax- and hammermen. Ten dozen bowmen. And there is the Crab's own army. Once rallied he can command two thousand."

Arlec nodded. "And there's a half-dozen Crosermen who once wore the cowls."

Cowlmen. Raina shivered; she was not the only one to do so. Cowlmen were legend in the clanholds, and the border clans east of Ganmiddich were known to have the best of them. Trained assassins, siegebreakers, crack bowmen, spies, and masters of concealment, they were named after the gray hooded cloaks they swathed themselves in on their missions. As far as Raina knew Blackhail had none of them. The big northern giants—Blackhail, Dhoone and Bludd—traditionally preferred might over ambushes, snares and assassinations. Smaller border clans could not afford the luxury of clannish pride. They were threatened by rival clans to the north and the Mountain Cities to the south, and had fewer numbers with which to defend themselves. Cowlmen were their way of evening the odds. According to the ranger Angus Lok their numbers were in decline and few young men were being trained to the cowl. Yet strangely enough this only added to their mystique. One glance around this hallway was enough to see that.

"Good," Mace said. "So the Crab heeded my advice."

Scarpemen and Hailsmen nodded judiciously, and Raina could tell that implication of Mace's remark—that he had been the one to advise Crab Ganmiddich to bring cowlmen into his house—sat well with them. Their chief was always thinking that extra step ahead.

For some reason Mace chose to look Raina's way just then. *Wife*, he mouthed for her eyes alone. She met his gaze, but it cost her. Instantly information passed between them. He was aware that she alone knew that everything he said here was a manipulation of the truth, including his remark about the cowlmen. He had never told any such thing to the Crab chief. How could he? They had never met man-to-man. To counter this damning knowledge, he simply let his memories of what happened in the Oldwood dwell for the briefest moment in his eyes. It was a weapon she had no defense against, that pleasure he took in what he had done to her, and she was first to break contact and look away. Every time they shared a moment like this it robbed a part of her soul.

He knew it too, and it was as if whatever vitality she lost *he* gained. Turning back to Arlec he asked, "And the repairs to the Crab Gate?"

"Done. But the riverwall needs—"

"The riverwall is of little consequence," Mace said, cutting the young hammerman short. "Drey and the Crab are sitting well. They should be able to hold out until we arrive with more men."

Several things happened to Arlec's face as he listened to his chief speak. First he had wanted to interrupt him, Raina was sure of it, point out that his chief was mistaken, and that the riverwall did indeed count and here was why. Second, he had begun to nod in agreement when Mace said that Drey and the Crab were currently secure. And third, his cheeks had flushed with excitement at the words *"until we arrive with more men."*

All around the entrance hall men uncradled their hammers and axes and unsheathed their swords. Someone—perhaps old and crotchety Turby Flapp—cried, "Kill Spire!" and then the thudding began. Hammer and ax butts were struck against the walls and floor with force. After a few seconds all the impacts fell in time and a single, thumping war charge echoed through the Hailhouse.

"Kill Spire! Kill Spire! Kill Spire!"

Feeling weak at the knees, Raina withdrew the few steps necessary to steady herself against the endwall. She had seen a similar thing happen six months ago, when Raif and Drey Sevrance had returned from the Badlands and the Dog Lord had been blamed for Dagro's death. *Kill Bludd!* they had cried then. A lot of good that had done, plunging the clan into war with Dhoone and Bludd.

Yet she could not deny that they needed this. For a week she had looked into the eyes of men and women who were lost. The Hailstone lay shattered and in pieces, and without it they were set adrift. Raina felt it, too, that feeling of no longer being anchored to earth and clan. The gods no longer lived here; the implications were too much to comprehend.

Here, though, was something Hailsmen *could* understand: war. Joy and rage and comradeship had come alive in this room. Mace Blackhail had turned a situation that was cause for despair into a rallying cry for the clan. It was, Raina realized with deeply mixed feelings, something she could learn from. Her husband had flawless instincts as a warlord.

Already the makeshift war parley was starting to head upstairs to the primary hall in the roundhouse, the warriors' chamber known as the greathearth. Bev Shank and his father Orwin passed Raina with barely a sideways glance. Orwin had his great bell-bladed war ax out and his swollen, arthritic knuckle joints were stretched white where they grasped the limewood handle. His oldest son, Mull, was at Ganmiddich. Ullic Scarpe, one of the many cousins of the Weasel chief, was brandishing his ugly black-tinted broadsword, making mock swipes at his companion Wracker Fox. Both men sneered at Raina, pushing closer to her than was necessary as they made their way toward the stairs.

Meanwhile, Ballic the Red was quietly pulling Arlec Byce and Cleg Trotter to one side and Raina could tell from the brevity of Ballic's expression that the master bowman had taken it up himself to explain to them the fate of the

Hailstone. Raina was glad they would hear the news from a decent man.

Mace was in the midst of a huddle of hammermen intent on escorting their chief up the stairs. As he drew closer Raina steeled herself. "Husband," she said. "If I might have a word."

He always marked her, even when his attention was pulled a dozen ways. His head whipped around and his strange yellow-brown eyes pinned her. "Corbie. Derric," he said to the two nearest men. "Go on without me. The war party will leave within five days."

Dent-headed Corbie Meese nodded. "Aye, Chief." He might have been a bit disappointed by Mace's schedule, but he was a better man than to show it. Bowing his head respectfully to Raina, he vaulted up the stairs.

Taking her cue from Longhead and Merritt—two people who never wasted an unnecessary word—Raina said to Mace, "Longhead awaits your decision on the guidestone. The remains must be laid to rest with proper ceremony."

"It is not your concern, wife. You are not guide or chief."

"Something must be done. Now. There's a scrap heap out there that used to be the Hailstone. How can we regain our dignity as a clan if we are forced to look at it every day?"

"Enough," Mace hissed. "I have made plans. Longhead will hear of them when I choose to tell him."

His words were like a slap to her face. He had made arrangements for the stone in secret, robbing her of the chance to have her say.

Detecting the heat in her cheeks Mace stretched his lips. "You forget your place."

She did, he was right. It was something she had to be careful of, that overreaching of her authority. A chief's wife had no dealings with the gods. It had been a mistake to claim the guidestone as her responsibility: it revealed ambition. Yet how could she not care? This was her clan and she was one of the very few people within it who could see beyond Mace Blackhail and his self-promoting war. A quick glance at her husband's face helped sharpen her mind. She could not give him too long to think.

"Will you at least do me the favor of letting Longhead know

you have the matter in hand? That way he might stop pestering me. I'm run ragged as it is." Raina waited.

Mace's expression slackened, the careful scrutiny of moments earlier withdrawn. Not forgotten. Withdrawn.

"I'll send a boy."

Raina nodded. Instinct told her she needed to put more distance between herself and the guidestone. "About the rehousing. There's close to two hundred families camping in the hallways, and more are arriving every day. It's becoming dangerous. Only last night a Scarpewife knocked over an unguarded lamp outside the great hearth. If Bev Shank hadn't acted as quickly as he did we would have had a fire on our hands."

Mace shrugged. "I'm sure you have it all in hand. The widows will doubtless give up the wall."

He watches you, you know. Little mice with weasels' tails. Bessie Flapp's words echoed in Raina's mind. How did Mace know what she had asked the widows in confidence? Unsettled, she pushed ahead. "The widows have agreed to give up their hearth for ninety days."

"You have done well, Raina."

The words sounded like genuine praise, and she could not stop herself from glancing around to see if anyone else was within earshot.

Mace did not miss her reaction or its implications, and muscles in his lean face contracted. "And will Scarpe families be allowed to stay there?"

Here it was. And yet again he was already ahead of her. She would not think of that now, though. Would not wonder who amongst the widows had turned against her and was whispering secrets to the chief. *I must learn from him*, she told herself before speaking her first lie.

"That was never an issue. We both know it wouldn't be wise to house Hails and Scarpes so closely. That's why I decided to let the tied Hailsmen use the widows' hearth. The Scarpes can have my quarters. There's a lot of unused space there—dressing rooms and sewing rooms and whatnots—it should be enough to keep them out of the halls."

Mace looked at her for a long time. She was certain that he

knew she was lying, but equally certain he would do nothing about it. What she had not imagined was that he would reach out and touch her.

"You'd make a fine chief," he whispered softly in her ear before he left to plan the war.

THREE

South of the Dhoonehouse

Rain trickled down the Dog Lord's collar, found a groove in his wrinkled old back and rode it all the way down to his smallclothes. Damn! He hated the rain. If there was anything worse than wet wool next to your vitals then Vaylo Bludd had not encountered it. Itched, it did. Felt as if an army of fleas were holding a tourney down there— and an underwater one at that. Not to mention the smell. Vaylo had never harbored much love for cragsmen—every clan chief he knew had trouble collecting the lamb tolls—yet he had to give them this much: Wet wool was surely one of the foulest-smelling concoctions ever cooked up by the Stone Gods, and every cragsman in the clanholds had to live with it.

Hunching his shoulders against the rain, the Dog Lord picked up his pace. The field they were crossing had a slight cant to it that Vaylo felt keenly in his knees. It was growing dark now, and the bit of wind that had been ragging them all day had finally shown its teeth. Sharp gusts sent rain sheeting into their faces. Nan had her hood pulled all the way down to her eyebrows. The color had drained from her lips, and her eyelashes were spiky with raindrops. The bairns were miserable. Pasha was hugging herself, teeth chattering uncontrollably as she rubbed her arms for warmth. Aaron hadn't said a word in over an hour. Vaylo didn't like the way he was shaking. Hammie didn't like it either, and had tried several times to pick up the bairn and carry him. Little Aaron was having none of it, and squirmed free from his grip every time.

Hammie himself seemed the least ill-affected by the storm,

and without gloves, oiled top cloak or hood there was no doubt he was bearing the worst of it. He was a Faa man of course, that had to have something to do with it. Faa men were stoics. If there was an unpleasant task to be done they'd simply tuck their heads low and get on with it. Slop buckets hauled up from the pit cells, elk fat rendered for soap, boils lanced, drains unblocked, holes dug: Faa men did it all. And none of them were complainers.

Vaylo sighed heavily. He'd been chief to so many good men. And where had he led them? Men were dead. Children were dead. Clan Bludd lay broken and in pieces. Gods knew they had deserved a better chief.

Stop it, Vaylo warned himself. What was done was done. Dwelling in the past was an indulgence best left to widows and old men. A chief could not afford to live there: the price exacted by self-reproach was too high. Oh, he knew he had done many things wrong—doubtless somewhere some god was keeping a list—but he could not let that stop him. This small band of four was his clan now. Nan, Hammie, the bairns. They were a short distance southwest of the Dhoonehouse, traveling through territory of an enemy clan, without horses, food or adequate clothing, and with only one good knife between them. The Dog Lord had no time to waste on regrets.

What had Ockish Bull said that spring when they lost ten hammermen in the mother of all fuckups that became known as Bull's Brawl? *Mistakes have been made. Gods willing I'll make no more.*

Vaylo grinned. Thinking about Ockish Bull always did that to him. Who else would have dared to insult the memory of Ewan Blackhail in a Hailish stovehouse filled with Hailsman? Who else would have had the jaw?

"Pasha. Aaron." Opening up his greatcloak, Vaylo beckoned his grandchildren to him. They wouldn't come at first so he had to bully them. The sight of their granda baring his teeth usually made them roll their eyes and groan, but tonight the bairns were subdued. They came to him, but more out of habit than anything else. Tucking a child under each arm, he hiked up the slope. Water squeezed out from the bairns' woolens as he hugged them.

Vaylo cursed their father, silently and with feeling. Pengo's treachery had led them to this. Pengo Bludd had been so eager for any kind of fight that he'd deserted the Dhoonehouse, taking everyone he could bribe, sweet-talk, or bully along with him. Only forty had remained behind, and a holding the size of Dhoone could not be defended by such numbers. When the attack came they'd had no warning. There'd been no one to spare for long watches. Robbie Dun Dhoone and his army of blue cloaks must have been laughing as they broke down the door.

The Dog Lord let the bile rise to his mouth, and then jabbed it against his aching teeth with his tongue. Where had Pengo been when the Thorn King came a-knocking? Riding south most likely, his nostrils twitching to the smell of city men's blood. The damn fool had chosen the wrong war! Thought he'd engage the Spire Lord's army in the south rather than pro-tect Bludd's holdings in the north. *Well I hope he finds some measure of glory fighting city men for he'll get nothing save a swift death from me.*

The anger warmed but did not comfort Vaylo. The rain kept coming, running down his face and streaming off the tip of his nose. It was hard to see, even harder to know what to do. As best he could tell they were crossing an overgrown graze. Stalks of gray, winter-rotted oats slapped his legs, and waist-high thistle burrs kept snagging his cloak. Everything was wet and getting wetter. Underfoot, the rich blue-black soil of eastern Dhoone was rapidly turning to mud. Vaylo swore he could hear the mos-quitoes hatching. The night had that smell to it; the soggy aliveness of spring.

The hill graze was one of dozens they had crossed since escaping the Dhoonehouse. The land east of the Dhoone was mostly grassland. Cattle and horses grazed here in summer and spring, sheep year-round. Yet numbers had dwindled, and Vaylo hadn't spotted a single black head in two days. Livestock had been seized. Dhoone's horses were now roasting over Bludd fires and swelling Bludd breeding stock. Their sheep were crop-ping grass in the Bluddhold. Without animals to care for, Dhoone farmers had either fled or were lying low until better times. And now that a Dhoone sat upon the Dhooneseat once more, those better times were about to start.

Word was already being spread. Twice now the Dog Lord and his small company had been forced to drop belly-down into the wet grass as mounted Dhoone warriors rode past. Both times Vaylo had spoken a prayer. *Please gods, let them not be man hunters.*

He would take all their lives—Aaron, Pasha, Nan, Hammie and then himself—rather than risk being dragged back to the Dhoonehouse and the man who ruled there. The Dog Lord had looked into the eyes of Robbie Dun Dhoone and seen what absences lay there. The Thorn King had jaw, no doubt about it, but it wasn't the hot, reckless jaw of Thrago HalfBludd or the muleheaded jaw of Ockish Bull. It was a cold and calculating jaw. The sort of thing that would drive a boy to pull the legs off a cockroach just to see what it would do, and a grown man to use others and then discard them like gnawed bones.

Vaylo shivered, not from cold but sheer relief. Robbie Dun Dhoone had not laid hands on his grandchildren. Thank the sweet gods for that.

It had been a hard five days since they'd escaped, no doubt about it. After the Dhoonehouse had been sacked their little party of five had been forced to retreat to the Tomb of the Dhoone Princes. Right then, with Robbie Dun Dhoone beating down the door, Vaylo wouldn't have given a tin spoon for their chances. Dhoone had retaken Dhoone, and Bludd—the clan who'd been squatting in the Dhoonehouse for half a year—had to be made to pay for their presumption. Robbie had ordered the *slaughter*, not capture, of Bluddsmen. Not a moment too soon, Pasha had located the secret entrance that led to the tunnels beneath Dhoone. *Mole holes*, Angus Lok had called them. Vaylo had not believed they existed.

Yet another thing he was roundly wrong about. The network of tunnels had deposited them in a dense copse of crabgrass and black willow, at the bank of a muddy creek just one league southeast of the Dhoonehouse. It had taken most of the night to travel the dark, underworld passages of Dhoone.

The ways beneath the roundhouse gave Vaylo chills. They were old and haunted, and they smelled of things other than clan. In some places the stonework was so rotted that you could poke it with your finger and watch as it dimpled like sponge.

Tree roots, pale and glistening like intensities, pushed through the walls and ran along the floor and ceilings in hard ridges. Hammie had to be careful with the makeshift torch he had fashioned, for most of the rootwood was long dead and the roots hairs crisped to black the instant they felt the flame. Some of the tunnel walls had collapsed, and they had been forced to backtrack several times. Originally they had been heading north, but collapsed tunnels drove them east and then south. Once, after pushing their way through a narrow opening, they had entered a cave used by hibernating bats. Every footfall raised clouds of chalky guano that smelled so caustic it brought tears to Vaylo's eyes. The Dog Lord had liked it not one bit, but he had been a leader of men for too long to let his discomfort show. Speaking a command to his dogs, he had sent the five beasts ranging ahead in search of a way out.

Nan had been a pillar of strength that night. Her calmness was catching. The way she held her head just so, her light way of walking, and the level tone of her voice created an atmosphere that affected everyone. The bairns had been as good as lambs; quiet, most definitely frightened, but so confident in Nan's calmness and their granda's ability to fix any problem — whether it be a broken top in the nursery or armed men in the hallway — that they never once lagged or showed fear. *Good Bludd stock there*, Vaylo thought with some pride.

If he were to be honest, the night in the tunnels had gone hardest on him. In his fifty-three-year life he had experienced many kinds of weariness, but nothing matched what he'd felt during the escape. Winning a battle made you feel immortal, capable of chasing down every last enemy and then dancing and drinking till dawn. Losing one crushed your soul. And for a man who had already sold half of that soul to the devil, that didn't leave very much left.

By the time the dogs finally found an exit and came running back to their master, Vaylo had fallen into a kind of dream walking. One foot in front of the other, and to hell with the pain in his knees and heart. His vision had shrunk to two separate circles that he'd long stopped attempting to force into a single view. To him it looked as if there were ten dogs milling around his legs, not five.

The dogs were scratched up and caked in mud. Two were soaking, and the big black-and-orange bitch had a gash on her left hind leg that was oozing blood. Yet devotion burned clear in their eyes. Their master had lost his human pack and been forced to flee the den, and now their sole desire was to ease his suffering. When Vaylo had finally set them a task they'd torn through the tunnels in their eagerness to complete it. They wanted so badly to please him.

Realizing this, the Dog Lord had made an effort. Forcing his vision to trueness and bringing his weight to bear on the knee that pained him the least, he patted and roughed up the huge, dark beasts. "Good dogs," he repeated over and over again as he took time to give attention to each of them. Relief made the dogs act like puppies, rolling on their bellies and baring their necks, all the while mewing needily like kittens. The youngest, a muscular black with a docked tail, dribbled urine onto a bed of white mushrooms that had sprouted in the darkness of the tunnel floor. *No one will be eating those in a hurry*, Vaylo thought dryly.

Standing upright, he had addressed the wolf dog. "Lead the way."

They all got caked in mud as it turned out. The dogs had found a tunnel rising to ground level—one that looked as if it had been dug by midgets—and everyone had been forced to drop to their bellies and shin through the icy sludge. Rainwater sluicing along the tunnel floor had mixed with the clay soil to produce a kind of potter's slip that poured into every nook and cranny and then set like cement against your skin.

For some time Vaylo had been aware that his small party was heading south, and he was dreading the journey ahead. When the wolf dog finally broke through to the surface, he was dead tired. Dawn light, filtering through an opening choked with willow and crabgrass, made his eyes sting. Despite everything his spirits lifted. His clan of four was free and unharmed, and now he could spend his days making those who had wronged him pay. That was when he saw the stone ring framing the exit portal. Hairs across his back rose upright, and even before he could name his fear the words from the Bludd boast sounded along the nerve connecting his spine to his brain.

We are Clan Bludd, chosen by the Stone Gods to guard their borders. Death is our companion. A life long-lived is our reward.

Part of him had known all along that the tunnels under Dhoone had not been built by clan. A chief might dig a hole in the earth as a last-ditch escape route, but no leader of clansmen would risk the scorn of his warriors by constructing a network of mole holes so extensive that a man could pass from one end of a clanhold to the other while never seeing the good light of day. Such measures ran too close to caution for that. No. These tunnels had been dug by minds that thought differently than clan. Minds that valued survival above all else. These tunnels had been dug by the Sull.

The exit had been braced with an oxeye of blue marble deeply veined with eggshell quartz. Unlike most of the other stone bracings in the tunnels this one had not crumbled or rotted. The marble had resisted the restless trembling of the earth and the stresses of hard frosts and sudden thaws. Its surface was lightly pocked with corrosion and lichen had begun to sink its root anchors into the stone, yet all of its massive quarter-circle segments had held their alignment so truly that the ring they formed was as perfect as the sun.

Or the moon. For there it was, etched deep into the hard blue stone, the moon in all its phases. Crescent, gibbous, full, and the new moon, which was no moon at all, simply a dark uncarved space marking the beginning of the cycle. That space haunted Vaylo even now, three days later. It said something about the Sull, he'd decided, something about their absolute foreignness to clan. He wasn't a man given to sudden fancies but that space, that stark *absence* in the design, spoke of hell and places unknown, and the darkness Ockish Bull had said existed before time.

The Dog Lord felt a shiver coming and shook it off with a sharp snap of his head. Damn Robbie Dun Dhoone and his high-stepping blue cloaks. Their roundhouse was stuffed with ghosts. Vaylo blew two lungs' worth of air through his lips. Who was he fooling? The entire Northern Territories were stuffed with ghosts. You couldn't build a doghouse or an outhouse without feeling the hard chunk of cut stone hitting your shovel the minute you began to dig out the ground. The Sull had been there first. They had built atop every mountain, hill and head-land, upon every lakeshore, riverbank and creek bed, and in every mossy hollow, barren canyon and dank cave.

Vaylo remembered his favorite fishing hole in the Bluddhold, a green pond no wider than a man could spit. It was set so deep amongst the basswoods and sword ferns that if you didn't keep your eyes lively you'd miss it. He'd stumbled upon it after old Gullit Bludd had given him a beating for some mis-demeanor or other, and cautioned his bastard son not to show his face in the roundhouse for a week. By the fourth day, Vaylo recalled, he was so hungry he was spearing wood frogs with his boy's sword and tearing tree oysters from rotten stumps. That was when he found it, the fishing hole. He was looking up at the canopy, tracking some scrawny squirrel that he hadn't a snail's chance in a salt barrel of ever catching, when he walked straight into the water. Icy cold and clear as emeralds, it was so beautiful that even a boy of nine couldn't help but catch his breath and admire it.

Of course, he did what every nine-year-old would do when faced with a body of still water; he found some pebbles and skimmed them. As the pebbles skipped over the surface they created ripples that attracted silver minnows in search of flies. "Fish!" Vaylo had shouted triumphantly, and promptly set about whittling a fallen branch into a rod. As he worked he invented fancies about the fishing hole in his head. He was the first living man to ever stand here, the first to blaze a trail through the impenetrable tangle of Direwood, the first to pull a two-stone trout from the hole's icy depths. When he got to the tricky part where he had to notch the stick to run a line, Vaylo was so absorbed in his daydreams that he lost his grip on the knife.

He'd been sitting on some bit of rock close to the water's edge, and the blade plonked into the silt at his feet. As he dug fingers into the sand to grasp the hilt, his gaze slid between his legs and onto the face of rock. Something was engraved in the stone. A crescent moon, cut so deep that a lizard had laid her milky eggs in the hollow, stood above a single line of script. Vaylo was no scholar, and he wouldn't learn to read until many years later, but he'd seen enough clannish writings to know that the script wasn't clan.

The quarter-moon was a sign of the Sull.

Vaylo recalled feeling many things at that moment: excitement that he had stumbled upon a site once held by the Sull; fear that some kind of danger still lurked in this place; and disappointment that he had not been the great discoverer after all. The Sull had been here first.

It had been a lesson that had stayed with him for close on fifty years. Clan had gained land at the expense of the Sull, and a chief's job was to insure they didn't get it back.

"Granda! Your nose is red!" Pasha's high, excited voice cut through Vaylo's thoughts, forcing him in to the present. Where he most definitely belonged.

"Granda's nose looks like beetroot," Aaron chimed.

"There's only one thing for it," Vaylo proclaimed loudly, glancing from one pale and shivering grandchild to the next. "Last man to the top smells like cow fart."

Pushing Pasha and Aaron from him, Vaylo charged up the slope. They had been heading along a creek bed that ran along the base of a small hill, and the first part of the climb was steep. His knees creaked, a muscle in his left thigh started cramping, and all seventeen of his remaining teeth gave him grief as blood pumped at pressure through the roots. But dammit he was going to make it to the top of that hill. Behind him, he heard the bairns' feet thumping as they scrambled to catch up. Pasha called after her granda to wait, while little Aaron squealed excitedly at Hammie Faa to get moving. Vaylo laughed out loud at the thought of Hammie being dragged into the race, then wished immediately he hadn't. Gods, but he was old. Lungs as holey as his had no business getting involved in anything faster than a brisk walk. And exactly which Stone God was responsible for making a man want to do a fool thing like win a race? Unable to decide whose domain it fell under, he cursed all nine just to be safe.

Pasha had the long legs of a colt and the sheer bloody-mindedness of a Bludd chief, and within half a minute she had passed him. Vaylo huffed and puffed and *willed* himself up the hill. Rain blasted his face, and the wind sent slimy, partially decomposed leaves splattering against his chest like bugs. It was getting so dark that he could barely see his feet. Just as he

thought he might at least come in second, his grandson over-
took him on the final stretch. Windmilling his arms and
whooping with delight, Aaron streaked ahead. The Dog Lord
growled at him as he passed.

"Granda!" Pasha shouted once she'd reached the top. "You'd
better hurry. Hammie's gaining."

That won't do at all, Vaylo thought. It was one thing to lose
a race to a young whippet of a girl, another thing entirely to lose
one to a chunky spearman with two left feet whose favorite
saying was "A thorough job beats a fast one every time."

Clamping his jaw together, the Dog Lord reached for his
final reserve of strength. He found himself remembering the
days he'd spent living at the fishing hole. The rod had worked
like a charm. And with the fish nipping like puppies and a
place to call his own he'd decided to stay away two weeks not
one. *That* would show his father. When his son failed to return
after the first week, Gullit Bludd would be beside himself with
worry. Vaylo imagined the scene of his homecoming over and
over again during the long nights camped out in the forest; his
father's gruff but relieved welcome, the playful cuffing, the
break in Gullit's voice as he said, "You had me worried for a
while there, son." It had felt so real that the morning he
returned to the Bluddhold, Vaylo had actually expected his
father to be standing on the redcourt, waiting for him.

Only Gullit Bludd had not been at the roundhouse that day.
He'd taken his two legitimate sons on a longhunt four nights
back, and had left no message for his youngest son, the bastard.

The old hurt burned within Vaylo like fuel. Once a bastard,
always a bastard. *Well, just watch and see what a bastard can do.*

Fists pumping, Vaylo attacked the final stretch of the hill as
if it were an enemy that needed beating. Hammie had to be
thirty years younger than he was, yet the Dog Lord refused to
think about it. Jaw was what counted in the clanholds, and no
one had ever had more of it than the man who had stolen the
Dhoonestone from Dhoone. One final push and the hill was
his. Hammie tried to keep pace but his short, sturdy legs were
designed for distance not speed, and he fell back when Vaylo
topped the hill.

As the bairns rushed forward to cheer them, both men

shared a long, weary "What the hell were we thinking?" glance before dropping to their knees. Hammie began to wheeze like a goat. The Dog Lord felt a familiar pain in his chest, but ignored it.

"Hammie smells like cow fart!" Aaron dove on top of the spearman, propelling him further into the mud. Laughing so hard she snorted, Pasha ran to join her brother and soon both children were jumping up and down on Hammie's belly, roaring with laughter and yelling "Cow Faa—rt!" at the top of their lungs.

Hammie endured this for about as long as any man could before firmly setting the bairns on their feet. Wiping himself off he rose with some dignity. "Seeing as I haven't had a bath in over a month, I'd say that cow fart might just be an improvement."

This statement started the bairns giggling all over again. Vaylo was concerned about the noise, but glad in his heart to hear it. Pasha and Aaron deserved this. They'd been as good as gold these past five days, and quieter than was good for any child.

"Hush now, little ones." Nan's voice was gentle but firm. She hadn't taken part in the race, and only now reached the top of the hill. The wind had dragged back her hood and sheened her face with rain. "It's late and we must be quiet."

Vaylo nodded his thanks. Somehow Nan knew that he couldn't bring himself to discipline his grandchildren just then. She was the smartest one of the lot of them, and the Dog Lord was glad she was his.

As he held out his hand so she could pull him up, he heard a low howl echoing from the south. Wolf dog. Even though he had heard the call of his oldest, best-loved dog countless times before, Vaylo felt a loosening of muscle in his gut. Some sounds bypassed a man's thoughts and entered his body directly, and the call of a wolf was one of them.

All five dogs had been ranging wide throughout the evening, forming a protective circle around the party and hunting small game for food. Just before sunset the oldest bitch had brought Vaylo a jackrabbit still in its winter whites. Vaylo had no appetite for raw meat and judged it unsafe to light a cookfire, yet he had taken the rabbit from her jaw all the same. A dog giving up its prey for you was no small thing, and only a fool didn't understand that.

The dogs were trained for silent patrol, and although all had been taught to alert their master to danger by issuing a single piercing howl, only the wolf dog ever sounded. The other four always deferred to him.

"Everyone down," Vaylo hissed, cursing himself for his stupidity. Thanks to him they were now standing on the most exposed point for leagues—and not a damn tree in sight. At least there was no moon to light them.

The mud smelled sweetly rotten, and when Vaylo scooped up a handful he could feel the dead matter in it. Beetle legs and stalks of grass scratched his skin as he smeared it across his face, blacking himself out against the night. Nan didn't waste a moment with feminine fussing and swiftly did the same to herself. Hammie was closest to the bairns and saw to them before masking himself. Both children submitted soundlessly to Hammie's ministrations, but Vaylo knew they were scared. Tears welled in Aaron's eyes.

Aaron was his only living grandson. Just seven years old, the boy had lost his mother and his homeland. And he hadn't seen his father in thirty days. Remembering his own tears as a boy— tears of hurt and loneliness and rage—Vaylo reached over and laid a hand on Aaron's back. The Dog Lord had spent thirteen years growing to manhood in Gullit's house, and not once during that time had anyone touched him with simple kindness. He was the chief's bastard son, begotten during the drunken revelry of Spring Fair, his mother rumored to be the lowest of the low: a common stovehouse whore. The only affection he'd received was from his father's hounds. Good dogs, who had treated him like pack.

Ahoooooooooo. The wolf dog's howl came again, pitched lower this time and closer. The Dog Lord's protectors were on the move.

Vaylo nodded to Hammie, and the small party began to belly down the east face of the hill. It was raining hard now and Vaylo's cloak was quickly soaked. About halfway down the slope, he spied a copse of spindly blackthorn and altered his course toward it. He was listening intently, but could hear nothing above the wind. The wolf dog's call had come from the south, and that meant Dhoonesmen riding out from the Thistle Gate.

"Granda, I can hear horses coming." Pasha tried hard to whisper, but at nine she hadn't quite gotten the hang of it and the words came out louder than if she'd spoken them in her normal speaking voice. Nan put a finger to her lip to hush her, but the damage was done.

Hammie and the Dog Lord shared a glance. The spearman had left his spear in the Tomb of the Dhoone Princes, where he had used it to bar the trapdoor that led from the roundhouse to the tomb. Hammie was still in possession of a good knife, though; a foot-and-a-halfer cast from a single rod of blued steel. The kitchen knife Vaylo now called his own was another matter entirely. The tang rocked loose in its handle, and three days of rain had cankered the blade. Of course Nan still had her maiden's helper—a slender dagger with a wicked double edge and some pretty scrollwork—but Vaylo would never consider taking it from her. A Bluddswoman had as much right to defend herself as any man.

Scrambling with his knees and elbows, Vaylo pushed toward the blackthorns. Finally he could hear what Pasha heard: horses at canter, closing distance from the south. *Dogs be good*, Vaylo willed. If the five beasts homed too quickly they would betray their master's position. Right now Vaylo needed them to stay put.

Reaching the bushes, he tugged off his rain-drenched cloak and threw it across the branches. It wasn't much protection against the needle-sharp thorns, but it was better than nothing, and Vaylo had the bairns' eyes and tender cheeks in mind. Gesturing furiously, he beckoned Pasha and Aaron to push through the tangle of winter-hardened canes and into the center of the copse. When they hesitated he fixed them with full force of his chief's glare and hissed, "*Now!*"

Not once in Vaylo's thirty-five-year chiefdom had anyone disobeyed an order spoken in his command voice and no one was about to start now. The children jumped into action, ducking their heads and plowing through the bushes as if they were being chased by wolves. Even Nan and Hammie moved smartly, Hammie pulling his cloak taut around his body and diving into the bushes like an otter into water. Vaylo took little satisfaction from their responses. He could hear horses closing distance from the far side of the hill, and the rhythmic beating of their hooves sounded like war drums.

Three, he counted. And they weren't slowing. That was something.

Vaylo ducked into the bush as the horses crested the ridge. As he gulped air to steady himself his knees touched Nan's. When he looked at her face he knew he was seeing a mask: firm and fearless, calm as if she were accustomed to crouching in a thornbush daily. Frowning, she rubbed dirt from the corner of Aaron's eye and tucked Pasha's black hair under her hood. Her instinct with the bairns was flawless. She knew that no-non-sense, oft-repeated gestures calmed better than soft words and protective hugs.

Vaylo edged about slightly, presenting his back to the chil-dren, and then slid the kitchen knife from his belt. Hammie knew the game and did likewise. The sharp odor of newly wetted ground acted like a drug on Vaylo's windpipe and he found himself breathing deep, clear breaths. The riders were almost upon them. When the pounding of hooves grew deaf-ening Vaylo spoke a prayer to his favored god, Uthred. *Not this time.*

Almost it was granted. The riders drew abreast of the bushes and continued southward, spraying clumps of mud against the blackthorns as they passed. Then suddenly there was a change in the rhythm of hoof falls, a subtle slowing, a pause as one man swiveled in his saddle and looked back. The sludge in Vaylo's boots curdled. *Sweet Gods, the cloak!* It lay there, muddy and nondescript, soaked in the rainy colors of the night, indistin-guishable from its surrounding in every regard. Except shape.

Vaylo imagined the rider's gaze sliding across the black-thorns. He heard the jingle of bit irons as horses' heads were pulled about. No words were spoken, but Vaylo imagined an exchange of wary nods. Hammie Faa looked to his chief.

The Dog Lord spun the moment, imagining all possible outcomes. Judging from the noise made by the horses' trap-pings, the riders were well-equipped. Harnesses tooled to support the hardware of war had a certain sound to them. The unusual quantity of buckles and D rings created a percussion of sharp snaps. For a certainty they were Dhoonesmen—they were traveling south from the Dhoonehouse in haste—but Vaylo doubted they'd been sent to track him. In his experience man hunters traveled light. Whatever their purpose they were dangerous. A small group of men did not stop to investigate a tiny discrepancy in the dark of night unless they were confident they could deal with surprises. Vaylo glanced at his grandchildren and then wetted his mouth. Pushing dank air from his lungs he whistled for his dogs.

A single note, diamond-sharp, ripped through the noise of the storm. All was given away in that moment, and while five dogs responded with a chorus of unearthly howls, horses were spun about and kicked into motion.

Vaylo nodded at Hammie. To Nan he mouthed the words, *Stay here and do not move.* For the children themselves he had no words. Nan knew what to do.

As the dogs homed, Vaylo moved free of the brush and caught his first sight of the riders. Three horses, three men. Dhoonesmen, lightly armored for travel but armed with full battle complements. They were clad in blue wool cloaks fastened with thistle brooches and shod in stiff boar's-leather boots. Two held nine-foot spears, and all had the sense to don battle helms before approaching.

Vaylo felt the old mix of excitement and fear as he prepared to face them. *Here I am again, outmanned and outhorsed. The Underdog Lord, they should have named me.*

Hammie Faa picked his position—three feet back from his chief. Even now he could not give up the habit of respect. Vaylo reckoned he was all of twenty-three.

"Who stands there?" came a hard, commanding voice as the riders approached. Hearing the accent, Vaylo revised his opinion. At least one of these men was Castlemilk dressed as Dhoone.

The dogs were rapidly closing distance, and Vaylo waited . . . waited . . . before speaking. When the first of the dogs—the big black-and-orange bitch—came within striking distance, he stilled her with a raised fist. Immediately the bitch sank to her haunches, her amber eyes glowing, a growl smoldering deep within her throat. Within moments the other dogs arrived, instinctively forming a circle around Vaylo's party and the Dhoonesmen. One by one, they followed the bitch's lead and bellied the ground.

The two riders bearing spears reined their horses within striking distance of Vaylo, whilst the third, the smallest in stature, hung back. Their thornhelms cast black shadow across their faces and Vaylo could not see their eyes. Both spearmen's horses were well-made and would outpace the dogs over distance, but the smell of the wolf dog made them nervous. Both animals were flicking their tails and tracking the wolf dog's position with their ears. The third rider's horse was past its prime, a dun mare long in the tooth and short-hoofed, but it wasn't nervous like the others. It stood its ground well, its ears forward, interested and alert, calm under its master's hand. Vaylo immediately reassessed its rider: any man who could command a horse to calmness in the presence of wolf musk had skills to be reckoned with.

"Answer the question!" The Castleman spoke again, puncturing his words with a thrust of his spear and a forward charge of his horse. He was tall, but lacked the shoulder breadth of a hatchetman. Dual scabbards holstered on opposing sides of his gear belt indicated his weapon of choice.

Vaylo regarded the spear tip pointed directly at his face. Absurdly, he thought he recognized it as one of his own. Then again it had probably been Dhoone's in the first place, seized by Bludd after the strike on the Dhoonehold. Such were the transitory possessions of war. Take himself. He'd once commanded three roundhouses, now he was down to exactly none.

Which means I have nothing but thin air to lose.

Grinning savagely, the Dog Lord spoke his name.

FOUR

Negotiation

Bram tried not to shiver when the Bludd chief spoke his name. They had all guessed the stranger's identity the moment they spotted the first dog, but it had not prepared them for hearing the man speak. The Dog Lord's voice was savage and calm; the voice of a man who had killed and would kill again. Bram thought of his brother's account of the one and only meeting between himself and the Bludd chief. "He's an old man," Robbie Dun Dhoone had pronounced, the morning after Dhoone had been retaken. "Past his prime and losing his edge, and if it wasn't for his hellhounds he would never have escaped."

Hearing the Dog Lord speak, Bram Cormac knew his brother's words to be a lie.

The dogs reacted to their master's voice by altering the pitch of their growls. Slow thunder rumbled deep within their throats, making Guy's and Jordie's horses blow nervously and flick their tails. Bram squeezed the mare's flanks with his thighs, coaxing the beast to calmness. Now if only he could calm himself.

"And exactly who do I have the pleasure of addressing?" The Bludd chief's voice came again, cold as the rain driving against his face. He wasn't a big man but his shoulders and chest were well-built, and he had something about him—a kind of iron-hard solidity—that gave him a powerful physical presence. His linen shirt was sodden to the point of transparency, and the woolen waistcoat he wore over it was so weighed down with rainwater it sagged. His long gray hair was braided into warrior queues, and grease had combined with rainwater to produce an oily iridescence. The blade he held was a foot long and badly cankered. Bram regarded it closely, wondering if it really could be the simple kitchen knife it seemed.

"I'll do the asking, *Dog Keep*." Guy Morloch brought the point of his spear to the apple of the Bludd chief's throat. Immediately, the big wolf dog to Bram's right lunged forward, hackles rising. Guy's stallion threw back its head, nostrils flaring, eyes darting wildly as it tried to track the wolf's movements. With a single twist of his free hand, Guy shortened the reins, forcing the bit into the stallion's tongue. Controlled, the creature quieted, but Bram could tell from its eye whites that it was still dangerously close to panic. The wolf, satisfied that the spear point was no longer threatening his master's throat, dropped its belly to the mud and bared its teeth.

Vaylo Bludd waited for quiet. Whilst Guy's horse was bucking he had shifted his ground slightly, moving away from the bushes that had first concealed him. The hefty armsman at his back quickly did the same. Bram found himself wondering about those two movements as the Bludd chief spoke.

"If I were you I'd ride on, Milkman. My dogs are hungry for white meat."

So he knows Guy isn't a Dhoonesman. Bram looked to the tall Castleman and wondered what else Guy was giving away. Guy Morloch was a crack swordsman on the tourney court, but he was inexperienced in field combat and although he was still wielding the spear, he had made the mistake of backing off. And while the Dog Lord stood his ground, coldly focused on the man he correctly judged to be the leader of the party, Guy was jumpy. Even through the deep shadow created by his visor Bram could see Guy's gaze springing from Vaylo Bludd to his armsman to the dogs and back again. Perhaps Jordie Sarson saw this too, for the young blond axman walked his horse forward a few paces and fixed the Dog Lord with a hard stare.

Vaylo Bludd didn't even glance in Jordie's direction. Addressing Guy he said, "You could have left of your own accord. Remember that, Milkman, as my dogs bid farewell to your throat."

With a small motion of his knife hand, he commanded his beasts to stand. Hairs along Bram's neck flicked upright as the five dogs rose in unison and began to close the circle. Golden eyes glittering, fangs dripping, they snarled and grunted like pigs.

Ride on! Bram wanted to shout to Guy Morloch. *We're not here for this. We're just traveling through.*

Then Guy's horse began to buck. The big black stallion kicked out with its back legs, throwing Guy forward in the saddle. Guy's head snapped back. His spear went thudding to the ground as he fought to keep his seat. Twisting the stallion's mane in his fist, he forced its head up. At the same time Jordie kicked his horse about face and charged the nearest dogs. They leapt back, shaking their heads so hard their eyes bulged. An instant later they sprang again. Sweeping his case-hardened spear in a half-circle, Jordie attempted to keep them at bay.

Leaping forward, the Dog Lord seized the fallen spear. With perfect violence he plunged the spearhead deep into Guy's foot. A choked cough puffed through Guy's lips as blood gushed from the punctured leather of his boot. The dark liquid steamed in the frigid air and for a moment Guy simply looked at it, seeming more puzzled than shocked. His stallion, terrified at the prospect of being caught between the Dog Lord and his wolf, lowered its head, humped its back and unleashed a massive, twisting kick. Guy was flung from the saddle headfirst. His thornhelm flew from his head and went bouncing toward the snarling wolf. Guy landed hard on his buttocks, and quickly rolled free from the stallion's hooves. Liberated from its rider, the horse whipped its head from side to side, desperately scanning for an escape route. When it found the way to the west blocked by a single black-and-tan bitch it charged. The bitch moved a beat too slow and Bram heard the sharp retort of bone breaking as the horse overran the dog.

Jordie Sarson moved immediately to protect Guy but was brought to a halt by the four remaining dogs forming a block around his horse. As he tried to force his mount to ignore the slavering beasts, the fat armsman charged him. Jordie danced back, swinging the spear point back and forth between the armsman and the dogs. Kept at bay, the young blond axman could do nothing as the Dog Lord hefted his spear over his shoulder and sprang forward to impale Guy Morloch.

"*Stay your weapon!*" Bram screamed. "*Or I'll run your grand-children through.*"

All heads turned to look at him. He was shaking uncontrollably, and the motion sent sparks of light bouncing off his watered-steel blade. *Don't think of the sword now*, Bram warned himself.

Forcing his chin up he met gazes with the Dog Lord. The man's eyes were black and full of fury. He was breathing hard and his gut fat trembled as he stilled himself. Bram watched the spear. Only when he saw the white-knuckle grip relax did he judge it safe to breathe. Nothing in his fifteen-year life had prepared him for a moment like this.

Whilst Guy Morloch and the Dog Lord had been trading words, Bram had been watching the copse of blackthorns. The fact that both the Dog Lord and his armsman had moved away from the bushes had set him to thinking. Such a small but deliberate act. It occurred to Bram that they were trying to draw fire . . . but from what? Possessions? A wounded comrade? What exactly lay in the middle of the dense tangle of thorns?

So Bram had watched. When the Dog Lord had lunged forward to stab Guy Morloch's foot, Bram had spotted a movement. Immediately the motion stilled, but it was too late. Bram was known for his eyes. When riding out in company he'd lost count of the times when Robbie or someone else had turned to him and said, "Tell me what you see, boy." During the retaking of Dhoone, Robbie had waited to give the order to charge until Bram confirmed that only one of the Thorn Towers appeared manned. Even this very night it had been Bram who spotted the cloak thrown over the bush, Bram who was convinced he saw the gleam of eye whites deep within the shadowy canes.

Neither Guy nor Jordie had wanted to stop. They had a task to complete and were anxious to be done with it. Jordie was simply eager to return to the excitement of the Dhoonehouse, where Robbie had created an atmosphere charged with gravity and purpose. Whereas Guy had made no secret of the fact that he thought the task beneath him. Indeed, if it hadn't been for the fact that Robbie Dun Dhoone had asked for a personal favor, the Milkman would not be here this night. Guy Morloch was nobody's nursemaid.

When Bram had forced a halt on the mud slope, stating his belief that someone was hiding in the blackthorns, Guy had punched a gloved fist through the rain. "We have no time for malingering, boy. If we stop to investigate every shepherd taking a piss between here and the Milkhouse we won't be done until spring."

Bram had nodded slowly, not expecting much else. He had used the time while Guy was speaking to study the bushes more closely. The cloak was brown as mud, but as the rain beat down on it some of the grime was washed away. After a few seconds he said, "I think the cloak is red."

It was enough to turn the party around to investigate. Red was the color of sunrise and sunset, raw iron and raw meat, eyes stung by woodsmoke and thoughts stung by anger. Red was the color of Bludd.

"Drop the spear," Bram shouted to the Dog Lord. His voice sounded small and puny to his ears, and it had clearly cracked over the word *spear*. To make up for it Bram stabbed at the blackthorns with his sword. *"Now!"*

The Dog Lord didn't move. Bram could see him thinking. The Bludd chief's portion of guidestone hung from his waist in a hollowed-out ram's horn sealed with a cap of crimsoned lead. His lore was suspended beneath it: three dog claws strung on a flax twine. Bram wondered about that. Three dog claws, yet the Dog Lord always commanded five dogs. Whenever one of the five died it was immediately replaced. Bram risked glancing over at the bitch that had been trampled by Guy's horse. The creature lay on its side in the mud. It was seizing, its chest and front legs jerking feebly as green mucus bubbled from its mouth. It would have to be killed, Bram realized. The Dog Lord would need a new dog.

"I canna set the spear down, lad," the Dog Lord said at last, "until matters are settled between us."

Bram was struck by how reasonable Vaylo Bludd now sounded. The spear he held was still clearly trained on Guy Morloch—one swift lunge and the Castleman would be dead—but something fundamental within the Dog Lord had changed. He was neither threatening nor threatened. His gaze did not stray once to the place were his grandchildren were concealed.

Bram had maneuvered his mare so he was almost directly above them. He could clearly see the boy and the girl, obviously brother and sister from their striking dark looks. They were shielded by a gray-haired Bluddswoman who clutched them tightly to her sides. The woman held a foot-long maiden's helper in her right hand, but Bram's new sword was four times that length and she had the sense not to engage him. Bram could see where one of the thorns had pierced her cloak at the shoulder. A perfect circle of blood was spreading through the wool. Seeing it, Bram recalled the tale told about Bluddwives: They would kill themselves and their children rather than risk falling into enemy hands. Something stoic and watchful in the woman's lined face made him believe she was capable of such an act.

Oh gods. What have I started? Bram felt the beginnings of despair. He wished suddenly to be gone, to ride away from the frightened faces of Vaylo Bludd's grandchildren and the jerking body of the dog, ride north as far as he could, past Dhoone and across the Rift Valley, right into the heart of the Want.

It was the sword. The damn sword.

He could barely look at it. "Bludd chief. Lay down your weapon or I'll cut the girl." Bram hardly knew where the words came from, but some anger meant for his brother made them sound like the real thing.

The Dog Lord must have heard it too, for although he didn't drop the spear, he raised its point so that it was no longer directly threatening Guy Morloch. "Let's not do anything hasty, lad. We're both here to protect our own."

"Run the brats through, Bram," Guy Morloch cried from the mud. "Don't listen to a word he says."

Bram and Jordie Sarson exchanged a glance. The young blond axman had had the sense to keep the visor on his thorn-helm lowered, which meant that the Dog Lord perceived only one boy in the party, not two. Jordie was barely eighteen, but you could not tell that from his build. Executing the smallest possible shrug, he gave command of the situation to Bram.

Jordie Sarson was over six feet tall, a sworn clansman with a third of his face covered by the blue tattoos. He'd been trained to the ax by Jamie Toll, who everyone called the Tollman, and he shared the fisher lore with Robbie Dun Dhoone. Yet he was only two years older than Bram. And he didn't know what to do.

Guy Morloch was breathing hard. Bram could not make out his face in the darkness, but he could see that Guy was curled up in the mud, nursing his bleeding foot. A stream of rainwater running downhill was hitting the Castleman's back and then forking into two to flow around him. The rain itself was finally slacking, and a bitter cold was setting in. Bram shivered. Realizing his arm had been pulled down by the unfamiliar weight of his new sword, he made a clumsy adjustment. Glancing up at the Dog Lord, he saw the weakness had been noted.

"You know what we've got here, lad?" the Dog Lord asked in a leisurely droll. Softening a cube of chewing curd between his fingers, he answered his own question. "We've got what city men call an impasse. Way I see it, neither of us wants to budge. Now that could mean we stay here all night until one of us gets spooked or frozen and makes the sort of mistake that ends lives, or we could come to an agreement man-to-man." The Dog Lord looked Bram in the eye. "Which is it going to be?"

All the time while the Dog Lord had been speaking Bram had been concentrating on keeping his features still and his sword arm up. He had watched his brother often enough to know that you had to keep your expression guarded during parley. Robbie Dun Dhoone rarely let his true feelings show. *So what would Robbie do here?* After he'd thought about it for a moment, Bram decided that Robbie would never have got himself into a situation like this in the first place. Which didn't help matters one bit. Bram took a deep breath and held it. He felt a bit light-headed, as if he might be sick. "I'll listen."

The Dog Lord nodded judiciously, as if Bram had been very wise. Indicating Guy with the butt of the spear, he said, "The Milkman called you Bram. You know my name. I'd appreciate the rest of yours."

Guy Morloch shouted, "Tell him nothing."

Bram frowned. Although he knew it wasn't very charitable

he wished Guy would just shut up. For a reason that he couldn't quite understand he wanted to say his name out loud. If he were to die here, on this muddy hillside in the middle of the southeastern Dhoonewilds, his remains torn apart by dogs, then he wanted the man before him to know exactly who he killed.

Holding his voice steady, Bram said, "I'm Bram Cormac, son of Mabb."

The Dog Lord pushed the softened black curd into his mouth and chewed for a while before speaking. Raindrops beaded on his five-day stubble as the downpour finally ended. "I knew Mabb Cormac. Your father was a fine swordsman. I fought against him at Mare's Rock. Had two pretty blades, as I remember. Called them his Blue Angels, on account of their watered steel." Vaylo nodded toward Bram's sword. "Would that be one of them?"

Bram could not reply. Looking down at the sword, he saw his reflection weirdly distorted in the folded steel. His face was pale and elongated and his lips had been warped to a bloody slash. Still the same brown hair and brown eyes, though. The silver metal would not change that. Abruptly, he looked away. The Dog Lord had to know by now that the boy he was talking to was brother to Robbie Dun Dhoone, yet he had made no mention of it. Bram found himself grateful for that, but he still did not trust himself to talk about the sword.

Here, Bram, take it. Bear it across your back when you go.

The words were too new and too painful, and Bram spoke quickly to bury them. "The sword is my own business, Bludd chief. We have matters here that need settling. You are an enemy to this clan and a trespasser on this clanhold. Withdraw your dogs and release my man."

As the final word got out, Jordie Sarson drew a sharp breath. Guy Morloch made a noise that sounded as if he were choking on a fish bone. Even the wolf dog stopped snarling. Cocking its head and raising its tail, it looked expectantly toward its master. Vaylo Bludd nodded slowly, as if such a declaration was just what he had been waiting for. For one crazy moment Bram imagined he saw a spark of approval in the older man's eyes.

"So you're Robbie Dhoone's brother after all." The Dog Lord spat out a wad of curd and ground it into the mud with the heel of his boot. "Well you're young yet and have a fair bit to learn about parley, else you'd know better than to issue demands." A quick glance at Guy Morloch. "Robs a man of his dignity, you see, makes him feel like a cornered bear. Now I can't speak for you, Bram Cormac, but I've seen a man mauled by a cornered bear. He lost his left arm and three fingers from the right one, and even though a sawbones stanched the wounds and saved him, he never thanked him for it. Woke with the terrors every night, you see. Drank himself soft every day." The Dog Lord paused a moment to scratch the rain from his stubble. "Me, I believe it wasn't the loss of a limb that ruined him. It was the memory of the attack. An old bear, down on his luck and baited to the brink of madness, is about the scariest thing you're ever likely to meet."

Black eyes twinkled coldly as the sentence snapped to a close. Bram felt the heat of the warning flush his cheeks. *This is the Bludd chief*, he realized fully at last. *The most feared man in the clanholds, and I'm sitting here threatening his grandchildren.* Bram tried to swallow but his mouth was too dry and his jaw just clicked queerly instead. At the same time he became aware that a muscle in his sword arm had developed the queasy ache of imminent cramping. He had to do something—*now*—before the heavy blade started wobbling.

"Lay down your arms and call off your hounds and I'll release the woman and the girl." The Dog Lord started to interrupt, but Bram plowed on, knowing full well that if he didn't get it out now he never would. "The three of you will walk east with the dogs. When a hour has passed and I'm satisfied that you've completed your part of the bargain I'll release the boy to your armsman."

"Give him nothing!" Guy Morloch cried from the mud. He was trembling violently; you could hear the shiver in his voice. "As soon as he gets his hands on the boy he'll send his dogs back to savage us."

"Not if he gives his word," Bram answered, looking straight at the Bludd chief. "And I give mine."

The Dog Lord watched Bram without blinking. The strength in his right arm—his hammer arm, Bram guessed—was so great that he held the nine-foot spear aloft with no sign of strain. Bram had handled Guy's spear; its shaft was rolled iron and its butt was counterweighted with lead. It had to weigh close to two stone. Just thinking about it was enough to make Bram's weapon arm start to cramp.

Oh gods. Clamping his jaw tight, Bram concentrated on keeping his sword arm level. From the blackthorns below him, the Bluddswoman watched with knowing eyes. His arm had begun to shake minutely and she read the motion in his sword. Slowly, deliberately, she released her grip on the two children. Her maiden's helper gleamed wickedly as she gave herself room to move.

Speak, Bram willed the Bludd chief as wire-tight muscle flooded his arm with acid. *Speak!*

The Dog Lord reached for a second piece of chewing curd and then thought better of it. As he returned the black cube to his belt pouch, the moon rose above the clouds and shone cold light upon his face. *He's old,* Bram thought. *And tired.* Worry about his grandchildren had made his jaw muscles bulge like sparrow eggs. Yet he still made no reply.

Bram could no longer be sure his fingers were adequately gripping the sword hilt. A sickening numbness was pumping through his fingertips. A foot away the muscle of his upper arm was burning. For an instant Bram was sure he was going mad, for all he could think was *If the numbness moves up quick enough it just might douse the pain.* Then he heard the soft click of joints as the Bluddswoman began to rise. Suddenly he could no longer hold up the sword and the flat side of the blade fell against the mare's rump.

"You have my word."

It took Bram a moment to realize that the Dog Lord had spoken, and another moment to realize what he'd actually said. The Bluddswoman knew straightaway and immediately lowered her weapon. Discreetly, she began to ease herself back into her former position between the boy and the girl. Her green-eyed gaze held Bram's for an instant, conveying no rancor or sense that Bram should count himself lucky. Instead she seemed to say to him *We have an agreement of our own, you and I.* She had kept her actions—and therefore Bram's vulnerability—hidden from the Dog Lord, and in return she expected him to keep his word. Bram was struck with admiration for her. She would have killed him, this woman with the sea gray hair who was old enough to be his grandmother. Robbie had taught him that such dignity was the sole preserve of Dhoonesmen. Robbie had been wrong.

Rainwater trickled from the sleeve of Bram's jacket down along his wrist to his thumb. He could see it but not feel it. Carefully, Bram rested the numb hand against the mare's neck. When he looked up he saw that the Dog Lord was waiting for him to speak. "You have my word in return," Bram said.

"You fool," screamed Guy Morloch. "No Bludd scum can be trusted."

It was difficult to ignore a sworn clansman, but Bram knew he must. A small nod to the Bluddswoman was all it took for her to rise, hand in hand with Vaylo Bludd's granddaughter. The girl was beautiful, dark-skinned with a perfect oval face. When her brother began to sob she turned to him and said quite clearly, "Aaron. You heard Nan. You must wait here until this warrior grants your leave."

Warrior? Bram felt shamed. He did not deserve such a title. He had not sworn a single yearman's oath to his clan. *And now I never will.*

The Dog Lord prodded Guy Morloch's thigh, not gently, with the butt of his spear. "Up, laddie," he commanded. "You're free to go."

As Guy struggled to his feet he threw Bram a vicious glance, one that promised all sorts of trouble later. Sensation was slowly returning to Bram's hand, and he found himself wishing that the numbness would now travel to his head. "Jordie. Dismount and help Guy." Seeing Jordie hesitate, Bram added, "The Bludd chief will call his dogs to heel."

For a wonder the Dog Lord did just that, issuing a short whistle that brought all four dogs to his side. The fifth, the wounded bitch, pricked up her ears and made a feeble attempt to stand. Her pelvis had been crushed and when she tried to roll onto her belly, her rear legs rocked loosely, without power. The Dog Lord spoke a command to the other dogs, and they sank to the ground as he made his way toward the bitch. Bram watched as he squatted and cupped her head in his hand. Even now, damaged as she was, the creature nuzzled his palm.

Abruptly, the Dog Lord stood. He was holding Guy's spear, and Bram looked away as he raised it above the dog. Some things were between a man and his gods.

When it was over the Dog Lord pulled a fistful of dead oat grass from the mud and wiped the blade clean. One of the four remaining dogs howled softly, and the wolf dog quieted its pack member by biting softly on its ear.

"Bram Cormac." The Dog Lord dropped the bloody grass into the mud. "Before I walk away from this place as agreed, I would speak with you in private."

Guy Morloch shouted, "Don't go. It's a trick." The Castleman was leaning against Jordie's stallion, whilst the axman knelt before him, attempting to yank off Guy's boot. "Bludd has no honor."

Bram wished it was all over. He was tired of thinking, and soaked to the bone. "Drop the spear and I'll talk," he said to the Bludd chief.

With a hard movement the Dog Lord drove the spear deep into the mud. The shaft vibrated as he walked a short distance downhill and waited for Bram to join him.

Bram considered staying seated on his horse, but the same sense of respect that had made him look away while the Dog Lord killed the bitch made him dismount. The Dog Lord might be his enemy but he was first and foremost a chief.

The Dog Lord wasted no time on small talk. "On your return to the Dhoonehouse I would have you deliver a message to your brother."

Bram kept himself very still. He could not trust himself to nod.

The Dog Lord took his silence for agreement. "I need you to tell your brother two things. First, you must tell him old grievances should be forgotten. Whilst we fight amongst ourselves the city men circle like wolves. When they spy weakness they will strike." He paused, waiting. Bram made the smallest possible movement that could be taken for a nod. "And there's another thing. Tell him days darker than night lie ahead."

The words touched Bram like a cold wind, making gooseflesh

rise on his arms. Almost he knew what they meant, but when he tried to capture their meaning his sense of understanding fled. Bram studied the Dog Lord's face. This close you could see the veins in his eyes. He was the longest-reigning chief in the clan-holds, a bastard who had slain his father and half-brothers, taken his sister as a wife and sired seven sons. He had seized the Dhoonehouse with the help of dark forces and lost it when his second son had deserted him. Once he had counted nearly twenty children as his grandkin. Now he was left with two. Bram knew the stories and thought he knew the man, but looking at the Dog Lord's face he realized there was more.

He made a decision. "I will not be seeing my brother for some time. Give your message to one of the other men."

"How so?"

It was a question Bram had hoped would not be asked. Looking down at his numb hand he said, "I am claimed by the Milk chief."

The Dog Lord nodded slowly and with understanding. "In return for a debt run up by Robbie Dun Dhoone."

Bram was glad it was not a question. He did not wish to speak ill of his brother. Robbie had sold him to Wrayan Castlemilk along with a dozen watered-steel swords and a fantastical suit of dress armor that had been forged for Weeping Moira. In return Robbie had received temporary command of six hundred Castlemilk warriors. Elite hatchetmen and swords-men who wore their hair plastered with lime and styled themselves "the Cream." With their numbers added to his tally, Robbie had finally commanded enough manpower to retake Dhoone.

Now that the Dhoonehouse was back in Dhoone hands the Milkmen were overdue to return to their clan, yet Robbie still held them in his sway. There were more battles to be fought: battles with Bludd to retake Withy, and Blackhail to retake Ganmiddich; battles also with the army of city men who were rumored to be invading the border clans from the south; and more battles still with the Dog Lord himself. No longer content simply with displacing Vaylo Bludd, Robbie had made it his mission to destroy him.

Even during the five chaotic days following the reoccupation,

Bram had observed a subtle shift in the Milkmen's loyalties. "Robbie has need of us," they said in low voices. "Best to hold out here until his enemies have been dispatched." Such thinking wasn't in Castlemilk's best interest, but Bram knew from experience that Robbie was hard to resist. He won, that was the thing. Whatever it took, he did.

Bram wondered when Wrayan Castlemilk would realize that she wasn't getting her men back.

It was hard to understand why Robbie still insisted on holding up the part of the agreement that meant delivering his brother to Castlemilk. Instinctively Bram knew it would not serve him well to think too hard about the answer. What Robbie valued, he kept.

The Dog Lord watched Bram closely. "Wrayan Castlemilk is a canny chief. I think she had the eye for me once."

Despite everything Bram laughed out loud. The Dog Lord laughed too; a roguish sound filled with self-mocking. When he stopped he looked Bram straight in the eye. "There's no shame in being fostered to another clan. I spent a year in Ostler as a bairn. My father had meant it for a punishment—it was the farthest he could send me without casting me from the clanholds—yet I had an honest time of it all the same. They didn't know me there. Didn't know that I wasn't allowed to play with the best boys. You know the ones; sons of warriors, nephews to the chief. Boys with purebred horses and their own live steel. I learned how to tickle trout and dance the swords, how to bring down harlequins with a bola and hedgehog a riverbed for defense. Cricklemore Carp, their old clan guide, even taught me how to read—me, a worthless bastard from a northern clan. I bawled like a babbie when I left."

The Dog Lord shook his head softly as he remembered. "A fostering is what you make it of it, Bram Cormac. Milk can be made into many things."

Bram nodded, feeling stirred despite himself. Perhaps going to live in the Milkhouse wouldn't be as bad as he thought. Perhaps there he wouldn't be Robbie's disappointing half-brother, small for his age and unable to train for the ax. Perhaps he might be something else. He could study the histories, learn about the Sull, discover why they had relinquished so much land to the clans. Stopping his thoughts before they ran away with him, Bram met gazes with the Dog Lord. He was beginning to understand why this man had been chief for over thirty-five years.

"And your message?"

The Dog Lord shrugged, but not lightly. "Give it to the Milk chief. Mayhap she'll need it more than Robbie Dhoone."

"Guy could bring it to Rob."

"Nay, lad. Some things depend as much on the messenger as the message." The Dog Lord glanced over his shoulder to where Jordie was helping the now bootless Guy Morloch mount his horse. "And I don't think the Castleman will do."

Even though part of Bram agreed with the Dog Lord's opinion, he tried hard to not let it show. "As you will."

The Dog Lord took a few steps up the hill and then turned. "By the way, lad, you did a fine job tonight. Kept your head. Kept the pressure on. If you were my kin I'd be proud."

It was too much. Bram felt the hot spike of tears in his eyes. Only four days had passed since Robbie told him he must leave and take up residence in Castlemilk. Four days and Robbie's words of farewell still burned a hole in Bram's chest. *"It won't be so bad, Bram. We both know you were never really cut out for Dhoone."*

"I'll be off now," the Dog Lord said. "I'm sure I'll be hearing more of you, Bram Cormac." With that he headed upslope, waving a hand in farewell to his armsman and calling his dogs to heel. When he reached the blackthorns, he knelt and said a few words to his grandson, and then put out his arms for Nan and his granddaughter. With the dogs milling anxiously around all three of them, the Dog Lord and his companions headed east.

He did not even warn me to keep up my side of the bargain and release his grandson and armsman as agreed. He simply expects it be done. That act of trust buoyed Bram as he hiked up the hillside toward Guy and Jordie.

The heavyset armsman looked uneasy as Bram approached. His knife had been lowered for some time, but his grip was unrelaxed. Poorly outfitted in a shaggy cloak, boiled-wool pants and a deerhide tunic, he was soaked through and dripping. His warrior queue was not nearly as magnificent as his chief's. Early balding had seen to that.

Bram said, "My name's Bram Cormac. What will I call you?"

"I'm Haimish Faa of the Bludd-Faas. Most people call me Hammie." The armsman spoke with a soft backcountry accent, and Bram guessed he was younger than he looked. Sometimes it was hard to tell when a man was plump and balding.

"Hammie. Why don't you bring out the boy and go and sit with him on the ridge while we wait."

"Aye, sir."

Bram had never been called sir in his life. It wasn't right, and he would have said so if he hadn't realized that right now Hammie Faa wanted to believe in him. His own safety and the safety of Vaylo's grandson depended on it.

Leaving the armsman to lift the small boy from the bushes, Bram crossed to where Jordie was binding Guy's foot. Jordie had just taken off his greathelm, and his face had that pink, steamed look of something left too long in the tub. He said nothing at Bram's approach, but smiled gently, letting Bram know that everything that had happened was just fine with Jordie Sarson. Bram felt absurdly grateful. He liked Jordie. The young axman was one of Robbie's favored companions, yet he had none of the arrogance that usually went hand in hand with the blue cloak.

"You're not just going to let them stand there," Guy Morloch said, gesturing toward Hammie Faa and the boy from his seat atop Jordie's gray stallion.

"No. You're right. I should take them a blanket to sit on."

Guy snorted harshly. "Think you're so clever, don't you? Negotiating with the Dog Lord." He made his voice mince like a girl's. "You do this and I'll do that and we'll all have tea and oatcakes when we're done."

"Guy, stop" Jordie tried to defend Bram, but Guy simply overran him.

"And as for you, Jordie Sarson. Hog-tie the fattie and the boy. I'm hauling them back to Dhoone."

Jordie's mouth fell open. After a moment of consideration he shook his head. "I won't do it, Guy. We both heard the agreement. Bram gave his word."

"Bram! What does he know. His mother was a rabbit-catcher from Gnash."

"It doesn't matter, Guy. When a Dhoonesman gives his word he gives . . . " Jordie struggled a moment. "His soul."

All three of them fell quiet. The sudden drop in temperature had made the mud begin to steam, and as Bram walked to his mare he could feel icy tendrils creeping up his thighs. Shivering, he took his sleeping roll from the harness. He could feel Guy watching him, and knew it was only a matter of time before the Castleman spoke. There was nothing Guy could do about the mutiny—without Jordie's help he couldn't even mount a horse—yet he had to assert his authority somehow.

"Boy. Move yourself and find my gelding."

Bram nodded. "After the agreed time has passed and I've released the hostages."

Guy didn't like this answer very much, but he had the sense not to challenge it and risk a second mutiny. The skin on the Castleman's face was gray and slack, and he was shaking in short bursts. Dark blood was seeping through the woolen bandage on his foot. "Fine, but if you can't find head nor tail of him I'll take the mare in payment."

"Here," Bram said to Jordie a few moments later, handing the axman a leather-bound flask. "Unbind Guy's bandage and clean out the wound with this. When you're done smear the wound with beef tallow before binding it. And give him a dram of malt before you start."

"Thanks, Bram." Jordie grinned in relief. Doctoring was beyond him. Guy simply looked disgruntled and said nothing.

Bram carried the blanket and a few other items to Hammie Faa.

Vaylo Bludd's grandson shied behind Hammie's chunky legs as the Dhoonesman who had threatened him with a sword drew near. He had to be about seven, Bram reckoned. Skinny as a stalk with large hands and a large head. "What's your name?"

When the boy made no reply Hammie elbowed him gently. "Come on, lad. When a clansman asks a question, you answer."

"Aaron Bludd," the boy said at last, not looking Bram in the eye. "But I'm known as Arrow."

Hammie lifted an eyebrow toward Bram as if to say, *That's the first I've heard of that*, but he allowed the boy his dignity and did not contradict him.

"I brought a few things. Salt beef. Cheese. Hardtack." Bram handed the armsman a small package, hastily wrapped in one of his old nightshirts. "And there's a couple of honeycakes." He hesitated, suddenly shy. "For the lady."

"Nan'll be grateful for them," Hammie said bluffly. Bram guessed he must be hungry—five days was a long time to go without proper food—but wasn't surprised when the armsman simply tucked the pack under his cloak, unopened. Pride would not allow him to reveal how much he needed to eat. When the boy began questing beneath Hammie's cloak, Hammie said firmly, "Later."

Bram and the armsman waited out the rest of the hour in companionable silence, stamping their feet against the cold and blowing on their hands. Hoarfrost was forming, and Vaylo's grandson amused himself by sliding across the mud on fragile rafts of ice. When Bram judged the time was up he nodded at Hammie Faa. "Have a safe journey back to the Bluddhold."

For the briefest moment Hammie Faa's face went blank. Recovering quickly he nodded and mumbled, "Aye. Gods be with you on the road." Placing a guiding hand on Aaron's back, he struck a course due east.

Bram watched them leave. As man and boy disappeared beneath the curve of the hill, a wolf howled in the distance. A reminder from the Dog Lord. *Set them free.*

Shaking his sword hand to get the blood flowing, Bram hiked up the slope. His entire body felt battered and used up, and the thought of spending the night searching for Guy's runaway stallion was almost too much to bear. Just to sit and drink some water would have been nice. When he saw that both Guy and Jordie were mounted, reins in hands and visors lowered, he guessed that he wouldn't be sitting down any time soon.

Guy trotted Jordie's stallion downhill. The left stirrup had been unbuckled and Guy's bandaged foot dangled loose against the creature's belly. Rainwater soaked into Guy's cloak had stiffened to ice, freezing the badly rumpled fabric into lumps.

When he spoke his breath whitened in word-length bursts. "You'll have to make your own way from here on, Cormac. We're heading for the Fly."

The Fly was a shallow river that crossed the Dhoonehold two days southeast of the roundhouse. The old watchtower that defended the raised crossing was known as the Stonefly. One of the first orders Robbie had given upon seizing the Dhooneseat was concerning the regarrisoning of the tower. A score of hatchetmen — hammermen and axmen — now patrolled both the north and south rivershores and the forest beyond. If Guy and Jordie rode hard through the night it was possible they could reach the Fly by dawn. Guy intended to set the hatchetmen on the Dog Lord's trail.

"We're not breaking the agreement," Jordie said quietly, drawing level on Bram's mare. "We agreed to set them free and not pursue them, and . . . and . . . " Frowning hard at the reins in his hands, Jordie stumbled to a halt.

"We're *not* pursuing them," Guy said firmly, some of his old haughter returning. "We're alerting others to their presence."

Bram could tell Jordie didn't want to catch his eye. There was nothing that interesting about his reins. Jordie knew that although they were upholding the word of the agreement, they were still breaking faith. And then there was the matter of an earlier agreement, one concerning the safe delivery of Robbie's brother to the Milkhouse. Both Jordie and Guy had promised to escort Bram on the journey southeast and protect him from the dangers that awaited lone travelers on the road. Maimed Men, city men, trappers, bandits, enemy clansmen and even enemy Dhoonesmen had been spotted on the Milkway. Not to mention the fact that a boy traveling alone might simply fall from his horse into a ditch, injuring himself so badly he couldn't get up.

Well I'll just have to be careful where I put my feet. Oddly enough Bram found himself too tired to care about being abandoned. "And my horse?"

Guy made an exasperated puffing sound as if the answer were glaringly obvious. "You'll have the best mount in the party — mine."

If I can find it. Bram considered mentioning the fact that

Guy's stallion had run loose over two hours ago and could be halfway to Blue Creek by now.

"It's not a gift, mind. I'll expect him to be returned within the month." Guy expertly turned Jordie's horse. "Jordie. We're off. The sooner Tiny learns the Dog Lord is alive and on his way back to Bludd the better."

Jordie shifted his weight forward in the saddle, preparing his mount for a swift start. "You can always follow us back, Bram," he said gently. "You know, run and try to keep pace."

Bram shook his head firmly. Even if such a thing were possible, Robbie would not want him back.

"Gods' luck, Bram Cormac." Jerking his head in farewell, Guy Morloch dug iron into horseflesh and sped off.

Jordie hesitated a moment and then gave the mare its head. The little horse raced down the slope, its hooves gouging divots from the mud in its eagerness to catch up with the stallion.

Bram sat down on his cloaktails and watched them. He was dead tired, and relieved to have them gone. After a time he began massaging his numbed hand. Strange tingles still persisted, and although he knew it was probably nothing he was a bit worried all the same. He very much liked his hand.

Part of him was still trying to figure out how Guy could have made such a big mistake. Hammie Faa had barely managed to cover his confusion when Bram wished him a safe journey to Bludd. The Dog Lord wasn't heading home. He was heading north to the Dhoonewall. Guy had assumed that the Dog Lord was south of the roundhouse because he meant to follow the old Ruinwood trail east through Dregg. Where in fact the Bludd chief and his companions were circling the roundhouse before eventually turning north. The tunnel leading from the Tomb of the Dhoone Princes must have deposited them some distance south, leaving Vaylo with the difficult job of guiding his party through land overrun by enemies.

Bram decided the Dog Lord was more than up to the task.

Knowledge was interesting, Bram concluded, rising. Once you were in possession of it you could choose to pass it along or keep it to yourself. Power lived there just as surely as it lived in a swinging hammer. Only you didn't need muscle to wield it.

Thoughtful, he headed uphill. His throat was raw with thirst. Luckily Jordie had thought to unbuckle the saddlebags from the mare, and Bram found a waterskin and other supplies. As he drank he began planning for the night ahead. It occurred to him that it would be a good idea to spread feed around his bedroll. That way if Guy's stallion decided to return while he slept it would likely stick around until morning. Unable to locate horse feed, he used porridge oats instead.

When he was done, he pushed a wedge of rye bread between his teeth and chewed. It tasted like wood. Swallowing forcefully, he drew the watered steel from its sheath. The edge needed oiling. Jackdaw Thundy, the old swordmaster at Dhoone, would whack a boy with the flat of his blade if he dared leave a sword untended after rainfall. Even the pride of Dhoone—hard and lustrous, twice-fired watered steel—was not immune to canker.

Frowning, Bram watched as moonlight flowed along the whorls and ripples in the blade. Robbie had given him the lesser of the two swords. The one he'd kept for himself was known as a horsestopper. A full-size battle sword with a two-handed grip that had the length and heft necessary to impale an armored warhorse, it was forged from the highest grade of watered steel, known as mirror blue. A blade made of mirror blue was paler and more glassy than one forged from traditional watered steel. Light shone through its point.

No light shone through the point of Bram's blade, but that didn't bother him. Truth was he preferred the smaller, lighter footsword with its simple cruciform handguard and the hare head surmounted on its pommel. His father had commissioned the ice-hare pommel as a tribute to his wife upon her death. Tilda Cormac had been the best wire-trapper in Dhoone, and when her husband was away for the winter on long patrols she had kept her family fed.

It was Robbie who had benefited the most. Tilda had always given her stepson the choicest cuts of meat: the fatty loin from the rabbit's back, the coon liver, the porcupine's heart. Robbie had been born to her husband's first wife yet she had reared him as her own. Bram often wondered what she had received in return. Robbie had treated her like a servant, never showing her the respect due to a stepmother. "Elena Dhoone is my mother.

Not you," he would scream when she wouldn't let him have his way. "You're just a rabbit-trapper from Gnash."

Even though he didn't much feel like it, Bram unhooked the weapon care pouch from his belt and began working yellow tung oil into the sword. Tilda's sword. Robbie had been set to hand it over to the Milk chief in payment for the Castlemen, and Bram wondered how his brother had managed to get it back. His memories of what happened that night in the Brume Hall after Robbie sold him to Wrayan Castlemilk were not clear. Perhaps Robbie had renegotiated the gift of swords, but Bram doubted it. A dozen watered-steel swords had been promised. A dozen had been delivered. Bram had a shadowy memory of Robbie kneeling quietly by the sword pile and sliding out Tilda's sword. If the memory was true he would have had to replace it with another blade. Why he had gone to such trouble was hard to know.

Bram decided not to think about it. Nerve endings in his fingers had begun to fire randomly as his hand came back to life, and he flexed the muscles to keep blood pumping.

He found himself imaging Guy and Jordie arriving at the Stonefly. Tired and breathless, they'd hasten through the garrison eager to speak with the head hatchetman, Tiny Pitt. Search parties would be dispatched. Messengers would be sent north to Dhoone: the Dog Lord was in the Dhoonewilds, heading east. The knowledge that Guy and Jordie would soon send a company of hatchetmen east when the Dog Lord was heading north should have made Bram feel something as a Dhoonesman. Yet it didn't.

Instead he felt a small stirring of something else. It was good to have knowledge that no one else but you possessed.

"Castlemilk." Bram spoke the word out loud, testing.

His allegiances were shifting and he no longer knew which clan he owed loyalty to anymore.

FIVE

The Racklands

A night heron shrieked in the distance as Ash March crouched by the shore and drank. Moonlight had transformed the Flow into a river of mercury, silver-black and shiny as metal. Hopefully not dangerous to drink. Ash tasted the river as she swallowed; oily and strange, not quite water anymore.

Standing, she wrapped her lynx-fur coat around her chest and shivered, though she wasn't really cold. It was an hour after sunset and the sky glowed dimly in the west. In the east a half-moon hung low between sentinel cedars. The moon was closer here, she'd noticed. Stars too. The night itself was blacker, richer, as if darkness had been distilled to its highest proof. Ash could feel it settling against her skin and siphoning through the lenses in her eyes. The land she stood in was ruled by the Sull: night and day had irrevocably changed.

A breeze set the cedar boughs swaying as she hiked up the shore. The sharp, spicy scent of their needles was released in a sudden burst, like a seedpod ejecting it spores. The smell reminded Ash of Mask Fortress, of closed boxes, locked chests. Secrets. She had never seen such massive trees. Their boughs swept wide in vast shaggy circles that claimed the space of a dozen lesser trees. None of their needles were green. Silver and blue and a shade of dusky purple she had no name for, they had abandoned the colors of normal growing things.

Switching her path to avoid the ice-dried remains of something that might have been a fox, Ash returned to her makeshift camp. She was muscle-tired but restless, and she did not want to sleep. Seven days had passed since the stand at Floating Bridge and not an hour, awake or sleeping, had gone by where she had not relived the events of that night in her mind. In a way the nightmares were easier. There was something to be said for watching everything unfold in painstaking detail in her dreams. At least she was asleep. At least her dream self wasn't constantly asking: *What could I have done to save Ark's life?*

Ash inhaled deeply, found herself glancing back at the fox. Ark Veinsplitter, Son of the Sull and Chosen Far Rider, was dead. Brought down by unmade pack wolves, torn limb from limb by creatures who no longer had red blood pumping through their hearts or warm flesh coddling their bones. *Daughter,* he had called her. She would never hear him say that word again.

Deep within the overhang of her coat sleeves, Ash's hands made fists. *I should never have stepped onto the bridge.*

The memory of that night was as clear and sharp as a splinter of glass. Their party of three—Ark, Mal Naysayer and she herself—had been pursued by creatures from the Blind. From the moment she had become Sull in the mountain cavern they had chased her, and two hours south of Hell's Town they finally brought her to ground. It might have been possible to outrun them if it hadn't been for the river. The wolves had cornered them on the north bank of the Flow, where the road met the Floating Bridge. Horses could not be ridden at a gallop across the four-foot-wide boards, so Ark and Mal had turned to make a stand. Her mistake had been to ride onto the bridge ahead of them. She could see it all: the wolves closing in, the Naysayer drawing his six-foot longsword and stepping forward; and Ark . . . Ark pulling the linchpin from the Floating Bridge, and telling her how she had made him proud as the bridge began to float away. She and her horse had sailed east on powerful river currents, buoyed by pontoons that bounced like fishing floats in the water, unable to do anything but watch as Ark and the Naysayer battled the Unmade.

Ark had fallen. Two she-wolves had brought him down as the pack leader sprang for his throat. The battle had lasted mere seconds after that. The Naysayer finished it. Ash had grown up in Mask Fortress, and for ten years her sole view was of the brothers-in-the-watch weapons courts, which lay below her bedroom window. Not once in all that time had she seen a man wield a sword like the Naysayer. He ended the battle in just four sword strokes, and then dropped to his knees by his *hass*. Ash had no longer been able to see clearly by then—the current had carried the bridge close to the river's south bank—but she had understood the motions performed by the distant shape that was Mal Naysayer.

The Far Rider had executed *Dras Morthu*. The final cut. With Ark hemorrhaging from mortal wounds, his strength failing and the light dimming in his dark brown eyes, the Naysayer had made a decision. Ark Veinsplitter might have been brought down by unmade wolves, but it was Mal Naysayer, his fellow Far Rider and *hass*, who had ended his life.

The Sull were deeply proud. Never let an enemy take a life.

Ash raised her face toward the night sky and inhaled. *The wolves were hunting me.* That was something she would have to live with, the absolute certainty that Ark had died protecting her life.

Exhaling, she closed her eyes. The blackness was absolute. *Daughter.*

Where was the other man who had called her by that name? Where was the Naysayer? Was he standing grave watch by his *hass*'s corpse? Had he crossed the Flow? Was he searching for her? Or had Ark's death altered his path, causing him to focus attention elsewhere? Perhaps there was family to inform? Or—more likely—missions of greater urgency to undertake? Mal Naysayer lived by the sword. He might have judged the task of escorting Ash March to the Heart Fires too passive.

She had turned her back on him that night on the Flow. A strong sense of invading his privacy had made her walk the gelding along the Floating Bridge to its anchorage on the southern shore. Even in darkness, across the width of a river, she could feel the weight of his loss. Mal Naysayer was close to seven feet tall, with densely muscled shoulders and a back as straight as a lodgepole pine. To see him bend was to see his grief.

I am on Sull territory now, she had told herself as she stepped from the bridge onto the road of crushed quartz. *Surely I can make it to the Heart Fires on my own?* It had made sense to leave him; that way he would not be burdened with the task of bringing her to his home. The decision whether or not to follow her would be his own. Perhaps he might come after her, but she could not rely on it. The first person to call her daughter had taught her that men could not be relied upon.

So where was Penthero Iss, Surlord of Spire Vanis, this night? Was he deep within the Blackvault plotting to kill those who would take his place? Did he miss the daughter he'd found as a newborn and adopted? Or did he miss controlling the Reach?

Ash opened her eyes. The stars were cold and blue.

Crushing layers of pine needles and old, yellow snow beneath her boot heels, she returned to the dry camp. The Sull horse watched her with anticipation, his tail raised, his ears forward, standing on the exact patch of ground where she'd unsaddled him. Ark and Mal had used him as a packhorse and a spare, and he had muscular legs and a deep chest. Stony white and dappled, with shaggy patches on his neck and withers, he wasn't nearly as elegant as the Far Riders' mounts. Yet all Sull horses were beautiful. It had something to do with the intelligence biding in the center of their eyes.

Ash felt a rush of pleasure as he snuffled her bare palm. It made thinking about her foster father easier. Would he have really gone through with his plans to imprison her? Surely not. She was his *daughter*. All she'd ever wanted to do was please him.

Leaning against the gelding, Ash tried to warm away the hurt. Iss had never loved her, she had to remember that. He had adopted her because she satisfied the requirements of a prophecy foretelling the birth of a Reach: a newborn left to perish in the snow outside Vaingate. *Your little hands were blue,* Iss had been fond of telling her. *And when I picked you up and tucked you under my cloak you barely made a sound.*

Why had her foster father wanted her so badly? If she hadn't run away from Mask Fortress what would have become of her? She knew Iss had planned to imprison her, but how had he intended to use her?

What had Heritas Cant told her in Ille Glaive? *"You will be able to walk the borderlands at will, hear and sense the creatures that live there, and your flesh will become* rakhar dan, *reach-flesh, which is held sacred by the Sull.*" It made about as much sense now as it did then. Yet she did not think Cant's words were false. Mistaken perhaps, but not false.

And why had Ark insisted she become Sull? *"If you are not with us you are against us, and as such no living, breathing Sull will let you live."* What did she possess that filled them with such fear?

Thoughtful, Ash rocked her weight back onto her feet. She was a Reach, and she did not know what that meant.

Leading the Sull horse by the cheek strap, she guided him toward the section of riverbank where rye and wild carrot had seeded between the scree. He deserved a treat. Once he'd eaten his fill he would head straight back to the camp. He would not stray, and if he heard anything that alarmed him he would immediately return to her side.

Ash didn't know what she would have done without him these past six days. He knew the way home. With a loose hand on his reins he headed east, following a subtle path along the rivershore that Ash could only occasionally discern. Together they had passed vast beds of ice-rotted bulrushes humming with black flies, sulfurous tributaries that dumped mustard-colored ore into the Flow, hedges of spiny bushes that formed defensive walls around beachheads, salt ponds ringed with game paths, and long stretches of shoreline where ghostly forests of needle-thin birches grew from the frozen mud.

She wasn't sure how far she'd traveled from the Floating Bridge. Sometimes she rode, but more often she chose to walk. Awake before the first cock crow each morning, she was on the trail before dawn. It was easier to keep going than stop. If she had been traveling alone she would have walked all day, swigging from her water bladder as she wove between the trees, only halting to catch her breath and pee. The gelding needed to graze though, and she was forced to stand and wait for long intervals as he cropped last year's grass.

Waiting was a kind of torture. It gave her time to think. Katia, her little wild-haired maid, dead. Ark dead. Raif gone. All three had risked their lives to help her, and she had not paid them back. Ash filled her lungs with night air, punishing herself with its icy sharpness. She lived in a world where she had not paid them back.

Camp was little more than a circular patch of kick-cleared ground twenty feet north of the treeline. Out of habit Ash had raised a guidepost, and now began laying stones for a fire ring. She had no tent hides and feared lighting a fire in this strange land, but it gave her something to do. The river stone was green traprock reefed with fool's gold, and it was cold and sharp. Ash had lost her gloves along with her supplies so she had to lay it bare-handed. Darkness rose as she worked, snuffing the wind and pulling up mist.

Intent on building the fire ring, stacking the stones in over-lapping layers as Ark had taught her, she did not hear the gelding approach. When it pushed its nose against her back in way of greeting, she jumped in fright.

"Bad horse," she scolded, feeling foolish. Suddenly everything seemed foolish: the guidepost and the fire ring. Traveling alone to the Heart of the Sull without even knowing why.

"What am I doing here?" she asked aloud, hearing the trem-ble in her voice and not liking it. "What am I good for except getting people killed?"

Nothing answered. Along the treeline the cedars swayed in long, rolling waves. The gelding watched her, its head cocked, straining to read her mood. Abruptly Ash sat. She was tired and hungry and quite possibly going insane. Frowning, she glanced at the near-perfect circle of rocks, thought about it for a moment, and then leaned forward and knocked it over with her fist. Feeling a bit better, she spoke a command to the horse.

The gelding moved closer, swinging about to present its flank. Ash reached into her coat, located her gear belt, and drew her knife. Two weapons Ark had given her: a sickle blade with a weighted nine-foot chain attached; and a slender hand-knife made of the rare white alloy that was more precious to the Sull than gold. Platinum. Case-hardened with arsenic and other strange metals, the blade was so fiercely edged that when it first sliced your skin you felt no pain. Angus Lok had possessed a similar weapon, also Sull-wrought, that he lovingly called his "mercy blade." Ash had never seen him use it, for although it had both the form and dimensions of a standard handknife it was not the sort of blade that lent itself to spearing meat or picking dirt from fingernails. It was too formal and deadly for that.

Ash held the knife as she had been taught; thumb on the riser, index finger on the dimple, edge out. The handle was lightly hollowed for balance, and a crosshatch pattern of overlapping flight feathers had been etched into its surface to form a grip. The metal was shockingly cold, and she waited for her body heat to warm it before she spoke.

"Ish'I xalla tannan."

I know the value of that which I take. Ark Veinsplitter had taught her the words: the first of the Sull prayers.

With a swift and practiced movement she ran the knife's edge across the short hair of the gelding's flank until she encountered the faint resistance of a surface vein. Tendons jerked in her wrist as she sliced through the vessel. The horse shuddered briefly, then stilled as blood jetted from its belly. Kneeling forward, Ash opened her mouth to catch the flow. Blood gushed between her teeth, hot and winy and smelling of grass. She swallowed, filled her mouth and then swallowed again. Massaging the flesh around the cut to keep the vessel open, she drank until her stomach was full. Satiated, she clamped her palm against the wound. The gelding stepped into her, increasing the pressure. They both waited. Once the flow had decreased, Ash pinched the horseskin together and removed her hand.

As she sealed the wound with the purified wolf grease she kept in a pouch at her waist, a twig snapped with force beyond the treeline. Ash sprang to her feet. The cedars were a trap for shadows, black and suddenly still. The only thing that moved was mist venting from their roots. Ash listened, watched, *smelled*, and then slowly unhooked the sickle knife from her belt.

When the second sound came it was not from where she was expecting it. This time it came from the river shore. The wet plunk of something dropping into water. Without thinking she spun about to face it, and even before the scythe's chain stopped swinging, she realized her mistake. Anyone, anywhere could throw a stone into water.

"Drop your weapon." The order came from directly behind her. It was spoken mildly, but Ash wasn't fooled. Her foster father was the Surlord of Spire Vanis: she knew how power sounded.

Without turning she opened her fist and let the sickle knife drop to the ground. The silver letting knife was back in its deer-hide sheath attached to her gear belt and she slid her left hand into her coat opening to draw it. A whirring sound and a shot of cool air against her ear stopped her dead.

"Place both hands by your sides and turn around. You do not want me to fire again."

No she did not. Instantly, she dropped both hands. The arrow had passed so close to her face the stiff feathers of its fletchings had scratched her cheek. *This man is Sull*, she decided as she turned to face him.

Yet when she saw him he was not clad in Sull furs and Sull hornmail. He was dressed in simple deerskins collared with marten, and cross-belted with tanned leather. The belts were buckled in brass, not silver. His hair, and any ornaments that might proclaim his race, was concealed beneath a marten-fur cap. Yet how could he not be Sull? The precision of his voice. His height. The deep shadows beneath his cheekbones. That shot.

Ridiculously, as she stood there facing him, the hair on the left side of her head floated upward, suddenly weightless. The arrow must have charged the strands as it passed.

The stranger inspected her for some time, his eared longbow resting easy in his grip. A hard-sided arrowcase made of over-lapping disks of horn was suspended, ranger-style, at a cross angle from his waist. Ash wondered how long he had been spying on her before he'd made his move.

"Who are you and what is your business on this path?" Again there was that voice: firm, resonant, its owner sure of his own worth.

Ash raised her chin. "My business is my own to keep. My name I give you freely. Ash."

It was full dark now and the stranger had his back to the moon. She could not see his eyes. "You are not Sull."

Pitched in the dangerous area between question and state-ment, the words were a trap. All possible replies damned her.

Deny being Sull and she was a trespasser. Claim it and risk being tested and fail. Ash took a breath, stealing extra seconds before answering. She was in Sull territory, south of the Flow and southeast of Bludd. That much she knew. Her foster father had possessed maps of this place. Onionskin scrolls, brown with age and dry as hay, that could only be unrolled when it rained. She had seen them once or twice, peering over Iss' shoulder as he studied them. Blanks, that was what she mostly remembered. Unfilled spaces that in other maps would be crisscrossed with mountains, rivers, place names. Even so, her foster father had found something within them that held his interest: the oxbow curve of a coastline; a border illustrated with the footprint pattern of a wolf; a warning spelled out in High Hand, "Here Be Where Sull Are Most Fierce."

Ash thought about that before she spoke.

"I am Ash March, Daughter of the Sull."

The stranger's chest expanded, sucking in the words. A long moment passed. Then another. Up until then Ash had not realized she was afraid. She had thought the looseness in her gut was just the horse blood finding its level.

No living, breathing Sull will let you live . . .

The river flowing behind them created drag, sucking the ice mist east. Abruptly, the stranger rested his bow. "I am Lan Fallstar, Son of the Sull and Chosen Far Rider." He bowed deeply at the waist and Ash finally saw his face. Acutely angled, golden-toned, with that faint alien sheen that meant Sull. "This Sull asks that you forgive his trespass."

Ash gave some of his silence right back to him. She didn't have any idea how to react, was unsure about the nature of his trespass, and was, if she were honest, disconcerted by his age. Ark and Mal had been mature men, their faces lined with experience, their gestures dignified and weighted, yet this person standing before her looked to be less than ten years older than she herself. He was young, and that confused her.

Unsure what to do, Ash found herself mimicking her foster father. *Take control of the conversation:* she could almost hear his voice. "Do you travel alone, Lan Fallstar?"

An eyebrow was raised at that. "I do."

"How long have you been watching me?"

The Sull Far Rider shrugged, raising slender, finely muscled shoulders. "It is not important."

Ash thought it was—she did not like the idea of him watching her as she bled the horse—yet there was exactly nothing she could do about that. Her instinct was to continue questioning him anyway; leave him no chance to question her. "Where do you travel?"

He began moving toward her, and something told her she had made a mistake. With a series of movements so swift Ash could barely follow them, the stranger reached behind her back, crouched, snatched the sickle blade and its chain from the ground and sprang away. "Far Riders answer to no one except He Who Leads. If you were Sull you would know that." With a snap of his wrist he sent the chain into motion. The metal links rustled crisply as the chain wrapped itself in perfect order around the sickle's handle.

Not even Mal Naysayer had done that.

The chain was weighted with a teardrop of metal studded with peridots. The stranger studied this for a moment, cupping it in his free hand and turning it toward the light. Without looking up he fired off a command in Sull.

The looseness in her belly shifted downward. She had only a few words of Sull and she did not know what he wanted.

"I said show me *Dras Xathu*." The stranger's voice turned sharp, and when he spoke something unpleasant happened to his mouth. "*Now!*"

The word hit Ash like a slap to the face. The only other person who had spoken to her in that way was her foster father, and she was surprised by the strong instinct to "be a good girl." Confused, she struggled to comprehend what the stranger meant. *Dras Xathu?* The First Cut? When understanding finally came she felt no relief. Just more confusion.

Taking a step forward, she tilted her face and raised her chin. The wound inflicted upon her many weeks ago by Ark Veinsplitter was now a rough scar. It had been an initiation of sorts, part of becoming Sull. "Before a child comes to manhood or womanhood," Ark had told her, "blood must be drawn in friendly combat. We wound ourselves so that we might deprive our enemies of the satisfaction of delivering the First Cut."

As the stranger moved forward to inspect it, Ash held herself still. She could not let him know he had upset her. A hand gloved in lizard skin grasped her chin, and suddenly she could smell him: pungent and powerfully alien. Immediately, something primeval at the base of her brain responded with a warning: *You will never be one of them.*

With careless force he thrust her chin up and back. A finger slid across the roof of her lower jaw, halted, then pushed up at the exact point where bone ended and soft tissue began. Ash coughed in panic. He was closing off her windpipe.

Abruptly the pressure stopped. Turning away from her, he slid the sickle knife into his buckskin tunic. "You will travel with me from now on, Ash March. Stow your equipment and saddle the horse. We do not sleep here this night."

Ash fingered her throat. She had never seen the wound Ark had inflicted, and for the first time it struck her that the scar felt strange. The raised tissue seemed to form a shape. Briefly, she traced it with her thumbnail but couldn't work it out.

Her attention shifted when a muscular black stallion trotted into view. The animal came at Lan's command, emerging from the darkness of the cedars. Tossing its head and kicking its skirted heels high, it moved with some knowledge of its own worth. It was trapped and harnessed for a long journey, with wide belly and rump straps for hauling camp gear and a leather hood to protect its eyes. Ash had spent time with Sull horses and thought she knew them . . . but this one. This was one fit for a king.

"Do not touch him."

She had been in the process of reaching out her hand to let the horse sniff her, and she halted awkwardly midway. Her horse trotted past her as she stood there, its head lowered in shy submission, eager to greet this splendid new creature. Was that why he hadn't alerted her to the stranger's presence? Did Sull never warn against Sull?

"Pack your equipment."

Ash rounded on the stranger. He wasn't her foster father, she told herself. She didn't have to obey him. "I choose to travel alone, Lan Fallstar. Do not trouble yourself with me any longer." The words were a mistake—she knew that—but the stranger rattled her. His hot and cold behavior reminded her too much of Iss. Clicking her tongue she beckoned her traitorous horse. *Raise camp and depart, that's what I'll do.* The best direction didn't seem immediately clear, but she'd think about that later.

The Far Rider's dark eyes glittered strangely. "This Sull believes you are owed a second apology. Sull do not command other Sull." A calculated smile revealed white, even teeth. "But we are all possessive of our mounts."

He wanted her to smile with him, and even though she knew it she smiled anyway. Angus Lok, Mal Naysayer, Ark Veinsplitter: good men all of them, but god help you if you harmed their horses.

"In my father's house we have a saying. A poor beginning is no excuse for a poor end. So forgive me, Ash March. This Sull has been on the road too long and needs to relearn good manners."

In my father's house we lie and lock people up, she wanted to reply. But didn't. Before she could form a proper response, Lan spoke again.

"Come. We must break bread before the journey." Without waiting for a reply he unbuckled a road-beaten saddlebag from the stallion's rump. Resting it on the ground, he pulled out a rolled-up carpet and an ivory box. Woven from midnight-blue silk, the carpet was old and very fine. A design of five-pointed stars and denuded trees was worked in silver thread. Ash had seen such Sull carpets before—both Ark and the Naysayer had possessed them—but she had never seen one as intricately worked as this. When she blinked the design stayed before her eyes, temporarily burned into her retinas like a light source.

"It is the skin of gods." Lan gestured to the carpet. "Sit."

Suddenly Ash felt very tired. Even her foster father hadn't switched from coldness to civility so quickly, and she placed the chance of Lan switching back as pretty high. Uncertainty is draining, she decided, sitting. At least by staying she didn't have to head off into the night, hungry and alone, with only a horse to guide her. Plus it knocked at least one uncertainty on the head: she no longer had to worry about an arrow in her back.

Kneeling, Lan unfastened the wrought-silver clasp on the

ivory box and opened it. As he drew forth items he spoke, revealing that he had marked her interest in the rug. "The carpet is very old, woven by the last of the great threadsingers. It comes from *Maygi Horo*, the Time of Mages, when threadsingers were blinded once they had served their apprenticeships. A spool boy would prime the loom and block the colors, following the threadsinger's orders. It is said that without eyes they saw farther, though this Sull does not know about that."

As Lan spoke the word *Sull* he struck a light. One of the items he had taken from the box was a small pewter lamp, and as he adjusted the valve at its base the light shifted from yellow to blue. Unguarded, the flame ripped fiercely, burning mist. Peeling off his gloves, Lan bared long, well-shaped hands. A bowman's callus on the middle finger of his left hand revealed him to be left-handed. On the middle finger of his right hand he wore what Ash first assumed to be two separate silver rings, but when he turned his palms upward, she saw that the rings were fused at the back by a gristled lump of solder.

He gestured toward the lamp. "This Sull asks if you will join him in paying the toll."

Ash looked from the flame to Lan's face. The Far Rider's expression was coolly neutral, but she suspected his motives. Her gaze flicked back to the flame. An icy violet corona shivered around a core of blue fire. She had once witnessed Mal Naysayer put his bare hand into a flame and hold it there for many seconds. It had frightened her, but at least she had understood his motives. The Naysayer had been demonstrating the power of *Rhal*, the perfect state of fearlessness that Sull sought in times of uncertainty and war. He had not been priming a trap.

Ash shook her head. "This Sull believes this is not her toll to pay."

Lan's cold clear gaze pinned her, searching for weakness. Ash stared right back, silently praying her eyes wouldn't give her away. She didn't fully understand what was happening—neither Mal nor Ark had ever paid a toll with burned flesh—but instinct told her she had been challenged. And when challenged it was best to challenge back.

Long moments passed and then Lan nodded firmly. "It is

so." Shifting his position he reached for the coupled scabbard at his waist. One fork of the sheath held his sword and the other held a dagger. Lan drew the dagger. Ice mist curled across the rug as he held the dagger's blade in the flame. Ash smelled the metal heating. Oil on the blade blackened then disappeared as the edge began to glow. The flame burned hot and clean, fueled by a substance purer than oil. When the knife edge became a wavering red line Lan removed it from the heat. Speaking the Sull words "*Gods, judge me*" he pushed the blade tip across his forearm. Fluid sizzled. Skin opened but did not bleed, instantly cauterized by the heat. Pumping his hand into a fist, Lan waited out the pain.

Ash held herself still, tried not to breathe in the stench of cooked meat. Why had he paid such a high toll? Letting a few drops of blood was one thing, but this. He'd burned through skin and into fat and muscle. What came at such a cost? She could tell from the many old and silvery scars on his arm that he normally opened veins, so what made tonight different?

He was no longer here, either, on the south bank of the Flow. His eyes were vacant and there was a hollowness to his presence that Ash felt, but couldn't explain. One minute she had been sitting opposite a whole and living man and in the next something integral, like the weight of his awareness, was gone. Excised.

The final thought that struck her was that Lan Fallstar was a Far Rider of a different make from Mal Naysayer or Ark Veinsplitter. At first she had thought it was just his age that set him apart, but now she realized there was more. The fine carpet, the city men clothes. And neither Mal nor Ark had ever paid a toll in burned flesh. What she couldn't decide was how these differences affected Lan's status. Did they add up to less or more?

An eerie hiss, like the sound of air being sucked through a crack, puffed through Lan's lips. It was traveling inward. The Far Rider's chest bellowed out and his clenched fist sprang open, and he began falling forward. Straightaway he stopped himself, slapping down his palm on the rug. Blinking, he took in his surroundings, his seared arm, Ash.

"Break the bread. We must leave."

Ash wasn't sure what she had just witnessed, but her instincts warned her to be cautious. Things were moving fast. An hour earlier this man had been a stranger to her, and now he was not only commanding her but doing so with possessiveness in his voice.

"And if I chose not to?"

"This Sull believes that would be a mistake."

Ash couldn't decide whether his words were a threat. Not waiting on a response, Lan unwrapped the bread. Studded with tiny black horsemint seeds and baked hard for travel, the bread was placed on a small wooden board. Lan sprinkled it with water from his hip flask, placed a palm upon it, and then pressed down with his free hand, breaking the bread into crumbs. He waited and after some time had passed he said, "You wish me to take bread before you?"

Ash nodded. She did not know the Sull custom here, but she had remembered one from her foster father: Always let your enemy eat first.

Lan chose a piece of bread the size of an acorn and brought it to his mouth. Ash waited until she saw him swallow before doing the same. The bread tasted bitter, the horsemint seeds like little drops of bitumen.

"Drink." He passed her his hip flask. Fluid was traveling to the burn site on his arm and his skin was becoming bloated. He watched her as she drank, his expression giving away nothing. When she was done, he stood and collected his things. As he rolled the carpet he said, "If you continue alone on your current route you will be lost. Your gelding is snow-, not iceborn, and he has not been bred to *thal axtha*, the path lores. That he has brought you this far is a testament to his intelligence and training. Do not make the mistake of believing he can take you further. Two days' walk from here lies the birch way. Every tree that grows there has been seeded from a single mother tree. What this means to you, Ash March, is that all look the same. Enter the birch way untrained and alone and you will fall into madness. All do. The birches are beautiful, but you will find no end to them. During the first day you will be hopeful. You will say to yourself '*I must simply stay on my course.*' The second day you will become afraid and the rattle of the birches will begin to haunt you. On the third day your mind will begin to wander and you will catch yourself forgetting your purpose. On the fourth day you will begin to love the birches, and take long rests to admire them. On the fifth day all is lost.

"No Sull has ever counted how many trees grow there. We do not concern ourselves with such things. But know this: the birch way is just the start. We are Sull and we are hunted, and we will not make it easy for our enemies to harm us."

Lan Fallstar turned away from her and began stowing the carpet and other items in his stallion's saddlebags. Ash watched him pull on his gloves and mount his horse. When he clicked his tongue and headed east she was not surprised.

He knew she had no choice but to follow him.

SIX

The Lamb Brothers

The dreams were like deep wells; once you stepped into one you kept falling. The sense of dizziness, and suspension of thought as you waited for the landing, was the same.

Most of the time Raif knew he was dreaming. Dreams had a texture to them, a vivid thickness, as if you were viewing them through an inch of clear glass. And they always had an edge, a point beyond which you could not see. Most of the time Raif didn't even think to look. He fell. Days passed, or perhaps they only seemed to, as he plunged deeper and deeper into a floor-less world.

All the people he loved were there. Da and Drey, Effie, Ash, Uncle Angus. The world made no distinction between those who were alive and those who were dead. Bear was there, watching with solemn interest as she chewed a mouthful of grass. Da told him never to leave his boots wet overnight. Shadows ebbing and swelling formed a cycle, not unlike night and day. When the shadows lifted, people came to visit him. Some watched, others spoke. Angus Lok usually had something to say. "A pretty shot," he offered more than once. "What's next?" None of it made much sense, but it was not unpleasant, just vaguely frustrating. Raif seldom had the chance to answer back.

When the shadows gathered and deepened, the nature of his dreams changed. Drey left, that was how the nightmares began. His brother would be there, at his side, and they'd be facing the danger together and it felt scary yet somehow good. They were brothers, and that was how it was between them. Then Drey would leave. One moment he would be there, his shoulder brushing against Raif's, and the next he would be gone. Disappeared. Raif's gut would clench. His hand would snap out in the darkness, and his fingers close around air.

He fell alone after that. Head spinning, fingers splayed like pinion feathers, he plunged deeper into the darkness. There was no going back, that was the true horror that lay waiting in the shadows.

Drey had gone, and there was no going back.

Time passed. Sometimes Raif would experience a deep bone-numbing cold and grow frightened as he lost sensation in his hands and feet. If the cold continued he would become certain that his hands and feet had broken off and his limbs now ended in stumps. Panic came then. Without hands, how could he break his fall?

An eyeblink could change everything. Cold could be replaced by heat, silence by animal howls. Things huffed and grunted on the far edge of his perception. Feeding. Shadows ebbed and swelled, creating an undertow that sucked him down.

Raif saw things he did not understand: a face staring up at him through a foot of pressure-formed ice; a wound smoking like a piece of kindling about to burst into flame; a thick and unlovely sword without fullers or decorations sinking to the bottom of a lake. Clan and kin loomed from the darkness, then fled.

Effie called out his name, and Raif's heart jumped in his chest. Where was she? He could not see her. *Effie*, he screamed at the darkness, *EFFIE!*

Bitty Shank came then, smiling with a closed mouth. He was dressed in armored plate bossed with iron studs and mounted with hammer chains. The chains rattled as he approached. He was shambling slightly, as if he'd had too much to drink or wasn't well. Raif smiled back at him. Bitty spread his lips in a death grin, revealing teeth pointed like fangs. Suddenly he lunged forward, and as his hand shot from his chest Raif saw a fist-size hole in Bitty's armor. The skin and rib cage were gone, and something black and gristled and not quite heart-shaped beat in Bitty's chest. Raif turned and tried to flee, but Bitty's hard, pincerlike fingers grabbed hold of his shoulders and bit into his flesh. Corpse breath pumped along Raif's cheek. Bitty hissed, "Where you running to, Raif? I've got a new heart for you to kill."

Stop! Raif cried, trying to wrench himself free. Bitty's armored fingers sank deeper and deeper, ten knives slicing his muscle like cheese.

From somewhere far in the shadows Angus asked calmly, "What's next?"

Bitty jumped on Raif's back. Stumbling forward, Raif struggled to keep his footing and failed. Air punched from his lungs as he landed hard on his stomach. Bitty clung to him like a spider, strong and inhumanly fast. Panicking, Raif bucked against Bitty's hold. Every time he took a breath Bitty squeezed him harder. Bitty's knife-fingers slid through the spaces between Raif's ribs, and Bitty was laughing, *laughing,* and Raif could feel the heart-shaped thing in Bitty's chest thumping against his back.

Leave us. The voice that spoke was chilling, an icy wind blowing through an open door.

Bitty froze, yet even as he stilled he became something *other.* Something dark and malleable, a heavy shadow spilling over Raif's shoulders and rolling across his face. Gasping for breath, Raif sucked in the shadows and breathed in the substance of Death.

Air crackled as she approached. Light failed her, sliding off her presence like dark wine poured over glass. The sweetly corrupt scent of spoiled pears preceded her as she leaned forward and laid a kiss on Raif's brow.

I believe I will call you son.

Noooooo, he screamed at her. *NOOOOOOOO!*

"Sshh."

Raif moved his head, tracking the new voice. As he shifted his attention one way, Death withdrew. Chuckling softly, she pulled her nightmare robes behind her, beckoned the darkness, and left. She always had the last laugh.

Droplets of lukewarm water pattered across Raif's face. As he scrunched his eyes tightly closed, he became aware that he was no longer falling. Somehow he had landed on solid ground.

Light filtering through his eyelids flickered as something moved between Raif and the source. *I am awake,* he said to himself, testing, his mind carefully calibrating each word. When water began to patter against his face a second time he cracked open his lips and let it fall into his mouth. His tongue soaked up the droplets like a sponge, and there was some pain as parched flesh expanded. As if that first pang had opened a door marked "Pain" Raif's mind began receiving signals from his body. His throat felt raw and scratchy, and his back and rib cage were stiff. A deep, unsettled ache in his left shoulder seemed the worst thing. It moved through his muscle like liquid.

Noises began to register. A strange chittering was followed by a rattling sound, like stones being shaken in a jar. Then footsteps, or rather foot*falls* for the sound was soft, subtle, owing more to the yielding of floor than the striking of feet.

Raif wondered whether he should open his eyes. Caution made him hesitate. The same instinct that told him his memory was working even though he had not probed it, told him his position here—wherever "here" might be—was vulnerable. So he listened and waited.

Time passed. The quality of light changed, the colors filtering through his eyelids shifting from blue to red. Air cooled. A sharp, burnt odor reached Raif's nose, followed by the scent of unfamiliar cookery. Bittersweet spices, licorice, clove and sumac floated upward with the scent of pungent smoke. Footfalls sounded again. A light was struck, then silence.

Raif waited, limbs still, body cooling. After a while it seemed to him that the silence had an expectant quality to it and he began to imagine he was being watched. As the hour wore on he grew more and more certain that someone was waiting for him to make a move. Raif wondered how long the watcher could keep silent, how long he or she could play the game.

More time passed, and aches and needs began to assert themselves. A muscle in Raif's damaged shoulder had tightened and needed to be flexed. Thirst gnawed at his throat, and he became aware of the fullness in his bladder. Quite suddenly he had to move.

He opened his eyes, and blinked against the light. It took

him a moment to understand what he saw. He was lying in a small, high-roofed tent braced with slender yellow bones that were double-curved like sycamore wings. The tent canvas was made from clarified hides; skins of stillborn animals that had been melted to the point of translucence. Clan did not have the knowledge to prepare them, and Raif imagined he was looking at great wealth. Rays from the setting sun shone through the hides, illuminating whorl patterns where fur had once grown. Raif could not guess what animal they came from.

Lines of silky blue smoke rose from three seaglass lanterns raised on longbone poles. To his left Raif saw a loose pile of saddle blankets dyed in colors of yellow: saffron, ocher, wheat. The tent floor consisted of thickly piled pelts and fleeces. Raif recognized the curly-haired fleece of a bighorn sheep and the dappled white pelt of a snag cat, but he did not recognize the others. One was orange with black circles, another was horse-shaped and striped black-and-white, and another still was stiff and ridged and green as pondweed. He was lying on a mattress of mounded earth overlaid with sheepskin, and he was covered by a single blanket woven from a wool softer and lighter than musk ox.

When he was ready, Raif turned his attention to the figure standing by the roped-down tent flap. The man was tall and lean. Sable-colored robes so dark and richly dyed they absorbed light were wrapped around his head and body in loosely twisted folds. The headpiece consisted of tiers of fabric hung from a curved hood. A single bow-shaped slit revealed his eyes.

The man bowed his head slowly but did not speak. He had been waiting, Raif decided, allowing his visitor time to grow accustomed to his surroundings. Squatting, the man poured green liquid from a copper pot into a glass cup with a copper base. The liquid steamed as he crossed the small, circular space of the tent and laid the cup on the hides by Raif's bed. The man's eyes were an inky brown and his eye whites had a faint bluish tinge to them, like a bird's. His skin was ash brown and there were three small black dots spaced evenly across the bridge of his nose that might have been tattoos.

Nodding once toward the cup and then to a wooden bowl close to Raif's feet the man withdrew. Night air purled through the tent slit as he raised the guide rope and disappeared. Raif watched the tent flap spool back down. Thick raw air circled the tent, dragging down smoke from the seaglass lamps as it sank.

Raif sat up. Pain shot along his left side, spiking in his shoulder. Blood rushed to his head, making his skin flush, and then rushed back down, leaving him faint. Planting his feet on the strange green hide, he rested for a moment before standing. A question that had been waiting just beyond the radius of his thoughts came sharply into view. *How long have I been here?* He had no answer, he realized, no experience to relate his body's condition to time.

Standing brought on a wave of dizziness, and he clung to one of the yellow bones as he waited it out. The bone echoed when he tapped it with his knuckle; hollow as a birdbone. When the tent stopped spinning, Raif reached for the green drink. It smelled of licorice and something his memory couldn't find a name for. He did not taste it, simply drank in deep gulps, swallowing rhythmically. Done, he glanced down at the wooden pot. Shaking his head, he decided to go outside rather than piss in a bowl.

He was still in the Great Want. The knowledge came to him the instant he stepped upon the gray, powdery earth. Overhead, the great wheel of stars blazed and turned. Knowing better than to gauge the passage of time in the Want by lunar phases, Raif ignored the rising moon. A light wind was gusting, shifting the dust into dunes and carrying the smelted-metal scent of new-formed glaciers. Raif was standing within a circle of five tents, all similar in shape and size to the one he had slept in. Outside the circle a corral consisting of tanned leathers hung from ivory tusks sheltered woolly mules and a single saffron-fleeced milk ewe. Inside the circle, at its center, four men squatted around a cook fire, spearing food from a black pot with sharpened sticks. No one spoke. All four glanced Raif's way before returning to the business of eating. They were dressed in similar robes of varying shades and it was impossible for Raif to tell which one of them had been in his tent. One of the four had plunged a lean copper spear into the soft earth, and it stood, point-up, within reach of his left hand.

Raif walked to the far side of the tent and urinated. From

what he could make out the Want looked flat here, with only dunes and boulders casting shadows against the moon. On impulse he bent down and scooped up a fistful of earth. The soil was pulverized pumice, and it poured through his fingers like cool, dry sand. Watching it he was struck with the idea that the Want had allowed him closer. Closer to what he could barely put into words. Something had happened long ago in this place. Sadaluk, the Listener of the Ice Trappers, had told how the Want had once been like any other land. It had a North and South and stars that could be relied on. Water flowed, trees grew, animals grazed and others hunted. People had lived here; if not Men, then perhaps another, older race. Raif had stood in one of their cities: *Kahl Barranon*, the Fortress of Grey Ice.

He shivered. Placing a hand on his left shoulder, he worked away at the pain.

A doom had been laid upon this place. Life had been destroyed. Time had been broken and now leaked. Space and distance had been stretched and folded, worn so thin in parts that you could see things on the horizon — mountains, hills, cities — that were thousands of leagues away, and so thickly gathered in others that you could spend all day walking and then turn to see your starting point less than a hundred feet behind you. Raif could not begin to imagine the magnitude of catastrophe that could break the bones of a continent, crush it so completely that its relation to nature and the heavens changed. He could not imagine it, but standing here, bare feet sinking into soft pumice as he watched the wind carve the dunes, he had the sense that its aftermath could be seen. Forces of heat and pressure had left scars. Angus had once told him that pumice was formed when mountains exploded and molten rock gushed up from the center of the earth. Was that what had happened here? Or something worse?

Raif headed back to the tent. The hooded men had finished eating and were now sipping hot liquid from glass cups. One man held the cup beneath his chin and let the steam roll over his face. No one spoke. Raif guessed the temperature to be just below freezing, yet they did not appear to feel it. Again, they noted him as he passed but did not halt him. They knew the

Want then. Knew that the phrases "free to go" and "you cannot leave" had no meaning here.

As soon as he was inside the tent, Raif felt his strength drain away. His body was tired and achy, and it seemed difficult to think. Turning, he spied a copper jug filled with ice melt. A hot stone from the fire had been dropped in the jug to thaw the ice, and the water tasted burned. After he had drunk his fill, Raif lay on the bed and slept.

He did not dream. At some point during the night he awoke. The lamps had burned out and it was wholly dark. A strange note, low and plaintive, rose outside the tent. At first Raif thought it was the moan of the wind over the dunes, but then other notes sounded. Slow and mournful, they joined the first note in harmony before glancing away. The song created was like nothing Raif had ever heard before, hollow and deeply resonant, and he was reminded of a story Angus had once told him about the great blue whales that swam beneath the frozen ledges of Endsea. "They travel the coldest, deepest currents where the water is heavy enough to crush men. Alone, they call out in the darkness, searching for more of their kind."

That was what the song of the hooded men sounded like to Raif: a cry in the dark. *Who is there?*

The song continued, solemn and questing. Raif listened for a while and then slept. When he awoke in the morning the memory of the hooded men's song had gone.

Dawn light, silvery and diffused by mist, shone through the tent's clarified hide walls. Inside all was cold and still. Raif lay and watched his breath crystallize in the frigid air. His body felt better. Rested. The pain in his shoulder was still there, but other things seemed more important. He was thirsty and hungry, and he wanted some answers.

Finding his belongings piled against the tent wall, he dressed himself against the cold. The Orrl cloak had been treated with some care, brushed and properly folded. No one in the clanholds could made cloaks like Orrl, cloaks that shifted color along with the landscape. They took months to prepare, the master furrier laying down countless layers of light-reflecting varnish on specially softened hides. Only white winter warriors were allowed to wear them, and Raif imagined the hooded men had never seen such a cloak before. He thought a moment and then drew his on. Unarmed, he went outside.

A shallow sea of mist washed across the dunes. The sky was pale and featureless, filled with haze. Two of the four hooded men were standing by the cookfire, gazing out through the tent circle toward the Want. They turned to watch as he approached. When he could see their eyes clearly, Raif greeted them.

"I am Raif Sevrance. Tell me who is owed my thanks."

Two pairs of brown eyes regarded him. Neither man spoke. After a moment the younger of the two turned to the elder, who nodded. The younger man headed away toward the tents.

Raif waited. The older man crouched by the cookfire and began turning over embers with a stick. From the little Raif could see of the skin around his eyes, Raif decided he was not the one who had first tended him in the tent. Over the bridge of his nose, he had five black dots, not three. Hooking the kettle handle with his stick, the man pulled the copper vessel from the fire. Flames crackled in the mist as he poured hot liquid into a cup and offered it to Raif.

Steam pungent with licorice and wormwood condensed on Raif's face as he accepted the glass cup. He did not drink. Wormwood was considered poison in the clanholds, yet he did not think this man meant to harm him.

A third man emerged from the farthest tent and made his way toward the fire. The ewe bleated as he passed the corral, begging for a milking. Raif set the cup on the ground. Within seconds it was swallowed by the mist. Coming to a halt before the fire, the third man nodded once to the elder. A dismissal. The elder rose with the aid of his stick and walked toward the corral.

Watching the third man Raif decided two things. One, it was the same man who had waited in the tent as he feigned sleep. And two, he, Raif Sevrance, would not be the first to speak.

The third man's gaze pierced Raif, passed through the holes in his eyes and saw inside. Raif felt known. There was a moment where something hung in the balance, as if a cup standing on a table had been knocked over and was rolling toward the edge. The cup might stop before it reached the edge or fall and break. Raif did not breathe. The brown-black gaze held him.

And then withdrew.

"Sit." The man spoke softly, long brown fingers uncurling to indicate the mist.

One word, yet Raif knew instantly several things. Common was not the man's first language. His accent was long and lilting, filled with smoke. Raif had the sense that he rarely used *any* language, that he was speaking solely for the stranger's benefit. Finally Raif knew that he had not been judged by this man. The cup had come to rest on the edge.

Raif sank to the ground. It was like diving into water; the coldness of the mist.

The man touched his chest. "Men once called me Tallal." Holding the back of his robe against the back of his knees, he dropped into a crouch. "If it pleases, you may use that name."

"And the others?"

"They are my lamb brothers. Their names are not mine to give." Absently, he made a slight stirring motion with his index fingers, rousing the mist.

"I owe you thanks. For saving me."

Tallal thought for a moment and then nodded. "Perhaps."

The word troubled Raif. He felt out of his depth, and wished he could see the whole of the man's face not just the slit containing his eyes. "How many are you?"

"Eleven."

It took Raif a moment to realize Tallal was including the animals in the count; six mules and the milk ewe. Four then. Yet five tents.

Tallal had tracked Raif's gaze as it moved from the corral to the tents. "In my homeland we have a saying: *God will only come if there is room in your house.*" He smiled; Raif could tell by the crinkling around his eyes. "My lamb brothers and I very much want God to come."

Raif became aware of a light pricking sensation around the small of his back. The mist was receding. For some reason he thought about the small gesture Tallal had made seconds earlier, the finger rousing in the mist. "Are you and your brothers lost?"

"No."

How can you be in the Want and not be lost? Raif wanted to ask yet didn't. A sense of propriety stopped him. It was too early in their acquaintance for such a question. "Where did you find me?"

Tallal shrugged. Anyone who hadn't spent time in the Want might take the gesture as a careless dismissal, but Raif understood it. *Anywhere. Nowhere. Who can say?*

"And my horse?"

The wind pressed Tallal's facepiece against his lips as he murmured. "The tide carried her away."

Raif nodded once. Now the mist had gone you could see the pumice dunes clearly. The wind was whittling them down, blowing streamers of dust from their crests. He let the icy particles scour his face awhile before turning back to Tallal. "How long have I been here?"

"Four nights as you and I count them." Tallal's voice was quiet. As he spoke he fed pale, barkless driftwood to the fire. "Much ailed you. My brothers and I did what we could to heal your body. We gave you water and tonics so you might sleep. I cleaned your wounds. If this breaks one of your holy laws I ask pardon."

Raif knew nothing of religions that forbade healing. "It does not."

Tallal nodded softly as if Raif were confirming something he had already guessed. "Strong gods guide you. They would not be petty, such gods."

A piece of driftwood hissed as moisture trapped inside it turned to steam. Raif imagined for a moment he could be anywhere: in a distant desert, a foreign shore, the face of the moon. Unfamiliar territory, and it was becoming his domain. Sometimes it seemed as if every step he'd taken since leaving clan had been a step into the unknown.

It was in his mind to say to Tallal that he had no gods, that he had broken an oath and abandoned his clan, and no gods that he knew of would keep faith with such a man. Yet he didn't. Instead he remembered the nightmare. It made him hope Tallal might be right.

"Where do you head?" he asked.

Behind his face mask, Tallal's expression changed. Raising his hand, he touched the dots on the bridge of his nose. Three separate movements. "Where the Maker of Souls leads."

Raif wondered what kind of god would lead his followers here. The Stone Gods had no dealings with the Want; their domain ended in the hard, fixed earth of the Badlands. "Your god claims this territory?"

Tallal lifted his gaze to the Want. "My god claims souls, not land. He commands us to search for souls in need of peace."

A compulsion out of his control, like an involuntary knee jerk, made Raif ask, "Dead or alive?"

Tallal looked at him, his dark eyes filled with knowledge. "We are lamb brothers. We care for the dead."

The wind moaned, skinning the dunes. Raif shivered deeply, his neck bones clicking. For an instant he had an image of himself as a carcass and the four hooded men as ravens picking at his dead flesh. He shook himself. You had to guard yourself against the distortions of the Want. All of them. Tallal and his lamb brothers had nothing to do with him, and to imagine otherwise was some kind of vain and crazy blasphemy. They were here to do the work of their gods. He was here because he couldn't find a way out.

Observing Raif's disorientation, Tallal said, "The buffalo women and the bird priests deal with *ayah*, the souls of the living. Their numbers are many. It is said that there is a herd of buffalo for every sheep." Tallal smiled gently; Raif could hear it in his voice. "It is not wise to get in their way. They can be fearsome when it comes to saving souls. When a man hears the rumble of many hooves and turns to see the buffalo stampeding it is not unlikely he will change his course."

Raif grinned. He was beginning to feel better, but he had a hunch it wouldn't last. "And the souls of the dead?"

A smoke ring of breath blew from Tallal's mouth. "*Morah.*" The word had power. Raif felt it pump against his eardrums. Slowly, rhythmically, Tallal began to rock back and forth on the balls of his feet. "*Morah* is the flesh of God. Every man, woman and child who passes through this mortal world grows a portion of God within them. This we call the soul. When someone dies their soul rises to the heavens and God claims it and sets it in place. The Book of Trials foretells the day when the Maker's body is whole and he will walk amongst us and we might look upon his face. We, the Sand People, await that day with hope and deepest longing. Yet if as much as a single soul is lost God's body will remain incomplete and he will be forever unknowable.

"The Book of Trials commands the lamb brothers to seek out the lost souls of the dead. All must be counted and released. They are precious to us beyond reckoning, for they contain the substance of God."

Raif stared into the flames whilst Tallal spoke. The wood burned green and white and gave off the cold and empty smell of high places. Listening to the lamb brother made him feel sad. Tallal had been set a task that would never be completed. His god would never come. There were too many men and women out there who had lost their way and died without peace or salvation. Generations of bodies had disappeared; flesh eaten by maggots, bones dried to husks then ground into sand. How could they be saved when there was no record of their existence?

And who would save the souls of the Unmade?

Heritas Cant had said that every thousand years the creatures of the Blind ride forth to claim more men for their armies. *"When a man or woman is touched by them they become Unmade. Not dead, never dead, but something different, cold and craving. The shadows enter them snuffing the light from their eyes and the warmth from their hearts. Everything is lost."*

Without thinking, Raif raised his hand to his shoulder. The wound had begun to sting. If Heritas Cant was right, then countless people over thousands of centuries had been lost, their souls claimed by the Endlords. Raif glanced at Tallal. Did he know this? Was he aware of the impossibility of his task?

Tallal's gaze was level. "Once a year in the hottest month of summer, when the sand snakes grow bold and even the blister beetles search for shade, the storms come. Day falls dark as night. Rain crashes from the sky and lightning strikes. Once in a very long while when lightning touches sand it turns to glass. This glass is very rare. A thousand thunderstorms may pass overhead yet everything—the sand, the wind, the moons and the stars—must be in accordance before lightning can transform sand into glass. Stormglass is a powerful talisman. Kings and shamans covet it. It is said that when you look into it you see other storms; storms that are gathering and may come to be, storms of thunder and storms of men. My people sweep the sands for it when we travel. Like gingerroot it lies beneath the surface, out of sight, and we use acacia branches to comb the dunes as we walk the cattle. We dream of finding the perfect unbroken piece, long as a sword and clear as water. In my lifetime I have never known anyone to find such a piece. Yet still we sweep."

Tallal paused, waited for Raif to meet his gaze. "To search is to be sustained by hope. Every morning we may wake and say *Perhaps today I will find what I seek*. A sense of purpose is like a meal of lamb and rice; it can fill an empty man."

Raif breathed in deeply, letting the cold air steep inside his chest. He wondered at what point Tallal had ceased talking about the search for stormglass and started talking about the two of them instead. Glancing down at his hands, Raif saw the cold had turned them gray. His fingers felt raw, and the stump on his left hand where Stillborn had chopped off the tip of his little finger looked bald and misshapen. The wound had healed months ago, but the ridge of scar tissue left behind by the stitches would never make a pretty sight. It was the price of admittance to the Maimed Men. You could not become one of them and remain whole.

Will you come back?

Raif thrust his hands into the folds of his Orrl cloak, hoping to thrust away Stillborn's words. Sunlight broke through the haze, giving off a weak silvery light that made nothing seem warmer.

Tallal rose to standing. A figure emerged from the farthest tent and headed toward the fire. Judging from the stoop of his shoulders and the slight rocking motion of his walk, Raif guessed it to be the elder lamb brother he had addressed earlier. The man was carrying a rolled-up prayer mat.

"We pray now," Tallal said.

Raif stood. He needed to think. Crazy ideas were getting tangled in his head. Did the lamb brothers know who they had rescued? *I watch the dead. They save them. Does it mean some-thing or nothing?*

Tallal walked to meet the elder man and the two of them exchanged a handful of words in a foreign tongue. Wind twisted their cloaks around their legs. The elder nodded once. More words were spoken and then Tallal headed back toward Raif.

"My brother asks if you will join us in prayer."

Raif was surprised by his desire to say yes. He had not expected to be included. Shaking his head, he said, "Perhaps tomorrow." As he spoke he knew it was a lie.

Tallal knew it too. "As you wish."

A moment passed where Raif wanted to say something but didn't. How could you tell someone that the reason you didn't want to pray to their gods was because you feared being struck by a bolt of lightning? Nodding farewell to Tallal, Raif headed back toward his tent.

The lamb brother stopped him with a question. "How long have you walked the Want?"

Turning, Raif smiled gently. A distance of twenty paces separated him from the masked and robed figure of Tallal. Pumice blowing from the dunes was already beginning to fill in his footsteps. "Too long."

Tallal did not return Raif's smile. His eyes were serious, and for the first time Raif noticed deep lines around them. "A man who does not know where he is headed will never find a way out."

Raif turned and walked away.

SEVEN

Twenty Stone of Eye

Marafice Eye thrust his good foot into the stirrup and hauled himself over the back of his horse. The steel gray stallion shook its head and stamped its iron-ringed hooves against the traprock, and Marafice the Knife had to shorten the reins and rap on its rump to take command. It was a fine beast, and the Knife didn't blame it for fighting. If someone thrust a metal bit between his teeth and forced two metal spurs into his belly he'd likely do the same.

Damn, but it was cold. The sky west of Ganmiddich was turning that mouth-ulcer color that meant snow, and the slow water on the inside edge of the river bend was quickening to ice. At least there was no wind. It wasn't an ideal day for an assault on the Crab Gate, but in Marafice Eye's experience it was always better to attack than wait.

He was careful as he tightened the waist and chest cinches on his breast and back plates. Small things like that could betray him; those little adjustments close to the body that everyone with two eyes could do without thought. And they were watching him, make no mistake about it. Those high-and-mighty grangelords and their sons; he could feel their sharp and critical gazes on his back. *Butcher son*, they called him—but never to his face. That wasn't their way. They preferred to smile and nod and "yes, sir" him man-to-man. They were scared of him, of course, but fear was an interesting thing, Marafice had noticed, and feeling contempt for what you feared eased the sting. So the lordlings were nice to him in person—though they choked on it—and in private they cursed him as a low-bred, savage beast.

Ignoring the squire waiting with his sword, Marafice Eye spun his massive warhorse and looked out upon the sea of tents that spread across the wooded upland north of the river.

It was a quarter past dawn and the strange mists had gone, but there was still something not to his liking about the light. The grangelords had claimed the best and safest ground, hard along the rocky cliffs of the Wolf, and their fancy silk and linen tents reflected the unlovely color of the sky. Breakfast was being cooked, and from the looks of things the grangelords weren't denying themselves one bit. Servants were stirring pots, plucking game birds, toasting cheese, and grinding peppercorns. Some fool had built a smokefire and was cranking an entire side of lamb. What did they think this was, a day at the tourney field?

Grimacing in disgust, the Knife began to turn his horse, but at that moment his attention was caught by a single figure standing in front of the farthest silk tent.

Ready, that was Marafice's first thought. Unlike most of his fellow grangelords, Garric Hews of House Hews, heir to the vast holdings of the Eastern Granges, was armed and armored. His chest piece was simply fashioned, with rolled edges around the neck and waist, and a reinforced plate above the heart. It had probably cost more than a house. Marafice knew subtle workmanship when he saw it. The enameling alone would have taken an armorer three months. Contrasting bands of white and silver ran along the turning edges and cloak pommels, and a coin-size decoration on the right shoulder had been jeweled and enameled in the shape of a rampant boar. The Whitehog of House Hews.

Garric Hews returned Marafice's stare. His war helm was tucked under his arm, revealing a soldier's close-cropped hair. He was nineteen. Yet it wasn't a normal nineteen. Being a grangelord bred arrogance. Being heir to the greatest house in Spire Vanis bred something more. Twenty-three surlords had called themselves Hews, and Garric Hews' desire to make himself the twenty-fourth could be read in the muscle mass beneath his face. The Knife had observed him on the practice court and in the barracks; he was a savage fighter and a cool-headed controller of men. A company of seven hundred hideclads rode under him. They were the best-equipped men in the entire army; each and every one of them horsed, and chain-mailed, and armed with dagger, horse sword and pike. Hews trained them daily in formation, and Marafice had to admit he did a good job of it. He knew the value of well-trained men.

They both did. Shifting a muscle close to his mouth, Hews showed a cold smile to his rival. Marafice received all the information delivered in the smile, and then turned his horse sharply and rode away. He would give the Whitehog nothing back.

The game trail ran southeast, following the river as it bow-curved upstream and Marafice took it through the camp. Jon Burden was crouching by the red fire, drinking breakfast. It was likely there was ale in his pewter tankard, but Marafice wasn't worried about that. The first captain of the newly formed Rive Company knew how to carry his drink. He and his second-in-command Tat Mackelroy, known as Mackerel, stood as Marafice rode toward them, but Marafice waved them down. He would parley with them later. Right now he needed to be alone.

The camp was spread over half a league, and it was already starting to smell. Horse shit, man sweat, woodsmoke, and lamb grease had combined to form a sharp-sweet scent that the Knife had come to associate with war. Here in the Rive section it was especially bad. For some bloody-minded reason known only to themselves, Rive Company had taken to burning horse turds as fuel. Rive Company had been formed three months earlier in Spire Vanis from volunteers and veterans of the city's Rive Watch. Through no coincidence whatsoever they numbered seven hundred. Marafice Eye hadn't been present when the decision to burn horse turds had been taken, but he guessed it had little to do with a shortage of fuel and more to do with camp politics.

Rive Company was directly upwind of the grangelords' encampment, and they gifted the grangelords with the smell. It was the way it had always been in Spire Vanis: that old, bitter rivalry between the grangelords and the watch. The grangelords held and sheriffed the land outside the city and the watch policed it within. Nothing, not one wormy apple or tin spoon, entered Spire Vanis without passing the inspection of the watch. And no one, not even Garric Hews or the High Examiner himself, could gain access to the Surlord without being escorted into his presence by the watch.

The grangelords resented those two facts with such intensity they all but frothed at the mouth like rabid dogs. Power was theirs. They were the ones with the wealth, the land, the titles and the private armies so misleadingly named hideclads. Outside the city they were as good as kings. Within it they were reduced to supplicants—by baseborn, low-bred thugs, no less. That was what galled them the most.

Marafice stretched his lips into a tight smile. They were his men, the watch. Good men, hard-fighting, hard-playing, down-to-earth. *They* weren't having roasted game bird for breakfast, that was for sure. It would be porridge with a dollop of lamb's grease—and a chunk of blood sausage if they were lucky. They were well-equipped though. Marafice himself had made sure of that. He wasn't about to send his brothers-in-the-watch to war unprepared. All seven hundred had Rive Blades, the blood-tinted swords fired in the Red Forge. The Knife had wrung money from the Surlord to pay for their pikes, and when he hadn't been able to wring more he had paid for their plate armor himself. It had cost him the entire dowry he had received from Roland Stornoway for the pleasure of marrying his eldest daughter. That, and half the savings he had on account with the tight-lipped priests of the Bone Temple. It wasn't fancy stuff like the Whitehog's, but it was solid, and if a lance blow landed just right it might make the difference between broken ribs and disembowelment.

Reaching the edge of the cliff, Marafice reined in his horse and dismounted. He was free of the camp now, hidden from hostile glances by a crop of spindly weed trees and some evil-looking thorns. Below him lay the great expanse of the Wolf River, its waters brown with tannin. Trees and bushes uprooted by an earlier thaw had logjammed to form an island midstream. Some kind of waterfowl perched atop one of the upturned root balls, but Marafice didn't know enough about birds to identify the breed. Abruptly he turned. The updraft funneling along the cliff had chilled his dead eye.

Cover it, advised the very few people who dared speak to him about the loss of his right eye. *Have a bridle maker cut out a patch and strap it over the socket.* He had nearly done just that, but something had stopped him. Some kind of fool pigheadedness that he had come to regret but would not now reverse. For better or worse it had become who he was. The hollow socket repulsed him, and he had not willingly looked in a glass in three months. On his worst nights he suspected that his exterior now accurately reflected what lay within. People had always thought him a monster. Now he had become one.

The strange thing was that sometimes he thought he could see through his missing eye. In his dreams he saw further. The colors were deeper and the edges as crisp as a line drawing. Even after he woke he was sure the eye was still in place . . . right until the moment when he reached for the water pitcher and poured himself a cup. It spilled. It always spilled. He could see well enough over distance, but those small judgments close to the body betrayed him every time.

Marafice rubbed the socket with his gloved fist. The coldness was hard to get used to, the chill so close it could freeze his thoughts. Damn Asarhia March. Her foul sorceries had robbed him of the skin of his foot and an eye. She had killed his brothers-in-the-watch, too. Five of them, blasted against the hard granite of the Bitter Hills . . .

Enough, he told himself. What was done was done. He was Marafice Eye, Protector General of the Rive Watch, the Surlord's declared successor, and husband to Liona Stornoway, Daughter of the High Granges. He had gained more than he'd lost, and you could not say that about most men.

True enough his new wife was a high-strung slattern whose belly was currently swelling with another man's brat. But she was rich beyond reckoning and she had the very great fortune of being born into one of the five Great Houses of Spire Vanis.

Stornoway could give Hews a run for its money. It was older than Hews, claiming an ancestor of the Bastard Lord himself Torny Fyfe, and although it could not match the sheer number of surlords spawned by House Hews, it more than made up for it in wealth. Stornoway held the two most important high passes south of the city, and all goods coming north across the mountains were subject to its tariffs. That, canny management of its holdings and rumors of Sull gold made Stornoway a byword for untold riches in Spire Vanis. The scale of the wealth took some getting used to. What did a butcher's son know of baudekin, emeralds, ambergris, perfumed cushions, and gilded prayer books? What did he care? Power was what counted. That Stornoway gold would need to work. Arms, fortifications, horses, guards, bribes: those were the only things it was good for.

Marafice squinted into the eastern sky. Behind the storm-heads the sun was rising. It was time to move out.

He returned to camp quickly, signaling to the hornsman to call arms. Jon Burden rode to meet him and together they inspected Rive Company as it formed ranks.

Helmets, Marafice thought dryly. *I should have forked out for some matching sets.*

The men of Rive Company were lean and hard and cloaked in red. Those who were wearing birdhelms looked frightening enough to appear in children's nightmares. With their faces entirely covered by steel likenesses of the Killhound of Spire Vanis, they could no longer fully rotate their necks and moved like beings awakened from the dead. A good third of the seven hundred did not possess birdhelms and wore whatever they could beg, borrow or scavenge. Many wore standard pothelms forged from black iron. Others had full visored helms complete with crests they had no rights to and feathers they had no need for. One man sported a helm with two enormous bullhorns forged to the sides, and another wore something that looked suspiciously like a wooden bowl.

"Weadie," Marafice called out to the man.

Will Weadie was in the process of binding his horse's tail to prevent it from flaying in the charge. Tall and veiny with a nose that was beginning to wart, Weadie was pushing fifty. Marafice remembered training under him as a new recruit. Weadie had been second to the master-at-arms, Andrew Perish, who was also amongst the seven hundred here today.

"Sir." Weadie rubbed his nose with the back of his hand.

"Is that a wooden bowl on your head?"

"Aye, sir." Weadie knocked on the crown, producing a hollow rap. "I drilled the holes meself and me sister made the straps."

"You should have come to me. I would have seen you got something better."

Weadie shook his head. "Wouldn't want it. After thirty years in the watch I'm done wearing the bird skulls. Call me reckless, but I'd rather take my chances with a flying ax than ride around with nine pounds of metal on my head."

Marafice believed him. He also believed that Will Weadie, like many men retired from the watch, was sorely in need of funds. The annual pension of ten silver coins barely stretched to a hot dinner every night. They needed plunder, and Marafice was going to make sure they got it. First spoils were theirs, by order of the Surlord, Penthero Iss. Marafice had insisted upon it, but he was no fool and they were a long way from Spire Vanis and the Surlord's words were no longer law.

The wrangling had already begun. Farms, mills, cottages, smiths and stovehouses had been plundered on the journey. Only yesterday they had raided a mining camp upriver. It was the only time Marafice could recall attending a raid where the fighting was worse *after* than during it. He'd been glad of his reputation then. Both the hideclads and mercenaries feared him in equal measure, and just the word that he was riding in to break up the feuding was enough to excite a spontaneous laying down of arms.

God only knew how the spoils had been divvied, but judging from the zealousness of the guards posted outside Rive Company's supply tent, his brothers-in-the-watch hadn't fared too badly.

To Weadie he said, "Put some metal under there. *Now!*"

Weadie jumped at the force of his voice. "Aye, sir."

Marafice turned away as the aging armsman ran toward the red fire in search of an iron pot or anything else that would do the job. Damn fool. Didn't he know they'd be shot from above with longbows? Those clannish arrowheads hit like axes.

"Jon," he said to the commander of Rive Company. "We split the men, fifty-fifty. Have them form shield walls on either side of Hog Company. Hews is taking the center."

"Aye."

The word conveyed all that Jon Burden did not like about this plan. They'd discussed most of it last night, but only today as he'd looked into Garric Hews' face and seen all the arrogance and challenge there had Marafice decided firm. Rive Company would flank Whitehog Company like a pair of armed guards. Marafice trusted Garric Hews about as much as he trusted a whore with open sores.

I am better than you. I am harder and more cunning, and one day when you hear the hiss of wind in your chest it will be me sliding out the knife.

That was what Garric Hews had said earlier with his cool, superior smile. They were rivals for the lordship of Spire Vanis, and this—this godforsaken wasteland ruled by animal-skinned clansmen—was where they would fight it out. Penthero Iss had named his successor, and Garric Hews did not like the sound of Marafice Eye, Surlord, one bit. What Iss had done was unprecedented, and not likely to stick once he was dead and gone, but that wasn't the point. Marafice had publicly declared himself for Surlord. Anyone who fancied that position for himself would have to deal with seven feet, twenty stone of Eye.

"I still say we keep our men together," Jon Burden said. "Take the left flank. Stay out of the river."

Marafice shook his head once, hard. They were riding between rows of open-fronted rawhide tents, their horses' hoofs sinking deep into the mud. Camp priests had been busy before dawn, spreading the sacred ash. The strange tingly odor of burned nightshade was released with every step. "If the gate falls the Whitehog could cut us off. A dozen horsemen placed just right, and he could hold us back while Hog Company rides through. This way we'll be on him. Garric Hews will be seeing so much red he'll think his head's split open."

Jon Burden grunted. He was a stocky, powerfully built man with thick blond hair and a full beard that was showing gray. The killhound brooch that fastened his battle cloak boasted two mosquito-size rubies for eyes. Those rubies denoted twenty years service as a captain of the watch. In his time Jon Burden had expelled the Forsworn from the city, quelled the hunger riots during the bitter winter following Penthero Iss' ascension to Surlord, led the force that rode against Hound's Mire at Choke Creek, crushed the Nine-Day Rebellion led by the Lord of the Mercury Granges, and foiled numerous assassination attempts on Iss. Jon Burden knew what it took to win. He had argued to take the center, and Marafice had nearly let him have it, but a conversation he'd had with Penthero Iss ten weeks ago in Spire Vanis had stopped him.

"How do I lead this army of misfits?" Marafice had demanded of Iss, his voice echoing across the marble-entombed space of the Blackvault. "The grangelords, the darkcloaks, the watch?"

"You have been Lord Protector of Spire Vanis for eighteen years," Iss had replied, cool as well water. "You already know how to lead. Now you must learn how to use."

Marafice shivered as he remembered his Surlord's words. Iss' brand of cold calculation was foreign to him, but of all the men he knew Penthero Iss had risen the farthest and stayed put the longest. That meant something to the Knife. Iss was the son of an onion farmer from Trance Vor; it served a butcher's son well to listen and learn.

So he would use Garric Hews and Whitehog Company by giving them the honor of taking the center during the assault. The greatest danger lay in the center—it was the spearhead of the attack, open to the worst Ganmiddich could fire at them— and Marafice's first instinct had been similar to Jon Burden's: we will take this peril as our own. Yet when he had asked himself *Would Iss have done this?* he had paused and changed his course.

The simple fact was that Whitehog had superior training and weaponry. Marafice knew it. Hews knew it. Doubtless Jon Burden knew it too but his pride got in the way. Whitehog Company had been training in battle formation for years. They were tight. Their captains had decades of experience patrolling the southern border against the Glaive, and their leader was sharp and aggressive. Rive Company were fine men, but a good third were over forty—and a high portion of that number hadn't seen active service in years. Much though he would have liked to cherry-pick the best seven hundred from the watch, Marafice had taken only those who had volunteered. The result was a motley band of seasoned fighters, thrill-seekers, zealots, old men dreaming of recapturing their glory days and scroungers in need of cash. It wasn't an ideal force by any reckoning, but Marafice took some pride in the fact that none were here against their will.

Besides, it was in his interest to keep Spire Vanis secure in his absence. Deplete the watch too badly and he put the Surlord's security at risk. An assassination while he was here, a thousand leagues and twenty-one days' hard travel from the city, was the last thing Marafice wanted. If anything ever happened to the Surlord he needed to be close to claim his prize.

"Lead an army for me, Knife," Iss had murmured all those months ago in the Blackvault, "and in return I will name you as my successor."

Marafice blew air from his mouth. While he'd stood here thinking, mud had turned to chalk on his horse's hooves.

"Jon," he said brusquely. "I will hear no more arguments. Split the men. We ride within the quarter."

He waited until Jon Burden met his gaze and nodded, and then kicked his horse toward Mud Camp, where the mercenary companies were forming ranks. This business of surlording won no friends. Even though Jon Burden had no love for Garric Hews and Whitehog Company, he could not be told the second reason Marafice had let them take the center. Hews would be leading his men. He had ridden at the head of the line on every raid and sortie Hog Company had undertaken since leaving Spire Vanis. Today that placed him at the center of the center—bull's-eye by Marafice's reckoning.

The Knife would not deceive himself. It would suit him well if Garric Hews was picked off by a sharp-eyed clannish bowman. No duels or backstabbing need be done. No risk of open grangewars between the Eastern Granges and the High Granges, no repercussions, ill feelings, or mistakes.

Marafice Eye shrugged shoulders the size of full-grown sheep. A man could always hope.

Mud Camp was situated at the north of the encampment, hard against the treeline. Two creeks, which the mercenaries had named the Ooze and the Pisser, ran like open drains through the ranks of tents. Within the camp the mercenaries had formed clans. The professional companies had chosen the most defensible ground, backing onto thick stands of stone pine. Upstream of the other mercenaries, they had the fresher water and higher ground. Their cover consisted of giant sheets of waxed canvas hung over birch poles. Sourwoods, uprooted for use as windbreakers, had been lashed into lines in place of walls. Marafice admired the design. It was trim and economical, and had the advantage of leaving the mercenary companies light on their feet. They didn't haul a dozen cartloads of tent supplies from camp to camp like the grangelords. They carried everything they needed on eight packhorses.

Marafice's gaze became less admiring as he scanned the lower tiers of Mud Camp. Professional mercenary companies were one thing. Freelancers were another entirely. Motley bands of ill-equipped foot soldiers were milling around the cook fires, sucking on sparrow bones, oiling spear heads with filthy rags, fastening on buckled and peeling body armor, scratching their flea bites, swilling from tin flasks filled with crude grain alcohol, and spitting with feeling into the dirt. Chicken farmers, street vendors, tallow makers, stablehands, fish picklers, lime boys, pot boys, bath boys, outlaws, thieves: they were all here and nervous as hens around the smell of fox. Their contracts promised one silver piece a tenday and a "just and equitable portion of all common spoils won during the campaign." Which meant they would probably get nothing at all.

Marafice felt some sympathy for them, but his disgust at their unpreparedness and the state of their camp was stronger. What sort of men let their animals stand in a lagoon of their own filth?

He was not pleasant as he gave his final orders.

Steffan Grimes, captain of the largest professional outfit and acting commander of the entire mercenary contingent, rode forward to discuss the last-minute changes. Born from scratch-farming stock on the brush flats east of Hound's Mire, Grimes had propelled himself far for a man who was still a good five years under thirty. When the Knife looked into Grimes' blunt, ice-tanned face he saw himself. Younger. Coarser. Still intimidated by the high-and-mighty grangelords.

"They have arseholes just the same as you and I," he had said

to Grimes at the start of the campaign, *"the only difference is, with all the duck livers, lark tongues, and raw oysters they eat, they use theirs a lot more."*

It had been exactly what he wished someone had said to him at that age, yet Grimes had not been ready to hear it. He was still unsure of himself around Garric Hews and his high-stepping brethren. When a grangelord barked an order, Steffan Grimes' first instinct was to obey. It was a problem. Grangelords came in all varieties, from shrewd, to middling, to full-blown raving idiocy, yet each and every one of them believed he had a God-given right to lead men.

That was where Andrew Perish came in. Marafice clasped Grimes' forearm and wished him "Profit on the battlefield," and then turned to meet his former master-at-arms.

Andrew Perish had removed himself from the bustle of the camp and was standing on the cliff edge, gazing south at the hazy purple mounds of the Bitter Hills. Smoke rising from a fist-size iron crucible at his feet warned mortals to leave him well alone. Andrew Perish was speaking with God.

The master-at-arms of the Rive Watch was sixty-one years old, yet he had the spread-legged, straight-backed stance of a man half his age. His hair was soldier-short and perfectly white. A shiny rash on his jaw and neck told of his habit of shaving twice a day. That same unbending self-discipline made him rise in the darkness of predawn every morning to prepare his kit, wash his small linens, cook his breakfast and tamp his own fire. He was a forty-year veteran of the Rive Watch, a man of fierce faith, and once long ago in a separate lifetime he'd been the second son of the Lord of the Wild Spire Granges.

In Marafice Eye's opinion he was the most valuable man in the camp.

The Knife waited for the communion to be done. He was little used to waiting and it made him grumpy. Watchful eyes marked the deference and judged it. That made him even grumpier. After a time he dismounted. Pain shot along his damaged foot as his weight hit the ground. He ignored it.

"It will snow and it will be bloody," Perish said at last, stamping his heel on the crucible and driving it deep into the mud, "but His work will be done."

Andrew Perish turned to face his commander-in-chief. Cataracts were beginning to whiten his brown eyes, yet it only made his gaze seem sharper. It had the force of a fist punching through a wall. "Every clansman we kill will be a prayer: *See how we love thee, Sweet God.*"

Marafice made his face like stone. True belief disturbed him. His experiences during the Expulsions had taught him to be wary of men who had the fuel of God burning in their eyes. You couldn't always control them. There had to be close to a thousand here today who had come for no other reason than to slay heretics. They were good men, hardworking, ordinarily loyal, yet you could not predict what would happen if their God fuel was ignited. The Knife had a strong memory of sitting his horse and looking on as his fellow brothers-in-the-watch hacked off the hands and feet of Forsworn knights. He had not forestalled that unnecessary cruelty, but it did not mean he had liked it.

He was all business as he spoke with Perish. "Inform Hews he'll be taking the center. We're splitting Rive—we'll flank him. I'll be leading the east flank. Burden will head the west."

Andrew Perish bit this off and chewed on it. As battle plans went it wasn't the brightest, but Perish wasn't the sort to quibble over details. He was the liaison, the bridge between the grangelords and their armies and the great unlanded rest of them. Perish could talk to the most foulmouthed, foul-smelling swine herder in Mud Camp and then turn around and parley with a pride of perfumed grangelords reposing in their silk tents. All respected him: He had foot soldier's muck on his boots and the blood of lords in his veins.

The Knife knew he could command the grangelords without Perish's help, but this way it was easier. Smoother. Tempers were held in check on both sides. The grangelords didn't have to receive orders directly from a butcher's son, and everyone else was spared the aggravation of dealing with the grangelords first-hand.

"Watch him." Perish's voice was iron hard. Between them there was no need to name names. "Once the battle is met he will abide by his own rules."

Marafice glanced east toward the river bend that concealed

the green traprock walls of Ganmiddich. The first snow had begun to fall, sleek and heavy flakes that entered the water like diving birds. "I have my own rule in this battle," he said. "Dog eat Hog."

EIGHT

A Cart Pulled by
Twelve Horses

"Raina. What d'you make of that?"

Raina Blackhail followed Anwyn Bird's gaze south across the Blackhail clanhold. They were standing on the ancient bowman's gallery that jutted from the roundhouse's southern wall. Longhead said no one had been up here in decades, and Raina could see why. The gallery had been built on to the exterior dome by the War chief, Ewan Blackhail. Ewan's son had slain the last of the Dhoone kings, and Ewan had feared retaliation. Amongst his many hastily built defenses was a ringwall that circled the roundhouse at a distance of two hundred feet, a six-story watchtower built atop Peck's Hill in the eastern pinewall, and a series of booby-trapped wells and earthworks that ran along the Dhoone-Blackhail border and that, as far as Raina knew, had killed a whole lot of sheep. Five hundred years later and few of Ewan's creations were still standing. Judging from the cracked stonework and faint rocking motion of the ledge this one didn't have long to go.

Still. It was good to be here. The strange eastern wind was blowing, snapping the blackstone pines in the graze and pushing around the last of the snow. A red-tailed hawk was riding the thermals, scanning for weasels and other small prey through the bare branches of Oldwood. The sky was clear, and a cold and a brilliant sun was shining. Standing high atop the roundhouse you could see for leagues.

And no one but the person standing next to you could hear you speak. Raina glanced at her old friend, the clan matron

Anwyn Bird. Anwyn was getting old. Her ice-tanned face was deeply lined, and her eyes had extra water in them. Not for the first time Raina found herself wondering why Anwyn drove herself so hard. She had never married, had no family that Raina was aware of, yet she had more strength of purpose than anyone in the entire clan. When she wasn't baking bread for two thousand, she was butchering winter kills in the gameroom, milking ewes in the dairy, gutting eels in the kitchen yard, plucking geese in the poultry shed, distilling hard liquor in the stillroom, or fletching arrows in her workshop. Clan was her life. Comparing Anwyn's dedication with her own, Raina found herself wanting. Yet it was she, Raina Blackhail, who had spoken up in the gameroom.

I will be chief.

"Over there," Anwyn said, nodding her chin southwest. "At the treeline."

Raina looked again and this time she saw something emerging from the black-green mass of the southern pines. A team of twelve horses was hauling a war cart toward the roundhouse. The cart was built from whole glazed logs that shone red in the sun, and its weight was so great that it needed six wheel axles to support it. Black smoke gouted from a chimney built into the center of the roof. A pair of archers, crossbows loaded, prowled the roof's flat timbers, and a dozen heavily armed outriders formed a shield wall around the cart and team.

"Can you see their colors?"

Raina shook her head. "Dark, is all I can make out."

They watched in silence as the great, smoking behemoth lurched and rolled along the uneven surface of the graze road. Raina wondered if Anwyn was feeling the same level of unease as she was. Ever since the clanwars started all roads into the clanhold had been heavily patrolled. Redoubts had been built at key bends and crossings. Nothing could get this close to the roundhouse without sanction. So who had sanctioned this? And why hadn't she and Anwyn been informed?

"It's probably some war contraption brought in to defend the Crab Gate." Anwyn turned her back on the cart and looked Raina in the eye. The sudden movement made the fox lore suspended around her neck jump out from beneath the neckline of her dress. "The first thousand leave at dawn. Mace just told Orwin he intends to ride at the head."

Raina nodded slowly, letting the news sink in. She had hoped her husband would lead the war party headed to Ganmiddich, but until now she hadn't been sure. Ever since Arlec Byce and Cleg Trotter had returned from the Crab Gate, the roundhouse had been gearing up for war. Weapons, armor, horses, mules, carts, supplies: all had to be assembled and coordinated. Mace had taken charge of the planning, but when asked if he intended to ride to defend Ganmiddich himself he had been evasive. He was a wolf, you could not forget that. Secrecy was one of his ploys. How could your enemies plot against you when they could not be sure of your plans?

"With Mace gone we should be able to restore some order to our house." It was the closest Anwyn had come to open criticism of the Hail chief since the night in the gameroom. She looked like she might say more, but Raina spoke to halt her.

"The repairs are going well. As soon as the remains of the Hailstone are removed we can seal the east wall."

"If they ever get removed," Anwyn retorted. "The one man who can decide the fate of the stone rides off into the sunrise at dawn. That's our soul, lying there and turning to dust. How can he stand by and watch as it blows away?"

"Hush," Raina whispered. Even out here she was nervous of her husband's spies. *Little mice with weasels' tails.* "If Mace rides tomorrow without reaching a decision it will suit us well enough. I will decide what will be done. I will see that the remains of the sixteenth Blackhail guidestone are laid to rest with proper dignity. Me, wife to two chiefs. And once it's done I'll send a party east to Trance Vor and command them to return with a new stone." Raina hardly knew where the words came from. Until the very moment she spoke them she had been dead set against interfering with the fate of the guidestone. *That's how power works,* she imagined. *See an opportunity and seize it.*

Muscles in Anwyn Bird's plump face tightened and Raina feared she had made a mistake. Yet the clan matron simply nodded. "Fair enough. Someone has to do it."

Raina searched Anwyn's gray eyes, but found them guarded.

I will lose friends, she realized. *Claim power and people will judge you.* Suddenly Raina wanted very much to run through the roundhouse, find Dagro and crush him to her chest. It was so easy to conjure up his smell: horses and tanned leather, and that fine earthy scent that was his own. Gods, how she missed him. She did not want this. Did Anwyn actually think that she wanted to be chief? She would give up everything to have her husband back, willingly go and live in a mountain cave with the wild clans and eat nothing but rabbit haunches and tree bark for the rest of her life. You couldn't turn back time though. As a child she'd been told stories of dragons and sorcery and giants, stories where forest folk abducted children while they slept and dragged them into enchanted worlds, where men were turned to stone by angry necromancers, and where the gods crushed entire armies in their fists and the next day built walls with the bones. Not one of those fantastical, unbelievable stories had ever mentioned turning back time. None had dared offer that false hope.

Anwyn could read people's thoughts, Raina decided, for she said, "The past months have not gone easy on any of us, Raina. Loved ones dead. War. Hardship. And now the stone. Yet we are Blackhail, the first amongst clans, and we do not hide and we do not cower and we will have our revenge."

Hairs on Raina's arms pricked upright. The clan boast. Sending out a hand to steady herself against the stone balustrade, she let the east wind roll over her face. She smelled pine resin and frozen earth. Yes, she wanted revenge. Her husband had been slain in cold blood. Her body had been violated. Shor Gormalin, the man who would have protected her, had been shot in the back of the head. And what had she, Raina Blackhail, done to right those wrongs? Nothing. She shared a bed with the man who had done them.

Sister of Gods what have I let myself become?

Letting out a long breath, Raina studied Anwyn. It was unusual to see the bleached cross section of fox bone. The clan matron normally kept her lore tucked away. People often made the mistake of assuming Anwyn's lore had to be some kind of bird—pheasant, turkey vulture, hawk—but it wasn't. Anwyn was a fox. Raina hadn't learned that fact for many years, for lores were private things and it was considered impertinent to ask someone outright what spirit claimed them. Instead you learned through friends and kin. The widows knew the most, keeping tally each night around the hearth. Bessie Flapp had been the one to tell Raina that Anwyn was a fox. "She's a queer one, is our Anny. All hustle and bustle on the surface, but quiet as a fox underneath."

Bessie was dead now, killed during the sundering. Raina had never known her to speak a word that wasn't true.

"Why do you push me, Anny?" Raina asked, surprising herself again. "Out of a whole roundhouse of people why should I be the one to overthrow him?"

Anwyn laid a hand on her skirt to stop the wind from getting under it. When she spoke the normal ruddiness dropped from her voice, revealing a deeper, clearer tone underneath. "Who else? Dagro wasn't the only one to die in the Badlands. Meth Ganlow, Tem Sevrance, Jon Shank: all could have been chief. Shor Gormalin was killed a month later. Who does that leave? Orwin claims he's too old. Good men like Corbie Meese and Ballic the Red are loyal to their chief. Someone has to oppose him. Blackhail must be saved."

"I was born at Dregg."

"Tell me you don't consider yourself a Hailswoman."

Raina could not. She had lived in this house for seventeen years. Blackhail was her life.

Looking out across the gaze she saw that the war cart was stuck in a rut. The teamster had dismounted and was lashing the rumps of the lead pair of horses as four of the armed guards pushed their backs against the tailgate. The cart jerked sideways and then sank back down. More armed guards dismounted. Raina still couldn't discern their clan. Bannen, Dregg, Harkness, and Scarpe all wore dark colors on the road.

Raina turned her mind back to Anwyn. Manipulated, she decided finally. That's how she felt. Anwyn's use of the clan boast had been a jab in the small of her back. Anwyn was the real instigator here. She was the one who had arranged this meeting today, and the meeting before that in the gameroom. It was she who had invited Orwin Shank and the chief's wife and then sat back and waited to see which one was willing to speak treason. Looking into Anwyn's open, doughy face it was hard to understand why.

"What do you want out of this?" Raina asked finally, tired of thinking.

"Nothing." Anwyn held herself steady.

Raina inspected her. You could tell the truth, she decided, and still leave room for concealment. In this case she couldn't be sure. "I need to know where you stand, Anny."

The clan matron pushed her long graying braid behind her back. "I am with Blackhail, Raina. As long as you are the best hope for this clan I stand beside you."

Raina shivered. Here was the whole truth, and it was not comforting. Anwyn would stand by her as long as she approved of her actions. Suddenly weary, Raina turned her back on Anwyn and moved toward the cast-iron half-door that led to the widows' hearth. Crouching low, she slipped inside.

The room was hot and filled with people. Hatty Hare put her foot on the loom break and turned to look at the chief's wife. Merritt Ganlow and one of the Shank boys were pushing a worktable against the wall. Two clan maids were kneeling on the floor, rolling up a carpet, a third girl was rubbing linseed oil into one of the stretching racks, and slender and lovely Moira Lull was crouching on the thick black hearthstone, feeding woodchips to the fire.

Raina moved aside to let Anwyn step into the room. Merritt nodded briskly at both of them. "Be ready day after tomorrow," she snapped.

It took Raina a moment to realize that Merritt was heading off questions about the preparations to accommodate the tied clansmen. The head widow had been dragging her heels for days, but Raina knew better than to mention it. The work was being done now; she would be grateful for that.

Anwyn put a hand on Raina's arm. "I best be heading back to the kitchen. I've a second bake to do today. The war party needs bread."

Raina followed her out of the room. When the carved wooden doors closed behind them and they were alone at the top of the stair, she said, "I will use Mace's absence to change things in this house, but do not push me. I have respect for you,

Anwyn, and we've been friends for many years, but don't assume that because you picked me for this I'm under your control. I will be my own master."

Seconds passed. Raina could hear the vast stone warren of the roundhouse grinding under its own weight. Anwyn's face was hard to read. In the time it took her to slip through the balcony's half-door she had tucked away her fox lore. Finally she pushed her lips together and nodded. "You need help, I'm here."

Raina hid her relief. Strangely, she didn't feel tired anymore. Mace would be leaving the roundhouse. Tomorrow. While he was gone she would take command of the clanhold. It was her duty as chief's wife. Once the hole in the east wall was sealed she would ask Longhead to build a great big fortified barn, and when it was done she'd quarter the Scarpes there. Get them out of her house.

"Thank you, Anwyn," she said.

Anwyn bustled. It was something she did with her shoulders and bosom, and it restored the matronly mask. "Can't stand around here gossiping all day. Busy times. Bad and busy."

She left Raina at the top of the stair. Raina felt giddy, light enough to float away. *That's another thing about power: it goes to your head.* Suddenly the day seemed like something to enjoy, not endure. She would go and speak with Longhead about the remains of the stone, hint that something would be done soon. Then she had to supervise the housing of Scarpes in her old quarters. Ventilation was bad there and she needed to be sure that no one brought in cook stoves. After that the day was her own. Maybe she'd saddle Mercy and take a ride out to the Wedge. Pay her respects to the dead horses that were being buried there. Later she would be needed by the sworn clansmen.

A thousand warriors rode out tomorrow. Her attendance was their due.

"Lady."

Raina jumped. Turning around, she saw Bev Shank emerge from the widows' hearth. He'd been helping Merritt move the heavy machinery into storage. Bev couldn't be over twenty, yet like all the Shank boys he was losing his hair. He was a yearman, trained to the hammer, and his lore was the white-tailed deer.

"May I speak with you?"

He was deferential, as was proper for a yearman when faced with his chief's wife. Raina replied soberly. "Of course."

Bev looked at his boots. The back of his neck was burned and peeling. Shank skin never did well in the sun. "It's about Drey . . ." He struggled for a moment and then spit it out. "Me and Grim ride to Ganmiddich tomorrow and we don't know what to tell him about Bitty."

The word had arrived from Black Hole five days back: Raif Sevrance had killed a sworn clansman in the mine. Drey's brother was a Maimed Man. Raina's stomach contracted softly. So much loss. When would it end?

"You must tell Drey the truth. Speak it plainly. You lost your brother that day. So did he."

This was a new thought for the young yearman, she could tell. Raif Sevrance was gone from this clan more surely than Bitty Shank. Bitty could be remembered, spoken of with respect and affection by friends and kin. Drey would never be allowed to speak his brother's name again. Raif Sevrance was a traitor to his clan.

Bev frowned, thought for a while, then slowly began to nod. "Aye, lady. Aye."

Raina laid a hand on his arm. "Bitty taught me how to tie lures, one morning when he came down to Sand Creek with me and Effie. We didn't catch a single fish, but it didn't matter. Bitty had us laughing. You know Effie: had to be dragged out of the roundhouse screaming. But she loved Bitty, and I swear that by the time Bitty waded knee-deep in the creek, singing that special fish-catching song of his, she'd completely forgotten she was outside."

Bev smiled with a closed mouth, swallowing. "The song didn't rhyme," he said after a moment. "Didn't really have a tune either."

"No. And it didn't help catch any fish."

Both of them laughed. There were tears in Bev's eyes. He was too young for this. So was she.

"Ride proud tomorrow, Bevin Shank," she said, lifting her

hand away. "We are Blackhail, and the Stone Gods made us first. When we die they welcome us back."

Bev's hazel eyes looked into hers. He surprised her by bowing at the waist. "You are good for us, lady. Good for this clan."

She wished with all her heart that he was right. Her doubts must be kept to herself, though. This boy had already lost three brothers. Tomorrow he would leave to reinforce Drey Sevrance and Crab Ganmiddich at the Crab Gate. She could not send him to war without hope. "Clan will hold steady until you return."

It was a binding promise, she realized as soon as she spoke it. A thousand men rode tomorrow: they had to have something solid to return to. She, Raina Blackhail, would make sure of that.

Bev accepted her words with a solemn nod. Taking his leave, he headed down the drafty stairs, doubtless making his way toward the greathearth and the sworn clansmen who were gathering there.

Raina held herself steady until he was long out of sight. She breathed and did not think, refilling. Time passed. Sounds of men calling out, children laughing, dogs barking, axes splitting wood, doors opening and closing, and footsteps, thousands of footsteps, filtered up to the top of the house. Someone exited the widows' wall, passing her right by. A gust of wind spiraling up the stair brought the scent of fried onions and grilled lamb chops.

That made her move. Hungry, she descended the stairs.

As always when she reached the lower levels of the roundhouse she had to cover her distaste. Once clean, echoing corridors had been turned into filthy camps. Scarpemen and their women continued to burn their foul oil lamps, let their mangy house dogs run wild, and squat and shit in open view. A group of Scarpewives were feasting on lamb chops, sopping up the gravy with Anwyn's fresh bread. Raina averted her gaze as she passed them but not before she saw what they were drinking: Gat Murdock's Dhooneshine. She would know that old goat's bottles anywhere: he'd filched them from her ten years ago. Four brown-and-tan glazed toppers that had once been filled with womanly unctions. Dagro had bought them for her during a clanmeet in Ille Glaive. She'd long been reconciled to the fact that Gat Murdock had claimed them. Gat was Gat, and every clan had someone like him. This was different. This was theft. Never in a million years would Gat let strangers drink his brew. Generosity was a concept the aging swordsman had never grasped. No. Someone had found, fancied and stolen it.

A Scarpe. They were like termites, eating away at Blackhail's house, undermining its foundations. Raina considered turning back and wresting the Dhooneshine out of the Scarpewives' bony hands. Five of them against one of her? Probably not the best idea. Even if she won, dignity would be lost. News of the chief's wife in a scrum with a bunch of Scarpers would provide the roundhouse with enough delighted gossip to last a week.

She hurried on. When she reached the ground floor, she found the fifteen-foot-high clan door drawn open and a crowd of tied and sworn clansmen milling around the entrance hall. Black, muddy snow carried in on boot soles had slickened the floor and grown men were slipping. Stepping back up the stairs, Raina searched for a friendly face. From the looks of things a messenger had arrived. A slender young clansman wearing a marmot-fur hat and a coat caked in road dirt appeared to be the center of attention. Spying the misshaped head of Corbie Meese, Raina beckoned the hammerman over.

"What's happening?" she asked as Corbie wended his way through the crowd.

Corbie was wearing the fine gray wool cloak his wife Sarolyn had made for him. Designed to be worn over battle armor and a full complement of weapons, it had taken three bolts of cloth to finish. When he moved it looked like his shadow. "Jamsie's come from Duff's. The Dhoonehouse has been taken by Robbie Dun Dhoone. Pengo Bludd's seized control of Withy, and is marching an army south to meet the city men."

Raina blinked. This was news. In the days since the Sundering Blackhail had grown inward, an animal licking its wounds. Yet the world didn't stop when a guidestone shattered. Here was proof. Struggling to make sense of what she'd just heard, she said, "I thought Withy was already controlled by Bludd."

"It was. Hanro, the Dog Lord's fourth son, has held it for the past three months. Seven days back Skinner Dhoone launched an assault—probably fancied Withy as a base to retake Dhoone. Looked like he might claim it, then along comes Pengo with his big army and crushes Skinner against the walls of the Withyhold. Jamsie says it was a bloodbath. Eight hundred Dhoonesmen dead. No word yet on Skinner. Some whisper he fled the field."

Raina went to touch the powdered guidestone at her waist and had to stop herself. The guidestone was dead: there was no comfort for her there. "Why didn't Robbie send men to reinforce his uncle?"

Corbie made a hard sound in his throat. "Robbie Dun Dhoone's a cold one. Rumor is that he planned it that way. While Skinner was busy attacking the Withyhold, Robbie was free to steal a march on Dhoone."

"No." Raina couldn't quite believe it. No clansman would knowingly send fellow clansmen to their deaths. It was evil, and the Stone Gods would not pardon it.

Corbie nodded solemnly, following her thoughts. "Pray he never becomes our ally."

Raina would.

"Pengo's seized control of the Withyhold," the hammerman continued. "He's older than Hanro and higher in the pecking order. Jamsie says he hasn't let the grass grow. Couple of days to rest his crew and he headed out for Ganmiddich."

"Dear Gods. That was fast."

"When the win's upon a man, Raina, it does something to him. Makes him fierce and resolute." Corbie glanced toward the greatdoor as a new group of warriors arrived. "And remember, Pengo will know by now that the Dog Lord's been routed. The Dhoonehold's lost. There's no going back."

"What will happen? Will we still ride to defend Ganmiddich?"

"What choice do we have? The Crab Chief swore an oath to Blackhail. Ganmiddich is under our protection. Hailsmen walk the Crab Gate this very hour."

Raina took a breath. This was turning into a dangerous swamp. Only seven months ago the clanholds were at peace. Old rivalries brewed, borders were in dispute, water rights were claimed and defended. There were skirmishes and cattle raids, but no open warfare. A year ago Dagro had stood in the chief's chamber beneath this very hall and told her that once the feuding between Orrl and Scarpe was over he'd count his chiefdom a success. *"The clanholds rest easy now. Our boys are fostered as far as Haddo and Wellhouse, we have traded gifts with Frees, the Dog Lord is growing old and tame. Soon there'll be naught for me to do but stay abed with my pretty young wife."*

He could not have been more wrong.

"We'll need to send more men," she said.

"Aye," Corbie agreed. "At least another thousand. Maybe more." His mind was no longer quite with her, she realized. He was thinking of Drey Sevrance, Bullhammer, Tom Lawless, Lowdraw, Rory Cleet and the two hundred other Hailsmen who were garrisoned at Ganmiddich. He was waiting for his chief, anxious to have the matter settled and be on his way to defend them.

It shamed her, for she could not stop herself from thinking, *Please do not let this delay Mace's departure.* It would be so easy for him to decide to send the first thousand south and travel with the second contingent. She might be damned, but she didn't think she could stand another day of him. Just to rest, to lay her head on a pillow and not have to worry about what the next moment might bring. Ever since the day in the Oldwood she had known no peace of mind. Always, it was: *What will Mace do next? Does he know what I'm thinking? Can he tell how much I despise him?*

Raina straightened her shoulders and willed her mind away from the dark place. If she stayed there too long he won.

"Where is my husband?" she asked Corbie.

The hammerman flexed the huge saddles of muscle on his upper arms. "As soon as he spied that big wagon out on the graze he took off. He's escorting it in right now."

Raina glanced at the door. She heard voices from outside but couldn't see anything beyond the great crush of clansmen on the threshold. She heard herself ask in a calm voice, "Do you know what the wagon's about?"

Corbie shook his misshapen head. "I best go, Raina. Meet him at the door."

The east wind was howling through the roundhouse now, pushing men's cloaks against their thighs and blowing out torches. From her place, three steps up, Raina could see the great circle of the entrance hall. She watched Corbie navigate the crowd, listened to the rumble of something heavy approaching.

Suddenly there was a great push toward the door. Raina thought she heard Mace's voice, but she couldn't be sure. Clansmen were shouting out the news.

"Bludd rides to Ganmiddich."

"Dhoone is retaken."

Raina's heart beat in deep powerful strokes. A lamp close by blew out, then another. She smelled the strong black smoke of extinction. On the other side of the doorframe a conference was taking place. She knew Mace was there now, for his presence could be detected in the silences. Men were quiet, listening.

A lone clansman cheered. Another followed, and soon over a hundred clansmen were shouting, "*Kill Bludd! Bill Bludd! Kill Bludd!*"

Mace had pleased them. He must have spoken again, for the noise quickly died. A group of hammermen broke away and headed through the roundhouse with purpose. Corbie Meese wasn't one of them. Raina resisted the urge to run after them and discover what was happening. She was desperate to know and desperate not to know, her mind rolling back and forth like a boat in a storm.

Orwin Shank was the next to make his way inside. His face and ears were flushed. As he crossed the hall he saw her, but quickly averted his eyes. Like a sleepwalker, Raina began descending the stairs. Men made way for her, opening up a passage to the door. She was chief's wife, and sometimes she forgot her value. Scarpes had no respect for her, but this was a crowd of Hailsmen, not Scarpes. Walking into the space they created for her, Raina felt the heat of their bodies. Big, powerful men they were, dressed in black wool and worn leather, their bodies weighed down with hammers and longswords, axes and gear belts, knives, ice picks, shovels.

"Do we still ride tomorrow?" she asked no one in particular.

A dozen replied, "Aye, lady."

Sunlight from the door blinded her. "And my husband, does he still ride at the head?"

Ballic the Red placed a steadying hand on her elbow. She had not realized she had begun to sway. "Mace will ride with the first thousand as planned," he told her in his rough burr. "The second force will be led by Grim Shank."

Ballic smells like beeswax, she thought inanely. *Probably uses it to waterproof his bow.* She stepped outside. For a moment she couldn't see anything, so great was the contrast between the dark, smoky entrance hall and the harsh sunlight of midday. Man-shapes coalesced from the brightness. The blocklike form of the war cart came into view. Seen this close it was bigger than she had imagined, a stovehouse on twelve wheels. The teamster was releasing the lathered and shaking horses from their yokes.

"Who'll be in charge of defending the Hailhouse while they're gone?" she asked the nearest warrior.

"Chief gave Orwin the honor."

She did not recognize the young Hailsman's voice, and did not turn to look at him. Her thoughts were like beads, connected only by the slenderest thread. So far so good. Orwin Shank was the best, most logical choice. He would not interfere with her plans.

When she was ready, she turned her gaze to her husband. Mace Blackhail was standing by the wagon's front axle, speaking with two men. One was the Scarpeman Mansal Stygo, who was never far from Mace's heels. Mansal had killed the Orrl chief with a hammer blow so hard it had driven Spynie's head into his chest cavity. A month later Mace had invited Mansal and his crew to overwinter in the Hailhouse. The second man had his back to Raina. He had the shoulder breadth of a hammerman, but something in his posture warned her there was more to know. His full-length cloak was narrow across the back and oddly formal. The fur collar was a deep, luxurious brown; she couldn't decide what animal it came from. By contrast the cloak's hem was in poor shape, tattered and black with mud. When the stranger noticed Mace's attention shift away from him, he turned to see who the Hail Wolf was regarding.

Raina Blackhail stared right back. The flesh on the stranger's cheeks had been scarified and tattooed to create the illusion of depth. Sunlight disappeared into carefully manipulated pits in the skin. He was a Scarpe, she saw that now, for black leather traces were woven into his shoulder-length braids and his fur collar was the fancy weasel known as mink. He appraised her, there was no other word for it, looked her up and down and decided what she was worth.

Mace spoke a word and the three of them moved toward her. Three Scarpes. One plan. Raina kept her shoulders straight as the pieces came together in her head. The wagon. The cloak hem. Mace's face.

"Raina." Mace's voice was tightly controlled. Beneath the hardened leather carapace of his riding armor, his lungs were portioning air. "I don't think you've met Stannig Beade, clan guide of Scarpe and counsel to its chief. He's brought us a gift from his clan."

Dear Gods. No. Wind knifed across the greatcourt. Hammer chains rustled, dry snow snaked over the stones. Everything that was Blackhail was being blown away, and she had been a fool to imagine that she could be the one to stop it. Raina glanced at the wagon. The sawn ends of the poison pines were oozing sap. Poor Anwyn. She had not seen this coming.

But the gods had. That's why they left.

Unable to find her voice, Raina nodded at the stranger with the darkly watchful face.

"Raina." He did not bow; she had not expected him to. Nor had he offered her the courtesy of "lady."

"Stannig has split the Scarpestone," Mace said, raising his voice so all gathered on the greatcourt could hear. "Today he brings us our half. Blackhail is no longer a clan without guide or guidestone. For a thousand years we've shared warriors and oaths with our brother clan, now we share their stone."

Silence followed. The wind blew. And then Mace Blackhail spoke again. "Stannig will stay in our house until the Stone Gods return."

NINE

The Crab Gate

The Ganmiddich roundhouse commanded a bend in the Wolf where the river changed course from west to south. Built from the same green traprock that formed the cliffs and banks of the river, it sat on high ground above a crescent-shaped gravel beach. The great dome of the roundhouse dwarfed the east and north wards, which had been added at a later date. The primary entrance to the dome was through a pair of ten-feet-high double doors known as the Crab Gate. Carved from seasoned oak and armored with plates of fossil stone, the Crab Gate was held to be one of the great wonders of the clanholds. How the fossils had been fixed to the wood, where they came from, and what creatures they revealed were sources of wonder and myth. Marafice had once seen them up close for himself and they had given him a chill. Segmented eyes, pronged claws, winged fish, cloven tails, serrated fangs, scaled birds, basilisk spines, kraken heads: all displayed in deep relief in bone yellow limestone.

It made for a good show, but not necessarily good defense. Marafice knew the gates were heavy and resistant to flames, but he suspected the fossil stone would crack if barraged with missiles, and double gates, by their very nature, were weaker than single ones. If he remembered correctly, there were two big couplets on the interior of each door that were large enough to accommodate the girth of a hundred-year oak. So a single tree trunk barred the entrance to Ganmiddich. Marafice saw it most nights in his dreams.

Now, though, looking north upriver toward the bend,

flanked by an army of eleven thousand hideclads, mercenaries and brothers-in-the-watch, he looked upon the Crab Gate's pale exterior a quarter-league in the distance and felt some measure of fear. He did not believe in the God of priests and knights, of temples and prayer books and a thousand fussy rules, but he did believe in something. Exactly what was hard to quantify, but if pressed he'd call it power. He spoke to that power now. *Guard me. Guard my men.*

Snow fell as the army of Spire Vanis advanced at slow march. The wind was from the east and it channeled along the river and through the bluffs. The Wolf ran shallow here, boulders and gravel banks slowing the flow. Birches and willows choked the water margin, and evidence of recent high water could be seen in uprooted trees, undercut banks and newly exposed stone. The frost that had begun in the early hours of the morning had claimed shallow pools and slow meanders, coating them with opaque crusts of ice.

Close to midday now, the temperature was barely warmer. Marafice felt his plate armor sucking away his body heat and did not much like the thought of donning the birdhelm. Like many in the lines he was putting it off until they were within fire range.

Shifting in the saddle, Marafice looked back over the ranks. The rear guard, led by the improbably named Lord of the Glacier Granges, had cleared the bend and was forming ranks. *Hideclads,* Marafice thought with some heat, *a man could be blinded looking at so much steel.* Which damn-fool surlord had been responsible for repealing the Hide Laws, that's what he wanted to know. The Hide Laws had prohibited private armies from wearing chain mail and metal plate unless directly under the command of the surlord. The law had given the hideclads their name. For hundreds of years the armies maintained by the grangelords to defend their granges were allowed to armor themselves only in hardened hide. It had been, as far as Marafice Eye was concerned, a very fine law, and one which he wouldn't think twice about reinstating. Nothing wrong with a surlord having the best army. Nothing wrong at all.

Facing forward, Marafice gave the command to sound the

drums. Tat Mackelroy, who was Jon Burden's second-in-command but today was riding at Marafice's right hand, stood in his stirrups and bellowed the order down the ranks. Seconds passed, and then the kettledrums began to sound. Slowly, rhythmically, forty drumbeats fell in time. The deep hollow booms sent waterfowl into flight and spooked the horses. Some shied and broke the line. One reared and threw its rider into a rank of foot soldiers. The teams pulling the scorpions and the battering ram were unaffected by the noise: they had been brought in from the south and were trained to stillness in battle. Marafice had thought his own mount trained, but training and experience were different things, and the great black warhorse was unsettled.

Da-dum. Da-dum. Da-dum. The noise hurt Marafice's ears.

"Shall I call horns?" Tat Mackelroy asked. He was a six-year veteran of the watch, an expert broadswordsman who'd been promoted so quickly through the ranks that some resented him for it. Mackelroy didn't care. He was too busy doing his job.

"No horns. Not yet." Marafice glanced east at the Ganmiddich Tower, perched atop the inch. Old beyond knowing, it was the tallest standing structure in the clanholds. On clear nights some said you could see the fire burning in its top-floor gallery from the far side of the Bitter Hills. Marafice didn't know about that. He looked and saw a five-sided tower erected on an overgrown rock in the middle of the Wolf. It was not constructed from the same traprock as the roundhouse and it did not resemble any structure built by clansmen. It was occupied, the darkcloaks had informed him of that. Close to a hundred longbowmen, mostly Hailsmen, lived in and patrolled the three upper floors.

Today, for them, there would be no going back to the roundhouse. Last night the darkcloaks had sabotaged their boats. Marafice could see the boats from where he sat, their keels drawn up high on the rocky beach. They looked fine, but they weren't. That was the way the darkcloaks liked to work.

"I won't have them," Marafice had roared at Iss two months back in Spire Vanis. "They're sly, skulking. They cannot be trusted. And the men won't stomach them."

"Don't be a fool," Iss had replied. "Stop thinking like a

butcher's son from Hoargate and think like a man with something to lose. You'll be commanding an army in excess of ten thousand. You'll be responsible for their food, safety, lives. You cannot afford to indulge your backwoods notions of what is and isn't right. Take the darkcloaks and use them. Put them to work, let them be your ears in the ranks and your eyes in the field. The things they know can tip the balance; tricks with fire and smoke, snares, bluffcraft, sabotage. They're trained to see what is hidden: weaknesses in buildings, concealed doors, animal tracks, strategies, men. If you must, use them only to gather intelligence. It will be little, but it may be enough."

"They are sorcerers!" Marafice had cried, punching his fist against the Blackvault's door. "How can I look my men in the eye knowing I countenance such foulness?"

Iss waived a pale hand, unconcerned. "Do not look them in the eye then. A surlord does what is best for a surlord, not what the majority of his acquaintances decree acceptable. You are going into Ganmiddich blind, with your enemies beside you. I'd say you need all the help you can get."

Even then Marafice had not relented. Fear of the old skills ran deep. There was a dirtiness to them, a sense that once you used them their stench clung to you and you were lessened in some essential way. It was only a week later, when Iss had visited him at the Red Forge and casually thrown a curl of parchment on the table, that Marafice had changed his mind. "What is that?" he had barked, unnerved at having the Surlord interrupt him as he ate his dinner of ham and beans.

Again, there had been a wave of the pale hand. "Read it," Iss had said, knowing full well that Marafice was barely capable of writing his own name.

Angry, Marafice had pushed away his plate. "Just tell me what it says."

"It says that last night Garric Hews met with Alistair Sperling, Lord of the Salt Mine Granges, in the back room of a small tavern south of the Quartercourts. They discussed you. Hews knew Sperling had just committed to riding to Ganmiddich with three hundred men, and he sought to discover how the esteemed lord might react to a possible mutiny on the road."

Marafice had stood. "What was Sperling's response?"

"Oh he was for it, bless his salty little soul."

"Then I do not want him or his men."

Iss had laughed then, a superior sound that did not let Marafice in on the joke. "You cannot exclude everyone who does not like you. You'll end up with an army of one. The questions to ask are these: How did my Surlord receive this information? And: How can I stay one step ahead of those who mean me harm?" Iss had paused, more for effect than to allow Marafice the opportunity to reply. "The answer to both questions is dark cloaks. These are men who love to spy."

So Marafice had taken them, a half-dozen in all, perhaps more. Their numbers were hard to pin down.

Already they had earned their keep. Most evenings he met with one of them in the privacy of his tent. Usually it was the man named Greenslade, a thin trapper with elaborately queued hair. That was another detail he'd learned about the darkcloaks: they often masqueraded as other things. Greenslade kept him well informed about loyalties in the camp. A day south of the Wolf, Hews had arranged something Greenslade called a tester. Hews' plan had been to separate Marafice from his brothers-in-the-watch during the river crossing, then stand back and observe if any other factions in the army of eleven thousand would step forward to protect their leader when it appeared he might be vulnerable. Knowing that one simple fact about the river crossing had been enough to foil the plan. Marafice had simply ordered the Whitehog to cross the river first and it was done. Even arranged to have one of the guide ropes break so the whole damn lot of them got a soaking.

It had been a very satisfying moment, and it had changed his opinion of the darkcloaks. Iss was right: Even though he was uneasy with their services, he could not afford to waive them.

Since then Marafice had learned other useful things. Greenslade had provided a headcount of the forces in the Ganmiddich roundhouse, and also disclosed information about messengers sent to Blackhail for reinforcements. By Marafice's calculation the reinforcements were at least five days away: more than enough time for him to gain possession of the house.

Today he rode to break the Crab Gate, and it was a strange

feeling to know the darkcloaks were in place and ready. Their aid made him less of a man and more of a surlord, and that was probably the way it had to be.

"Quick march," he commanded Tat Mackelroy. It was time they started the dance.

As the order was relayed down the ranks, Marafice looked over his left shoulder toward the center. The line was good, you had to give the Whitehog that: he knew how to marshal men. Hog Company formed a solid column, a hundred wide and seven deep. A dozen in the fore carried pennants of snow-white silk embroidered with the likenesses of fat, mean-looking pigs. There was white silk also on the men's backs: short half-circle dress capes that were attached to the plate armor by spiky little horns. They were a fair and deadly sight, impossibly proud, splendidly accoutered. Every clansman's nightmare.

Hews himself forwent the pleasures of the cloak, creating an island of steely sparseness amongst the white. Aware that he was being inspected, Hews turned to look Marafice in the eye. Over the heads of seventy-five men they appraised each other. Just as Marafice thought he would be the first to look away, the Whitehog bowed his head. "Helmets!" he commanded, and Marafice watched with amazement as seven hundred men donned their helmets in perfect synchronization.

It was a chilling sight. And a lesson. Any confusion regarding which company had superior training had just been cleared up.

Now, of course, Marafice could not give a similar command himself. Of his crew of three hundred and fifty, he reckoned at least four of them would fall off their horses attempting to place the nine-pound closed-visored birdhelms correctly on their heads. Even putting on his own helmet at that moment would have made it look as if the Eye was taking orders from the Whitehog. Still, it had to be done, damn it. At this distance a shot from the roundhouse would fall well short of the line, but there was no telling how a shot from the top of the tower might fare.

Clansmen were watching. Marafice could feel their attention in the hollow of his dead eye. The curved walls of the roundhouse might look as blank as stone, but peer closer and you'd see the crude arrow slits, the embrasures, the murder holes above the door. Smoke rising from vents, not chimneys, gave the impression the entire dome was steaming. River water lapped on the empty beach, and Marafice marked the drag lines of boats hauled up the hill to the roundhouse for safekeep.

This house had been taken twice in half a year. First by Bludd and then Blackhail. It was not easy to secure. It looked it—with its implacable stone walls and defensible position above the river—but it was a crab, and once its shell was broken there was soft meat inside.

As the line accelerated to full battle march Marafice put on the birdhelm. It was like wearing a lead coffin on your head. Snowflakes had found their way inside and Marafice felt their icy sting against his cheeks. Once the neck cinch had been tightened his head movements were severely restrained and he had to twist at the waist to check on the column he commanded. Good, most helms were in place.

Da-dum. Da-dum. Da-dum. The kettledrums boomed and the line advanced, fanning out as the land opened up. Protected by a twelve-deep rank of cavalry and foot soldiers, the archers and boltmen readied their bows. It had been Andrew Perish who had advised Marafice of the one-in-seven rule.

"Every company, no matter their numbers or purpose, needs to assign one man in seven to a bow. The grangelords will fight you on this, but ignore them. Range weapons may not get the high-and-mighties excited—too humble, no glory, little chance to deck out the body in fine and expensive plate—but a good bowmen is worth his weight in gold on the field."

It had been surprising advice coming from a former master-at-arms whose specialties were the sword and pike, but that was Perish for you: hard, practical, inclusive.

As long as you believed in God. From his position at the the head of the east flank, Marafice could not see Andrew Perish back down the ranks. The master-at-arms was ahorse, picking up the rear and keeping a watchful eye on the two hundred mercenaries directly behind him and the Lord of the Salt Mine Granges' hideclads. Marafice reckoned it was a good fit. High and low. Perish could handle them all.

Suddenly a cry went out to Marafice's right. Cursing his

birdhelm he swung wildly in the saddle, searching out the source of noise. A brother-in-the-watch, one of his own men, was slumped over the neck of his horse, a perfectly placed arrow stuck deep into the strip of vulnerable flesh circling his neck where his birdhelm and backplate failed to meet. *Should have had mail collars,* Marafice thought angrily. The Surlord should have ponied up the cash.

"*Easy,*" Marafice roared down the line. "Break rank at your peril." The poor sod with the arrow in his neck would just have to lie there and die.

As he spun to face forward, he glanced at the tower. Someone within its black granite walls knew how to shoot.

Snow blew against his horse's flank as the wind quickened. The fancy silk pennants snapped against their poles and the even fancier cloaks fanned out like bells.

"The Whitehog commands the charge," came the call from the center. "We move on his say."

Marafice didn't like this one bit, but if you gave a man the center you didn't have much choice but to let him lead. As a reluctant nod of acquiescence was relayed back up the line, Marafice studied the sky. It had to be midday by now, and by the look of things it would get no lighter. Now was not a good time to wonder why he was here, yet he could not seem to help himself. What did Iss want from the clanholds? It barely made any sense for Spire Vanis to claim land here. True enough the border clans were well stocked and wealthy, but if Spire Vanis occupied Ganmiddich it would be a sitting duck. There was a lot of angry clansmen out there, not to mention the lake men from Ille Glaive. All were closer to the Crab Gate and had better access to supplies.

Was it just a glorified raid then? Eleven thousand men chasing spoils? Marafice did not think that was the whole answer. It did not fully explain why the grangelords were here. Yes, they liked livestock and plundered swords as much as anyone, but they were also using this campaign as a chance for self-promotion. Returning to Spire Vanis with the glow of victory would raise a grangelord's status amongst his peers. For ambitious grangelords like Garric Hews, Alistair Sperling and Tranter Lennix, grandnephew to the old Surlord Borhis Horgo, it was a convenient field of play. For his own part Marafice knew what he was getting out of today—the sponsorship of his claim for surlord—but what Iss sought to gain was a mystery. Perhaps he hoped each and every one of his rivals would die.

That made Marafice crack a smile. Glancing again at the tower, he decided to steal a little of the Whitehog's thunder. "Sound the horns!"

Tat Mackelroy relayed the order and within seconds the first blasts of trumpets could be heard. The battle for the Crab Gate had been engaged.

You could not hear the horns and not be stirred. Marafice felt it. His men felt it and pushed against the line. Garric Hews was no fool and knew better than to fight the moment.

"Charge!" he screamed. *"To the gate!"*

The charge was like being propelled forward on a crashing wave. The noise was deafening, the colors blurred, the danger of tumbling out of control real. Air and snow rushed through Marafice's eye slit as his armor creaked and sawed, shaving skin from the back of his neck. He could no longer risk glancing at the tower, but the signal had been given. It was in the hands of the darkcloaks now.

As the charge moved forward, the line spread, opening up space in the interior for the machinists and bowmen to work. The scorpions had been carried in pieces to the clanholds and assembled at the camp: once they were set down and loaded they'd be ready to deploy.

Da-dum. Da-dum. Da-dum. The drums boomed and the horns wailed as a wall of arrows shot from the tower rained down on the east flank.

Marafice stared ahead. The Ganmiddich roundhouse and its square ugly outbuildings were still a blank. As the charge grew closer the risk of looking foolish increased. A city-men army at full charge was a fearsome sight, but if the clansmen did not engage the charge would break on the walls and they'd be forced into a siege. No one on the line wanted that.

What was taking the darkcloaks so long? Marafice could see the fossil stone on the Crab Gate clearly now, see brief shadows of movement behind the arrow slits and embrasures. Part of the east flank had spilled into the river shallows—easy targets for the bowmen in the tower. One man fell. Then another; his foot catching in the stirrup as he slid from his mount. The panicked horse bucked and reared, trying to shake itself free of the body. The momentum of the fall had dragged the saddle down the horse's torso and the belly strap was now pressing against the stallion's scrotum. *Poor beast*, Marafice thought before yelling, "Either kill it or cut the straps."

An arrow pinged off the right side of his birdhelm, grazing his horse's leather rump armor as it continued its flight. An instant later a second arrow buzzed right past his left ear. It took him a moment to realize it had come from the direction of the Crab Gate. The roundhouse had opened fire.

Behind him the first wave of crossbolts were loosed against the roundhouse. *Thuc, thuc, thuc, thuc*: hundreds of times in Marafice's still-ringing ear. When the bolts met the traprock walls they simply stopped and fell to the ground. It was not a reassuring sight. Bolts first, cavalry next.

Insanely, Hews was still holding the charge. They were less than two hundred yards away now. Did Hews think so little of clannish buildings that he imagined horses could knock down their walls?

Suddenly there was a scream from within Hog Company. Two lines deep, a hideclad's cloak was alive with flames. Fire arrows, and even as Marafice realized the cause, the sky blackened with smoke as a volley of flaming missiles was loosed from the roundhouse. Swatting one away with the flat of his sword, Marafice watched as Hog Company started to panic. Hideclads began tearing at their fancy white capes and driving their horses away from the center where the greatest concentration of arrows were falling. Hews spun in his saddle to calm them, but he could only do so much. Men afraid of fire made poor troops.

As the line met the hill the charge slowed. The horses were tiring. Nerves were worn. It was hard to look at the blank walls of Ganmiddich and not be discouraged. Hews had been counting on the famous jaw of the clansmen, the pride that demanded fight, not hide.

But not Marafice Eye. As they scaled the base of the hill and the first stone ball was loosed by the scorpions, a cry went up from the ranks.

"Fire in the tower! Fire!"

The stone ball smashed into the top of the hill, cratering the slope and throwing up a hail of dirt and snow. Horses in the line shied, some halted. Marafice's own mount shook out his head, but kept its pace. "Fine beauty," he murmured, angling his upper body toward the tower.

Black smoke gouted from the narrow windows and upper gallery of the Ganmiddich Tower. Weird green flames shot from one window, swiftly followed by a fountain of sparks. A short explosive crack sounded, and the stench of sulfur and smelting metal drifted over with the smoke.

"Mother of God," Tat Mackelroy whispered. "What's happening?"

Marafice did not look him in the eye as he replied, "Call it a lucky break."

Tat waited to hear if his Protector General would say more, and when the great man said nothing, returned his attention to his mount.

Marafice barked an order into the center to halt the charge. He did not like himself much just then.

For a wonder, Garric Hews minded what he'd said and broke the charge. The steepness of the hill made for a surprisingly short stop and for a few minutes there was chaos as six thousand reined-in horses scrambled for space. Marafice used the time to monitor events in the tower. It was telling that all missile fire had stopped. Smoke was pouring from every window in the stone structure. If there were flames it was now too dark to see them. The sole entrance to the tower was by way of a small rounded door plated with lead that directly faced the roundhouse across the water. Marafice sent out the order to bowmen and machinists to target the door. Reckoning he now stood within hearing distance of the roundhouse, he made sure his voice rang clear.

The Crab Gate remained closed, but Marafice imagined it wouldn't stay that way for long. At midwinter he'd visited this very roundhouse and met with clansmen firsthand. He'd come away impressed. They were fighting men, fiercely loyal, and he did not think for one instant they would stand by and let their fellow clansmen die.

Behind the roundhouse the oldgrowth forest known as the Nest clicked eerily in the rising wind. The trees were gnarled and ancient, crippled by the weight of overgrown limbs. The darkcloaks said there were paths running through them leading north toward Withy and west to Bannen. According to Greenslade, the paths were always vigorously defended.

Marafice's attention was drawn back to the tower by the retort of a half-dozen crossbolts splitting wood. The door had moved. Those inside wanted out.

Quietly now, Marafice sent an order propagating down the line. "On your guard. Be ready." He did not know exactly what the darkcloaks had done to fill the tower with fire and noxious smoke, and he decided now he would never ask them. Let them keep their bags of tricks to themselves. Spying ashes on the flat of his sword, he wiped the blade clean against the back of his sheepskin mummah.

All was silent for the longest moment and then the Crab Gate swung open and the battle was met.

Mounted clansmen rode out of the roundhouse: Hailsmen, Crabmen, Withymen, and Bannenmen. More poured from behind the outbuildings, as stable doors were flung apart.

"Kill Spire! Kill Spire!" they chanted as they used the downhill momentum to steal a charge.

"Spears out!" screamed Garric Hews, scrambling to harden his line. Marafice's own line was hard, though he knew his men felt fear. Clansmen were like animals, wild and brutal, wielding hammers as big as children as they bellowed at the top of their lungs for their enemies to die. Heads low, battle cloaks streaming out behind them, they met their enemies full-on.

A great clash of metal sounded. Men gasped. Horses squealed. Blood jetted through Marafice's eye slit and into the socket of his dead eye. Where it came from he could not tell. His great bloodred Rive blade was up and cutting. He figured as long as he did not let it rest he would be safe.

Clansmen came at him in hordes, hammers and axes swinging. They had the advantage of high ground and superior maneuverability, but the city men had heavy-gauge plate and four times their numbers. It was hard to remember that in the fray. The sheer relentlessness of the clansmen was something

Marafice had not counted on. You wounded a man, he should fall away. Not clansmen though. They smiled grimly and attacked again.

Marafice became a machine. One mailed fist on the reins to drive the stallion forward, the other on his sword hilt to thrust the blade. At his side Tat Mackelroy was fighting two-handed. In his left hand he braced a spear against his horse's flank, protecting his Protector General's right flank, and in his right he wielded the Rive blade. The reins were between his teeth. Marafice had several occasions to be grateful for his chief aide's spear. Sometimes when a hammer came close to his body he could not see it. There were blind spots with his one good eye.

In the center, Garric Hews and Hog Company had fallen back and then rerallied. This might have been the Whitehog's intention, for it had created space for the clansmen to charge into, which Hews slowly began to close off. Jon Burden had disengaged the west flank and was pursuing the clansmen who were pouring from the outbuildings. It was in the east, in Marafice's turf, that the fighting was fiercest. Clansmen were desperate to break through the Eye's line to reach the shore and save the tower men.

Trapped within the birdhelm, Marafice's sweat began to steam. Between gaps in his stallion's armored plates, lather was rising. He no longer had the time or energy to monitor events on the inch. Perhaps the tower men had risked the door. Perhaps they were still inside. One thing was sure: they were not visibly dead, for the look in the clansmen's faces told him they still hoped to rescue their men.

The day darkened as the battle wore on. Bodies piled up on the field. A man's severed head was rolling between the horses like a kickball. The machinists were still launching missiles at the Crab Gate and the outbuildings, cracking stone walls and flattening the odd clansmen. The bowmen had been charged with targeting the lines of clansmen leaving the outbuildings, but the mass exit had ceased and now the bowmen were still. In any other battle they'd be assigned to pick off runaways. But these were clansmen . . . and clansmen didn't run away.

Marafice's armor was black with blood. The pain in his sword arm was so intensely ingrained that it actually hurt more when he rested it than it did when he just kept thrusting. So he kept thrusting. His voice was hoarse, but he barely knew what he'd been screaming. His line still held, so he imagined he'd been screaming something right. At some point during the long hours of fighting, he realized that the battle had turned in their favor. Hews had successfully drawn out and cut off their center, Jon Burden had killed their side guard, and Marafice's men had held the water margin. All that remained was to finish off. Down the ranks, the foot soldiers and mercenaries already knew this and began a serious push for the Crab Gate.

With the luxury of more time the machinists actually managed to align one of the scorpions perfectly with the double doors, and launched a stone that bowled down the left door. Fossil dust shot up in a great cloud and although Marafice didn't much fancy breathing in those old and freakish remains he knew he didn't really have a choice. He wasn't the only one to spit a lot after that, he noticed.

With the door gone there was no chance of retreat for the clansmen, and the part of Marafice that respected honest fighting men felt for them. It did not prevent him joining the final charge.

As he kicked his horse forward two things happened that seemed strange. The first was the sight of a lone horseman, freshly mounted and lightly armored, galloping along the river and up through the ranks. A Spireman, no doubt about it, and from the looks of his kit some sort of messenger. The army hadn't received word from Spire Vanis in several weeks, and Marafice wondered at the wisdom of a messenger riding onto the battlefield. If the news had waited that long, a couple hours more would make no difference.

The second thing was a horn call from the north. It sounded so quickly, Marafice had to glance over to Tat Mackelroy to confirm that he had really heard it. Tat's brief nod had told him all he needed to know. At first Marafice assumed that the call must have come from a crew of Hailsmen in the Nest, sounding a retreat, but when he looked into the unguarded faces of the enemy he saw confusion and something that might have been fear.

Troubled, Marafice put all his energies into the charge. The sooner they took the roundhouse and secured it the better. Glancing over his shoulder, he saw the Whitehog was also preparing for the final push. Just this morning Marafice had planned to kill the Lord of the Eastern Granges if a suitable opportunity presented itself. The rush for the gate would be as good a time as any. While an army of eleven thousand attempted to wedge itself through a nine-foot opening there was no telling what mischief a man could do. Yet Marafice knew he would not act. Not here. Not now.

The Whitehog had fought like a demon. He'd made mistakes—they all had—but he'd never failed to watch his men, never paused to rest, never once issued an order that excluded himself from danger. The clansmen had a saying, "You are worthy of respect," and it summed up how Marafice felt as he watched his rival on the field. You could not fight all day with a man and then turn around and kill him. Marafice hadn't known that this morning, but now he did.

Strange, but he felt lighter than he had all day. It was as if a weight had been removed from his chest. Good fighting men: that's what counted. Tomorrow he would send the darkcloaks home to Iss. The Surlord could keep them.

The charge for the gate was poorly planned but enthusiastic, with foot soldiers, hideclads and mercenaries moving forward in a disorganized line. Even as he approved of their high spirits, Marafice worked to restrain them. Many of the men pushing to the front had not seen hand-to-hand combat with the clansmen and didn't realize the remaining force, while small, was deadly dangerous. As the Whitehog appeared distracted by something in the center, Marafice decided to head the line himself. He was Protector General of Spire Vanis and leader of this army: it was right and fitting that he claim this territory first.

The final push was surprisingly hard. The clansmen who were left were mostly Hailsmen and they fought like cornered wolves. Helmets were off now and their braids banded in silver snapped against their necks as they moved. Marafice was so intent on the fight that he didn't immediately register the softening. He was so close to the door now he could see individual scales on the kraken's ugly hide. Tat was at his back, blade long abandoned, fighting solely with his spear. Worrying noises sounded, but as long as Marafice didn't hear the horn from the north he figured he could let them pass. Then Tat touched his arm.

"Hog company and the grangelords are withdrawing."

This sentence made so little sense to Marafice that he ignored it, and chopped his Rive blade into a clansman's hand, cutting off two fingers at the tip. The man's heart was beating wildly and there was a lot of blood. In the small pause that followed, Tat grabbed his Protector General's forearm and yanked him out of the line.

"They're going. The grangelords are leaving."

Marafice tried to catch his breath. "Going?" he repeated stupidly.

"Yes. Look." Tat was taking no chances and physically spun Marafice around.

Blinking, Marafice attempted to take in what he saw. Over half the army was leaving the field. All those who were retreating were mounted. All were grangelords and grangelords' men. Lord of the Salt Mine Granges, Lord of the Glacier Granges, Lord of the Two River Granges, Lord of the Iron Hills, Lord of the Spirefield Granges . . . Lord of the Eastern Granges, Garric Hews.

"What is this?" Marafice asked, blood draining from his skin.

Andrew Perish trotted his horse forward. The former master-at-arms was bleeding from a wound to his foot. A small gobbet of flesh was glued to his ancient breastplate; it did not appear to be his own. "Messenger from the city. The Surlord is dead."

Sweat and blood dripped from Marafice's helmet to his neck. At the door the battle was still waging, but more and more men were congregating at the top of the hill.

Iss dead. It made no sense. Who could have slain him?

Marafice watched the retreating forces gain momentum, accelerating from walk to trot to gallop, rushing to get back to the city and stake their claim. A surlord was dead. A new one would be made.

Me, Marafice thought. *Me*.

He looked at Andrew Perish, stared straight into his occluded eyes.

"I will not leave the field until His work is finished," Perish said, "and I have a thousand men here who'll back me."

The believers and fanatics. About two hundred of them were Rive Watch, Marafice reckoned.

Perish did not wait for a response. Extending his Rive Blade forward he cried solemnly, "For His glory!" and joined the charge for the gate. Others followed. Marafice didn't blame them. Victory was so close you could smell it. It smelled like a broken door.

Scanning the motley remains of his army—the mercenaries, machinists, foot soldiers, drummers, retired brothers-in-the-watch, and walking wounded—Marafice wondered what to do. He, Marafice Eye, should be the one rushing back to Spire Vanis. The surlordship was his. The whole point of being here was to secure that one glittering jewel.

Yet he could not leave men unsupported on the field. He was not Garric Hews.

If Perish was right and he did indeed intend to lead a thousand into the roundhouse, then that would be a thousand men at grave risk. Marafice glanced at the one remaining door. A great chunk of fossil stone had broken off, revealing plain old oak beneath. Marafice thought of the clansmen, and the dark-cloaks, and Garric Hews. Nodding softly to himself he made a decision.

"We take the house as planned."

Even as he spoke, the unfamiliar horn sounded from the woods directly behind the roundhouse. Whoever they were, they had arrived.

TEN

Parley in the Thief's House

Crope moved with as much stealth as he could manage. It wasn't much—seven years in the mines had turned his joints to creaky doors—but it was enough to sneak up on the fly. It was a big one. A biter. Most people called them black flies, but if you looked real close you see they were really brown. This one had landed on the wall next to the strange shiny stain that smelled of snails. It was the perfect position from which to launch an attack upon the figure on the bed . . . and that wouldn't do. Crope dove forward and snatched it into his fist. That wouldn't do at all.

The fly bit the tender center of his palm as he opened the door and stepped into the hall. Crope couldn't really blame it, but it did hurt, and he decided to release the fly in the hallway and let it find its own way out. The house had four stories and he was standing on the topmost floor. "Fly down," he advised as the insect buzzed away.

Crope took a moment then just to settle his mind. It wasn't that he was upset or anything . . . just things got a bit much from time to time. The light in the hallway helped. Late-afternoon sun shone red and golden, warping floorboards and stirring dust. Quill said that the man who had originally built the house had been a sea captain who'd once plied the trade routes between the Seahold and the Far South. "Missed the ocean, he did," Quill had reported. "So he built himself a ship." With its round windows and plank decking the house did look a bit like a boat, but mostly it just looked like a house.

It wasn't home, though. Crope couldn't guess how long he

would have to hide out in the cold and stony city at the base of a mountain. It made no difference: it would never be his home.

Quietly, he let himself back into the sleeping chamber. Entering the cool, low-ceilinged dimness was like passing into a cave. His lord could not bear bright light. Even in his sleep he shied away from it, screaming from his fever dreams that it burned. Boiled-wool curtains, dyed black and double-lined, concealed the chamber's only window, yet some portion of light still got through. Crope used this to navigate the room as his eyes grew accustomed to the dark.

His lord was still sleeping. Baralis' slight, misshapen body lay curled in a fetal position on the bed. The sour, grassy scent of fresh urine was leaking from the mattress and Crope fretted over whether it was better to let his lord sleep or waken him and strip down the sheets. Crope was not good with choices. Choices could lead to mistakes.

Dimwit, Halfwit, Nowit. Couldn't pluck a half-bald chicken.

The bad voice was like an itch inside his head and he tried very hard to ignore it. His lord was sleeping quietly, at rest in his mind. Perhaps it was best to let him be. Crope could not recall many hours where his lord had simply slept. Mostly he shook and clawed the sheets and repeated the same word over and over again in different ways. *No. No.*

No.

Crope shivered, though the room was warm. Not hot, not cold. Lukewarm. His lord could bear no other temperature on his skin. His lord was broken and needed mending. Crope had experience with mending. He'd fixed chickens and dogs and squirrels before but there was so much profoundly wrong with his lord that he wasn't sure it could ever be made right.

But it would not stop Crope from trying. Silently he crossed the room to where the driftwood table with the charred legs stood. The water he'd fetched earlier had now reached the same temperature as the room and he soaked some of it up in a heavy cloth. Cupping his free hand beneath the cloth to catch the drips, Crope moved toward his lord. As always when he neared him, Crope felt the anger knot in his chest. He did not understand how one man could have done this to another. During his first year at the tin mines he had pulled a digger from the rubble of a collapsed seam. The man had been smashed by falling stone, his body torn and punctured in a dozen places by sharp edges of quartz. A fluke upward shearing of rock had punched out his eye and replaced it with a shiny chunk of tin. His left leg had been disjointed at the hip and the tendons in both his feet had snapped. Unable to inflate his lungs, he had lived for about an hour. Crope thought of the digger's broken body whenever he saw his lord.

Crushed, that was the word. And it was one thing for a lode-bearing seam of tin to do that to a man. Another thing entirely for someone to do it to someone else. It was evil, and Crope lived with the real and secret fear that even though he had killed the man who had harmed his lord the evil that had been created still lived on.

Crope was gentle as he dripped water on his lord's brow. Baralis' eyes were almost destroyed, the corneas folded inward, the whites scarred and crisscrossed with strange veins. Even the lids were scarred, Crope noticed as he washed his lord's face.

"You are with me," he murmured softly as Baralis stirred, "and you are safe."

Eighteen days had passed since he'd rescued his lord; Crope knew this to be so because Quill kept an account. Quillan Moxley was a friend and thief. He was also a man of business, and Crope worried about the cost of hiding out in his house. Eighteen days of food, medicine and shelter added up—especially, Crope conceded rather sheepishly, when it was him doing the eating. Quill had asked for no reckoning, but Crope knew how these things worked. Obligation had been created, and obligation meant debt.

Still, Crope respected Quill. He was a man of his word. He'd promised to help Crope free his lord from the chasm below the pointy tower and had gone ahead and done just that. And Quill would never run to the bailiffs to settle a grievance. Men who enforced laws in this or any other city were not friends of Quill, and that suited Crope fine. Just the thought of bailiffs was enough to make Crope scan the room for likely escape routes. When a bailiff locked you up you never got out.

Jangly music rose through the floorboards as the girls in the floor below began to prepare themselves for the night's work. Crope worried about the girls. Some of them wore too little and might catch chills. Others drank too much and Crope would find them passed out on the stairs in the morning. Quill called them prostitutes though the girls never used that name themselves. He rented out the two middle floors to them in return for a portion of their take. Crope was shy around the girls. They reminded him of wounded animals who needed mending, but he knew it wasn't his place to try and fix them.

He required all his mending skills for his lord. Methodically over the past eighteen days he had tended Baralis' ailments. Open wounds were the most pressing problem and Crope cleaned them with alcohol and rubbed them with a salve made from aloe and sweet fennel. The ulcers and pressure sores had to be washed with a tincture of calendula twice a day, and Crope was careful not to let his lord lie in the same position overlong else the skin break up and become worse. There was deadnettle for the bladder, horehound for Baralis' weakened lungs, and butcher's broom for his enlarged heart. Ewe's milk so thick with cream it coated your hand like a glove helped restore his weight. Then came the potions that dulled the pain and dimmed the night terrors: blood of poppy, skullcap, devil's claw. Crope tried not to think too long on their names; they were a warning, he left it at that.

What he could not drive from his mind were the things wrong with his lord that could never be made right. Bone had been broken, allowed to partially reheal, and then systematically broken again. What was left was a body that would never bear its own weight, a spine riddled with bone spurs, vertebrae that had fused around the neck, a femur with a head so misshapen that it no longer fitted squarely in its socket, finger joints that would not bend, a wrist that could not rotate, a rib cage that lay like the collapsed hull of a shipwreck beneath the skin.

It was something worse than torture, something that went beyond the desire to disfigure and cause pain. Crope was not good with notions, and he'd had to puzzle the evil for a long time before he realized its purpose: the creation of absolute dependency.

Baralis could not have lived without the aid of his persecutor.

He had been stripped of the ability to fend for himself. Everything required for survival—food, water, warmth and clothing—had to be brought to him by another. Unable to draw a cool glass of water to his lips or move to ease the pain of the pressure sores, Baralis had been forced to wait in the darkness until his persecutor brought relief. Crope had lived in the sulfurous darkness of the tin mines. He'd been locked up in root cellars, back rooms and cages. He knew what it was to be frightened and alone. What he didn't know was what it felt like to be helpless. He was a giant man, and when chains needed breaking all he had to do was take them in his fists and pull.

His lord could not have pulled; that was the thought that undid Crope.

Feeling the bad pressure building behind his eyes, he took a step away from his lord to calm himself. The giant's blood in him pumped hard when he got angry and he had to be careful to keep his chest from getting tight. One of the last times he'd given in to the giant's blood he'd brought down a tavern in a fortified town north of Hound's Mire. Bringing down buildings wasn't good.

The smell of hot grease distracted him. The girls downstairs were preparing supper: hare fried in duck fat, if he wasn't mistaken. The girls had set up a little stove in the hallway and cooked whatever Quill or their customers brought to the house. Crope's mouth began to water at the thought of crispy hare skin, which was mostly a good thing. Feeling hungry was better than feeling mad.

As he washed his lord's wounds, Crope noticed the sunlight begin to fail. The strange, circular marks on Baralis' thighs and buttocks didn't bother him so much now. Crope had imagined his lord being branded with hot irons and that made him mad, but Quill had said no, that wasn't the case. According to him, Baralis had lain on his chains for so long that iron had leached through his skin and laid down pigment like a tattoo. Crope thought that Quill was about the smartest man he knew—excepting for his lord, of course.

A knock on the door made Crope freeze. What was he to do? Answer it? Ignore it? Hike out the window and escape? Quill had warned him many times of the need to keep a low profile.

"Keep your head down, your door locked, and your mouth shut. You're in the worst kind of trouble: you good as killed a king." Crope had no argument with that. "Worst kind of trouble" could have been his middle name.

Frowning at the little circular window set at shoulder height in the west wall, Crope decided escape wasn't going to be quick. Grease would be needed. Bulk of this magnitude didn't go through openings of that . . . smallitude without a considerable amount of help.

"It's me. Grant me ingress."

Quill. *Stupid, scuttle-brained fool. Should have known it was him all along.* Crope nodded softly, relieved. The bad voice was usually right.

"A moment," he called out. Bending deep at the waist, he attended his lord.

Baralis was in the half-world between sleep and waking. Blood of poppy pumped through his arteries, slowing the workings of his heart and liver, and clouding his brain. The terrors had been bad last night and Crope had been frightened that his lord might injure himself. Baralis had writhed on the bed, arching his spine and clawing at the shadows in front of his face. *No,* he had cried again and again. *No.* The blood of poppy had stilled him, but now, half a day later, he was beginning to stir. Crope knew his lord. He could tell from a few tiny movements—the flick of an eyelid, the contraction of muscle below the jaw—that Baralis was becoming aware.

Swiftly, Crope tucked pillows beneath his lord's head and straightened the sheets. With the little whalebone comb he had carried with him all the way from the diamond pipe, he groomed Baralis' night-black hair. There was no time to banish the sour smell of urine so Crope scooped a packet of dried mint from the table and crushed it hard in his fist. On his way to the door he scattered the pieces randomly about the room. It didn't disguise the sourness exactly, he decided, reaching for the door bolt. Just made it smell as if someone had drunk a bucket of mint tea before pissing.

It would have to do. One quick glance back assured Crope that his lord was now in possession of his dignity, and he was free to pull back the bolts.

"Took your time," Quill said, stepping through the doorway, his gaze shooting into all the dark spaces. "Sleeping is he?"

Crope nodded, thought, then shook his head.

Quill appeared to understand this and jabbed his chin in response. Medium height and lean as back bacon, he shrank to almost nothing when viewed from the side. His hair was dark and greased close to his skull and his eyes were an uncertain color that Crope could only describe as "murky." As befitted a thief, Quill's clothes were unremarkable in fit and color, offering no information worth repeating to a bailiff. Brown. Gray. Worn. It was his custom however to wear "a spot of cream." Cream was gold that was nine-tenths pure, Crope had learned, and it advertised Quill's status to others like him. Today he wore a heavy-gauge chain circling his left wrist at the cuff mark. You could see it only when he extended his arm in a certain manner . . . which was exactly as he planned.

Sliding himself against the far wall, Quill said, "Close the door. There's business to discuss."

Crope did Quill's bidding, hoping Quill wouldn't study the room too carefully while his back was turned. The rough plank walls had sponged up years of damp, and holes of varying sizes told of long-standing infestations: woodworm, termites, mice. A rug woven from bulrushes had partially unraveled on the floor, and overhead in the roof beams fiddlehead spiders had crocheted a killing field for flies. Crope tried to keep the room clean, but no matter how much he swept and scrubbed the shabbiness remained.

"Watch'll be coming door-to-door tonight," Quill said, flicking his gaze away from the figure on the bed as Crope turned to face him. "A carter hauling tallow up Lime Hill swears he saw a giant as tall as two men heading east towards Rat's Nest at dawn."

Crope felt his face grow hot. He had been out last night, walking in the chill air and watching the stars fade as the sun rose from behind the big mountain. He knew it was a risk, being out at dawn, but seventeen years interred in the darkness of tin mines and diamond pipes changed a man, and there was no one alive who could keep him away from the light.

Quill studied the color in Crope's face before nodding

shrewdly with understanding. Perhaps he'd been locked up too. "Here's what we know. The watch has had their drawers in a dither ever since the night the tower fell. They don't look good. The Splinter comes crashing down, destroys half the fortress, wakes up every doomed and deluded soul in the city, and covers every rooftop, walltop and tabletop with a layer of dust as thick as me thumb. Eighteen days later and they're still pulling bodies from the wreckage. And to make matters worse they haven't found the Surlord." Quill paused to give Crope a speculative look. "All things considered it's a fuckup of historic proportions. Half the city's scared arseless and the other half's busy as bees trying to fleece them. We've got grangelords running wild with their hideclads, Rullion's whitenecks igniting one unholy fire under the faithful, and Mask Fortress under siege.

"Blunders left and right. Bollockings for all. The watch needs to be seen doing something. And that something, my friend, is finding you."

Crope looked at his feet. "Not as tall as two men," he said.

Except for blinking a few times, Quill ignored this. "Rumors are running like cheap ale. The mountain moved, ancient evil's awoken, the Surlord's in hiding, the Surlord's dead. Only one man alive knows the truth of what happened—and I'm looking straight at him and it ain't a reassuring sight."

Crope stared at his feet. *Chicken-brained fool. Brought down the whole henhouse now.* "Go away," he offered, "take lord and never come back."

Tutting impatiently, Quill peeled back the curtain and glanced down at the street. "As I said, hardly reassuring." He seemed to be speaking to himself. Letting the curtain drop he spun around to face Crope. "Look. Leave the city and you might as well light a signal fire and holler at the top of your lungs *Come get me.* Last time I counted, giants hauling cripples on their backs were few and far between. Dozens saw you that night. Now granted some may have exaggerated your considerable charms, but there's two things they all agree on. One, that the man seen escaping from the collapsing tower was an unnaturally big bastard. And two, he's as guilty as sin.

"Every watch brother, bounty hunter and bailiff in the city hold is looking for you. You're as easy to spot as a pig in a snake basket, and neither you nor his lordship there should be going anywhere anytime soon."

Once again Quill's gaze rested upon Baralis. The thief was deeply interested in him, Crope had noticed, but pretended otherwise. Baralis lay silent and unmoving, his eyes closed, breath hissing faintly from his lips.

Listening.

Quill continued. "Matters may have died a death if the carter hadn't sang his song with you as chord and chorus. Now the watch is at our heels and they're knocking door-to-door. They're going to be on that stoop this very night and unless we do something sharpish we're all gonna hang."

Crope knew some kind of response was called for, but he was having difficulty keeping up. Quill spoke fast and fancy, and the word *bailiff* had been spoken and it was getting hard to think. "No hang."

"Too right no hang." Quill was beginning to get animated. "I haven't sneaked these streets for twenty years to get a necking for mischief I didn't make. Abetting a friend of a friend, I was. The King of Thieves himself, Scurvy Pine. That's the way things work in the back alleys: you help someone, I help you, and when time comes when I require a little assistance meself my dues are paid in full. Course the system starts to break down when one good deed turns into an ongoing concern. I have to ask myself 'What's in it for me?' and from where I'm standing now—between an eight-foot stack-o-hay and death on two sticks—it ain't looking good."

"No good," Crope echoed in deep agreement.

This response appeared to exasperate Quill, who began to pace the room. "So all the time you hauled rocks in the diamond pipe you never stashed a little cream for yourself?"

Morose now, Crope shook his head. "Had diamond . . . lost it."

"And what about his lordship there. Lord of what? Lord of where? Has he holdings, land, goods?"

Crope continued shaking his head. Baralis had been a powerful man once, in the land south of the mountains. Kings had waited upon his word. But the old kings were dead now and those who had taken their place had ill-liked Baralis and his methods. All had been lost. It hardly seemed real. A castle had burned to the ground and Baralis had burned along with it, and while everyone else was fleeing the flames, Crope had run toward them. It was the smoke, he remembered, thick and hot like boiling wool. The first time he breathed it in, his gums had shrank away from his teeth. Eighteen years later and they still hadn't sprung back.

Nothing had sprung back. Crope had pulled Baralis from the flames but even though his body had been saved the losses were still being counted. Crope believed he would never know all the ways in which his lord had shrunk. Land and titles could be counted, a body seared by flames and then broken could be seen and reckoned, but the other things—the mind, the will, the *power* of his lord—were beyond his ability to comprehend. Some of his lord was still there, lying behind the slow-tracking gaze, but how much was impossible to know.

Even though Crope knew it was a mistake to think of the bad man, the one with pale eyes who Quill called the Surlord, he couldn't seem to stop himself. That man had destroyed his lord. Ridden them down, he had, coolly keeping his distance while his armsmen had drawn swords. *Wittle-wattle. Wittle-wattle. Chicken jowls for brains.* Crope flushed with shame as he remembered his lord's capture. It was all his fault. After he'd rescued his lord he could have gone anywhere in the Known Lands. Flee, that was the important thing. Escape from the walled city and the men who were enemies of his lord. North, south, east, west: it hardly mattered which way. So why had he chosen to head north into the mountains? Because he was stupid, that was why. Any other direction and they would have been high and dry. Wet and low was what they got though. Eighteen years of wet and low.

The pale-eyed man's capture of his lord had just been the beginning. While Baralis was hauled off to the pointy tower, Crope had been left for dead in a dry gully. Arrows, four of them, had punctured his giant man's hide. Crope could not say how long they rendered him unconscious, but what he did know was that his first and only thought upon waking was *Now I must rescue my lord.* The hijack had been sprung in foothills northwest of Hound's Mire and Crope knew with certainty that his lord had been taken west. So west he went, toward the city with the gray limestone walls he stood within this very night. Within less than a day he'd run afoul of the slavers. Years later, Crope learned that slaving companies regularly patrolled the lawless country known as the Mirelands. According to Scurvy Pine, anyone crossing the mountains on their own or in small, undefended companies was judged fair game. Hobbled, blindfolded, and harnessed to the back of a wagon, Crope had been hauled east to Trance Vor. The Vor was an outlaw city financed with diamonds, tin, mercury and gold—anything that could be dug from the earth. Scurvy Pine said that slaving was illegal there, just like in most other cities in the North, but the Vor lords turned a blind eye to it. Slaves were needed to break the stone.

Crope had been sold to the tin mines. Eight years later when the seam had run dry, he'd been traded along with his chain brothers to the diamond pipe north of Drowned Lake. Rumor had it that mining diamonds was easier than mining tin, but Crope soon learned those rumors were false. Eighteen hours a day you broke rock. An hour to eat and piss, and five to sleep. After nearly a decade of living underground, working in the open pit of the diamond pipe had first seemed a blessing. Then autumn's cool sunshine fled and half a year of winter began. Ice storms, blizzards, northern winds and freezing fog: rock had to be broken through it all. Crope had watched men's hands turn bright pink and then white, and known that within a week they would rot and have to be amputated with the pipe surgeon's bone saw. Bitterbean called it the miner's farewell, for everyone who went under that green-toothed saw died.

In the eight years he mined the pipe, Crope had seen all the ways a man could die. He knew he was lucky to be here, lucky to have a hide so thick it defied freezing, lucky to have a back so strong that after eighteen hours of breaking rock, it would straighten like a bivouacked birch. He'd been lucky to have Scurvy Pine, the King of Thieves, as his protector, and lucky to know that one day he would escape and find his lord.

That knowledge had sustained him better than warm blankets and lamb stew. When Scurvy Pine had come up with the escape plan, Crope had agreed to everything he'd asked. His job had been to break the leg irons that bound the slaves into a line. *"Don't you go forgetting, giant man. You be ready when I give the word."* When the word came Crope had been ready. He and Scurvy had escaped, and while the King of Thieves fled north, Crope had headed west.

Come to me, his lord had commanded. Now Crope was here and his lord was free, and things were still wet and low. Stupidly, he had imagined that once he and his lord were reunited their problems would disappear.

Crope looked at his boots—yet another thing he owed to Quillan Moxley. The thief had deemed his original diamond boots "lacking in mediocrity" and had purchased a superior, more forgettable pair.

"Lord has nothing. Crope has nothing," Crope said, feeling deeply wretched. "Can break rocks and fix things" He struggled for more. "Once acted in a mummers' show as a bear."

Quill appeared genuinely puzzled at this and paused for a moment to consider it. With a shake of his head he continued. "His lordship must have friends in high places. Stashes? Influences? Favors waiting to be cashed? You don't end up with a surlord as your personal jailer unless you're valuable, or dangerous. Or both." A thoughtful look charged Quill's features. "You're going to have to leave this house tonight, my friend. I'm not your protector. I'm a thief, and I don't want to hang."

Suddenly things had become deadly serious. It was almost dark in the room now. Oil lanterns burning in the street lit the ceiling with a flickering orange glow. The north face of Mount Slain was breathing, moving banks of mist across the city. Crope felt their chill, and his instinct was to light the little brass stove in the corner. That had just become an impossibility though. You couldn't fault Quill for looking out for himself. If it wasn't for his lord, Crope imagined he would have done the same. Still, it was hard to know what to do. Why was there never enough thinking room in his head?

Quill let the silence be, his long thief's fingers twitching.

Suddenly the sound of horse hoofs rang out in the street below. The Rive Watch. Few in the Rat's Nest owned horses— nags to pull barrows, donkeys for hauling soft goods and drunks. It had to be the red cloaks.

Crope's gaze jumped from the blacked-out window to Quill. A delicate adjustment of neck muscle was all it took for the thief to send his face into shadow.

Here it was then. Quill had called in his marker, and Crope had no means to pay. Nodding softly, Crope said, "Go now. Take lord out back." Who knew where they would go? Not north, that was the only thing he was sure of. No good had ever come to anyone from heading north.

Quill bowed his head gravely. "May your nights always be long and moonless."

Crope tried to respond with matching dignity, but the panic was building. His lord was too sick to travel. What would they do? Leave the city? Stay? Quill said everyone in Spire Vanis was searching for them. How could they even walk to the nearest gate without being seen? Crope tried, but he imagined the plea "Help me!" was writ clear upon his face.

If it was the thief didn't acknowledge it. With a swift movement Quill crossed to the door. The bolts were pulled with expert skill. Even the one that needed oiling made no sound. Light from the hall poured into the room. "I'll send the dog up," Quill said in parting. "Best be quick."

Just as the thief's shadow slid across the threshold a word sounded.

"Wait."

It was a command, issued quietly but filled with force, and it halted the thief in his tracks. Baralis had spoken.

Quill reacted so quickly, spinning around and stepping back across the threshold, that for a moment Crope wondered if he hadn't anticipated such a response all along. Pushing the door closed behind him, the thief fixed his gaze on the bed. "I'm listening."

All the time Quill had been in the room, Baralis had not moved. He moved now though, using his elbows to pull himself up a fraction on the bed. Crope's instinct was to rush forward to aid him, but his lord sent a look from the distant past. *I will deal with this.*

Thwak. Thwak. Thwak. The sound of a spear butt thumping a door sounded from the street below. Crope couldn't tell if it was Quill's door or the one before it. Incomprehensibly, neither

Baralis or Quill seemed to care. Each was looking at the other in a manner that reminded Crope of the way free miners appraised newfound diamonds for flaws.

After a moment Baralis spoke, and to Crope's ears his lord's voice sounded more beautiful than it had eighteen years earlier. It broke on some of the words and sometimes faded, but its power was still there. All that had been lost could be heard, yet that only added to the richness. Crope's heart ached with love and sadness. The essence of his lord had always lived in his voice.

"Deliver us safely from the watch and you will be rewarded."

"How so? Your friend here says you have nothing."

Baralis's reply came quickly, but to Crope's ears it was not as fast at it would have been eighteen years earlier. "My servant speaks the truth as he knows it. *I* know where the Surlord's secret stash lies."

Quill's eyes widened, yet he forced them back down to two little strips. "Secret stashes? Do you think I was born yesterday?"

"You were born thirty-one years ago in a town so small it didn't have a name. You lived in a lean-to built by your grandfather, who beat you with a fire iron. You left home when you were nine. No one came after you, but you never stopped hoping."

"Enough." Quill was shaking. "Where is this stash?"

Shouting sounded from down below as Baralis rocked his mangled body forward on the bed. Sheets fell from him like shed skin. "I will not reveal the whereabouts of Iss' stash, but know this: I have moved beyond deception. I want nothing but shelter for my servant and myself. Hell knows me, and you cannot understand what that knowing brings. Every hour that passes I become less. The things that I want are beyond your power to hoard or steal. Help me and you will receive what I no longer desire."

A moment passed where if Crope was asked he would have said he felt as if the earth beneath his feet was turning, and then the thief nodded slowly, without eagerness. "The deal is done. God help us all."

Crope gathered his lord's possessions together as Quill went ahead to fetch the dogs.

ELEVEN

A Raven's Call

Raif opened his eyes. All was still and dark. The Want had thickened while he slept, there was no other way to describe it. Sometimes it felt loose and full of space, a vapor that might blow in the wind. Now it felt like sediment sinking to the bottom of a glass.

Without thinking, he raised his hand to his chest. He had been sleeping on his back, yet something had pushed the raven lore deep into the V of his throat. As his fingers pried the hard piece of bird ivory from his skin, his mind became aware of something his body already knew. Danger. His muscles were already charged, his sweat glands open and excreting oil. Even before he opened his eyes his night vision had been engaged.

Unknown territory, that was what his life had become. Yet what choice did he have but to embrace it?

Rising, he made swift decisions on what he would need. The dimness of the tent did not slow him, and he located clothes, boots and weapons, readied himself, and then stepped outside.

A piercing frost had cracked down on the Want while he'd slept. No wind could live in such cold and the air was paralyzed. The cookfire in the center of the tent circle had shrunk to a dim, red glow. Frozen smoke accumulating around the base was slowly suffocating the last of the flames. The lamb brother on night watch was away from his post. Raif tracked his footsteps to the corral and spotted him calming the milk ewe.

The animals knew.

Raif crossed to the fire, closed his fist around the lamb

brother's bone-and-copper spear and tugged it from the earth. "Here," he said, as the man approached him. "Take it."

He was the youngest brother, the novice. A single black dot was centered over the bridge of his nose. The discipline of his brothers was something he had not yet mastered, and in the unobserved darkness of his watch he had tied a horse blanket over his dark brown robes to keep out the cold. He shed this now as he took the spear. Whatever he read on Raif's face was enough to sober him. In the seven days he'd stayed in the lamb brothers' camp, Raif had never heard him speak. Raif couldn't even be sure if he understood Common, but he spoke to him anyway. Probably to calm himself.

"With me."

The man's gaze flicked to the clarified hide tents, where his fellow lamb brothers were sleeping.

Raif shook his head. "Leave them."

The lamb brother seemed to understand and fell in step beside Raif. He handled the nine-foot spear well, Raif observed, balancing it lightly at his waist. Raif's own weapon felt strange in his hand. Plunged deep into shadowflesh, the Forsworn sword's weight had shifted downblade. He knew he should probably knock out the crystal mounted on the pommel to restore balance, but he couldn't bring himself to deface the Listener's gift. Besides, he had the Sull bow. Slung crossways over his back, the six-foot longbow slapped against his right shoulder blade and buttocks as he walked. The horn case containing his arrows should have been suspended high on his left shoulder for ease of draw, but instead hung from the gear belt at his waist. The shoulder wound still bothered him. He could feel it now. It was tight.

Heading away from the tent circle, he tried to make sense of what was happening. The raven lore, given to him at birth by the old clan guide Beardy Hail, felt like a chunk of fuel ice at his throat. *Here it is, Raif Sevrance. One day you might be glad of it.* Beardy's words echoed in the hollow space between Raif's thoughts.

Drawn, that was the word. He'd been woken by something and drawn outside.

Back at the tent circle one of the mules began to bray. Raif glanced at the lamb brother. *Easy*, he mouthed. Again, probably to himself. Cold muscled in to his chest, freezing the little pockets where air waited to slip inside the blood. Underfoot the pumice dunes were as soft as flour. Every step raised a puff of dust.

Starlight blued the Want. Raif looked over a seabed landscape where shadows did not exist. It occurred to him that he should be afraid of walking too far from the camp, but his mind was rationing fear. Odds were he would need it later. If he was unable to return to the tent circle then so be it. There was no choice here. The raven lore had called.

At his side, Raif could hear the lamb brother breathing hard. In cold this intense it took effort to expel the breath. Raif was glad the man was here, grateful not to be alone in the twilight world that had become his life. Tallal had said the lamb brothers search for the lost souls of the dead. *Morah*, he called them. The flesh of God. Raif did not know whether that meant tracking down rotting corpses and defleshed bones, or hunting ghosts. He did know they were here to do their work. Tallal had told him as much yesterday as they had walked the perimeter of the camp looking for driftwood. Raif had asked him why they called themselves the lamb brothers, and Tallal had replied, "To my people the lamb is a symbol of hope. Lambing season is a time of celebration. Spring comes and life is renewed after the long hardship of winter. Without lambs there would be no milk, no wool, no meat. Our bodies would perish. We who seek *morah* honor the lambs. Every morning when we leave our tents we offer thanks. May the nourishment they provide give us strength to continue our search."

Raif found it surprisingly easy to imagine why the lamb brothers were here. The Want seemed as good a place as any to find lost souls.

"*Shayo!*"

The lamb brother's urgent whisper cut off Raif's thoughts. The word was unknown to him, but the meaning was clear. Following the lamb brother's gaze, Raif peered into the eerie blue landscape of dunes.

Nothing moved. Both men came to a halt. The lamb brother held his breath. The silence was immense, unlike any other silence Raif had experienced. Stand and listen long enough and you might hear the stars burning.

Firming his grip on the sword, Raif scanned the horizon. At the far edge of his vision the mounded pumice gave way to rubble and crumbling cinder cones. The cones' shapes reminded him of frost boils in the Badlands. Tem said boils were formed by frozen earth pushing up rock. They were hollow in the center, Raif knew that much. As boys he and Drey would play charge the castle in them, and a game they'd made up themselves called double death to Dhoone that involved, as far as Raif could recall, a lot of shouting and throwing sticks. Raif swallowed the memory before it could hurt him, and replaced it with something else.

What came to mind was the frost boil Sadaluk, the Listener of the Ice Trappers, had shown him many months ago in the west. Sadaluk had made him scrape at the ice that had collected in the hollow center of the boil. Something dread had died there. A creature from a time of nightmares, its grotesquely enlarged jaws sprung open and packed with ice.

Raif shook himself. While his mind was wandering he had not blinked and his eyeballs ached with cold. Blinking now made them sting.

As his eyesight cleared he spotted a movement at the base of one of the dunes. A puff of powder rose from the surface. The skin across Raif's back pulled tight. At his side the lamb brother flexed his spear. They watched the dust mushroom lazily in the still air. Raif wished for more light. The Want was as dim as murky water. Where was the damn moon?

Something glinted. A beam of starlight ran along a straight line and disappeared. The lamb brother spoke the name of his maker and began to move forward. Raif made his best guess of the distance between himself and the puff of dust. A hundred and sixty paces.

He remembered the *Shatan Maer*. Sword or bow? The Listener had advised him to learn how to kill with a sword, look his victims in the eyes as he took their lives. Raif had learned. He could list the men he had killed with his sword. Chokko of Clan Bludd. The Forsworn knight. Bitty Shank. Deep in his core Raif knew the Listener had been right. It was too easy for him to kill with a bow. It was swift and uninvolved and he could do it from a distance of a hundred and sixty paces.

Yet the Listener had been speaking of men. Raif had slain the *Shatan Maer* with his sword. It had been sickening and exhausting, and it had not made him a better man. Heritas Cant had told him the Unmade were already dead. They might look like men, but they were not men. Their flesh had been claimed by the Endlords, and changed in ways Raif did not understand. They had hearts, he had learned that for himself, but those hearts did not pump blood.

A tingle of pain sounded in the muscle of Raif's shoulder. Ignoring it, he sheathed his sword. As he reached for the Sull bow he glanced briefly at that lamb brother walking woozily across the dunes. The man had his spear lightly balanced above his shoulder, but his mind was on his footing and he'd allowed the point to droop. Better to stay put, Raif decided. Let whatever was out there come to you.

"To me!" he called out, running numb fingers over the finely waxed twine that braced the bow. When the lamb brother's course failed to change, Raif yelled, "Get back." The lamb brother heard him this time, acknowledging the noise with a slight sideways motion of his veiled head, but he did not stop. He'd halved the distance between his original position and the puff of the dust, and was accelerating down a dune. Raif guessed the lamb brother had understood the instruction well enough, and had chosen not to heed it.

He did not know then; had no experience to warn him what might be out there. Raif thought starkly, *Who has?*

Unable to warm the wax with his fingers, he settled for smoothing the twine. The Sull bow felt as light as a stalk of grass. Out of habit he flexed the belly before drawing. Nights as cold as this killed bows. Self bows, those made from a single stave of wood, could simply snap. Built ones would curl and come unglued. The Sull bow was a built recurve, constructed from layers of horn laid down in alternating strips. If it were a clan-made bow it would have felt stiff and brittle and a clans-man might think twice about using it. The Sull bow bent as easily as a dancer's spine, ticking once as the recurve popped out. Made for nights like this, it was ready.

Raif slid an arrow from the case, laid it against the riser. The action calmed him, and he found himself remembering his father's voice.

"So, will you be a hammerman like your brother Drey?"

"No, Da. I choose the bow."

Hooking the twine with his three middle fingers, he pulled back the Sull recurve. Straightaway his focus shifted. Background blurred. Individual stars bled into stripes. The outlines of the dunes sharpened. Raif searched for and found the foot-size mound of settled pumice that seconds earlier had been dust in the air. Fist on level with his right shoulder, he held a full draw as he tracked the surrounding space. The lamb brother was approaching the mound, caution slowing his pace. Hard breaths made the cloth panel covering his mouth move like bellows. Raif briefly sighted the man's heart. Its rhythm was unfamiliar to him, but he could still read the fear. With a small mental tug, he pulled away.

Raising his sights he scanned the cinder cones beyond the dunes. He did not expect to spot anything amongst the ancient, deteriorating vents. That wasn't the point. Something was waiting in the dunes. Until it moved it could not be spotted . . . and it would not move until it could strike.

The cones were still. The peculiar quality of starlight made it impossible to accurately gauge their height or distance. To Raif they were evidence of the doom that had been laid on the Want. The earth's crust was not stable here. Fissures undermined it, molten rock charged it, and things had a nasty habit of forcing their way out. *Kahl Barranon*, the Fortress of Grey Ice, had been built on flawed mountain rock. It could be a thousand leagues from here, or maybe less than ten. Slowly, Raif was coming to understand that distance didn't matter in this place. What mattered was the Want was wounded. Its skin was riddled with cracks and the *Shatan Maer* had tried to push itself through the largest. Raif had sealed that breach, but looking out across the cones he guessed it was not the only one.

"Go no further," he murmured, dropping his gaze to the lamb brother on the dunes. The man was about twenty paces from the disturbed dust. Both hands were on his spear and he was moving forward slowly, stabbing air. Raif scanned the space directly in front of him. Nothing. As he panned wider, muscles in his draw arm started to quake as the twine began to slice into the joint of his index finger. Ballic the Red had once told him that holding a longbow at full draw was the equivalent of lifting a grown man one-handed. *"Release quickly,"* the master bowman had advised. *"Every second you wait power and accuracy are lost."*

At the edge of his vision something moved. A section of air rippled and for an instant a shape was revealed. Behind the lamb brother's back, dust smoked from the dune.

"Watch out!" Raif screamed, angling his bow. As the lamb brother spun around, the dunes exploded. Dust sprayed up in a footstep pattern heading straight toward the lamb brother. Pumice glittered in the air, making it difficult to see. Raif glimpsed something dark and not quite human. As soon as he had it in his sights it was gone. The lamb brother's robes began to flap as air rushed against him. Bracing himself he distributed his weight evenly between his legs, stabilizing the spear at his waist.

A high metallic screech sounded, and then everything was obscured by whirling dust. Raif fought down panic. He couldn't see. Part of him wanted to run away, save himself while he still had time.

Noises spat from the dust cloud like sparks. Something grunted. A wailing gasp was followed by the weird harmony of metal meeting metal on a sweet spot. Blades clashed. Raif spied the shadowy outline of a head between curling lanes of dust. Dropping his sights, he searched for a heart.

An invisible line spooled from the center of his eye, slipping effortlessly through the swirling pumice. Straightaway it found a heart. Hot and red, it hammered in imperfect time. Raif recognized it and switched his gaze. The lamb brother. Both combatants were moving frantically, their torsos jerking back and forth. Raif felt the sickening suction of an unmade heart, but as he tried to lock it in his sights, the lamb brother stepped across his line of view.

Move, he mouthed, experiencing something close to shock as utter cold was replaced with heat.

Suddenly the hot heart faltered. A thin cry sounded, and for a moment all fell quiet. Raif knew he could not afford to think about what it meant. Pushing his awareness forward, he locked on to the second heart. It was like plunging into icy black water. He could not see or breathe; just feel the coldness seize his chest. His first instinct was to get out—this was not a living organ and he had no place here—but the suction he'd felt earlier pulled him in.

A river of darkness flowed through the heart's malformed chambers, its slow, muscular current animating the meat and teeth and membranes of the Unmade. Raif's own heart fell in time so quickly it was as if it had been waiting all along to match the rhythm of the dead. The moment loosened. He thought of Drey and Effie, and could not imagine a time when loving them wouldn't hurt. Follow the current and it would no longer matter. He wouldn't have to feel or think.

Ma-dum. Ma-dum. Ma-dum. The current tugged him under. Downriver all was shadow, a darkly welcoming place. Raif's middle and index fingers twitched, easing his grip on the arrow. All he had to do was let go.

"Will you come back?" Stillborn's question, spoken all those weeks ago at Black Hole, broke the rhythm.

Raif blinked. He was bone cold, almost frozen in place. The unmade heart contracted strongly, powering the surrounding flesh. Raif smelled the raw blackness of the void . . . and remembered what he had to do.

Closing his eyes he released the string. The twine whipped forward and lashed his wrist. Concussion from the recoil passed through his left arm and into his shoulder. Pain jabbed at the scarred flesh. It barely registered. The arrow had entered heart-meat.

The creature from the Blind buckled and collapsed. Hitting the dunes, it raised a coffin-shaped cloud of dust. Raif thought he heard a noise, a sort of sucking crackle, as its heart collapsed.

In the quiet seconds that followed Raif stood and breathed and did not think. Coppery saliva collected in the bottom of his mouth. Behind him he was aware of movement as the remaining lamb brothers crossed the dunes. Directly ahead, the dust began to settle and two fallen bodies emerged. Scrubbing a hand over his face to brush off ice crystals that had accumulated on his eyelashes and facial hair, Raif made his way toward them. Deep within, he fought the impulse to name the Stone Gods. He would not claim the comforts of clan.

The first body was part sunk into the pumice. The lamb brother had fallen on his stomach and a small wet slit in his sable robe was his only visible injury. It was an exit wound; he'd been gored through the gut. Raif dropped to his knees and gently turned him. The body was already growing stiff. Dark vapor curled from the wet and ragged hole that had been torn in his lower abdomen. The impact of the fall had dislodged his headpiece and Raif got his first look at the lamb brother's face. His youth came as a shock.

"Leave him," Tallal ordered, approaching. "It is forbidden for *jinna* to touch our dead."

Raif bowed his head, not understanding fully what the lamb brother meant, but hearing enough in his voice to realize he was upset. With an effort, Raif rose to his feet. He was exhausted, and the pain in his left shoulder was rapidly draining what little strength he had left. He did not want to look at the second body, but didn't know what else to do. All three lamb brothers were on the dune now, silent men wrapped from head to foot in dark wool robes. They did not want him here, he could tell that from the way they moved to separate him from the body. Perhaps they blamed him for their brother's death. Perhaps they were right.

The creature from the Blind had fallen on its knees, and by some strange alignment of its spine its body still knelt upright. As Raif drew near he detected the same raw, alien odor he'd smelled earlier. The creature was naked and its head and part of its chest were covered in fine scales. It was not quite human. Oversize blood vessels running along its arms and legs fed bulbous humps of loosely slung muscle. A bone spur on one side of its jaw protruded through its skin. Raif shuddered and moved away.

The creature's weapon had landed a small distance from its body, and he walked over to inspect it. The thick, night-black sword was burning a hole in the dune. It had already sunk two feet. The walls of the hole gleamed softly as pumice was transformed into glass.

Voided steel.

Raif glanced at the lamb brothers; two were kneeling by the body while the third was prayer-walking at the base of the dune. Raif crossed over to Tallal. The lamb brother was rewinding the cloth around his slain brother's face.

Not knowing how to soften what he was about to say, Raif coughed to get Tallal's attention. "We must burn the body. Quickly."

Tallal's long, slender hands ceased moving. "Leave us," he replied without looking up. "Return to the camp while we prepare Farli for the journey."

Farli. Tallal had slipped and spoken his brother's name. Raif repeated it to himself, committing it to memory. You did not forget a man you had fought alongside. When he spoke, his voice was hard. "Your brother has been killed by voided steel. The metal does not belong in this world. If you leave your brother's body intact it will be consumed by dawn, claimed by the same evil that created that thing over there. He will become one of them, and once that happens I cannot say how long he'll be damned."

All three lamb brothers looked at him. The elder brother who was prayer-walking stopped midstep.

Raif pressed on. "I have seen it with my own eyes. Forsworn knights, slain by the same make of weapon. Their bodies were stripped. Despoiled." He halted, remembering the Forsworn redoubt, the black stains the four bodies had left on the floor. "We must destroy the body. Now."

Tallal shook his head. "We do not burn our dead."

"If you do not burn him I will."

Raif did not know whether it was the words or the threat behind them that got through to Tallal. The lamb brother looked first at the elder and then at the brother who was kneeling on the other side of the body. Both men nodded almost imperceptibly, letting it be known they acceded to whatever decision Tallal made.

Tallal closed his eyes, took a breath, and then opened them. In the seconds that it took he had aged. "We must cleanse him first."

"Be quick," Raif warned, before heading back to the camp.

The mist began to rise as he traced the lamb brothers' footsteps to the tents. Darkness held. The animals were quiet as he approached, the cookfire dead and smoking. Raif slipped inside his tent. Sitting on the mattress he pulled the wool blankets around him. He just wanted to get warm. After a while, he rose, fearful of falling asleep.

His hands felt big and dull as he poured himself a cup of water. Clumsily, he spilled liquid down his cloak. Exhaustion was making him shake. Although he did not much want to he forced himself to go outside and search for oil. Aware that the lamb brothers kept most supplies in the corral, he headed toward the animals. The milk ewe bleated as he stepped over the hide barrier and entered her tiny domain. She was a fine-looking animal, with bright eyes and a curly coat. Her udder was swollen with milk. To comfort her Raif unhooked her honey log from the ceiling and placed it within her reach. The mules poked their heads over the partition wall and watched as he searched for oil.

Once he'd found a brick of sheep's butter and a carafe of lamp oil, he nodded farewell to the animals and left. A sharp breeze pushed him forward. The great dome of stars was paling, and the mist was on the move. Raif spent most of the journey looking at his feet. He did not want to get lost. As he studied the footprints leading to and from the dunes he realized that one of the lamb brothers must have made his way back to the camp and then returned to the bodies. The thought that someone had been at the camp at the same time he was there bothered him. Why had they not made themselves known?

When he reached the dune he saw that all three men were standing over the body of their slain brother, heads bowed, face cloths moving as they prayed. Something had been done to the body. An L-shaped incision had been made to open the chest, but Raif was only allowed a fleeting glimpse. As Tallal stepped forward to bar his approach, a second brother hastily covered the corpse.

Feeling unwelcome, Raif indicated the things he had brought. "I'll prime the fire."

"No." Tallal faced him and said no more.

Raif said, "I would help you." Even beneath the gravecloth, he could see the corpse was smoking.

"You have slain the wrall. That is enough."

Raif was surprised to hear the world *wrall* from Tallal. It was the same one used by Heritas Cant all those months ago in Ille Glaive. He would have liked to ask to what the lamb brother knew of them, but the time wasn't right. Placing the carafe and butter on the ground, he said, "It must be done now."

"As you wish." It was a dismissal, and Tallal stood and waited until Raif realized that fact.

It was a long walk back to the camp. As he approached the tent circle Raif smelled burning oil and felt some measure of relief.

Knowing he would not sleep, he set about rebuilding the fire. The discipline of peeling sticks, packing kindling and stacking logs helped clear his mind. *"It's no small thing to build a fire,"* Da always said, and Raif decided he was right. When the flames grew fierce enough to sustain themselves, he sat back on his cloak and watched. The heat felt good. It burned, and that was fine.

Dawn came. The mist drained, and clouds began crossing the sky. The lamb brothers did not return. Raif rose, deciding he would milk the ewe. She was bleating plaintively now, in need of release.

Tomorrow he would leave this place. He barely wanted to admit it, but some small childlike part of himself had hoped that he might find a home with the lamb brothers. They searched for the lost soul of the dead; he watched the dead. It had seemed . . . fitting. Right. Only it wasn't, and he'd been a fool to imagine otherwise. He did not blame them. How could he? They had healed and sheltered him. They deserved his thanks and respect.

Who he was, what he did, had shocked them. They dealt in spirits. He dealt in flesh.

Raif caught the raven lore in his fist and turned it. The hooked piece of bird ivory felt as rough as if it had been scoured by the dunes.

Will you come back?

Strange as it was, the Maimed Men had accepted him. Stillborn, Addie Gunn, even the Robber Chief himself, Traggis Mole: none cared about his past. They had used him, but perhaps he was made to be used. And they needed him. The Rift was the deepest canyon in the North. Its greatest flaw. Maimed Men would be the first to die if it were breached. After tonight he understood that what had happened in the Fortress of Grey Ice had slowed, but not changed, things. The Unmade were still pushing through.

Someone had to push the other way.

Letting the lore drop against his chest, Raif went to milk the ewe.

Yes, I'm coming back.

TWELVE

Along the Wolf

Effie Sevrance sneezed. It was a big thick one with lots of snot. In the old days she would have been mortified; there'd be Letty Shank and Florrie Horn squirming and crying "Eeeew!," Raina shaking her head and saying, "Really, Effie, get a cloth," and Da warning, "Wipe that on your sleeve and I'll tan your backside. I didn't trade two unopened fawn carcasses for that dress to be spoiled within a year." Da never tanned her backside, not once. She knew he didn't mean it. He knew that she knew. It was the thing that came after that hurt. "What would your mother think?" Effie reckoned those five words held more power than an entire armory of swords. They were like a spell: speak them and he who hears them will change.

They worked even if you had never known your mother, if she had died giving birth to you. Effie wiped her nose on a scrap of ragging left behind when the cheese it contained had been eaten. It smelled like feet. The men from the Cursed Clan had the worst kind of food.

They were over by the shore, pulling their long lightweight boat up the bank. Last night's frost had surprised them with its depth, and even though only two feet of stern had been left in the water, the entire boat had frozen in place. Waker Stone and his tiny, aging father had worked for the past hour to free the craft from the ice. Fourteen feet long, the boat consisted of mooseskin stretched over a wooden frame. It was so light that the two men could haul it over their heads and carry it right up the mud beach. Setting it down, keel up, on the dry reedgrass above the highwater mark, Waker called for Chedd to help him.

Chedd was doing something stupid with a stick and centipede, making the ugly thick-bodied insect scuttle up the same mound over and over again by pushing it back down every time it reached the top. Effie had warned him centipedes could bite, but Chedd was two years older than she was and from Bannen and he wasn't about to listen to anything a nine-year-old Hail girl had to say. Served him right if he got poisoned. Might even stop him stuffing his fat face for a day.

"Got a greenie hanging," he said to her as he coaxed the centipede onto the stick.

As soon as she raised her hand to her face, Effie knew she'd made a critical mistake.

"Got you!" he cried, tossing the centipede toward her. "Nothing there."

Effie was so mad at herself she stamped her foot. Chains rattled. Chedd's annoying laugh—it sounded like a dog being sick—went on and on until a single word from Waker stopped it.

"*Boy.*"

Chedd's face froze and he dropped the stick. Lurching into motion, he hopped and shuffled down the beach as fast as his leg irons would let him. His tunic was too short and Effie could see the roll of fat around his waist jiggling. She must be a bad person, she decided, for her thought at that moment was *I'm glad it's not me.* Waker Stone was not a man you wanted mad at you.

Shivering, Effie tramped her way back to the firepit—passing a somewhat disoriented centipede along the way. It was about an hour past dawn and the clouds that had hung over the Wolf for the last five days were beginning to break up. Yesterday it had snowed. Today that snow was on the ground, frozen into little icy pellets that crunched when you stood on them. Ahead, the river seemed sluggish. The Wolf was not pretty here, one day east of Ganmiddich. Waker said they were in flood country. The land north of the river was flat and choked with bog willow, frog fruit, reedgrass, and great big bulrushes with exploded heads. There was a lot of mud. Luckily it was frozen—yesterday when it was oozing it had smelled really bad. You could see it in the river, turning the water an unpleasant murky brown. Waker wasn't pleased with it at all. He said it made the river acidic, and acidity was the enemy of his boat.

He and his father would spend at least an hour a day tending the boat. Its skin had to be patched and stretched, waxed and tied, the sprayrails and gunwales oiled daily, the load removed before beaching. It was, Effie had to admit, a beautiful vessel, with skin the color of old parchment and a gleaming cedar frame. The only time Waker and his father spoke to each other was to discuss the condition of the boat. Which made the fact they'd left it overnight in the water pretty strange.

Effie glanced upriver toward Ganmiddich. Although she was several leagues east of the roundhouse, she could still see the tower. The fire had gone out now, but smoke still puttered from the open gallery on the top floor. The tower was probably the reason the boat not been properly beached. Yesterday at noon when Chedd had spotted the strange green fire, Waker had immediately steered to shore. They'd been camping on the frozen mudbank ever since.

No one had slept much last night. The first fire hadn't lasted very long, but the smoke it produced poured from the tower's windows all day. Then, after it had grown dark and there was nothing to see in the west except sky and stars, a second fire had ignited. This one was different. It was red.

Blue fire of Dhoone, black smoke of Blackhail, red fire of Clan Bludd, that was the litany Effie had learned as a child. Clan Bludd had seized Ganmiddich in the night. Blackhail was defeated and unhoused.

Drey. Effie scooped out her lore from beneath the neck of her dress and held it in her fist. Her lore was a round piece of stone with a hole drilled through it given to her by the old clan guide Beardy Hail. As far as she knew she was the only person in the clan who had an inanimate object as her lore. It just wasn't done. People had birds and animals and fishes, and occasionally—but not often—trees. No one had a piece of glass or a chunk of coal, it just wasn't . . . clannish. When she had first been given it as a newborn, her da had told Beardy to take it back. "Her mother's body is still cooling," Da had said. "This child has enough to bear." Beardy wouldn't hear it. Beardy had never retracted a lore, not even Raif's.

Effie didn't mind it much now. She no longer cherished fantasies about the fawn lore or the swan lore. Fawns were nothing but wolf bait, and swans were great honking birds that had to run half a league to take off. At least when a stone sank it sank fast.

Yesterday she had been glad of her lore. The small lump of granite had told her about Drey. She'd known he was in danger even before Chedd had seen the fire, and later she'd known when the danger became worse. Drey was in command of Blackhail forces at Ganmiddich: he would have been on the front line. Effie did not know how the battle had fared or what had befallen Blackhail. That wasn't the way her lore worked. It pushed warnings through her skin but not much else. About three hours after midday it had jumped against her breastbone and instantly she knew Drey had been hurt. There had been nothing after that; the stone was still. Through the evening and the night she kept checking, taking the stone in her fist and squeezing hard, but she could not force anything out of her lore.

It was difficult not knowing what happened to Drey. Effie Sevrance loved her brothers very much. Both of them, Drey *and* Raif, and she didn't give a swan's bottom about what anyone at Blackhail said. Raif wasn't a traitor. Raif had killed four Bluddsmen outside of Duff's defending Will Hawk and his son Bron.

Aware that her chin was sticking out, Effie tucked it back in. Dropping the lore against her chest, she went to sit by the dead fire as the men of the Cursed Clan fixed the boat.

Clan Gray, that was where Waker Stone and his father came from. The clan in the middle of the swamp. Effie didn't know much about Clan Gray, didn't even know if they had a roundhouse still standing. She knew it was the farthest west of the clanholds and it shared borders with Trance Vor and the Sull. Just thinking about that made Effie glad to be a Hailsman—Blackhail's only vulnerable border was with Dhoone. Still, the swamp probably kept invaders at bay, always supposing there *were* invaders, of course. A clan with a curse laid upon it would hardly make a grand prize. They had a good clan treasure though, if Effie remembered rightly. A steel chair that had been carried across the mountains during the Great Settlement.

We are Gray and the Stone Gods fear us and leave us be. That was their boast, or part of it. Inigar Stoop had told her it over-reached the boundaries of boastfulness and stepped right into blasphemy. Perhaps that was why they were cursed. No one at Blackhail ever mentioned the reason behind the curse, and Effie had come to the conclusion that there were two possible explan-ations why. First, they didn't know. Or second, a curse might be catching. Clansmen were nothing if not superstitious.

Effie had considered asking the present company about the origins of the curse, but Waker and his father, who Chedd believed might be named Darrow, were hardly the kind of people who could be questioned. Father Darrow barely said a word, just kept his beady-eyed gaze bouncing from Effie to Chedd and back again, and Waker was just plain scary. He looked like something that had been left too long in the water. Once, when he'd been pulling off his otter-fur coat, Effie had got a glimpse of the pale, grayish skin around his waist. You could see the organs through it, the dark purple lobe of the liver and the coiled sausage of the intestines. It was enough to put Effie off her food for an entire day. Waker had the jelly eyes as well, that's what Mog Willey used to call them. Eye whites that protruded too far from their sockets and were so full of fluid that they jiggled when they moved. Waker's father didn't have them so Effie imagined they'd been passed down from his mother's side. The thought of meeting a woman with eyes like that made Effie hope the journey to Clan Gray lasted an especially long time.

At least she assumed that's where they were going. Waker had made it clear to her from the very first night he would answer no questions from a child.

"You'll be quiet, girl, unless you fancy the gag."

Effie did not fancy the gag. Even in the confusion of all that had happened that night, she knew she didn't want that wet and moldy ball of ragging thrust in her mouth. "I will not cry out," she had told him quite calmly. "I doubt if the men crossing the river would aid me even if I did."

Waker Stone had glanced across the Wolf at the city men army crossing on barges. "You're a smart one," he told her, "but don't make the mistake of imagining you're smart enough to fool me."

It had been ten days since she'd been abducted from the clearing by the waterfall. That first night Waker had dragged her north through the brush that choked the riverbank to a camp set up in the tumbled-down ruins of an old stovehouse. Part of the stove was still standing, and although its iron door had long since gone, the big wrist-thick hinge pins that had held it in place were still sunk into the brick. Waker had shackled her to them while he explained the rules she would now live by.

"You'll be fed and treated fair as long as you are silent and obey me. The first time you attempt to run I will capture you and cut off your left hand. Try it again and my knife moves up to your elbow. If you're foolish enough to attempt a third time you will die — not because I will kill you, because no one's ever survived having their arm hacked off at the shoulder." He looked at her hard with his pale, bulging eyes. "Do you understand?"

She did and nodded.

"Good. Tomorrow I put leg irons on you. Once they are on there is nothing in my possession that can remove them. I carry no ax strong enough to cut the chains or no pick with the correct bore to punch out the pins. Do you understand this also?"

Again, she had nodded.

"Very well. I'll send the boy over with some food. You will eat it and then you will sleep."

The boy had turned out to be Chedd Limehouse, a big lumbering redhead from Bannen who she had been surprised to learn was only eleven. He'd been taken three days earlier, he explained the next day when they were finally alone. Her leg irons were on by then — ankle cuffs forged from matte gray pig iron strung together by a two-foot chain — and Waker had gone off to sell Chedd's horse. Chedd had been taken by the river too. Not the Wolf, but by its northern tributary, the Minkwater, that drained the uplands above Bannen. Chedd had been turtling in the rock pools close to the bank. It'd had been a good day for it, he explained. Warm enough to have roused some snappers from their winter sleep. He had been alone except for his horse. "Waker came out of nowhere, he did," Chedd whispered. "One minute I'm turning over a great big dobber, the next I'm being dragged by the hair through the reeds." His horse had been taken too, and while Chedd and Waker's father had paddled upriver on the boat, Waker had ridden parallel to the shore. "He's not much of a horseman," Chedd confided knowingly. "Kept bending forward in the saddle and losing his stirrups."

Chedd didn't know why he had been taken, but he feared the worst. "They're going to eat us—roasted whole on sticks. Either that or sacrifice us to the marsh gods: tie stones around our ankles and throw us over the side."

Effie wasn't having any of that. "There's no such thing as a marsh god," she'd told him, "and clansmen aren't cannibals. They're more than likely selling us to the mines."

To hear Chedd wail about that one you'd think he'd prefer to be eaten alive. "But it's not clan! They can't take us to Trance Vor . . . it's not . . . *right*."

Nor was being shackled and kidnapped, but Chedd did have a point. It was hard to imagine any clansman anywhere—even one who was cursed—selling clan children to the mine lords. Perhaps Waker was up to something else, but Effie couldn't imagine what that might be. Only two things were clear: they were slowly heading east toward Gray; and Waker wanted her and Chedd alive.

So far the going had been slow. It wasn't just that they were paddling upstream, it was the need for caution. With all sorts of armies fighting over Ganmiddich, the Wolf River had become a dangerous place. Waker's father had knowledge of the water-ways, and sometimes they would leave the main river and portage to the backwaters; the streams and meanders, the flood-season creeks and pools. They had circumvented the Ganmiddich roundhouse entirely, and Effie still hadn't quite worked out how. She just knew they left the Wolf for a day, poled up a fast-running tributary, portaged through an over-grown shrub swamp and then floated the boat on a second tributary, following the current downstream to the Wolf.

Waker always paddled from the bow while his father guided the boat from the stern. Chedd paddled from the center, though he wasn't very good at it, and tended to cheat after a while when his shoulder got sore. So far Effie had not been assigned any tasks. Which was just as well really, as it was hard getting used to the boat.

It was a new and distressing experience, being afloat. Hailsmen had never been rivermen—probably because no navigable river flowed close to the roundhouse—and it wasn't unknown for clansmen to live and die without once setting foot in a boat. Effie hadn't really given them much thought before, even when she'd stayed with Mad Binny out on Cold Lake. Just being outside was trial enough, let alone being outside on dangerous, changeable, death-dealing water. She couldn't swim, even though two summers ago Raif had tried very hard to teach her at the beaver pond in the Wedge. It would have helped, she had to admit, if she'd actually got in the water. Poor Raif tried everything to coax her in—letting her know how warm the water was, promising to keep hold of her at all times, and then finally attempting to bribe her with cakes—but she wasn't having any of it. So she had watched from the rocks as he did swoopy things with his arms and kicked his feet. It didn't look very hard, and she'd decided it was a bit of a worthless skill, like dancing, and promptly dismissed it from her mind.

That had all changed five days ago when Waker had made her step into the boat. "Easy, girl," he'd warned as he held the gunwales to steady the long, thin watercraft. "Bend at the waist, keep yourself low."

That was all very well, but it was only her second day in leg irons, and she was still working on the techniques required to walk with only two feet of slack. That was one thing Chedd excelled at, the shuffling, the sidling and—when all else failed—the one-legged hop. He was pretty quick on his feet, she had to give him that. In the end she couldn't manage to step in the boat and had to be picked up. Waker had not been gentle as he plunked her down on the seat.

Things were getting a bit better now, but there was always the fear of falling in the water. The boat rocked and swayed, especially when Waker and his father stood to use the poles. Chedd said farther upstream there were rapids where the water frothed and bucked like a rabid raccoon. He said they'd probably die trying to pole against them. There was a lot wrong with those two statements, Effie decided. Waker and his father obviously had experience of the river, and if they could circumvent an entire roundhouse they could certainly find a way around some rapids. Plus she doubted very much that either one of them would attempt anything that placed themselves and the boat in danger. And finally, if there was anything less like water than a rabid raccoon Effie Sevrance would like to see it.

"Girl. Cover the fire. We leave within the quarter."

Waker didn't even look at her as he spoke. They'd finished repairing the ice damage and the boat was now back in the free-flowing water beyond the ice. As Waker's father held the craft in place, Chedd and Waker began to load the supplies. They traveled light, without tents or fireirons, and it made for swift camps and departures. No comforts were afforded. Waker's father had a distrust of fires and let one be lit only for the time it took to boil a kettle for the trail tea. Yet even when the fire burned for only half an hour and left the smallest possible footprint, Waker was meticulous about covering all traces of it when he left. Effie had a feeling she knew why.

She'd been observing the way he and his father traveled for the past few days. They were sneaks. They knew the back ways and the side ways, the ways through the reeds and the ways under the deeply shaded canopies of weeping willow. They knew exactly where they would stop each evening. Campgrounds and hideaways, stock ponds for fishing, mussel beds for musseling, duck-nesting banks for fresh eggs: they knew them all. And did not want to share them. Leave a burned-out fire or any other trace of habitation and their secret places might be lost. They inhabited a world right under the noses of a dozen clans yet floated by undetected. It was a type of power, Effie recognized, to possess such stealth.

For a wonder the sun came out as she raked over the fire coals with a willow switch. It even felt a bit warm if you squinted. The wind had started chopping up the water and Effie reckoned they'd be in for an unpleasant day afloat. Normally they got a much earlier start, but the business of the tower had thrown everyone off. Plucking at the lore suspended around her throat, Effie checked on Drey. Still nothing.

"Girl, in the boat."

Effie released her lore, but not before she saw Waker's sharp gaze skim over it.

Boarding the boat was still somewhat of a problem. She'd never been the most graceful girl—even when she'd had the full use of both legs—and she just couldn't seem to manage the combination of water, boat and leg irons in a single flowing movement. Her dress always got soaked and then she'd have to sit on it all day. It got wet now, despite the fact that she hiked it up to knee height in knee-deep water. She couldn't quite work that one out. With an awkward little move she'd named "the storker" she lifted her right leg as high as the leg irons would permit and then took a one-legged hopping jump into the craft. Positioning was everything. Land low and in the center and you were all right. High and off-center and the boat started rocking like a rabid raccoon in a storm.

Luckily today she got it just right. Chedd was already sitting on his seat, one down from the stern, and he turned around and aced her with the double thumbs. Grinning, she thumbed him back. He really wasn't bad. For a boy.

Waker's father stepped in next and she was pleased to see he had a paddle, not a pole. That meant he wouldn't be standing, and that made for a more stable day in the boat. Waker pushed the boat into motion and then vaulted onto his seat. They were off.

Father and son worked well together, paddling in perfect time on opposing sides. Waker's strokes were deep and efficient and you could feel the power of his shoulders pulling the boat. He was not big and bulky like a hammerman but he had an efficient and enduring type of strength. He could paddle upstream all day. His hair was black and flat and he pulled it back at the nape of his neck with a fine moonstone clasp that was not clan-made. It was his only jewel. His thigh-length moosehide boots were thickly waxed and shed water, and his pants and coat were cut from dense, velvety otter hides. The only way to discern his clan was through subtleties in his gear and person. He did not carry a sword—that in itself was telling—rather a long spike-like knife that he kept in a sheath made from the green and scaleless skin of the salamander. Riding next to the spike-knife on his gear belt was a second, shorter knife, this one sheathed in leather covered with frogskin. Frog and salamander: the twin knives of Clan Gray.

Once Effie had spotted them she noticed other indicators of his clan. His powdered guidestone was kept dry in a swim bladder that he wore on a thong around his neck. The brass buckle of his gear belt had been stamped with water marks, and the little fingernail on his right had been excised, exposing a pad of purple flesh. At the time of their first yearman's oath all Graymen had one fingernail removed. Effie didn't know whether Graymen were allowed to choose which of their nails would be taken. She did know that Waker's father had the exact same scar: little finger, right hand.

On impulse Effie spun around in her seat to look at Waker's father. He was staring straight back at her, as if he'd anticipated her turn. *Anticipate this then*, she thought, feeling slightly unbalanced. "What's your name?"

Both Chedd and Waker Stone turned at the sound of her voice. Generally there was no speaking in the boat: it was one of the rules. Waker's father continued paddling in smooth, uninterrupted strokes. His jaw was slack, but he looked at her as if he knew exactly what she was up to. Which was strange as she wasn't even sure herself. Frowning, she turned around to face front.

"Girlie, girlie, girlie, girlie. Wonder why it wasn't early?"

Hearing the croaky, gleeful voice coming from behind, Effie spun back, but she was too late. Waker's father's jaw had already fallen slack. His little beady eyes were triumphant.

Gods, he's weird. Disgruntled, Effie turned her back on him and fixed her attention on the river.

The boat had found its channel and was moving upstream. They were about thirty paces from the north shore, which still consisted of mud banks glazed with ice. You couldn't see the southern shore because of the densely wooded island midstream. Effie spotted a ruin amidst the fire pines, and wondered what clan, if any, claimed it. Chedd had sworn blind there were river pirates living on the islands, but Effie didn't believe him. How would pirates make a living? Waker's boat was the only craft in sight.

As the morning wore on the going became more difficult.

The wind fought the boat and they were forced midstream by tree debris and rocks. Waker and his father muscled the boat forward, their paddles cutting parallel troughs through the water. Gradually the mud banks and reeds gave way to woods. Trees grew right up to the river's edge. Some were actually standing in the water. Effie wondered how long it would be before the river level dropped and they got some relief. When she spied a fisher eagle diving in water just off the shore, she couldn't help but speak again. "Chedd," she hissed. "Over there. It's got a fish."

Chedd had been engaging in fake paddling for the better part of an hour and was glad of the distraction. "She's a beaut," he whispered with appreciation. "Look. On the island. You can see her nest."

Effie glanced at Waker's back, checking that this hushed conversation didn't offend him. He had to be able to hear it— they were only separated by a distance of seven feet—but perhaps because they were keeping their voices extra low he'd decided to tolerate it. The back of his head, decorated with the palely beautiful moonstone clasp, held steady and did not move.

"How do you know it's a she?" she whispered, gaze following the line of Chedd's pudgy finger to the eagle's nest.

Chedd shrugged. "Just do."

Effie shrugged back. The eagle had what looked to be a green pickerel in its hooked talons. The fish wriggled wildly as the eagle flew toward her nest. Once she was overland, she released her grip and let the fish plummet toward the beach.

Chedd turned his neck to look at Effie and they both executed a collected shoulder-scrunching wince at the moment the pickerel hit the rocks. "Eew," Chedd sighed with feeling.

"Double eew," Effie agreed, watching as the eagle swooped down to retrieve the smashed fish.

"Uh-oh. Trouble coming."

"*Ssh*," Effie hissed. In his excitement Chedd had forgotten to lower his voice. Waker had to have heard that, but a quick glance at the back of the Grayman's head told Effie nothing.

Color crept up Chedd's neck. "Sorry," he muttered. "I forgot."

Finally Effie understood what Chedd had meant by trouble

coming. As she looked on, a pair of ravens broke through the trees and swept in toward the kill. The eagle saw them coming straight for her, plucked out a piece of the pickerel's belly, gobbled it down and sprang into flight. She was nearly twice the size of the ravens, but Effie guessed she was a smart bird who knew when she was outnumbered. The ravens, night-black creatures with oily wings, fell upon the fish carcass and started cawing and squawking and battling each other for the best pieces.

"What happened to females first?" Effie whispered, fascinated.

Chedd corrected her in a voice so low it took her a moment to understand him. "They're both female too."

"How do you know that?" she demanded.

Again Chedd shrugged. "Dunno. Just do."

Effie fell silent, thinking. She looked at the back of Chedd's chubby neck and then out toward the island and the ravens. Out of habit she reached for her lore. The stone was wind-cooled and heavy. It told her nothing. Waker's father steered the boat toward the shore, taking advantage of the deepening channel. The shoreline was still heavily wooded, but the land was beginning to rise and rocky draws and undercuts lined the bank.

"Chedd," Effie said after a while, leaning forward so she could whisper in his ear. "How did you know about the ravens before they broke the trees?"

"Didn't know," he replied, defensive.

He was a bad liar and Effie wasn't about to let him get away with it. "You did know, because you said trouble was coming when there was nothing there."

Chedd shrugged expressively, his shoulders moving upward in three separate stages.

"Has anyone ever said anything bad about you?" Effie persisted. "Like you might be . . . " She lowered her voice to its absolute minimum. "Chanted."

Chedd nearly jumped off his seat. He shook his head so vigorously he rocked the boat. "No. No. No. I'm training for the hammer," he said, as if this automatically disqualified him from suspicion. He thought for a moment and then added, "My da's a hammerman too."

Effie frowned. She could tell by the set of his shoulders that

Chedd had entered what Mog Willey called "the clamdown." Once someone had entered the clamdown the only thing to do was leave them alone. They would open up only in their own good time.

Light goldened as the sun moved to the west. The wind died and the chop left the water. Effie couldn't see anything but water and trees. Pines and hardwoods warred for space along the shore. Over time her legs had grown stiff and she raised them a little bit to get the blood pumping. The chains were wet and dripping; there was always an inch of water in the boat. As she watched the chains swing between her feet she thought of Chedd and Waker and Waker's father. Something was lying at the far edge of her memory and she was trying to make it roll toward her. Of course as soon as she tried it rolled the other way. Memories were tricky little animals to catch.

Feeling the boat pull strongly toward the right, she glanced over her shoulder at Waker's father. His face told her nothing, but she could see from his strokes that he was guiding the boat ashore. Wondering why they were stopping so early Effie scanned ahead. Smoke lines, three of them, rose above the tree canopy in the distance. Effie wondered what roundhouse or settlement they came from. A handful of tiny ancient clanholds lay along the river between Ganmiddich and Croser. The country was wild here, thickly forested and overrun with vines. It was known as "tree country" and Inigar Stoop always said it was nothing more than a hatchery for flies and a feeding ground for bears. Effie took it to mean he disapproved of the wild clans that lived here.

When she saw Waker set down his paddle and draw out the pole from its place in the hull of the boat, Effie realized they weren't going ashore after all. They were going to pole up a creek.

Even though she looked really hard she couldn't spot the tributary until they were right on top of it. She could feel its waters, pushing against the stern of the boat, even perceive the cross eddies swirling where the two channels met, yet could see nothing but choked-up willow and sumac ahead. Anyone looking on would have thought Waker and his father were about to pole right onto the shore. But no, at the last instant Effie spied a telling shadow beneath the trees. Crouching low and tucking their heads against their chests to avoid being hit by branches, Waker and his father steered the boat through the canopy and into the creek.

A pretty nifty move, Effie thought, slapping at a willow twig that was aiming right for her eye.

The creek was narrow and winding, a line of brown water leading through the trees. Waker's breath came harder as he poled against the quick-moving current. Effie kept herself still. The boat was rolling from side to side and she didn't like it one bit.

Girlie, girlie, girlie, girlie. Wonder why it wasn't early? For some reason Waker's father's stupid rhyme kept playing in her head.

They headed upstream until the light failed, and then Waker's father guided the boat to a narrow pebble beach surrounded by black oak and hemlock. It was nearly dark by the time Effie stepped into the water. Her legs were a bit numb so she didn't feel the cold much. The memory was back again, playing hide-and-seek in her head.

"Girl, gather sticks for the fire." Waker held the boat for his father to alight and then began to unpack the load.

Effie's feet were still in the water. The bottom of her dress was wet. She was shivering and all she wanted to do was wrap herself up in a blanket and sleep. "I have a name, you know," she said to Waker. "It's Effie Sevrance. And that over there is Chedd Limehouse."

Chedd, hearing his name mentioned, looked up from his task of laying bedrolls, saw Effie facing off against Waker Stone and decided to make himself disappear. "Off for a piss," he said to no one in particular, darting into the trees.

Waker had been in the process of unloading the waxed sack containing the food. Gaze staying on Effie he walked to the shore and deposited the sack on the beach. It landed with a crunch. "Your name won't mean nothing where you're going. So drop your proud little fancies and build the fire."

Effie felt heat rise to her cheeks. Waker's father passed her in the water, his malignant ferret face twitching. Effie waited for him to walk up the beach before addressing his son. "Are you selling us to the mine lords of Trance Vor?" There. She'd spit it out.

Waker Stone's eyes bulged a fraction farther from his skull. His head went back and a high braying noise exploded from his lips.

Effie stepped back. The noise continued and she realized quite suddenly that he was laughing. Behind her, Waker's father sniggered once in solidarity and then went quiet.

After a moment Waker calmed himself and looked her straight in the eye. "Girl, I promise you you're not going to no mine."

She waited but he said no more, simply picked up the sack and went about his business on the beach. As Effie watched him the memory she'd been grasping for all day rolled into place. Automatically, her hand reached for out for her lore.

Girlie, girlie, girlie, girlie. Wonder why it wasn't early?

Of course! Her lore hadn't warned her the night of the kidnapping. Her lore always alerted her to danger. Always. But not then. So why?

It was a question she tried to answer as she gathered sticks for the fire.

THIRTEEN

Stormglass

Raif dreamed he was awake and could not sleep. When he woke he lay on his bed, eyes closed, and rested. Today he would leave the Want.

Or try to.

Light angling through the clarified hide walls filtered into his mind's eye. Silvery rings floated across his vision. It was peaceful just to watch them for a while. Soon he found it was one of those rare times when he could picture Drey, Effie and Ash without feeling the pain of losing them. No hurt, no longing, just memories of their faces. Effie grinned, showing him a great big hole where her front baby teeth used to be. Drey was still, offering himself for inspection, his large brown eyes vigilant and unblinking. Ash was still also, but unlike his brother and sister, Raif could not see her clearly. Wind was moving through her long silvery hair and she smiled gently as her image faded.

Raif rose and dressed, scrubbed his teeth with pumice, drank a full pitcher of water, combed and rebraided his hair, shaved. Forming a pile of his possessions in the middle of the tent, he carefully inspected his weapons, waterskin, gear belt, the Orrl cloak and half a dozen other lesser things. Those items requiring care he carried outside.

Diffused sunlight shone across the dunes. A net of high clouds drifted overhead, and at ground level the wind was mild and halting. A lamb brother just beyond the tent circle was skinning a large carcass, rolling back the hide with one hand as he pared the pink, fatty flesh. With a shock, Raif realized they had slain the dead brother's mule.

He crossed to the fire. Three prayer mats were laid out side by side upwind of the smoke. Raif settled his possessions in the pumice and went to look at them. They were simply woven, made from dyed and polished wool. The background of the closest rug was the same deep brown as the lamb brothers' robes, and only two other colors had been used to weave the design: warm amber and silvery yellow. Raif recognized the buffalo and lambs from Tallal's story. The animals were lined up along the top border, as if ready to journey down the length of the rug. His gaze tracked the design. Exotic trees and animals he could not name formed small islands along the way. Suns picked out in the amber thread were shown rising between the cleft of two hills and setting on a flat desert plain. Resting atop the bottom border was a shining expanse of silver, worked to look like water. No, ice, Raif corrected himself, for some kind of bird stood atop it, pecking at the surface. The bird was worked in the same brown as the background and its features were hard to see. The only way to make them out was to study the over-weave created by thread being placed on top of thread. Hairs rose along Raif's neck as he made out the shape of the bird's bill.

Briefly, he scanned the other two rugs. The designs differed but the story remained the same: the lambs and buffaloes on a journey toward the ice. He saw no more ravens and was relieved.

Returning to his equipment he studied the sky. He knew it was futile to judge time from the sun's position in the Want, but he could not break the habit of eighteen years. The air was like crystal today, revealing the landscape in sharp-cut lines and crisply focusing light. The dunes had shifted while he slept and things that had once been covered were now revealed. Rocks as round as eggs, petrified tree limbs and a rack of antlers had emerged from the pumice overnight. Raif wondered what had become of Farli's body. Was there anything left for the dunes to cover? Did he want to go and find out?

No, he did not. Squatting by the fire, he picked up a birch pole and hooked the brass kettle that was resting on the edge of the coals. There were no cups, so he did not drink, just let his hands warm against the metal. When they were limber enough he set to work. The tension in his bow needed correcting, so he restrung it. Dry air had warped some of his arrows, so he whittled back the shafts. Last night's extreme cold had cracked part of the finish on the Orrl cloak, and Raif wondered if it could be fixed. As he ran his fingers over the surface, little chips of pearlized varnish fell off. Deciding he would need to consult with someone who knew about such things, he set the cloak aside and began oiling his leather goods instead.

From time to time, out of the corner of his eye, he was aware of the lamb brothers moving around the camp. One went to consult with the man butchering the mule carcass, stayed for a while and then left. Raif thought it was probably Tallal. Later the same brother crossed to the corral and tended the ewe. It looked as if he were washing her mouth and teeth. No one approached the fire.

After a while Raif stopped and ate. Gluey rolls made of wheat and whey were warming in the cookpot. Curds of sheep's cheese with chunks of dried apricot stuffed inside made them taste both salty and sweet. The kettle was cooler now so he lifted it above his head and poured the sharp, greenish tea into his mouth. The movement sent a spasm of pain through his left shoulder.

When he was ready, Raif stood and made his way to Tallal's tent. In the eleven days that he'd been here he had learned many small things about the lamb brothers. One was the protocol for entering another's tent. Bending, Raif scooped a handful of pumice from the ground. With a light movement he threw the sand against the tent wall.

"Come," came Tallal's voice after a moment. It was telling that he had not spoken in his own tongue.

Raif entered the dim smokiness of the tent. Smudge lamps suspended from longbones ringed the room at waist height, giving off dull red light. Raif had not been in any other tent beside his own, and the differences drew his eye. Lambskins overlapped across the floor. The curve of a painted chest perfectly matched the curve of the tent and sat snug against the wall. There was no mattress, only a nest of thin yellow cushions piled around the central support. Hanging from the ceiling by lengths of wool thread were dozens of small leather pouches. Raif had to duck to avoid knocking them with his head.

Tallal was kneeling on one of the lambskins. His head was bare, the hood placed on a little bone stool by the door. Surprised, Raif hesitated to move farther into the tent.

"Sit," bid Tallal. "Look."

Holding his chin high, he watched Raif look at him. Proud, that was Raif's first thought. Tallal's black hair was cropped close to his skull. His cheekbones were wide and prominent and his brown lips were full. The three black dots above his nose were repeated on his chin. Just as with Farli, Tallal was younger than Raif had thought. Not young exactly, but far from old. Tallal's deep dark eyes with their strangely bluish whites tracked every shift in Raif's gaze.

"Would you like to see my teeth?"

Raif thought Tallal might be gently mocking him, but couldn't be sure. "No."

Tallal bowed hid head gravely. "Eat," he said, indicating a silver platter no bigger than Raif's hand that was neatly laid with spiced nuts.

Recognizing the formality of a long-practiced custom, Raif slipped a nut into his mouth. It was sharp and salty, like the sea. After he swallowed, he surprised himself by asking, "Why did you butcher the mule?"

"Ten is an unlucky number for my people."

Raif thought back to his first conversation with Tallal when the lamb brother told him there were eleven in the party. His headcount had included the animals. So they were nine now.

"It is the number of the Dark One's children," Tallal continued. "Whenever ten are gathered it draws His eye."

But we are ten, Raif thought. *Including me.*

Tallal watched as the implications of his statement finally dawned on Raif.

"You knew I would leave today?"

"We hoped."

Raif took a breath and held it. The smoke from the lamps burned his throat. Of course they wanted him to go: they had seen what he was.

"I'm sorry about your brother."

Tallal did not blink. "So are we."

Raif stood. Pouch things swung wildly around his head.

"You cannot leave," Tallal said. "You do not know how."

He was right.

Rising, the lamb brother removed his hood from the stool and offered the seat to Raif.

He hadn't brushed against a single pouch, Raif noticed, sitting. "What's in them?" he asked, jerking his head toward the roof.

"Souls."

Raif closed his mouth, looked up at the plain brown-and-tan pouches and then looked away.

Tallal smiled softly, with understanding. "This lamb brother asks to be forgiven. He did not mean to surprise you. The sacs are our way of keeping count. Each one represents a soul we have reclaimed for God. When we return to our people they are opened with great ceremony and the *morah* is released."

The pouches were the size of plums. "The *morah* is in there?"

The lamb brother shrugged. "Some believe so. This lamb brother thinks perhaps the flesh of God is too powerful and impatient to be contained in such small things."

"When will you return?"

There was no shrug this time. Tallal's gaze lengthened as he looked beyond the walls of the tent. "I think perhaps not for a very long time." The lamb brother turned his head a fraction and looked straight at Raif. Understanding passed between them. "Sometimes a purpose must be a man's home."

Raif inhaled the smoke; funny how it no longer burned. "What if you are unsure of your purpose?"

"You ask yourself. You ask others." Tallal indicated the Want with a slight movement of his wrist. "You search."

"Until last night I believed I could help you. It seemed as if our purposes were close." Raif stopped, fearing he had said too much.

Yet Tallal simply nodded. "The Book of Trials speaks of the raven. It tells us that when we see one we should follow it, for ravens feed on opened carcasses. They find the dead."

Raif could think of no reply.

"The lamb brothers believe you need a new sword." Tallal's dark eyes glinted. "Last night it was noted that the *wrall* was brought down with a bow. Our elder brother thinks perhaps this is not good. He believes some things are too powerful to be killed in such a manner. He says there are creatures so far removed from the world of flesh that no blade forged by man can kill them." Tallal frowned. "Our elder brother worries about such things."

A stray draft set the smudge lamps jittering, suddenly brightening, then darkening the tent. Smoke funneled around the walls, its scent strengthening as if something within it had reacted to the wind. Raif felt his mind circling with the smoke. Tallal was leading him somewhere as surely as if he had attached guide lines to Raif's belt. Almost against his will, Raif's hand sought out the weapon holstered at his waist. *Did you really think this would be the sword that makes you?* The Listener's words, spoken all those months ago in his hut by the sea, suddenly seemed dangerous. Like a curse.

Tallal continued; Raif knew he would. "It is written that thirty hundred years ago our people nearly died. A drought was visited upon the Sands and no man felt rain upon his back for thirteen years. When the rains came they brought no relief for the sky had grown too dark and the rain was full of ash. In the charcoal years that followed it was sung that wralls walked the sand and claimed us. We were simple people, without weapons to best them, and we had grown weak. When the Outlanders came and offered us the chance to meet the wralls in battle as their allies, ten thousand of our people marched north with the Outlander horde. They were never seen again.

"After the charcoal years ended the barren years began. We do not know much about those times for there was no one to sing the histories. Gradually my people revived. Daughters were born. Water holes were replenished. Dates and lambs grew and we were fed. Finally one was born to us who was named Meesa, Needs To Know. The buffalo women tried to claim Meesa for they knew she was strong and would save many living souls, but she denied them and went in search of the ten thousand missing men. Meesa left the Sands as a girl and returned bent and gray. Some say a hundred years had passed while she searched. The lamb brothers ran out to meet her. 'Tell us what you know,' they pleaded. And Meesa told them and the lamb brothers sang her knowledge into the histories, and many generations later those histories were written down."

Tallal paused, took a nut from the tray and ate it. He was confident now, Raif saw, sure that the end of his story was being anticipated. It was. Even though he knew he was being manipulated, Raif still needed to hear it.

"Meesa traveled north during those hundred years and talked with many people in many lands. Piece by piece she learned what had become of the men. The Outlanders had driven them far north, promising that tomorrow the battle would be met, yet when the next day came there was no sign of the enemy horde and the Outlanders lied again. Wralls took many on the long journey, claiming the *morah,* stealing from God. My people feared to return to the Sands without fulfilling their promise of ending the plague of wralls. They believed that by staying away there would be more food and water for those who were left behind.

"Finally they arrived at the Valley of Cold Mists. 'Here,' the Outlanders said, 'is where their armies will rise.' My people had heard those words many times before and did not believe them. My people made a mistake. The wralls rose that night in vast hordes. Their armies spread across the horizon like the sea. My people were caught unawares in their sleep. As quickly as they took up their bows and spears they were ridden down, run through with blades as dark as the night. The histories tell of many dread beasts that could not be killed by men. Even the Outlanders with their forged steel could not match the wrall kings. My people were slaughtered. The Outlanders were decimated, down to their last thousand when the raven lord rode through. The raven lord was not one of us and our histories do not record his name or his people. We know he wielded a sword that was as black as well water, and that he used it to slay a wrall king.

"After the battle ended the raven lord was dead. He had driven back the wrall hordes but his body was broken, ravaged by many cuts. The few Outlanders who still lived walked to high ground and slept, and in the morning when they awoke they found the valley below had been flooded and frozen. A lake of red ice now lay in place of the battlefield, and every man and every beast who had died there was now frozen beneath the ice."

Raif shivered. As Tallal had been speaking, a gusting wind had set the leather pouches rocking overhead. They rocked now, out of time with each other, swinging like pendulums back and forth. *I need to think,* but Tallal didn't plan on giving him time.

"When the lamb brothers heard this tale from Meesa they began to keen. Thousands of our souls lost, taken by the wralls and impossible to reclaim. Meesa told them to quiet their grieving for the souls had not been claimed by the Dark Lord. The souls were frozen with their bodies and as long as the lamb brothers found them while the ice still held we could claim them and set them free."

Tallal looked at Raif, looked into the substance beyond his eyes. "Last night, Raif Sevrance, you showed us what we must do when we find those bodies: we must destroy them as soon as they are released from the ice. It is not a lesson that pleases us, for our most sacred law prohibits the desecration of the dead: God asks that when we come to Him we be whole."

Raif bowed his head. He could not look anymore at the sorrows revealed in the lamb brother's eyes. "How do you know the ice is still frozen?"

"We hope."

More sorrow there. Remembering the patterns on the prayer mats, the raven pecking at the ice, Raif said, "You search for this place, the Valley of Cold Mists." It was not a question. Understanding was coming. The lamb brothers' purpose was not the same as his own, but there was a point where they intersected. The Red Ice. That was why Tallal had led with the sword. It had seemed to come out of nowhere, the lamb brother's concern for his blade. Now Raif saw it for what it was, a carrot to lead him to the other side. Tallal sought to recruit him to the search.

Stirred but cautious, Raif said, "All was frozen, good and bad?"

Tallal nodded.

"What happens if the ice melts? Would the Unmade . . . the wralls . . . come back to life?"

"I do not know."

It was not a reassuring answer. Raif moved on. "You are sure the sword is there?"

"Yes, frozen on the raven lord's chest. It is said that it was once wielded by Sull kings."

Raif licked dry lips. "What made the valley flood?"

Tallal shook his head.

"And you do not know where it is?"

The lamb brother glanced at the tent flap, at the thin sliver of light coming through. "We believe it lies in the north of this continent. East, west, center: we are unsure."

"You hope for help," Raif said, thoughts still forming, "yet you do not want me in your party."

"Ten is an unlucky number."

"With the mule it would have been eleven." Raif was surprised at the heat in his voice. "Why will you not have me?"

Tallal's nostrils flared as he took a deep breath. Absently, he reached up and steadied one of the leather sacks that was still swinging. "You may not much like the answer."

Raif had not imagined he would. "Tell me."

"Two of our party are dead. You killed neither but you drew their deaths as honey draws the sand flies." Tallal stood and lifted a small glazed jug from the floor of the tent. Walking the circle of smudge lamps, he poured a drop of oil in each one. "If you journey with our party we fear more deaths. The lamb brothers do not judge you, for we are taught all creatures born of God have a purpose, but the path you walk is dark. The raven must feed."

One by one the smudge lamps sizzled, releasing the crushed-grass odor of wormwood. Raif wondered if it was mildly poisonous, like the drink. Even though he had guessed what Tallal might say, it was not easy to hear it. When people learned what he was and what he could do would they always push him away? What of the Maimed Men; would they be any different?

"If I were to find the place you seek, how would you know? You and your brothers might be anywhere. How would I find you?"

Tallal set down the jug and crossed over to the painted chest.

Kneeling, he said, "Let us find you." He pushed open the lid of the chest and searched for something inside. Raif noticed three more black dots at the back of his neck. "Here," Tallal said, flinging something toward Raif.

Raif snatched it from the air. It was a leather pouch similar to those overhead, with something flat and jagged in it.

Tallal smiled, delighted. "If my mother were here she should be grateful for your quickness." Seeing Raif's confusion, he shooed his hand at the pouch. "Open. It is a gift."

The leather was old, darkened by many oilings. A length of undyed wool formed the drawstring. Raif pulled it back, and discovered a piece of glass.

"From me."

The glass was the size and length of a fingerbone. One end was blunt while the other narrowed to a delicately curved point. Raif rolled it between his fingertips, watching light tumble within it. He wasn't sure, but it seemed as if the light and reflections moved a fraction slower than the glass itself.

"Stormglass," Tallal said, his smile softer now. "Just a little broken piece found by my great-great-grandfather—on my mother's side."

Raif closed his fist around the glass. "Thank you."

"When my brothers and I were young we would turn our mother's hair gray by tossing it to each other across the date yard. We were bad sons. After the beatings we were better." The memory stopped Tallal for a moment, his brown eyes looking inward. Shaking himself, he said, "Even a piece this small is good luck. Kings and rich men may crave unbroken rods and whole branches, but as long as you have a tip you have the *nagi*. The essence. When stormglass is formed it mirrors the lightning that created it. Sometimes it branches as it shoots through the sand. When that happens there can be several tips—the point where the lightning's power comes to rest. This is one such piece."

Raif did not know what to say. Tallal's pleasure in giving him the piece seemed genuine, but a gift this precious usually came with a price.

"It is said that if you carry a piece of stormglass you will never be alone in a storm." Tallal voiced the words lightly, but

Raif knew they were not light. Here it was: the cost. "Keep it close to your skin when lightning strikes and the lamb brothers will find you."

Tallal held Raif's gaze. Pride and something almost opposite to pride existed in the muscle tensions of Tallal's face. He was waiting, Raif realized, upon an answer.

A wisp of wormwood smoke floated across Raif's knuckles as he glanced down at his fist. Perhaps the smoke was not poisonous as much as numbing. Perhaps it prevented deep thought. He opened his fist and slid the stormglass into its pouch. "I give no promises," he warned, tying the pouch to his gear belt. But he did, he knew he did.

The lamb brother carefully controlled his face. Crossing back toward the cushions, he said, "Let me tell you what you must do to leave the Want."

FOURTEEN

The Copper Hills

Vaylo Bludd did not want to admit that his knees were sore and he needed to rest. In the past fifteen days he'd had enough walking to last a lifetime, and his heart, his knees and all seventeen of his teeth ached persistently with every step. Gods, what had he come to? A warrior without a horse. A chief without a clan. What was next? he wondered. A Bluddsman without kneecaps or teeth?

"Vaylo. We should halt for a minute. The bairns need to pee."

The Dog Lord looked long and hard at his lady, Nan Culldayis. It was an hour past noon and they were on their third hill of the day and this one was the steepest yet. It was pretty enough, the blackstone pines giving way to winter heather and wild oats that had been tidily cropped by rogue sheep, but the climb was tiring and monotonous and the wind that was blowing south from the Rift cut you like a blade. Vaylo tucked his long gray braids under his coat collar as he said, "No, Nan. We carry on."

He left her looking at the back of his head. The Dog Lord was nobody's fool and he knew what his lady was about. She thought to provide him with an excuse to stop and rest, and he wasn't having any of it. Bairns need to pee indeed! Those bairns had peed their way north across the entire length of the Dhoonehold. Another couple of hours wouldn't hurt.

Indignation oiled Vaylo's knee joints and he worked the hill hard, stabbing its thin rocky soil as he climbed. This was Copper Hill country and the slopes were pitted with old mine shafts and vent holes. As far as Vaylo knew there was only one copper mine still open—and that was far to the east, sunk deep beneath Stinking Hill. Copper hadn't been seriously mined on the Dhoonehold for five hundred years, and only cragsmen and raiders walked these hills now. You could still see the copper though; a certain greenish tint to the soil made everything that grew here look healthier than it really was. Many of the little rills and creeks that drained the hills sparkled with red ore. Copper had made Dhoone rich at one time, and paid for the construction of the finest roundhouse in the north. Dhoone copper had once been carted overland all the way to the Far South, and strange kings and warlords had forged mighty weapons from it and sent back all manner of treasure in payment. Copper's glory days had long passed though, and it had been fifteen hundred years since a copper weapon had bettered a steel one on the field. Still, copper had its uses even now. Vaylo had heard that in the Mountain Cities people liked to eat off it, and he knew clan maids like to wear it in their ears and around their wrists. Copper was stretched into wire and hammered into pipes, fired with tin to make bronze and zinc to make brass. At the time Vaylo had taken possession of the Dhoonehouse, the mine at Stinking Hill was still producing a hundred tons of raw ore a year. He had shut it down of course, then thought better of it and ordered it reopened. Gods only knew what was happening there now. One thing was certain: after all the looting and cattle raiding carried out by Bluddsmen over the past six months, Robbie Dun Dhoone would need all the hard cash he could get.

That was a thought that never failed to make Vaylo smile. Robbie Dun Dhoone might have won back his roundhouse, but Bluddsmen had stripped it down to the bare walls. Vaylo had no idea where the loot had gone—he hadn't taken anything for himself except a half-dozen kegs of fine Dhoonish malt—and he found he didn't care. Gone was enough. Gone would slow the Thorn King down.

"Hammie," Vaylo said, turning about to address his armsman Haimish Faa. "When did you last see the wolf dog?"

Hammie was huffing and puffing his way up the hill. He was thirty years younger than the Dog Lord but about four stone heavier and Faa men, like Bludd chiefs, had never been walkers.

Hammie wiped his red and wet nose with his coat sleeve, wincing as raw flesh met coarse wool. "He left as soon as the bairns awoke. 'Bout dawn."

The Dog Lord nodded, his mind eased. He'd seen the other three dogs throughout the day as they ranged back and forth, patrolling, guarding, hunting. The big black bitch had brought down two jackrabbits and carried them straight to his hand. The young male had brought back a sick-looking woodrat and Vaylo had taken it from the dog's jaw and flung it as far as he could. Unhappily it hadn't been the last he'd seen of the rat as the dog kept finding it and bringing it back. Every time this happened the worm-infested vermin looked a little worse for wear, and Vaylo thought to himself, *Do I really have to touch this?* Touch it he did though. The young male's eagerness and joy were two things he didn't want thwarted. You couldn't have a dog love you unconditionally and not give anything back.

The wolf dog had been with him for seven years and of all the dogs Vaylo had loved and owned it was the wolf dog who was closest to his heart. The Dog Lord did not show it, he did not need to, for the two of them knew what lay between them. The Dog Lord's worries were the wolf dog's worries. His kin was the wolf dog's kin. That the dog had stayed up all night guarding Aaron and Pasha was as it should be. The wolf dog had been present that terrible day when Vaylo had found seventeen of his grandchildren dead and buried in the snow above the Bluddroad. The dog knew how precious the two remaining grandchildren were. Still it wasn't like the wolf dog not to home every few hours. All the dogs ranged wide and then returned at various times to insure their human pack was safe. Vaylo hadn't seen the wolf dog since last night when he'd scolded the beast for snatching a rabbit from the fire. It was good to know that after the wolf dog skulked away in shame and anger he returned later to guard the bairns.

Truth was they were all hungry and short-tempered. Rabbits alone did not make a meal. If you ate too much they gave you the runs and if you didn't eat enough you starved. It was, as Ockish Bull would have said, a choice between the ugly and the just plain bad. Nan and the bairns got the best of it. The organ meat could stay with you for half a day, but the muscle meat, which Vaylo and Hammie enjoyed, only hung around long enough to bid a fond farewell to your gut. The dogs didn't mind it, but then what did dogs know about decent food? Vaylo was grateful for what they caught, but after fifteen days of jackrabbit, woodrat and opossum his gratitude was wearing thin.

It was turning out to be a hard journey, harder than he had imagined when he'd first decided its course the night they escaped from the Tomb of the Dhoone Princes. The distances involved were longer than he'd anticipated and the hardships more wearing than he could have foreseen. Nothing to eat except lean meat, no clothes except what lay on their backs, no weapons except a kitchen knife, a longknife and a maiden's helper. Until yesterday when they finally entered hill country, they hadn't even been able to cook the meat brought down by the dogs, so wary was Vaylo of lighting a fire. Man hunters were out in the Dhoonehold, searching for the Dog Lord and his party, and all it would take for them to spy their prey was a lone line of smoke on the horizon or a flickering orange glow amidst the trees. Twice now Vaylo had spied mounted men in the distance and each time he'd known they had Dog meat on their minds. Man hunters had a look to them: lightly armored, finely horsed, *hungry*. Vaylo feared them, for he very much doubted whether Robbie Dun Dhoone cared if his enemy was taken dead or alive. The man hunters carried crossbows and would shoot at distance, and there were nights when Vaylo could not sleep for the thought of Pasha and Aaron being shot in the back.

Yesterday had brought an easing of his fears. The Copper Hills were a no-man's-land of bleak moors, wind-stunted pine forests, heather fields and rocky peaks. They had seen no sign of habitation in over two days and last night Vaylo had finally judged it safe to build a cookfire. They had been weary, but merry enough, and for a wonder Hammie had produced a small wedge of red cheese. "The laddie from Dhoone gave it to me," he said by way of explanation, "and I was saving it for the right moment." They had all taken a bite, though Aaron had spit his out, declaring it tasted like chicken wattles, and *that* had caused a huge scrap amongst the dogs. While three of them fought over Aaron's chewed-up leftovers, the wolf dog had sneaked in and stolen the rabbit from the fire.

Vaylo had roared at all of them then, the bairns included, and ordered everyone except Hammie to go to sleep. His nerves were not what they had been, he realized later as he lay atop his cloak and looked out at the dim, starless night. The loss of forty good men at the Dhoonehouse followed by the rigors of a fifteen-day journey had worn him thin. How old was he now? Fifty-three, fifty-four? Too old to be starting from scratch, yet what choice did he have? Last night, before beginning his watch, Hammie had said to him, "Chief, we're living through bad times."

Vaylo had not replied, though he knew well enough what his response should have been: "Hammie, I created them."

Gullit Bludd had not taught his bastard son much, but by default Vaylo had learned certain things at his father's hearth. The first amongst them was that no one would look out for him save himself. The second was that if he made a botch-up of things—be it letting the dogs out when one of the bitches was in heat, forgetting to haul the warriors' leathers in from the rain, or failing to skin a deer carcass before it froze—it was no one's responsibility but his own. Break it, you fix it or get a beating. That was the way Gullit's hearth had worked.

It had not been a bad lesson all in all, though it had come back to haunt him in recent months. He, the Dog Lord, had brought the clanholds to its knees, and Vaylo had the uncomfortable feeling that there was no one to set it to rights only him. Gods, why had he ever accepted Penthero Iss' offer of aid? He should have taken the Dhoonehouse alone. The invasion was damned from the start, from the very first moment when Vaylo had said to Iss' emissary, "Do what you must, halfman. Just spare me the details so I can deny them."

Suddenly tired, Vaylo stopped climbing and sat on a loose hump of rocks. Below him, Nan and Hammie were shepherding the bairns along a particularly sharp draw. The wind had tugged Nan's sea gray hair from her braid and flushed her cheeks with blood, and she looked young and a little bit dangerous. She'd taken to holstering her maiden's helper crosswise on her back like a longsword, and Vaylo knew that the little pouch at her waist that used to contain her portion of powdered guidestone now held henbane instead. She'd come across it ten days back, growing on the banks of a melt pond near the Dhoone-Spur border, and picked it and dried it for self-protection. It was deadly poison and she had enough to kill all of them, save the dogs, and the only place she trusted to store it was her powder pouch, for no child would ever dare touch that.

"Pasha. Aaron. Slip behind those bushes and relieve yourselves. Quick about it now." When Aaron hesitated Nan set him in motion with a pat to his backside. Hiking quickly up the remaining slope, she left Hammie to pick up the rear.

"The Dhoonewall can't be that far away now," she said to Vaylo as she sat beside him on the rock and gazed south across the rolling highlands of Dhoone. "And then this journey will be done."

Nan Culldayis was no talker and she spoke only when she had something to say. Vaylo waited.

"A hundred and eighty men await you at the Dhoonewall," she said finally, still looking ahead. "That's exactly three times the number you commanded thirty-five years ago on the raid to steal the Dhoonestone from Dhoone."

She was right, and Vaylo understood all she meant by those words. Somewhere not far north of here lay the fastness known as the Dhoonewall. It had been the Dog Lord's destination right from the start. His eldest son Quarro commanded the Bluddhouse and Vaylo knew enough about the greed and ambition of his seven sons to guess that he would never be welcomed back. The Bluddsmen at the Bluddhouse would be loyal to Quarro now, and a failed and aging chief arriving home with a single armsman as escort probably wouldn't be allowed through the gate. Worse, he might even be shot during the approach. So no, not for one minute had Vaylo considered returning to the Bluddhouse—he would not debase himself by appealing to his eldest son for shelter. He would head north instead to the Dhoonewall, where the longswordsman Cluff Drybannock stood ready with a hundred and eighty men.

It had seemed like a lifetime ago when Vaylo had sent Drybone north to defend the two major passes in the Copper Hills. The Dhoonewall was a defensive rampart spanning the six leagues that separated the passes. It had lain unused since the time of the River Wars, and only one of the original six hillforts remained livable. Vaylo had feared Dun Dhoone using the fort as a base to gather men and launch an attack on the Dhoonehouse, so had decided to garrison it with Bluddsmen. His original plan had been to kill two birds with one stone—send his troublesome second son Pengo far away from the Dhoonehouse where he could do no harm. Pengo would have none of it though—threatening to take the bairns with him if his hand was forced—and Cluff Drybannock had offered to take his place. Vaylo had regretted letting Drybone go. Cluff Drybannock was the best longswordsman in the North. He was a bastard, part Sull, part Bluddsman, and when he'd turned up at the Bluddhouse twenty years ago Vaylo had taken him as his adopted son. He missed Dry, and feared he had made a mistake by sending him away.

That wasn't what Nan was about here, though. She had watched him these past days, seen his spirits fall and his temper rise, and she sought to tell him in her own way that all was not lost. If he had managed to carry out the most audacious raid of the past hundred years with a crew of sixty men, then imagine what he could do with three times that number. That was what Nan meant to say. He could not deny the logic of it, but he had been young then and filled with certainty. He was old now and the only thing that he was certain of was that he had made mistakes.

Vaylo glanced down the hill, checking on Hammie and the bairns. Pasha and Aaron were in good spirits, whooping and hollering at one of the returning dogs. The bitch looked to have another rabbit in her jaws. That made three in under a day.

To Nan he said, "I must be sure who my enemy is before I send good men to fight. My sons are scattered across the clanholds—some hold houses, some don't. If I were to attempt to take their holdings from them by force then Bludd would be killing Bludd. As for Dhoone, the Thorn King can keep it. I sat on the Dhooneseat for a while and I canna say I enjoyed it. That seat is cold, Nan, and it was won at too great a cost to my soul. Anything I win now will be hard-fought and hard-defended. Yet what that prize might be I canna say. Always in the past my next move was clear to me: raid, invade, ambush, crack down on my rivals, attack. Yet things have changed for me, and I'm no longer sure what comes next."

At his side Nan breathed evenly and did not speak. Clouds

were breaking up in the south and bands of sunlight swept across the hills. It was too windy for frost, but it was cold enough, and Vaylo felt the wind tears sting his eyes.

After a while Nan stood. Turning so that she was opposite him, she said, "You knew my da, Nolan Culldayis. He swung hammers with Gullit during the River Wars. Took up carving wood after your father died, used to make foxes and blackbirds and other fancies. I asked him once what he was working on. It was new block of cherrywood and he'd just started whittling. He said to me, 'I don't know what it is yet, Nannie. Knowing would ruin the surprise.'" Nan raised a finely shaped eyebrow at Vaylo. "It was the possibilities, you see. As long as he didn't know what he was carving there were more of them."

Vaylo bowed his head at his lady, acknowledging the wisdom of her story yet not sure if it meant anything to him. A clan chief with jaw *sprang* surprises; he was not doing his job if he himself was surprised.

Rising, he held out a hand to accept the bitch's third rabbit of the day. She'd been waiting all the while Nan had been speaking, halted by a small gesture of Vaylo's hand, and now she came forward, wagging her tail so forcefully it rocked her bony rump right along with it. "Good girl," he told her, taking the bloody fur-covered sack from her jaw. He inspected it, frowned, and then gave it right back. "Eat," he commanded. And she did, opening her jaw wide and wolfing it down whole in a unlovely, jerky motion that looked like a dry heave in reverse.

Vaylo was glad to have it gone. One more rabbit and there was no telling what he might do: run back to the Dhoonehouse and bunny-kick Robbie Dun Dhoone in the head.

"Nan," he said, holding out his arm for her to come to him. "Did I ever tell you about the day your da taught me his special move?"

Aware that he was shutting down all talk about the future, Nan nodded knowingly and let him put his arm around her. "The Culldozer?"

"Aye. The one where he'd let his hammer lie flat against his horse's belly just so and then present his left flank to the enemy so they couldn't tell he was armed. Then once he got close enough, he'd swing about and uppercut them in the jaw."

Nan shook her head in bafflement. "I suppose it saved the pulltooth some work."

Vaylo grinned. Pasha ran up to them and wriggled under her granda's free arm, and he got to tell his two best girls about the day he dropped his newly minted warhammer on Nolan Culldayis' left foot whilst attempting the special move.

The wind wailed as they walked, blowing in their faces and scaling their skin. Silvery spikes of heather undulated in waves like the surface of a lake. Ahead the Copper Hills grew taller and more desolate, and Vaylo could see sunken holes in their faces where ancient and unsealed mine shafts lay. Ockish Bull had told him once that the deepest hole ever dug by a clansman could be found in these hills. "Harlin Dhoone ordered its excavation. Had an old mineshaft reopened, climbed down to the deepest level, and pointed to the ground. 'Dig there,' he commanded his men, 'and do not rest your spades for one year.'" Vaylo recalled asking Ockish what the hole was for; had Harlin reason to believe that a new lode of copper lay beneath? Ockish had shaken his large bland head. "Copper, no. Harlin dug it as a warning to his enemies. Cross me and you'll end up down there."

Vaylo frowned. With Ockish Bull you could never quite be sure what was and wasn't true. He could spin tales with the best of them, and possessed a facial expression so inscrutable that it never helped to look at him while he spoke. Vaylo smiled to himself, remembering. Gods, he missed him.

"Granda. Over there. Look."

Vaylo followed the line of his grandson's arm, squinting to make out detail in the distance. "What is it, boy?" he barked, unable to see anything in the valley except heather and shrunken pines, and feeling the first stirrings of fear.

"Mounted men, Granda. Dozens of them."

Dear Gods, no. "Get down," he hissed. "*Now!*"

"Granda," came Pasha's voice, cool as cream. "They're Bludd. I can see the red banns."

Cluff Drybannock. Vaylo had dropped to his knees—he was the only one who had done so—and Hammie came forward to offer him a hand. Preferring to stand on his own, Vaylo slapped him away. "What do you see?" he asked.

Hammie frowned in concentration as he scanned the valley. "Bairns are right," he said eventually. "There's over a hundred clansmen down there. It's definitely Bludd, I can see their cloaks. They're heading right for us."

"It's Drybone!" Aaron said excitedly. The boy began jumping up and down and waving both hands over his head. "We're here! We're here!"

Vaylo and Hammie exchanged a glance. Hammie shrugged. Vaylo pressed his knuckles against his heart; some tightness there. "Warriors do not jump up and down when they greet each other." He gave his grandson a long, reprimanding stare. Dropping his arms, the boy fell silent. "Good. Chin up. You too, Pasha. One on each side of me."

As the bairns fell in line, Vaylo looked ahead. He could see the horsemen now, see the rich blackness of sable cloaks and the oily sheen of well-groomed horses. Most of the men had spears couched upright on saddle horns and all had longswords holstered so high on their backs that the crossguards and hand-guards were visible above their shoulders. They had moved into the formation known as "rule of all," where a single line curved inward forming a reverse C shape so that the farther a man stood from the center the more forward he was. It was a little-used formation and Vaylo wondered what, if anything, it meant.

Cluff Drybannock rode at the center of the line. He was bareheaded and his waist-length braids streamed behind him as he closed distance across the valley floor. Opal rings bound his hair, and as he drew closer Vaylo saw other signs of the Sull: a quarter-moon painted on the shaved portion of his skull, owl feathers sewn on the collar of his cloak, hands gloved in darkly iridescent moonsnake.

Vaylo did not move from his place on the hill. He had formed a line of his own with him at the center, a bairn on each side, Nan at one end and Hammie at the other. Nan and Hammie had taken their cue from what Vaylo had said to the bairns, and stood, chins high, as they waited. Vaylo wondered if they felt the same apprehension as he did, wondered if they also strained to make out the expression on Cluff Drybannock's red-clay face.

Spying a streak of black and gray at Dry's right stirrup, Vaylo understood what had brought these men out. The wolf dog trotted at Dry's heels, tail up and in motion, its yellow eyes alert. It had raced ahead to the Dhoonewall and returned with the mounted might of Bludd.

Vaylo swallowed. Several outcomes occurred to him, and he found some comfort in the fact that there wasn't one in which the bairns came to harm. He could see Cluff Drybannock's startling blue eyes now; all the Sull Vaylo had ever met had eyes that looked as if a light shone through them. *What does he see when he looks at me?* Vaylo wondered. *An old man? A failed chief? An encumbrance? A rival?*

As the wings of the C hit the hill and began to climb, Vaylo recognized many men: Mogo Salt, Midge Pool, Big Borro, Odwin Two Bear. He looked all of them straight in the eye. They looked right back, he was glad of that, but their faces were hard to read. In a matter of seconds the formation closed around him and he found himself facing Cluff Drybannock. Expertly, the longswordsman reined in his horse. The line halted. For a moment the wolf dog was the only thing that moved as it trotted across the thirty paces that separated Drybone from its master. Vaylo paid it no heed. His gaze was fixed on Cluff Drybannock.

The two men stared at each other, the chief's bastard and Sull bastard. Overhead a V of geese passed north, their calls dull and labored as they fought the wind. Soon they would cross the Rift, Vaylo realized, and wondered what they would see when they looked straight down into the abyss.

Cluff Drybannock did not blink or speak. Raising his left fist, he issued a prearranged command, and one hundred and sixty men—Vaylo knew this because he had counted them—stood in their stirrups and dismounted. Drybone did the same, and perhaps of all the people gathered here this day only Vaylo could tell that Dry forced his movements to slowness to match time with the other men. When a perfect half-circle had been formed a second command was issued, again with the raising of a fist.

As one a hundred and sixty men raised their arms and gripped the handles of the swords. As one they drew them. The snick of metal shaving leather rang out as a single sound. All waited. The wind died. At Vaylo's side, the wolf dog howled, confused.

Then Cluff Drybannock, the greatest longswordsman in the North, exploded into motion. Drawing a form in the air with the point of his sword, he leapt forward, his movements so swift his cloak crackled like lightning. He spoke a word and it was no word that Vaylo knew, and then, halting, he raised his longsword to his chest, took it in both hands . . . and sent it plunging into the earth.

That was the signal for the other hundred and sixty men to come forward and lay down their swords before their chief. Kneeling, they laid their weapons, point-out toward him, forming a semicircle of steel around Vaylo Bludd.

The Dog Lord stood and accepted them. Dry's sword vibrated right in front of him, its blade a foot deep in the stony soil. Dry himself was breathing hard, yet his face was still.

"Son," Vaylo said to him.

"Father," Cluff Drybannock replied, using that word to address his chief for the first time in his twenty-nine-year life. "We have waited long days for you to come."

FIFTEEN

The Mist Rivers
of the Want

"No man or woman can ever hope to navigate Mhaja Xaal, the Land of Unsettled Sands. Once he or she has accepted that as truth it is possible to find a way through. Sun and stars must be ignored. Instinct set aside. That which is considered by most to be wrong and foolish must be embraced. A man or woman wishing for passage must be like the kit fox, scarab beetle, and rattlesnake: they must travel solely at night.

"Only in darkness can we find our way through. What the light shows cannot be trusted and is therefore without value. We must learn to honor that which we touch, not see. Know that, and you have the secret of leaving *Mhaja Xaal*.

"On the darkest nights when there is no moon to light the way the mist rivers flow. The mist rises in the darkness, filling arroyos and canyons. To leave *Mhaja Xaal* you must find an arroyo large enough to stand in and walk against the current. All the mist rivers in the Land of Unsettled Sands flow inward toward its heart. Why this is so, the lamb brothers do not know. What lies at the heart of *Mhaja Xaal* is not a mystery we cultivate. We do know that it is not enough to judge the course of the mist rivers from their banks. What you see will deceive you. The surface currents may run contrary to that which lies beneath. To leave you must stand in the current and feel the pressure of the mist against your skin. Touch alone will lead you out."

Tallal's words ran through Raif's head as he walked. The lamb brother had spoken them earlier that day in his tent. It was evening now, crisply cold with a red sky fading to black. Raif had taken his leave of the lamb brothers an hour earlier and by now he could no longer look back and see the lights of their tents. This was it then. He was once more adrift in the Want.

He could not say that he liked it. It wasn't easy not to think about Bear. The hill pony had died, and if he had been a better, wiser person it would not have happened. He should never have taken her with him, that was his first and greatest mistake. When you go to the Want you go alone. It didn't matter to Raif that the lamb brothers came here in numbers. Let them do what they choose to do. He, Raif Sevrance, would never bring another living thing into this place.

Strange, but it was beautiful tonight. The remains of the sunset glowed on the horizon and the great open flatland spread wide in all directions. The pumice dunes had been replaced by baked rock and it looked to Raif as if he were walking on a dry inland sea. On impulse he bent down and scraped the pale, scaled rock with his thumb. When he brought it to his lips he tasted salt.

As he stood he noticed his shadow was fading. A band of hot white stars had emerged in the sky opposite the sunset, and Raif spun a full circle as he scanned for the moon. No moon. Not yet.

"Where is the nearest place to join the mist river?" Raif had asked Tallal, half a day ago at the camp. The lamb brother had begun shaking his head even before all the words were out.

"My memory is good and if you walk with me to the fire I can point out the direction from which the lamb brothers came. Your memory, however, is bad."

Raif had grinned wryly. Only five minutes earlier Tallal had told him directions could not be trusted. "I'm still learning."

"My people have a saying: 'There are two ways to learn. Listening is the easiest.'" Tallal smiled. "Come, let us find you some supplies."

They had been generous, and Raif had found himself touched. The fine, soft blanket he had slept with since the first night had been waiting for him, neatly folded, by the fire. Fresh sheep's curd, butter, honey, dried dates, almonds, unleavened panbread, preserved apricots, lentils and a packet of herbs for tea had also been set close to the fire. Raif had never asked how long the lamb brothers had been away from home—it had seemed an indelicate question—but he had imagined it was well over a year. By now supplies brought from their homeland must be sparse, yet they had given their food freely. With grace. For some reason Raif found himself thinking about the Hailsman Shor Gormalin. Shor had been the best longswords-man in the clan, a scholar of clan history, and a friend to Tem and Dagro. Shor had taught Raif about grace. Looking at the neatly laid pile of supplies, given without fuss or show, Raif imagined that Shor Gormalin would approve. "Grace is a pow-erful force," Shor had said, one morning on the practice court as they were wrist-to-wrist on deadlocked hilts. "It lifts men."

That was how Raif felt receiving the gifts of the lamb broth-ers: lifted. During the brief time he had stayed with them he had forgotten one important thing. These men had saved his life. Gods knew how they had found him. Passed out on a ridge in the middle of the Want, lips black, tongue swollen, sword bloodied to the hilt, Bear slain beside him: it could not have been an appealing sight. Yet four men had judged him worth saving.

"Farli." Raif spoke the slain lamb brother's name out loud. The sound was small in such a big place, instantly sucked away by space and darkness. The question was there in the back of his mind, waiting to be asked. *Could I have saved him?* Raif knew he had been slow in his responses, slow in finding his target and letting the arrow fly. If he had ran across the dune with Farli and fought with him side by side would it have been different? Probably, yes.

Grow wide shoulders, Clansman. You'll need them for all of your burdens. Sadaluk's words blew through Raif's head as the weight of that "yes" settled on his shoulders.

For no good reason, he changed his course. He'd been head-ing into the sunset and veered off at a tangent, picking a distant boulder as his destination. The light was nearly gone now and the temperature was dropping fast. The big double-chambered waterskin given to him by the lamb brothers bounced against his back. Its heaviness was reassuring. There was no guarantee he would find the mist river tonight or any other night, and even if he did there was still the question of how long it would take to leave the Want once the river had been found.

"It will take as long as it must," Tallal had said before they parted. "And where it leads is something that cannot be known. Out, that must be enough."

Raif glanced at the sky; still no moon, but the stars were teeming. The seabed was lit by a dome of silver light, and he could clearly see the salt scale that covered every rock and piece of debris underfoot. It stopped hoarfrost from forming.

As he neared the boulder his perception of its shape changed; one side was rounded yet he saw now that the opposite side was curiously straight. Closer still he realized that the front of the boulder was projecting forward, the curve and straight line meeting at a point. It was a boat, he understood quite suddenly, fallen on its side and sunk partially into the seabed. A small fishing boat or rowboat with a simple hull that had once consisted of steamed planks. It was quartz now, petrified by ash and mud into flaky iron-colored plates. Raif knelt and ran his hand across the crumbling ridge that had once been its keel. Chips of quartz broke off and fell to the seabed without a sound. Inside, the seats and most of the gunwales had collapsed and lay like blocks of cut stone in the bottom of the boat.

Abruptly, Raif stood. It would be spring in the Hailhold now. The oaks would be budding in the Oldwood, the sword ferns uncurling above the snow, the first bluebells would be peeping up around the basswoods, and the air would be vibrating with the sound of bird calls: geese, ducks, pheasants, ptarmigan, chickadees, cardinals, horned owls. Life—not stony, desiccated deadness—and he wanted some of it for himself.

He walked for several hours, holding the setting that he'd picked with the aid of the boat. The seabed rolled out before him, flat and unchanging, a landscape of dry ghosts. As the night grew darker his vision was reduced to the shadowy pendulums of his feet. If the moon rose it did so behind the thick tide of clouds that had washed across the far edge of the sky. Raif scanned for ravines as he walked, but as long as he remained on the seabed he wasn't hopeful. Few cracks split the earth here. The entire seabed was one vast depression, easily deeper than most canyons. When he stopped to drink he knew that he wouldn't find the mist river that night. An almost imperceptible lightening of the sky in the left quarter told of the inevitability of dawn.

Deciding he would walk until morning he continued on course. As the light grew his spirits fell: every increase in brightness revealed more seabed. Nothing else. When the sun finally pushed free of the horizon, it was tempting to carry on walking—put in some distance while he could. For a while he sprinted, aware as he did so that he was making a lot of noise. Each footfall echoed like the *chunk* of a chopped log.

Finally out of breath, he halted. Hot-faced and sweating, he put a hand on each knee as he waited for the hammering in his heart to subside. Peering through the gap between his legs he saw the path he had taken outlined with clouds of salt dust: one for each step. The sky was a piercing blue and the sun rode pale and low, like the moon. Looking ahead, he realized that the long run had got him nowhere. All he could see was the flat chalk-colored plain of the seabed. Not even a boulder in sight.

"Only in darkness can we find a way through." Recalling Tallal's words, Raif sat. No point looking for cover or a suitable place to camp. Although he didn't much feel like it, he pulled out his bedroll and set about making preparations for sleep. He had no fuel for a fire and wondered if that was good or bad. Clan had no rules to govern sleeping by day. Deciding he probably wouldn't sleep anyway, he lay down and covered himself with the lamb brothers' blanket.

Aware of his vulnerability, he rolled and circled, straining his neck to keep watch in all directions. Hours passed. The sun shone. Nothing moved. Of all the empty places in the Want this seemed the emptiest. Nothing even pretended to grow here. There were no mountains on the horizon, no ice lenses to refract the light, nothing except shimmering air and seabed. Raif stared at the shimmers. He was sure that he would not sleep.

When he woke it was dusk and the final slice of sun was sinking beneath the horizon. Feeing vaguely stupid, he checked the seabed for changes. If the landscape had changed it was in subtle ways he could not discern. Kneeling, he stowed his supplies and ate a light meal of dried fruit, bread and nuts. The

234 †   J. V. JONES

water tasted of the lamb brothers' spices and charred wood. After he'd taken his fill he cupped some in his hand and let it trickle over his face. Hoping it was a luxury he would not come to regret, he broke camp and headed out.

This night would be different, he could tell that straight-away. Warmer and darker, insulated by clouds swiftly moving across the sky from Want-north. Within an hour it was full dark and he could barely see his feet. Raif walked cautiously at first, gradually moving faster as the ground beneath him remained unchanged. Soon he was jogging in short steps, his waterskin, daypack and longbow thumping against his back. He had to get off the seabed. It was a good night for mist, but this was not a good place to find it. The salt would suck it right back.

He ran faster. Hours passed and he covered leagues. Twice he stopped to drink and catch his breath. Both times he studied the sky. Clouds were consolidating into a mass in the Want-north and it was getting difficult to spot even the brightest stars. He hurried on. The visual world was shrinking. He couldn't even see his fists as he ran.

When the ground dropped beneath him, he felt a moment of indignant surprise—there was no place to land his foot—and then went plunging into the black.

He lost time. Pain roused him and he opened his eyes, blinked, and then opened them again. The difference between eyes open and eyes closed was nonexistent. The blackness on both sides was absolute. He was lying on his back, with his left leg twisted at the ankle beneath him. Something jagged and stony lay beneath his thighs and buttocks. Beneath his back the waterskin was slowly deflating; he could feel its water soaking his cloak and sealskins. It had probably saved his spine.

A breeze was blowing gently against his face, and he won-dered how long he had been unconscious. If he'd had to guess he would have said less than a minute, yet his perceptions couldn't be right for even in the Want the weather didn't change that quickly. The air had been still and now it was moving.

Rolling onto his side, he removed the pressure from his bent ankle. Pain made him woozy. *Gods, may it not be broken.* Grasping his booted shin with both hands he straightened his knee and foot. Once both legs were laid flat he sat for a moment and thought, unwilling to test the ankle just yet. The only thing he could hear was the sound of his own breath. If the sky was still overhead he could no longer see it. He had no visual way of telling how far he'd fallen, but the fact that he was alive and could move his back and hips had to be a sign that the drop couldn't have been more than ten feet.

He checked his weapons next. The longbow had been loosely cross-strung against his back and had ridden up during the fall. The string was now around his neck and the bow was on top of the ledge created by daypack and waterskin. It was sound. He exhaled, relieved.

The Forsworn sword had been suspended from his gearbelt by a G-shaped brainhook and had landed beneath his right leg. Inadequately holstered in uncured sealskin, the sword hadn't fared as well as the bow. His weight must have come down hard on the flat, for the blade was bent at the midsection. As he ran a hand along the badly warped steel, the old clan joke shot through his mind. *What do you call a man without a sword?*

Bait.

Raif stood. Splinters of pain exploded in his ankle as his foot accepted weight. Inhaling sharply, he bit back a cry. Tears welled in his eyes as he pushed his left foot into the correct position beneath his hipbone. He'd heard somewhere that if you could wiggle your toes then your foot wasn't broken. Concentrating hard, he forced messages along his nerves. He'd be damned if they weren't going to wiggle.

It was hard to tell, but he thought his toes were moving. Something down there was responding—he couldn't see what—but he thought it might be the toebox of his boot. To test the foot, he applied more pressure. At about seventy pounds the ankle gave, bucking like a horse refusing a jump. It was probably the ankle then, not the foot. That was good.

That was very good. What next?

For a few seconds after that he blanked. He was awake and conscious, aware that he should marshal his thoughts but temporarily incapable of doing so. *Think*, he ordered himself, pushing a hand through his hair. *Think*.

The hand came away damp. Inanely, he turned his palm

toward his face and looked. Pure darkness stared back. Frowning, anxious about the sword, he tried to formulate a plan. He was in a hole. Did he need to get out or was he better staying put? He could probably walk as long as he didn't put too much weight on his ankle, whereas climbing one-footed in the dark was a skill he'd never mastered. That was settled then: he had no choice but to stay here until daylight. If it was a ravine he could navigate it using his bow as a stick, and there was always a chance it could lead to something deeper where the mist river flowed.

Raif shivered. The cold down here was different, more penetrating. The breeze kept forcing it against his skin. Reaching behind his shoulder, he unhooked the Sull bow. The familiar glassiness of the lacquered horn calmed him as he untied the string and let the bent stick rest in his hand. Shifting his weight onto his good right ankle, he sent his left foot sliding across the ground. Stones and uneven rock pushed against the side of his boot. It was rough, but seemed walkable.

Come to us.

Raif's head shot round, tracking the noise. Every hair on his skin swayed as if his body were floating in water. He listened, but could hear nothing except silence buzzing in his ears. "Who's there?" he challenged. Detecting a break in his voice he didn't like, he tried again. Harder. "Who goes there?"

Nothing. Seconds turned to minutes as he stood, motionless, in the dark. The breeze, which earlier had seemed cool and reviving, crawled against his skin like silverfish. His teeth started chattering and the noise they made echoed weirdly, batting back and forth against the rock. Quite suddenly he remembered the leaking waterskin and shucked it off his back. It came away dripping, close to two-thirds of its contents drained. Running his hand along the bottom, he probed for leaks. Only part of his mind was on the job, the other part was listening. Afraid.

Unable to detect the leak, he settled for upending the skin so that the remaining water settled against the spout. His hands shook as he strapped the wet skin awkwardly against his back. Perhaps he was still reeling from the fall. Perhaps he'd just imagined the voice.

His left ankle burst into pain with its first step, but Raif gritted his teeth and forced it to take the weight. Swinging the longbow before him, he moved forward. *Tap. Tap. Tap.* The ear of the bow knocked against rocks, stones, hard earth? He couldn't say. It revealed a path forward and that was enough. Some critical, logical part of his brain knew that he was no safer on the move than he was staying in one place, but he'd been brought up at Tem's hearth as a clansman . . . and a clansman always met his enemies head-on. The breeze was blowing at his back now and he could feel it chilling the bare skin of his neck. Oddly enough he seemed to make good time. The ground was flat here and there was a little push to the breeze that kept him moving.

Come, Twelve Kill. We await you.

Raif froze. Instantly the silverfish were back, scuttling over his face and eyeballs. *"Who's there?"* he roared.

His words echoed in the darkness, breaking up and growing weaker and weaker until all was left was the word *there*. It came back sounding like a direction.

There.

Crazily Raif swung around. Forgetting his damaged ankle, he put all his weight on his left foot. Pain made him see light as the ankle buckled and he dropped to his knees.

The echo returned and this time it sounded like an admonishment.

There.

Raif breathed deeply as he searched for the will to stand upright. The breeze was stronger here, a persistent light wind dampening his skin. He wondered what was left of the night. It seemed more than ten hours since the sun had set. Surely the darkness couldn't go on much longer? Smiling grimly, he reminded himself that this was the Want. The darkness could continue for as long as it liked.

How had the voice known his name? That was what he wanted to know. Twelve Kill was his Rift name, the one given to him by Yustaffa the Dancer. Who else would know that beside the Maimed Men? Suspecting he was better off not thinking too long about the answer, Raif hauled himself to his feet. His left foot felt so loosely connected to his ankle that he wondered if it might fall off. Something perverse in him made him force his weight back onto it and stand, teeth bared, as the pain subsided.

After that there was nothing to do but continue walking. The darkness rode on, black and oily, providing no traction for his vision. Underfoot, the rockbed grew smooth and he had an overall sense that he was descending. Slowly, the path's course began to curve. Raif became aware of a second breeze blowing against his back. It hit at a different angle than the first, and it smelled of frozen kills set by the stove to thaw. Raif knew the smell well, all hunters did: fresh blood, black blood and ice. He turned his head, tracking the scent. Two breezes now and they met here, where he stood.

Aaaaagggghhhh.

Raif jumped at the sound of a faraway scream. It had come from directly ahead, where the two breezes commingled and became one. As he waited, listening, something brushed against his right arm.

"No," he cried, spinning around, his heart thumping. "Who's there?"

Raif unsheathed the Forsworn sword, tugging hard to force the bent blade from the scabbard. Water from the split waterskin trickled down his back.

Come.

The word was spoken in the softest whisper and it slid right past his ear.

Raif swung the sword in a circle. "Keep away," he warned.

That was when he felt the fingers trailing across his face.

Raif hissed. Shrinking back, he dropped all his weight onto his left foot. Immediately the ankle buckled and his leg gave way beneath him. Releasing his grip on the Sull bow, he used his left hand to break the fall.

There.

Raif sat on the rockbed and drew the sword to his chest. His heart was beating so rapidly it felt like it might seize and stop. Cautiously he brought his free hand to his face. A line of ice was rafting down his cheek. Not gently, he scrubbed it away.

At ground level the breezes were firmer, muscling against his back and side. He was wet all over he realized; his hair, sleeves, pant legs.

Oh Gods, he thought, understanding slowly dawning. *This is it, the mist river. And I've been heading downstream.*

Less than two days ago Tallal had warned him the only sense he could rely on was touch. Raif had listened but not heard. He had imagined the mist river purely in visual terms—a sort of moving channel of clouds—yet he hadn't once paused to consider what it would feel like to be in it. Foolishly, he had disregarded the full meaning of Tallal's words. "Touch alone will lead you out."

Ha, ha, ha.

Soft laughter echoed along the ravine. Raif imagined he deserved it. How long had he been traveling with the current, toward the heart of the Want? Too long, that was the answer. Every step downstream was a mistake. Raif shivered. He had been deeply, recklessly stupid. The Want was an unsprung trap with invisible tripwires humming in all directions. He'd been caught in one of them and it nearly killed him, and here he was less than twenty days later walking straight over another wire.

Anger at himself made him hard on his body and he hauled himself up, not much caring about the pain he inflicted on his twisted ankle. When he remembered he'd dropped the bow, he scrambled for it in the jet black darkness. Relief flooded over him when the tip of his sword touched horn, and he wondered at what point his peace of mind had come to depend solely on possessing weapons. Sword and bow. They had become his armor, his comfort, his fate.

Yet there were things upstream that were immune to them. The voices did not fear him . . . or at least did not fear his weapons. He thought about that as he oriented himself against the flow.

Deciding he would not take the second, stronger channel but retrace his steps upstream, Raif turned to face the oncoming mist. Its icy wetness slid between his teeth and down his throat. He sniffed deeply, making sure that he was heading into the fresher-smelling of the two streams, and then took his first steps into the black.

Noooooooooooo . . .

The howl cracked through the ravine like lightning, but this time Raif did not pause. He felt the mist pushing against him, felt ragged foggy shackles condense around his ankles and wrists. Strong steps broke them. They re-formed again and he broke them again, and the wet sucking noise they made as they snapped accompanied his every step. An hour passed and then another and still there was no increase in light. Holding his bow out before him like a blindman with a cane, Raif walked the mist rivers of the Want.

Occasionally there would be forks in the stream and he would have to pick a course using nothing more than instinct. Other currents might be colder or swifter, wider or narrower, they might smell of glaciers, ozone, raw iron and burned rock, and each time he bypassed one he wondered if he had made a mistake. He had a vision of himself as a rat in a water maze, paddling furiously to stay afloat while trying to find the cheese. Those above could look down and see everything, see the grand scheme of tunnels and turns, know instantly the best route, and then laugh amongst themselves as the rat missed one opportunity after another, propelling himself deeper into the maze.

"Out," Tallal had said, "that has to be enough."

Raif walked against the current and hoped that the lamb brother was right. When he grew thirsty, he drank without halting, holding the waterskin high above his head. He never grew hungry and never stopped to relieve himself. He had a fear of standing still. He did not want to feel those ghost fingers on his face—or anywhere else—ever again.

The night spooled out, growing impossibly long. Either that or he had lost the capacity to judge time. Sometimes the voices spoke to him, but he had a sense that they were farther away now, separated from him by great lengths of mist. As he worked his way around what seemed to be a U-shaped meander, he became aware of a change in the current. It was weakening, and for an instant he thought he smelled damp earth. He picked up his pace, desperately sniffing the air, but could detect nothing beyond the hailstone odor of the mist. When the path finally straightened he heard a noise. Scratching, followed by a short, high-pitched squeak.

Rats. Raif allowed himself to hope. Rats did not live in the Want. He was moving quickly now, shambling forward, favoring his right foot over his left. The summer he was eight years old he and Drey had spent hours belly-down in the underlevels of the roundhouse searching for rats. It had been an unusually warm spring and the rats had bred like . . . rats and the entire Hailhouse had been overrun. Longhead had set traps and poison and even hired a verminist from Ille Glaive. A month later, with numbers unabated, the head keep had come up with the bright idea of drafting the clan youth into the cause. He set a bounty: for every five whole rats brought to him, dead or alive, he would pay out a copper coin. This was unheard-of wealth — coin was rarely used in the clanholds — and Raif and Drey had set about trying to capture enough rats to make themselves rich. Other boys wasted days showily trying to spear rats with swords and shoot them with arrows, but he and Drey had decided on a different approach. "Stealth," Drey had intoned, his voice deadly serious. "We must live with them and smell like them and once we've earned their trust we spring our trap." The trap was a big square of fisherman's netting given to them by their uncle Angus Lok.

Raif grinned as he remembered the three days he and Drey had lived in the underlevels, sleeping on the damp, muddy floor, eating trail meat like proper hunters and strategizing endlessly about rats. It had been a good time. Raif couldn't recall earning the rats' trust, but he did remember deploying the net. Constantly. In the end they caught eight whole rats and an angry raccoon. When they brought their bounty to the head keep, Longhead had scratched his head. "I didn't say anything about coons." Seeing their faces fall he added, "But now I come to think of it one coon is more of a nuisance than two rats. A rat can't lift the lids and get into the grain bins. Coon can. A copper for both of you — and this stays between you and me."

A whole coin each. Raif couldn't remember what he did with his, maybe swapped it for some rusty piece of weaponry from Bev Shank. Drey had given his to Da. He had always been the better man.

Raif let the memory fall away from him, forcing himself back into the present. Straightaway he realized something was wrong. The air was still. No mist washed against his face, no breeze lifted his hair. Without a current to walk against he had no guide. Halting, he tried to pin down his mistake. When he'd first heard the rats he was pretty sure the current was still push-ing against him. What had he done then? Thinking about Drey had distracted him. Had he veered off course? He turned his head, knowing as he did so that to look behind was useless but unable to break the habit of a lifetime.

Then he realized something strange. He could see the barest outline, a black-on-black edge about ten feet above him. Blinking, he waited. One grain of light at a time, the world came into view. Raif's eyes protested the growing brightness, sending out weird blooms of color and floating dots. Sky emerged above the edge, gray and pearly, swamped with clouds. The ravine appeared below it. Blue sandstone walls rose on two sides, their surfaces riven with cracks, their ledges collecting grounds for deadwood and loose scree. Underfoot, the porous stone was venting skeins of mist that quickly dissipated in the dry air. Ahead, where the ravine wall met the bedrock, a bony bristlecone pine lay twisted and on its side, its needles a pale ashy green.

Raif glanced down the length of the ravine. It was still dark back there. Turning, he walked toward the bristlecone pine. It was alive, he could smell it. As he knelt, rubbing the fragrant needles between his fingertips, the light increased and the way ahead became clear. Sourwood bushes, rock oak and hornbeam choked the foot of the ravine where it dovetailed into a large dry riverbed. No, Raif corrected himself, the river wasn't dry. A line of green water glinted in its center.

It was canyon country, west of the Rift. He had been here twice before. He knew the lay of the land, its faults and under-cuts, its shrunken willows and yellow sedge. It was probably less than two days' walk to the city on the edge of the abyss.

As Raif stepped from the ravine and into the dry riverbed, a final cry echoed from the dark place behind him.

Keep away from the Red Ice.

He did not look back.

SIXTEEN

Crouching in the Underworld

Raina Blackhail crouched in dank and fetid underlevels of the roundhouse and prayed her light wouldn't go out. It was one of those horn-covered safelamps that was supposedly impervious to the wind. The lamp's bulb-shaped brass reservoir was pleasingly full and felt good in her hand, but there was no getting round it: the flame was jumping.

Darn thing. And what on earth was she doing down here anyway, when she could be upstairs enjoying a fine midday meal with Anwyn Bird in the good light—and fresh air—of day? Instead the smells of rotten leaves, night soils and dead mice were assaulting her senses as she paddled through a half-foot of standing water. The underlevels of the Hailhouse stank like an old man. They were shrinking like one too. According to Longhead, who was one of the very few people in the clan who cared about such things, the Hailhouse sank a little each year. "It's the weight of the stone," he'd explained to her many years ago. "When the spring thaws come the earth softens and the walls begin to sink. Not much, but certainly enough." He had wanted to show her the marker he had scribed on the base of the roundhouse in order to monitor the rate of sinkage. Raina had declined. She'd been twenty-two at the time and madly in love, and she wouldn't have cared if the entire Hailhold had sunk ten feet in a single day.

Well it's sinking now. And the irony was that she, Raina Blackhail, had turned into Longhead: a person with a marker, monitoring the decline. Raina smiled at the thought. It made what she did seem less grim.

Noticing a flattening-out of an overhead ceiling groin, she straightened her spine and rested a moment. Her back was aching with the strain of carrying her lode and she wondered if she should have asked Jebb Onnacre to help. No, she shook her head. Jebb was a good man and she trusted him, but this risk must be hers alone.

Pushing herself off from the wall she concentrated on remembering the way ahead. The standing water was deeper than when she'd been here last and she was glad she'd had the sense to put on her knee-high leather riding boots. As she moved, the pack strapped to her shoulders kept sliding out of place and she had to constantly reach back to recenter the weight. She wasn't sure how much longer she could carry it. Sweat was trickling past her ears, and two dark stains were spreading across the armpits of her dress. The sopping wool felt like itchy mush.

Shunting the weight sideways, she slipped between two stone columns and entered the dark airless labyrinth of the foundation space, the bottommost level in the roundhouse. It was surprisingly warm and some kind of rain was falling—the ceiling must be saturated with groundwater. The safelamp began to hiss and Raina brought it close to her body for protection. Bending at the waist, she cleared the entrance tunnel and followed the passage as it led down.

It wasn't long before oily water started flooding over the tops of her boots. Awkwardly, she hiked up her sodden skirts and tucked them under her belt. As she worked, the safelamp swung lazily in her free hand, sending an egg-shaped beam of light rocking across the walls.

A fuzz of blue-black mold covered the stone. In the corner where the sandstone walls braced the ceiling, moths had laid their eggs. Thousand of white maggots fed on the mold. Some had pupated into pod-shaped cocoons that hung suspended from the ceiling by dusty threads of silk. When a breeze came they clicked together, making a noise like rustling leaves. Raina averted her eyes and resumed walking.

Built solely as a buffer between the roundhouse and the cold earth, the foundation space had not been designed for walking. Raina reckoned the ceiling height was under five feet, and looking ahead she could see it was dropping. The strange thing was she wasn't as afraid of this place as she had been in the past. Old fears were falling away. Fear of rats and other small things now seemed like a silly luxury, like wearing a lace bonnet on a windy day. Vain too, a demonstration of delicacy, an announcement that one has managed to steer clear of the hardships of everyday life. Same with spiders and darkness and thunderstorms: girlish fears for girls who did not know the real things they should fear.

Raina could tell them. Sometimes she would like to yell them out loud just to get them off her chest.

Spying a T-junction ahead, Raina took a moment to rest the weight and run over the directions in her head. She did not want to make a wrong turn. Effie Sevrance had shown her this place. That girl knew the roundhouse like the back of her hand. Strongrooms, crypts, wet cells, mole holes, clay pits, ice pits, well heads, dungeons: Effie knew all the dark and secret spaces beneath the roundhouse. She would go missing for entire days and no one, not even her brothers, could find her. When she finally emerged, blinking and baffled at all the fuss, she would say simply, "Sorry. I forgot." Raina had come down hard on her after the time she'd gone missing for three whole days. "You will stay here in my chambers, within my sight, for the next ten days. And you'll spend that time composing apologies for all those you have worried and inconvenienced." Poor Effie had done just that.

Raina became aware of the water in her boots, lukewarm and turgid, congealing like jelly. Effie *was* alive; she had to be. Raina was sure she would know if it wasn't true. A messenger had come from Dregg only two days ago, and the word was still the same: no sign of the cart containing Effie Sevrance, Clewis Reed, and Druss Ganlow. Raina understood that something must have happened on their journey—a detour, a mishap, a mistake—but it didn't mean that Effie was dead. Just waylaid.

Breathing heavily Raina took the turn. *How am I going to tell Drey?* She had put off sending a message to Effie's brother three times now. Between his responsibilities defending the Crab Gate and his heartache over his brother's treason, Drey

Sevrance had enough on his shoulder. Besides, she owed it to him to deliver the news in person, to look into his eyes and accept the blame. *I was the one who thought Effie would be better off at Dregg.*

Besides, Drey was gone now, called to war. It was not a good time to give a Hailsman bad news. The rumors from Ganmiddich were worrying: whispers of city-men armies on the march from the south whilst Bludd forces were cracking down from the north. Hailsmen would die. Drey might die. If the gods truly loved her Mace Blackhail would die.

Raina shivered at her own coldness. Her clan was marching south to defend the Crab Gate, and here she was wishing that some steel-plated city man would thrust his blade through her husband's heart. What was it Bessie Flapp always said? *Be careful with wishes. Once in a blue moon a god will grant them and show us just how selfish we are.*

Bessie was right. The clan would not benefit from losing its chief. Not now, with wars against Dhoone and Bludd to be fought. It wasn't even certain that she, Raina Blackhail, would benefit from her husband's death. If Mace were to die in battle his title would be up for grabs. She had told exactly two people of her plans to be chief—Orwin Shank and Anwyn Bird—and their support, while gratifying, was hardly enough to claim the prize. Anyone with enough jaw could step ahead of her.

Shaking her head in frustration, Raina set the matter aside. She could not afford to be distracted. Her destination was drawing close and if she wasn't alert she would miss the entrance.

After Effie's three-day disappearing act, Raina had forced the girl to show her the paths she took below the roundhouse. That way, if Effie ever went missing again, Raina would know exactly where to find her. Effie had frowned and tutted and looked critically at Raina, before finally saying, "It will ruin your dress."

A ruined dress was a small price to pay for an education. Effie moved around the roundhouse like a mole in a set, diving beneath footstones and through holes in the walls, and scurrying between cracks. Raina had been afraid to blink lest she lose sight of her. She had still been afraid of rats back then, and remembered getting cross and a little bit shaky and commanding Effie to *Slow down.* Still, it had been worth it. Blackhail was the oldest clan in the North and it had the oldest roundhouse, yet most of the time when you were aboveground you didn't see its age and its history. Belowground was different. There were no plastered panels or tapestries concealing the rough stone walls, no wooden boards laid over floors. No chief, dissatisfied with what he saw, had ordered its halls to be knocked down and rebuilt. The underlevels of the roundhouse had been left alone and disregarded. Oh some clansmen stubbornly maintained cells here and the great open space of the cattlefold was still in use, but mostly this was dead space. Rats swam in the standing pools. Bats nested overhead between the ceiling groins. History lived here, quiet as dripping water.

If she had taken a left turn instead of a right one at the T-junction Raina knew that she would have ended up in a room full of grave holes. Nearly two hundred people had been interred in the dome-shaped chamber, their bodies inserted head first into narrow, deeply dug holes. Stones so heavy Raina wondered how they had been transported here capped every grave, and if you walked into the room with good lighting you could discern a pattern in their placement. The stones formed a map of Bannen's clanhold.

Fifteen hundred years ago the great Bann chief Hector Bannen had launched a surprise assault on the Hailhold. Blackhail was in decline and infighting had left it vulnerable; Hector had seen an opportunity and seized it. That wasn't his sin though, and no one judged him for it. No, what Hector had done to deserve being buried on his head along with his two hundred best warriors was break his oath to Blackhail. Only five years earlier Hector had sworn allegiance to the Hail chief Dowerish Blackhail. Dowerish was still chief at the time of the assault—though his younger brother Eagon was pursuing that position for himself—and with a cleverly staged mock-surrender Dowerish had lured Hector's front line into the roundhouse, cut them off, and then cut them down.

It had not been a proud moment for either clan, and most current histories did not include it. But the stones did not lie. Raina had stood and watched as Effie Sevrance skipped between them, attempting to locate the stone under which Hector Bannen had lain for fifteen hundred years.

Feeling her thigh muscles begin to shake, Raina picked up her pace. The lode was digging into her back and it was becoming difficult to inhale two full lungs of air. She couldn't go much farther. Where was the opening?

A breeze hitting her cheek made her turn to look down a corridor. Iron bars, thickly crusted with rust, flickered in the light from the safelamp. Down that way lay Blackhail's ancient and derelict dungeon, the Hellhold, and that meant she was getting close. Another breeze confirmed it: the narrow passage to the left led to the chief's chamber. Effie said it didn't look like it would, but if you took the ramp instead of the stairs it led straight to a secret entrance. Raina shook her head. How could Effie have possibly learned such a thing?

Taking small, slow steps through the water Raina began to study the sandstone walls. Every few paces brick stanchions stood out from the stone at right angles, bracing the great weight of the roundhouse. The shadows and hollows they created had to be carefully inspected. Not all sunken panels were as they seemed.

Spying the faint outline of a palmprint on an inset block of stone, Raina halted. This was it. She placed her hand on the palmprint and was glad to see it matched perfectly—no one else had been here since Dagro's death. Pressing firmly against the stone, she pushed her hand sideways and drew the stone aside. It was a tile set on a track lubricated by superfine sand. Once it was in motion it moved with ease. A line of sand spilled from the edge of the track as air trapped in the darkness for five months rushed through the opening.

Am I doing the right thing? she wondered, knowing there was no one to give her an answer. Sometimes she imagined there weren't any right answers, just things men and women did and the talk they used to justify them. Could she justify this then? Yes, she could.

The opening was at hip height and Raina realized she could not climb through it with the load on her back, so she set down the safelamp and shouldered off the pack. It was a lot heavier in her arms than it had been on back and as she lifted it through the opening her arm muscles wobbled. Quickly, she lowered the pack to the ground.

The water in her boots ran up her thighs as she hiked into the room. It was not a pleasant sensation. By some unexpected piece of luck the ground here was dry. Good. Turning, she slid the tile facade back in place and then took a moment to enjoy the relief of no longer bearing a five-stone weight on her back. She would pay for it tomorrow, but right now she felt strong and capable.

She, Raina Blackhail, had carried the largest remaining piece of the shattered Hailstone to safety whilst thirty feet above her Scarpemen were working to grind the remains down to nothing and dump them in Cold Lake.

It was an outrage and she was powerless to stop it and the only way she had of fighting back was to steal a piece of the stone before it was destroyed and hide it in a place where Scarpes would never find it. Here, in this ancient strongroom outfitted by the Silver chief Yarro Blackhail to conceal his treasures, was where the last piece of Hailstone would come to rest.

Raina did not know much about the gods, had never understood their secret motives, and had not once in her thirty-three-year life felt touched by them, but she had been moved to act by a strong sense of wrongness. Stannig Beade, the new clan guide from Scarpe, had not wasted any time asserting his power. "The Hailstone is dead," he had told the crowd assembled on the greatcourt five days back, "and just like a corpse we must mourn and bury it."

The word *bury* had been a mistake. This was Blackhail, not Scarpe, and a Blackhail corpse was left to rot above ground in hollowed-out basswoods, and the crowd had grown restive. Stannig Beade had a sharp eye and a subtle mind and had quickly realized his mistake. "Just as a slain Blackhail warrior is left in sight of the gods, we will do the same with the stone. We will grind it down to powder and scatter it over the earth. I know it is hard to hear. I look before me and see good men and women who loved the Hailstone like a god. But make no mistake, the Hailstone was never a god. It was a place where the gods rested, and now it has been shattered they have nowhere to dwell when they come to Blackhail. Do you want that, Hailsmen and Hailswomen? Do you want the Stone Gods to pass by your roundhouse and your clan?"

No they had not, and many in the crowd began to nod their heads in agreement. Stannig Beade was a clever speaker; his voice had been sharp and rasping, but his words had got him exactly what he wanted.

Already he had made a lie of them. The remains of the Hailstone were being dumped in Cold Lake, not scattered on open ground as he had claimed. The first cartload had been hauled west yesterday at dawn. Raina had seen it leave. She had asked questions and got no answers, so she had saddled Mercy and followed the tracks left by the cart. Tarp had been roped over the rubble, but a wormhole in the cartbed leaked dust. Raina was not given to fancy, but there had been a moment when she had first spotted the trail of granite powder lying lightly amid the yellow winter grass where she felt as if the Hailstone was letting her know where it was and what she must do.

The trail of Hail dust led all the way to the east shore of Cold Lake. She had watched from a careful distance, concealed by the boughs of a two-year hemlock, as the Scarpeman driving the cart had backed the bed up against the lake, released the tail-gate and let the cart roll down to the shore. The rubble had gone crashing into the water. Raina had not waited to see the dust cloud settle and had promptly turned Mercy and galloped home.

At first she had wondered about the lie. Why would Stannig Beade risk being discovered in such an obvious deception? The answer came when she got back, and it surprised her. There were people in the roundhouse—Hailsmen and Hailswomen—who were already aware of what Stannig was doing. Merritt Ganlow was one of them. "Oh come on, Raina," the head widow had said after Raina informed her of what she had seen. "Of course the Hailstone was never going to be scattered—it'd cause dust storms for a week. Best place for it is the lake. That way it'll stay in one place. Whole almost. Stannig told me that after he made the announcement to the clan he spent time with Scarpestone, alone, and the gods told him he'd made a mistake. The Hailstone wasn't a corpse and should not be treated like one. The remains should be shown deeper respect."

Raina had actually laughed, a bitter sound not much to her liking. "You don't actually believe that, Merritt? Stannig Beade doesn't care about the Hailstone. He wants to see it destroyed so thoroughly it can never be resurrected, and all its power becomes his."

Merritt Ganlow had jumped on her words. "The Hailstone *is* destroyed. He didn't do that. We did, as a clan. All Stannig's doing is trying to dispose of the remains in a decent manner. Tell me, Raina, what else is he supposed to do?"

They were both shaking. They had been standing outside the closed door of the widows' hearth and Raina felt weary and exposed. She had not expected this from Merritt. Edging farther away from the door, she said, "Why does he insist on grinding every bit of the stone to nothing? I've seen what's he's doing, not even a chip as big as an apple core will remain by the time he's through."

The head widow had already begun shaking her head whilst Raina was speaking. "We are clansmen. We grind our stone. That's what we've done for centuries. Stannig Beade is doing what every guide since Ballard the Scared has done before him: he loads the stone in his mill and breaks it."

"No," Raina protested. "It's not the same."

Merritt Ganlow raised her chin. "Tell me why."

She could not. The words needed to convey the complex and ephemeral ideas in her head were beyond her. What Stannig Beade did was wrong, she felt it in her gut—he'd come here and looted the heart of clan—but if she said that she would sound like a peeved child.

All the while Raina was thinking Merritt watched her with keen green eyes. When the silence had stretched overlong, she said, "Your nose is put out, Raina. Simple as that. With your husband away you thought the mice would play, but now there's another cat in the house."

Raina had to give it to Merritt: the woman was sharp. It was true, Raina had been hoping to run things while Mace was away. Return some order to the house, banish the Scarpes to outbuildings, make plans of her own for Hailstone. She'd wanted the chance to guide Blackhail back . . . to clan.

Breathing deeply, Raina tried to replace her waning strength with air. A woman whom she had trusted and called friend had been cleverly turned against her. Almost it was too much.

She tried one last time. "You are right, Merritt, I'm not happy that Stannig came here. He's Scarpe's guide—let them have him. We're paying tribute to a foreign stone whilst Scarpemen are grinding down the Hailstone and carting it away."

Merritt must have heard something close to breaking in Raina's voice, for she was gentle in her reply. "Who better to do that job? Name me one Hailsman who would relish breaking down the ruined stone? Stannig hopes to spare, not deceive us."

How had he got to her? Raina wondered. What tales had he spun? What promises had he whispered in her ear? Whatever he had done it was subtle, for Merritt was too clever to fall for obvious ploys. Did he know how close Merritt was to Raina herself? Was he trying to isolate the chief's wife? Raina tucked that thought away for later consideration. To Merritt she said the only thing she had left. "Stannig Beade is a Scarpe. I thought you were my ally against them."

Tutting softly, Merritt shook her head. "Think clearly, Raina. My position on Scarpes in the Hailhouse is unchanged. Tomorrow, through that very door, two hundred Scarpes will come and kick me out of my hearth. They've done some sort of swap-around with the tied Hailsmen who were due to take it. It's a disgrace, and you underestimate me if you think that Stannig Beade can convince me otherwise. He hasn't tried to. I doubt if he'd dare. What he did do was come to me and ask my opinion on some things. And for a wonder he actually listened to the answers. That, I respect. It's fitting that a new clan guide acquaints himself with matters of clan, and also fitting that he takes the time to introduce himself to its widows. He knows there are things wrong in this clan. But right now he doesn't have time for that. His priority is the new guidestone—and rightly so. We must be settled as a clan before we can move forward, have a heart beating before we can breathe. You know that and if you would look beyond his colors, you would see that Stannig Bead is guide first and foremost. Not a Scarpe."

Raina felt a little stunned, as if someone had knocked her with some force on the head. How on earth was she to deal with this? At least now she knew how Stannig Beade had got to Merritt: he had flattered her and opened up a channel to power. It was telling that Stannig Beade had made no such overture to the chief's wife, no cozy little talk, no confessions of uncertainty, no delicate request for information. He wouldn't dare. Five days ago on the greatcourt they had met eye-to-eye, and she had seen through him and he through her. Stannig Beade knew the chief's wife for his enemy, and Raina Blackhail knew that before her stood a man who coveted Blackhail's power.

It was then, looking into Merritt Ganlow's superior face, that Raina had decided to steal the Hailstone. She'd be damned if she'd stand by and let some clever, scar-faced Scarpemen have his way with the remains. And Merritt could go to hell too.

Now, one day later, Raina had lost the bravado she'd felt outside the widows' hearth. Strange, but when she had actually stolen the stone from the rubble that was heaped against the roundhouse's east wall, things had begun to change for her. She had chosen her moment carefully, for the night crews were still working on the wall and her only opportunity to be alone was when one of Anwyn's kitchen girls had called the crews inside for ale and supper. Oil lamps and guarded candles had been left burning on poles and on makeshift pedestals of piled stones. A big vat of tar was bubbling on a slow green flame and buckets of white lime had been arranged in a loose half-circle around it. Timber boards and split logs were strewn across the ground, and Raina could smell the itchy, dry-skin odor of sawdust. A second scaffold was now in place, bridging the gap between bare ground that had once held the guidehouse and the shattered remains of the stable block. Raina had to be careful to duck her head as she crossed toward the scrap pile of granite.

Stannig Beade's mule-powered stone mill cast its big blocky shadow against the remains of the Hailstone. The new clan guide was wasting no time and Raina could see that the largest chunks of stone had already gone under the mill. What remained were pieces no bigger than a man's head, and even these had been sorted and were lying in a separate pile close to the millstone. Stannig would be grinding at dawn. A charge of anger ran down Raina's spine. How could Merritt Ganlow not see what this man was about? Snapping her head once, as if to shake off some unpleasant insect that had alighted upon it, Raina approached the remains.

She had thought, wrongly, that it might be difficult to tell Hailstone from roundhouse stone: the explosion had blasted and commingled both types of rock. Yet there was no mistaking guidestone. If she was ever asked what the differences were, she would not be able to provide an answer that would satisfy anyone other than a clansman. It was guidestone. It was different.

She picked the largest piece, how could she not? And struggled to lift sixty pounds of dead weight to her chest. She had not thought to bring a saddlebag or pack, and had only her shawl to conceal the stone. Now that she no longer had fine chambers to call her own she slept in one of the dry cells beneath the kitchen that Anwyn used for storing herbs. She took the stone there, walking around the exterior of the roundhouse and not through it. When she rapped on the kitchen door Anwyn answered. The clan matron did not know what Raina carried and did not ask.

Later Anwyn brought her supper, hot onion soup and a wedge of fried bread, and nodded briskly at Raina's request for white spirits and a shoulder pack sturdy enough to carry a small child.

Something had already begun to change for Raina that night, but when she poured white spirits onto a soft rag and began to polish the largest remaining piece of Hailstone, she finally realized what it meant. This was no longer about spiting Stannig Beade and thwarting his plans. This was about Blackhail. This was about preserving its heart. Someone someday would need this and when they did Raina Blackhail could tell them where to find it.

Crouching amid the flickering shadows of Yarro Blackhail's hidden strongroom, Raina Blackhail slipped the Hailstone from its bag. It was an edge piece from the exterior of the stone and the old chisel lines were still upon it. Raina thought of Inigar Stoop; his body had never been found. Would he be glad she was doing this?

I do not know.

Glancing around the small rectangular-shaped room, Raina wondered where to stow the stone. Over in one corner, perched atop a wooden market crate, were the items she had taken after Dagro's death. Small things, tokens for herself; gifts of modest jewels he had given her, his personal handknife, his belt buckle, a letter Norala, Dagro's first wife, had written to them both before her death. Raina had not been able to bear the thought that Mace Blackhail might claim them as his own, so she had removed them from her chambers and his gaze. Once he had asked her quite pointedly about Dagro's handknife, for it was well made and handsome with a translucent ivory handle and double-edged blade. She had told him that Dagro must have taken it with him to the Badlands for she hadn't seen it in over a month. She had been new to deception then and it had been a very bad lie. He never challenged her on it: any mention of the Badlands left him cold.

Mace had been gone five days now, riding for Ganmiddich with a thousand men. Tomorrow a second thousand would leave with Grim Shank at their head.

Realizing she needed to attend the departing warriors, Raina made a quick decision about the stone. She would leave it in the far corner, uncovered, and in full sight. To slide it back in the pack and conceal it would only draw attention to it if it were found. This way it would just be a wayward chunk of stone. She doubted very much that any Scarpeman besides Stannig Beade would be capable of recognizing it as Hailstone. But a Hailsman or Hailswoman would know it, and that was perhaps enough.

The wedge-shaped piece of Hailstone fitted perfectly in the corner and to Raina it seemed as if it were drawing shadows around itself, for when she stepped back she could no longer see it clearly. It had become part of the foundation, a slightly irregular chunk in the wall. She had thought she might speak a prayer but now that it came to it she had none to offer. The Stone Gods either knew what she did, or didn't. They either judged it right or wrong. No poorly worded prayer would change that.

Scooping up the shoulder pack and the safelamp, Raina crossed to the entry portal. The stone tile was easier to set in motion from inside for a small depression cut into the face provided traction for the fingers. Within seconds Raina was back in the foundation space, once again knee-deep in water. Freed from the weight of the stone she felt oddly light and miscalculated the force needed to walk. The water sloshed a lot and twice she nearly tipped over. *Drunk*, she decided. Alcohol optional. Now she came to think of it though, a good strong dram of Anwyn's twenty-year malt would be just the thing. Her nerves deserved it.

Reaching the narrow gap between stone pillars that led up toward the living spaces, Raina let down her skirts. It wouldn't do for a chief's wife to be seen baring her thighs. It wouldn't do for her to be seen down here at all, but once she reached the upper cellars where the dry cells were located she was in the clear. "Just checking on the butter stores for Anwyn" would do it, either that or "Longhead's still worried about flooding, and I thought I'd take a look at it for myself."

When she reached the stairs she sat, pulled off her boots and drained the water. Her toes were white and wrinkled. The boots were drenched and would need to be carefully stretched as they dried. Once they were back on her feet she ran up the stairs and along the landing, the safelamp swinging giddily in her hand. One more flight of stairs to go and she'd be aboveground in the land of the living.

"Woman."

She spun in the direction of the voice. Along the corridor all was shadow. The person who spoke did not carry a light.

Stannig Beade stepped into the halo created by Raina's lamp. As always she was surprised that he was a clan guide, for he had the shoulder breadth and muscle of a hatchetman. He was wearing his ceremonial cloak, the black boarskin burned ragged at the hem. His tattooed and needle-pocked cheeks trapped the lamplight and gave you nowhere to look save his eyes.

"Stannig." Raina was pleased with how strong her voice sounded. Resisting the urge to draw the shoulder pack behind her skirts she said, "If you will excuse me I have work to do in the stables. Good day." She turned her back on him and nearly got away, but he stopped her with a question.

"Did you fall?" He waited until she had turned back to face him before dropping his gaze to her sopping skirts.

She shrugged. "Work."

He let the silence spin out, breathing possessively, claiming the air between them. "I see." His hands twitched. Raina could see the stone dust wedged beneath his fingernails. "I have been looking for you. Someone said they had seen you slip below-ground at noon." He paused, letting her know that it was now a long time after noon. "I had not thought to find you here."

"Yet still you looked." It was a mistake to challenge him and she wished she could take it back.

Again his hands twitched. "I believe you are unhappy with the removal of the Hailstone."

Merritt Ganlow. Raina could hardly fathom it. She and Merritt had been friends for twenty years; their husbands had shared a tent the day they died. How could Merritt do this? How could she talk to this man about their private conversations?

Stannig Beade watched Raina compose herself, his expression fixed, his dark eyes gleaming with animal triumph.

Raina took a deep breath. Think, she told herself. *Think.* "I have some concerns, I will not hide that. To grind the stone to nothing and dump it in the lake seems . . . unceremonious."

Stannig Bead brought a hand to his face and tapped his chin. "Unceremonious," he repeated, giving the word a sharp little twist. "A chief's wife concerned with matters of the gods . . . how . . . unusual."

Raina felt her face grow hot.

It appeared to be the outcome he was hoping for, as he nodded once, to himself. "Seems I have chosen the right person after all."

She would not give him the satisfaction of asking what he meant. Stomach sinking, skirts dripping water onto the floor, she waited.

Stannig Beade was unperturbed. Moving his powerful shoulders in a relaxed shrug, he said, "The ceremony to hallow the new Hailstone requires a person of high honor to light the Menhir Fire. Commonly it is custom for the clan chief to hold the torch, but as you are aware your husband is a-war. I have given long thought to the matter of who should stand in for him, and spoken with many people in the clan. Time and time again a name came up. She is the one held in deepest respect. She is the one whose presence is most valued. She is the who will bring the highest honor to the ceremony." The clan guide of Scarpe and now Blackhail looked Raina straight in the eye. "I know you would not want to disappoint your clansmen and clanswomen, Raina Blackhail, so I will assume on Menhir Night you will stand at my side and aid me in presenting the new Hailstone to the gods."

He did not wait for her answer, just bowed a sharp dismissal and left her standing in the corridor alone.

She watched dust roused by his footsteps settle and knew she had been outmaneuvered by an expert. Stannig Beade would use her standing in this clan to strengthen his position and validate the new guidestone. She could hear her clansmen now:

"Well, I was against it, I admit. But there's Raina at Beade's side and we all know she's not a woman to give her support lightly."

"Aye. If the new stone's good enough for Raina Blackhail it'll do for me."

Aware she was swaying slightly, Raina sent out a hand to brace herself against the wall. She could not refuse Stannig Beade, for she had heard the warning in his voice: *Refuse and all will know it. You will fracture the clan and reveal your ambition . . . and what good will that do you on Mace's return?*

If Mace ever did return. If he died in battle it would suit Beade well enough. The Scarpe guide was already beginning to act like a chief.

Raina gave a little cry of fright as the flame in her safelamp went out.

SEVENTEEN

The Clan That Walks Swords

It was two hours past sunset and the Milkhouse's primary door was closed and unlit. Bram Cormac hesitated to approach it and demand entry. The ferryman who had transported Bram and his horse across the Milk River was poling his barge away from the shore.

"Do'na dawdle, boy. The longer you leave it the harder you'll have to knock." Laughing as if he'd said something amusing, the ferryman floated away.

Bram looked at his feet. They were wet; the barge had taken in water once the weight of Guy Morloch's stallion had settled upon it. Still, it was better than having to swim across. Last time Bram was here there had been no ferryman to provide crossing.

Gaberil, Guy's horse, nosed Bram's side, playful now that the trauma of the crossing was behind him. "Easy, Gabbie," Bram murmured, absently running his hand over the horse's mane as he stared at the massive glowing dome of the Milkhouse. "I just need a moment to decide what to do."

It wasn't the truth. He knew what he must do—there was no decision involved—but it didn't mean that he couldn't stand here for a bit and just wait.

He had been lucky in a way, for the journey here had been his own. Once Guy Morloch and Jordie Sarson had left for the Stonefly, running off to alert Dhoonesmen to the Dog Lord's presence, Bram had no one to answer to but himself. Such a thing had never happened to him before and it had been scary, but also good. He'd remembered falling asleep that first night, crazily bedding down on an exposed hillside without fire or tent, thinking *Gods, what am I going to do?* Now he knew the answer.

Go slow.

Without anyone to shepherd him to the Milkhouse, Bram Cormac could take his time. It did not change his obligation to this clan, just delayed it by a few days. It was freedom and the Dog Lord of Clan Bludd had bought it for him, and Bram thought he'd better enjoy it while it lasted.

The best possible thing had happened that next morning. Bram had been woken by a bored horse. The night before Gabbie had fled in terror and panic as Vaylo Bludd's dogs closed in on him. He'd thrown his rider, Guy Morloch, and trampled one of the dogs. Bram thought he'd seen the last of him—a spooked horse far from home might simply take off and never come back—but Gabbie was smart, and although he'd spent only a short time on the hillside southeast of Dhoone, he'd found his way back overnight. Wasn't a bit sorry, either.

The two of them had shared a good breakfast of cheesebread and raw leeks, and once Bram had sorted out Gabbie's saddle—it had ended up beneath him, hanging from his belly—they'd taken a ride south. It had been a perfect day, Bram remembered, with a fresh breeze and just the right amount of cloud. It wasn't long before they'd run into the Fleece, a deep and narrow tributary of the Flow. They'd followed the Fleece west for a while toward Wellhouse, but when Bram spotted a settlement of tied clansman's cottages on the shore ahead, he turned Gabbie around and began looking for a crossing.

The land south of Dhoone was dotted with limestone farmhouses. Barely, wheat, oats and rye were grown here, and squares of burned stubble poking through thawing snow became a familiar sight to Bram. He'd spent two nights camping on the north shore of the Fleece, enjoying the unfamiliar sensation of being master of his own time. Mabb Cormac had taught both his sons how to fish, and Bram had whittled a pole and unraveled the border of one of his woolen blankets for twine. He didn't catch anything, but he learned why men loved to fish. You could do nothing and something at exactly the same time.

The weather changed and it rained a bit, then snowed. Gabbie shivered until he was given a blanket, and then began to chew on it. Bram thought about taking it away, but didn't. He decided it was quite possible for a horse to digest wool.

Eventually they crossed the river. An ancient hog-backed bridge spanned the Fleece just west of Clan Camber. The tiny clanhold defended the crossing with a stone and timber redoubt and a system of pulleys and river chains, but for some reason they weren't manned. Later that day Bram ran into a tied Camberman driving a pair of white oxen with a stick. The man had taken one look at Bram's Dhoone-blue cloak and driven his cattle from the road.

After that incident, Bram had considered taking off the fine cloak given to him by his brother Robbie and switching it for his old ratty half-cape. The cloak identified him not only as a Dhoonesman, but also as one of Robbie's elite crew of warriors. Bram didn't want to get into any fights. Still, he had to admit he'd felt a small thrill when the Camberman left the road to make way for him—such was the reputation of Robbie Dun Dhoone.

In the end Bram had decided to continue wearing the cloak. His reasons were complicated and not all of them were noble. Soon enough he would wear the cream wool of Castlemilk.

He tried not to think of it, and mostly that worked as a strategy. Castlemilk later. Travel in the now. Once several years back, before Bludd had seized the Dhoonehouse, and while Maggis was still chief, a visitor had come to the roundhouse. Maggis spent half a day in conference with the stranger and later walked with him around the clanhold, introducing him to various clansmen and women. Bram was curious about the stranger, but had assumed he would not be introduced—he was twelve at the time and small for his age and of little consequence to anyone except his mother, Tilda. Yet the stranger had spotted Bram spreading hay for the horses in the stable. The stranger had been talking with the swordmaster Jackdaw Thundy in a manner that suggested they were old and good friends. "Is he one of Cormac's boys?" the stranger had asked Jackdaw, nodding his head toward Bram. "Aye," Jackdaw had replied. "That's Mabb's youngest, Bram. Come over here, boy, and meet the ranger Angus Lok."

Up until then Bram had never heard of such a thing as a ranger, yet the unfamiliar word had caused a flutter in his chest. Angus Lok greeted him soberly man-to-man, and for a wonder he didn't ask any of the questions that Bram normally dreaded: *How come you don't look like your brother Rab? Did Bodie Hallax pull you from hammer training, or did you just drop out? Is it true your brother's related to the Dhoone kings?* Instead Angus Lok inquired about Bram's mother, asked Bram's opinion on his new sword—drawing it smartly on cue for Bram's inspection—and told Bram he should not neglect his studies; sword and pen was better than sword alone.

Bram had been mightily impressed. The meeting had lasted only scant minutes, but it left him with a good feeling that had endured for months. He recalled seeking out Jackdaw Thundy some time later and asking him about the ranger. "Angus is a dying breed," Jackdaw had said. "Circles like a hawk, waits like a spider. Knows the North like it's a wheatfield he's planted, and spends so much time in the saddle that it's a wonder he's not got wishbones for legs." It was a curiously vague answer, but Bram hadn't realized that at the time. Instead he was taken with the romance of a man crossing the country on a horse, alone, and watchful as a hawk.

That was how Bram had spent most of those free days after Guy Morloch and Jordie Sarson had left him; riding and being watchful, a hawk and a spider.

He wished he knew more about the histories. Every day he passed lengths of standing wall, broken bits of fortifications, paved roads gone to seed, burned-out barns, dismantled river dams, ancient way markers, sealed wells, burial mounds. Ruins, all of them. Whenever he spotted something interesting he stopped to inspect it, brushing away moss or snow, dead leaves or cobwebs: whatever had accumulated over time. Occasionally he spied faint signs scribed into the stone, but mostly the surfaces were blank. Markings had been worn away, dissolved by rain and tannins, and scoured by the wind. History had been lost. Who had built the perfectly placed dam on the Fleece? And who had destroyed it?

That was the recurring theme of the ruins, Bram had noticed. Something built, then destroyed. Thinking about it made him restless. Who would know such things? Who could tell him what had happened in the past?

Angus Lok, the ranger. He would know.

Bram had lost a whole day to the ruins he'd found in the north-facing lee of a hill in the pinelands above the Flow. Something circular—a watchtower, granary or small fort—had once stood in the shadows thrown by the hill's steep ridges. Something looking north. Scrambling over the shattered remains of cornerstones, footing blocks and lintels, Bram wondered who had erected this here and why. The nearest clanhold was Wellhouse. Its roundhouse was built from traprock. This structure had been built from hard and lustrous bluestone. Although he looked for identifying markers in the stone, Bram could find nothing to confirm his secret hope. If the structure had been built by the Sull, its ruins were keeping that knowledge to themselves.

That night he made camp against the small section of wall that was still standing. And dreamed of secrets and the Sull.

The next day he and Gabbie arrived at the Easterly Flow. The largest river in the clanholds had swollen above its banks and its waters were murky and swift. To the east Wellhouse maintained a crossing and to the west Dhoone commanded the Cinch, a narrow river gorge between two cliffs that could be strung with ropes to form a bridge. Most people crossed by boat; it was the horses that were a problem. Bram walked the stallion east along the shore, aware as he did so that he was heading away from Castlemilk. The Milkhouse now lay directly south of him. It was difficult to put his heart into finding a crossing. Gabbie was not a horse who took well to water and it was easy to say, *He's not going to swim across so I might as well take the crossing at Wellhouse.* Bram knew it for a lie. At some point during the journey Gabbie had become his horse, not Guy's, and if forced he would take the crossing for his master.

They wasted a day traveling to Wellhouse and paid a silver coin for the crossing. Bram had avoided the roundhouse and steered clear of Wellmen but he could not evade their stares. All knew him as a Dhoonesman and all were greedy for news of their sworn clan. The name Robbie Dun Dhoone was on everyone's lips, spoken in hushed tones, with fear. By now word had spread about Skinner Dhoone's crushing defeat at the Withyhouse. Rumor had it that Robbie Dun Dhoone had lured his fellow clansmen to their deaths. Little did the Wellmen realize that the slight, dark-haired youth who rode through their clanhold at dusk had been the one Robbie had sent to Skinner to set the trap.

Robbie didn't intend for Skinner and his men to die, Bram repeated to himself stubbornly. *He just wanted to insure that Skinner didn't steal a march on the Dhoonehouse, so fooled Skinner into attacking Withy instead of Dhoone.*

After the crossing at Wellhouse Bram wasted a second day heading south when he should have turned west. The land south of the Flow was old and wild and there were parts that had been lost to clan. Ancient forests of dead and dying trees formed impenetrable masses known as the Ruinwoods. *Keep to the trails:* that was the prevailing clannish wisdom concerning the Ruinwoods. Bram tried to adhere to it, but sometimes the temptation to explore long-abandoned cabins half-glimpsed through the trees was too much. Curiosity hadn't killed him, but he'd gotten lost, had his right pant leg ripped open by a blackthorn, stepped knee-deep into a sinkhole filled with wood tar and collected enough moose ticks to keep him busy with a handknife through the night. Often he saw deer and sometimes bears. One time Gabbie had shied and Bram couldn't understand why until he spied fresh snagcat tracks in the mud. From the looks of the prints it was a big male. And it was close, because Gabbie had either seen or smelled it.

"Make a lot of noise." Bram could not recall who had given him that particular nugget of information, but it sounded good to him and he began to half shout, half sing the Dhoone boast while striking the handle of his sword against Guy Morloch's fine pewter tippler.

Not long after that Bram decided to head west. It was time. Castlemilk was owed Bram Cormac.

He had miscalculated and headed too far south, so now he had to cross the Milk. Poor Gabbie, three rivers and he had to cross every one of them. River crossings, bears and snagcats: it probably didn't get much worse for a horse.

Luckily the Milk was calm. Spring thaw did not affect it in

the same way as other rivers. Its waters ran white, not high. Legend had it that the Milk ran through a gorge where the Sull had once mined milkstone. No living clansmen knew if this were true or not as none had managed to penetrate the tangle of Ruinwoods through which the Milk flowed. "Why can't someone simply pole upstream?" Bram had asked Guy Morloch once. Guy had tutted in disgust at Bram's ignorance. "Have you ever tried poling up a river fall? You know what happens? You get wet."

Bram shook away the memory of Guy's unpleasant laughter. While he was standing and thinking by the rivershore a full moon had risen above the Milkhouse. It was a heartbreakingly beautiful sight; the pearl dome of the roundhouse beneath a red moon. Bram clicked his tongue for the horse. "C'mon, Gabbie, let's see if we can wake some Milkmen and get you some hay."

It was strange to Bram that he could arrive at the door of the Milkhouse unchallenged by guards. Yet just as he was about to rap on the oyster-glazed wood, the door swung open, and he realized that unchallenged and unwatched were different things.

A big hard-bitten Milkman with shorn gray hair and tattoos tacked along the muscle lines of his bare arms greeted Bram. "You Robbie's kin?"

Bram nodded, surprised that he was both known and expected. The Milk warrior held a fiercely burning kerosene torch and Bram was startled by how close the man let the flames get to his skin.

Looking over Bram's shoulder, he nodded, "I see you've brought one of our horses back. Leave him there. I'll send a groom."

Of course, Gabbie was Guy Morloch's horse and Guy was a Castleman. Or had been.

"Inside now," the warrior said, yanking his chin back to indicate the roundhouse's interior. "No one'll see you tonight. I'll get you sorted with food and cotting."

Bram followed the man inside. It did not take much light to illuminate the small horn-shaped entrance hall, just a few covered candles suspended on chains from the walls. Milkstone was a strange thing. In the day it seemed to store the light; in the night it gave it back. Bram had little time for wonder, for already the warrior had disappeared around a corner and Bram knew that if he didn't follow closely he'd be lost. The groundfloor of the Milkhouse had been built as maze to confuse enemies, and to the untrained eye every turn and corridor looked the same. He had been here before, on the night his brother had negotiated for manpower with Wrayan Castlemilk, the Milk chief, but it still looked new to him. Somewhere on this floor he knew there must be halls and chambers but all he saw was endless corridors and a single white door.

The warrior led him through the roundhouse and then out the other side to a kitchen block that had been built on to the exterior wall. A half-dozen long oak tables were laid side by side with plank benches running between them. About a third of them were occupied by Castlemen, women and children, eating supper, rolling dice, drinking beer, shining armor, honing blades and stitching cloth. Mothers were braiding their children's hair, talking with mouths full of pins to other mothers. Some were coaxing babies to eat spoons of lumpy oat mush. A handful of clan maids were sitting prettily, buffing their fingernails with raw felt and popping stars of sugared anise between discreetly stained lips. All stopped what they were doing to turn and look at Bram.

"For Ione's sake! It's Robbie's brother alright. You've had a good look now get back to . . . your," words failed the warrior accompanying Bram and he made an all-inclusive gesture with his big, muscled arm, "dooderlings."

Laugher erupted from the table containing the Castlemen warriors. "Dooderlings, Pol?" chipped up some large, grizzled hatchetman, "that'a new one to me." More laughter followed, and this time women and children joined in.

Pol glared back; he didn't seem especially annoyed. "C'mon, boy," he said to Bram. "Supper. Set yourself down over there and I'll see what cook can manage."

Bram did just that, walking past the table of clan maids to the place at the back indicated by Pol. His cheeks were hot and he felt a bit dazed by all the life spread out before him. It had been a long time since he'd been in an informal kitchen hall like this one, and the presence of women befuddled him. One of the maids, a round-faced girl with raven-dark hair, shot out a hand and poked his leg as he passed. High, pretty laugher followed. Bram reckoned she must have done it on a dare.

Bram found his place and sat. When he looked back at the clan maids he found them all staring at him. With little titters of delighted embarrassment they looked away.

"Here you go." Pol slid a wooden board in front of Bram. "It's fry night. We're in luck."

Fried radishes, fried bread and rabbit fried in breadcrumbs were piled high in two bowls. Pol took the largest for himself and began to eat. Bram, suddenly realizing how hungry he was and how little he had consumed these past seven days, did likewise. The food was good and hot and plain. Watered ale helped it down.

As Bram was sucking on the last of the rabbit bones, a Castleman detached himself from the group at the far table and walked over toward them. It was the head warrior, Wrayan Castlemilk's right hand; Bram recognized him from the night in the Brume Hall. Bram put down the bone and stood to greet him. Such a man was due respect.

"Set down now," the warrior said evenly. He was of middle height and middle age, and he was powerful around the chest and beginning to loosen in the gut. A vial containing his measure of milkstone suspended in water hung from a waxed string around his neck. "I'm Harald Mawl and on behalf of my chief I welcome you, Bram Cormac son of Mabb, to this clan."

Bram's throat tightened; he wasn't sure why. The head warrior of Castlemilk stood before him and he didn't want to make a mistake. With a small cough, he replied, "I thank you, Harald Mawl. Castlemilk is the clan that walks swords and I am glad to have come."

Harald nodded once, gruff but satisfied, and then turned with some formality and walked away.

"C'mon," Pol said, standing. "Let's find you a cot for the night."

Bram was led back into the dome of the roundhouse. The clan maids were quiet as he left. After climbing a narrow flight of stairs and walking along a circular gallery that was open to the hall below, Pol halted and nodded his head toward a plain white door. "Chief expects you at dawn," he said in parting.

For a moment Bram just stood and looked at the door. The wood was fine-grained birch stained with lime. A pull ring forged from powdered iron was fixed to the wood by a fox-head plate. The White Fox of Castlemilk. Pulling the ring back he discovered a tiny fan-shaped cell with a wooden sleeping box laid with a thin mattress and two goatskins. A single covered candle burned on the near wall, and the only other items in the room were a filled water pitcher and leather bucket. Bram entered and closed the door. As he sat on the bed he wondered if feeling glad to be alone was a character flaw.

After spitting on his fingers he reached toward the candle. And then killed the light. He thought he'd better try and sleep, but his words to Harald Mawl worried him and he hoped he hadn't spoken a lie. *I am glad to have come.* Yet Bram wasn't sure how he felt. Arriving, he had expected . . . less. He had not anticipated this living, breathing clan. When he had spent time here during the winter it had been at the Tower on the Milk, a league to the east. Outfitted as a makeshift barracks, the broken tower had been far removed from the warmth and vibrancy of the Milkhouse. And Wrayan Castlemilk had shrewdly limited the Dhoonesmen's access to her hearth.

Bram pulled the goatskins all the way up to his chin. They were old and no longer smelled of goats, just dust. As he lay there, looking out, he realized it wasn't wholly dark. The milk-stone glowed. He fell asleep, and for once he did not dream about his brother Robbie. Just the milkstone.

He awoke to the strange thuds and calls of a foreign clan. Close by a door was shut with force. Someone shouted, "Blade court at dawn!" Someone else shouted back, "Go away and let me sleep!"

Bram rose and scrubbed the sleep from his eyes. His possessions were in Gabbie's saddlebags, so he couldn't do much about his hair, clothes or teeth. Plucking at the front panel of his tunic, he brought it to his nose and sniffed. Not good. And today he had to meet a chief. Drastic action was called for. Lifting the water pitcher high, he emptied its contents over his head. It felt cold and good. Maybe it would help with the smell.

After he aired the goatskins and relieved himself Bram headed downstairs to find the Milk chief. Clanfolk were up and about, sweeping corridors, dousing torches, chasing children, carrying buckets of fresh water up through the house and slop buckets down to the river, buckling armor as they raced toward weapons practice and hauling packs as they made their way to the stables. Most people ignored Bram, though one or two glanced at his blue cloak. Last night as Pol was showing him to his cell, Bram had made sure to memorize the route. It was an easy thing for him, for once he saw something he seldom forgot it, and he had no problem finding his way back to the kitchen. From there he headed left toward the entrance hall. Outside the sun was rising, and he quickly learned how to orient himself in the maze that formed the groundfloor of the Milkhouse. Exterior walls appeared brighter to the eye than interior, dividing walls. It was a fact that wouldn't do him any good at night, he realized, but was surprisingly useful at dawn when you knew the sunlight was coming in from the east.

The Oyster Doors were flung wide open and a stiff breezing was blowing off the Milk. A crew of swordsmen had gathered on the wide steps outside the entrance hall and Bram looked to see if one of them might be Pol. They were big men, with graying hair and deeply lined faces, their bodies toughened by decades of hard work. Some were wearing cloaks pieced together from white fox pelts and others had fox-head brooches fastened at their throats. All carried the one-handed fighting swords Castlemilk was known for, the curved knuckleguards and finger rings clearly visible above the tops of their scabbards.

Unable to locate Pol, Bram asked the nearest swordsman where he might find the chief. The man was sitting with his back against the doorframe, picking gravel from the sole of his boot. He did not look up as he said, "Chief's out back, paying her respects."

Bram hiked over the man's legs and went outside. Sunlight glinting off the river dazzled him and it took a moment for his eyesight to clear. The white sand on the landing beach was blowing across the grass and onto the gravel road that led from the river to the roundhouse. On the far shore, hemlocks and black spruce murmured as they moved in the wind. Turning his back on the dark and glossy trees, Bram headed up the path that ran along the roundhouse's exterior wall. He could feel his hair drying as he walked.

When he rounded the rear quadrant of the Milkhouse he spied Wrayan Castlemilk, the Milk chief, in the distance, standing alone. A quarter-league north of the path, beyond the orderly beds of the kitchen gardens, the hard standings, training courts, eel tanks, pigsties and cattle pens lay a large, white-walled enclosure. The gate leading to the enclosure was open and Wrayan Castlemilk stood just beyond the threshold with her back to the roundhouse. Although the wind was still high, her silver cloak did not move: stones must have been sewn into the hem.

Muscles in Bram's stomach loosened. He had heard of Castlemilk's gravepool and wondered if it was proper to approach it. The sheen of water was clearly visible on either side of Wrayan Castlemilk, and as Bram watched she knelt down and leaned forward. He continued walking toward the pool, curious and cautious, passing a children's court that had been colored with orange and blue chalk, and a mulched and caned vegetable bed, before coming to a halt thirty paces before the wall.

Unlike the roundhouse, the wall enclosing the gravepool was built from simple baked bricks, not milkstone, and it had not aged well. Green mold grew at the base and mortar had worn away leaving deep cracks around the bricks. One of the gateposts was listing, and the gate itself had been hastily stained with the same matte limewash as the wall. A fox head, deeply carved into the wood, was its only decoration.

Beyond the gate, Wrayan Castlemilk rose to her feet and brushed dirt from her cloak. Her right hand glistened with water. Turning, she saw Bram. With a small crook of her wrist she beckoned him forward and then waited, motionless, as he approached.

"Welcome," she said once he had come to a halt. "I had expected you sooner."

Bram's face flushed with blood, and he was about to apologize when he remembered his brother Robbie's contempt for people who tried to explain their actions. *A king has no use for sorry.*

Wrayan Castlemilk watched Bram, her brown eyes shrewd and thoughtful. She was the second-longest-reigning chief in the clanholds and had ruled Castlemilk for nearly thirty years.

Bram could not guess how old she was. Her face was unlined, though her waist-length braid was equal parts red and gray. "Our guide, Drouse Ogmore, is acquainted with Robbie's new guide at Dhoone. Both men keep birds, in the manner of the old clans, and it is not unknown for messages to pass between them." The chief raised a cool eyebrow. "So if a boy was to leave Dhoone for Castlemilk and arrive ten days late Drouse, and therefore I, might know it."

Aware he was being reprimanded, Bram bowed his head.

"Come, Bram Cormac," Wrayan said. "Take a walk with me around the pool." She did not wait for him, and began walking a circuit of the artificial lake.

It was a perfect circle, about eighty feet in diameter. Only a three-foot grass verge separated the lake from the wall that enclosed it. Bram was nervous as he followed the chief's footsteps, worried that some errant impulse might make him leap into the water.

And that was one place he did not want to be.

He could see the lead coffins, dozens of them, lying beneath nine feet of water. Round and encrusted with mussels, they looked like pale, ghostly boulders. Bram wondered how the bodies of the Castlemilk chiefs had been fitted inside them, and didn't very much like the answer he came up with.

"Skerro Castlemilk, the Winter chief, used to farm the mussels and eat them." Wrayan came to a halt by the edge. "He went insane. Some say it was the lead."

Bram could think of no suitable response. He frowned at the water, hoping to look serious and alert.

Wrayan Castlemilk did not appear to notice. "The milkstone silt at the bottom is nearly a foot deep. At one time it was custom to have a boy stir it every day with a paddle so it looked as if the caskets were submerged in milk." She smiled flatly at Bram. Sunlight sparkling off the shoulders of her silver cloak threw a strange brightness upon her face. "My brother Alban lies here, though he swore every day of his life that he did not wish to end up in this pool. Once a chief is dead, though, he has no say over his clan, his body. His sister."

She had ordered her brother buried here against his wishes, Bram realized.

Wrayan acknowledged Bram's expression with a small nod. "Someone will do it to me one day, order my body cut and sunk. It is the Milk way, and a clan is nothing without its ways. Dhoone, Blackhail, Bludd: what do you think makes them different?" A tiny movement of her wrist indicated that Bram need not bother formulating an answer: the Milk chief would supply one for him. "Our customs are the only things that separate us from other clans. We worship the same gods, abide by the same laws, want the same thing. It is in the small details that we forge an identity as clan; boasts we speak, weapons we carry, the manner in which we dispose of our dead. Twenty-eight years ago, when given a choice between betraying Alban and betraying the customs of this clan, there was only one answer for me. I am chief. If I fail to uphold the old ways I diminish us." She gave him a cold look, a warning, before continuing.

"Castlemilk is an old and proud clan, Bram Cormac, and I am an old and proud chief. We dance the swords, and mix our guidestone with oil and water and drink it like milk. Our best warriors fight with two swords and name themselves the Cream, and our girl children are taught one new way how to kill a man every year until they reach sixteen. We have been sworn to Dhoone for four hundred years but before that we stood alone. If you believe you have come to a lesser clan you are mistaken and you can march yourself right back to Dhoone. I will have you only on one term: and that is absolute loyalty to Castlemilk. Drouse is in the guidehouse, waiting upon my word. He expects to hear an oath and so do I."

She paused, her chest rising and falling beneath the fine silver weave of her cloak. For the first time Bram noticed the elk lore, fastened to the cinch of her braid. A thick hoop of spine. "I will leave you now," she said, her voice calm. "You have a quarter-hour, then you will either make your way to the guidehouse or collect your belongings and depart this clan."

Bram nodded once in understanding and she left him standing by the man-dug lake. A moment passed and then something—a fish or an eel—broke the surface of the water, flashed briefly, then was gone. Bram wasn't sure but he thought he saw teeth.

Clouds heading in from the north were moving swiftly

toward the sun and he could tell it wouldn't be long before they killed the sunlight. For no good reason whatsoever he drew his sword and stood on the grass and inspected it in the last of the full sun. Light on the watered steel moved upblade toward the point. He tried angling the sword in different directions but he could not get it to move the other way.

"It won't be so bad, Bram. We both know you were never really cut out for Dhoone." Robbie's parting words sounded in Bram's head.

No going back.

Abruptly, he sheathed the sword and headed out of the walled enclosure. He had made his decision.

EIGHTEEN
The Birch Way

It was the fourth day amongst the birches. The mist that had formed overnight rolled through the forest in breaking waves. It was a landscape of ghosts, pale and silvery, with nothing green or blue to be seen. The trees disappeared into the clouds, their straight white trunks the same thickness from base to crown. Hundreds of thousands of birches had seeded from a single mother tree, and the dark charcoal-colored scars where limbs had broken off were the only way of distinguishing one tree from another. Minute differences in spacing and light had produced branches at differing angles and heights, and the marks they'd left behind dappled the bark like pawprints. Lan Fallstar read these prints, and they appeared to provide him with enough information to navigate the unchanging landscape of the birch way.

Ash March tracked the Far Rider's gaze as it jumped from tree to tree, noting the birches it settled upon and attempting to discern a pattern in Lan's choices.

They were walking their horses through the mist. The sun was a diffused steel disk low in the east. The air was damply cold. Underfoot the snow was wet and uneven. Ash had learned it hid potholes and pools of standing water. She was cautious as she placed her feet. The birches had grown on low-lying saturated topsoil, not all of it frozen. Often brown water oozed from the snow as she stepped upon it. Other times her feet would sense give followed by traction followed by more give, as the soles of her boots pushed through sloppy layers of snow, sedge, water, mud and dead leaves. Today she could not see her feet and relied upon following Lan's path as closely as possible.

She had not realized it would be such a long journey through the trees. Nor had she imagined that walking through them could make her feel as if she were imprisoned. The birches were like iron bars. Fifty feet tall and stripped bare of leaves, they stretched in all directions as far as the eye could see.

She could not escape them, not on her own. While she was here she was dependent upon Lan Fallstar. If the Far Rider were to walk away and leave her she could be lost forever in these trees. Every birch and square foot of land looked the same. She had tried to apply what little she knew of the Sull path lores, looking for chips in the bark two feet off the ground, double nailheads sunk into the wood that looked like beetle holes until you stopped and inspected them, and subtle yellow burns in the tree moss where flames had been brushed against them in curving motions to form moon-shapes, but she had yet to spot anything so far. Most blazes did not seem to apply here. She knew the Sull often selected a single branch on a tree, stripped it bare of twigs and leaves and used it as a signpost to point the way of a trail, but the spindly crowns of the birches were as good as bare to begin with. And the slim, branchless trunks would be almost impossible to climb without spiked boots or ladders. They offered no footholds or handholds to aid an ascent. Rock blazes, bush blazes and fallen log blazes did not seem to apply either, as there was not a single fallen log, bush or rock to be seen in the entire forest. Snow, sedge and trees: they were its only features.

She had noticed osprey nests in some trees, big whirlwind-shaped constructions built out of twigs and scraps of sedge, and had spotted frequent elk and bear tracks, but although she suspected there was something to be learned from their presence she was unsure what that might be. Ark Veinsplitter would have helped her if he'd lived, explained how it was possible to navigate this land of phantom trees. He had made her Sull, drained her human blood to make way for Sull blood. He would have trusted her with the secrets of the birch way.

Lan Fallstar did not. She had asked him outright last night as they'd made a miserable and tentless camp in the mist. The fire had slowly reddened and died, suffocated by the film of mist that coated every log. "How do you find your way here?" she had said. "I should know in case anything happens to you."

The Far Rider had been rubbing clarified horse fat into the crusted and canyonlike burn on his left arm. He stopped and turned his deeply angled face toward her and said, "Nothing will happen."

"That's no answer."

The horse grease was stowed in a horn of fossilized ivory and he sealed it before speaking, thumping a stopper into the opening with the heel of his hand. "This Sull does not believe he has need to answer questions."

She had not argued with him. The tone of his voice was clear enough. He believed her to be an outsider, and he was right. In a way she could not fault him. The one clear thing she understood about the Sull was that they believed themselves to be a people under threat. They had once claimed the vast continent to the south; glass deserts, warm seas, city ports, rain forests, salt flats, marble islands, grasslands, high steppes, vast snaking rivers and mountains so tall their peaks could only be seen on a handful of days each year. And then there were the places beyond this continent, places with names that sounded alien and threatening to Ash. The Unholy Sea. Sankang. The Spoiled Lands. Balgaras. The Ore Islands. All this and more had once belonged to the Sull. Now they were reduced to a strip of land in the Northern Territories, perhaps a third of a continent.

And they lived in fear they would lose it. Ash had grown up hearing stories of the Sull's ruthlessness. Tales of the bloody battle at Hell's Core, where the Sull slaughtered the Vor king's son and ten thousand of his men and then refused to allow Vorish priests onto the battlefield to collect the bodies; tales of the massacre of innocents at Clan Gray where eight hundred women and children were killed in under an hour for daring to set foot on Sull land; and tales of the great burning of ships on the Sea of Souls where thirty-one vessels went down with all hands. What she had not heard at Mask Fortress was the other side of the tale. Of Sull dispossession and defeats, and of their great and driving fear they would one day lose their home. Every slaughter they carried out was defensive.

Ash raised a hand as she passed one of the trees and touched its flaking and silvery trunk. These birches were part of the Sull's defenses. They were an impenetrable wall guarding a vulnerable portion of its western border, and it wasn't surprising that Lan Fallstar would not share their secret with someone who claimed to be Sull, yet neither acted nor looked like Sull.

Glancing at the Far Rider, she wondered why she hadn't told him about Ark Veinsplitter and Mal Naysayer, about the mountain pool where she had been made Sull, and about her journey east across the margins of the Want. There was still a chance that the Naysayer was tracking both of them . . . and she hadn't mentioned that either. Lan had not asked about how she had come to be in the Racklands south of the Flow, and she wondered about that also. What did he know or assume about her? She tried to think back to the moment she had given him her name. She had been so nervous, so determined to stand her ground, that she had not thought to read his reaction. Had it meant something to him? Had word of Ash March, the Reach, traveled ahead of her?

Lan Fallstar was walking beside his fine black stallion and occasionally he would raise his hand to touch the horse's neck. He was dressed in serviceable riding clothes, deerhide coat and pants, a cloak collared in marten, and stiff boar's-hide boots. If he had been wearing a hat he might have passed at distance for a ranger or hunter. His black hair, gleaming with bone oil and part braided with lead clasps, gave him away. A bluish tint flashed when the sun hit it. That, together with the lead clasps that had weathered to a color and texture not unlike the surface of the moon, pronounced him as Sull. Only when you drew closer did you see the faint goldenness of his skin and the deep triangular shadows cast by his cheekbones upon his cheeks.

He knew she was minding him, yet said nothing and did not turn. Ash wished she were the sort of person who found conversation easy, who could say the kind of interesting and clever things that left people wanting to reply. Right now she could think of nothing but trees. Trees and more trees. And as they all looked the same she could hardly say, *Look at that one. Isn't it unusual?*

Frowning she kicked up the mist and watched as it swirled like grease on water. She wondered why she didn't trust him.

And he didn't trust her.

"How long before we leave the birches?" she asked.

Something about his shrug made Ash think he'd had it ready and waiting. "The birch way is long and not all paths are open. We travel as we must."

Snow squelched beneath Ash's feet and she lifted the hem of her lynx fur off the ground. The Far Rider had told her nothing, and she doubted whether the subject was worth pursuing but went ahead and spoke anyway. "How long did it take you last time?"

He turned to look at her, his expression cool. It took a moment before she realized that this look was to be his only reply.

Just like her foster father. Penthero Iss seldom deigned to answer questions he judged beneath him. It was a fact she had realized early on. As a young girl she'd worked hard to ask her foster father intelligent questions. Why did the ambassador from Ille Glaive ask not to be seated next to the Whitehog at dinner? If the crop fails in the eastern bread plains where would the city buy its grain? She'd wanted to please him so badly, wanted desperately to hear those rare words of praise: *Almost-daughter, you're such a good girl.*

Halting memories of her foster father before they could hurt her, Ash rubbed the nose of her gelding. On a whim, she held the horse back, opening some space between herself and Lan Fallstar. Gray mist poured in to fill it.

Why did she feel the need to talk to him? And why was she disappointed when he dismissed her? She didn't understand it. His coldness should be repellent, but it wasn't.

Suddenly she missed Ark and Mal very much. While she was with them she felt as if she were part of something. Included. They might have only revealed a small portion of their knowledge and secrets, but it was enough to give her hope that over time she would learn more. Ark Veinsplitter and Mal Naysayer were the reason she had become Sull. The two Far Riders were honorable and full of purpose, and she had assumed that all Sull were the same. Lan Fallstar was different. He kept her on the outside, withholding information. Keeping secrets.

She'd played this game before with Penthero Iss. Her foster father had been a master at keeping secrets. For seventeen years he'd concealed the true reason he'd adopted her as his daughter. Was something similar happening here? Did Lan know she was the Reach?

Ash watched as Lan rode ahead of her into the mist. If he suspected she was more than she appeared, he was doing a fine job of feigning ignorance. He treated her as if she were a lesser being; someone just pretending to be Sull. Last night when she had asked Lan to raise the small wolfskin tent he carried in one of his saddlebags, he had told her they would sleep out in the open. "If you want to lie in this mist then go ahead," she had replied. "I'll sleep in the tent."

"No," he had told her coldly. "Sull need no cover on a full moon."

It had felt like a slap in the face. If there was a custom here she was not familiar with, why could he not simply explain it? Why did he treat her with contempt? And why did she let it hurt her?

She had spent a miserable night, rolled in her cloak and drowned in vapor. When she'd woken, her hair was glistening with thousands of tiny drops of moisture. The Far Rider was sitting on his saddlebag, facing southeast. Fingers of mist were curling past his blank and open eyes. As soon as she moved he stirred. His face was pale, the skin around the jaw oddly slack. He asked her to tend to the horses while he rebuilt the fire. She had been eager to do his bidding.

By the time she'd returned from feeding, watering and brushing down the horses Lan was back to his normal self. He did not speak to her as they ate their breakfast of dried horsemeat and raw and fertilized snipe eggs.

Disappointed, Ash had looked out at the prison of trees and wondered when she would see the end of them. The first night she had met Lan Fallstar, he had warned her about the birches. What day had he said the insanity set in? She knew he had been referring to a person traveling alone and without knowledge, but she felt it anyway. He rarely spoke to her, and as she had no understanding of how the forest was laid out she was left with the dizzying sense that she was walking the same path over and over again. It was as if the birches were revolving in a great wheel around her. She had no way of gauging her progress.

Today, with the mist swirling at knee height and the clouds low and hazy, the world had been reduced to a band of stakes. She couldn't even carry out her normal job, which was to collect any stray branches that had snapped from the trees—she could not see the forest floor. From time to time, she would step on a branch, snapping it in two, and would pick it up and add it to the bundle on the gelding's rump. She had a sense that by gathering the fallen branches she was doing more than merely collecting firewood. The task had the feeling of housekeeping about it. It was as if by removing any identifiable marks, she was maintaining the birch way. When she had asked Lan about this his only reply had been "It is forbidden to cut down the birches."

Ash wished she knew more about the Sull. Her lack of knowledge made her vulnerable. Right now she existed at Lan's mercy, and she did not know enough about men and Sull to judge whether this made her safe or unsafe. She did not know her own worth.

She knew he watched sometimes; when she slipped off her cloak and dress to wash and sleep, when she rubbed grease into her arms and legs, and loosened her hair. During her final year in Mask Fortress, she had grown accustomed to frank attention from men. Some had told her she was beautiful, others had whistled as she rode across the quad. She had not disliked the attention. Sometimes she had even invited more of it. It gave her an intoxicating little thrill of power.

Whenever she caught Lan watching her she made a point of prolonging whatever action she had been doing. She was not fully Sull and he disdained her for that fact; but here was something that she had that he desired. There was more to it than that, though. That was the confusing thing. She felt attraction toward him too.

Whenever they shared the small wolfskin tent she found herself thinking about him. The tent was raised on a frame of hollow canes and the skins had been expertly cut and stitched to fit it snugly and seal out rain and wind. When you were inside you felt closed off from the world. Light coming in through the skins was amber and golden and strangely shaped; the skins acted like stained glass. The sleeping space was small, perhaps eight feet by six, and when they were both lying within it, Ash became herself acutely self-aware. Roll over just half a foot and she would touch him. The thought disturbed and excited her, and two nights back when they had last shared the tent she had spent several hours awake, resisting the urge to push herself closer. Even through the thickness of her blankets and furs she could feel his warmth. Or imagined she felt it. She also imagined that he was in the same state of awareness that she herself was. There was a false evenness to his breaths, not unlike her own, and a stillness to his body that seemed too controlled for someone who slept.

When Ash awoke in the morning she saw that the half-foot of space separating them from each other had been expertly maintained.

They had not shared a tent since then, but even this morning as she washed her face and neck with snow he had watched her through the flames of the fire. Later as he helped her saddle the gelding he had leant in toward her as she leant toward the horse and she had felt his hand touch her hip. It could have been an innocent miscalculation, but Lan Fallstar did not strike her as the kind of person who would mistake what he did with his body.

The touch had left her in a queer state of shock and restlessness. She was beginning to think the birches were getting to her. Nothing was making any sense. If Lan had wanted to touch her why hadn't he just come out and done it openly? And why had he treated her with contempt since then, answering her questions with the shortest possible responses and sometimes not even answering at all?

Ash ran her hands down her long blond hair, wringing it free of mist. The gap between her and Lan Fallstar had widened and she found herself not anxious to close it. It had to be close to midday now yet the sun remained a distant and shadowy presence keeping pace with them through the trees, and the mist continued to thrive. She was only just beginning to comprehend how little she knew of anything in the world beyond Mask Fortress. Her maid Katia had coupled with dozens of men—and she had been a year younger than Ash. Katia would have known what to make of Lan Fallstar's behavior. She would have taken charge of things and turned the situation to her best advantage. Ash paused to think about that. No, Katia wouldn't have really acted that coldly. She had enjoyed coupling with men. "Sweet and delicious as peaches," she'd told Ash once. "You should try it when you get the chance."

Flustered, Ash set aside the subject. She glared at the trees. She was beginning to hate them. The ground was spongy here. It was strange to crunch through hard snow and then feel the earth spring back. Perhaps that was one way Lan navigated, the texture of the earth beneath his feet.

Deciding she'd had enough walking, Ash stilled the gelding and mounted. The sound of leather snapping and metal striking metal broke the silence like a series of small explosive charges. She had not realized how quiet the forest was until that moment. Birds weren't even calling.

"Stay where you are." Lan Fallstar's voice came from a white and hazy point in the distance.

She could not see him, even with the extra height of the horse. With an expert adjustment of the reins she turned the gelding in the direction she hoped was east. Away from Lan Fallstar. The sturdy little horse seemed up for a trot and struck a path through the mist. The crowns of the birches were so high that hitting branches wasn't a problem, and the birches themselves were spaced well enough apart that a way through could be navigated at a trot. It felt good to ride away. She had agreed to become Sull at an unknowable cost to herself and Raif Sevrance. She had not agreed to trot behind a Sull Far Rider like a dog.

She was Ash March, foundling, left outside Vaingate to die. That had not drained away with her blood. She was almost-daughter to a surlord, and that had not changed either.

Ark Veinsplitter and Mal Naysayer had treated her with respect. *Daughter*, Ark had called her. Lan Fallstar didn't even use her name. So why was she so anxious to please him?

It was all very confusing. Like the birch way. Glancing around, Ash realized she had no way of telling how far she and the gelding had come. Every tree looked like the one she had just passed. A stirring of wind had made the mist choppy, and clouds sprayed up in loose waves. Slowing the gelding to walk she breathed it in and tried to calm herself.

She could hear no sound of pursuit. Now that the heat was leaving her she felt foolish and a bit afraid. Would it be possible to retrace her steps? A look over her shoulder revealed a landscape of haunted trees. If Lan Fallstar stood amongst them he was hidden by the mist.

The stubborn part of her wanted to continue on her path, just carry on going and somehow muscle her way out, but the practical part warned her to go back now while she was still pretty certain how far she had come. This was Sull land, she reminded herself. She could not be entirely sure that the mystery of the birches was purely physical. Strange sorceries might be woven between the trunks. Ark had told her about the Sull *maygi* and necromancers, men and women who birthed ancient magics by the dark of moon and lived apart in high sea caves and open towers. It would be only natural that such powers be used in defending the one thing they cared about above all others: defending their borders. What if she could never escape?

"Come on, boy," she said, kicking her heels into the gelding's belly and making the creature turn. This wasn't going to be pretty, having to return to Lan Fallstar with her tail between her legs, but it would be a lot less pretty if she turned insane and started loving the trees.

It took her over an hour to find him. Lan Fallstar was leaning against a birch, peeling an apple with her sickle knife. The knife's weighted chain swung lazily between his legs as he cut a continuous strip from the fruit. He studied Ash as she approached but did not speak. Ash pressed her lips together and made herself busy dismounting the gelding, removing its bit, and loosening its belly cinch.

"This Sull hopes you enjoyed your ride."

Ash had been in the process of unfastening the saddle straps and she had her back toward the Far Rider. She paused, fingers on the brass buckles, and thought of several ways to reply. None of them friendly. He had known she would come back. This annoyed her. She was annoyed also by the fact that he was using the knife that had been given to her as a gift by Ark Veinsplitter.

As she turned to give him a piece of her mind, he held the

peeled apple and the knife out toward her and said, "They are yours." His sharply beautiful face was hard to read. "Take them."

Ash came forward and stopped a few feet before him, suddenly awkward. He pushed himself off the tree and took the remaining steps to meet her. Holding out his palms he offered her the apple and the knife. The exposed meat of the apple was starting to brown. If there was a trap here she could not discern what it might be. Quickly she took the items from him. Their hands and wrists touched briefly, and the contact and the whole situation felt so confusing she had to turn away.

"You can give the apple to the horse. This Sull will not be offended."

Surprised by the humor in his voice, she looked over her shoulder. Lan Fallstar was smiling, and it was such a warm and unexpected sight that she smiled right back at him. She was aware of an immense sense of relief, but hardly knew why.

"When two people are parted in the birch way it is best if one stays close to the original point. That way it becomes possible for the second person to find her way back."

Ash nodded softly. After days of short and impatient replies, his explanation seemed like a kindness. Now it was she who had nothing to say to him, and she wrapped the chain carefully around the sickle blade's handle and went to feed the apple to the gelding.

Not long after that they headed on their way. The mist was finally breaking up and cold white sunlight slanted through the birches. Lan's pace was a fraction slower than before and she found herself drawing abreast of him more often. Briefly Ash wondered why they had to walk the birch way and could not ride. She thought about asking him, but stopped herself. She did not want to test this new goodwill between them.

With the mist gone the birches began to gleam like bones. Thousands became visible, layers and layers of trees stretching toward the horizon on all sides. Ash was glad to see her feet and found herself looking at them often. The variety of materials squelched by her boots was the only thing that changed in the landscape. The air smelled faintly of methane, and she wondered if part of the birch way was a bog. If they strayed too far off course here might they sink? For a while she tracked Lan's gaze as it slid through the trees, hoping to discover something about his methods of navigation, but she lost interest after a while.

Her hands and wrists still felt hot where he had touched them.

Lan said, "Let us stop here."

It was earlier than they would normally stop, but Ash was glad. She was hungry, and tired of looking at trees. As she unstrapped the fallen timber she had collected, the Far Rider set about unpacking his saddlebags. When she realized he was sliding out the tent, muscles in her stomach contracted in a way that made her feel half sick and half excited. Fumbling with the logs, she managed to drop a couple against the gelding's back hoof. "Sorry," she told the horse, kneeling awkwardly to pick them up.

After she'd built the fire and lit it she waited to feel more relaxed. The ground was dry here and she threw down her saddle and sat on it. Lan had finished pitching the tent and was now preparing their supper. She had come to him empty-handed—her saddlebags had been lost south of the Flow—and she was dependent upon his cooking utensils and food to eat. When she had met him she had been living on horse blood for seven days.

Lan cut up slices of cured horsemeat and dried mushrooms and put them in a pot with rich yellow kidney fat, cardamom seeds, and snowmelt. He worked quickly and with precision, using the same knife he had burned his skin with the night they first met. When he was done he cleaned the blade with oil that smelled of cloves, and a scrap of deerskin, and then sat in silence while the water in the pot came to a boil. A full moon rose as they waited.

"Take," Lan said, holding out a bowl of steaming and fragrant soup. She took it and their fingertips touched across the smooth glazed warmth of the bowl. The Far Rider watched her take her first drink. "Good?" he inquired, his voice almost gruff.

She nodded. It was bitter and rich with fat. She drank it all and then took her knife and speared the meat and fleshy mushrooms left at the bottom. It must have given her courage, for she said, "Why put up the tent? The moon is still full." Blood came to her face as she asked the question and she wished she could take it back. It seemed bold and reckless. And he would make her pay for it.

Lan set down his soup, long fingers carefully cupping the bowl. The lead clasps in his hair clicked together as he moved. "It is the first day of the full moon that is most sacred. We cannot count ourselves Sull unless we feel its light upon our faces thirteen days a year." His voice was stiff but she recognized he had made an effort.

She wanted to know more, but had no way of gauging how long his new patience would last so she said nothing further. When she leaned toward the fire and poured herself more soup it seemed to please him. Absurdly she felt glad.

Later, as she rose to tend the gelding, he stood also. "I will feed and water your horse," he said. "It is owed."

From this morning? How could such a small thing incur debt? Baffled, she bowed her head, and watched as he crossed to the area where the horses where pulling seaweedlike sedge from beneath the snow. After a few moments her gaze jumped to the tent.

She breathed deeply and went for a pee. Squatting in the shadows behind the tent, she hiked up her cloak and dress and relieved herself. When she was done she took a handful of snow and rubbed it between her legs.

When she emerged into the light of the campfire her face and neck were icy and dripping; she had washed them for good measure as well. Glancing at the Far Rider she saw that he was intent on picking out twigs from the hoofs of his stallion. He did not look up as she slipped inside the tent.

It was cool in here, and smelled of wolf. Light from the moon pierced pin-size holes in the skins. Quickly Ash stripped off her clothes and made a bed for herself out of blankets and furs. Snuggling down she curled into a ball. And told herself she wasn't waiting.

She felt peculiarly excited by her makeshift preparations. Their practicality seemed audacious. In her mind she had borrowed some forwardness from Katia. It seemed necessary.

Time passed and the pinholes of light changed angles. Noises occasionally sounded from outside; horses blowing air, the hiss of snow on the fire, the mournful call of the great white owl. Ash listened intently at first, her body shivering with rest-lessness and cold, but when every new sound failed to produce Lan Fallstar she gave up. It didn't seem possible but eventually she slept.

Her dreams were of the grayness that touched everything yet no one but she could see. The creatures that bided there uncurled their rotting limbs and claws as she passed. Some hissed. They watched her with narrow and glinting eyes, glad that she had not come in the flesh. Beyond them, a dark and immense presence was moving just beyond her perception. She felt its great age and momentum, and perceived the utter coldness of its purpose. *Mistressss*, it called through shadows that swarmed it like wasps. *Do not wake*.

Ash awoke. She was not alone. Lan Fallstar lay beside her, his body still, his breathing metered. The moon had set but it was not wholly dark; starlight blued the tent.

What am I? Ash wondered. She had been told she was a Reach by Heritas Cant and Ark Veinsplitter, but she did not know what that meant. She was shaking, she realized, her chest and stomach vibrating intensely. *Do not wake*. The words had been a warning. Did that mean the creatures in the Blind were afraid of her? Why? Ark had hinted that she could track the shadow beasts, perceive them over distance. Was that reason enough?

Teeth chattering, she rolled over, twisting the blankets and lynx fur around her body. She felt icy cold. The nightmare had sucked away her warmth.

Do not wake.

She reached for Lan Fallstar in the dim blue light of the tent. She hardly knew what she was doing but she craved his warmth and was desperate to feel his live body pressing against hers. He gasped as she touched him, and she felt him hesitate. He had not been asleep, she was sure of that. A moment passed where he might have moved away from her, where his hands were up and touching her hands and it would have been a small thing for him to push back. He did not push back. Instead he sighed sharply, parting his hands and sliding them down to her waist. A quick, almost violent flexing of muscle brought her next to him. Ash smelled him, the alienness of his skin and sweat. As he thrust through blankets and furs to grab her buttocks she kissed him. Her mouth was wet and full of saliva and it coated his lips before he opened them to kiss her back. Their teeth knocked together with an odd dissonance, and it slowed her for a moment. Lan's hand was moving between her thighs now and she could not understand why it was taking so long to reach where it needed to be. Her sex was hot and wet. It ached, literally *ached*, to be touched.

He did not taste human and that excited her. As she curled her tongue against the roof of his mouth he slid his hand against her sex. Ash opened her legs wider. Her tongue stiffened. Hot pulses passed along her belly. One finger found a sweet spot and rubbed it softly but insistently. She could hear the wetness *swish* against his hand. Grabbing him firmly she arched her hips toward him. The finger moved faster, its pressure increasing. With his free hand he squeezed her buttocks, his fingertips jamming into the point where they met. Ash gasped. All she wanted him to do was not stop. The finger was creating delicious friction deep beneath her skin. Suddenly the tension broke and her legs and hips started jerking. Heat pulsed down her thighs and up through her belly and she lost control of herself, grasping at his ribs and pushing against his hand. She did not breathe until it stopped.

Afterward he pulled himself on top of her and pressed his hard sex against her own. As he broke the fine membrane of skin that protected her body and entered her, he murmured, "*Ish'l xalla tannan.*"

I know the value of that which I take.

Outside the tent the wind began to rattle the birches.

NINETEEN

Hunting Prey

Raif reached the city on the edge of the abyss just as the sleet started. Smoke from the cave fires blew in his face. He could not say the familiar scent of burning sedge and willow canes made him glad to be back. He had a strong desire to set down his kit, rest, and not enter, but it was already too late for that.

"Twelve Kill on the ledge!" came the cry from a watcher on the high wind-carved cliff above him. Raif acknowledged the man with an open hand, yet did not look up. Already he could hear the call being relayed across the ledgerock, echoing from cave to cave and ledge to ledge, moving up cane ladders and rock-cut stairs, along tunnels and stone galleries before finally plunging down into the Rift.

"*Kill. Kill. Kill*," Raif heard. His name reduced to a single word.

The children came out first. Skinny and clothed in fine silks and brocades gone to rags, they kept their distance and stared at him with big eyes as if they had reason to be afraid. One older boy bounced a stone in his cupped fist, his tight little mouth twitching. Raif looked him in the eyes, looked long, and the boy caught the stone, closed his fist, and dropped his hand against his side.

The Maimed Men and their women came out next and they were not a lovely sight. Dressed in dyed leather shirts and tunics, animal skins with the heads still attached, armored cloaks, spiked helms, rat-fur hoods, scaled breastplates, steel gauntlets, burned dresses, boned bodices, goat-fleece collars and kilts and all manner of straps, belts, packs and chains, they did their name proud. Every one of them was lacking: a missing eye or arm, a clubfoot, a deformed spine, a cleft palate, a claw hand, a wine-stained face, absent flesh, extra flesh. Things not present at birth and others taken away later. Raif became aware of his own missing flesh—the tip of his little finger, cut off at the knuckle—and wondered if he would ever lose enough of himself to feel at home here. He had a brief but intensely strong desire to run, turn and flee back to the canyonlands and Badlands—places were the land was the only thing that was wasted. The cragsman Addie Gunn's words came back to him. *"None of us are whole."* He had not been speaking about flesh.

Raif walked steadily through the growing crowd, matching gazes only when he had to, when faced with the choice of meeting a challenge or backing down. Beneath the ledge of green rimrock, the Rift was trembling. The vast fissure in the earth was as dark and wet as a fresh wound and it gave off the same metallic odor. Last time he was here he remembered watching birds in flight below him, kitty hawks and swallows and turkey vultures. Today the Rift was full of nothing. It was the deepest hole in the earth and no man alive had ever returned from it. Its bottom could not be seen or known. On the clearest day with the sun directly overhead there was a point beyond which the eye could not see. Raif Sevrance had looked down on such a day, his gaze tracking the cracked and uneven cliffwall, past layers of ironstone, sandstone, limestone, hermit shale, granite, green marble, pyrite slate and schist, past the dark recesses of undercut caves, steam vents, and well heads before finally coming to rest at the point where the darkness rolled and swirled like hot tar finding its level. Raif found it hard to watch and soon looked away. It struck him that it was a moat defending a fastness: a layer that could not be penetrated without sanction.

His shoulders jerked in a single, deep shiver. His clothes were wet and he was sick of traveling. For the past two days he had done nothing but walk. Within the hard shell of his leather boots his feet were wrapped in rags and dried grass. His left ankle was still badly swollen, and a blister on the heel oozed watery blood into the makeshift padding. He knew better than to show this, not here in the city of Maimed Men, and walked without limp or stiffness, keeping his back straight and his hand close to the hilt of his bent sword.

Light was beginning to fail as he approached the center of the rimrock. A firepile had been stacked and primed, and the crowd began to gather around it. Raif spotted the dark and unfriendly face of Linden Moodie, the Rift brother who had led the raid on Black Hole. The garrote scar circling his neck was partially covered by a silver and black wool mantle. Raif met Moodie's gaze, confirming to himself that he was not mistaken. Linden Moodie had deliberately worn his spoils from the raid on Blackhail's silver mine. *I dare you,* his brown eyes challenged, *to show a reaction to the colors of your once and deserted clan.*

Raif did not know what expression was showing on his face, only that it did not change when faced with Moodie. He breathed deeply and allowed only surface thoughts to work upon his brain. He had not expected much coming here. No surprises so far.

"Raif! Over here!"

Tracking the sound of his name, Raif spied the big, powerful form of Stillborn wending his way through a group of Maimed Women. The Rift brother was dressed in a sleeveless buckskin tunic trimmed with rabbit fur. His bare forearms were wrapped in matching bullhorns. Breaking free from the crowd, he brought Raif to a halt by standing in front of him and enveloping him in a giant, smothering bear hug.

"I told the Mole you killed that Hailsman on your way out 'cause he challenged you for the gold," Stillborn murmured insistently in Raif's ear while he gripped him. "And that you told me you were off to take care of a spot of personal business and that you'd be back within a month."

The two men separated, but Stillborn caught Raif's forearms in his fists and held Raif at arm's length while he inspected him. The Maimed Man's hazel eyes were knowing. The puckered flesh that ran along his face and down his neck quivered with strong emotion. "Know two things before this dance starts," he said, his voice low and husky. "One: I am glad you are back. And two: I am your man."

Raif breathed and did not think. *Later*, he told himself. Aware that Stillborn was waiting upon a response, he forced himself to nod. "It's good to see you, Still," he said, knowing it was true only as he spoke.

It was little but Stillborn nodded, satisfied. He was a man well-used to little. Releasing his hold on Raif's ams he said, "I see you bent my sword."

Raif laughed. Of course, ownership of the Forsworn sword had always been a fluid concept between them. When Raif had first met the Maimed Man in the canyonlands, Stillborn had simply taken the sword as his own. Weeks later, on that dark day in Black Hole, Raif had taken it back. "I'd be grateful if you could lend me another one until I can get it straightened."

Even before he'd finished the sentence, Stillborn said, "Done."

"Azziah rin Raif! Well coddle my ravens' eggs and serve them with vinegar. Who'd thought we'd see your fine, handsome face again this side of damnation."

Yustaffa. The fat man with the swordbreaker danced lightly around the firepile, his breast and belly rolls jiggling beneath a fantastical outfit of yellow silk spotted with tufts of horsehair and belted, priestlike, with golden rope. He was carrying something in his chubby fist that he took care to hold level.

Raif did not greet him, but this only caused Yustaffa further delight.

"Lost a little weight, I see," he said, approaching. With a theatrical narrowing of his eyes he reversed himself. "No. I am mistaken. You've gained a little something upon the shoulders." For a moment the eyes were shrewd, and then the veil of spite returned. "What, no kiss? And here was I thinking you'd have missed me."

Some in the crowd tittered. One low-breasted hag shouted, "Ask him where he's been."

Yustaffa threw his free hand in the air and issued a big, showy shrug. "The people have spoken, and who am I to ignore them?" And then for Raif's ears alone, "Such a pathetic little bunch, don't you think?"

Raif reached behind his back and released his pack. Swinging it forward, he let it come to rest in front of his feet. He did not know what to say to Yustaffa, and felt something close to dizziness attempting to track the fat man's words.

Sleet falling on Yustaffa's yellow tunic created dimples in the fabric. He waited, eyebrows raised, in a pantomime of expectation, before swinging suddenly about and launching the item he'd been holding in his fist at the base of the firepile. A small explosive *thuc* sounded and hot white flames rolled out across the wood. The crowd aahed in appreciation.

Yustaffa executed a trim bow and then looked Raif straight in the eye. "Now we're all cozy around the fire you really should tell us where you've been."

Raif gazed out on the faces of the Maimed Men. About four hundred had gathered around the firepile, and they were armed with a motley of weapons; rusted iron spears, beheading cleavers, hooked pikes, scimitars, wooden staffs, clannish hammers, broadswords, list poles, knuckleguards, knives. Most of the women and every boy old enough to walk had daggers or other hilt weapons at their waists. They lived in fear, Raif realized, and he could not fault them for it. It was a hard life on the edge of the abyss. Nothing but tough grass and weed trees would grow here. Children had to be maimed by their parents, else risk strangers taking issue with their wholeness. Whatever was needed was stolen from the clanholds . . . or one another. The cragsman Addie Gunn had once tried to keep sheep on the upper rim, but they were snatched one by one for meat. Stillborn had once called the Maimed Men desperate, and warned Raif that desperate men didn't make good friends.

Raif saw that desperation in them now. They were lean and scaly and hollow-cheeked and he knew he had made a mistake by not stopping to hunt in the canyonlands and bring meat. He had come empty-handed. Just one more mouth to feed.

"There you go." Raif opened his hand and accepted a felt-sheathed sword from Stillborn. He must have run down to his cave to fetch it. "It's not pretty but it should do you for a while." With a quick salute he slid away.

As he clipped the sword to his gear belt, Raif searched the faces of the Maimed Men for Traggis Mole. The leader of the Maimed Men was nowhere to be seen, but at the back of the crowd, his face almost hidden by rising flames and black smoke, stood the outlander, Thomas Argola. He did not blink as Raif regarded him, just held his small, olive-skinned face level for inspection. Argola had been the one who had pushed Raif into the Want after the raid on Black Hole. Why? Raif wondered. Why had he readied a horse and supplies? What had he known, or guessed?

"Come now, Twelvester. Didn't your mother ever tell you it's churlish to keep people waiting?"

Yustaffa's piping voice broke through Raif thoughts. As the fat man finished speaking a stone hit the small of Raif's back. Snapping around, Raif pounced toward the crowd. People shied away from him. One woman, a tired-looking mother with a baby at her teat, cried out in fright. Raif felt muscles in his jaw pumping as he fought the itch to draw his new sword.

Yustaffa tutted with mock disapproval, deeply gratified by Raif's reaction. "Shame on you, my fellow Rift Brothers. You know the procedure. Story first. Stones later." He smiled winningly at Raif. "Don't worry, I'm just saying that to keep them quiet."

The flames were fierce now, leaping and crackling, firing off sparks. Darkness was rising, and it didn't take much to imagine it was originating in the Rift. On the edge of the rimrock Raif spied one of the windlasses that were used to lower bodies into the abyss. He swallowed, wished again he had thought to bring meat.

Glancing once at Thomas Argola, he said, "I journeyed into the Great Want and was lost for many days. I nearly died, but a group of men called the lamb brothers found me, healed my wounds, and set me on my way."

Several things happened as he spoke. When he named the lamb brothers both Thomas Argola's and Yustaffa's faces registered a beat of surprise. The outlander concealed his surprise better, but Raif detected a momentary loosening of his jaw. Most of the crowd listened in silence, drawing in breath when Raif had named the Great Want, yet even before he'd finished wonder had been replaced by suspicion.

"No one gets out of the Want," shrieked the low-breasted hag who'd spoken earlier.

"Aye," agreed many in the crowd.

Someone else called out, "What was you doing there anyway? Only madmen go the Want."

"Never heard of no lamb brothers," pitched in a shaggy bear of a man near the front.

Yustaffa sucked in his cheeks with relish. "Such suspicion. Makes you wonder how they sleep at night."

"I've heard of the lamb brothers."

All turned to look at the tiny cragsman Addie Gunn who was making his way across the rimrock. Addie had once been a Wellman, and you could still see the clan in him. He wore a pouch around his waist, but it contained salt, not guidestone. The habit of carrying powder was a hard one to break. "The lamb brothers live in the sand deserts of the Far South and they survive on ewe milk and lamb meat and dress themselves in wool and fleeces."

Addie was fierce about matters pertaining to sheep and no one in the crowd doubted his word. As a cragsman at Wellhouse he had maintained his own herd. Raising a quick hand in greeting to Raif, he addressed himself directly to Yustaffa. "You come from the glass desert due north of the sands. Tell me you haven't heard of them too."

As he watched Addie Gunn standing in the firelight, arms folded across his chest, daring Yustaffa to lie to the crowd, a muscle close to Raif's heart contracted. He had forgotten the goodness here.

For once Yustaffa was lost for words. Coiling the end of his belt rope around his fat middle finger, he hmmed and aahed and tutted. Finally, he let the rope go. "Well now that you mention it," he said sulkily, "I do have a recollection about them. Course it doesn't prove that they were in the Want or that Twelve Kill actually met them."

Men started to jeer. He'd lost the crowd and he knew it.

Addie shook his head slowly, frowning at Yustaffa and the Maimed Men. "The lamb brothers live on the dunes. League upon league of nothing but sand. Every hill looks like the next, and by the time you've topped one your footprints have been blown clean away and you can't even be sure which way you came. I ask you: how much more difficult could the Want be than that?" The cragsman's gaze darted from man to man, defying anyone to disagree with him. None did. Addie Gunn was well respected here. His know-how brought in goats and sheep. "Good," he said with a fatherly nod. "That's sorted then. Now as for the fact of what the lad was doing there in the first place I say this: sometimes a man's business is his own. He didna harm any Rift Brothers, and before he left I watched with my own two eyes as he fought long and hard in the raid. You don't have to take my word for it. There's Linden Moodie and Stillborn and others who'll tell you just the same. Now granted the lad's made a mistake not bringing supper for the pot, but I for one will go out with him tomorrow. And between his fancy Sull bow and my own two sheep eyes I have an inkling we'll bring something back. He's useful, don't forget that. Twelve Kill by nature as well as name."

The crowd nodded. Most were quiet. A group of older children broke away from the fire to kick around a leather ball. Stillborn chose that moment to return to the space before the fire. He was carrying a small burlap sack on his back and he shrugged it forward, letting it drop onto the rimrock.

"Trail meat," he said with some wistfulness, still looking at the sack. "Cured it myself last autumn. Spiced it real good too. If there's babbies around with milk teeth it'll knock 'em clean out." Unable to actually come out with the words *Trail meat all round* he walked away from the sack.

The Maimed Women pushed forward first. One woman, a blond-haired maid with a cleanly excised left ear, shoved Yustaffa in the backside to get to her share of meat. The fat man spun around and smacked her face and she smacked him right back.

Raif, Stillborn and Addie Gun moved to the side. Glancing over his shoulder, Raif looked to the place where he'd last seen Thomas Argola. The outlander was gone.

"Addie," Raif said. "Thanks. You saved my head."

The cragsman smacked his lips. "'C'mon now, lad. It was nothing."

Raif nodded solemnly. "Nothing."

Addie seemed pleased by this. "You'd better get some sleep. We'll have to be up and out afore dawn. We'll have to cover a lot of ground. Bad time of year to go looking for game."

"Worse time to come back with nothing." Stillborn also

seemed pleased. "Guess I might come with you. Someone'll have to wheel back the cart."

Addie looked at Stillborn as if he was exactly the kind of person you didn't want on a stealth hunt. Which was probably true. "If you're not at the east rim an hour afore sunup I'm not waiting" was all the cragsman said in reply.

"Where's Traggis Mole?" Raif asked, instantly killing the easy camaraderie between them.

Stillborn's large deformed face, with its seam of flesh and black bristles running from the temple down to the neck, sobered. "He's about all right, though I've seen him less of late. He'll have been told you're here, but you know the Mole. Chooses his own time."

Raif nodded. It was probably a mistake to feel relief at that statement, but he couldn't help himself. Right now he wanted to pull his aching feet from his boots, and sleep.

Perhaps seeing this, Stillborn said, "C'mon, lad. Let's get you set for the night. You'd best stay with me. Addie. You didn't do half a bad job up there. I never knew you had the gift of the gab."

"Nor did I," Addie replied lightly before slipping away.

Stillborn picked up Raif's pack as if it weighed exactly nothing. Silently, he led Raif down the series of rope ladders and stairs that led to his cliff cave. Raif was grateful not to be probed or forced to think. He was dead tired and had stood so long in the sleet that his hands and face were tingling.

The Rift music started as they arrived on the lower terrace. Grass lamps had been lit and the city was aglow with orange lights. The Rift music made the flames flicker. Bass murmurs, low whistles and door-hinge creaks rose from the hole in the earth, punctuated by long silences and sudden rock tremors. Raif could no longer see the Rift, and was glad.

Stillborn's cave was accessed by a narrow ledge that was separated from the rimrock by a drop of three feet. The Maimed Man jumped down, careless of the hell that lay below him. Raif couldn't manage such recklessness just then. He moved with care, favoring his right foot, fearful of the drop and of his own ability to manage the simple maneuver. Stillborn went ahead to light lamps.

"Raif," he said a few minutes later as Raif stood in the mouth of the cave. "Sleep. There's blankets and a bowl of water for your feet. I'll be out on the ledge, scratching up a bit of a fire. I'll see you in the morning." Moving briskly, the Maimed Man passed Raif and left him to the dim quiet of the cliff cave.

Raif sat on the pile of blankets and pulled off his boots. Not looking too carefully, he sank his feet into the shallow bowl of cool water. Bits of rags that had stuck to the blisters slowly soaked free.

You are safe tonight, Stillborn had said in his own way. *I will stand watch while you sleep.*

It was a gift, and Raif took it. Making a rough bed from the blankets, he closed his eyes and slept.

When he awoke the next morning it was still dark. Mist washing in through the mouth of the cave had coated every surface with a film of moisture. A single grass lamp burned on the rock floor by Raif's bed, its damp wick giving off as much smoke as light. Raif felt stiff but good. Rested and hungry. He could smell fatty meat charring and stood to investigate. His left ankle took weight with only a mild spasm of protest, though if anything it looked worse than it had in three days. The bruising had turned black and purple and for some reason his big toe had started to swell. He ignored it. It was a skill he was getting better at.

Stillborn was out on the ledge, hunched around a tiny little fire, a red blanket pulled tight across his shoulders, browning a length of cured sausage on a stick. He was shivering and talking to himself, saying the words, "Bloody, bloody, bloody. Sod it, sod it, sod it," in a weary voice that might have been intended to keep him awake. He wasn't aware of Raif standing at the mouth of the cave.

The sky had cleared and the stars were out over the clan-holds, and Raif realized it was the first time he had seen stars that could be relied upon in over a month. The nights he'd spent in the canyonlands had been overcast. Starlight lit the domes of the Copper Hills and the sea of mist surrounding them. The Lost Clan was out there, and Dhoone. Quietly, Raif turned and stepped back into the cave.

This time he made more noise, banging the bronze bowl

that contained the water and rifling through his pack for the items he meant to give Stillborn.

"You up, lazy-days?" came Stillborn's grumpy voice. "Come out here and watch the fire while I take a quick kip before we leave."

Raif understood the language here. Watch the fire meant simply *watch*. Crossing to the ledge he greeted Stillborn.

"What's this?" demanded the Maimed Man, staring suspiciously at the small packs and pouches that were squashed against Raif's chest.

Raif sat, letting the packages spill forward onto the rimrock. "Cheese, honey, dates, almonds, butter, dried apricots, lentils. Not the sheep's curd and the tea herbs, though. They're for Addie."

"Give him the lentils too," Stillborn said magnanimously, reaching for the largest pack. "Little orange buggers make me fart."

They had a good breakfast of sausage dipped in honey and nuts dipped in melted sheep's butter. The minute he stopped eating Stillborn fell asleep. His chin dropped against his chest, his massive shoulders slumped, his mouth fell open, and he began to snore vigorously and, oddly enough, in tune.

Raif drank water and watched the fire. The mist was receding and the flames brightened as he poked air between the sticks. The Rift was silent now. A slight shimmering of the darkness at eye level told him that it was venting heat. Time passed and after a while Raif reached inside his tunic and pulled out the pouch containing the stormglass.

It was beautiful to look at in the starlight. Light reflected and refracted, twinkled into existence. Moved. Its rounded sides felt good in his hand, like a talisman, and as he held it the glass warmed.

I give no promises. Raif mouthed the words he'd said to Tallal. Disturbed by their hollowness he said them again out loud.

"I give no promises."

"What? Where?" Stillborn said blearily, his head snapping up from his chest. A line of drool rolled down his chin as he look accusingly at Raif. "A man can't sleep nowhere nohow in this place." Standing abruptly, he said, "Fuck it. We'd better get going."

They got their gear together and killed the fire and the lamp. As they climbed up through the city, air rising from the Rift cooled the exposed skin on Raif's neck and face. Maimed Men walked and climbed through the thinning mist, heads hooded against the damp, torches swinging before them on long poles. Stillborn greeted some with curt nods. Others he ignored. He was wearing a tunic sewn from pieced wolverine skins edged with black leather, and a flat-paneled bearskin kilt. His arms and lower legs were bare, though they looked as if they'd been rubbed with lard for warmth. He carried no hunting bow but had brought a single, case-hardened throwing spear, five feet long and tapered at both ends. He used the spear as a walking stick, tapping the rimrock as he walked.

Raif was wearing the Orrl cloak and he noticed that some men did not see him until he was right upon them, so perfectly did the cloak match the mist. The Sull bow was strung crosswise against his back and his arrowcase, containing the scant half-dozen arrows he had left, rode high on his right shoulder. The borrowed sword swung from his waist. He had not drawn it yet, so could claim no firsthand knowledge of the blade, but judging from the ring pommel and iron crossguards, it was probably a basic cut-and-thruster.

As they made their way east the sky began to lighten and the smell of grass and willow smoke grew stronger. Children emerged, rumpled and sleepy-eyed, from lean-tos built against the cave mouths. Some caves had been closed off by cane screens or animal hides. Others were open to the night. Custom demanded that you did not peer into those spaces as you passed them. Maimed Men expected privacy in their caves.

Addie Gunn was waiting on the easternmost point of the city, a jagged granite promontory that extended fifty feet over the Rift. He was alone, cloaked and hooded in plain brown wool and leaning upon an oak staff. His lips pressed to a thin line when he saw them and he declared without greeting, "You are late."

Stillborn said, "And a fine morning to you, Addie Gunn."

Addie ignored this and said to Raif, "You're looking better, lad."

"Looked like hell last night," Stillborn said, clapping Raif hard on the back. "A night's sleep prettied him up quite considerably."

The cragsman nodded, thoughtful. "We'd best head off."

Stillborn bowed, somewhat creakily, at the waist. "Lead the way."

The sun floated beneath the horizon as they headed north from the rim, turning the sky red and then pink. Breezes snapped at groundlevel but there was no real wind. Raif had never traveled east or north of the Rift and was interested in the paths Addie chose. The cragsman led them across a rocky headland strewn with boulders and overgrown with spiny yellow grasses, juniper and holly. Small, dun-colored birds flew out from beneath bushes as they passed. Raif spotted hares in molt, ground squirrels, rats, mice and voles. As always it was difficult for him to tell if he actually saw the animals, or simply felt their beating hearts. He'd pass a loose pile of rocks and know that a vole was hiding within the shadows, quivering.

"Does anyone set traps?" he asked Addie as they made their way along a brush-choked draw.

Addie shook his head. Now that the sun had risen he had drawn back his hood, revealing his closely shaved scalp and big ears. "A few do. Mostly it's not considered worth it. Land's like dry bone."

Raif wanted to disagree, but didn't. A reluctance to reveal how different he was to other men stopped him. Instead, he made a mental note about traps. Hungry men and women would be glad of squirrel, vole and hare.

The morning wore on. The sun shone with cool brilliance in a blue cloudless sky. After leading them north for an hour or so Addie turned east and they were now descending into a trough-shaped valley carved by some long-retreated glacier. Huge erratic boulders and heaps of gravel peeked out through the thick ground cover of willow, fireweed and black sedge. A series of small green ponds arranged like beads on a thread ran along the center of the valley floor.

"Goats have gone to high ground for the kidding," Addie said, poking bushes with his stick as he searched for prints and scat. "Might see deer if the luck's with us. Elk'll have gone west.

Coons and pines: they'll be here, all right. Trick is spotting 'em. Bears, now . . . " He shook his head. "Better chance of cats."

Raif listened to the cragsman's litany, interested and alert. They were at the head of the valley on a steep downslope where he could see for leagues due east. The oily smell of sedge filled his nostrils and icy breezes lifted his hair from his scalp. Creatures were alive down there, moving beneath the willow, and he, Raif Sevrance, would hunt them. Life was simple and clear, and once Addie Gunn had finished speaking, Raif braced his bow and set off alone for the valley floor.

Glancing down at the Orrl cloak he saw the glazed leather now reflected the gray-green colors of the sedge. Briefly he wondered if the cloak also masked his man-scent, for he had noticed that as long as he moved quietly he was nearly impossible to detect. His first kill was a three-foot garter snake just emerging from her winter sleep. She was sliding between two ground junipers when he speared her with his new sword. Deciding to leave her whole with the gut intact, he slipped the snake between the waxed folds of his makeshift gamepouch. As he wiped his swordblade clean with a fist of fireweed, he was already scanning his next kill.

A raccoon, her belly swollen with soon-to-be-born kits, had denned in a shallow depression beneath a loose pile of rocks. Raif sent an arrow straight into her heart. It beat and then stopped. The unborn kits continued living for a while and then, one by one, their tiny, perfectly formed hearts ceased pumping. Raif sawed through the arrowshaft, unwilling to pull it and risk the head coming loose. Left inside it would hold the carcass intact. After that he decided to form a game pile, and chose an exposed spot on top of one of the boulders. That way if vultures or other opportunists spied the carrion, either Addie or Stillborn could cover it. Might even bag a fat bird for the pot.

Raif pushed off again, searching. It wasn't a good time of day for deer but he had a feeling that the water and the lush growth surrounding it might bring them out, so he made his way deeper into the valley. An hour passed, and then another. The sun moved overhead and flies began buzzing around the gamepouch. When Raif became aware of a large heart close by, watchful and beating with strong, easy strokes, he thought at first it was a brown bear. Then knowledge came to him and he was surprised he could have imagined it was anything other than a cat. Raif moved at the same time the cat did, bringing the bow to vertical as he drew back the string. The cat sprang away, leaping into the deep cover of willows and rocks. It was a full-grown male, heavy as two grown men with a pale silver coat free of markings. Raif loosed his first arrow and watched as it sped wide. He could sense the creature's heart but in the time it took for the arrow to leave the riser and cross the distance between Raif and the cat, the cat was already gone. His second arrow grazed the snagcat's rump. And then, just as Raif brought a third arrow to the plate, something sped past his face. He heard a whoosh followed by a thud of impact and knew instantly that the snagcat had faltered. Keeping his hands firm on bow and bowstring, he aimed the arrow and loosed it.

The big cat stopped. Dead. Raif's heart pounded and a familiar liquid pain rolled across his left shoulder—the first time he'd felt it in days.

"Is he down?" came Stillborn's call. The Maimed Man was standing high above Raif on a bank of stratified rock. Until the moment he had thrown the spear, Raif had been unaware of his presence. Raif was surprised by his own failings. Without Stillborn the cat would have got away. And he should have known Stillborn was there.

Stillborn jumped down onto the valley floor and walked toward the cat. The distance he had thrown the spear was impressive, a length no shorter than two hundred feet. "Saw you fire off a couple of arrows," he said. "Looked like you needed some help."

Raif nodded, attempting to conceal the confusion and irritation he felt.

Stillborn saw it anyway. "Best go look for your arrows, lad."

He did just that, leaving Stillborn to the kill. Two arrows had gone astray, and after searching for a quarter-hour in the brush Raif realized he wasn't going to find them. That had never really been the point.

Calmer, he returned to Stillborn and the cat. The Maimed Man had opened up the carcass, split the ribs and was in the process of removing the organ tree. The bloody, glistening flesh was steaming.

"Took your arrow out of the heart," he said in greeting as he cut through greenish back fat. "It's over there, on the rock."

Raif nodded, though Stillborn was not looking at him. "The liver's yours."

Slowing his knife, Stillborn said, "I'm glad to hear it. Come here and help me with the gut."

Together they cleaned and drained the carcass. The liver, the prize awarded to the hunter who brought down the kill, sat darkly on a bed of plucked fireweed, seeping blood. The sun, beginning its slow descent into the west, gave off something that felt like warmth. Addie Gunn reached them just as they decided to trophy-cut the snagcat's hide. The cragsman was dragging a yearling kid by its hind leg. He seemed happy enough to set his own butchering duties aside to advise on the best cuts to preserve the tail and legs.

It was hard work, and Addie built a spotfire so they could be be refreshed with tea. The little cragsman was delighted when Raif handed him the muslin pouch containing the lamb brothers' herbs.

"Treasure," he said, holding the pouch to his nose and inhaling deeply. "Smells like all the places a man could ever want to be."

Raif felt stupidly pleased. Sweat was dripping from his nose and dried blood reached all the way up to his elbows. "There's sheep's curd too, but I left that back at that Rift."

"Now that *will* be interesting," Addie said, sprinkling a few of the precious herbs into the pot. "I used to make me own back . . . back in another life."

Raif and Stillborn nodded soberly. All three of them had once lived lives as clansmen. Addie had been tied to Wellhouse as a cragsman, Stillborn had been born dead into Scarpe before being revived by a midwife, and Raif had spoken an oath to Blackhail and broken it. They were quiet for a while after that, setting their backs against the rocks as they sipped on wormwood tea.

Finally, Raif set down his cup and asked the question he needed to ask. "What has happened in the Rift since I left?"

Addie and Stillborn exchanged a glance. Stillborn nodded almost imperceptibly at the cragsman. *You take it.*

"Harmful times, Raif," Addie said, taking a stick and breaking up the fire. "Mole's getting nervous and it's making him quick with his knives. If you're not loyal to him you'll be paid a call in the night. Ten days back a half-dozen men were murdered in their beds. Throats slit from ear to ear, tongues sliced down the center. They call it the Vor king's kiss. Kill them and then split their tongues so even their corpses can't squeal. All six of the men had been heard complaining about the Mole. You know the sort of thing: Where's the food? Why did the last raid fail? What's the Mole doing for us? Harmless stuff in harmless times. But times aren't harmless anymore, and it serves a man well to shut up and starve."

"Why's Traggis Mole afraid?" Raif asked.

Again, there was that look, passed between Addie and Stillborn.

The cragsman took a deep breath, set down his fire-poking stick. "Mole's worst nightmare's happening and he's powerless to stop it. Night after we returned from Black Hole something godless broke free from the Rift."

At Addie's words both Raif's and Stillborn's right arms twitched. The ghost of clan, that desire to reach down and touch your measure of powdered guidestone whenever you felt a beat of fear. Addie must have seen and recognized the impulse, but he continued speaking his rough, backcountry voice low as if he feared to be overheard.

"Something not whole walked on the rimrock. Those that saw it said it was like night made into a man, dark and rippling, like it shouldn't have weighed anything at all. But I myself saw the cracks that it made in the stone. Rift brothers tried to stop it—Linden Moodie hacked off an arm—but it couldn't be stopped. Took thirteen before it left. Women, bairns, men." Addie shuddered. "The bodies blackened like they were burned, then they were gone."

Raif thought of the lamb brother Farli, and the Forsworn knight in the redoubt. "Next time the bodies must be destroyed."

Addie Gunn studied Raif's face, understanding much from the little he had said. "Aye," he said softly, spinning the word into confirmation of his worst fear.

Next time.

"What did Traggis Mole do?"

"What could he do? Took a swipe at the thing with his longknife, received a cut to the ribs. Ordered everyone back to their beds. Was set to take care of the bodies . . . afore the bodies took care of themselves." With that Addie seemed to run out of strength.

Stillborn, noticing the slump in the cragsman's shoulders, took over. "Mole's been telling everyone that it won't come back. The Rift Brothers are scared out their wits. Those men the Mole killed? Sent to the Rift the next morning, as if somehow that could help. Throw enough bodies down there and you stop the evil getting out." Stillborn blew air from his lips. "People are starting to say that the Mole can't help them. Mole's saying right back, 'Step out of line and you're dead.' He's made mistakes, and that's not like him. Two of the six men he killed were good hunters. Means less meat, more discontent. Who knows how long Addie and myself are safe? I used to think being a good hunter counted for something. Now I'm thinking if the man-thing from the Rift doesna get me Traggis Mole will."

Raif nodded slowly. It was worse than he had thought. Whatever he had done at the Fortress of Grey Ice had been nothing more than shoring up a crack. Pressure was building. First the Unmade in the lamb brothers' camp. Now this. *They're searching for weak points,* he realized. *They discovered one in the fortress but now that's sealed they're finding other ways out.*

He lost himself in his thoughts for a while, remembering snatches of conversation from his past. Addie Gunn had told him the Rift was the greatest flaw in the earth. If it were to be ripped open life for the Maimed Men and the entire clanholds would be over. Hundreds of thousands of Unmade would ride out.

And the Endlords.

Just their name alone sent a knife of fear into Raif's heart. *Why me?* Why was he the one who must fight them? The two things he had wanted from life were to be a decent clansman and a good brother to Effie and Drey. Now he would be neither. Now he was *Mor Drakka*, Watcher of the Dead. How had that happened? When? He didn't suppose the answer mattered much in the end. What choice did he have here? What man or woman, knowing the things he did, would walk away?

Raif Sevrance could not walk away. And perhaps, just perhaps, there was a glimmer of hope in that. Perhaps from a distance, in a most terrible and dread way, in a manner he could never have anticipated, he could still be that good clansman and brother. It was a hope. And it was his only one.

Coming back to the present was like emerging from icy water. He was cold and disoriented and it took him long moments to realize why Addie Gunn and Stillborn were watching him intently, *waiting*.

Raif glanced over at the bloody carcass of the snagcat and then said what he had to say.

"I will become Lord of the Rift."

And so it begins.

TWENTY

Pike

Effie Sevrance was rubbing boat oil into her ankles. It felt good and not at all boaty, cool and soothing on her chafed skin. The smell left something to be desired and it might possibly be a bit rancid, but it was pretty interesting the way it turned her legs all slick and green. Of course Chedd had to come over and take a look.

"What you doing?" he asked. Possibly the stupidest question in the entire world. He had eyes. He could see.

Effie said, "I thought if I put enough boat oil on my ankles I could slip my feet through the cuffs." For good measure she raised her legs above the deergrass and shook her leg irons. "What do you think?"

She felt a bit bad when Chedd actually considered this theory, squinting so hard it pushed his cheek fat up against his eyes. Then immediately regretted it when he said, "No. Your feet are too big."

"Dare you to drink it," she shot back at him, nodding toward the calfskin flask containing the boat oil.

Chedd Limehouse was champion of the worm-swallowing, vast-quantity-eating dare. He glanced down toward the river-shore where Waker Stone was pulling in his fish trap, and then at the beached and upturned boat. "Hand it over," he ordered tersely, like a surgeon requesting his saw just before he chopped off someone's leg to save a life.

Rolling forward onto her knees, Effie handed Chedd the flask.

"For Bannen!" he proclaimed, holding it high above his

head. Popping off the stopper with his thumb, he brought the nozzle to his mouth. And drank. Effie watched his throat apple bob up and down, up and down, as he swallowed large quantities of boat oil. Green grease began to spill from his mouth and roll along his chin, yet he continued drinking.

Finally she could take it no more. Punching the flask from his lips, she shouted, "Stop it."

Chedd grinned and belched. His jaw and neck were slick with oil, and the collar of his fine wool cloak was black. "Tasty," he said with deep satisfaction.

Effie glared at him, while secretly hoping that boat oil was some sort of harmless plant oil. Like linseed or castor. She didn't want to kill anyone, and she really did like Chedd.

Wiping his chin with shirtsleeve, he said, "See that cliff over there. If you climb it you can see for leagues. It's all open ground, heaths and rocks and things. Wanna take a look?"

Effie felt a pinch of the old fear. "No," she replied, knowing straightaway that she had disappointed him. "Bring me a rock back from the top."

It was a good thing to give a person something to do, she had learned. Chedd nodded. "Big or small?"

Effie brought both of her hands together and cupped them. "This big."

After committing the size of the requested rock to memory, Chedd set off. Halfway to the base of the cliff, without looking around, he raised an arm in silent salute. Effie was impressed that he had known she would still be watching.

Rising a little awkwardly to her feet, she started searching for the flask's stopper. Gods knew how Chedd was going to get up that cliff with his feet connected by two feet of iron chain. Hop, probably.

It was not going to be a nice day today, she could tell. The Wolf River, which was usually brown, was gray, and it had a little angry chop to it that made the surface matte. Thunderheads were shipping in from the south of all places and the hemlocks and blackstone pines on the riverbank were beginning to sway. To make matters worse Waker's father was just sitting by the boat, watching her with eyes that were double-beady. Sometimes she imagined that the little old man knew just what she was thinking. Clan Gray, that was where he and his son were from. It was a strange clan and not much was known about it. Perhaps the elders there had learned how to divine unguarded thought.

Even though she knew she was being silly, Effie made a face at him. It really was too much, all the staring and silence and *I-see-what-you're-about-girl* knowingness. For want of something better to do she shuffled down to the shore and offered to help Waker Stone head the fish. At least she had the pleasure of surprising him.

Waker had set the fish trap the night before after they'd pulled ashore. He'd caught three fish in the wicker basket; a shiner and two small trout. They were still skipping. "Take the shiner," he said, handing her the trap. "Show me how you mean to do it."

She did just that, handling all three fish with confidence. The shiner wasn't much longer than her hand and it was what Mad Binny would have called a "no-biter": you either ate it whole or threw it away. It wasn't worth heading or gutting, and Waker Stone knew it. Still, she laid it against the cutting stump, pinned its tail fin with her middle finger, and began making a scraping motion with the edge of her free hand. "Scaling," she informed Waker calmly. "Best done before you open the gut and chop off the head."

"So you know fish then," he said, looking at her with interest for the first time in all the days that she had known him. Abruptly, he turned his back on her. "Take it," he said over his shoulder. "Don't go lighting no cookfire."

Effie didn't very much want the shiner, but the habit of good manners, drilled into her over many years by Raina Blackhail, was strong and she took it. After the time she'd spent hiding in the waterfall hollow west of Ganmiddich she no longer cared for fish. Especially raw ones. Trouble was, she'd stopped hearing Raina's voice in her head and begun hearing Da's instead. *You kill it. You eat it.* He could be hard, Da. Hard but right.

Better than boat oil, she thought as she raised the wriggling shiner above her head. She had wanted to make a dedication, like Chedd, but the words "For Blackhail!" didn't mean very much to her. Perhaps she'd been gone too long from her clan.

Suddenly inspired, she cried "For Drey!" and dropped the silver fish into her open mouth.

It took some swallowing, but now that Drey's name was attached to it, it simply had to go down. She still didn't know what had become of her elder brother after the raid on Ganmiddich and in some hopeful and superstitious part of her brain she thought that if she got the fish down in one gulp then Drey would be made alive and well. The shiner went down. She could feel it bucking as her gullet muscles pushed it into her stomach. After that she needed to sit.

Waker's father, who might or might not have been named Darrow, followed her progress with jablike movements of his eyes. She knew, in the weird and unspoken rules of the mutual game they played, that if she broke down and hid herself deliberately from his sight—say behind a tree trunk or a rock—somehow it meant he had won. And Effie Sevrance did not want to give him the satisfaction. So in plain sight she sat, away from the boat and up high against the hemlocks.

From here she could see Chedd climbing the cliff. He was close to the top now. His technique of pulling himself up by his arms and then swinging his lower body behind him was pretty impressive for a fat boy. Now she wished she had agreed to go with him, but the old fears still had a grip on her feet.

Open ground. See for leagues. She shuddered, though not nearly as strongly as in the past. A year back she wouldn't have left the roundhouse unless bullied by Raina or Raif, enticed by the thought of Shankshounds, or driven out by the word "Fire!" Effie Sevrance had never liked outside. The more open it was the less she liked it, therefore woods were better than fields, low ground better than high. She couldn't say why this was so. Well maybe she could but the explanation was so . . . illogical that she didn't like to admit it, even to herself. You were exposed outside. Revealed. You could see the lay of the land, the age of it, the gnarled rootwood and weatherbeaten stones. And it smelled too. In the morning, that first wash of mist: that was the real true smell of the earth. It was old and watchful and tricky. It looked wide open, but all that air could be hard to breathe. The sky above was big and loose and if you looked long enough you could see it spin. Outside everything was moving, watching, growing, changing. Inside all was still.

And no eyes could find you there. Here was the strange bit—oh she knew the other stuff was odd, but this was odd on a different level—Effie thought something without good intentions was trying to seek her out. What that might be, she would be hard-pressed to come up with. She'd once overheard Orwin Shank talking to Jebb Onnacre about Mace Blackhail's mean-spirited dogs, "They're a malevolence, Jebb. They'll watch and wait, and then they'll bite you right on the knuckle so you drop the lock and they can escape."

That was how the searching thing seemed to Effie: a waiting malevolence. For as long as she could remember, right the way back to being a toddie when Drey and Raif would toss her, squealing and happy, from one to the other, she had believed that something was trying to find her. No one knew this—though Raif might have guessed something, for he was always extra protective whenever he took her outside.

What this thing might be, what it wanted, if it really existed or was just a thought that had got stuck in her mind, like a splinter, she did not know. All she knew for certain was that the feeling was strongest when she stood on open ground. Hollows, glades, even river channels that were lined with trees were preferable to high places and open places where Effie Sevrance might be exposed.

Things had got a lot better since she'd left the roundhouse. Poor Raina, she had thought to send Effie to a better life at Dregg. It hadn't worked out that way at all, but strangely enough it had still worked out. Effie knew that when Raina looked at her she'd seen a child who was too quiet and solitary, too interested in the Hailstone and the guidehouse and the dark, damp spaces beneath the roundhouse. After the trouble with the Shankshound being burned and Effie being accused of being a witch, Raina had feared that Effie would never be able to live a normal life at Blackhail and had sent her off to live with relatives at Dregg. Raina had hoped that Dregg would turn Effie around; Effie knew this for a certainty because Raina had come right out and told her. "You'll be able to dance there and make friends. Learn to cook and sew and fight with swords if it pleases you. They have lovely gardens, Effie, with waterfalls and box hedges and roses. You need to dig in them, get some sun on the back of your neck and dirt between your fingers. Run out to the plunge pond and grab fish, roll on the grass, laugh, suck hay, play."

Effie felt bad when she thought of Raina's words, as if somehow by being here she had let Raina down. Sometimes she thought it would be a good thing to send Raina a note. *Caught fish, rolled in the grass, made a friend. Still waiting to learn how to sew.* That was the funny thing, you see, by getting waylaid, first by Clewis Reed and Druss Ganlow and then by Waker Stone and his father, she was changing in the very sort of ways that Raina had hoped to bring about. Effie Sevrance in a boat, camping, cooking, laughing with Chedd, wading into the river to look for mussels and skimmers: those things would make Raina glad.

Thinking about Raina made Effie's heart feel heavy. There was no way to let her know that things were all right . . . and no way to be certain that those words would hold true.

As the first spits of rain landed on Effie's dress, Chedd did a victory wave from the top of the cliff. He was shouting and holding something up, but she couldn't make out what he was saying. Standing, she waved back. On the shore, Waker had finished cleaning the trout and was wrapping the fillets in dock leaves to keep them fresh until tonight. Waker's father had risen and was flipping the boat. Off soon then, Effie concluded. Another day on the river heading east.

What surprised her about river travel—at least river travel upstream—was how slow it was. A man could trot faster than two men could pole. The times Waker and his father got up to their best speed was when they were in a deep, slow-moving channel, using their paddles. Yet for some reason they usually stayed off the main river, choosing streams and tributaries that were either shallow, frothing, narrow or twisty. And that meant using poles, not paddles.

Effie often wondered how far they'd come. She'd been with Waker and his father for many days now and had fallen into an easy routine. Up at dawn or some time before it, breakfast, load the boat and float upstream until dark. The sparsest of camps would be raised, with neither tents, a proper campfire or latrines. A cold supper might be occasionally supplemented with lukewarm fish, and then to sleep, and the whole thing would start up again in the morning.

Effie had to give it to Waker and his father: they ran a tight ship. Waker wasn't even especially mean to her and Chedd. Mostly he treated them like cargo. As long as they did what he told them, sat still in the boat and stayed within sight of the camp, he did not raise his voice or touch them. Waker's father was something different. Effie thought of him as an evil little marsh man who delighted in other people's discomfort. She had noticed that when she was near him her stone lore felt muffled, as if it had been wrapped in thick blankets or plunged into water. It was alive and present, just unable to get enough air.

"Boy. Hurry now." Waker Stone called out to Chedd. "We set off within the quarter." The riverman's otterskin pants were wet to the knee and the water bought out their blue-green iridescence. Tight bands around the tops of his mooseskin boots prevented the riverwater from pouring inside them as he and his father floated the boat. "Girl. Cover the fire. Stow the pots and blankets."

Effie jumped to do his bidding. Waker wasn't to be ignored when he was preparing the boat.

Camp was a wooded and reedy inlet north of the Wolf. Chedd reckoned they weren't far from Croser now. Thinking about that Dhoone-sworn clan with its roundhouse of giant riverstones gave Effie a little thrill. She was a long way from home, heading into territory hostile to Blackhail. If they continued east they'd pass the Dhoone-protected lands altogether and enter territory defended by Bludd. It was a long way from home, and the river, headlands, trees and rocks were all changing, becoming wilder. According to Inigar Stoop, the east was a barbarian place that the Stone Gods claimed but never wholly possessed.

"Look out." Chedd Limehouse came running toward Effie with his right hand at his shoulder as if he were about to launch a shot put. "Catch!" he cried, propelling his hand forward with force.

Effie made a little cry and ducked.

Chedd began laughing heartily, rocking back and forth at the waist as if what he had done was so funny it had caused his lungs to seize. "Got you!" he gurgled, actually becoming a little red in the face. "Never threw it." Holding up his hand he revealed the stone he had brought down from the top of the cliff.

Effie was denied the pleasure of giving Chedd a piece of her mind by Waker barking, "Here with you both. Now."

Chedd helped her carry the bedrolls and pots to the boat. Once he'd handed them off to Waker he tried to give Effie the rock—a dog tooth of yellow halite—but she wasn't having it. A sharp look from Waker was enough to make Chedd drop the rock in the water.

As they pushed off rain began to fall heavily. Effie wished she had thought to save a blanket from the bedrolls, for her boiled-wool cloak was quickly soaked. If she turned around she could see the bedrolls—they were stowed beneath Waker's father's seat—but some kind of pride stopped her from asking for them. As they headed into the main river channel, Waker handed back a tin cup and told Effie to bail once the water covered her toes.

The water soon covered her toes. Thunder rolled from the south and the first of the big gusts hit the boat side-on. The long and narrow craft tipped wildly. Waker's father plunged his paddle deep into the water and turned in to the wind. Effie bailed, glad of something to do. The surface of the water was like a pincushion stuck with a million pins. The trees along the southern bank of the Wolf whipped back and forth as clusters of pine needles spun free. Directly ahead of Effie, Chedd Limehouse paddled with real force. Rain ran down Effie's face and into the neck hole of her dress as she fell into the urgent rhythm of bailing.

The river was wide here, a league across without a single island to block the view. Wooded hills formed the southern shore, and to the north lay impenetrable tangles of hardwoods, pines and winter dead vines.

Waker's father had set them on a course that was a fraction short of due south and she thought his intent might be to sit out the storm on the southern shore. That seemed like a good idea. With the bow of the boat facing the wind the going was steadier, yet every once in a while a rogue gust would get under the curve of the hull and for an instant the boat would rise, vertical, from the water. Waker would immediately stand, swinging his weight forward and stamp down the hull.

Neither he nor his father seemed much perturbed. They were both working hard and concentrating, yet Effie could tell that paddling through high winds did not stretch them. Effie envied them their waterproof clothing. Even Chedd was faring better than she was, as his cloak was lined with fine doeskin.

Rain was making it difficult to see. The southern shore became a murky grayness of darkly moving trees. The river itself appeared to be widening, for even as they headed south the shore did not look to be getting much closer. More river just kept spooling out. Effie tried to remember the maps of the clanholds that Dagro Blackhail kept, rolled and cased, in his chief's chamber. As best she could recall the Wolf split into three separate rivers above Croser—or rather three separate rivers merged to form the Wolf. Effie was unsure of the correct phrasing, also unsure of the course and names of the higher streams. Gray was south of here. She knew that.

"Chedd," she hissed, leaning forward. "Where are we going?"

Turning his head to look at her he said, "Don't know." His voice sounded a little weird. "I'm feeling a bit sick."

"Look at the water," Effie told him firmly. "Eyes ahead."

Chedd did just that. He had stopped paddling, she realized, and was bracing himself with a hand on each gunwale. His face was green.

Waker's father skipped a paddle stroke, allowing Waker's right stroke to steer the boat. The craft tuned a few degrees east, and Effie saw they were no longer heading ashore. Only river lay ahead.

Almost immediately the boat began pitching. The wind was hitting at an angle, yet also the river itself seemed to be pulling in a new way. Waker and his father settled into a rhythm of quick shallow strokes, not holding their paddles too long or too deep in the water. Brown foam rushed across the surface, and the wind sent it slapping against their faces. Effie reached for her lore. The stone felt sluggish and unsteady, half asleep. Dissatisfied, she let it drop against her chest.

Another wind gust got under the boat and the bow went up. Lightning forked on the south shore. Thunder exploded right on top of them. The boat rolled and pitched, suddenly unstable on both planes. Waker called out something to his father, and Waker's father set his paddle in the water and turned the boat due south.

Effie felt a moment of relief. Rain was coming down with force and no matter how much she bailed the water kept rising. The wind was head-on again; she could feel it flattening her cheeks. From the seat in front of her Chedd made a small noise. And then two things happened at once. A powerful gust got under the boat and Effie was knocked backward. As the bow came up so did Chedd, flinging his head and shoulders over the side. *Oh no, he's throwing up*, she thought with disgust as the the boat tipped slowly toward Chedd. Waker sent his weight snapping in the opposite direction but it was too late. Effie's bottom slid along the polished wood seat, and she hung for the briefest instant, parallel to the water, before plunging in.

The river seized her chest. It was shockingly cold and dark. A paddle whacked her chin. As she gasped in pain her lungs took in water. Where was the surface? Was she underneath the boat? Panicking, she began thrashing her arms. When she tried to move her legs her body jerked with such force it was as if the floor had been snatched from beneath her. The leg irons snapped with the jolt of a returning bowstring. Stilled by the concussion she began to sink. Now that she looked up she saw that yes, she had been under the boat. Its peapod shape was a receding darkness against the light.

She fell deeper, and began to understand that strange currents were at work. Three rivers met here. She could feel them spinning her body as they emptied her brain of thoughts.

Swoopy movements, she thought inanely, *that's what you're supposed to do with your arms to swim.*

One of the bedrolls she'd packed that morning floated past her face. Breathing, she took in more water. The boat had become a thin line and she could no longer remember why it was important. It grew dark, or perhaps she closed her eyes: the difference hardly seemed important.

It was all easy-peasey now.

Down she went into the Wolf's maw, deep into the cold brown water. There was only one little niggle that surprised her. Who would have thought that the very thing she had avoided all her life would be down here? The seeking malevolence was moving through the water to intercept her. It was forming itself into a pike; elongating, solidifying, glittering as it conjured scales. The malevolence swam with great assuredness and growing strength. It didn't just prowl the open spaces, it knew the dark depths as well.

It was a revelation. Inside, outside: it didn't matter where she was, it would find her wherever she was weak.

A small quiver of fear passed through her, moving up from her feet to her head. The pike was almost upon her. She could see its pearly, razored teeth.

Suddenly she was yanked up and sideways. The pike's jaw snapped closed. Something broke. Effie Sevrance was pulled the long distance to the surface. It felt as if she were being sucked from a tube.

Afterward she didn't remember much of the time that followed. Waker's jelly eyes loomed big as he worked her chest like a water pump. Waker's father actually said things. Proper words, helpful words. Chedd Limehouse shivered and looked afraid. He was told a dozen times to *Sit down and hold your place*.

Effie smelled the good scent of woodsmoke and slept. Waker roused her in the night, made her drink water she did not want and felt her hands and feet. "She's bone cold."

She realized she must have been dreaming then, for Waker's father actually said, "We must build a bigger fire."

Some time later in the orange glow of firelight, Waker's father's face appeared above her own. He had the sneaky, pleased-to-be-himself look in his eyes as he leaned close to her ear and whispered his real name. He knew she would not remember it tomorrow.

Morning came, and even though the sun shone in her face and she was swaddled in the best and thickest blankets she could not stop shivering. Waker's father brought her purple tea and insisted she drink though its temperature was close to scalding. It tasted like fat.

Chedd came over and knelt by her head. After looking both

ways to check that no one was in earshot he told her what had happened and where they stood. "South shore of the Wolf, on land claimed by Morning Star. Last night we could see the lights of a village."

Effie didn't have the energy to pull herself up and look around. The sky seemed nice and blue, and she could see that some of the trees were oaks and water chestnuts waiting to bud.

"Waker pulled you from the water. You'd been gone forever and we thought . . . I thought . . . " Chedd looked down. Tears squeezed from his eyes and he wiped them away with his shirtsleeve. "I had to hang on to the boat, Eff—I couldn't come and get you because of these." Rolling on his side, he brought his feet all the way up to her face so she could physically see his ankle chains. "I'm a good swimmer. I could have done it."

She believed him.

"Anyhows. No one knew where you were. Waker was in a state, diving and coming up. Waker's da tells him to hold on a mo' while he thinks. Waker's da's face gets all white and goosey and he points to a piece of water and says, *She's down there.* You should have seen Waker dive, like an otter after fish. He was down a long time, Eff. Me and his da started getting afraid. His da turned the boat and held it while I got in. Then he got in himself. And only then, when we were both sitting steady, did Waker break the surface with you."

Chedd wanted to tell her how she looked, but she stopped him; Effie did not want to know. Realizing she would soon need to pee, she asked him to help her to her feet. Gallantly, he squatted beside her and wrapped a thick arm around her waist. As she came to standing a wave of dizziness hit her. One hand came out for Chedd, who took it like a rock. The other hand went up for her lore.

But her lore wasn't there.

The pike had taken it.

TWENTY-ONE

Alone and Armed in the Darkness

Traggis Mole's cronies were waiting for them when they returned from the overnight hunt. It was late afternoon and the light was deeply golden. Due to some subtle seasonal shift, the sun was perfectly aligned with the Rift in the west. Red radiance poured along the fissure, casting shadows that had no end.

Addie Gunn and Raif were dead tired. Both had stayed up late in the night hunting deer and then woke before dawn to try for more. Stillborn on the other hand had fallen asleep at sunset and stayed asleep until breakfast, when the smell of Addie roasting goat's heart had finally roused him. He'd been lively all day, even though he was the one hauling the majority of game. A full-grown doe was balanced, yokelike, across his shoulders. An impromptu sled made from lashed willow poles that held the snagcat pelt, various cuts of snagcat meat and a partially butchered fawn, was being pulled on a leash attached to his waist. Addie carried the butchered goat and its pelt in a game sack slung over his shoulder, and Raif carried a mixed bag of ribs, spines, pelvises and longbones that could be boiled and scraped for meat, marrow and fat. All three of them smelled like blood, but Raif found he did not much dislike it. It reminded him of longhunts with with Da and Drey.

"At least he sent the pretty ones" was all Stillborn said as they approached the eastern ledge.

Two Maimed Men awaiting them on the rimrock were armed with thick spears of blackened and case-hardened iron. One wore an armored cloak; a half-circle of boiled and pleated leather mounted with coin-sized metal rings that had to weigh at least twenty pounds. The other man wore chainmail that had rusted around the armpits and a wool kilt over wool pants. Both men appeared whole, but Raif knew better than to be fooled by that. Everyone in the Rift was missing something, and experience had taught him that imperfections that did not immediately meet the eye were usually the worst kind.

Some instinct, perhaps fear or simple habit, made Raif stretch out a hand to read the air. The headwind was light and from the north. Updrafts rising from the Rift were fitful and without force.

Shucking off the bag of bones and letting it drop onto the green granite of the ledge, he said to Addie and Stillborn, "Take the meat. Go on ahead."

The little cragsman shook his head and was about to tell Raif exactly what he thought of that idea when Stillborn also shook his head. A single, curt shake aimed at silencing Addie Gunn.

"Come on," Stillborn said, somehow managing to clap Addie on the shoulder while still balancing the deer. "Lets make sure our Rift Brothers get the meat."

Addie hesitated. He knew how important the meat was, knew also that the Maimed Men needed to see with their own eyes who had brought it. Finally he asked Raif in a whisper, "Will you be all right, lad?"

Raif stared at the man with the armored cloak as he said, "I'll be fine. If you want to do me a favor find me arrows. Two dozen with feather fletchings."

The cragsman nodded. "If you're not back by midnight we'll come looking." Bending at the knee, he picked up Raif's sack. It was still dripping blood.

As Addie and Stillborn walked ahead, Raif let his right hand come to rest on the crossguard of his borrowed sword. It was a small thing, but it drew the attention of Mole's men away from Addie and Stillborn and to himself.

"You're coming with us to see the chief," said the man wearing the armored cloak. Now that he spoke, Raif saw he was missing front teeth. When Raif failed to move, he thrust out his spear. "Get walking."

He thought they would lead him down to Traggis Mole's cave but they led him up to the high cliffs instead. Ancient crumbling steps cut deep into the rock wound up through the city and out onto the headcliffs where the Maimed Men maintained their watch. The cliffs bulged above the city like wasps' nests, round-walled and tapering, connected to each other by a series of gangplanks known as the Cloud Walk. Raif had not been up here before and he saw that the rock was older and softer than the ledgerock below. Birds had made and abandoned nests in the potholes, and dwarfed pines had grown and died, leaving skeletons that rattled in the wind.

Both men were well-accustomed to the Cloud Walk and navigated the wood-and-rope walkways with ease. Raif tried not to look down, *did* look down and began to sway.

"We got a spinner," commented the armored cloak man without rancor. Neither he nor the chainmail man raised a hand to help.

Raif closed his fist around the guiderope. Two ropes suspended at waist height and a foot-wide plank of wood were all that was preventing him from crashing to the rimrock ninety feet below. Wind set the ropes swaying, and the weight of three men on the plank made the wood creak and bow. It would be easy to kill him. A near forceless movement of the hand would be all it would take. Raif tried to calm himself, but the world was tipping, and he was unsure what to do with his body to counter it.

"Walk."

It was both an order and advice. He had been holding too long on to the rope and had begun to lean into it—into thin air. Blinking as if that could somehow help, Raif rocked his weight onto his other foot and eased his hand from the rope. Giddy nausea filled his head. It felt as if his brain had detached itself from his spinal cord and was spinning like a top in his skull. Drunkenly, he took a step forward. More spinning. Seen from above, the city on the edge of the abyss looked like a chunk of driftwood riddled with wormholes. After thinking that bit of nonsense he took another step, followed by another one. Walking.

Two more gangways, a short tunnel, and a drawbridge had to

be navigated before they reached the western watch. Raif developed a technique he called "looking at the stray hair hanging down in front of my eye." To know its name was to know how it worked. At some point during the second gangway he realized what Traggis Mole was up to. Yet the knowledge that it was the Robber Chief's intent to throw him off guard and render him weak at the knees was strangely worthless. It didn't make the gangways any easier.

The sun was setting by the time the two men delivered him to the stack of freestanding rock where the Maimed Men conducted their western watch and Traggis Mole stood waiting. Wind and glaciers had carved out the stack, forming a structure that protruded from the cliff wall like a thumb. The top was flat and slightly canted toward the Rift. A fine down of sugar lichen covered the rock.

As the two men withdrew they pulled on the hoist ropes, raising the drawbridge and leaving Raif and Traggis Mole alone and trapped on the stack.

The king of the city on the edge of the abyss stood with his back turned to Raif, looking south beyond his domain toward the clanholds. Dressed in a floor-length greatcloak of horsehide edged with black swan feathers, nothing of his body was visible below the neck. A bricked-in fire was burning close to the center of the stack, and the Robber Chief must have tended it recently for a stick close to his feet gave off a silky line of smoke.

"Night falls," he said in greeting, not looking round.

The sun, no longer aligned with the Rift, sank beyond the canyonlands sending out a dying breath of red light. Raif looked down and saw the Orrl cloak reflecting the color perfectly, looked back up and saw the sun was gone.

"Right now below us Stillborn is presenting a snagcat to the Rift Brothers, claiming he brought it down with a throw spear." Traggis Mole spun and pinned Raif with his stare. "Does he lie?"

While the Robber Chief was in motion Raif fought the desire to step back. No one he had ever met in his life moved as inhumanly fast as Traggis Mole. The chief's wooden nose was strapped in place above his air hole and as the first dew of dusk formed his breath smoked white.

Raif said, "The blow that brought down the cat was Stillborn's."

"Brought down and kill are not the same," Traggis Mole replied, whip-fast in his harsh Vorlander voice. "His credit is undue."

"Stillborn's blow slowed the cat. Without it mine would have gone wide."

Traggis Mole made no reply. Minutes passed and silence stretched to the Rift and back before he called it in. "Do you know he took your gold?"

Raif blinked. For a moment he felt just as he had on the first gangway; as if the world were tipping sideways and he was unsure how to right himself within it.

The Robber Chief's small round eyes took in all, and gave nothing back. "The fifteen men who took part in the raid on Black Hole were each given a gold rod to reward their success. Ask Stillborn where yours is."

"I will not." The coldness of those three words surprised Raif.

There was a blur of motion, too fast to be tracked wholly by the eye, and then Traggis Mole was standing by the bricked-in fire, his cloak swinging at his heels like a child who could not keep up. "Perhaps he assumed that riches do not interest you."

Something in this statement seemed off-the-mark to Raif. A fraction too much space separated the words and it seemed to him that the Robber Chief was questing. Caution kept Raif silent.

Traggis Mole held the smoking stick in his gloved hand, though Raif had no memory of him bending to pick it up. Walking a circuit of the firepit, he scraped it along the wall. "Did they tell you about the Rift wrall that walked amongst us? How many fought it and how many it killed? Did your fine friends tell you that they arrived too late and the beast had already passed? Did they also tell you that every night I stand watch here, high above my city, and look down into the Rift? And did they tell you that once you start watching it never ends?"

The Robber Chief threw the stick into the fire, where it flared bright for a moment and then was gone. "Night falls and the shadows gather, and to watch you must grow accustomed to the dark. Bide where I stand, Raif Twelve Kill—alone and armed in the darkness—and ask yourself is this a prize worth winning, or a hole without end that will suck away your life?"

Raif made a gesture with his head; he did not know what it was nor what he meant.

"You did not think you could come here and keep your intent hidden?" Traggis Mole asked, turning so that the fire lit the down-facing planes of his face. "No subtlety conceals Stillborn's plans for you. You should ask him why he would not take the city alone, and then listen very hard to the answer. He's a good hunter and liked as well as any man is liked in this god-spurned place. If you had not returned two days back do you think he would have challenged me?"

Rather than say anything against Stillborn Raif did not speak, but the truth lay in the shadows between them.

"Fifteen years is a long time to spend complaining."

Raif moved his legs apart to spread his weight. Whilst Traggis Mole had been speaking he had the sense that he was standing in a fixed position above the darkness. All he could see below him was night sky. Once when he and Drey had been at the swim hole in the Wedge, Drey had wedged a board underneath a rock to use as a dive platform. Somehow it was different from diving off boulders; there was a bounce and you were suspended a couple of feet over the water. You didn't have to step *out*, just down. That's what Raif felt now, as if the jump would be easier here. A move forward was the same thing as a move down.

Everything Traggis Mole said had the hard ring of truth about it, even the stuff about the gold. Raif did not care about the gold, nor did it change his opinion of Stillborn. The Maimed Man had warned him early on that this was not the clanholds and he was no longer clan. Raif frowned. If that had been an attempt by the Robber Chief to switch Raif's allegiance it had failed. What had not failed were the other things Traggis Mole had said.

You must grow accustomed to the dark.

Those words described his life.

Walking the short distance to the edge of the cliff, Raif look down at the city, forced himself to see it. A bonfire had been lit on the main ledge and Maimed Men were gathered in numbers, probably roasting the meat Addie and Stillborn had brought them. No other fires burned brightly. The glows of dozens of grass and willow fires flickered weakly, a single stick or blade of grass away from extinction. Traggis Mole had once called this place a termites' nest, and that's how it looked to Raif as the dark forms of men and women scuttled below him. He did not care about these people, so why had he told Stillborn and Addie Gunn that he would make himself their chief?

In the light of day it was easy to say things and have them sound like sense. The night was different, full of dark spaces where doubts could grow. Words could get spun back on you. Traggis Mole had found the flaws in Raif's plan and hurled them back like darts. Raif did not want to spend the rest of his days on the edge of this abyss, battling whatever came out.

As if reading his mind, Traggis Mole said, "This flaw in the earth is mine. I've ruled it for seventeen years and I've found it gets no lovelier over time." Somehow the Robber Chief was now beside Raif on the edge, his finely shaped mouth pouring cold words in his ear. "Men whine amongst themselves, throwing blame. What's the Mole doing for us? Why haven't we got more food? Why doesn't the Mole act and change things? They forget where they are. They grow lazy, burn grass instead of wood and slaughter their ponies for meat. You tell them to go hunting and raiding and they look at you as if you're cursing in a foreign tongue. This is the Rift. People here do not work toward the well-being of their fellow men. To rule here is to be king of a hole. Once you fall in there is no digging yourself out. Are you prepared for that, Twelve Kill, prepared to feed these ungrateful wretches, break up their knife fights, dispose of their dead? And all the while you have to stand here and watch, one eye on the Rift and the wralls that walk there, and the other eye on your back, marking the men who would slit your throat?"

The Robber Chief's gloved hand closed like a vise around Raif's arm. "I will not let you slit my throat."

Raif swallowed. He could smell the Robber Chief, a smell of sweat and minerals and something else just short of sweet. The man's fingers were like nails being driven into his flesh. Below, the city and the Rift seemed to be tipping toward them. Raif was acutely aware of the slope of the rock. If you were to set a ball by the firepit it would roll off.

"Tell me you will not slit my throat," demanded the Robber Chief. The force of his grip made both of them shake.

Raif's arm was beginning to numb. Something about the Robber Chief's smell was familiar and vaguely disturbing, but his mind could not grasp what it was. For some reason he kept thinking about Drey's dive board. Moving forward was the same as moving down.

"I will not slit your throat," he cried out.

Instantly the same force that held him, yanked him back and he fell backward onto the rock, landing on his butt. He sat there a moment, planting his palms on the ground and breathing hard. Sharp tingles rose up his arm toward the wound made by the *Shatan Maer*, and suddenly Raif knew what the Robber Chief smelled of.

He wished he had recognized it sooner for it might have prevented him from taking a step forward.

And down.

I will not slit your throat. The words were a lie; he had spoken them knowing he would defy them. Oh, he would have been sure not to use a knife and take it to the Robber Chief's throat, but in all other ways the statement was false. Raif would have, and might still, kill him.

Break an oath, kill a clansman, lie to a man's face: the list of his sins had just grown longer.

Raising his chin, Raif gazed at the stars. Perhaps, hundreds of leagues to the southwest at Blackhail, Drey and Effie were doing the same. He liked to think of them safe. It gave him something, not strength exactly, more like a solid surface to rest upon . . . as he fell.

Raif glanced over his shoulder toward the Robber Chief, who had come to rest by the fire. A gloved hand, angling out from his greatcloak and grasping the edge of the firewall, told everything. Raif wondered how he had not seen it sooner. He, of all people, should have known.

"So you will not slit my throat," Traggis Mole repeated, a soft bitterness edging his voice. "I will make myself grateful for that."

Rising to his feet, Raif said, "The Rift Brothers should be taught how to set traps. There's small game to the east of here. Rabbits, ground squirrels, coons. Lean meat, but a man could do worse."

A strange light glittered in Traggis Mole's black eyes. "Do it," he said.

That cost him, Raif thought, unsure whether or not he had been right to bring it up. Traggis Mole's pride ran deep.

"Linden Moodie leads a sortie into the clanholds at dawn tomorrow. You will not be expected to go along."

Raif and the Robber Chief regarded each other carefully, searching for the truth behind one another's statements. Just once Traggis Mole pulled his wooden nose free of his face and took a clear breath.

"Why here?" Raif asked as the wind picked up, sending the flames in the firepit shivering.

The robber chief did not shrug or hesitate as other men might. He said, "I fought the pits in Trance Vor; if any life could prepare a man for this it would be that one."

Pit fighting. Raif had thought it was a legend. Two men flung into a pit and not allowed out until one of them was dead.

"The walls were always eleven feet high, do you know why?" Raif shook his head.

"Any higher and the gas lamps wouldn't be able to throw enough light into the pit and the crowd would be unable to see. Any shorter and a man could jump up and pull his way out." Traggis Mole watched Raif shiver. "The winner always had to wait for the rope to be lowered. One day I decided I no longer wanted to wait."

It was getting colder, Raif realized, yet the Mole did not appear to feel it. He was moving again, this time toward the north edge of the stack where a ridge of rock stretched down and back to join the cliff wall. "My story is no different than a dozen other men and women will tell you here. We're all lost, desperate. Chased. My mistake was in killing the man who lowered the rope to me that final time. He didn't deserve it, but I can't say that worried me much. He turned out to have the sort of brother that would not let the death rest. His name was Scurvy Pine and he called himself the King of Thieves. Took my nose from me and would have taken more if I hadn't escaped him. Next day he set a thieves' bounty on my head. A thousand pieces of gold, can you imagine it? Enough money to build a marble pool and drown yourself in riches. Every stableboy, man-at-arms, shopkeeper and villain in the city wanted to find me and chop off my head. And it didn't stop at Trance Vor. Word of Scurvy Pine's bounty spread west to Morning Star, Hound's Mire, Spire Vanis and Ille Glaive. Soon there was nowhere I could rest easy at night. I took to the roads and then the woods, spent a year scratching out a living at a lumber camp deep in the Trenchlands, and then, by some miracle of misfortune, I ended up in the Rift."

Traggis Mole's hand came up as he lightly touched his ribs through the fabric of his cloak. "And here is where I stay."

He knows, Raif realized, hearing the bleakness in his voice.

Traggis Mole met gazes with Raif, breathed hard through his wooden nose and then looked away.

"Everyone who saw you shoot against Tanjo Ten Arrow at the test of arrows saw what you could do with a bow. The outlander Thomas Argola reckons you can do more. He came to me the day after the wrall passed through the city, and you know what he said?"

Raif could imagine, but he shook his head.

"He said if I were you, Mole Chief, I'd pray for Twelve Kill's return."

The Mole moved and in an instant was directly in front of Raif's face, his gloved hand grasping the collar of the Orrl cloak. "What did he mean by that?"

Updrafts were rising, and the first hollow notes of Rift Music sounded. Raif smelled cat meat cooking nine stories below him. "You must have asked him."

For a moment Raif thought Traggis Mole would pull out one of his famous longknives and stab him in the throat. Yet he didn't. With a springing motion of his hand he released Raif's cloak. "I am asking you."

The calm in his voice sounded dangerous to Raif. "I can't tell you what the outlander knows. I've only spoken to him a handful of times and what he said made no sense. I can tell you that I have seen and fought those beings you call wralls. I have killed some. I can do it again."

Here was the knowledge he had been waiting for, the one thing that this meeting was about. Raif saw it now, saw the world of fear living behind the Mole Chief's black eyes. Saw it and knew it wasn't for himself. *We are alike*, Raif realized with a small start. *Both watching.*

Both wounded.

Traggis Mole said, "Will you defend your Rift Brothers?"

The words were formal, and to Raif they sounded like an oath. He thought before he answered. He did not want to speak a second lie. Some wary part of his brain checked for clauses. The words sounded like a simple request; they did not appear to conceal a trap. Only yesterday he had spoken a promise to Stillborn and Addie Gunn. *I will become Lord of the Rift.* Surely the two were one and the same?

Raif glanced at the Robber Chief, Traggis Mole. Why did he not ask for anything for himself?

The answer was beneath his cloak. Perhaps not even realizing he did so, Traggis Mole stood bent at the waist.

"I will defend the Rift Brothers." Raif tried, but could not keep the ring of oathspeaking from his voice, and the words bounced off the cliffwall and echoed across the Rift to the clanholds.

Oathbreaker, that was his Blackhail name.

But the Robber Chief did not know it.

Traggis Mole nodded once, and then called to some unseen watcher down below, directing him to lower the drawbridge.

He and Raif stood feet apart, watching each other as men climbed stairs and loosed ropes.

"Go," the Robber Chief commanded once the narrow wooden drawbridge was seated upon the lip of the stack.

The instant before Raif turned he saw a single curl of black smoke rising through the gap in Traggis Mole's horsehide cloak.

The wrall's sword had sunk deep into the meat between his ribs, and now he was being eaten alive.

Raif felt the wound in his shoulder twitch in sympathy as he crossed the drawbridge in the dark.

TWENTY-TWO

The Menhir Fire

Raina soaked in the copper bath and let her thoughts drift with the steam. It was good to be weightless. Her breasts floated on the surface, hot and pink, as her hand idly passed between her legs. Later her presence would be needed at the Hallowing of the guidestone, but for now she could simply float.

Jebb Onnacre had brought the tub to her chamber and Anwyn had drawn a bath with rosemary and precious ambergris. The scent was sweet and peppery, like baked fruit. Oil swirled on the water, trembling as Raina breathed. Dagro had liked to watch her bathe, and she had learned over time to enjoy being watched. Boldly she would raise her legs from the water and ask if he found her clean.

Pushing her toes against the base of the tub, Raina rose to standing. There was too much confusion down that path. Mace Blackhail had robbed that pleasure from her, the remembering of her first husband's lovemaking. She could glimpse it but if she looked too long, newer images were overlaid over the old ones. Son instead of father. Dead leaves between her legs. Stepping out of the bath, Raina twisted her wet hair into a knot and wrung it dry. She had never returned to the Oldwood. When she was chief she was going to have it chopped down.

Anwyn had laid out all manner of pretty things for Raina to dally with. Shell combs, silk ribbons, perfumed unctions, a silver mirror, rouge—how in the name of Ione had she come by that? Toweling herself dry with a yellow shammy Raina frowned in mild puzzlement. There was a message here, in all these maiden's gewgaws and paints, and if she thought about it long enough it wasn't flattering. Yes, Anwyn meant to treat her. The clan matron was one of the very few people in this roundhouse who knew what Raina felt about being forced to participate in tonight's events. Yet a hot bath alone would have sufficed as a treat. This armory of prettiness laid out on a crisply pressed sheet was something more.

Anwyn must have called in some favors, for she was a woman who when presented with a pot of rouge would use it to grease cow udders. The one thing she had in her corner was her total mastery and control of the clan kitchen. The clan maids might turn up their noses at mutton stew and boiled pork, but they'd hand over valuable equipment for honeycakes, dried and sugared apricots and plum wine. Raina sat on the corner of the bed and picked up a weapon at random. It was a needle of bone with a flat end that felt like sand paper. A buffer? Experimentally, Raina brushed it against her teeth. Dear gods, either Anwyn had made a mistake and included a woodworking tool amongst the trinkets or maids today had declared tooth enamel outdated. Raina put it back in its place and picked up the hairbrush instead. Her hair was tangled from lack of care so she rubbed a little unction on the toothcombs. That was better. It even smelled nice. By the time the waist-length, honey-colored locks were finally combed out the ends were beginning to dry.

Still naked, she reached for the rouge, sniffed it, tested it on the back of her hand, rejected it, then put some on her cheeks anyway. And then rubbed it off. Crucial seconds passed as she inspected herself in the mirror. No, she did not look like a city bawd. Her face actually looked better with some color, as if she'd been out riding or had an hour or two of sun.

Of course now that she saw herself she realized Anwyn's point. Tonight everyone in the clan would be gathered to watch the Hallowing of the new Hailstone. It was a ceremony you could live entire lifetimes and never see. People would be excited and expectant. It had to go well; the future of Blackhail depended upon it. Many clansmen and women would partici-pate in the Calling of the Gods, but only one person would bear the Menhir Fire, and up until an hour ago that person had been walking about the roundhouse as pale and grubby as a cellar maid. Even if she did not honor the stone she must honor her fellow clansmen: that was the catch of tonight. Wisely, Anwyn had understood this and given Raina a gentle push in the right direction.

Raina Blackhail, wife to two chiefs, must welcome the new Hailstone with reverence, properly groomed and attired. Everyone in the clan had sons, fathers or brothers at war. She must honor them. It was as simple as that. She must think of Blackhail, not Stannig Beade and Scarpe, must imagine the wishes of her first husband Dagro, not those of her second husband Mace.

Fanning her hair over her shoulders to encourage it to dry, Raina crossed to the cedar chest that she'd ordered brought down from her old chambers. It contained cloaks, dresses, shawls, smallclothes, blouses, boots, stocking, skirts, heeled shoes and other items of clothing. Dust rose as she pushed back the lid. The layers were packed with dried wheat seeds, though she could not recall why. The seeds created a snowfall of gold as she pulled out one dress after another. It had been a long time since she'd cared about how she looked. The old Raina—the one that existed before Dagro's death and the rape in the Oldwood—had been young and carefree and had not realized her own good luck. Raina felt tender toward her, indulgent of her girlish taste in dresses. Periwinkle blue silk! Such finery had probably cost Dagro an entire horse at the Dhoone Fair.

She would never again be the woman who wore this dress to the Spring Lark and pretended not to notice clansmen's admiring glances as she whirled around the dance floor. Such delight had forever passed. Prettiness and the politics of attracting, yet appearing to disdain, male attention seemed like child's play. The blue silk would not do. She rummaged further, thrusting arm-deep into the seeds. Finally she found it, right at the bottom keeping company with dried-out spiders, a dress spun from finely woven mohair, russet-colored, with a panel of silver tissue that peeked through a split in the skirt.

"*I know it's not to your taste, Ray. But mayhap one day you'll grow into it.*" Raina heard Dagro's voice as clearly as if he were speaking into her ear. He had gone to parley with Threavish Cutler in Ille Glaive and spent the night in the Lake Keep. At the feast he attended, he spotted a fine city lady wearing a dress much the same as this. "*She was dancing, and it flashed silver when she moved and I thought to myself: Raina must have one. It was the first time I'd ever looked at a dress and thought of Blackhail.*" Raina swallowed. He was a man so he had got the details wrong. A local seamstress had run it up for him, using the fancy city fabrics he had brought her. Raina had never liked it and worn it only once, when the ancient clan chief Spynie Orrl had come to visit. It had seemed old to her and fuddy-duddy, though it fit well enough around the bodice.

Seven years later it seemed just right. Stately and beautiful, heavy as a king's cloak. She pulled it on and struggled for some time with the lacings. Her waist was the same size but her breasts appeared to have gotten larger—had she always worn her dresses this tight?

Her hair was close to dry by the time she'd donned stockings and suede boots and a belt of silver chain, and she set about pinning it back. No matronly, serviceable braids. Not tonight. She would wear her hair in thick, loose hanks at her back, banded with silk ribbon.

She felt strange by the time she was done, not quite herself. The dress stiffened her spine, made her walk with her chin up and chest out. As she lifted the latch of the little cell beneath the kitchen that she now called her own, she realized her fingernails were rough and chipped. *That* was what the bone thing was for, she realized, smiling as she let herself out.

People fell silent as she made her way through the kitchens. The women punching down dough for tonight's bake stopped what they were doing and turned to look at her. The boy sweeping the floor actually started sweeping his feet. Raina thought for a moment, then halted close to the big center worktable where kitchen girls were assaulting vegetables with wicked-looking knives. The heat from the bread ovens was nearly unbearable.

"Everyone, " Raina said briskly. "Stop work and prepare for the Hallowing. All will be expected to attend."

Clanswomen stared at her, blinking, their hands either powdery with dough or wet with carrot and onion juices. "But the ovens," said Sheela Cobbin, one of the bare-armed women kneading the dough. "They're already fired and hot."

"Close them down," Raina said to her. "There'll be no bake tonight."

It was like using a muscle, exercising power. The more you did it the easier it became. Everyone obeyed her, setting down knives and mops and ladles, the dough women throwing damp cloths over their balls of dough, the oven boys closing the air holes with long metal hooks. "Borrie," she said to the boy who had been sweeping his feet. "When everyone has left I want you to stay behind and seal the kitchen door."

He understood exactly what she meant and nodded. "I'll let myself out of the back."

"Good." She'd be damned if any Scarpe would steal into this kitchen and sneak away with food from her clan tonight.

She was a little breathless by the time she made her way into the entrance hall. Part of her was a bit worried about stepping on Anwyn's toes, yet the clan matron was nowhere to be seen, and ultimately Raina knew that her own authority must usurp that of her old friend's. *Do and be damned*, that was what Dagro used to say at moments like this. The words had barely concealed his joy at doing exactly what suited him, and Raina only hoped that someday she might feel the same.

"Lady." Corbie Meese fell in step with her as she crossed the hall. The hammerman had elected to stay behind to defend the roundhouse while Blackhail's armies rode to war. His wife Sarolyn had just given birth to her first baby, a daughter, and although the child was doing well Sarolyn was still abed. "You do us proud."

She stopped to look at him, and saw that he was dressed in formal battle gear, complete with hammer chains, gleaming leather fronts, and armored gloves tucked beneath his hammer harness, high on his left shoulder. Glad and sad she smiled at him. "Tonight is for us—for Blackhail."

He read her face carefully, his hazel eyes earnest. She knew why he had sought her out to speak with her. He wanted to know what she felt about this evening. Could it really be legitimate, this hacked-off stone from another clan? By speaking to waylay him she had prevented them both from having to hear those damning words spoken out loud.

He bowed to her—hammermen who had trained under

Naznarri Drac, the Griefbringer, were always courtly. "The warriors follow you in this."

She held herself steady as he turned and left, realizing that the stiff formal dress with its silver panel and waist chain had turned her into a symbol of her clan. And little was required of a symbol save to evoke pride in that which it represented. Only when he was out of sight did she allow herself to breathe. She had not realized how much had rested on her statement. Corbie Meese had not acted alone. Even as she stood here, breathing the quick shallow breaths necessary to survive in such a dress, the hammerman was carrying word upstairs to the great-hearth and the men who waited there. *Raina Blackhail supports the Hallowing.*

Heart do not break, she warned it sternly. All she had to do was get through this evening with dignity. She could not allow herself to think of Stannig Beade and his perfect manipulation, must focus solely on the drawing together of her clan.

A group of Scarpe women with dyed black hair and dresses of various shades of red watched her with cool insolence as she stood and thought. The women had been cracking open hazelnuts with armorer's pliers, and Raina was willing to bet that the pliers had come straight from Brog Widdie's forge. Unable to stop herself, she marched right up to the women. "Leave this hall," she commanded. "Only Hailsfolk are allowed here this night."

A girl who might have been pretty if it wasn't for her dyed hair and ugly sneer, shot back, "That's not what we heard."

Raina felt the blood rush to her face. She wanted to smack the girl and grab the pliers from her skinny little friend. Luckily the dress would not allow it; its fabric would not accommodate stooping so low. Keeping her head level, she spoke one word. "Go."

Until that moment Raina had not known she possessed such a voice. Utterly cold and hard as nails, it served up exactly what was ordered. After snatching brief glances at each other, the four women turned and fled.

Raina just blinked. She felt as if she had discovered a secret power.

I must wear this dress more often, she thought as she went outside.

Torches as tall as two men were already burning in a great circle around the roundhouse. Phosphorus had been sprinkled on the oil-soaked twigs and the flames shooting up were silver. Hot sparks sailed on the breeze, and the crackle of burning minerals filled the air. It was just beyond sunset and natural light was receding, and despite everything Raina found herself stirred. The scent of boiling pig's blood triggered primal urges in her brain. She wanted to feed. And flee.

The large paved greatcourt in front of the roundhouse was where the ceremony would take place. Stannig Beade and his helpers were busy with preparations. The almost square-shaped chunk of Scarpestone had been raised on a platform that had been entirely plated in silver. Brog Widdie and his assistant Glynn Goodlamb had spent the past four days hammering the sheet metal into place. Glynn was still there now, lying by the foot of the platform, polishing the silver with white vinegar. The stone itself was covered with rich skins; sable, bearhide, musk ox and lynx. The skins were held together by an intricate network of silver wire that glittered along the seams like running water. A deep, rectangular-shaped trench had been dug around the platform at a distance of seven feet. Raina could only imagine the work it must have taken, for the baked clay stones that paved the greatcourt were huge.

Stannig Beade was squatting by the trench, pouring in fluid from a wooden cask. He was dressed in Blackhail colors, his pigskin coat dyed black and freshly collared with a roll of silver cloth. Raina had heard that he had commissioned a new line of tattoos to honor the ceremony. As he finished his task and turned toward the light of the torches she saw it: a band of scarified flesh stretching across both eyelids. She had to fight the urge to step back. Some of the pinholes were still oozing blood.

The clan guide of Scarpe noted Raina's revulsion and turned his back on her. Raina felt dismissed. She moved away, past the platform and the smokefires and the vat of boiling blood. People were gathering now, spilling through the greatdoor and around the sides of the roundhouse. Raina walked against the crowd. People made way for her, moving from their paths so she need not veer from her own. Faces were grave and excited. Torchlight and blood fumes charged the air.

Children and pregnant women were forbidden from attending the ceremony. Rumor had it that Hallowings had taken place where the unborn had dropped from women's wombs. Raina herself knew little of what was to come. Two days back Stannig Beade had summoned her to his stonemill and told her what she must do. It was a simple task—just carry the Menhir torch to the guidestone—and she found herself much relieved.

It was a good night for it. No clouds marred the sky and the stars were scattered in immense and sparkling waves. A faint and shifting band of green to the north might have been the Gods' Lights; Stannig Beade would be happy as a crow about that. It was hard not to be bitter. All the fine preparations; the sea of silver plate, the clanfolk in their rarely used finery, the wild call of the pig's blood. Stannig Beade had done an excellent job. Perhaps he believed the gods would come.

Perhaps I should try believing that myself.

Smoothing down her hair, Raina headed over to the small crowd that had gathered around Anwyn Bird and Jebb Onnacre. The clan matron was handing out the booze: a half-dram of her five-year malt to anyone who fancied it. She was dressed rather curiously in many layers—a dress, a bodice, an overtunic and an elbow-length cape—all sparkly and richly embroidered and bearing no resemblance to each other. Two peacock feathers were stuck like pins in her hair. Acknowledging Raina with a flat nod, she said, "I believe you shut down my kitchen."

Raina's instinct was to apologize but she she stopped herself and there was an awkward silence as the two women faced each other over the upturned barrel containing the half-drams.

"You look like a queen," Jebb Onnacre said shyly to Raina, breaking the silence.

"She does," Anwyn agreed, her light blue eyes still intent upon Raina. "So we must forgive her for acting like one."

Poor Jebb. His two favorite women in the world were regarding each other coolly and he didn't know what to do about it. He made a hmmming noise, opened his mouth to speak, thought better of it, and then reached for a half-dram and downed it.

Raina and Anwyn laughed at exactly the same time. "Thank you for the bath and the pretty stuff," Raina said to her.

"Good luck," Anwyn replied.

It would do. Raina left them and mingled with the growing crowd. People seemed to know not to greet her and offered instead brief bows of respect. It was getting cold now, the air dry and crisp. The green lights in the northern sky tantalized: *Now you see us, now you don't.*

Suddenly there was a soft popping sound and a ball of white light shot straight up into the air.

"Blackhail!" screamed Stannig Beade. "Attend the stone!"

Everyone fell silent, and began moving like a cinched thread toward the center of the greatcourt. Raina hurried around them, anxious to take up her position.

Stannig Beade's helpers kept the area twenty feet around the stone clear of people. They were Scarpes, Raina noticed, but wisely wore no tokens of their clan. When they spotted her, they let her pass.

Stannig Beade had made Brog Widdie silver-plate a second, smaller platform that had been dragged into position before the Scarpestone. Stannig Beade stood upon this metal dais, flanked by iron torches that hissed as they burned gas. The clan guide noted Raina's presence but did not greet her. He glared at the crowd, a big man once trained to the hammer, with bloody, eyes and twitching neck muscles.

"Blackhail!" he cried out when all were still. "Tonight we are gathered to present our new guidestone to the gods. It is not enough that it be delivered into the clanhold. The gods must be called to judge it."

His voice was grinding and terrible, filled with accusation as he prowled back and forth between the torches. "Look to yourselves, Blackhail, look into the center of your hearts and ask if you have cause for shame. The gods will come this night and they will know you. They will know this clan and every man, woman and child within it, and if they judge the sum of Blackhail unworthy they will reject its stone.

"Do not expect to fool them." He shot a brief, unreadable glance at Raina. "The gods come from stone and are stone hard. They will crush you down if you are false, smash the foundations of this clan." At the word *clan*, Stannig Beade's arm shot backward. Air rushed in toward the Scarpestone and the trench ringing its platform ignited in a sheet of flames.

Raina's ears roared. Heat beat against her cheeks. The crowd stepped back, fearful. One clan maid, Lansa Tanner by the look of her golden hair, fainted and had to be carried away.

The fire burned more fiercely than any fire Raina had ever seen. It dragged air from her lungs to feed itself and its flames shivered and leapt upward, *alive*. Stannig Beade's raised dais was only a few feet in front of the trench. Raina wondered how he stood the searing heat. He had become a dark profile against the light. A bear against the sun.

Screaming, he named the gods. "Ganolith, Hammada, Ione, Loss, Uthred, Oban, Larannyde, Malweg, Behathmus. Hear me! See me! Come to this clan."

The words were Raina's cue and she took the simple torch of green wood from the Scarpeman Wilder Styke, but she was confused, for she was supposed to approach the Scarpestone and light the Menhir stack that lay primed and ready by the foot of the stone. Beade had said nothing about a wall of flames. Unsettled, she took a step forward. From his position upon the second platform, Stannig Beade glared down at her.

"Walk forward and light the Menhir Fire so the gods will know where to enter the stone."

Raina felt the pressure of thousands of gazes upon her back. Her face and neck were slick with sweat. A spark from the torch fell upon her hand, sizzling as it scorched a tiny black hole in her skin. She took another step forward.

Stannig Beade called out to the gods. "Behold Raina Blackhail, the chosen emissary of this clan. Judge her and allow her to step through the flames."

Raina could feel the silver thread in the front panel of her dress growing hot. She was almost abreast with Beade now and had a choice between walking over the dais he stood upon, or around it, to get to the Scarpestone.

The Menhir Fire illuminates the hole I will drill deep into the rock, he had told her two days back. *If all goes well I will tap into a vein, and the gods will be able to make their journey to the heart of the guidestone. When they are present I will seal up the hole.*

She did not know what to do. Instinct warned her not to take another step, that once she passed Beade's dais the heat would be too great to bear. Yet her clan was watching, needing her to step forward. Stannig Beade had manipulated her once again. Had he actually told everyone that if the gods judged her worthy they would kill the flames? The guide scowled ahead, giving nothing away. He was a man who knew how to intimidate a crowd.

And she was his enemy, and he had placed her in a position where he could not lose . . . and she could not win. Flee and she would let down her clan on this most sacred of nights. Stay and she would be burned.

Raina took the step required to raise herself onto his dais. She turned her head and looked at him, but he would not acknowledge her.

He was a coward then, in the end.

The silver plating on the dais had been so highly polished that standing upon it was like standing on a mirror. Raina glanced down and saw her face staring back. She looked like a puzzled child.

Taking another step, she moved behind Stannig Beade. One more would bring her down on the other side of the dais. She was perhaps two feet off the ground, yet the flames in the trench towered over her. They burned ruthlessly, lashing and curling like blazing whips. Their heat dried Raina's eyeballs, and blew back the hair from her scalp.

Not one sound came from the crowd. She knew what they would see: the rigid black silhouette of a woman bearing a torch. What did they know of such a ceremony? Blackhail hadn't had a new guidestone in seven hundred years. For all anyone knew Stannig Beade could be making it up as he went along.

Raina began the forward motion that would take her off the dais. Of all the thoughts that were swirling in her head, one came to rest.

Do and be damned.

Rotating her hips, she shifted her momentum and stepped sideways instead of down. Suddenly she was right there, beside Stannig Beade, in the center of the dais. Before he had chance to react, Raina held her torch aloft and addressed the crowd.

"Blackhail," she cried. "Our old guide, Inigar Stoop, had

hoped this day would never come. Yet he swore to me that if it did he would walk through the fire with his chief. The gods must judge the guide as well as the clan. So I call upon our new guide to accompany me through the flames."

A moment of quiet followed, where the only noise Raina could hear was the pounding of her heart. Stannig Beade made a jerking movement, and filled his lungs to speak.

Someone in the crowd murmured something. There was a gentle push of people forward. And then quite crisply, Anwyn Bird's rang out from the back.

"Yes, guide as well as chief. Inigar always did say that."

"Raina and Stannig," came a second voice, very possibly belonging to Corbie Meese. "Raina and Stannig. Raina and Stannig."

Others took up the chant and it spread like its own kind of fire, rolling out across the crowd. Even one of the Scarpemen near the front began to mouth the words.

"Raina and Stannig. Raina and Stannig."

Stannig Beade's neck muscles were twitching like scorpions as he turned to look at her.

Raina did him the courtesy of looking back. "Shall we?"

This was her clan and he had misjudged her influence here, but after this moment he would never underestimate her again. She saw this in him and perhaps later it would make her afraid, but for now she felt triumphant.

She just hoped she wouldn't burn.

Beade did not take her offered hand. Instead he punched a fist into the air, silencing the crowd. "Blackhail! You dishonor the gods. This is not a horse race. Yes, I will walk with the representative of our chief, but beware the ire of the gods." He seared the crowd with a stare, replacing anticipation with shame. "They ill like clansmen thwarting their plans.

"Woman," he commanded Raina, "step in time with me."

She was not a fool and knew not to challenge him any further, and they began a solemn walk toward the fire. Flames jumped at them. Once they were down from the platform the heat hit their faces in waves. Raina kept in perfect time with Beade, matching his stride length and swing. She held the torch high between them, following his example of making a show for the crowd.

Dagro's dress would be forever ruined with sweat, she thought sadly, as perspiration poured from her body into the fabric. Perhaps it was just as well. It made her act like someone else when she wore it.

Stannig Beade knew something Raina did not, for when they drew close enough to the flames to smell their hair and clothes crisping, he made a small gesture with his finger and stepped ahead of her.

As he moved forward the flames died and he entered a world of smoke. Confused, Raina followed him. The stench of burned soil was sickening, and the ground she stepped on was hot. Fire had dazzled her eyes and she thought she saw a figure slipping away from the opposite side of the trench.

"Light the Menhir Fire," Beade ordered, his voice ugly now that they were out of earshot of the crowd.

Raina was glad to get away from him and crossed the short distance to the platform. Fire had tarnished the silver, and the platform's walls were almost black. Above them, the hides covering the Scarpestone were smoking. Bending at the waist, Raina pushed the torch toward the small stack of sticks laying on the platform's edge. With a jolt of surprise she realized the hides did not reach all the way down to the hole. The foot of the Scarpestone was visible and she could clearly see the pale circle of new stone that had been exposed by Stannig Beade's drill. The hole in its center was the blackest thing Raina had ever seen in her life. It was the color of all things forsaken.

Stannig Beade is right, she realized with a chill. *This is no game we play.* That hole was a passage for the gods, and if they did not like what they saw tonight they would not take it. Yes, Stannig Beade had his tricks—someone had flash-doused the flames for him—but this was no trick. And he and she wanted the same thing: the gods to return to Blackhail.

Sobered by her thoughts, Raina lit the Menhir Fire and prayed for the Stone Gods to notice.

TWENTY-THREE

Hard Truths at the Dhoonewall

The only remaining hillfort in the Dhoonewall that remained livable was a kidney-shaped mound of dressed stone that had a second roof built on top of its original slate roof. The second roof consisted of massive panels of copper soldered together and bent in place, that were secured, as far as Vaylo Bludd could see, by man-size needles that had been driven through the copper and between the slates and into the original wooden beams underneath. Had to be about a hundred of those iron rods sticking out of the roof, Vaylo reckoned, and he wouldn't be surprised that if he actually decided to take the roof stair all the way up to the top, walked across the scaly green carpet of verdigris and stood by one of those black needles he would see it was a spear. Fighting men had erected this roof, using whatever resources they had at hand; copper stockpiled from the mines to the south and clumsy spears they did not need. Vaylo could imagine it. Their roof was leaking and they were wet and miserable. They'd applied to their chief and been ignored. Attacks were coming from the north, their equipment was rusting, their clothes black with mold; a supply wagon had failed to arrive. Pissed off, they'd forged this roof, using a fortune of Dhoone's precious copper in its making and sending an angry message to their chief. Behold us, we are sons of Dhoone. The force with which the spears have been thrust into the roof, punching great dents in the metal, told all.

Of course the second roof barely worked better than the first. The soldiers never did seal up the dents, and rain found its way through them and ran down onto the first roof and along well worn paths to the mold-barrel fortress below.

Vaylo didn't like to breathe the air. He frowned at the slimy black film on the walls and found it surprisingly easy to imagine it invading his lungs. He had bid Nan do what she could, but she was one woman fighting against a horde of spores and quick as she flung back shutters to let in the wind the little black devils were invading her mop bucket, infiltrating the very agent of their own destruction. Nan laughed about it, and staunchly refused help. Vaylo had a feeling she liked being the only woman amongst a hundred and eighty men.

Well close enough to a hundred and eighty . . . but he would think about that later, when the sun wasn't shining in squares upon the flagstone floor that were almost warm when you walked on them, and the laugher of the bairns wasn't tumbling down the spiral-cut stairs.

Vaylo passed through the hillfort's central hall and into its northern ward. The building and part of the wall it defended was wedged between two hills. It was a basic structure with three rounded wards at groundlevel, three smaller ones on the floor above, and a warren of cells and store rooms on the upper level. Upwall, about two hundred feet to the east, a broken bit of watchtower with a partially collapsed roof remained standing. Vaylo hadn't gone up there yet, but he intended to do so soon as he had noticed Cluff Drybannock spent much of his time there. Drybone had visited the other five hillforts in the chain and pronounced them larger and better sited, and wholly destroyed. "Tumbled stone and freestanding walls are all that are left," Dry had said. "The roofs are gone and fox pines have seeded in the wards."

The hillforts still made little sense to Vaylo, though he was glad for his own sake that Dhoone had built them. Situated on the northern edge of the Copper Hills, they looked down over the scrubby fellfields, heaths and uplands that lay to the north. They had seen hard fighting in their time, that much he could tell, for there were places in the curtainwall where you could see the ghosts of long-past impacts: spider cracks of the kind that were caused by heavy shot, sections of stone that had melted to glass, craters and burn rings. The sight of them gave Vaylo a queer feeling in his chest. He knew the Maimed Men controlled a broken city somewhere to the north, but he wasn't sure if they had ever been capable of such a violent assault.

The Dog Lord chided himself as he passed through the ward door and onto the battle terrace. He should have learned the histories from Molo Bean and Ockish Bull. It would be reassuring to know exactly what the deal was here. It could be that a thousand years ago some bold Blackhail chief had launched a fiendish attack from the north. Maybe, gods bless them, the Lost Clan had been in ascendancy and Dhoone had felt threatened by their closeness. The clanholds were nothing if not stingy with their histories. Withy and Wellhouse kept tally, so the stories went, and there was something about a locked room at Castlemilk that was said to contain precious scrolls. For fifty-odd years now the Dog Lord had—in the deep and longstanding tradition of Bludd chiefs—disdained learning the history of the clanholds, but he was beginning to regret his ignorance.

Mistakes have been made. Gods willing I'll make no more. Thinking of Ockish Bull made the Dog Lord smile. His words performed the alchemy of placing contrition right next to defiance.

Vaylo's smile held as he spread his hands wide on the stone balustrade and leaned out into the fresh air. He was looking north over the fort valley and the headlands beyond it. The afternoon sun was blocked by the fortress at his back. This was the best spot in the entire building, this broad, half-roofed battle terrace that extended out from the northern ward. Standing here a man could imagine he was sailing north on a great ship through a strait that passed between two islands. The wind blew in your face no matter what time of day or night you came here and you could not see the earth below your feet.

Nan had commandeered part of the terrace as a playground for the bairns, and pretty much every man in the entire hillfort came out here a couple of times a day to breathe some good air instead of moldy foulness. A couple of men were out here now, sitting on the crates Nan had brought out for the bairns. Mogo Salt and Odwin Two Bear were sitting with their backs against the fortress wall, spearing carrots from a copper bowl with the tips of their swords. At the opposite end of the balcony a man whom Vaylo did not recognize was keeping watch, armed with a beautiful limewood self bow.

Vaylo called across to him. "Where is Drybone?"

The man turned, revealing the high cheekbones and finely sculpted bonemass of the Sull. "Sir, he is in the tower."

He was accoutered with tokens of Bludd—the red leather grip on his sheathed sword, the hollowed-out bone containing his measure of guidestone, the carbuncles of garnet on his cloak brooch—yet Vaylo did not know him.

"What is your name?"

"I'm Kye Hillrunner, once of Trenchland, now of Bludd." His voice was proud but Vaylo detected the nervousness underneath it. He was young, and this was the first time he had met his chief.

"Drybone took your oath?"

"Yes, sir. Eight months back while I was housed at Bludd."

Now that he had gotten a better look at the boy, Vaylo saw that his features lacked the icy perfection of full-blooded Sull. "How long have you been with us?"

"Five years. I worked on Ockish Bull's horse farm. That's where I met Cluff Drybannock and he began to train me."

Vaylo nodded; he thought the young man needed it. "So you met Ockish?"

"He died soon after I got there. His son let me stay on."

So Ockish had taken the boy in as a tied clansman. It fit, for all Sull, even Trenchlanders, were known for their skill at breeding horses. And Ockish always had a soft spot for strays. Vaylo knew better than to ask Kye who his father was or what claim he had to Bludd. If he was a bastard that was his business. Subject closed.

"Keep the watch for Bludd," the Dog Lord said to him in parting. "We are chosen by the Stone Gods to guard their borders."

It was part of the clan boast and Vaylo hardly knew what made him say it, yet if he was surprised by his own words, he was surprised more by the young man's response.

"I know it. That is why I am here."

A cold finger of fear touched the base of Vaylo's spine. He

looked at the young warrior, saw the slow burn of purpose in his inhumanly bright Sull eyes. It was not easy to turn away from it, yet Vaylo did, and headed back into the dampness of the fort.

What was happening here? he asked himself as he headed for the east ward. What trick was Ockish Bull playing from his grave? And what was Drybone's part in this? How many more Sull Bluddsmen would he stumble upon within these walls? Oh it was true enough Bludd had always taken in its share of Trenchlander mongrels—they shared a border after all—yet Vaylo could not set aside his agitation. The boast, the damn boast. *We are Clan Bludd, chosen by the Stone Gods to watch their borders. Death is our companion. A life long lived is our reward.* Fifty-three years he had lived with those words, fired by their hard-driving pride. When had they changed on him? How could words mean one thing one day and then the next day something else?

The blond swordsman Big Borro opened the fortified east door for him, tugging back the greasy hank of leather that hung in place of a pull ring. "Snow tomorrow," he said as Vaylo stepped out onto the Dhoonewall.

Snow? Vaylo frowned at the sun and cloudless sky. It didn't seem possible, yet he was wise enough not to voice a contradiction. It had been sixty years since a Borro man was last caught in a storm.

The Dhoonewall was cracked and weather-beaten. Its northern edge had been carved by the wind, and the breakwall had tumbled so there was nothing to stop a man from stepping over the brink. Entire sections of stone walkway were missing, the gaps overlaid with loose planks. In others areas the stone had buckled and erupted upward, forming shambling mounds where weeds thrived. Vaylo was careful where he put his feet. From where he stood he could look both north and south, and the great breadth of the earth was visible. The Copper Hills rolled out around him in purple and rust-brown waves, a sight to thrill a clansman's heart.

Now the tower was another matter, and as Vaylo closed upon it he had some fear for his head. Chunks of stone had fallen recently. Others looked imminent. Unlike the main building, the tower had not been capped with copper and its collapsed and black-rotted roof timbers still gripped a tinkling deathtrap of slates. Vaylo made a dash for the door. Reminding himself that when he'd held the finest structure in the clanholds—the Dhoonehouse at Blue Dhoone Lake—he'd never much enjoyed it, the Dog Lord entered the collapsed tower.

It smelled like a wellshaft, and echoed like one too. Both the tower and the Dhoonewall sank their foundations deep into the cleft between the two hills, and the first thing Vaylo spotted was a way down. *Should have brought a torch*, he thought, for although the roof had fallen in, six stories still came between him and the light. A single arrow slit high on the west wall provided the only source of illumination. Vaylo moved cautiously. Underfoot, the mold was as slick as ice.

"Dry!" he called out, frustrated. "Are you there?"

The sound of footsteps echoed along the tower's rounded walls. A line of masonry dust sifted from the ceiling. Vaylo's gaze tracked a movement across a dark space he had assumed was solid stone and Cluff Drybannock came into view.

"I apologize for not lighting a lamp."

Vaylo huffed. "You did not know I was a-coming. Here. Take my arm. Lead me up."

It did not occur to Vaylo to doubt Dry's ability to see in the darkness. From boyhood Cluff Drybannock had always fared best by night. Whilst boys older than him slept peacefully in their beds, he was out on the redcourt, practicing his forms. Vaylo remembered spotting Dry once when he didn't realize he was being watched. A boy of twelve rendered blue by the moonlight, repeating the same sword stroke a hundred and twenty times.

Cluff Drybannock took his chief's arm and guided him up the stairs. At some point between the first and second story the light increased, yet neither man made the motion to pull apart. Vaylo told himself that Dry was probably worried that his old chief would slip and break his neck.

Wind drilled through the tower. Vaylo wondered how much longer there was to go. The soft and familiar pain below his heart was letting him know that it resented stairs. Finally Dry slowed the climb and led his chief through a stone arch into a circular, vaulted chamber with boarded-up windows. The center of the vault had collapsed and a heap of stones, black lumber and roof tiles lay on the floor beneath it. Vaylo peered up through the hole and saw sky.

"The floor above holds up the remains of the roof."

This did not seem like an especially comforting statement. Vaylo ignored it and crossed to the north-facing window. It seemed odd that Drybone had removed the middle boards from this window but not the one facing south. "I met one of your new men today," he said. "Kye Hillrunner."

Cluff Drybannock nodded, but did not speak. Vaylo supposed he had no reason to; no question had been asked.

Dry was dressed in serviceable gray wool pants and a tunic of gray suede. The quarter-moon he'd painted just beyond the crown of his hairline had faded, and although opal rings still bound his waist-length hair, Vaylo was gratified to see that his wrist leathers and the grip of his longsword were red.

"It is clear enough this day to see the Rift." Drybone's fine and powerful hand fell again on his chief's arm, his touch light as he directed Vaylo to the exact direction. "It is the dark line on the break of the horizon."

Vaylo saw it. Without Dry he would never have recognized it for a gap in the world so little did the line in the far distance give away. "Is that where the Maimed Men live?"

"No. They lie east of here where the Rift is at its deepest."

"You watch it."

Again there was no question and Cluff Drybannock was silent.

"I set off for the Rift once," Vaylo said, his gaze still ahead. "I was nine and I was mad at Gullit. Decided to take off and never come back. Rode all the way to the Deadwoods, three whole days, before the anger finally left me and I turned for home with my tail between my legs. Had an idea about joining the Maimed Men."

"This Bludd warrior is glad you did not join them."

Vaylo was glad he was facing forward. Tears spiked in his eyes and he could let the wind blow them away. Seven sons and not a kind word or touch from one of them. He had been a bad father, he knew it. Obsessed with matters of clan, short-tempered, selfish, but surely he had never been cruel? *You were,* countered a hard voice in his head that sounded suspiciously like his father's. *You resented your sons for being born legitimate, for not having to fight tooth and nail as you did.* It was true enough, that was why things were different between him and Dry. They were bastards, and they knew all the small and big things that meant.

Keeping his voice level, Vaylo said, "Tell me why you watch."

Seconds passed and the wind blew and then Cluff Drybannock replied, "My blood makes me."

The same cold finger that had touched Vaylo earlier touched again in the exact same place. He had not expected such an answer, but now that he heard it he could not claim surprise. All along he had known his fostered son was made of a different, older substance than he himself. Others had known it too. Ockish Bull had helped rear Dry, and upon his death had left him a small purse. The great swordmaster Vingus Harking, great-uncle to the HalfBludd chief Onwyn HalfBludd, had come out of retirement, wheeling himself north in a cart pulled by dogs, just to train Dry for one year. Vingus had worked with others during his time at Bludd, but it was word of Cluff Drybannock's burgeoning skill that had roused him from his fossilage at HalfBludd. You could not meet Cluff Drybannock and not realize his worth.

Something glinting in the headland beyond the fort valley drew Vaylo's gaze. "Is there a stream over there?"

Drybone followed his gaze. "No. It is the Field of Graves and Swords. I have walked there. Most swords no longer stand. Those that do are rusted and no longer have their points."

A myth made true. As a boy Vaylo had heard of the Field of Graves and Swords, a graveyard where warriors were buried with their swords sticking up through the soil. He had thought it a fine thing, for the field was said to form the first line of defense for a legendary fortress—even in death the warriors guarded the fastness. It was strange to learn that this small hill-fort was the site of such a legend.

"What happened to the nine missing men?" Vaylo asked, no longer sure if he even changed the subject.

Cluff Drybannock touched the container made of bone at

his waist. "I sent them on a sortie northeast. They never returned."

"What was their purpose?"

"To gather intelligence on the Maimed Men, and hunt freely if they so chose."

"You rode out to find them?"

Silence, and then as if by pre-arrangement both men moved out from the window and turned to look at each other full-on. Dry's brick-colored face was grave. "I headed a search party. Their tracks were not hard to follow and we found . . ." he struggled for a word, "their remains within the day."

Vaylo touched his container of powdered guidestone. "Who died?"

Cluff Drybannock listed their names in perfect formal ranking beginning with the longest-serving sworn clansmen, Derek Blunt, and ending with the yearman, Will Pool, brother to Midge, who had taken his first oath seven months back. Vaylo knew them all. "Gods keep them."

Knowing he had no choice but to press on, he said, "Their horses?"

"Also gone."

"Dead or taken?"

Dry's nostrils flared. "Both. This warrior does not know a word to describe what was left of the men and their horses. Their shadows were left behind, burned into the grass."

Oh gods. "How long ago did this happen?"

"Sunset will mark the eleventh day."

Vaylo had to walk, and began to circle the vaulted room. His brain twitched as shocks ran through it. Bluddsmen dead. Derek Blunt had been forty-three, an experienced headman and an expert mounted swordsman. How could a heavily armed party come upon him without warning? "Was there sign of the enemy?"

"Big Borro found something close by, a sword-shaped hole cut into the turf. We dug and tried to find what had caused it. Six feet down we hit rock, but the sword-shaped object had burned through it and could not be reached."

Halting by the pile of roof debris, Vaylo turned over a rotten timber with the toe of his boot. Wood lice scuttled away from the light. "What's happening, Dry? What is the threat we are facing?"

Cluff Drybannock stood to attention, shoulders straight and chin high. "I fear the worst, my lord and father. In the days before I came to Bludd I heard things. The Trenchlands are full of whispers. Some say the trees start them. I was a boy and much ignored. Men and women would talk freely in the tavern where I served them. They did not believe a boy of seven had ears. Most were Sull or part Sull, and sometimes when the hour grew late their talk would turn to the threat growing in the darkness. They spoke of *Ben Horo*, the Time Before, and *Maer Horo*, the Age of Darkness. War had visited them in the past and would again. Most agreed the auguries were bad. *Xalla a'mar*, night is rising, they would say. *Li'sha mut i'scaras*. We must grease our swords.

"The words pulled the iron in my blood like a magnet. Why, I cannot say. A thousand years have passed since the shadows last rose, and the Sull believe they are due to rise again. I fear those shadows, my father. I fear our clansmen died by hands that were formed from *maer dan*, shadowflesh. I fear we stand at the closing of an Age and if we are not vigilant and fail to fight, the Age will see an end to the Stone Gods and to clan."

Vaylo breathed steadily and showed no reaction to his fostered son's words. Many things struck him at once, yet in the silence that followed it was sadness that took hold and grew. It had been unsettling to hear Dry speak those Sull words with such casual precision. Twenty-five years in clan yet it seemed the language of his birth was undiminished. Unsettling also to hear him speak for the first time about those years before he came to Bludd. Vaylo had known nothing about Dry's boyhood in the Trenchlands, save that when he arrived at the Bluddhouse he was badly beaten and close to starving. Yet even unsettled, Vaylo had been stirred with pride. Cluff Drybannock was a man worthy of respect. *My eighth son.* And much though Vaylo wanted him to be clan, he was not. A divide stood between them and if Vaylo looked forward he saw a parting in the distance, a dark line on the horizon. Like the Rift.

Not realizing he was massaging the pain beneath his heart,

Vaylo said, "Tell me what killed my men, Dry. If we encounter them again we must understand what we fight."

Shadows in the tower vault lengthened and grew richer as Dry spoke. Light shining between the slats of the boarded-up west window threw horizontal stripes across the walls as the wind died to a murmur.

"It is told that what the universe creates it will destroy. Gods are birthed with stars to give us light, and *Xhan Nul*, the Endlords, are birthed into the void of space to bring destruction. These powers are locked in a war that is finite. For many Ages, the gods and the light have prevailed. Earth has thrived. The sun shines and makes life. Civilizations grow and people have inhabited all lands that can sustain them. The Sull are taught this cannot last. From the moment of its creation the world was doomed. It exists and therefore must end. The destiny of the Endlords is to bring about that destruction.

"The destiny of the Sull is to stand against them. Many Ages ago, after the War of Blood and Shadow, the Sull sealed the Endlords and the creatures they had taken in a prison named the Blind. How they did this, I do not know. The walls of the prison are said to exist in a place beyond the physical realm. We cannot see or touch them. Once in a thousand years one is born, *Jal Rakhar*, the Reach, who can approach these walls and break them. I have heard whispers from the forests east of Bludd. The Reach exists and she has caused a crack in the wall between worlds. And the Sull make ready for battle as the first of the Endlords' creatures force their way out."

It took a moment for Vaylo to realize Cluff Drybannock had stopped speaking, for his words lived on in the quiet of dusk that followed. How long had they been in this tower? To Vaylo it felt like days.

I am an old man, he told himself. *A chief in search of a clan. This battle is not mine.*

It took an effort to speak. "These are the creatures you believe slew Derek Blunt and his men?" After the words spun with cool beauty by his fostered son, Vaylo's voice sounded harsh and world-weary to his ears. "What are we dealing with here?"

Cluff Drybannock did not appear to notice. All the while he

had been speaking he had not moved from his place by the north window. He did not move now as he replied. "The Endlords are voids that can spin matter around themselves and take on living form. They walk the earth to claim men and other living beasts for their armies. One touch of an Endlord and you are taken. Unmade. Men become *other*, their flesh sucked dry of life and replaced with an absence of light. The Endlords arm them with *Kil Ji*, voided steel, which is said to be forged from the strange metals of time itself. If you are killed by voided steel you are also taken."

Vaylo was beginning to understand things now. "The sword-shaped pit in the earth?"

Dry dropped his gaze from his chief. "This warrior believes it was made by *Kil Ji*."

Dragging a hand over the stubble on his chin, Vaylo looked through the hole in the roof at the sky. It was the color of deep mountain lakes. *Underwater*, that was how he felt, plunged from a world that allowed him to stand upright and see ahead, into one that was murky and had no place to rest his feet. Nine men lost, and if Cluff Drybannock's fears were true they weren't even dead. Did that mean they would never rest in the Stone Halls of the gods?

"Yet they died fighting," Vaylo said quietly, barely aware he was speaking out loud.

You could not be a clansman and fail to comprehend the full horror of those words. Dry nodded softly. "The Stone Gods have long memories. If the men are ever freed from the thrall of the Endlords the manner of their deaths will not go unrewarded."

The Dog Lord found he had to think about this statement for a moment. Light was leaving the tower quickly now, making way for the chill of night. "How can my men be freed?"

Straightaway he could see this was a question that Cluff Drybannock had hoped not to answer—perhaps not even to himself. He turned to look out the window and fill his lungs with fresh air. "Once a man or woman is unmade they join the ranks of the Endlords. They too will wield *Kil Ji* and unlike those who are imprisoned, they have no need to force their way out. They are here, amongst us, and they walk by night. To reclaim them for the Stone Gods we must slay them through the heart."

"Mother of Gods," Vaylo murmured.

They both fell silent after that. Vaylo could see Dry's profile, see him blinking as he worked the air in and out of his chest. After a while Vaylo asked him, "How do you know so much? A boy eavesdropping in a tavern would not have learned all this."

Dry turned so he could look directly at his chief. "The ranger Angus Lok told me much of this last winter, when we held him in the pit cell below Dhoone."

Of course. Vaylo should have guessed. He knew the ranger well. When they'd met all those months ago in the Tomb of the Dhoone Princes, Angus Lok had tried to tell him some of the very same things. He had certainly warned him. "*Return to Bludd and marshal your forces and wait for the Long Night to come. Forget about Dhoone and this roundhouse and your fancy of naming yourself Lord of the Clans. Days darker than night lie ahead.*" Vaylo had barely marked the words at the time, so intent was he on holding onto the Dhoonehouse. Yet Angus Lok had found someone else nearby who was willing to listen, someone whose blood pulled him toward the Sull and their causes, someone who was hungry to *know*.

Vaylo searched for how he felt. Almost you could not blame the ranger—bring a snake into your house and you will end up bitten—but he was less certain about Dry's role. Should he have listened so eagerly? How could you stop a man from wanting to know the history of his people? You could not, and to do so would deprive him of his freedom. That was that, then. There was no disloyalty on Dry's part, only listening. Yet it still hurt.

Dry stood waiting and Vaylo knew him well enough to know that he was anxious about his chief's reaction. Vaylo made an effort. "Angus Lok's information is usually sound, though he is particular in how and where he metes it out." It was the best he could do for now, and Dry sensed it.

Dry could have pointed out that Angus Lok only told him what he would have eventually discovered for himself, yet he did not. Instead, he said, "A half-moon is rising."

It was a truce. Cluff Drybannock was part Sull and he could

not deny it—did not want to deny it—and Vaylo knew he had little choice but to accept it. Neither man wanted to dwell on what it meant for the future: Sull goals and clan goals would not remain the same. For now they were both united in defending the hillfort: leave it at that.

"Let us walk in the moonlight back to the fort," Vaylo said.

Cluff Drybannock crossed the chamber and took his chief's arm, and they were both comforted by the touch for a while.

TWENTY-FOUR

The Weasel's Den

The march was grueling on both men and horses and Marafice was glad they had thought to bring the carts that the grangelords, in their haste to return to Spire Vanis and enter the contest for surlord that was surely taking place there, had left behind in the camp. The grangelords had left behind a lot of things without value—servants included—and it all added to the general motley of Marafice Eye's crew.

The carts now, they were a good thing. Saved the badly wounded having to be thrown over the backs of horses, or even worse—God forbid—being dragged behind them on sleds. The first thing he'd done after the rout was to set those fancy grangelord servants hitching the carts. It all had to be executed in haste of course for it had not been clear then whether or not the Bludd army would mount a full pursuit. Luckily they had not, preferring instead to chop down most of the remaining Hailsmen, chase the city men off the Crabhold and occupy and secure the gate. It was a miscalculation, Marafice reckoned. For any war chief with experience could have taken one look at the tired and bloody city men army and known it for easy pickings. The Bludd warrior in command was lazy, Marafice concluded. He had the swaggering looks of his father, the Dog Lord, but he was not half the man.

Marafice shuddered as he forced his great black warhorse down into the rocky stream. That moment after the horn sounded and the front line of the strange new army broke free from the woods behind the roundhouse, the Knife had known fear so concentrated it had stopped his heart. *Clan Bludd*. He had recognized their colors and their trappings straightaway and he knew instantly that he must call a retreat. He had met the Dog Lord man-to-man, looked into his eyes, and heard the timbre of his voice. Marafice Eye, with twenty years spent in the Rive Watch protecting three successive surlords, had never met anyone who had impressed him like Vaylo Bludd.

He had assumed that the Dog Lord would be leading the Bludd army. He was wrong. That wrongness was why his army of three thousand men was alive today. If he hadn't felt such fear of the Dog Lord he might have been ambivalent about retreat. Certainly Andrew Perish and his God-fearing nine hundred had wanted to stay and fight. They held the gate. Almost. It may have been possible to secure it. They had the numbers. Even with those bastard grangelords stealing away with half the army, superior manpower was theirs. Two factors were not in their favor though. One, they were unfamiliar with the Crabhouse, and it would have taken time and trial to secure it. And two, they had been fighting from noon to sundown and were flat-out spent. Even Andrew Perish, whose zeal gave new meaning to the phrase 'second wind' had been forced to admit that his men were flagging. That last hard fight with Hailsmen for the gate had been devastating. Many of Perish's faithful had fallen.

At least it had doused their God fires, and made it less of a fight to call a retreat.

It was hard to know how many had died in the rout. Numbers had been fluid, bodies already strewn across the roundhouse steps and its river hill. Marafice could not take such matters lightly, and he had played the retreat over and over again in his head. It was a hard thing for a warlord, a retreat. Did you command the front or bring up the rear?

He had brought up the rear, because that seemed like the way he had lived his life. When you were born a butcher's son in Spire Vanis you started at the back.

Still, even if the retreat had not gone as well as it might, Marafice believed the men who marched with him this day would live longer lives because of it. Bludd, Blackhail, Dhoone: all three northern giants had their eyes on Ganmiddich. It would have turned into a killing field. Three thousand city men holed up in the most bitterly contested clanhold in the north? How long before the real might of Blackhail turned up? And what about the self-crowned Thorn King, Robbie Dhoone?

Marafice shook his head as he shortened the reins and encouraged his mount to take the shore. They would not have been supported. Who the hell in Spire Vanis cared about this rabble of fanatics, mercenaries, and aging brothers-in-the-watch? No one now that the grangelords had upped stakes and headed south. Indeed it would suit most of the high-and-mighties in Spire Vanis if the Protector General of Spire Vanis simply never returned home.

The Rive Watch was always a tricky proposition for an aspiring surlord. The eager candidate would almost certainly be a grangelord, reared from birth to be hostile to the Rive's power and the rough-necked men who wielded it. A swallowing of pride was usually called for. Some were smart about it—Iss, a grangelord by fosterage, had planned ahead, and joined the watch as a young man. Marafice had respected him as a leader, but he had always known Iss held him in contempt. Brothers-in-the-watch might be lacking in finery and titles but that did not make them stupid. They controlled Mask Fortress itself: the seat of the Surlord's power. Some courting was called for if you fancied calling that fortress home. No one could take it without the Rive Watch's support.

Now that the watch's leader was a thousand leagues away from home, stuck on the wrong side of the Wolf for fear of making a crossing, that courting had suddenly got easier. Some bright and ambitious brother-in-the-watch had doubtless declared himself in command while Marafice was away. He would be insecure, not wholly supported by men who were loyal to the Eye. That meant the aspiring grangelord could play a hand of divide and conquer; set one faction against the other, whisper promises to both and keep none of them. Marafice knew how it would go down. He had seen the same kind of dealings several times before.

That was why he should have been there. If he'd been in the city the day that Iss died no one could have matched him. The watch was his. Thanks to a quick marriage to the Lord of the

High Grange's sluttish daughter, a grange and its titles were as good as his own. Even Iss himself had declared Marafice Eye as his successor. It was a rock-strong foundation that had now been rendered worthless.

First come, first take: that was the law of Spire Vanis. Mask Fortress did not hold open its doors until all contenders had been assembled and accounted for. It wasn't a tourney, governed by the rules of polite engagement. The doors were closed the instant someone claimed the surlordship for his own. Prising those doors open again was a long, bloody and frequently futile task. It was the difference between rolling a boulder down a hill and carrying it up again. You needed a hundred times the force.

What am I doing even thinking of it? Marafice chastised himself. Here he was, stuck in the godforsaken clanholds, in some wild river territory eight days west of Ganmiddich, with three cartloads of badly injured men on his hands and another two hundred walking wounded, unable to find a safe place to cross the high and swift-moving Wolf, all the while constantly having to check over his shoulder lest crews of heathen clansmen attack his rear.

Marafice frowned at the sky. At least there was some sun about, not like yesterday when the thunderheads blew in from the south and turned the Wolf into a chop field of flying branches and jagged water. Damn the river to hell. They had tried to take the same crossing that they'd used coming over, but the ferryman had upped and gone and taken his ropes with him. Iss had arranged the crossing, and Marafice hadn't taken much interest in it at the time. The only thing he recalled for certain was that Clan Scarpe was somehow involved.

It had been a very stupid mistake, not insuring that the retreat to the city hold was properly covered. It made Marafice angry with himself just to think of it. Who knew or cared how the grangelords had crossed the river? They didn't have injured—anyone not able-bodied had been thoughtfully abandoned on the field—nor did they have carts, tents or supplies. Mounted men, all of them, they had probably used the dozen boats that were tied up back at the camp and swam across the horses. The boats had been scuttled, of course. That order would have given the Whitehog no end of delight.

There was the bridge of boats at Bannen, but Marafice knew no welcome would be offered to city men there. Bannenmen had fought with Blackhail for Ganmiddich, and Marafice had felt nothing but anxiety during the two days they spent crossing Bannen lands. Ban scouts had watched them as they headed west along the rivershore. Potshots had been taken, and there was a short exchange of fire. About two hundred swordsmen had appeared on the river cliff above Marafice's column the next day. The Bannenmen had sat their horses, gray cloaks blowing in the wind, mighty longswords holstered at their backs, and sent Marafice a message he received loud and clear. *Keep walking.*

It was another piece of luck, Marafice reckoned. That Ganmiddich roundhouse was like honey to the bees. Word of Bludd seizing it had doubtless mobilized the might of Bannen, and the forces that remained behind were safe-keepers, insufficient in number to mount an attack on three thousand city men.

"God is good," Perish had claimed the next night as they made a light and nervous camp on the Wolf. "He will see us home."

Marafice had declined to tell Andrew Perish exactly what he thought of that. Home for God was heaven and to get there you had to be dead. Instead he had told Perish of his still-evolving plan to approach Scarpe.

When not talking about the One True God, Andrew Perish was as sharp as an iron tack. The white-haired former master-at-arms had leant in toward the fire so that that the crackle of burning pine needles stopped his words from traveling where he did not want them. "Iss had friends at Scarpe. He paid them good coin to secure that crossing. They must have pulled those barges all the way east to Ganmiddich—upriver, no less—and that's the kind of service that doesn't come cheap."

Marafice nodded. He had already worked out some of this for himself. "Scarpe's sworn to Blackhail—one of their former sons is the new Hail chief. How will it sit with them to aid the army that attacked Blackhail at Ganmiddich?"

Perish pushed his lips together and breathed deeply through his nose. Slowly and gravely he began to shake his head. "Not nearly as bad as it should. Do not forget they let us cross in the first place. What did they think we were going to do? Make parlor visits? Someone at Scarpe knew what we were about, and either wasn't much concerned, or even worse it suited them." Perish's cataract-burdened gaze rested long on Marafice Eye. "If you're asking me is it worth making overtures at Scarpe my answer is yes. If you're asking me how to go about it I say use caution and be prepared to move out quickly. No clansman fears our God and all are damned, but some move in deeper hells than others."

Marafice stood. The heat from the fire was hot upon his face and the blackening pine needles suddenly smelled like embalmer's fluid. At that instant he wished he had something to crush between his fists, so deeply and completely did he hate the grangelords who had abandoned this army. How dare they? How dare they leave these men injured, unsupported, and cut off?

Aware that he was pacing and that his fists were pumping, Marafice made an effort to calm himself. Not for Perish's sake—the man had taught him how to protect his balls from sword thrusts when he was seventeen; there was little room for pretense between them—but for the sake of others who were standing and sitting close by, marking the conversation between their commander and the former master-at-arms.

Finally, Marafice had been able to speak. "I hear your warning," he told Perish. "We'll be there in a couple of days. We will see how Scarpe lies."

Looking around, Marafice reckoned there was a very good chance they were in Scarpe-held territory right now. He could see smoke in the not far distance, rising above ugly purplish pines that looked half burned. The river was not bonnie here. Dozens of streams and creaks drained the headlands, and the waters they transported ranged in color from gray and scummy, to tarlike black. Upshore, an abandoned and improperly sealed mine head leaked yellow fluid into a shallow river pool that had a dead raven floating on the surface. Everyone had to be careful with their horses, for the ground was littered with sharp-edged slate and seeded with devil's thorns.

Down column, they were having difficulty pulling one of the

carts up the stream bank and Marafice rode down the line to help them, nodding once to Jon Burden along the way. *The command is yours.*

The carts had originally been designed to transport those dozens of little luxuries that grangelords deemed necessary to life; silk pillows, perfumed oil, wooden salt scrapers, beeswax candles, back itchers, preserved fruit, field armor, war armor, riding armor, red wine, white wine, fine liquors and all manner of cured and exotic meats. A lot of that stuff had been left behind and it made for poor eating but good comradeship. Fruit fights had occurred. Pillows had been commandeered as targets; and the salt scrapers had found a brief but deeply satisfying use as firewood. The alcohol had run out three days back: it was the only taste his men and the grangelords shared.

Seeing that one of the rear cartwheels was wedged in the crack between two hunks of slate, Marafice ordered the horses to be unhitched. Forward was not going to work here: the cart needed to roll back. As the driver and others close by set to work on the horses, Marafice and a dozen other men dismounted to brace the rear. The driver had a steady hand and was able to warn those in the water the instant the hitch was released. Marafice accepted the great weight of the cart, and began barking out orders. Shoulder muscles shaking in intensive bursts, he and the other men controlled the backward roll into the stream.

It was smallest of the three carts, he was grateful for that. They'd padded it with blankets and a decent pile of sword-shredded silk cushions, but it was not an easy ride for the twenty-five men within it. As he looked over the tailgate he saw this was the cart containing the clansmen they'd taken as captives. Two Hailsman and two Crabmen, all wounded and chained to the posts. It wasn't much of a headcount, but Marafice was close to glad there were no more. Captives were a headache. They needed to be watched, fed, doctored, and, in this particular case, protected from the zealous tendencies of Perish and his faithful who would like to see them burn.

The Hailsmen stared at Marafice with proud and wary faces. The two hammermen were big men with silvery stretch marks across the skin of their arm and shoulder muscles. One of them had been responsible for the deaths of a dozen brothers-in-the-watch; Marafice knew this to be so because he had watched the man fight with his own eye. He was young, with an unscarred face and clear brown eyes, yet Marafice had the feeling that he had been the one in command at the gate. He had been an untiring fighter and good rallier of men. Marafice doubted if they would have been able to take him if one of Steffan Grimes' crossbowmen hadn't softened him with a quarrel to the ribs.

All five of the clansmen had turned stone cold in protest when Tat Mackelroy had tried to remove their pouches of powdered guidestone. Marafice himself had issued the order to remove all weapons and personal effects from the captives, but seeing something akin to desperation in the eyes of the clansmen as Tat cut away the first man's powder pouch, Marafice had modified the order. He knew fighting men and he knew desperate men. Let the five keep their clannish tokens: it would go easier on everyone that way.

Later Marafice had had to battle the point with Perish who counted it as an offense against God that men in this column were carrying, how did he put it? The ashes of pretender gods. It had not been a comfortable conversation for Marafice, for at some point he realized he was dead set on having his way. To tell the man who had first taught you how to correctly balance a sword that you were favoring an enemy at his expense was hard. Yet something deep down in Marafice would not move. Strange enough, Perish had let it be and had not referred to the matter since.

It had been Jon Burden who brought up the subject of interrogating the captives. The commander of Rive Company had rightly pointed out that they needed to know the names and ranks of the five men. Marafice had allowed him to question them without use of force but that had yielded nothing. Burden now wanted to be free to rough them up and scare them. Marafice agreed that such measures were necessary, but told him to hold off until the worst of their wounds had healed. Who cared about clannish ranking anyway? They had chiefs, but not much else.

"Driver! Hitch the horses!" Marafice wanted to be gone. He and the other men had made the small adjustment necessary to take the cart on a different course up the bank and now they held it steady while the driver positioned the team and fastened the cinches and chest bars. Rusty water ran over the toes of Marafice's black boots. Some got in. A clannish sword had pierced the leather during the final charge on the gate.

"Ride on," Marafice commanded. The driver was back on his seat and he clicked his tongue, setting the team into motion.

Marafice realized he was sweating as the weight finally moved off his chest. The young hammerman stared at him as the cart climbed the bank and Marafice frowned back. *Damn captives. More trouble than they're worth.*

When he was back in the saddle and riding up the column, Marafice found himself snapping out orders. The machinists were falling behind with their contraptions, a wounded mercenary had slumped over the neck of his horse and nobody had bothered to aid him, and a handful of free pikers looked drunk. The Knife was in a bad mood and the sight of that smoke above the rise north of the river did not do anything to improve it. It was one thing for the great Penthero Iss to do dealings and double dealings and dickerings—he enjoyed them—but not Marafice Eye. He feared being tricked.

Yet even as he joined Jon Burden at the head of the line he spied a movement between the sickly purple trees. The river was well used here, he noticed. As they followed the curve of the river north, plank jetties and worn paths came into view. Draglines told of boats hauled up the bank and concealed in the woods. A wooden gutting hut sat on piles at the water's edge, and everywhere there were signs of men: burned out fires, moldy tarp, tattered fishing line, whittled sticks, apple cores, trout bones.

Marafice knew they were being watched and kept his chin high and back straight. He had told no one other than Perish about his plan to deal with Scarpe and he was glad of that because it meant no one in the column slowed. Iss' advice moved like a cold mist through Marafice's brain. *Let them come to you.*

The Scarpe roundhouse was a couple of leagues north of the river and you could not see it through the trees. The smoke from the house smelled oily and slightly poisonous—not good for children or asthmatics. Marafice wondered about Scarpe's system of watches. How long had they known the city men were coming? Certainly long enough to abandon the riverbank and hide the boats. Was it long enough to plan a surprise attack? The Knife gave a silent order to Jon Burden to relay down the line. *Stand ready.*

He meant it for himself, he realized, for the column had already fallen into a quiet, jumpy watchfulness. None dared draw weapons without his say, but they were thinking about it. He could see it in their eyes. A quick glance down the ranks revealed that mounted brothers-in-the-watch were now heavily flanking the two carts that contained their wounded. The third cart, containing mercenaries, a handful of hideclads and the captive clansmen, deserved no such consideration apparently, and trundled along unguarded save for a lone spearman stationed there by Steffan Grimes.

When arrows were loosed from behind the trees, Marafice jumped in his saddle. Even expecting a surprise he had been surprised, and watched the missiles fly with something between panic and amazement. Long arrows, nearly four feet in length, pierced the dirt and grass in a near perfect line twenty paces ahead of the column, forming a barrier to the way ahead. Dozens and dozens of them continued striking the same thin stretch of beach until a wall of sticks was formed. The arrows' feather fletchings riffled in the wind as the shafts vibrated, sending their message to the city men.

Do not pass.

Marafice and Jon Burden exchanged a glance. The head of Rive Company waited for his commander to speak. The wall was four feet high, two deep and eight long: any fool could pass it. Marafice raised an arm, calling the column to a halt. It was a technicality; most men had already stopped.

The woods surrounding the river were quiet. Marafice could not see anyone move within them. He waited, waited. A red-tailed hawk rose on the thermals above the river and swooped south in search of prey. Men in the column began to cuss and spit in mild shows of disapproval. Marafice ignored them.

He heard the mounted men before he saw them, horse hoofs pounding dully in ground softened by yesterday's rain. Thirty warriors dressed in black cloaks and black leathers rode through a break in the trees. They were lean men, tall and pale, with thin braids fastened in complicated arrangements and gleams of silver at their throats and ears. Their weapons were couched, but as they drew to a halt all men save their leader drew swords.

Marafice's hand shot up, commanding his army to stillness. It was an order he would never have given in the past. People who drew weapons in his presence usually ended up dead.

"Our chief denies you passage through this clanhold," called out the head warrior. He had stopped about fifty paces upshore, insuring high ground and a quick retreat for his men.

Marafice forced himself to remember the bowmen concealed in the woods. Otherwise he would very much like to hack these men down. "I want passage south, not west. Take me to your chief."

The head warrior showed no surprise. A hand gloved in expertly tanned black leather patted his horse's mane. "Choose two men to accompany you. Your weapons will be ransomed but held within your sight."

What the hell good will that do me? Marafice thought. Aloud he said, "Pick three of your own to stand as hostages for our safe return." After taking a long and pointed look down his column, past crossbowmen, pikers, swordsmen, *more* swordsmen, spearmen, machinists and foot soldiers, he added nastily, "They can keep their weapons out and swinging."

Two spots of heat colored the head warrior's cheeks. He chose three of his men who couldn't have looked less thrilled and directed them to stand by the wall of arrows. To Marafice, he said, "Follow me."

He was a fine horseman, turning his horses with grace and precision and building up to a canter as he headed for the trees. All the Scarpemen moved swiftly, putting Marafice and his chosen at a distinct disadvantage: their horses were nervous of picking up speed in the woods.

Marafice had picked Tat Mackelroy and a mercenary from the ranks he did not know to accompany him. It was a decision made in an instant, but he was pleased enough with it. Perish and Jon Burden were too precious to lose—they would know what to do if he didn't return. Cut their losses and force a path west. Tat was a good man, and Marafice had become used to having him at his back. As for the mercenary . . . well, the poor sod might learn something. Or die.

The head warrior cut a tight path through the pines. The tree boughs had been sheared off to a height approaching twelve feet to enable men mounted on horses to ride freely. Marafice felt a tightness in his chest all the same. His deepest fear was to lose his remaining eye. Sunlight razored through the pines at sharp angles, creating bands of light and shade. Seeing the way ahead was difficult. Marafice lagged behind. Tat and the mercenary stayed close, confused but loyal.

When Marafice took a hand from the rein meaning to push away a drooping pine bough, Tat warned him not to touch it. "Poison pines," he murmured softly. "Scarpe's known for them."

They were led not to the roundhouse but a large clearing in the woods that had been seeded with dark green grass. A canopy made from the same fine black leather as the head warrior's gloves had been erected in the center. Under its shade sat the Scarpe chief, waiting.

Yelma Scarpe was small and sharp-shouldered with thin lips and dyed black hair. She wore a sword like a man, and every one of her ten bony fingers glittered with oversize jewels. Once Marafice and his two men were in open ground, she scribed a shape in the air, and two hundred men stepped from the shadows, swords drawn, points out, forming a circle of blades around the glade.

Marafice forced himself to calm. He had thought it would be a small thing to put himself in danger, but he realized now that it was not. Riding through the pines had thrown him off center and he could not recall what advantages he brought here. Part of him had assumed that once he was here he would know what to do. Iss had made negotiation seem effortless, like breathing, but this air was too rich for Marafice's lungs. He wanted only to be gone.

The chair occupied by the Scarpe chief was high-backed and solid, made from a single block of oak. The armrests were carved in the shape of weasels and Yelma Scarpe rested her rubied and sapphired hands upon their heads. "You stand in my clanhold without my leave. This does not please me."

Marafice was unsure whether or not this statement required a reply. He had remembered one piece of advice given to him by Iss and he held on to it like a talisman. *Listen twice before you speak.*

Yelma Scarpe drummed the weasel heads. "My nephew tells me you need to cross the river. I command the last crossing between here and the Storm Margin. That means you must make terms with me. It is possible that you would be able to force a path west through my clanhold, but that would cost us both men, and leave you farther away from Spire Vanis, searching for a crossing that does not exist. Five rivers drain into the Wolf beyond this point, three of them from the north. What this means to you and your army is that even staying *on course* along the Wolf will be difficult, and you may be forced into the northern woods."

She paused, favoring Marafice with something so hard and joyless he doubted if it could be named a smile.

"My scouts tell me you have injured. Three cartloads."

Marafice said nothing. Sunlight reflecting off one of the Scarpemen's swords was bouncing into his good eye. A black rage was simmering within him and he imagined kicking the Scarpe chief in the head and crushing her against the chair. Finally the pressure became too much. "What if we just steal your fucking boats? You can't match us for numbers—half of your men are at Blackhail."

"You'll be stealing burned wood if you try it," she said back to him, relaxed now that he had stepped into the hole she had dug for him. "The barges have been primed with lamp oil. One word from me and they're up in flames."

Marafice felt like a fool. All of it could be bluff and he would never know it. The five rivers, the last crossing, the barges wet with oil. Iss would have never walked into a meeting ignorant of such things. Knowledge was power. And lack of knowledge meant that you could be backed into a corner and made to pay to get out.

"Shall I name my terms?"

He did not know how he managed not to choke on the words: "Go ahead."

The Scarpe chief made a small satisfied sniff. "I want the war machines, the battering ram. Two hundred horses and their saddles, two hundred suits of armor including leg pieces, and the clansmen you hold as hostage."

Her scouts were good, he had to give her that. She waited for an answer, her purple tongue flicking out once to wet her lips, her jeweled fingers stroking the weasel heads. How had it got so hot in this damn glade? Marafice glanced at the overhead sun and then wished he hadn't. Circles of light burned his eye. That moron with the sword was flashing him on purpose as well. He needed to think but all he could see in his mind's eyes were weasels and blistering light.

With a biting motion of his teeth, Marafice forced himself to weigh the chief's demands. The war machines? She could have them. They only hit their target one time out of five, as he recalled. And the battering ram would be a pleasure to leave; its wheels got stuck more often than the carts'. Steffan Grimes might kick up a fuss—it was his company's ram, after all—but in Marafice's experience professional mercenaries were usually inured to the vagaries of war. People died, possessions were lost, others were gained: such were the norms for professional soldiers.

The horses, though. They were different. Two hundred was a greedy little demand and she knew it. If he met her on this it would cost his army dear. Brothers-in-the-watch would be deprived of their mounts, for Marafice could not see a way to take horses solely from the mercenaries. The cost would have to be borne fairly, else mutiny was risked. As for the armor—well, she could have his riding plate, for a start. Thing chafed like all the hells when you tried to move in it. The other hundred and ninety-nine suits shouldn't be much of a problem either, though the pieces would not necessarily match.

He said, "A hundred horses and I'm keeping the clansmen."

"A hundred and fifty and *I* keep the clansmen."

She was nothing if not fast. Marafice looked into her small black eyes and told her, "The clansmen are not negotiable." He barely knew why he did it, for up until that point the clansmen had been negotiable—they were captives, their purpose was to be pumped for information and then sold. It even made sense that she, as a clan chief, would want to buy back members of her liege clan, Blackhail. Yet he did not think her purpose here was a moral one. Anything this woman gave you would end up costing more than its worth.

Just as Yelma Scarpe opened her mouth to speak, Marafice stopped her. He had remembered something about the Scarpe roundhouse and thought, *To hell with it, I'll let it fly.* "I heard there was some burn damage to your roundhouse. Must make it hard to defend."

That closed down her pinched little face. She had just been about to insist on the clansmen, he was certain of it, but now she paused for a moment to rethink. Around the glade, two hundred swordsmen shifted their weight from foot to foot. Some let their sword points dip, others exchanged brief glances.

"A hundred and fifty. Done." Yelma Scarpe rose to her feet. "I'll send out a bargeman to run the ropes. Be ready with your tribute within the hour."

Tribute, that was a nice word for it. Marafice did not bid her farewell, indeed said nothing as he watched her bony rump slip away between the trees. She was a weasel all right. He did not think he had bested her, but at least he had held on to something. Fifty horses and five clansmen to be exact.

The thought gave him some pleasure, and when a lone cloud puffed across the sun he actually smiled at the man who had been trying to blind him with the reflection from his sword. Apparently the Eye smile was not a pleasant sight for the swordsman looked quickly away. *Blinded you back with ugliness*, Marafice thought with satisfaction.

"Come on, boys," he said to Tat and the mercenary. "Let's get out of this weasel's den and make our way home."

Spire Vanis was calling his name.

TWENTY-FIVE

Stormbringer

Wet and low, that's what they were, and Crope didn't like it one bit. Whoever had said that thing about not appreciating what you had until you lost it was wise enough to be a king.

Or a thief. Crope tried not to think bad things about Quillan Moxley, he really did. Business was business and a deal had been struck and Quill had fulfilled his part of the bargain—moving Crope and his lord out of the Rat's Nest and into a second location where they were bound to be safe as long as Crope kept his big stupid self out of sight—but it seemed to Crope that the spirit of the agreement had been underserved. With his lord supplying Quill with information leading to profit you might have thought that the thief would have arranged a move up for them. Not down.

Crope frowned at the two tiny and perfectly square windows high above him. He did not like being down. Down meant mines and diamond pipes, groundwater, sludge, mold, gases, dead mice and fear of being trapped. He could tear down a wooden wall—it was dusty and a bit dangerous and it made his back ache—but when you were underground the walls were made of stone, and even if you did knock one down you wouldn't find freedom on the other side. You'd just find earth instead. It was the kind of thought that could lead a man to panic, and Crope had spent considerable mental energy attempting to set it aside.

In fairness to Quill he had provided several luxuries. Crope's lord now had a proper horsehair mattress and pillows filled with pigeon down. And the blankets the thief had brought three days back were so soft that when you slept in them it was like taking a warm bath. Stools, candles, clothing, a pine chest, tin bowls, pewter spoons, a flowery blue pitcher for water, chamber pots, an hour glass, dice, sheepskin slippers, a sheepskin rug, a wooden thing with hinges of uncertain purpose that Crope was too shy to ask about and a small pig-shaped stove had all been smuggled down to the cavernous depths beneath the Quartercourts.

"There's a world of rats down there," Quill had said that first night as they made their way southeast through the back alleys of the city, fleeing the red blades, "and the very few individuals you're likely to encounter will have more reason than yourselves to keep their distinguishables hidden."

Pulling the handcart containing Baralis, Quill had led them toward the center of the city where the legal wranglings and public executions took place. Quill had ordered Crope to walk behind him at "a distance no less than thirty paces." That way, Crope supposed, passersby would not mistake them for a group. It had been a difficult journey, for Crope had feared losing sight of his lord. Every time Quill rounded a corner, Crope's five-chambered heart would thump against the inside of his rib cage like a reverse punch. He trusted Quill—nearly, almost, completely—but danger could strike around any bend and wipe both men out. At least he'd had the dogs to calm him.

Town Dog and Big Mox had spent most of the journey quiet as lambs, content to let the slack in their leashes flop against their backs. It was only when Town Dog, with her considerably shorter legs, decided quite suddenly she was done with walking and plonked down her rump in the mud that Big Mox had started acting up. Crope didn't think Big Mox realized he was just too big to be picked up and slipped inside the space between a man's tunic and his undershirt like Town Dog. Big Mox was a fierce and oversized match bull who became grouchy when he thought he was losing out. Crope had had to spend the final quarter of the journey yanking on his leash to prevent him pissing against every hitching post and barrow leg they passed.

Crope already knew the Quartercourts by sight, for he had

walked around the giant limestone edifice several times in the days before he rescued his lord. It was a place where instinct told him not to dally. A circle of gibbets lay directly across from the courts' wide and impressive steps, and whenever Crope had passed by, bodies in various states of mutilation had been hauled up like ragged flags. By day the courts teemed with red blades and finely dressed men who were so rich they had no need to hitch their horses. They were either carried there in covered chairs lined with cushions, or had servants stand outside and hold their horses' reins while the lords went inside to conduct business. A lot of men wore thick chains of office draped across their shoulders. Quill said those men were grangelords dressed for session. Crope wasn't quite sure what session was but he had a feeling it was something to do with lopping off men's heads.

It had seemed a strange choice of hideaway, but that night when they had fled Quill's townhouse Crope had been in no state to ask questions. Besides, at least they weren't heading north, the direction of all terrible things.

It had been a relief to get off the streets. The area around the Quartercourts was strangely quiet at night; the grand halls and places of learning closed up. There were no street vendors plying their trade on corners or street girls huddling around charcoal braziers for warmth. It wasn't that sort of place. Business was done by day here, and when darkness fell all the fine men in chains, and the judges, officials, armsman, ushers, scholars and grooms moved elsewhere, out of sight of the gibbets and into those parts of the city where you could sup cool ale and feast on sweetmeats and linger over life. Walking the empty and echoing streets, playing tug-o'-war with Big Mox while trying to keep his lord and Quill in his sights, Crope had felt exposed. Actual paving stones had been laid underfoot and his footsteps retorted like crossbolts. He felt only relief when Quill had executed one of his rakish turns into an arch sunk deep into the shadows of the Quartercourts' western facade and rapped lightly on a miniature door carved from a single chunk of hickory. After a brief exchange of whispers, Quill and his motley band of misfits and dogs was allowed entry into the limestone halls of Spire Vanis' public courts.

Quillan Moxley was the sort of man who had friends in all kinds of places. Associates, he called them, men and women who owed him favors, were involved in various illegal activities with him, or were the sort of people whose silence could be bought for a price. Crope did not know which category the night warden of the Quartercourts fell into, but he did know that the man had gone to considerable lengths to ensure he had not seen Crope.

"Self-protection," Quill had told Crope later, after the thief had led them to the second underlevel beneath the limestone compound. "What a man doesn't know for certain he can lie about with impunity."

Crope didn't know what the word *impunity* meant but he figured it had something to do with being interrogated by bailiffs. They couldn't force knowledge from you that you didn't own. Crope had seen the back of the night warden's head a few times over the past days and concluded that he had clean hair.

"I used to store fruit and vegetables down here at one time," Quill had said, walking through the series of dank stone cellars that would become Crope's home. "It was a good little earner until the Lord of High Granges opened his passes to cheap produce from the south."

Crope had frowned and nodded, attempting to demonstrate to Quill his understanding of the finer points of business.

"Better off without it, really. Carts loaded with cabbages were getting difficult to smuggle past the watch." Quill shook his small head with feeling. "And God help you if you made the mistake of taking possession of perishables. They had to be up and out within a day."

More frowning and nodding was called for, though in truth Crope had got stuck on the word *perishables* and was no longer quite certain what the thief meant.

Quill had appeared to appreciate the sympathy regardless. "Well. I'll be off for now. You have the use of all the space right up to the ice-house door. Only time anyone comes down here is to pick ice so when you hear footsteps move sharpish and lock yourselves in the big stockroom at the back. Night warden's the only one besides yourself who has the key."

The big stockroom had turned out to be the best room out of

the lot of them. It was situated against the Quartercourts' exterior western wall and although it was low-ceilinged like the other cellars, two window shafts provided light from the ground-level windows in the room overhead. If you stood just underneath the shafts, which Crope was currently doing, you could look up and see the sky through iron bars. Sometimes Crope saw flashes of people's feet and legs as they hurried down the street. Once he'd looked up and seen a raven tapping against the bars.

It was good to be able to keep Town Dog here. The small room at the top of Quill's townhouse had not been big enough for master, servant and dog, so Town Dog had had to go and stay with Quill. Crope had missed the busy little creature with her off-white coat and stubby tail. She'd followed him around a town he'd once visited far to the east of here, and when he'd had to leave in a bit of a hurry—owing to an unfortunate incident concerning the removal of a support beam from a tavern—she'd trotted through the gates, right on his heels. Town Dog had been with him ever since. She'd even been with him the night he'd gone to the pointy tower to free his lord.

She hadn't been allowed in this room at first, of course. His lord slept here, in the best, driest and airiest spot, his mattress raised off the floor by a wooden pallet and separated from the damp wall by a nailed-up sheepskin. Crope had been nervous about how his lord would react to the dog for he had no memory of Baralis treating any animal beside his horse with kindness. Plus, Town Dog was an energetic scrap of dogness, disinclined to sit and with a tendency to smell. Deciding it was best to keep them apart, Crope had made a point of keeping the stockroom door shut so that Town Dog couldn't gain access to his lord. This had meant that Town Dog spent a lot of time at the door, scratching, digging and mewling suspiciously like a cat. Crope had been mortified. How would his lord ever sleep? Measures had to be taken, and Crope had begun to leash Town Dog to one of the many iron rings that lay rusting against the cellars' walls. Then a strange thing had happened.

Every night in the darkest and quietest hours before dawn, Crope slipped out of the Quartercourts to walk the streets. He knew what he risked, yet he could not stop himself. For seventeen years he had been chained inside the mines and he had a hardness in him now that would not bow to anyone in matters of his freedom. Going outside each night was his sign to himself that he was a free man and that his comings and goings were his own.

As a precaution against detection he had taken to wearing the special cloak Quill had commissioned from the tailor who created clothing for the Surlord's secret intelligencers known as darkcloaks. *Gray for day. Brown for sundown.* Falling all the way to his feet, it was longer than he liked in a cloak, and its wool was unaccountably itchy, but if it could help him steal across the main courtyard in Mask Fortress without raising an alarm it probably wouldn't do any harm to wear it on his outings around the Quartercourts. Crope had an inkling that it made him more . . . *shadowy* than he normally was. Not invisible or anything fancy like that, just a tiny bit more difficult to see. Like a brown lizard on a brown wall.

He didn't like to put the hood up—itchy arms were one thing, itchy ears quite another—but forced himself to do so during those tricky moments leaving and returning to the Quartercourts. *Ingress and egress,* that's what Quill would have called it. The thief knew many fine and impressive-sounding words. To leave the Quartercourts, Crope had to open the door to the ice house where big blue blocks of lake ice were stored between bales of hay and pass through to the other side. Next he had to climb the steps to the servants' level that was used by the Quartercourts staff in the daytime to service the finely dressed lords. This was the tricky part, for sometimes potboys and scrubbers would hide from the night warden during his rounds so they could stay in the courts overnight.

Crope aimed for stealth when crossing the servants' level. He *aimed*, but suspected he fell short. A woman had screamed at him once, and he'd very nearly screamed back. She'd been sleeping on the bench near the door, covered by a scrap of blanket, and had woken when he'd stepped on a creaky board. Crope had hightailed it up the stairs and out of the Quartercourts, and had then spent an anxious hour walking the streets wondering how on earth he was going to get back. As it turned out, the night warden had heard the commotion, informed the woman that she was drunk and had seen a ghost, and turfed her from the building. Crope knew this because Quill had scolded him about it the next day. "Warden gave me a real fishwifing, I can tell you. Next time you ignore my excellent advice make sure no one is around to see you do it."

Crope felt bad about that, but it didn't prevent him from going out. Most nights he took Town Dog and it was their great mutual pleasure to walk the streets of Spire Vanis side by side, Town Dog taking eight steps to every one of Crope's.

The night when the strange thing had happened, Town Dog wasn't feeling up to going out though. Crope thought she may have eaten a bad rat, for her tummy was swollen and she'd refused food. He left her with some water and a stern warning about being a good girl. When he returned two hours later she wasn't in her place and the length of string that bound her to an iron ring on the wall had been severed. Crope checked the strange warren of rooms that Quill had secured for them; the peat cellar that still held the moldering remains of ancient bricks of turf, the star-shaped servants' chapel with its six stone mortars for grinding amber, the cold room for hanging game that still had hoists and brain hooks suspended from its ceiling, the room with the bathing pool sunk into the floor that was filled with crusty black water, and the cavernous space with the iron racks, iron wheels, and iron tables whose purposes Crope had no wish to guess.

Town Dog was nowhere to be found. Crope worried about the bathing pool, wondered how a man would set about dredging a body of water. Deciding he'd better check on his lord first, he headed back to the stockroom.

The door was open. The door was never open. He had closed it himself on the way out. Immediately Crope felt the bad pressure behind his eyes as the giant's blood moved at force through his brain. Muscles engorged and his sublungs which normally lay dormant beneath his major lungs sprang open to suck in air.

Baralis.

Crope threw himself through the doorway. Head whipping around to take in the details of the room, he saw his lord lying quietly on the bed, his body curled in its normal position, his broken and swollen-jointed hand resting on Town Dog's neck.

"Calm yourself," came Baralis' beautiful smoky voice. "We have been here all along."

Crope had stood there, heart thudding like a hammer against an anvil, his entire body vibrating with power that needed to be discharged, and stared at his lord and his dog. Town Dog raised her head a little and stared back, but quickly lost interest. Tucking herself against Baralis' arm, she headed off to sleep.

Baralis' darkly distorted gaze was steady, though his skin had that sheen to it that meant the poisons he was taking to kill the pain were sweating out. "I called her. She is not to blame."

She had chewed through the rope to get to him. And what of the door? Crope glanced back at it accusingly. His lord could move himself, but very slowly and at great cost, using his arms and shoulders to drag his weight. Crope did not believe he could have made it across the room.

"You did not close it," Baralis said, perfectly tracking Crope's thoughts. "It was ajar. The dog pushed through."

Crope took the door in his hand and tested its swing. Yes, it did catch a little at the last moment. Pushed without an extra spin of force it would not close. Crope nodded, satisfied. It had always been easy to agree with his lord.

That had been about five days back, and it had now become habit for Town Dog to spend a portion of her day sleeping or lying quietly on Baralis' bed. After the first shock of it, Crope was glad. They were three now, and there were times when they were all in the stockroom together, when Crope was mending a piece of clothing or mixing up a batch of medicine or just sitting under the window shafts to get some light that he felt content. If the moments could be caught and spun out they would make an agreeable life.

Baralis had grown stronger since they had moved from Quill's house. Some of it was the superior medicines, foods and comforts now brought regularly by Quill. The most expensive medicines were those that dulled pain—blood of poppy, skull-cap and devil's claw—and Crope had been sparing in their use. Now his lord could be given sufficient skullcap to insure he slept through most of the night. Better rested, his health had improved. The open wounds on his back and shoulders were slowly drying up as flesh knitted itself into puckered ridges. Bedsores had been eased by the new mattress, and now that Baralis' muscles were a little stronger he could shift his weight when they began to bother him. The damp air of the stockroom appeared to suit him better than the dryness of Quill's attic and his breaths were less labored, and there were fewer panics brought on by his failure to take in sufficient air. He had started to eat a little solid food—oatmeal with marrow butter, and raw eggs—and that made him more robust. Even his sensitivity to light had improved, and he no longer called for blankets to cover the window shafts at midday. Not that it was ever bright in the stockroom—sunlight rarely found a way in.

Little improvements in his lord's health encouraged Crope. He knew his lord would never be able to walk or properly use his hands, but now he had hope that some kind of life was possible. There had been days in the attic when Crope had feared his lord would lapse into unknowing and die.

Now Crope dreamed of leaving the city, of buying a horse and cart and heading off in one of the good directions and not stopping for a very long time. Once Spire Vanis was far behind them they would find a good piece of land with well-drained meadows, a hard standing for milch cows and a field hoed for beans, and purchase it from an obliging farmer who would be so pleased at the offering price that he'd throw in his barn goat for free. Then he, Crope, would set about fixing and planting and milking, and Town Dog would be at his heels and his lord would be on the back porch, in the shade, beneath a warm blanket, looking up from his book now and then to tell them all what to do.

Crope glanced from the windows to his lord. Baralis was resting not sleeping, though his eyes were closed. Quill had brought fresh linens a few days back, and the sheets were clean except for a few sweat rings and some dog hairs. A series of small dark stains on the pillow might have been blood of the poppy or simply blood. Baralis' breathing moved the tan blankets at a steady rate, and because they were pulled high around his neck a casual observer might assume the man lying beneath them was whole. If you were to look closer, though, you would notice the old white scars on his eyelids and the burn circles around his nostrils, and the melted cartilage in each ear.

They shut down his senses, Quill had said once with a small shudder. *Deprived him of sight, sound and smell to break him.*

"The thief comes," Baralis said, opening his eyes.

Disconcerted, Crope nodded; there didn't seem much else for him to do.

"Do not leave while I speak with him."

Crope repeated the words back to himself so he would not forget them. His lord was different now, harder and purer like a metal that had gone through the fire. Only words that needed to be said were spoken, and the very few items he requested were necessary for survival. Crope had the sense that he was both less and more. Less of body and less of self. More of mind.

It upset him if he thought about it too much. How could his lord ever sit on a porch and take part in a normal life?

Crope resisted the answer and busied himself with the small attentions Baralis required. Pillows and bedding had to be straightened and Baralis himself had to be gently elevated to a more upright position. Muscles in his lord's jaw tightened like wires as he was moved, yet he made no reference to the pain. Crope lightly combed his hair and drew a short wool cape across his shoulders. Satisfied that his lord had his dignity, but not sure how much that now mattered to Baralis himself, Crope stepped back and prepared to wait.

It was just past midday, and a failure in light told of an approaching storm. Belowground all was still and warm. The pig-shaped stove, set on the side of the stockroom opposite from Baralis' bed, radiated heat through its thick iron casing. Town Dog, who had been ratting in the big room, began to bark. Crope went to silence her and greet the thief.

Quill let himself through the ice-house door. A burlap sack was slung over his shoulders and the first thing he did was swing it forward and set it on the ground before his feet. "Commodibles," he said in greeting.

Crope had a feeling it was a dismissal. *Take the commodibles—whatever they might be—and make yourself scarce for half an hour.* Recalling his lord's words Crope picked up the sack and carried it through to the stockroom.

Quill, realizing the way things were, wisely made no objection. "Storm's coming," he said to Baralis as he entered. "Not going to be much of one, though. Reckon it'll be up and out before sunset."

"Sit," Baralis replied. Now that he had more strength in his lungs his voice sounded richer and more resonant. He had regained his ability to send a word softly yet make it act like a command.

The thief pulled up a stool, using the time it took to send his gaze darting around the room. "You'll need more coals," he said, "for the stove."

Crope was on the verge of agreeing with him heartily, but a tiny flick of Baralis' eyes stopped him. Quill had taken the stool Crope usually sat on to feed the stove and care for Baralis, and Crope had nowhere to sit. Awkwardly he shuffled backward so he could rest against the wall, hoping all the while that once he was there they'd both forget about him.

"Tell me the news in the city," Baralis said to the thief.

"Stornoway holds the fortress. Fighting's mostly done. There's been some trouble at Almsgate but the other gates are sealed."

"What trouble?"

"Lisereth Hews' hideclads stormed it. Word arrived yesterday that her son's on his way back from the clanholds, and she needs to control at least one gate so the Whitehog can enter the city."

Baralis closed his eyes for a fraction longer than a blink, and Crope knew he was dealing with a spasm of pain. "Will she succeed?"

Quill thought about this, one of his long thief's fingers circling his chin like a sundial. "All she needs do is keep fighting until her son arrives—some are saying that might be as early as tomorrow. She's managed to get hold of a battering ram and she's a tough mother of a bitch; I think she'll do it."

"And Stornoway?"

"The watch is his. As long as they're loyal to him it's going to be difficult to break the fortress. The old goat's sitting tight.

He's told the watch that by supporting him they're supporting Marafice Eye—them being father and son and all now that the Knife's wed his daughter—and his hideclads are running the city."

"Are we safe here?"

The thief sucked in air through his lips. "If Hews makes it into the city no one's safe. We've been lucky so far. Roland Stornoway was quick on his feet, took the Fortress while the city was still reeling over the Splinter's collapse. If Hews wants it from him there'll be no end to the blood."

Let's leave, Crope wanted to shout. *Tell Quill to buy some horses and go.* Yet his lord didn't say those words and Crope could tell by the look on his face that he wasn't thinking them either. Baralis' burn scars were silvery in the stormlight, and right now his dark eyes looked almost clear.

"Stornoway's son-in-law is on his way back."

Quill did not seem to notice this wasn't a question, or perhaps Crope was mistaken and it *was* actually a question, for the thief answered it like one. "Marafice Eye commanded the army that went north. Word is that he separated from the Whitehog and is still in the clanholds."

Baralis breathed and did not speak. Last night he had slept soundly, which was a good thing as far as Crope was concerned for it always unsettled him to hear his lord calling out in his sleep.

No.

Such a small word. Crope was not sure why he thought about it now.

"Thick snow will dampen the fighting at the gate."

Nine words, Crope knew because he counted them, and the world shifted. The crumbly coals in the stove burned steadily as if nothing had happened and flecks of dust and burned matter sailing in the air continued on course. Yet the light changed, as it would need to, draining away like water down a culvert. Crope expected it would be dark within the hour.

And his lord would be reduced.

Already he could see it, a subtle shift from resting actively against the pillows to simply lying there. Not slumped, for the thief was still in the room and the appearance of control must be maintained. Baralis' skin grayed as Crope looked on, and poisons began to ooze from his pores. Crope's instinct was to rush forward, set his lord to rest properly in the bed, drip the red tea of the hawthorn berry between his lips to strengthen his heart and cool his face with damp cloths. Yet he could do nothing until the thief was gone. His lord's will held him in place.

Quill sat motionless on the stool, yet Crope was struck with the notion that if he were to touch the thief he would feel him vibrating. Energy hummed through the stillness. Quill's gaze rested at a point directly in front of Baralis' face. His pupils were enlarged with revelation.

He had been promised things, gold and treasures—access to the deceased surlord's secret stash—yet Baralis had been slow to deal them out. Hints had been dropped, a piece of information leading to the discovery of a small cache of gold had been disclosed. Crope knew how these things worked. His lord was keeping the thief on the hook. Quill hadn't known it that day in the attic, but any man who struck a deal with Baralis stood on quicksand. What Crope didn't know now was his lord's purpose. Power had been Baralis' sole motivation in the past. He had striven to control a kingdom and then a continent, and failed. Those days had gone though, and Crope felt a knife of fear slide in his neck when he thought about the new days to come.

Evil had been born in the monstrous iron chamber beneath the tower. The man who had clamped it with faucets and pulled it out was dead, but the thing he had brought into this world lived on.

Hell knows me and you cannot understand what that knowing brings. Crope knew his memory wasn't good, but even if he lived to be three hundred years old he doubted if he would forget his lord's words.

Crope wondered if the thief was thinking of them too. Certainly he was thinking of ways to profit from the information that a storm meant to pass through the city in a couple of hours would take an unexpected turn for the worse. Perhaps he was also thinking there was use in knowing that the fighting at Almsgate would be slowed. Or perhaps, like Crope himself, he was wondering if by holding the storm at unspeakable cost to himself, Baralis was serving or resisting hell.

Quill stood. "I'll see you get those coals for the fire."

Baralis nodded, accepting the complicated acquiescence of the thief.

Once Quill had let himself out, Crope went to tend his lord. He feared what Baralis would lose this day.

TWENTY-SIX

The Outlanders

"**W**here does Thomas Argola live?" Raif asked.

Stillborn did not much like this question. They were standing on the shell-shaped ledge in front of the Maimed Man's cave, shoveling snow. A storm had hit in the night and spring had rolled back into winter. When Raif looked south to the clanholds he saw a world turned white.

"Don't get close to him," Stillborn said, his breath making icy clouds from the words. He was dressed in his normal garb of a sleeveless tunic and a kilt over pants. His concession to the cold was a glossy black sheepskin draped over his shoulders and tied in place with string. Reaching the area where his firestack was buried, he stopped shoveling and began to scrape. He wasn't about to waste good wood. "The outlander's not one of us."

That meant he wasn't clan. Raif chucked snow into the Rift. None of them were clan. "I'll find him for myself."

Stillborn harumped. Straightening his back, he said, "Come here."

Raif crossed to his side and looked up. Above him the buckled and uneven layers of cliff rock, caves and ledges rose for over two hundred feet.

"See that small gray door, near the same color as the cliff?" Raif nodded. "That's where he lives. Only man in the Rift to have an actual, hinged, godforsaken door." Stillborn scowled at it. "And a lock."

Raif broke away from him and went back to shoveling.

Stillborn was disappointed that no plans had yet been made to seize control of the Maimed Men from Traggis Mole. He did not know what Raif knew. Raif wasn't even sure what he knew himself. The Robber Chief had been badly wounded by one of the Unmade, and for more reason than one Raif needed to find out what that meant.

He could feel it as he put his back into digging out the snow; the liquid tingle in his left shoulder where the *Shatan Maer's* claw had punctured him. Abruptly, he set the shovel against the cliff wall. "I'll be back later," he said.

Stillborn showed his teeth. "Be sure to knock."

Snow had stopped falling from the clouds but it was still moving in the air around the Rift. Ice crystals sparkled on the updrafts and blew off ledges in plumes. Raif stayed close to the cliffwall and took short steps. Men and women were out shoveling snow, building fires, visiting one another and taking fresh air. A group of children on the rimrock were building a ghoul out of snow. People were in high spirits, glad that the storm had passed by quickly and the temperature was rising.

The rope ladders were slick and dangerous and Raif was glad of the rough pads on his boarskin gloves. Rock grit had been sprinkled over some of the more dangerous spots — narrow ledges, wooden gangplanks and landings around ladders — and for the first time Raif realized that the Maimed Men were capable of working together. He even found he was less disliked: no one glared at him or threw stones. Despite what Traggis Mole had predicted, Addie and Stillborn had shared credit for the meat brought back from the overnight hunt, and all who ate that night knew that Raif Twelve Kill was owed part of their thanks. The snagcat pelt was different. Set apart. To bring down a cat was a feat demanding praise and Stillborn had claimed all laudings for himself.

Raif lost sight of the gray, unfinished wood door as he worked his way up through the city, but he had a sense of its general location and headed east on one of the long ledges. As he neared a rope hoist he slowed down and considered whether to take it. The hoist bypassed an inset ledge and headed up to the next broad plateau of rimrock.

"No need to go any further, my dear boy." Yustaffa stepped

out from the shadows of a cave mouth. "As you can see I'm already here."

He looked like a fat snow bear who had rolled in jewels.

"You like?" he said, glancing down at his outfit. "Should I spin?"

"No," Raif told him. The jewel things were dazzling. They seemed to be suspended in invisible netting over the white winter pelts he was wearing. The feather-light fur of ice hares formed a tunic that looked made of fluff.

"Twelve Kill Joy I should call you," he said, and then went ahead and spun anyway. "Yustaffa must haffa spin. Care to talk?"

"No."

The expression on Yustaffa's smooth plump face hardened. "Wouldn't hurt the future king to play nice."

Raif stared at him, blinking and dazzled, as he spun again and walked away. Were there no secrets here?

The pleasure he had taken in the day gone, Raif stepped into the hoist basket and pulled on the thick rope. Snow had not affected the pulley's motion and he ascended quickly, placing fist over fist. The basket had been woven from tough wicker and it creaked and sawed but held firm.

Alighting on the rimrock, he looked for the gray door. Almost certain it was on the inset ledge just below him, he searched for a place to make the jump down. Once he'd found a suitable cut in the rimrock, he squatted to inspect it, then made the leap. On landing he felt a jolt of pain in his still-tender ankle and had to stand a moment to relieve it. As he pivoted his foot left and then right to test it, he became aware that someone was watching him. Turning his head he saw a young woman standing by a cave mouth holding a handful of snow.

She was wearing a moss green dress of felted wool with a black bodice laced snug against her waist. Her skin was deeply, almost greenly, golden and her dark hair, which was caught loosely in an amber band at her neck, fell in waves to the small of her back. Seeing Raif look at her she rotated her wrist and let the snow fall from her hand.

Raif looked away, put his weight on his throbbing ankle, and then looked back. She was still watching him. He could not decipher her expression, nor could he think of anything to say. Here was the last place on earth he would have thought to find beauty.

Knowing he would have to walk past her to search for the gray door, he became acutely aware of his movements. He cursed his ankle, for even as he took his first step he knew it would make him limp. Glancing ahead, he spied two other cave mouths, one closed off with a bamboo screen and one that stood unguarded. He continued walking. To attempt to swing back up to the rimrock while the woman watched seemed an action loaded with potential for embarrassment. As he neared her he couldn't decide where to look, and his gaze jumped from her face to the way ahead and then, inexplicably, to her feet. She was standing in a half-moon of roughly cleared snow.

He missed the fact that she was also standing *in front* of an open door. The door opened inward and had swung into the shadows of the timber-framed cave mouth. Only when he passed the woman and stole a quick glance back did he see it. Faced with a choice between stopping, turning and speaking to her, or continuing to walk along the ledge, he was uncertain. The fact that the ledge came to an end just beyond the unguarded cave helped clear his mind. He had to go back.

She watched him as he came toward her a second time. The cuff of her green dress was wet where she had held the snow.

"Does Thomas Argola live here?" he asked, satisfied that his voice sounded normal.

"He does." She looked at him with eyes that were darkly, greenly, brown.

Raif waited, but she offered no more. "Is he here? Can I see him?"

"He is here. I will ask if he will see you." She did not immediately move like others would. Instead she created a deliberate pause and did nothing to fill it.

Just when Raif thought he should speak again, she whirled around and headed for the door. As he waited he searched for, and found, the pile of snow she had dropped. The imprint of her fingers were still upon it.

"Raif." The slight and loose form of Thomas Argola appeared in the doorway. "Come."

Raif followed him into the cave. Two copper lamps set on recesses in the wall were glowing with smokeless light. The cave was small and nearly round. Its ceiling was strikingly uneven, the rock dipping low in concertina-like folds and then muscling into high vaults. A natural flue had formed at the apex of the tallest vault and Raif could feel its draw. At least two other chambers led from the cave where the rock wall bored down into the cliff. Their entrances were screened with lengths of faded gold and green brocade. One of them was moving. The girl was gone.

"Sit." Thomas Argola spread a long-fingered, olive-skinned hand toward the cushions and rugs arranged around a small brass brazier set at knee height.

Raif resisted the direction, preferring to move about the space, looking at glazed boxes, straw baskets, frayed silk rugs and tarnished metal bowls piled with rolled parchments, hollow eggs, cards of silk thread and dried yarrow heads that lay on the cave floor. He was too keyed up to sit.

Realizing that Thomas Argola was waiting for him to speak, Raif searched for a way to start a conversation. The girl had thrown him off center. "We're lucky the storm didn't stay longer."

Thomas Argola executed a movement that looked like a controlled drop, collapsing his body onto one of the silk cushions. "Our luck is someone else's misfortune." He spoke the words with a pointed lightness that Raif suspected was intended to convey meaning. He waited, and the outlander spoke again. "The storm was disturbed, its course deflected south."

Raif halted by the brocade screen that had been moving when he entered. A design of dragons and pear trees was woven into the cloth. "How is that possible?"

"It very nearly isn't." Thomas Argola bit each word as he said it.

Feeling his skin cool, Raif turned to face the outlander. Argola's expression was flat and challenging. A speck of blood was caught between his cornea and the white of his eye. Seeing it Raif abandoned the hope they were talking about natural forces.

"We live in dangerous times," Argola said in confirmation. "Sit and I will pour us some broth."

Raif sat. It was hard to comprehend what he had just heard, and he took the small bone cup offered by the outlander without acknowledgment. A storm could be made to alter its course? Surely not.

"To our health," Argola said, raising his own cup, "and sanity."

They seemed good things to toast just then. Cups struck, Raif and the outlander drank deeply. The broth was well made, salty and rich with marrow and thyme. The outlander seemed pleased to pour Raif a second cup.

"Mallia makes it, though she must do without the ginger from our homeland. Thyme serves as its substitute."

Raif drank and did not speak. He told himself he wasn't waiting, but he didn't think he fooled Argola.

"My sister," the outlander revealed eventually.

Now he had said it, Raif saw the resemblance; the coloring, the hair. But not the eyes. They were different. Needing to change the subject, he asked, "What do you know of Traggis Mole's . . . health?"

Argola set down the cup by his foot and watched as the liquid it contained steamed. Seconds passed, and then he said, "He has shown you the wound?"

"No."

"Be glad of it," Argola retorted quickly. "I have treated it and continue to dress it, and it is not a sight I would wish on anyone."

Shuddering, Raif felt a twinge of pain in his shoulder. A little icy jab. "How bad is it?"

"Answer that and I give you the keys to this city."

Raif worked his way through the outlander's words, caught off-guard by their slyness. *Remember the mist*, he told himself. The man sitting before him had pulled fog from a lake on a still dry night at Black Hole. While everyone else in the raid party was fighting to gain entry to the mine, Thomas Argola had been packing Bear's saddlebags with enough supplies to carry Raif into the Want. *It's a hard journey north*, he had said, knowing that for every hundred who went there only two or three ever returned.

And here he was now, breaking the confidence of his chief and arming his rival with information. Raif stopped himself and forced a correction. The outlander was not clan and Traggis Mole was no clan chief; the expectation of loyalty did not exist.

The cushion Raif sat on had tassels on its corners and he caught one in his fist. So Traggis Mole was in a bad way. "What happened?"

Argola made a movement with his hand. "The thing that got onto the rimrock that night was never human. Even when it lived in flesh it had been some kind of monstrosity. More dog than man. It barely knew how to wield a blade, but it was strong—and fast. No one could get near it. Eventually the Dancer caught its blade in his swordbreaker, and as Linden Moodie came in to attack its unarmed flank, Traggis Mole took the side bearing the sword. Something happened. The creature's blade slid free of the breaker and it whipped around and tore through the Mole's side. Moodie cut off its arm. But it was too late. The damage had been done."

Raif nodded softly to himself as he compared Addie's account of the attack to Argola's. "The Mole kept the severity of his injuries hidden."

"Wouldn't you?"

The flatness in Argola's voice irritated Raif. He stood. "What happens when someone is injured by the Unmade?" As he spoke he heard the false note in his voice—the forced casualness of the question—and he imagined Argola would hear it too.

The outlander looked at him carefully. "It depends on the extent of the injury. The Mole took a hit to the chest with voided steel. The blade missed his heart but passed through some of his lung. It didn't kill him . . . but it will. Not from infection, not as you and I know it. The wound is clean, if you can call it that. It's what the voided steel left behind . . . some of itself. It's a blackness eating away at him, incinerating his flesh like acid. I can only suture the wound so far. It needs to . . ." he hesitated, "vent."

Raif closed his eyes and took a breath. It was the same as the Forsworn knight in the redoubt; the dark, silky substance leaking from his wounds. Half liquid, half smoke.

"Traggis Mole is being taken. The wound is too deep. He is strong and fights it, but his flesh is cankered with a substance beyond evil and to cut it out would kill him."

The outlander rose from the pile of cushions. "You'd better show me what you've got."

Raif stepped back. His heel struck one of the metal bowls, producing a note that vibrated through the cave.

Argola regarded him with some impatience. "It's why you came here, is it not? Something in the Want injured you?"

Again, Raif felt himself irritated by the outlander's assumptions. The fact that they were correct only made it worse. He had nothing to lose now—certainly not privacy as this meeting so far had been a demonstration in how little Thomas Argola valued discretion. With a snap, Raif unhooked the Orrl cloak. Yanking his undershirt and sealskin up around his neck he showed his back to the outlander. "It's low on the left shoulder."

Argola approached him. He looked and said nothing.

The pull from the flue lifted hairs on Raif's skin. After a while he could stand the silence no longer. "What is there?"

"Three puncture wounds. All are scarred over and dry. The middle one looks to be the worst of them. May I touch it?"

No. Out loud, Raif said, "Go ahead."

Two things happened then. First he felt a bite of pain where Argola's finger touched him, and second he saw that the cloth screen with the dragons and pears had been pulled partway back and Argola's sister was standing behind it, watching him.

Raif tugged down his shirt. He could feel his color rising and wanted nothing that moment except to be gone. The outlander shooed his sister with a flick of his wrist. He did not seem much concerned.

"They were not made with voided steel," he said to Raif, a question in his voice.

Glancing at the screen, Raif saw that Mallia Argola had disappeared. He wondered if she was just beyond the screen. Listening. Coming here had been a mistake. He started toward the door.

Argola moved with him. "Stop," he said, his voice flat yet somehow compelling. "If you will not speak hear me out."

Raif halted by the door; the farthest point from the dragon-and-pear screen. Argola understood him and edged close, and for the first time it occurred to Raif that the outlander appeared whole. No obvious abnormalities or cuttings marked his flesh. What was his place here? Maimed Men would not tolerate an undamaged man or woman in their realm. The outlander did not hunt and was not well liked. Raif supposed he had his uses. He had tricks; the revealing of the suspension bridge across the Rift, the raising of mist during a raid.

The speck of blood in Thomas Argola's eyes floated toward his iris as he said quietly, "Underlying the middle wound there is some discoloring and a small pocket of inflammation. I thought it would be soft, but when I touched it I found it hard. I'm assuming something raked you with its claws—it's what it looks like—and I'm also assuming that the creature who did it was unmade." A pause while Raif nodded. "I believe you were lucky and unlucky. Lucky that it was *maer dan*, shadowflesh, not voided steel that punctured you. Unlucky in that a small piece of claw broke off in your flesh."

"Cut it out," Raif said.

Thomas Argola was already shaking his head. "It's embedded in the muscle. Cut it out and you will loose function in your arm and shoulder. It must be drawn, not cut."

Raif did not understand why the outlander was playing games with him. "Then draw it out."

"That skill is beyond me."

More games. "You tend Traggis Mole."

"And I can do nothing for him. He dies."

Raif punched the meat of his hand against the door. Left shoulder. Left arm. Two hundred pounds of pull in a fully drawn longbow and the left shoulder and arm must brace against it. "Why do you manipulate me?"

"You know why."

Raif's gaze met the outlander's. At least he did not bother to lie. "Who are you?"

"Thomas Bireon Argola, from a city you've never heard of called Hanatta. I lay small claim to the old skills and have some experience as a healer. I came north three years ago with my sister, for reasons that are not yours to know. And I do not lie about the drawing of the *maer dan*. It is an art practiced by races older than mine and the Sull."

"Are you whole?"

"Do not make me show you all the ways that I am not."

Raif's anger collapsed. Suddenly he felt tired and out of his depth. His shoulder seemed to ache more now than it did before Argola's pronouncement, and he remembered that he had hurt his ankle. And now it hurt.

Argola looked tired too, the corners of his mouth were turned down, the lips pale. Raif wondered if his thoughts were similar to his own: it would be good to have some peace.

"Can I live with the *maer dan* inside me?"

"You do," Argola said, almost gently. Then, in a stronger voice, "It is situated in the muscle above the back of your heart. If it moves inward there is no bone to stop it."

Oh gods.

"The closest Sull settlement is due east of here, in the great taiga where the Deadwoods meet the Sway."

Here it was, the manipulation. Raif felt it in the hollow center of his bones. It was a funny thing, manipulation; even when you knew someone was doing it and they admitted to doing it, it could still work. *It is a hard journey north*, he had said last time. Now east.

"Have you heard of the Lake of Red Ice?"

"I have."

"Do you know where it is?"

"All I know I have said."

Raif looked at the blood in Argola's right eye and imagined how it had got there. "Look for me," he commanded.

The outlander's face registered surprise, and then—Raif would remember for the rest of his life—*satisfaction*.

"If you are to watch you must be prepared when they come."

Raif thought about all these words revealed. Argola knew about the sword. Knew also about the name he had taken for his own. *Mor Drakka*. Watcher of the Dead. How did he learn these things? What did he know that Raif did not?

Thomas Argola's small, sharp-featured face gave nothing

away. His plain brown robes reminded Raif of what the monks in the Mountain Cities wore to demonstrate they had no interest in worldly things.

"Did they tell you the name of the sword?"

It was as if the outlander had a stick and kept poking him harder and harder to see what he might do. Raif's back was against the door; he could not be driven any farther. "No they did not."

Argola received the warning, seemed pleased by it. Again there was that lip stretch of satisfaction. "The sword that lies beneath the Red Ice is named Loss."

Loss.

"There are some things in the Blind that will not fall by any other blade."

It was too much. Raif punched back the door bolt and let himself out. He did not look back or close the door.

Sunlight streamed against his face and he could barely make sense of it. Bouncing off the snow on the ground, it came at him from every direction. Bright, razoring light. It should have dispelled the dark seizures in his brain, yet it just seemed to feed them.

Loss.

He headed toward the upper ledge. A knotted rope hung from the ledge he had jumped and he yanked himself up it. He had left behind his gloves and cloak in the outlander's cave, and the cold and the rope burns added to the strange energy of pain and twitching thoughts he had become.

I will not slit your throat. I will defend the Rift Brothers. I will become lord of the Rift. Every time he spoke these days he seemed to take on another oath.

He had given none to Argola, though. Yet he had allowed the man to push him. Releasing his hands from the rope, Raif landed on the rimrock. Snow crunched as he flattened it. Had he allowed Stillborn to push him too?

Deciding no good would come of knowing, he switched his mind away from all of it. Argola's motives. The puncture wound. The sword. It was just past midday and the sun was at its highest point above the clanholds. Raif walked to the edge of the broad table of rock and sucked in the sight of his homeland.

Seven hundred paces, that was the distance that separated the clanholds from the Rift in this place. A man could cross it in a matter of minutes—east of here there was a hidden bridge. Yet there might as well be a wall as tall as the sky. Raif Sevrance could never go back.

He stood and let the sun warm him and the snow cool him. And when he was ready he looked down into the Rift.

For the first time ever, Raif was aware of beating hearts deep within its depths.

TWENTY-SEVEN

A Castleman for a Year

Dalhousie Selco, the swordmaster at Castlemilk, kept an hourglass slung around his neck on a chain and used it as a torture device. If you as much as glanced at it he'd grab the chain and twist it, turning the hourglass from vertical to horizontal. Stopping time. Only when he was satisfied that you and the other young men he was training had been suitably punished did he twist the chain back and let time run.

Bram was learning fast: best not even to look at the swordmaster, let alone his glass. That path led to double trouble. Trouble from Dalhousie now. Trouble from the other boys later. *You made him give us an extra fifteen minutes—in the snow.*

It was true enough. They were training on the smallest of the three swordcourts at the rear of the roundhouse, and when they'd trudged out before noon and Dalhousie had directed them to the only court that had not been cleared of snow they all thought he'd made a mistake. No one had dared say so. Though Enoch had whispered to Bram, "Either Housie's off his nut or he's going to make us shovel snow." Whispering was a grave error in the swordmaster's presence. If he heard you he would whack your shoulder with his wooden scabbard. Luckily for Enoch there *was* snow: five pairs of feet crunching through it on their way to the swordcourt had provided sufficient noise to camouflage his offense.

Even when it had become obvious that Dalhousie had not made a mistake and did indeed intend to put them through their forms while making them stand in two feet of snow, the full extent of his evil plan had yet to be revealed. Bram had trained with Jackdaw Thundy, the old swordmaster at Dhoone, and he knew that any swordmaster worth his salt was tough and demanding. He hadn't known they were capable of torture.

"Castlemen," Dalhousie had shouted when they were all assembled on the court. "Pull off your left boots and let's get moving."

Bram Cormac, Enoch Odkin, Trotty Pickering and Shamie Weese, known as Beesweese, had looked at each other, round-eyed and blinking.

"*Now!*" roared Dalhousie.

At first Bram had been glad he had his socks on—tube-shaped sheaths of rabbit skin rendered bald by constant use—but after five minutes of plunging his foot in and out of the snow the material had become wet and icy and he ended up pulling it off. At least the bare skin could dry off a bit between dunkings. Dalhousie had set them in pairs—Bram against Enoch, Trotty against Beesweese—and made them stand opposite each other while they took turns executing and defending forms.

"Swan's neck! Bluddsmen's farewell! Hammer cut! Harking's needle!" Dalhousie Selco marched from one end of the court to the other, shouting out the forms. Every so often he would explode into motion, and his chosen victim would have to defend himself against a series of attack forms while screaming out their names. Occasionally Dalhousie would throw in a new form, and Gods help you if you mistook it for something else.

"If you don't know it *cover you body and step back*!"

It left Bram's ears ringing. Dalhousie had the loudest voice he had ever heard.

"Cormac. What's the difference between a swordsman and a man with a sword?"

Bram had been moving through a series of high blocks, defending against Enoch's head blows, while trying to keep his bare foot out of the snow. He was still not accustomed to being called Cormac and it took him a moment to realize that Dalhousie was addressing him. The rule on the swordcourt was that you never broke away from an engagement to answer questions. You shouted out as you fought.

"Training," screamed Bram.

"No," Dalhousie bellowed. "Experience. A man knows nothing until he's been in a genuine blood-spurting, puke-making, knuckle-bursting sword brawl. You can train every day between here and damnation and you'll still be a fool with a sword. You have to get out there and fight, see a man's eyes and know he's scared shitless, and realize he's seeing the exact same thing staring back." With that, Dalhousie launched himself at Bram.

Sword high from countering head blows, Bram was forced into an awkward lower-body block. Elbow up and extended, wrist pivoting inward, he lost control of his sword the instant the first blow hit. Metal screeched as Dalhousie used Bram's sinking blade as a fulcrum to turn his sword point into the center of Bram's gut. As Bram felt the hard jab of blunted steel against his navel, a second blow cut him on the side of the neck. Enoch Odkin.

"Good work," Dalhousie told the lanky Castleboy. He had nothing to say to Bram.

Enoch gave Bram a little shrug when the swordmaster's back was turned. He was older than Bram, probably sixteen or seventeen, with blue-black hair and thick downy eyebrows that met in the middle. He'd rolled his left pant leg up to the knee, revealing stupendously hairy legs and the kind of scars that stableboys got from being kicked by unfamiliar horses. His foot was bright pink with cold.

Bram decided he held no grudge against him. He also decided he'd had enough of defending and went on the attack. Enoch raised his sword and stepped back, sending his tender pink toes into the snow. Bram cut sideways with his sword, forcing Enoch to set down his entire foot. A second cut, a perfect mirror of the first, caused Enoch to shift his weight to the side. His bare foot lost traction for the briefest instant; Bram knew this because he saw the momentary loss of control register in Enoch's eyes. It was a small thing then to slide under his guard and stick him in the ribs.

That was when Bram had made the mistake of looking at Dalhousie and his hourglass. He wanted to see if the swordmaster had watched the exchange between him and Enoch, and unfortunately his gaze fell short of Dalhousie's head. They were, at that point, well into the last third of sand and probably had less than a quarter to go before they could pull on their boots and defrost their feet. Yet when Dalhousie saw Bram looking in the direction of the glass, he smacked his lips and stopped time. Trotty and Beesweese slowed their sword strikes to look over at Enoch and Bram. Enoch put his eyebrows to work, raising them up and sideways in the direction of Bram Cormac.

"Fight on," Dalhousie warned. He didn't start time again for fifteen minutes.

By the end of the session Bram's toes were so numb that he could no longer tell when they touched the ground. He had to look. The pain in his heel where chilblains were forming felt strangely unrelated to the cold. It was as if someone had taken a razor to his foot and chopped it into squares. When it came time to put his boot on, he couldn't do it, and just sat in the snow and looked at it.

"Put it on," Dalhousie said approaching, his voice pitched at a volume below loud. "I know it's only a wee walk back to the house, but do it. A swordsman never neglects his body."

Bram wrung out the rabbit sock and pulled it on. It felt like slime, but he didn't think he'd get the boot on without it.

"Good. Do you know why I made you take it off?"

"No."

Dalhousie squatted on the flattened snow. He wasn't a big man, but it was easy to forget that. His hair was short, and so thick and curly it seemed to have muscles. Unlike his beard, it showed no gray. "You never know what you're going to get in a melee; mad men not caring if they get ripped to pieces as they come at you, a one-to-oner turning into a one-to-three, acid thrown on your back, pants falling around your ankles, blood in your eyes, open wounds, frostbite. Me facing you and politely exchanging blows is not how it happens. A good swordsman knows how to fight through surprises. He's prepared to be unprepared."

Bram nodded.

Dalhousie had upended the hourglass around his neck and yellow sand was running through the globes. "You're quick, I'll give you that. And you can make your size work for you. Come see me in the Churn Hall at dawn and I'll show you a couple of knee stickers."

Bram eased on his boot as he watched the swordmaster cross over to Beesweese, exchange a few words on his technique, and then head off to the house. He was tired and beaten up and he knew he would get a big bruise on his neck where Enoch Odkin had sneaked him. It would go with the others he'd gotten over the past days. And then it would simply go.

Hauling himself up from the snow, he realized his pant seat was soaked through. This, together with his half-numb foot, didn't make for a pleasant walk back. The sun was behind clouds and the air hovered just above freezing. The kitchen gardens, walled garden, stable court, playground and cattle standing were lumpy with new snow. Two grooms were trying to force the stable doors open through thick drifts. A big white dog was barking at them.

A *Castleman for a year.* Bram reached into his tunic and slipped his new, alien guidestone from its hidden pouch. The gray liquid was suspended in water, and held in a stoppered vial made of cloudy glass. At one time Bram had believed that only the head warrior wore his Milkstone in this manner, but now he knew that all Castlemen and women wore theirs in much the same way. The difference was that Harald Mawl was allowed the privilege of display. All others, including the Milk chief herself, must show discretion when wearing their portion of powdered guidestone. It was a small thing, but Wrayan Castlemilk had been right when she said such small things made a clan.

Bram had seen her little since that day by the gravepool. She had attended the swearing of his First Oath, causing no small ripple of surprise when she stepped forward to accept Bram's swearstone and act as second to his oath. Bram had at first been relieved. Every yearman worried about that moment—who, if anyone, would step forward and back him? No one wanted to stand before his clan, alone and in silence, unclaimed. Yet afterward Bram had thought about it and wondered if he really wanted a chief holding the stone that was under his tongue as he spoke the Castlemilk oath.

"I will keep the Castlewatch between the Milk and the Flow

and stand ready to fight for one year." It was a simple oath, unlike Dhoone's, and it did not claim that extra day.

The ceremony had taken place outside the guidehouse, in view of the Milk River, with the sun setting between ships of crimson cloud. It was the first oath Bram Cormac, brother to the Dhoone king, had spoken. He was a clansman: it would not be his last.

His days had been busy since then, filled with names and customs in need of learning, and the three separate and distinct pursuits that filled his day. Pol Burmish, the warrior who had greeted Bram at the door on that first night, had taken him to meet the swordmaster the morning after First Oath, and his training had begun in earnest. Swordfighting was taken more seriously here than at Dhoone and the level of swordcraft was higher. Bram had thought himself proficient with the longsword. He was wrong. At Dhoone he had been judged too small to train for the hammer and ax, and had taken up the sword instead. He was Mabb Cormac's son and people said he had some of his father's skill. It was a confusing time. Mabb promised to train him, then died. Jackdaw Thundy, the old swordmaster, had a stroke and retired, and was replaced by Ewall Meal, who had been Mabb Cormac's old rival. Ewall had liked the son little better than the father, and the training sessions had not gone well. *"You're too small, boy. Step aside and let the next man have a go."* Bram had stopped attending the sessions. After that he trained alone. Sometimes Mabb's old comrade-in-swords, Walter Hoole, would spend an hour or two with him in the evenings, putting him through his forms as he retold old stories about the glory days of Mabb and Walter. Often he was drunk. Bram had no way to gauge his progress, and had no longer been sure that he wanted to continue training. And then the Dog Lord invaded Dhoone.

Bram let himself in to the creamy maze of the Milkhouse. He had worked out the orientation of most of its corridors and doors and no longer had to figure direction by sunlight. Which was good. It meant he could get around on overcast days, and at night. But he had noticed things, absences where there should be chambers, or rather a lack of access *to* those chambers. He saw the ground floor of the roundhouse clearly in his mind's eye and knew there were spaces he had yet to enter.

Those spaces played on his mind. Rumor had it that histories were kept there; secrets about the clanholds and the Sull that had been hidden for hundreds of years. Bram had worked out the location of one of the secret chambers—it was located behind the west stairwell and adjacent to the women's solar— but a sense of honor kept him from searching for the entrance. Still, he would dearly have liked to see what lay inside it. And sometimes he thought that honor was a sham.

Realizing that he was hungry and late for his work in the guidehouse, Bram glanced toward the kitchen. Breakfast had been fried apples and veined cheese, but that had been half a day ago. He could smell baking, and frying—Castlemilk's cook worked frequently with boiling oil—and decided not to resist. Limping at full speed, he made his way through the roundhouse and out the other side.

The kitchen was bustling. The benches were filled with women, children, seasoned warriors and old-timers taking their noonday meal. The noise was close to deafening. Cook and his helpers were clanging pots and trivets, pitchforking sides of venison from vats of sizzling fat and stoking the ovens with giant pokers. Heat and steam and cooking smells combined to form a force that pushed through the air like wind. Bram hurried to the food tables, glad to see that no full-sworn warriors were waiting to be served. Men with lifetime oaths to their clans were always fed first. Pol waved a greeting from the back, and the head dairyman, little crotchety Millard Flag, shouted something about the skimming needing to be redone by the end of the day. Bram nodded an acknowledgment. There was no fooling Millard: do a hasty job and he knew it. Grabbing a fried pastie filled with lamb and onions, Bram tucked his head low and prayed to make it to the guidehouse without anyone stopping him to give orders.

The pastie was hot and juicy and it burned his tongue when he bit into it. Once he'd made his way through kitchen's east door and outside, he scooped a handful of snow from the ground and packed it into his mouth. His numbed toes were just beginning to come alive in his boot and they felt grossly swollen, like they could split the leather. His limp got worse and he had to slow down to manage the short climb up the embankment to the guidehouse.

Castlemilk's guidestone was housed in a separate building two hundred feet east of the roundhouse situated on a raised bank above the Milk. It was a large timber-framed structure that looked like a barn, and had the same double-size two-story doors as most barns. And a door within the door. A brick chimney had been built against the north-facing wall and Bram could see black smoke rising above the tarred wood roof. A single set of footsteps stamped lightly into the snow led from the roundhouse to the guidehouse. None led back. Finishing off the last of his pastie, Bram followed the footsteps like a path.

The door set within the door was closed but unlocked, and Bram lifted the polished pewter latch and entered. Dimness and smokiness enveloped him. It was like entering a building after a fire. The smell of charring seedpods and river weed was sharp and throat constricting, and Bram had to fight the impulse to cough. As his eyes grew accustomed to the dark, he marked the red glows of smokefires placed at regular intervals around the perimeter of the room. This was the stone chamber, yet he could not yet see the stone.

"You are late." Drouse Ogmore, clan guide of Castlemilk, stepped from behind a wall of smoke. Dressed in unfinished pigskins with the hairs still attached and the worm rings and slaughter scars visible, he looked like a member of the wild clans. Short and powerfully built, with black hair and dark skin, he was holding a shovel as if he meant to harm someone with it.

"Take it," he said to Bram, thrusting it toward him. "Clear the area outside the door."

"The small door?"

Drouse Ogmore answered this question with a single, withering look.

Both big barn doors then. As Bram's hand closed around the handle of the shovel and began to move back, Drouse Ogmore pulled in the opposite direction. "The past two days you have been late. You will respect this stone. You will not be late again."

Bram nodded, and Ogmore released his grip on the shovel. "Come and see me when you're done."

As he moved toward the door, Bram saw two green eyes watching him from the shadow of the guidestone. Nathaniel Shayrac, Drouse Ogmore's assistant, and the one who had made the footsteps in the snow, stepped forward and opened the door for Bram. And then shut it hard against his back.

Bram frowned at the snow. He felt bad about what Drouse Ogmore had said and wished he hadn't stopped at the kitchen for food. Ogmore had taken his oath and offered him occupation in the guidehouse. *"When your brother wins back Dhoone come and see me. The future might not be as dire as you think."* Those were the words Ogmore had said to him all those weeks ago on the Milkshore when had they laid Iago Sake to rest in the manner of the Old Clans. Ogmore had acted as guide for Dhoone that day, floating the oil and igniting it, incinerating Sake's corpse. Bram had not spared the meeting a thought while he was at Dhoone, but the Castlemilk guide had not forgotten him.

Eight days ago after Bram had spoken First Oath, Ogmore had invited him back to the guidehouse. "Come view the stone," he had said, "and I will prepare your yearman's portion."

Bram had only ever seen one guidestone before and that was Dhoone's. The Dhoonestone was less than forty years old and its edges were quarry-sharp. Vaylo Bludd had stolen the old stone, and Sumner Dhoone, the Dhoone chief, had moved swiftly to replace it. Bram had not known what an old stone looked like, the scars, the cavities, the oil and mineral stains, the fissures, and cutting faces, and molds. The Milkstone was an ugly chunk of skarn mottled with iron pyrites and flawed with chalk. It was not level and its west face was braced with a scaffold made from bloodwood logs. Bram had stood and looked at it, astonished that a stone could look so . . . used.

"Approach it," Ogmore had said. "You've earned that right." *By speaking the oath?* Bram wondered. He had stepped toward it, immediately feeling the coolness it cast on the surrounding air. Up close he could see the rasp marks and drill holes and he had the sense that this was a living, working stone.

The Dhoonestone lay like a fossil in the guidehouse; ill regarded and barely viewed. It was the shame of it, he believed. No Dhoonesman could look upon it without knowing they'd been bested by a seventeen-year-old boy from Bludd. The Milkstone was different, proud and aging, no longer steady on its feet but still useful, still aware.

Bram had been unsure whether or not to touch it. *This is my guidestone*, he told himself, forcing his hand up. When his fingers were a pin's length from the stone he felt a force, like a magnet attracting metal, pull them in. Sucking in his breath he made a small, astonished sound, and watched as his hand homed to the stone.

It showed him things, flooding them into his thoughts in waves that hit in quick succession. A river fork. A man in a bearskin hat. Wrayan Castlemilk bouncing his swearstone in her hand. Robbie smiling and saying, *Do it*. Bram saw a dense forest of trees and something rippling through them. *Water?* he questioned uneasily, before the stone snatched the vision away. After that he could not keep up with the flood of images, they crashed against him and fled. Parchment unrolling. A room cased in lead. A second river forking . . .

His hand snapped back, jolted and released, and his arm whiplashed with the shock. Exhaling in a great push he realized he had been holding his breath. For a minute he just stood there, breathing and staring at the palm of his hand, as the jolt the guidestone had given him dissipated through muscle and bone.

Drouse Ogmore's voice had broken through his daze. "You will spend half of each day here, working for me. Tomorrow I will expect you at noon."

The guide must have seen some of what had happened, Bram realized later, for he was standing all the while by the door, yet he had never mentioned it, and never again urged Bram to touch the stone.

Deciding he'd better get started, Bram put his good foot to the shovel and started digging out snow. He'd been helping at the guidehouse for seven days now and it was not the sort of work he would have imagined. He had thought he would learn secrets and history. Surely guides must know the clan histories?

Legend had it that when the clanholds won their territory from the Sull the guides drove giant warcarts into battle. Some said that the guidestones themselves were loaded onto those cartbeds. Bram got excited just thinking about it. Such a sight would have been wondrous to see. Why didn't Ogmore talk about that?

The Milk guide just broke rock. He spent most of his days up the stepladder chiseling rock from the stone's northern face, or at his work bench breaking, grinding and sorting the fragments. Sometimes he would use the bow drill, bracing it against his chest with a wooden tile, as he yanked it back and forth. At the rear of the roundhouse there was a stone mill, the kind that could be driven by an ox, but Bram had yet to see Ogmore use it. When Bram asked him about it, the guide had favored him with one of his withering stares. "At Castlemilk we do not waste the gods' breath unless we must."

Considering this statement later, Bram had decided Ogmore was referring to the dust that would get blown away in the wind if the guidestone fragments were ground outside. Certainly Ogmore was obsessed with collecting every last mote that dropped on the guidehouse floor. Bram was allowed to sweep only when all doors and windows were closed, and when Ogmore was drilling through one of the hallowed planes of the stone, Bram had to be sure to set down a sheet to capture the sacred powder.

That was another thing he'd learned: not all parts of the stone were equal. Ogmore divided the Milkstone into faces and planes, and used different sections for different purposes. Ogmore did most of his work on the stone's north face, where the powdered guidestone was mined. Two days ago when word came from Dhoone that a Castlemilk warrior wounded in the retaking had succumbed to his injuries and died, Ogmore had taken his chisel to the southeast corner and cut out a heart-size wedge of stone. The stone there was rich with pyrites and difficult to work and Ogmore had to use pliers at times to cut through the metal. By the time he was finished he had produced something beautiful and gristly, a fitting substitute for a warrior's heart.

Yesterday Bram had watched as Ogmore tapped off a chalky

segment from the guidestone's bulbous south face. "Swearstones," he'd replied when asked.

None of it so far had been what Bram expected. It was strenuous work, and he'd fall into bed at night, aching and sweating, his eyes and throat scoured by dust. So far Ogmore had not allowed him to grind or sort the stone. He hauled it, swept it, oiled and cared for the tools, spread the dust sheets, split timber for the smoke fires, cleaned the workbenches, fetched water from the river, scrubbed the collecting basins and shoveled snow. Nathaniel Shayrac was permitted to grind and pan-sift the fragments, though no one but the guide himself ever took a chisel to the Milkstone.

Bram paused in his shoveling to survey his work. The double doors of the guidehouse now had a ten-foot space cleared around them, and some fairly neat mounds of chucked snow lay off to the sides. The question was: would ten feet be enough? Bram thought of Ogmore, frowned and then resumed shoveling. Another five were called for.

He thought about the clan guide's riding to battle as he worked. *That* would be a fine thing, he decided. To be able to fight and possess knowledge all at once.

He was faint with exhaustion by the time he was done. His knees were loose and wobbly, and the sword blister on the right hand had swollen to the size of an eyeball and split. He had to use his little finger to work the doorlatch.

Switching from the afternoon dazzle of snow to the shadows of the guidehouse took some adjustment, and Bram was caught off-guard when Nathaniel's pale face loomed close to his.

He tutted, shooting out missiles of bad breath. "How does it feel to have your brother sell you?"

Bram swung at him. Nathaniel was prepared and jumped back. Bram tried to track his shape in the murky dimness, thought he detected a movement and took a second swipe. Striking air, he fell off balance and couldn't get his treacherous knees to save him. As he fell Nathaniel punched him in the head.

"Young men," hissed Drouse Ogmore, "control yourselves."

The guide stood at the southeast corner of the guidestone and glared at them. Bram blinked. The guidehouse was rocking and he needed it to stop. For some reason he smelled skinned rabbit—the smell of his mother's workroom growing up.

"Take it," Ogmore said.

Bram wondered what he meant, and then something skin-colored and fan-shaped dropped into view. A hand. Nathaniel's hand. It would help if he could keep it still. Tentatively, Bram sent up his own hand and watched as it swayed back and forth like pondweed before Nathaniel's came and gobbled it up.

The pain of the split blister being squeezed of its juice brought Bram round. Yanked to his feet, he sent everything he had to his knees. It was barely enough to keep him upright.

"I'll have no fighting in this guidehouse, do you hear me?" Ogmore's gaze darted between Bram and Nathaniel.

"He was—"

"No excuses," snapped the guide, silencing Nathaniel. "You shame the gods with petty blame."

Nathaniel's long face, with its uncommon amount of space between the nostrils and upper lip, colored hotly.

"Go to the roundhouse and fetch my supper." Ogmore stared hard at Nathaniel until he moved. Then, turning to Bram, "You. In the back with me."

Bram concentrated on his knees as he followed Ogmore's swirling pigskins around the eastern face of the Milkstone.

The rear section of the guidehouse had been partitioned off from the main hall and several small rooms had been framed. Ogmore's private sleeping chamber was located here, as well as a small dining area, and stockrooms. Leading Bram into the dining area, Ogmore said, "Sit. Take some water."

Bram sat on the polished birch bench with great care, like a man who had drunk too much and was trying to conceal it. The table was rocking and he thought he might be sick.

Perhaps realizing that it was going to take Bram some time to get to the water, Ogmore poured a cup and handed it to him. "Do you know why this guidehouse is made out of wood and not stone?"

Anticipating that it would be better to speak than shake his head, Bram said, "No."

"The old clan guide, Meadmorn Castlemilk, designed it so

that if it's ever besieged we can torch it and burn alive those who would steal our stone." Ogmore paused and then told Bram, "Drink."

Bram did. The water was cool and gritty.

"The Milkstone would not be burned. Changed perhaps, but not destroyed. Meadmorn reckoned it worth the risk." Drouse Ogmore looked straight at Raif, his deep-set eyes gleaming in the light of the half-shuttered window. "A flaming can sometimes stop things from falling into the wrong hands."

Water gurgled in Bram's stomach as he realized that Ogmore was talking about Robbie.

"Count yourself lucky, Bram Cormac, that you are here."

He didn't come out and say it, but Bram knew what he meant. Better to have been burned than stay in Robbie Dun Dhoone's hands. Bram made no reply. Robbie was his brother and he would die rather than speak a word against him.

Ogmore knew this. Resting his powerful, scarred and callused hands on the table, he seemed satisfied at what he had said.

As the rocking in Bram's head subsided, he realized that the guide must have overheard Nathaniel's words. Why else speak of Robbie at this moment?

Ogmore was capable of reading thoughts, for he said, "Nathaniel is worried you will take his place as my apprentice."

Bram heard the rise in the guide's voice, and understood what it meant. He waited.

Ogmore stood and crossed the short distance to the window. Bram assumed he would close the shutter as the sun was fading and a frost was setting in, yet the guide threw it back. "Castlemilk needs two things above all else," he said, looking east toward the Milkhouse and the broken Sull tower where Robbie Dun Dhoone and his men had garrisoned over winter. "Our numbers of young warriors are depleted. They have been wooed away by the promised glory of Dhoone, and we wait, and they do not return. Above all things a clan must be able to defend its borders and protect its house. I am clan guide and I do not say this lightly so hear me well: when a clan is under threat the gods must take second place. Our gods are hard and dread, but they made us what we are. And what we are is clansmen. Given a choice we will fight. The gods know this, and even if they do not forgive, they understand."

Turning from the window, his shoulders limned by failing light, Ogmore searched Bram's face. "So now you know the rankings. Warriors first. Guide second. Yet there are many warriors . . . and one guide. Tell me then, Bram Cormac, who is most important?"

Bram could not. He remained silent.

Ogmore appeared unsurprised yet at the same time stirred. "As we stand here and speak Blackhail fails. Do you know why?"

"Their guidestone shattered."

"No." Ogmore spoke with force. "A new stone can be quarried, new powder can replace the old in warriors' pouches. It is possible to recover over time from such blows, yet the Blackhail guide failed his clan so absolutely he sent it spiraling down into hell." Bram felt hairs prickle along his arms. "He trained no replacement. He died with his stone in the darkness of night and the next day Blackhail was doomed. There was no one to step in and guide the clan in the days when it most needed guiding. Fatal mistakes were made. The remains of the Hailstone were left to lie on open ground, in plain sight of clan. The Walk of Secession was not performed, and clansmen and clanswomen walked with the tainted powder at their waists and did not know it was tainted. A new clan guide was brought in from Scarpe and hauled half of the Scarpestone north in a cart. This monstrosity was hallowed five nights back. The crimes against the gods are many and continue, and while Blackhail lives with an alien stone at its heart it will never rise from the hole dug by its own guide."

It was close to dark now and Bram could no longer see Ogmore's face. He wondered how the guide knew so much about Blackhail, then remembered Wrayan's speech about the birds.

"Tell me now," Drouse Ogmore said, his voice spun with small prickles, "who is most important: warrior or guide?"

Bram bowed his head. The motion started the room rocking one final time. "Guide."

Drouse Ogmore left the word in silence so Bram could feel

the waves it created. Minutes passed as they stared at each other and only when it was full dark and the only light in the room came from smokefires next door did Ogmore speak.

"Castlemilk needs an apprentice guide. If I die we need someone to continue the ways of the stone. The mistakes of Blackhail cannot be ignored. The Milkstone must be protected. And known. I must teach someone the places to drill and not to drill, the weak points, the oil reservoirs, the hollows that must never fill with ice. Knowledge of the old ceremonies must be passed on, for someone in this clan must always know how to mount a Chief Watch, replace and hallow a new guidestone, accept the oaths of its warriors, choose lores for its newborns and chisel hearts. Such are the dealings of a guide, and I would pass them on to you."

"Will I learn the histories?" Bram asked.

Ogmore looked at him strangely. "Scholars do not make good guides."

Bram opened his mouth to ask why, but Ogmore forestalled him with a raised hand.

"We will speak no more. Do not give me your answer now. I know you work hard at your swordsmanship under Selco and Burmish. I also know you spend two hours in the dairy each morning, performing the simple tasks necessary for feeding clan. Both of these endeavors are right and fitting. For now I would have you continue all of them, including assisting me in this house, but know this: I will ask for a choice. When sufficient time has passed for contemplation I will call you into the presence of the Milkstone and an answer must be given." Drouse Ogmore walked to the edge of the table and leant across it so that his face was inches away from Bram's. "I saw you that day when you touched the stone—it reached toward you. You must decide if you are willing to reach back."

The guide pushed himself to upright and left the room. Bram sat alone in the darkness and watched as smoke poured under the door.

TWENTY-EIGHT

The Rift Awakens

Raif was awaiting delivery of the Forsworn sword. Stillborn had sent it to Piggie Blesdo for a refiring four days back and had gone off this morning to retrieve it. Piggie was an ex-Dhoonesmen and blacksmith who had built a tower furnace on one of the high eastern ledges, and did most of the steelwork for the Maimed Men. Stillborn had gone to retrieve it three hours back, but Raif wasn't worried by his absence. Stillborn was an expert at whiling time. Besides, it was good to be alone.

Yelma, Stillborn's sand-filled quintain, was creaking on her iron chain that was suspended above the fight circle. For reasons Raif could not guess, Stillborn had dressed up the practice dummy in ugly iron turtle armor and a red skirt. She didn't have a head, but the top of her torso boasted a fleece hat with ear warmers. Stillborn had nailed it in place. Raif had taken a few swipes at her earlier, but had quickly lost interest. He had not yet found the balance of the sword Stillborn had lent to him, yet even with that disadvantage it was too easy to spike the quintain's heart.

Stillborn's cave consisted of a single chamber shaped like a wedge of cheese turned on its side. The rock ceiling above the cave mouth and fight circle was high and vaulted, but toward the back of the cave, the ceiling lowered sharply and ended, thirty feet into the cliff cave, in a point. The point was where Stillborn stowed his least-used possessions; rusted spears, heaps of old clothing, an iron bathtub, a stool with a broken leg, a preserved bear head, several saddles, a silver urn decorated with enameled balls, and other trophies from his raids and hunts. Raif sat among them, the rock ceiling less than a hand's length above his head, and tried to decide if it was worth sanding the rust from one of the spears.

The spear he had in his hand was good and heavy, its shaft made from a single piece of rolled iron, its head bladed with a rusted but decent point. Stillborn had told him to help himself to anything he found here. "Except the bear head," he'd added thoughtfully, squinting into the possession pile. "I might have a go of tacking that on Yelma."

To remove himself and the spear from the tight wedge of the back wall, Raif had to walk in a crouch, holding the spear horizontal at his waist. Ahead, he saw a figure step into the light surrounding the cave mouth. Raif moved through the shadows toward it.

Mallia Argola gave a small scream as she spied him coming toward her, armed.

"No," Raif cried out, holding the spear away from his body. "I . . . I'm just going to clean it."

She glanced from the head of the spear to his face, lips pressed together, forehead knitted into a deep frown. "You scared me."

"I'm sorry." Raif set down the spear and moved forward with his back hunched. Twice he'd seen her now and both times he was walking like an idiot. "What do you want?" Right away he realized it was an ungracious question, but it was too late to take it back.

Holding out a package wrapped in some silky kind of cloth, she said, "Your gloves and cloak. You left them at our home." Her voice was faintly accented, and prickly with the emotions that followed unjustified fear. She was wearing a long-sleeved dress of a color that fell between deep green and deep blue, and the same black bodice that had snugged her waist yesterday on the ledge snugged it again now. An airily woven black shawl covered a narrow strip of her arms and shoulders. "Take them."

Raif approached her, and they shared a few awkward moments as the package was transferred between them. She smelled like marsh fern, spicy and green.

"Are you not going to look?"

Puzzled, Raif glanced down at the package. It had been tied neatly with black cord.

"The cloak," Mallia said, as if she was stating something that should be obvious to him. "I repaired it for you."

The Orrl cloak had been damaged in the Want; he had not given it much thought since then. Seeing that she was waiting, he tugged on the string and unraveled the package. The silky cloth fell to the ground, revealing his black boarhide gloves resting on top of the cloak. She watched him carefully as he tucked the gloves into his gear belt and then inspected the cloak. He could not remember exactly where the varnish had started to chip and grew more anxious as he searched and couldn't find the spots. He knew she was expecting him to praise her work. After a minute or so he gave up and looked at her, preparing an apology in his head.

She was smiling. "Maybe I have done too good a job."

Raif felt relief and strong attraction.

"Here." She took the cloak from him. "Just there by the hem. See? And there in the front." She moved into him to demonstrate her work. Now that she pointed it out he could see where she had applied something—lacquer, varnish, metallic paint—over the bald spots, carefully overlapping and matching, nearly perfectly, the original finish.

"Thank you," he said, pleased. She had shiny spots of pigment on her fingers.

"It took me most of the night to match it. I have never seen anything quite like it."

She was so close he could see the fine golden down on her cheeks and temples, and see how quickly and wonderfully it became deep brown at her hairline. He spoke to distract himself. "It's made by the clansmen at Orrl. They wear them to hunt in winter."

"Orrl," she repeated, as if committing the word to memory.

"It's the most westerly of the sworn clans." His voice sounded wooden to his ears but he couldn't seem to stop speaking. "Its territories border Scarpe and Blackhail, and its warriors hunt as far as the Storm Margin."

"Storm Margin. I have heard of that." She smiled again, and he could not tell if she was stating a fact or gently mocking him.

Her breasts were full and round beneath the fabric of her dress. Her waist was cinched small enough to be circled by his hands.

Crazily, Raif wanted to grab her and squash her against his chest. Afraid that he might actually do so he stepped back.

She stepped with him. "Your cloak." As she handed it back to him her fingers touched his wrist.

Raif breathed sharply. He had no experience of women. Was it possible she expected him to touch her back?

Mallia Argola looked at him with green-brown eyes. She was older than he was, perhaps by four or five years. "Give me your hand," she said to him.

Maneuvering the Orrl cloak over the crook in his left arm seemed to take forever. He was sure she must think him a fool. When he was done, he held out his right hand and was surprised to see it didn't shake.

She took it firmly, forcing the fingers up and also forcing him to move toward her. Raising his hand to her face, she studied its scars and bow calluses. He could feel her breath wetting his skin. Slowly she pushed his palm to her lips and kissed it.

Wildness threatened him then. He wanted her and could perceive her heart, and somehow the two things got crossed in his head and the only thing he knew for sure was that given long enough he would harm her. He could not tell the difference between desire to kill her and desire to her. Fearful of losing his mind, he wrenched back his arm.

In that final instant of contact he felt her teeth nip the base of his thumb.

"It is done," she said to him, calmly. Her eyes glinted with something that might have been triumph—whatever it was, she blinked it away. "Tooth and hand. In my land that means we will be more than friends."

He turned away from her, stirred and barely sane. Blood was ricocheting around his body. The Orrl cloak was on the floor.

"I must leave," she said, her voice trailing toward the cave mouth. "My brother sends a message: come see him tonight."

With that Mallia Argola was gone.

Raif told himself not to look around. He paced to the back of the cave and found himself soon thwarted by the low ceiling, Casting around for something to . . . *use* . . . his gaze alighted on the rusted spear. Hefting it over his shoulder he took a run at the quintain. The spear's point was cankered and blunt, and the force required to punch it through iron plate was immense. Raif drove it through Yelma's chest armor, yanked it out, and then drove it through again.

He was still stabbing the quintain a quarter-hour later when Stillborn sauntered into the cave holding an oil lamp on a pole.

"Gods, lad. What are you doing?" he asked, setting the lamp down on the cave floor.

Raif stopped. He was shaking and drenched with sweat. One of his fingers was bloodied; he had sliced it on a jagged edge of plate.

Stillborn came over and took the spear away. Laying a hand on his shoulder, he guided him firmly around. "Come and rest for a while."

Raif allowed himself to be led to the sleeping mattress. When Stillborn thrust a cup in his fist, he drank. It wasn't water. He told himself he'd just lie down for a while to calm the pounding in his head. The sun was setting and rich pink light filled the cave.

He dreamed of Ash. She was floating on a plate of ice carved from a glacier. He was standing on the shore, and at first the current moved her toward him, and there was a moment when, if they'd both reached out their hands, they might have touched. He called her name and reached for her, his hand touching space she had just occupied. Yet Ash March no longer looked at him, and the current carried her away.

At first he thought the clanging was part of a new dream. A bell was tolling in the distance and he knew, as you knew things in dreams, that the sound was coming from a place where he did not want to go. He struck a path in the opposite direction, telling himself that the faster he moved the quicker the sound would decrease. He jogged and then sprinted. Someone called his name.

"Raif. Better be up. The Mole's sounding the alarm."

Opening his eyes, Raif saw it was full dark. The pole lamp Stillborn had brought earlier was the only illumination in the cave. Stillborn was squatting next to him. The spare tooth embedded in his neck tissue was biting.

"The alarm," he repeated, his hazel eyes glittering like cut stones. "Something's out there."

The noise was barbaric. A great clashing of tempered and untempered metals, beating out of time and driven by fear. Raif had never heard anything like it; the boom of gongs and peal of bells, the rasp of ridged metal being sawn across rock, the bedlam of iron plate smashing against iron plate like cymbals, and the hammer of hundreds of cook pots as the Maimed Women came out upon their ledges and tried to beat back the dark.

Standing upright, Stillborn cinched his gear belt. Two swords, a nail hammer and a knife hung there. "I best get going. Follow when you can."

Raif swung his feet onto the floor.

Nodding at Yelma as he passed her, Stillborn said, "Looks like she's got a case of exploding boils."

"Still," Raif said. "The sword?"

"Foot o' the bed, my old friend. Foot o' the bed."

The Forsworn sword had been wrapped in a length of cheesecloth and laid at the end of the mattress. Kneeling forward, Raif tore off the fabric and uncovered the blade. The flat had been polished so finely it reflected his face like a mirror. Drawing his thumb along the edge he tested for sharpness. It opened the skin but drew no blood. Good. The point was like a diamond, hard and brilliant, and the only thing he saw that was not perfect was a slight warping in the pattern of the steel where bent metal had been fired and hammered back to true.

Raif removed Stillborn's borrowed blade from his sealskin scabbard and replaced it with the Forsworn sword. The rock crystal surmounted on the pommel flashed as he moved across the cave. As he clasped the newly repaired Orrl cloak around his throat he felt some shame about what had happened earlier with Mallia Argola. He did not understand himself.

Grabbing the pole light on his way out, Raif Sevrance headed toward the greatest concentration of noise.

The night was clear and lit by stars. Snow glowed blue. The moon had not yet risen, but Raif calculated it was due. He moved quickly, leaping from Stillborn's ledge to the one above and then up the rope ladder to one of the longer ledges that ran east. Others were moving too. Maimed Men, their faces blank, their knuckles white where they gripped scythes, stone-bladed axes, sharpened and fire-hardened wooden staves, cruciform halberds, forked spears, swords, knives. The frenzied clangor of the alarm worked on their bodies like a drug, making arms twitch and neck tendons spring out like wires. The clash of metal chopped Raif's thoughts into slices. He could no longer think of whole things, was incapable of formulating or retaining a plan. Instead he thought in pulses. *I must go up this ladder. I must avoid the hoist lifts. Too many people: Get out of my way.*

He drew his sword. Two women kneeling on the ledge, beating cauldrons against the rock, cried out his name. Naked, their bodies obscenely shadowed and missing flesh, they hissed as he stared at them. Slowly they began beating out a new rhythm on the rock.

"Twelve Kill. Twelve Kill. Twelve Kill."

He turned his back on them. Maimed Men made way for him as he landed on the lowest of the three great rimrocks that spanned the city. Hiking on top of a boulder, he tried to see the way ahead. Armed men were moving across the snow. A watch fire had been lit by the mouth of the pool cave, but the flames were sluggish and needed pumping. A blind man beating a sheet of scrap metal by the fuel pile had caught the rhythm of the hags above and now fell in time with them. *Twelve Kill. Twelve Kill. Twelve Kill.*

Raif shouted to someone, anyone, no one, "Feed the fire."

People looked at him and did not move. Perhaps their thoughts were like his own, and while they heard his voice, the sense of its meaning would come later.

Raif jumped down. Below him the Rift lay like an absence in time and space, a crack of perfect darkness in a night drawn blue by snow and stars. He felt hearts moving deep within the earth where rock softened and ceased to be; unmade flesh pushing with inexorable force against the barrier that divided worlds.

Tongue wetting with saliva, Raif made his way up to the next ledge.

He heard the fighting before he saw it; heard heavy thuds and sudden inhalations, squealing swords and the compressed murmur of frightened men. His mind picked the sounds out of the clangor like jewels in the sand. Raif shouldered his way through the crowd. His name had traveled before him and the alarm beating on the middle level of rimrock hammered it out for all to hear.

Twelve Kill. Twelve Kill. Twelve Kill.

A darkness above the heads of the men drew his eye. Something lashed out. A child screamed. Raif laid his hands on people and pushed them out of his way. Linden Moodie, Stillborn, Yustaffa the Dancer, Traggis Mole's big guards, and other unwhole fighting men formed a loose circle around the shadow beast. It was eleven feet tall and moved like a serpent, snapping and weaving, launching attacks with its head. Unarmed except for talons as thick and black as turkey vultures; it was not the kind of being capable of wielding a sword.

Raif thought of the *Shatan Maer*, imagined this was one rung down in the level of creation. It moved like liquid shot at force. A crack of its tail sent Linden Moodie to his knees. Plunging its head around, it snapped off both his legs. Blood fountained onto the snow. The crowd stepped back. One of the Mole's cronies stuck the monster's hide with his spear. And could not get it out. Thrown off balance by his own thwarted force, he stumbled backward, right hand cupping air. The shadow being leapt forward and thrashed him with its claws, tearing up skin and ribs and genitals.

The guard's spear was lodged in the back of the creature's neck where it swung back and forth like a tuning fork. The dark matter of unmade blood smoked from the hole. A series of high squeals shot from the being's jaw as it spun a half-circle and lashed out at the nearest Maimed Man. A sickening crunch was followed by the sound of vertebrae popping like knuckles as the creature bit off a man's head.

Raif glanced across the clearing at Stillborn who was slowly moving forward, sweeping his sword in a defensive half-circle with every step. Their gazes met and agreement passed between them. Raif attempted to meet Yustaffa's gaze, but the Dancer gave a little snort and looked away. His swordbreaker had been abandoned and in its place he wielded a scimitar with a thickly rounded blade.

Stillborn made his move, yanking the nail hammer from his

belt and flinging it at the back of the shadow beast's head. The
creature whipped around. Prepared, Stillborn was already moving
away. Raif hurled himself at the being's darkly scaled back, leaping up to sink the Forsworn sword into its heart. Shadowflesh
opened with a hiss. There was give, the point slid inward.

And then the blade failed.

The break in the pattern. Raif felt the collapse and tried to
muscle through it, but the sword could no longer be driven
forward. Just bent. Releasing his grip on the hilt, he kicked a
foot into the creature's hide and sprang back. Almost he made
it, but as he flung his body out and around, he felt the air-push
of imminent impact followed by a massive, battering ram of a
blow. It propelled him forward into the crowd. The creature's
shadow fell upon him and he thought his life was done, but
something happened—what, he would not find out until
later—and the creature spun around and moved away.

Raif saw people's feet through a watery haze. He smelled the
snow. It stunk like gas. Dimly he was aware of something happening behind him, of shifting weight and shadows.

The pain in his left shoulder had no end.

"Give me your sword."

The words did not seem to come from him, yet he must
have spoken them, for a big brute of a Maimed Man hauled
him to his feet and handed him a weapon. The weight of the
blade was shocking. It was forged like an iron bar. The man had
a malformed spine; extra bone bulged from the back of his
neck. "God's speed to you," he said with feeling.

Raif had no reply for him. He had turned toward the clearing and saw a killing field of snapped and disemboweled bodies
and blood. The snow was stained black. A dozen spears stuck
from the creature's shadowed hide and the holes they created
vented smoke. Raif's gaze darted to the few men left at the
other side of the clearing, searching for Stillborn. When he
spied the swish of a tan leather kilt, he allowed himself to
breathe . . . and move forward.

Twelve Kill. Twelve Kill. Twelve Kill. A thousand pieces of
metal and rock tolled his name.

The being was screeching. The end of its tail was gone,
loped off by a sharp blade. Its eyes burned cold with hate.

Raif and Stillborn performed the dance. Each knew the other's mind without having to meet glances. When he was ready Stillborn rushed the creature from behind and stuck his sword deep into its tail stump. An unearthly scream split the night. Raif's eardrums crackled. The being snapped around like a whip. Raif rushed in, his gaze searching, *searching*, as his body flew through air. He landed like a demon on the being's back, and guided the ugly, borrowed, good-for-nothing-but-bashing sword into the puncture hole created by the Forsworn blade. Hide and muscle had already been penetrated. The borrowed sword was solid. All he had to do was ram it through the heart.

The blade slid into muscle. Raif thrust deeper, driving his fist through the hole in the creature's hide. The creature jerked. Raif twisted the blade with all his might, coring its heart like an apple. The breath was sucked from his lungs as the vacuum produced by the collapsing heart created the opposite of a shock wave. Raif pulled his fist free from the hide. It was coated with oily blackness. Leaving the sword in place, he sprang back and ran.

The being failed, Raif didn't think any other word could quite describe it. One moment it was upright, vital and craving, and the next it sank to the rimrock. Gone.

Bloody snowflakes thrown up by its fall seesawed through the air as Raif made his way to Stillborn. The big Maimed Man rushed forward and caught him in a massive hug. Raif let himself be supported. His ears were ringing. Pain rolled across his shoulder in waves. Stupidly, his teeth were chattering.

The creature's dead body twitched and hissed, diminishing.

At last there was silence. The alarm petered out and then stopped. Maimed Men seemed little relieved. None approached the being's carcass, but people started gathering around something small and ragged lying on the rimrock. A body? Whispers and urgent calls sounded through the crowd.

"He saved your life," Stillborn said in Raif's ear.

Raif stepped away from him. He needed space to breathe. "Who?"

"The Mole."

Raif steadied himself for a moment and then glanced toward

the body. The ragged black shape looked too slight to be a man. *Oh gods.*

Stillborn wiped the sweat from his temples through his hair. "As soon as you fell backwards the creature was on you. There was nothing anyone could do. I came forward . . ." He shook his head. "Wasn't fast enough."

"But Traggis Mole was."

"Aye. Came out of nowhere, like lightning. It was a fine sight. Took off the creature's tail with his knife, shifted its attention from you to himself. It was as if he had no mind for his own safety. You couldn't get that close to the creature and not get . . ." Stillborn shuddered. "Torn."

Raif left him and made his way toward the body. He could smell the blood as he moved through the crowd. It was possible that some of it was his own. People opened a space for him and he moved into it. He was shaking intensely, but he no longer felt any pain.

Traggis Mole lay in a drift of snow close to the cliff wall. He was not yet dead. What was left of his body was wet and twitching; Raif could not look at it. Wisps of dark shadow fed upon the exposed organs. The Robber Chief's face was untouched. His eyes were open and watching Raif.

Raif knelt. He understood much that was dread and good. The truth of Traggis Mole was there to see, and Raif wondered why he hadn't recognized it sooner. He and Traggis Mole were alike. The Maimed Men were all the Mole had. They were his clan, and keeping them safe from harm had been his life. Something close to pure love touched Raif then, and he knew the things this man would ask for were owed.

The moon rose over the Rift, spilling silver light upon the dying man and the man who would kill him. Traggis Mole spoke the few words that mattered. Raif Sevrance spoke another oath.

Quietly and without ceremony, using Traggis Mole's own longknife, Raif Sevrance stopped the Robber Chief's heart.

TWENTY-NINE
Chief in Absentia

Stannig Beade had begun holding meetings in the chief's chamber. The guide of Scarpe and now Blackhail had let it be known that because there was as yet no guidehouse he needed a place to rest and contemplate, one befitting his rank in the clan. Raina tried not to let it bother her, though in truth she knew that Blackhail's carpenters could have had a building up and framed within a week. Granted the walls would take another week, and when it was done it would be made of that decidedly second rate material—as far as clansmen were concerned—wood. But a building was a building, and if Stannig Beade had truly wanted to be alone in a place befitting a guide he could have had a guidehouse erected within twenty days. Raina had once heard something about Castlemilk having a wooden guidehouse, but wasn't quite sure of her facts. Else she might have confronted him with them.

Beade had requested that she attend him in the chief's chamber at noon. He had sent this message by way of one of those silly clan maids who had the habit of attaching themselves to powerful men. "The guide commands me to tell you," Jani Gaylo had begun. Raina had stood there, amazed. Since when did a guide command a clanswoman to deliver his messages? Inigar Stoop had had the use of a boy who brought him supper. If he wanted to speak to anyone he left his guidehouse and found them.

Once she had delivered her message, the red-haired Jani Gaylo had dashed off in the direction of the chief's chamber, anxious to tell Stannig Beade the deed was done. Raina had half a mind to stop her, to tell the girl she would be better employed in the kaleyard digging carrots and onions, or out in the woods setting traps.

Blackhail needed food not meetings. The Scarpes were like rats, gnawing away at Blackhail's supplies. When they first came they had brought tributes—piglets with runny eyes, damp sacks of grain, sheep that walked in circles, barrels of wormy fruit—yet even these imperfect goods had dried up. Hundreds of Scarpes had been here for months. They ate food, drank ale, burned lamp oil and timber. What did they bring for their keep? Anwyn was beside herself toiling to feed them. And more arrived each day. Just this morning, when Raina crossed to the makeshift stables to brush down Mercy, she'd spied another of their poison-pine carts rolling in.

Knowing that if she thought about it any more she'd drive herself into the kind of state where she'd be likely to challenge the first Scarpe who crossed her path, Raina calmed herself. She had been working in the grain drum, helping the tied clanswomen turn the grain. It was hard, dusty work, standing knee-deep in millet as you shoveled it from one place to another like snow. Some of the women had fastened linen strips across their noses and mouths to prevent the fine millet dust from settling in their lungs. Raina realized she should have done the same, for her throat felt itchy, and when she sneezed into her hand little specks of kernel sprayed against her skin. Turning grain wasn't a job she was used to, but after Stannig Beade's message had arrived this morning she'd needed to do something to work off her indignation.

It hadn't quite succeeded, though she had enjoyed the company of hardworking farm women. None of them, including herself, had mentioned the high grain mark that circled the wall twelve feet above their heads. A spoken reminder of Blackhail's hardship would have spoiled the easy camaraderie.

Raina left the women to their cheese and ale. Now that the dust had settled they reclined on the grain like queens. Waving farewells as she exited the perfect circle of the grain drum, they called her by the name "Chief's," short for "chief's wife." Raina felt both pleased and worried by it. The word was uncomfortably close to chief.

The grain drum had been built abutting the roundhouse's northwestern wall and its main door, located two full stories off the ground, faced north. Emerging into the chill grayness of midday, Raina stood for a moment on the stone landing and gazed across the pine forests of Blackhail toward the Balds. Blackstone pines, bristlecones and black spruce were shedding snow in the quickening wind. Hunters' tracks cut between the trees led north in white strips. Turning east she saw the Wedge, the great forested headland that rose on granite cliffs. The snow had already fled from those trees, which were a mixture of hard and soft wood. A swath had been logged ten years back, but the new growth had come in so quickly that unless one rode amongst it, it was difficult to tell where the clear-cut had been.

Raina knew the paths through the woods; knew where the clan boys staked claims over fishing holes and swim holes, knew the secret green pool where the clan maids bathed naked and obsessed over boys, knew the hollows where the old women set their traps, and knew the fruit trees where a hunter dressed in field gear might spend a day, waiting for deer. She had been thirteen when she came here from Dregg. Twenty years of her life had been spent here, and looking back now she could not pinpoint the moment when she'd ceased being a Dreggswoman and become Hail instead. Not her marriage to Dagro, for she remembered wearing the hotwall roses in her hair and carrying her portion of Dreggstone in a filigreed silver locket that overhung her tightly laced breasts. Perhaps later then, when she became established in her role of chief's wife and fell into the rhythm of working hard and receiving respect. But no, if she were honest she still held part of herself back. *I will go home to Dregg when I am old and widowed,* she had told herself, and the thought had given her comfort. Even when word of Dagro's death had come south from the Badlands she had borne the ill news by making the sign of the rose. So no. The most likely moment she had become a Hailsman to her core was when she'd spoken the words in the gameroom.

I will be chief.

Descending the steps Raina fought the wind's desire to tug away her blue wool shawl. People had said that once the storm was over the temperature would come up and the snow would melt so quickly you'd hardly remember it had been here at all. People were wrong. This was the fifth day the snow had failed to melt—and spring planting was due.

Aware that it was as close to noon as it was ever likely to be, Raina decided she'd go and check on the progress of the east wall. She'd be damned if she were going to attend Stannig Beade's parley as promptly as if she were an apprentice tool-maker the first day on the job.

The path that led east around the Hailhouse had been cleared of snow by Longhead and his crew. The wooden gates of the kaleyard had been flung open and a couple of men stood in the large walled kitchen garden, digging soil or snow or both. Raina waved at them and they waved back. The east face of the roundhouse was where the majority of its outbuildings were located—dairy sheds, hay barns, eel tanks, styes, the oast house, the remains of the stables and guidehouse—and Raina encountered many clansmen as she made her way toward the scaffolding.

The hole blasted in the east wall was visible as she drew close, and it gave her an uneasy tick of surprise. Surely by now they could have sealed it? Blackhail was not wanting in stone. Approaching the frame of ladders and plank platforms, Raina hailed the nearest man. Squatting at the top of the scaffolding, he was busy carding mortar. His fingers were wet with slurry.

"When will it be finished?" she asked him.

"Tomorrow," he said chopping the mortar into squares and then flattening it. "Though it'll be a week afore the curing's done and we can start the new ward."

Raina stared at him and then the hole, and had the sense not to ask: *What ward?* Now that she was closer she could see that the hole had been framed into an arch, enlarged in parts and built up in others. A border of polished granite slabs rimmed this new portal, and as she looked on the workman buttered another slab and plugged it into place. When had this happened? Five days back she had been out here and just seen a hole. Had she failed to look properly? Leaving the man to his work, Raina went in search of Longhead.

It took a while to locate the head keep, as he was performing one of the more obscure tasks of his office: batting. Now that the horses were housed in the dairysheds, the high lofts had to be cleared of bats. Apparently the cows didn't mind the winged rodents flitting around at night, or at least had grown used to them, whereas the horses took fits and started bucking whenever one of the little devils squeaked by. Raina was with the horses, and found herself surprisingly reluctant to climb up the tall ladder to the hayloft.

"He went up there an hour ago, lady," said one of the grooms helpfully. "You can smell the smoke."

Raina nodded doubtfully. She was having trouble understanding what people were saying to her today.

"For the bats," the groom added, proving that he was a smart young boy, capable of reading his chief's wife's face. "He's making 'em drowsy."

Raina turned and smiled at him. He was one of the Lyes, a cousin to slain Banron, and you could see the family similarities in his broad cheekbones and wide-set eyes. "Isn't that something?"

"Yes, lady," he agreed. "It certainly is."

The pleasure of that small exchange stayed with her as she hiked up the ladder and landed in the hayloft. The air was warm here and it had some of the same itchiness as the grain drum. Blue smoke rose in bands from two brass smudgers. Longhead was crouching amongst the bales, plucking drugged bats from the hay. With an efficient twist of both wrists he broke their necks and threw them in a steel bucket. As Raina walked toward him a bat dropped right in front of her, landing at her feet. Its leathery wings trembled as its tiny red eyes rolled back in its head. It had a snout like a pig, she noticed, stepping around it, and ears the size and shape of mussels.

"Is it all right to breathe the smoke?" she asked Longhead.

Longhead spun around to face her, and for the second time that day Raina realized she shouldn't be inhaling the air. The head keep of Blackhail was wearing a black felt mask. He shook his head, chucked another bat in the bucket and then picked something from the nearest hay bale and threw it toward her.

It was a mask just like his, and she slipped it over her nose and mouth and tied it tightly.

"Nightshade. It'll make you sleep," the keep said, his voice muffled by the felt.

Raina came and knelt close to him, trying hard not to look at the dead bats in the bucket.

"They'll go to the Scarpes," he said flatly. "They eat them."

Hay pricked her knees through the fabric of her dress. "Was it true they wanted the horses?"

Longhead nodded. The black mask made his long pale face seem even paler and longer. Bat's blood was drying beneath his thumbnails. "They came to me, seeing if I could stop the burials. Said it was a waste of good meat."

A dozen horses had died when the Hailstone exploded and five more had to be destroyed because of their injuries. Raina had arranged the burials. She had heard a rumor that the Scarpes wanted the carcasses, but had given it little credit. Butchering horses reared for meat was one thing, but eating riding horses was a practice abhorrent to Hailsmen. She was glad now that she'd had the carcasses carted to the Wedge—she wouldn't have put it past Scarpes to dig up the graves.

Another bat dropped from the overhead rafters as Raina leant in to the keep. "What's happening with the eastern wall? I thought it was being shored." Distorted by the mask her voice snaked over the "s" sounds.

Longhead glanced over his shoulder, checking the long dim roofspace, before answering. "Beade stopped the work ten days back. Says there's no point in sealing the hole as he intends to build a guidehouse and a ward to house the Scarpes off the eastern hall."

Raina pulled down her mask and sucked in drugged air. "He's *guide*. He has no right to direct the making of this house." *You should have told him exactly where to stick his plans.*

Longhead's bunion-knuckled hand came up in self-defense. "He says he discussed it with Mace Blackhail before he left. Says the chief gave the go-ahead."

Realizing she was starting to feel dizzy, Raina planted the mask back in place. "Why did you not come to me?"

The head keep puffed air into his body and then let it deflate. "He said not to bother you with it, that you already had enough on your hands . . . " Longhead hesitated, reluctant to continue speaking. After frowning hard, he spat it out. "Said you might start fussing and putting your foot where it had no place."

Raina sat back, letting her butt sink into the hay. Dagro had once told her about the time Ille Glaive besieged Bannen. The city men had set their tents in bold sight of the Banhouse, and then spent the next ten days building cookfires, holding tourneys and mounting curiously halfhearted attacks. All the while their miners were digging a tunnel beneath the roundhouse. One of the tents had masked the mine head, and when the city men were ready they lit fires in the tunnel and collapsed Bannen's western wall. Undermining it was called, and Stannig Beade was doing it to her.

Knowing better than to reproach Longhead, she said simply, "I am never too busy to hear what happens in this house."

Blackhail's head keep pulled down his mask. He looked older and more serious without it. "I hear you."

She hoped it was a promise to come to her next time Stannig Beade tried to force one of his schemes. Pushing herself onto her feet she bid him farewell.

As she took the ladder down through the hayloft floor and into the newly boxed stable space she was aware of a little giddiness, a looseness in her joints and a delay in her vision. The Lye boy offered his arm to help her down the last steps.

"A messenger has arrived from Ganmiddich," he told her, full to bursting with the news. "The guide is meeting with him on the greatcourt."

Raina knew she disappointed the boy by not responding, but she dared not move a muscle on her face. Stannig Beade overstepped his office. If the chief was away the most senior warrior met with messengers. That meant Orwin Shank, not Scarpe's clan guide.

Raina left the dairy-turned-stables and made her way to the roundhouse. Ever since the night of the Menhir Fire Stannig Beade had slowly been claiming privileges in the clan. It was as if he had been holding himself back until the tricky maneuver of installing half the Scarpestone into the heart of Blackhail had been successfully completed. He was guide now. He ruled the stone. Time to show his teeth.

Raina was still finding singed hairs amongst her tresses. Part of her left eyebrow had gone, crisped off by the flames in the trench, and the metallic panel in her mohair dress had been burnished black. She did not think the Stone Gods had come that night, but a show worthy of their presence had been mounted. After the stone had been unveiled people in the crowd spotted signs; a series of green lights falling from the heavens, the sudden and inexplicable smell of bitumen, the line of smoke rising from the Menhir Fire, forking so as not to pass the drill hole, and the sound of distant drums beating to the north, seeming to come from a place beyond any seeable horizon. Tricks the lot of them—except possibly the forking of the smoke—carefully stage-managed by Stannig Beade to awe the crowd. He had worked assiduously to get the new Hailstone, and therefore himself, established.

It had been a relief to most in the clan, Raina realized later, to have all uncertainty about the guidestone ended. A ceremony had taken place. The gods had been called. Stannig Beade had done a decent job. Just yesterday in the kitchens Raina had heard Sheela Cobbin say to another woman, "It's time we put it all behind us."

Raina almost agreed with her. But she had walked out on the greatcourt three times since the Hallowing, and each time she touched a stone bereft of gods. Even when the old guidestone had been dying you not could place your fingertips on its surface without sensing the immense and ancient power withdrawing. Even when gods were barely there you could feel them.

Right now, as she passed under the scaffold and through the new archway to the east hall, she could feel the pull of the charged metals they had deposited as they left. Her maiden's helper, suspended from the leather stomacher at her waist, skipped toward the wall. She put her hand on it, flattening the foot long knife against her hip. The gods had left Blackhail, and despite all of Stannig Beade's fancy footwork they had not come back.

On the night of the Menhir Fire she had made the mistake of imagining he was as concerned as she herself—without a doubt he had been anxious during the ceremony—but now she realized that anxiety had more to do with his desire that the ceremony go well and the crowd be suitably impressed with eye-popping spectacle, than any real care about the state of

Blackhail's soul. Stannig Beade might call himself a guide but Raina did not believe he was a man of god.

Yelma Scarpe was probably laughing in the burned shell of the Scarpehouse. Either she had rid herself of a rival for her chiefdom, or sent a trusted agent to run Blackhail in the absence of its chief.

Finding herself in the entrance hall, Raina headed for the door. She could not say why she had chosen to travel through the house rather than around it, other than a vague notion that she did not want Stannig Beade watching her as she crossed open ground. One of the clan widows hailed her from the great stairway, but Raina waved her away. She could see them now, the small group on the greatcourt, and it should have eased her mind that Orwin Shank's fair, balding head was clearly visible amongst the other, darker heads, but new worries sprang to life.

Word from Ganmiddich. Two thousand Hailsmen at war. Had the army reached the Wolf yet? And what about the three hundred Hailsmen who were entrenched at the Crab Gate?

She had meant to be commanding, serene, yet her joints were still loose from the nightshade and her eyesight had not fully corrected, and all she wanted to do was hear the news. "Orwin," she called, knowing she could count on him to make way for her.

The patriarch of the Shanks lifted his head toward the sound of his name. His pale blue eyes were slower to focus than they once had been and it took him a moment to realize who had spoken. "Raina," he said, taking a step away from the huddle of men.

She knew then that the news was bad. His voice was soft and shocked. A fleck of spittle lay on his bottom lip. Crossing over to him, Raina held out her hand. Orwin Shank had lost three sons. Bitty, Chad, and Jorry. *Please Gods may he lose no more.* The aging hatchetman did not register Raina's hand on his arm. He was shaking and his flesh felt cool. The big silver belt buckle he always wore polished and gleaming was stamped with fingerprints.

Quickly, Raina noted who was here. Corbie Meese, ancient and one-armed Gat Murdock, Brog Widdie, the master smith who had once been a Dhoonesman, Ullic Scarpe, brother to Uriah and nephew to the Scarpe chief, Wracker Fox, also Scarpe, and Stannig Beade. Other men hovered in small groups around them, hands swinging in loose fists, gazes darting between Corbie Meese, Raina and Stannig Beade.

The clan guide was dressed in sparrow skins and black leathers and he wore a thick silver torc at his throat. The pig hides were gone. He spoke her name and it did not sound like a greeting.

She ignored him. "What has happened?" she asked Corbie Meese.

The big hammerman with the dent in his head glanced once at the guide before speaking. "The Spire army took Ganmiddich. Then they themselves were routed by Bludd. Between the two attacks every Hailsman at the Crab Gate was lost."

No. Cold prickles passed up her legs to her womb and stomach. Mull Shank. The Lowdraw. Rory Cleet. Bullhammer? Had Bullhammer been there? Dozens more.

Drey Sevrance.

Raina Blackhail held herself very still. She was no longer touching Orwin Shank. All were watching her. She could feel the blood behind her eyes. "Where is Mace?"

"He camps on Bannen Field with the two thousand and plans to retake what has been lost."

She told herself she was not disappointed that her husband was still alive. "And the Crabmen?"

"No survivors. The Crab chief is dead."

Crab Ganmiddich gone. "Who is the new chief?"

Stannig Beade sucked in air with a small hiss. As if driven to scorn by such trivial questions he told her, "The new chief is also named Crab."

She had a choice then for she could have fired back *Do not tell me what I already know. Who was this man before he declared himself chief and took the name Crab?* Instead she thought of the dead clansmen, and gave them her silence and respect.

The silence passed from her, breathed out with her breath like Longhead's drowsy smoke, and passed from man to man to man. Within seconds everyone on the greatcourt fell quiet and the silence passed through the greatdoor and into the house. People milling in the entrance hall stilled. Stannig Beade watched this happen, his eyes cold and flat.

He is my enemy, Raina understood then. And in some ways he was worse than Mace. At least her husband did not covet the power she held in Blackhail's house. Mace was warrior and chief—let his wife take care of matters of home and hearth. Stannig Beade was different. He could not rule men in fields of battle. His power existed only in the confines of clan walls, and that put he and Raina at odds.

She saw all this in the silence, and then let it drain away. It would snow again, she decided, glancing at the clouds. Let it snow.

Drey Sevrance dead. He had brought her Dagro's last token, the brown-bear pelt Dagro had been skinning when he died. "Lady," Drey had said, standing at the door of her private chambers, "I have finished it for you." In all the days of horror that followed, that act of chivalry had stayed with her. In the long dark night after the Oldwood she had clutched the bearskin to her breast and belly, lost. If she had not had the skin for comfort she might have passed beyond lost, to the place where insensibility and insanity waited to trap your mind. Since then Drey had brought her small tokens every time he returned to the roundhouse, little things he'd won or bartered; a pebble of amber fine enough to be drilled for a pendant, a pair of mink skins that could be cut for gloves, an embroidered noseband for Mercy. Drey Sevrance had handed these gifts to her without words or ceremony, and she had understood that to him she represented something worth returning to in clan.

Raina inhaled deeply, drawing back the silence she had spun. "Orwin," she said. "Come into the house."

With a light touch she guided him round. His swollen, arthritic fingers grasped her dress sleeve, pinching the skin beneath, but she did not think he was aware of it. Nor did she mind the pain. Corbie Meese stepped from the group, meaning to follow them, but Stannig Beade halted him with a question.

"What of the women and children of Ganmiddich?"

Raina felt the words like stones flung against her back. *Here is the question you should have asked, chief's wife. Shame on you for not inquiring about the innocents.*

Corbie replied that most of the women and children had been transferred to either Bannen or Croser. Few had been at the Crab Gate on the day of the attacks.

Raina listened until she moved beyond earshot. Orwin's fingers continued pinching her arm as she led him into the roundhouse. Anwyn Bird was there, waiting at the foot of the stairs, and Raina found herself so happy to see her plain yet pleasing face that idiotic tears sprang to her eyes.

"Hush now," Anwyn said to both Orwin and Raina as she approached. And though neither of them was making a sound they understood what the clan matron meant. *I will care for you.*

The three of them climbed the broad stone steps to the greathearth and passed beneath the granite doorway. Sworn clansmen stood to attention as they entered the great circular space of the warriors' hall. "Put more logs on the fire," Anwyn commanded, and three men sprang into action to do her bidding. One of them was a Scarpe, Raina noticed. A young man whose hair had that greenish tint to it that meant Scarpe's black dyes were fading.

Anwyn pointed and nodded with force, and things were done. Blankets were brought, her twenty-year malt rushed up from the stillroom, Jebb Onnacre, Orwin's son-in-law, sent for. Men who had no relation by friendship or kin to Orwin Shank were dismissed. Soon the room was warm and peopled only with Hailsmen and Hailswomen. The vast, vaulted space with its stone benches arranged in concentric circles and its horse-size central hearth had probably never known so few to stand within its walls. Berta Shank, Orwin's only surviving daughter, sat next to her father and Anwyn wrapped a single blanket around both of them. Orwin was numb. He had not said a word since he'd spoken Raina's name on the greatcourt. When Anwyn handed him a dram of malt he took it from her but did not drink. Raina sat next to Jebb. Her arm was smarting and she knew she would have an ugly bruise by morning.

"Here," Anwyn said, passing her a wooden thumb cup filled with malt. "Drink."

Raina did, throwing the golden liquid to the back of her

throat in a motion that would normally have the clan matron up in arms. You did not gulp a twenty-year malt. You sipped and savored. Raina enjoyed the burn as the hard liquor slid down to her gut.

Drey Sevrance dead.

She watched the fire. All in the room were quiet now, their movements subdued. One of the double doors opened and Corbie Meese stepped in. Quickly assessing the mood, he found himself a seat, not close to but within sight of Orwin Shank, and settled down for a long stay. Gat Murdock came next, and although Raina had never felt much affection for the crotchety old swordsman, she could not fault him this day. Silently and without fuss he chose a seat near the back. Others came, Hailsmen and Hailswomen, and over the course of the next hour those who had at first been exiled from the greathearth were allowed back.

Raina felt moved by a strong and invisible force. Goodness, she decided later. Everyone watched the fire. Anwyn moved between the benches like a nurse bringing blankets and water and malt. No one wept, though many had taken losses. It was understood that Orwin Shank's loss was the greatest and respect was paid by minding his expression and his silence. Even the bairns who were allowed in later upheld the quiet of the hearth.

How long they sat and mourned as a clan was hard to say. The fire was kept stoked and there were no windows in the greathearth to let in light. When Raina felt someone sit next to her on the opposite side of the bench from Jebb Onnacre, she glanced around, prepared to give a silent nod of greeting. She expected the mourning to continue into night and to be present until its end.

Sitting next to her was Jani Gaylo. "The guide wants to see you," she whispered. "He awaits you in the chief's chamber."

The parts of herself that had been buoyed by the dignity shown by her fellow clansmen sank and Raina stared at the girl coolly. She stood. Motioning to Anwyn that she was fine and nothing was amiss, Raina Blackhail took leave of the great-hearth. Jani Gaylo, dressed in pretty orange and blue plaid, followed her from the room.

"Do not," Raina warned the moment the door was closed

behind them, "make the mistake of accompanying me to the chief's chamber."

The girl actually took a step back. "Yes, lady," she mumbled, as Raina turned and left her standing at the top of the stairs.

The wall torches had been lit and the greatdoor was closed. All was quiet in the entrance hall and the few Scarpe warriors who were standing in groups, drinking ale, averted their gazes in something approaching respect as she passed. They must have lost men, too, she realized. It made her wonder where Blackhail's and Scarpe's armies stood this night. Did they intend to retake the Crab Gate? Were they bivouacked in one of the spruce forests northeast of Ganmiddich, hunkered down in three-foot snow?

The narrow steps leading to the chief's chamber had been freshly swept of cobwebs and dust, and Longhead or one of his crew had actually installed a wooden handrail along the tricky part where the steps buckled forward. Raina abstained from using it. She had not been here in several months and did not want to be here now.

The door was ajar and she did not knock, simply pushed it back and entered the chamber. Stannig Beade sat behind the big chunk of granite known as the Chief's Cairn, studying a chart. A mat covered with blankets lay close to the far wall, and Raina realized with a shock that he was now sleeping here.

Beade rolled up the scroll as she moved forward, but her eyes were quicker than his hands and she saw it was a map of Blackhail and its bordering clans.

"Welcome," he said, pushing aside the scroll.

He must have trained for the hammer in his youth, Raina decided, for his shoulders were powerful and two big muscles sloped down from his neck. The tattoos across his eyelids had healed, but whoever had punctured them had done a hasty job and the pigment-filled holes looked like bird tracks.

"You know why I have summoned you?"

She could not begin to guess. "What do you want?"

He stood and crossed over to the sole lamp in the small oval chamber and rolled back the wick. Light decreased. "Your behavior in this clan does not befit a chief's wife. People have noted your forwardness and brought it to my attention. Raina

Blackhail overreaches herself, they say. She makes decisions she has no right to make. I have tried to let it pass. If you had attended me at noon as I requested I would simply have reminded you of your place. But after the scandal you created on the greatcourt I must take action. I am guide, and my responsibility is to the well-being of this clan. As Blackhail's armies are away I have arranged for those newly housed in the widows' wall to move into quarters vacated by sworn clansmen. This will leave the widows' hearth free once more for the widows. After you leave my chamber you will move your belongings there, and from this night forth restrict your activities to caring for the bereaved and the sick."

"How dare you."

Stannig Beade responded to the ice in her voice by moving closer. "Never interrupt a warriors' private parley again."

"You are no warrior."

The blow was so hard and shocking Raina stumbled backward. She lost a second of consciousness, and found herself crumpled by the door.

Stannig Beade was standing over her, breathing hard. He drew back his hand to strike her again, but the sound of footsteps bounding down the stairway halted him in his tracks.

The high, girlish voice of Jani Gaylo called out, "Did Her High-and-mightyness come? I gave her your message but you know what a bitch she is."

"*Get up,*" Stannig Beade hissed at Raina. And then to Jani Gaylo, who had just rounded the corner, "Raina is overcome with grief, help her to her feet."

The girl's red eyebrows went up and her cheeks turned pink. She stood for a moment, taking in the scene of the chief's wife on the floor with her skirts and braid in disarray, and then dashed forward to help. "Lady, I—"

"Hush," Raina told her, looking into Stannig Beade's cold glittering eyes. "I can help myself."

They watched as she rose to her feet. Shaking and with the imprint of Beade's open hand flaring on the side of her face, Raina fled.

THIRTY

Three Men and a Pig

The river was named the Mouseweed and it flowed between gorges and through brush-choked valleys in the Bitter Hills and Stone Hills. Herons fished in its shallows and moose picked paths along its gravel banks as they came to eat tender water weeds and drink. Bears patrolled the shores, and cracked open the overnight ice on beaver ponds in search of sluggish fish.

Yesterday Effie and Chedd had played a game of dams, which meant that whenever you saw a beaver dam you cried, "Damn!" It had been extraordinarily satisfying at first, the cussing without seeming to, but there were just so many dams along the river that within a matter of hours the game had gotten old, and Chedd had started repeating the word so quickly it made a noise like buzzing flies. *Damndamndamndamndamn.* She had poked him in the back to make him stop, which of course just made him do it more. Then she had to think of another game to distract him, but nothing quite matched the—if she did say so herself—sheer brilliance of dams, and the only thing she could come up with was bear: *naked.* Chedd had sniggered at this, and she wished straightaway she could take it back. Naked was not a word you used around eleven-year-old boys. She hadn't known it then. But she did now.

"Otter," Chedd Limehouse said now, swiveling his fat neck toward her. "*Naked!*"

Effie glared at him. There was no otter. This was the second day she'd had to put up with him naming nonexistent animals and declaring them naked. As they were paddling through a narrow stretch of the Mouseweed in broad daylight, Effie had some hope that Waker would silence him, but the Grayman appeared distracted. His large bulbous eyes were fixed on the way ahead.

They were making good time, Effie observed. The channel was deep here and the current logy. Good paddling conditions, she thought, taking some pleasure in the knowledge and vocabulary she had picked up from traveling with Waker Stone and his fiercely odd father, who might, or might not, be named Darrow.

They let her paddle now, and she was surprised by how hard it was and how much she needed to rest after even the briefest series of strokes. The pain in the back of her shoulders and forearms would strike quickly and once it was there it nagged continually. Waker told her she would grow into it as long as she paddled every day. Effie had taken him at his word, and had fallen into the rhythm of brief paddles followed by long rests. Three days now and the pain just got worse.

At least she didn't fake-paddle like Chedd, who could be seen even now rotating his paddle as it entered the water so that it sliced more than it pushed. Waker's father must have known what Chedd was up to. Manning the back of the boat he could keep an eye on all three of them—Waker, Chedd and herself—yet he never did anything to correct Chedd's idle ways, and Chedd had the good sense never to look around and catch his eye. Effie decided she must have less good sense, for sometimes she couldn't seem to stop herself and spun around in her seat to look at the tiny old man. Every time without fail he was ready for her, triumphantly, malignly, staring back.

The night she had been saved from drowning by Waker, the old man had told her his name. Or at least she dreamt he had. The name was hiding in her memory like a flea in a crease, and she told herself that if she just waited long enough it would spring right out. Darrow didn't ring any bells, she knew that much. Chedd had come up with that one, and now she came to think on it he might simply have overhead Waker telling his father, "Da, row."

"Naked," Chedd said for no good reason. "As a bear."

Effie watched his shoulders chuffing up and down with delight. It was enough to put you off boys for life.

More paddling was called for, and she took the wooden paddle from her lap and plunged it deep into the brown water. She might have splashed Chedd on the first stroke, but not on the ones following. Paddling was too serious a business.

It was a calm but cold day and the sky was uniformly white. The Mouseweed was passing through a series of gorges and high-cut banks, and thin, silvery falls emptied into the river at every bend. The cliffs were red sandstone, mined with hollows and crevices, and grown over with chokeberries, black birch and vines. They had left the main artery of the Wolf three days back, following a long camp whilst Effie recuperated from the near-drowning, and without a doubt they'd passed beyond the Dhoonelands and into territory protected by Bludd.

As far as Effie could tell they were heading southeast. The Bitter Hills were a slowly lowering barrier to the south. Stony and jagged, their chutes packed with new snow and their skirts dark with hemlocks, they cast long shadows on the river as they dumped snowmelt into its depths. The most easterly section of Bitter Hills was called the Stone Hills by city men, and Effie had to admit it was a pretty decent name. When she was resting between paddles she imagined the city on the far side. Morning Star. Having no experience of cities whatsoever, she fancied it as a grand collection of roundhouses with many outbuildings and several towers. The people would wear linen and silk, not wool and skins, and their voices would be high and fluting.

Ahead and to the north lay the Bluddsworn clans: HalfBludd, Haddo, Frees, Otler and Gray. Chedd said the only roundhouse they'd be likely to spot was Otler's and that was days east of here, but Effie thought he might be wrong. HalfBludd shared borders with Morning Star; depending upon what river branch they were on they might see it once the hills shrank away.

The Mouseweed felt different to Effie than the Wolf, older and more secretive. Last night she had seen a lynx withdrawing through the trees behind the camp. The wild and beautiful cat with its pointed ear tufts and blue-gray pelt did not seem to belong in the world of clan. She had tried explaining this to

Chedd—who had matter-of-factly informed her the lynx was female—and Chedd had surprised her by agreeing. "It's the Sull who wear their pelts," he said. Sometimes he could say things that were exactly right. Clan did not wear lynx because they did not know how to trap or hunt them. Those skills belonged solely to the Sull.

Deciding she'd had enough of paddling, Effie shook the water from her oar and rested it against the gunwales. Hands free, she reached for her lore.

It was something she always did, that absentminded checking, that quick motion upward to see how things stood in her world. Stupid. *Stupid*. You'd think by now she'd have gotten used to the fact that her lore was gone, gobbled up by the pike that was more than a pike, lost for ever and eternity in the Wolf.

She had tried to make them go after it—spread nets, dive into the river, build dams—and in fairness to Waker Stone he had not dismissed her pleas out of hand. "It's gone," he had told her firmly. "Even if I dived for it how would I know the difference between that a thousand other stones?"

She had not told him about the pike. She had lived for a month with Mad Binny on Cold Lake, and knew the importance of sounding sane. The words *A pike ate my lore* were too close to *My sheep knows how to fly* for comfort. Instead she had commandeered Chedd Limehouse, forcing him to search the rivershore and set fishing lines. Guilt had prevented him from asking too many questions about the fishing lines—if he hadn't vomited the boat would never have capsized—and he had worked diligently for two whole days on the task of locating Effie's lore. On the third day she'd felt well enough to join the search and had waded thigh-deep into the now calm water, but her restored health had worked against her. When Waker saw her chastising Chedd for setting the lines in the wrong place, he had decided she was fit enough to return to the boat, and they were out upon the river by midday.

She held no ill feeling toward Waker for his haste. He had saved her life, and although she knew that he did so because she was in some way valuable to him—like gold—it didn't alter the fact that her life *was* saved. Effie was very much fond of her life. She wasn't one of those silly girls who heedlessly put their lives in danger by riding horses over high hedges, or sticking their heads underwater and counting how long they could hold their breath. Tree climbing, rock scaling, bridge swinging, roof walking, pool diving and even the wearing of insufficient layers in the cold were not things that Effie Sevrance did. Granted she used to sleep with the shankshounds, but even if they had torn out people's throats, they were good as lambs around her.

Waker had treated her a little differently since the near drowning and she had treated him a little differently back. She understood now that the abduction and journey were nothing personal. Waker Stone was doing his job. She and Chedd were cargo, and what a man wanted in his cargo was simply that it be easy to stow. If she did not fight against the stowing, which by her reckoning was the equivalent of getting into the boat promptly each morning, Waker was satisfied. Freedom could be had in a sideways kind of manner. She and Chedd could do whatever they wanted at the camp—as long as they remained in sight. They could now talk in the boat—as long as woodsmoke wasn't in the air. Nothing much was expected of them—they weren't even forced to paddle—and that meant they were free to enjoy the river and its sights. And as long as you ignored old crazy Waker Senior and forgot that you were being hauled east against your will the journey wasn't bad. She had even begun to think that she *owed* it to Waker to be good, what with him saving her life and all and she being precious cargo.

It was this realization that she *ought* to behave well that had made all the difference. Waker had recognized this shift in her, which was mostly detectable in the quickness she responded to his requests and her determination to show him she was a good paddler, and he had responded in some kind back. Just this morning he had thrown her a small pouch of dried spiced peas. No word, barely any warning that she needed to get her hand ready to receive a catch, just a white bag chucked at her chest. Spiced peas were strange and set your gums tingling, and it took her a while to realize they were meant to be a treat. Once she understood their specialness they began to taste better.

She had the feeling now that if Waker had possessed a pick with the correct bore to knock out the pins in her leg irons he would have freed her.

"Stoney broke. Brokey stone. What's it like, girlie, to be all alone?"

Effie spun around in her seat and glared at Waker's father. He was sitting on the stern seat, calmly pulling his paddle through the water. His lips were closed and his green eyes sparkled with spite. He was wearing the shaggy brown otterskin jacket he always wore, but today he'd thrust a bunch of club-moss though one of his string holes.

"I know what you said," she told him.

He looked at her and started moving his mouth like a fish. Spittle wetted his lips as his old pink tongue jabbed out.

Disgusted, she faced front.

"Nothing to like about pike."

She did not turn back. Suddenly cold, she decided to warm herself up with another bout of paddling. Mounds of hackled snow capped the rocks and gorges, and the river water had that thickness to it that meant it wasn't far above freezing. Chedd had fallen asleep in his seat and was snoring. Effie used her own paddle to hook his back in the boat. The clump of wood hitting the gunwales roused him, and he shook his head like a dog shedding water. Within five minutes he was back asleep.

Effie tried not to think about her lore, but Waker's father had a way of getting under her skin. *Stoney broke.* It was considered the worst kind of luck to lose your lore, like a doom. Inigar Stoop told chilling stories of those clansmen unfortunate enough to lose their lores. Jon Marrow had accidentally dropped his squirrel lore down a well shaft east of the Wedge. He was jumped by Dhoonesmen the next day, so the story went, and while he was defending himself against their hammer blows something horrible happened to his man parts. Effie thought they might have froze. Then there was the tale of little Mavis Gornley, who had lost her lore whilst riding to the Banhouse to wed her betrothed, a dashing Bann swordsman with teeth filed to points. As soon as she realized her grouse lore was missing, Mavis had dismounted and retraced her steps, carefully inspecting every hoofprint made by her horse. Mavis was so intent upon looking down that she hadn't seen the big grizzly who came loping out of the woods and tore off her head. The only way to save yourself from similar misfortune was to rush back home to your clan guide and beg him to replace the missing lore. This was a tricky business apparently, and could take several months. During that time you were left vulnerable and unprotected and were advised to stay inside.

Well, Effie thought, glancing up at the crumbly red walls of the gorge and the hemlock forests that lay beyond them. *There's exactly nothing I can do about that.*

In a way the stories didn't bother her. Bad luck was something she didn't believe in. It was the actual *missing* of the stone that felt bad. She hadn't realized how much she had relied upon the ear-shaped chunk of granite until it had gone. Her uncle Angus had once told her how bats were able to fly in the dark. "They listen for their cries bouncing back off trees and walls." "But they don't make any sound," she had replied. "Not any that you can hear," he had countered. She'd thought about that conversation many times since, as it seemed to her that her lore was a bit like bat ears: able to detect sounds that no one else could hear. Vibrations caused by changes. Stirrings in the air. Course when you put it into words it also sounded a bit . . . pikish, but Effie Sevrance knew what she knew.

And she missed knowing it. That was the worst thing, the absence of reassurance, the forewarning of danger. Now bad things could happen and she would only know about them at the same time everyone else did.

It was like losing a sense. And a tooth. The hole was there, new and strange, and she kept poking it in disbelief.

Realizing that she'd been paddling for too long on one side, Effie switched her oar to the right. It was getting colder and her breath began to make clouds. She thought she detected the pitchy green sharpness of burning pine and searched for woodsmoke above the tree line. She couldn't see any, but Waker Stone's father wasn't taking any chances and steered the boat closer to shore.

The curved prow of the boat glided over the still water, and for a while the only sound to be heard was the muted splash of paddles as they broke the surface. Oddly enough the silence seemed to waken Chedd and he jerked forward in his seat and had to scramble to steady himself.

"Looks like we're going ashore," he said to Effie, glancing around.

"Silence," Waker warned, muscling the paddle. The walls of the gorge were closing in on them, and Effie could see rocks beneath the water. Red spruce and birches extended out over the river, their limbs fingering the surface. Effie could not see how it would be possible to go ashore. The cliffs were too high and there was no place to beach the boat. She thought perhaps that Waker was using the cliffs for cover, that by pulling close to them he was making the boat less visible from above. It was no use asking questions, that was for sure. Spiced peas and information were two separate things.

Using his paddle as a tiller, Waker's father steered around the rocks with ease. As they rounded the river bend, Effie saw that the gorge wall was lowering and wedges of forest had forced their way to the shore. Undercut cliffs had toppled forward and sheets of sandstone lay half-submerged in the water, bleeding sand the color of rust. Waker was paddling with long, deep strokes and the boat moved quickly around the ledges. Both he and his father appeared to know this stretch of the river well and anticipated problems before they reached them. Just as they were moving out from the shore to avoid some willow-choked shallows something dropped into the river about thirty feet ahead of them. Effie had been minding her paddle strokes, and didn't catch what it was, but she saw the splash. A big crater in the water.

Waker turned around and nodded at his father. The Grayman's eyes were bulging with force, but he looked more displeased than afraid. Effie noticed that just before he dug his paddle into the water for his next stroke his right hand slipped away to check on his twin knives.

Once they'd passed the shallows they headed to the nearest landing. As Waker and his father maneuvered the boat parallel to one of the collapsed sandstone ledges, Chedd glanced back at Effie, his eyebrows high. Effie shrugged weakly. It would have been a pretty good time to have her lore.

Waker tied the mooring rope around a fist of rootwood that no longer had a tree attached, and then draped the air bladder over the side of the gunwale to act as a buffer against the rocks.

"You two," he said, looking from Effie to Chedd. "Stay here. Keep your mouths shut and don't try anything." Waker's eyes jiggled like gut fat as he waited for them to nod. Satisfied, he sent a hand signal to his father, plucked his daypack from beneath the bow seat, and alighted onto the ledge.

As Effie braced herself against the roll of the boat she checked upshore. The cliff wall that had been exposed when the ledge collapsed was deeply, damply red. Trees had not yet found their way into its crevices, but ropy vines were creeping down from the woods above. Two ravines split the cliff. The largest was running with meltwater that frothed over big sandstone boulders. The second appeared to be a path leading up. Waker headed toward it, jumping across a break in the ledge along the way. Within seconds he had passed out of sight.

Chedd, Effie and Waker's father sat in the boat and waited. Effie put her booted feet against the back of Chedd's seat to give them a rest from the standing water. Just as Chedd turned around to complain about them, men's voices sounded overhead. Someone shouted, "Weapons on the rock." In the silence that followed, Effie imagined Waker pulling out his twin knives, the frog and the salamander, and placing them carefully on the appointed ledge. Her gaze tracked the path Waker had taken into the narrow, winding ravine.

Suddenly harsh laugher exploded from a point lower and closer to the shore. Metal was rapped against rock. Something squealed. A command was issued in a low, guttural voice and the sound of footsteps tramping brush and crunching stone soon followed. Behind her, Waker's father drummed his fingers lightly against the flat of his paddle.

As the footsteps grew louder and closer, Effie realized that Waker was being marched back down the ravine. Someone was holding a spear or a stick that scraped against the sandstone with every step. What she saw next was hard to fathom. A blackand-pink pig came into view. It was haltered like a horse with a bit between its teeth and someone was leading it on a leash. The pig's eyes were small and mean and its hairy chewed-up ears flopped around the sides of them like blinkers. Snuffing wetly, it snouted through the sedge and berry canes at the bottom of the ravine. The man holding the leash came into view next. He was nearly as ugly as his pig. His nose had been broken so many times it looked as if it had knuckles. Hefty but turning to lard, he was dressed in a stripy red-and-gold cloak and donkey-hair pants that were too tight. His weapon was a two-pronged spear that he held upright like a pitchfork. A slack iron chain, not unlike a hammer chain, connected the spear head to a leather band at his wrist.

Waker followed next, and two other men brought up the rear. Both men were armed with evil-looking four-bladed spears. The smaller man wore a cloak that had been embellished with iridescent disks that flashed like fishskin. Effie could not tell if any of them were clan.

"What 'ave we here, my little piggy?" the man with the broken nose said, spying the boat. "Livestock, by the looks of it. Good and healthy."

Waker came forward. He was unrestrained and Effie saw that his knives were riding high in their sheaths. Tar oozed over their hilts. The strangers must have poured it on the blades to disable them. "They're mine, Eggtooth. I've paid the toll on them."

The pig trotted over the sandstone to investigate the boat. The man named Eggtooth followed. "That was before I had me a proper look at 'em." His eyes were pale, almost colorless, and they were now focused on Effie. He licked his lips. The pig began to squeal. Reaching the boat, it pushed its wet, pine-needle-encrusted snout against Chedd's arm. Chedd jerked away and the boat rolled. Waker's father made a quick adjustment. Steadying.

Eggtooth glanced at him. "Good day to you," Effie leant forward, thinking, *Here it is: Waker's father's name*, "old man."

Waker's father made no reply. The pig would not go near him, Effie observed.

"And what 'ave we here?" Eggtooth jabbed her chin with the butt of his spear, forcing her to raise her head. "A little scar I see. The stitcher did good work."

Effie resisted the urge to touch her cheek. She had forgotten the scar existed. No one had mentioned it to her since the day Laida Moon had winkled out the stitches. Cutty Moss's knife had cut deep, but Laida had told her she was lucky because the luntman had picked the one spot on her cheek where there was no muscle underlying the skin. When Laida had held up the glass and shown Effie her handiwork, Effie remembered thinking *Is that all?* She had expected something . . . grander.

Unsure what to do she looked at Eggtooth evenly. His nose was covered in broken veins and there was some kind of insect bite on the left nostril.

"Cool as milk," he commented, throwing the remark backward to his men. "Pretty hair. A man could make good coin just in the scalping."

Effie frowned. Why was he trying to goad her? The pig, finished with examining Chedd, turned its flat pink face toward her. She wasn't about to have any of it and clapped her hands right in front of its snout. With a loud grunt, the pig closed its tiny black eyes and launched itself at her throat. Eggtooth snapped on the leash, lassoing the pig in midair. Ungodly squealing followed. Chedd plugged his fingers in his ears.

Under cover of the noise, Waker's father leaned forward a fraction in the boat and whispered in Effie's ear, "To get rid of scum, best play dumb."

Eggtooth twisted the leash so that the metal bit dug into the corners of the pig's mouth. The creature's eye bulged and it began to wheeze pathetically. After a few seconds, Eggtooth released the slack.

"On your way to the Cursed Clan, eh?" he said, still addressing Effie. "Know what they do to young uns there?"

Effie nearly, but did not, say *No*.

"Feed 'em to the bog," Eggtooth said with a nasty laugh.

A strangled, airless sound came from Chedd's throat.

"Tie stones to their chests and sink 'em," Eggtooth said, switching fire from Effie to Chedd. "Pull 'em up a week later and eat what the fish didn't want."

Chedd fainted. One moment he was sitting upright, if a little forward on his seat, and the next he keeled right over, falling straight into the prow of the boat. Something cracked. The boat rocked wildly. Effie dug her heels into the deck to stop herself from sliding forward.

Eggtooth and his men roared with laughter. The one with the fish-scale cloak slapped his side. The pig sneered at Effie. Waker's father stretched his arm to work out a cramp. On the sandstone ledge fifteen feet away, Waker watched his father's arm. Effie felt her mouth begin to tingle.

"I told you these two were no good," Waker said, speaking over the laughter. "A fattie and a mute. You've had a gold piece for them—they're not worth any more."

Eggtooth tapped his forked spear against the rock. He seemed to be thinking. The pig had found a lump of duck crap and was licking it.

"She's no mute," Eggtooth declared finally, staring straight at Effie.

A long pause followed, and then Waker Stone said quietly, "Go ahead, look for yourself."

All the while Eggtooth had been tapping his spear, the strange tingly numbness had been growing in Effie's mouth. It felt like she was being pricked with dozens of needles, only there was no pain, just weird pricking. By the time that Chedd had pulled himself up from the prow and lumped himself down on the seat, the numbness had turned into thickness and now she no longer recognized the landscape of tumorous ridges that had become the insides of her mouth.

Suspecting a trap, Eggtooth made a signal to his men. Lowering the points of their spears, they sheared fur from Waker's otter-skin coat. Eggtooth took a step forward and carefully brought the twin points of his spear to the roof of Effie's jaw. "Open up," he told her.

Effie opened her mouth. Something darker and thicker than air smoked out.

Eggtooth leant toward her. Peered inside. Frowned. Everyone was quiet, even the pig. Eggtooth's own mouth fell open. "Sweet gods. She doesn't even have teeth, let alone a tongue." Shuddering with feeling, he withdrew the spear.

Effie closed her mouth. The thickness was wearing thin. Behind her, Waker's father's seat creaked.

"Get going, the lot of you!" ordered Eggtooth with a mighty stamp of his spear. "Sodding freaks."

Waker wasted no time in jumping into the boat and pushing off. Not bothering to recoil the mooring rope, he left it trailing behind in the water. Instinctively Effie knew that she had to steer more than paddle, and she plunged her oar deep into the starboard side, guiding the boat away from shore. Directly ahead of her, Chedd paddled with real force. Directly behind her, Waker Stone's father hung on grimly to the gunwales, exhausted.

Chedd and Waker quickly fell into a strong rhythm, and the three men and the pig were soon left behind on the northern shore. When the boat finally rounded the riverbend and they passed beyond sight, Chedd turned to Effie. A square welt on his forehead marked the place where he'd hit the deck.

"Pirates without boats," he said with satisfaction and relief.

Effie decided that now wasn't a good time to remind him what Eggtooth had said about Clan Gray.

Floating east on the Mouseweed, she tried very hard to feel saved.

THIRTY-ONE

A Journey Begins

"Give me one more day," Thomas Argola, the outlander, had said. "Do not leave in the morning." They had been standing in his cave, the only one with a hinged door in the entire city, and Raif kept his hand on the bolt to keep the door from closing. "No," he had replied. "I go tomorrow. Tell me what you've learned."

Raif thought about that conversation now as he and Addie Gunn headed due east along the rim of the Rift. They had been traveling for the better part of the day and the going was hard and rocky. Stony bluffs, mounds of boulders and steep and sudden drops had to be navigated with care. Ground snow was a problem, concealing cracks and loose stones, but at least it wasn't hard with ice. Weeds poked through the white. Mounds of black sedge concentrated the warmth of the sun, turning the surrounding snow into mush. The air was clear and smelled of stone, but Addie warned that come nightfall there'd be mist. "Air's dry. Land's wet. Fog'll rise with the dark." There was not much the small, fair-haired cragsman did not know about the land, and Raif accepted his words without question. It did not mean they would stop though. When you've given a dead man your word you only stop to sleep.

Topping a cracked shelf of granite, Raif turned to see if Addie needed a hand up the slope. The cragsman was wearing his brown wool cloak and carrying his oak staff, and he waved Raif away as if he were a bothersome fly. "Been scuffing the crags since afore you were born, laddie. And most days I was toting sheep. Only time I'll need a hand from you is to stir the beans while I make the tea."

He was only half joking, Raif realized, and nodded somberly. "Sorry, Addie."

Addie Gunn grumbled something that sounded like "Glad we've got that sorted" before hiking solidly onto the ledge.

The granite was weak here, veined with softer limestone. The limestone that had been exposed to the surface had worn away, creating dimples in the surface that were now filled with snowmelt. The shelf jutted out over the Rift and both men paused to look south. Snow had melted at a faster rate in the clanholds and most of the hills were bare. Winter-rotted groundcover made the north-facing slopes look burned. Raif wondered what Addie was thinking as he stood there and minded his former homeland. Wellhouse was likely due south of here; the cragsman's old clan.

"Lambs'll need stabling this year," the cragsman murmured softly, to himself. Turning to Raif, he said, "C'mon, lad. If we can get on the headland afore dark it'll make for an easier start in the morning."

Raif let Addie Gunn lead the way.

They had departed the Rift at dawn, at the exact moment the sun had appeared in the east above the rim. Arrangements had been made the night before, many of them while Raif slept. The attack by the unmade beast had left him exhausted and unable to fully catch his breath, and he had slept through most of that night and a good portion of the next day. When he had awoken at noon he had told Stillborn what he meant to do. "I'll need supplies for the journey," Raif had told him. "Pull together what you can. I have to meet with the out-lander."

Stillborn had been bewildered and hurt. "Supplies for both of us you mean?" he had asked. At some point that morning he had shaved his face, and the bristles that normally stuck out of his facial scars were neatly clipped. "I will be going with you."

Raif shook his head. "I need you here, leading the Maimed Men."

No argument carried weight against the stark fact that Traggis Mole was dead, and Stillborn knew it. "But they want you," he had said. "Not me. It was you who killed that beastie right in front of their eyes. You who laid the Mole to rest."

"I know what they want," Raif said. "Tell them they'll have to wait." He made his voice hard because he had to, because he would not be thwarted in this. As long as he had known Stillborn, the Maimed Man had complained about Traggis Mole's leadership, and lusted after taking his place. Now that place was vacant and it was time for Stillborn to step up and lead. He had a look on his face like he'd thought he'd been trapped, but Raif ignored it. Stillborn should count himself lucky he'd been trapped only once.

"There is no one else," Raif told him. "The Maimed Men respect you. You're the best hunter, the best blade fighter. And it wasn't just me who brought down the Unmade. If you hadn't distracted it I could never have gotten close enough to place my sword."

The two had stared at each other, the air between them charged with tension. Raif had not blinked. Nor had Stillborn.

"Very well," Stillborn had exploded, throwing himself back as if he'd been physically repelled. "If this is how it is then so be it. I will guard them while you are away. But I will tell every single one of them you'll be back."

Raif heard both the warning and the plea in Stillborn's voice. It touched him, but he did not show it. "Do as you must."

Stillborn waited to see if there would be more, and when there wasn't he dragged his hands across his hair and face. "Gods, Raif. We're living in hell. How are we going to survive?"

"Kill everything through the heart."

Raif had left Stillborn then. He had the sense that if he'd stayed longer he would say things counter to his purpose. And his purpose was to depart. The next meeting with Thomas Argola in his doored cave had gone no easier.

Mallia Argola had let him in. Sunlight shone right onto her face, turning golden upon her skin, and for the first time Raif wondered what was missing. In what way was Mallia Argola not whole?

It was a question he had no time for. "Leave us," he told her. "Take a walk."

She had meant to withdraw into the cave, into the shadows

beyond the dragon-and-pear screen where she could watch and listen in, but quickly realized this was something he would not permit. Her green-brown eyes had looked at him carefully, and he felt shame at the way he had behaved toward her in Stillborn's cave. If that shame showed on his face she did not react to it, merely saying, "I will return after you are gone." As she passed him in the doorway, she lightly touched his arm.

It was confusing, that unexpected show of understanding and goodwill, and it took him a moment to refocus his mind.

That was when Argola had tried to shut the door. Raif balked him, shooting out his hand and barring the space around the doorframe. He had not meant to do so, but could not seem to stop himself. Thomas Argola was a man who worked best on the periphery of crowds and in the shadows of closed rooms. Raif Sevrance decided he would conduct this interrogation in the light.

"When did you tell Traggis Mole about the sword?"

The outlander glanced nervously at the open door. Sunlight, which had made his sister's skin look spun from gold, made his own skin look yellow. "The night after we talked I went to see him. He . . . *was* our chief."

Raif heard the excitement in Argola's voice and was repulsed by it. "You told him everything?"

"I believe I never said I would not."

Were you paid for it? Raif wondered, glancing at the worn treasures in the cave. The silk rugs and copper bowls. The screens. It was not a question that mattered, he realized. A man must use what skills he had to live.

Trying to recall all that had been said four days back in this cave, Raif said, "What did you tell him about me?"

Argola shrugged. "He already suspected much."

"That is no answer."

"Close the door."

"No."

The outlander took a sharp breath. Backing away, he found himself a place to stand where he was no longer exposed to direct sunlight. "I told the Mole you were the Rift Brothers' only hope. No one else can hope to stop the Unmade when they break through in numbers. No one. Look at what happened the other night. You were the only one who knew what to do, the only one who could stop it."

"Someone else could have put a blade through its heart."

"*Really?*" Argola blasted. "You could barely put it through yourself."

In the silence that followed, Raif leant against the back of the door. His shoulder was throbbing, and he felt scarcely able to cope with the hard truths spoken by the outlander. He had come here for information, and, if he was honest, the chance to use up some anger. It seemed to him that Thomas Argola deserved it. He had been the one who was pulling the strings. He had been the one who had framed Traggis Mole's second-to-last words.

"*Swear to me you will fetch the sword that can stop them. Swear you will bring it back and protect my people. Swear it.*"

Raif had sworn. A man was dying. The man who had saved his life.

The final words Traggis Mole had spoken were between a man and his gods, and Raif would never repeat them.

Now he wondered only one thing: would Traggis Mole have sprung forward to stab the beast if Thomas Argola had not told him two nights earlier that Raif Twelve Kill was the Rift's only hope? Had Traggis Mole made the decision that Raif's life was worth more than his own?

Raif glanced at the outlander. Thomas Argola had manipulated the Mole chief, just as he had manipulated Raif the night after Black Hole. What was the outlander's purpose? Did he realize his manipulations had brought death?

But Traggis Mole was dying anyway; those were words Raif needed to avoid hearing at all cost. If Thomas Argola ever said them he would kill him.

Suddenly weary, Raif said, "I leave at dawn. Tell me what you have learned about the Red Ice."

Argola had protested, asking for more time, but he of all people had to know that once you set a top spinning it was was out of your control. Raif guessed he had discovered something, for he had not forgotten Mallia's words. *My brother sends a message: Come see him tonight.*

In the end what Thomas Argola had been able to tell him

was little. He was one of the few people in the Rift who could read and write, and had managed to collect many parchments that had been seized by Maimed Men on raids. They saw no value in them and traded them gladly, though it was known that all manuscripts containing maps were to to be surrendered to the Mole. Argola had discovered little from searching his own collection and wanted time to search the Mole's. The thought of the outlander rifling though Traggis Mole's possessions was distasteful to Raif and he hoped that Stillborn would not allow it.

"If you are determined to leave tomorrow then all I can advise is this," Argola had said at last. "It is written that the Lake of Red Ice exists at the border of four worlds and to break it you must stand in all four worlds at once."

Raif had been frustrated. The words sounded like nonsense, designed only to confuse. "You said east."

Argola's smile had been indulgent. "Yes, there is that."

Raif had turned and left him. He had not spoken any word of farewell. Thomas Argola knew either less or more than he claimed, and Raif could not decide which was worse: to know more and not reveal it? Or fake what you didn't know?

Maimed Men hailed him as he returned to Stillborn's cave, and Raif had no choice but to ignore them. Acknowledge their calls of "Twelve Kill" and he risked undercutting Stillborn's position. Raif Sevrance was not yet ready to declare himself Lord of the Rift. That thankless job went to Stillborn, and Raif knew that the best way to support Stillborn was to remove himself from the Maimed Men's attention. And not run the risk of anyone naming him "Chief."

Briefly, he had looked for Mallia as he climbed to the higher ledge, but Argola's sister was nowhere to be seen.

Once he had arrived back at Stillborn's cave he'd eaten the small meal of smoked meat and panbread that had been left for him, built up the fire at the cave mouth, and then lay on Stillborn's mattress and slept. He dreamed there was a black worm living in his shoulder, gnawing its way through his flesh.

The next morning he was awakened by Stillborn in the dark hours before dawn. "Addie's waiting outside," he had said, handing him a cup of water.

It took Raif a while to understand this statement. He swallowed a mouthful of water. "No."

Stillborn was ready for this. "You tell him then. He's been camped there for the past five hours. Won't listen to a thing I say. Doubt if he'll listen to you."

The Maimed Man was a bad schemer, Raif reckoned, for all the time he was speaking, Stillborn had not once looked him in the eye. It made a refreshing change from Argola.

"It's nothing to do with me," Stillborn continued, compelled to fill the silence. "Just told him when you were leaving. Didn't put no ideas in his head."

Raif rose and went out onto the ledge. He noticed Yelma now had two iron pots for breasts.

"You cannot come with me," he had said to Addie before the cragsman had chance to speak. "You are old and you will slow me down."

Addie Gunn had been sitting on a camp chair with his back to the fire and the cave mouth, and did not bother to turn at Raif's approach. "Fancy a journey east," he said, looking straight out across the darkness of the Rift. "Got a hankering to see trees—real ones not piss-thin bushes. I imagine I'll set off soon. 'Magine when I do no one will try and stop me, it being a free world and all and a man being free to travel where he pleases."

Raif breathed softly and deeply. It occurred to him that all you had to do to know a man's resolve was look at the back of his neck. "Addie, I do not know where I go. How can I allow someone to accompany me when I don't know the dangers or how long I will be gone? Traggis Mole took a fatal blow to save my life. His death weighs on me. Do not put me in a position where yours might too."

The cragsman continued staring ahead. Time passed. The fire crackled and spat as a willow knot filled with pitch went up in flames. Eventually Addie Gunn stood and turned to face Raif. "I hear you, lad," he said, "but do you ever wonder if some might feel the same about you? Your death would not be a weight this Rift Brother is willing to bear."

Raif had bowed his head, defeated and heartsore. He had needed this and didn't even realize it: someone to stand second to his oath.

"We travel light and take no animals."

Addie nodded wisely. "I imagined we would."

It was hard to believe that conversation had taken place less than twelve hours ago. Already it seemed to belong in the past, in the city they'd left behind. Look west now and you could not see it. Not even the smoke from the grass fires.

With Addie leading the way they made better time. He had a goat's instinct for the ways between the crags. Raif was content to follow, glad to have no responsibility for a while beyond the placement of his feet. The sky grew bluer as they moved to higher ground and subtle changes took place in the air. Below them the Rift was a trough filled with shadows, narrower here than in the city of Maimed Men.

The discussion as to whether or not to take the hidden bridge across to the clanholds had been a short one. Raif had not been for it, and the cragsman had acceded to his choice. "It means a couple of days on the journey," he had told Raif, so there was no misunderstanding. "The path to the north is rocky and we'll have to put our backs into it. After the third or fourth day it should begin to level off."

To Raif it was a price worth paying. He had a strong preference for not walking on land claimed by clan.

Addie wasn't much for conversation so they climbed in silence. Sometimes the cragsman would whistle a few notes of one of the old lambing songs, and other times he would pluck dried grass heads from the snow and chew on them. He kept an even, unhurried pace, and did not look around to check on Raif. Every so often he would halt to check the depth of a snowdrift with his stick.

Even though the light was failing they made good progress, and they topped the tiered and fractured cliff face just as the mist began to rise. Raif shivered as the sweat beneath his sealskins cooled against his skin. For the last quarter they had been moving northeast to the Rift and when they paused at the cliff top he turned around and saw that the crack in the earth had filled with cloud.

"Happens quick," Addie said, following his gaze. "We won't be able to continue much longer."

Raif took the lead from him. He did not want to stop. While

his mind was occupied with walking he did not have to think about the look in Traggis Mole's eyes as he died.

Swear it.

As the hour wore on the shadows disappeared, driven away by the mist. Islands of cloud rose from the Rift and drifted slowly in circles. The rocks underfoot slickened and the surface of the snow mounds turned to grease ice. Raif had to bend his head to see his feet, and after a while he could not see them at all. Sunset had taken place some time back, but the light remained strangely, quiveringly white. Behind him he could hear the steady pad of Addie's thinly soled boots. The cragsman was not whistling anymore.

"Lad." Addie's voice pierced the mist like an arrow. "I'm done here."

The words carried an authority that Raif had not expected. They did not mean *I.* They meant *We.* Raif put up no argument, and tracked Addie's footfalls through the mist. The cragsman had in mind somewhere he meant to go.

He and Stillborn had probably hunted these cliffs, Raif realized, stalking mule deer and wild goats. Addie slipped between a crack in the rock and into a pocket in the cliff wall. It was not a cave, for the clouds floated freely overhead, but it offered some protection against the mist. Addie set about making a camp. It was darker here than out in the open, but still not as dark as it should have been. Raif wondered if the moon had risen.

He made a circuit of the small clearing, hiking up slabs of granite and leaping between boulders. When he came across a dried-up sage bush wedged into a depression in the rock, he hauled it up for kindling. It had surprisingly tenacious roots.

Traveling light meant there were no tents, only sleep mats and blankets. Each man carried his own water and supplies and although they would not stray from the path to hunt they would keep an eye lively for game. Addie kept his supplies strapped to his torso in a series of tanned leather pouches that helped distribute the weight. This meant he took some unpacking, and Raif found himself smiling as he watched the cragsman struggle with an underarm pack.

Raif did not offer to help, but he did set about making a fire.

One thing he had learned from his short time raiding and hunting with Addie was that the cragsman was fanatical about his tea. The sage flared quickly and smelled like winter festivals and stuffed game birds. Raif placed a smooth rock into the center of the flames and went in search of willow. He had to squeeze through the gap in the cliff to find it, and by the time he had returned Addie had already boiled water for the tea.

"When you're short on fuel it's always best to use water from the canteen instead of snowmelt," he said, noting Raif's surprise. "If it's been wedged in your armpit all day it'll be nice and warm."

Raif had no reply for that, and fed his willow sticks to the fire.

"Tea?" Addie asked when the herbs had steeped.

Raif surprised himself by saying, "Yes."

Huddling close to the flames they drank their tea from tin bowls. Addie had laid strips of smoked meat upon the stone to warm and now dropped two wrinkly apples in the pot containing the dregs of the tea. It was good to sit there and draw in the smells and heat from the fire, good also to be physically exhausted.

And away from the hell of the Rift.

"I smoke it with the fat on," Addie said after a while. "It doesna keep as long but it's juicier."

Raif agreed. He'd been on many longhunts in his time and knew the quiet rhythms of camp talk. After they'd eaten the meat, he asked, "Is there a moon up there?"

Addie glanced up at the banks of mist. "Aye."

Stewed in the tea, the apples had plumped up and had to be cooled before eating. Raif mashed his in his bowl with a spoon. It tasted tart and honey-sweet. Earlier he had intended to ask the cragsman some questions, but now he decided to hold his peace. From where he sat he could neither see nor perceive the Rift, and it seemed no small blessing to spend a night free from the burdens he carried and the oaths he had spoken. When Addie stood and said, "I'm off to sleep," it sounded like a good idea. Not bothering to find a flat stretch of rock to lie upon, Raif tugged the blankets from his bedroll and made his bed near the fire.

He slept lightly. On the way back from gathering willow he

had jammed some branches into the gap in the rock, and his ears listened for the sounds of rustling. None came. Addie snored. The mist began to fail, and the moon shone through gaps in the haze before setting. Nagging pain in Raif's shoulder made it difficult to sleep on his back, and he rolled onto his side. Sound, dreamless sleep followed.

When he awoke at dawn Addie was already up. The crags-man had two strengths of tea; the morning variety was darker and thicker. Today it tasted of apples. "Boiled it down from last night," Addie said, frowning into the pot. "Has its good and bad points."

Raif took a cup and slipped through the crack and out onto the cliff. The rising sun shone silver through the filmy remains of the mist. Ahead the clanholds were washed in gray light, their hills and valleys and forests rendered in shades of gray. A hundred feet below, a pair of swallows were in flight. Raif drank his tea. Thinking of it as medicine helped. After he stretched out his shoulder and relieved himself he returned to the camp.

Addie had killed the fire and packed. He was sitting on a saddle of rock, working a lump of goat fat into the belly of his bow. Thickly carved from a single plank of yew, the cragsman's weapon fell a good foot short of a true longbow. "Are you set?" he asked, folding the remains of the fat into a small sheet of waxed hide.

Raif gathered his blankets and waterskin. "Yes."

They ate their breakfast as they made their way east. Addie had stuffed strips of smoked meat with goat cheese and they held them in their fists like rolls. The cragsmen took the lead, setting the same unhurried pace as the night before. Raif was frustrated at first but after a while he came to understand that Addie was pacing the journey so they would need fewer rests. About an hour after they broke camp they were swooped by a pair of birds, little dun-colored creatures that dive-bombed their heads. Addie declared, "Eggs," and waved Raif ahead while he searched the base of the cliff wall for nests.

Raif struck a path that led him closer to the edge of the Rift. The split in the earth was perhaps four hundred feet across here, nearly half the distance it was in the city. If he looked straight down, he could see tiers of rock like giant steps below him. Rotting snow was sending needle-thin waterfalls trickling into the abyss. Watching them Raif wondered how deep the Rift really was. What happened to that water?

"Look at these beauties," Addie said, coming to join him on the edge. He was carrying a nest woven from willow and pine needles. It was not much bigger than his fist. Five speckled brown eggs lay in the center. "Take one."

Raif tilted his head up and cracked the egg into his mouth. It was creamy and thick, newly laid. When he was done he threw the shell into the abyss.

"How deep is it, Addie?" he asked.

The cragsman had taken one of the eggs himself, and was now packing the remaining three in his chest pouch, carefully spacing them between lumps of cheese. "I canna say, lad. In its own way it's a mystery as big as the Great Want." He glanced at Raif. "At least a few of the souls who enter the Want come back."

"No man's ever tried to climb down and see?"

Addie snorted. "Show me a rope long enough to lower a man into hell. You *fall*. And keep falling. Simple as that."

Raif thought of Traggis Mole's body and shivered. Today at noon the Maimed Men would lower it into the Rift. Stillborn would be the one who touched the flame to the rope. The Robber Chief's body would rock, suspended above the abyss, until the flames burned through the rope fibers and it plummeted into the depths.

I will not slit your throat, Raif had told him. Instead he had put a blade through his heart.

Raif glanced down at his sealskin scabbard, where he now kept Traggis Mole's two-foot longknife. Stillborn had attempted to lend him another sword—a pretty hand-and-a-halfer with a double guard—but Raif had declined. The Forsworn blade had failed on him, and now he would not trust another sword.

Until . . .

Raif set the thought aside. The Mole's knife was wickedly double-edged and made from dense Vorish steel. It would do.

"Snow's coming again," Addie declared, looking east. "I can smell it." He fell silent, and Raif imagined him worrying about the lambs that would be born in the snowfall. "Best get off," he said after a while.

"Addie." Raif stopped the cragsman from returning to the trail. Nodding toward the Rift, he asked, "How long before it closes?"

The cragsman looked at him with some surprise showing in his gray eyes. "It never closes, not wholly. North of Bludd it narrows so that men can cross it, but it's always there, a black crack running through the forests between here and the Night Sea."

Raif reached for his lore. Holding the hard piece of raven in his fist. He continued east with Addie Gunn.

THIRTY-TWO

A Lock of Hair

"Cut me a lock of your hair," Lan Fallstar said to her. "I would keep it. For luck."

Ash knelt by the lake, cupped its cold and green water in her palms, and splashed it against her face. The shock made her shiver and she scrubbed her cheeks, nose and forehead to warm them up. Briefly, she considered stripping off her clothes and tumbling into the water. She recalled that every winter in Mask Fortress a handful of aging grangelords would break through the ice in the Fountain of Bastard Lords and frolic—there was no other word for it—in the freezing water. She and Katia had watched them one year, giggling uncontrollably at their flabby, yet somehow slack, naked bodies. Katia had called them "insane old coots" and Ash had agreed, thinking it a fine assessment. Now she thought she understood the impulse. There was a kind of wild freedom to be had in being naked in defiance of winter. And it would certainly get some kind of reaction from the Far Rider.

"Your hair," he said again to her, his voice light but insistent. "If you will permit I will cut it for you."

Ash turned to face him. The bodice of her dress and the hair around her face were damp and cleaved to her skin. The snow was deep here and her booted feet were sunk into wells. It wasn't snowing yet, but the air had that tingle to it and the sun had been missing for hours. They stood within a woodland of giant white spruce feathered with clubmoss, and cold cedars with corklike trunks. Swordferns and licorice ferns poked through the snow, brown and wiry after the long winter. Moss and silvery lichen grew on the rocks around the lake and on the north and west faces of the trees. The lake itself was small and darkly green. Much of its water was open, and Ash wondered if it was stirred by underground springs.

She did not know what to make of Lan's request. Part of her felt flattered. It seemed the kind of thing that warriors in epic poems would beg from their secret loves before heading off into battle and getting themselves horribly and unexpectedly killed. Ash remembered reading such poems to Katia, and them both agreeing it was all a bit silly. Then they'd go ahead and reenact them anyway. Because as well as being silly the poems were also dreamily appealing. What was never in doubt was the fact that a lady should count herself lucky to be asked for such a token. Yet it didn't quite fit. Lan Fallstar never acknowledged what happened between them in the tent at night, not by day, and he had not proclaimed his everlasting love for her. She was still not sure he even liked her. Even now, as his gaze lighted on the pink swell of her breasts revealed by the damp fabric of her dress, he looked disapproving as well as interested. She had a notion that Lan Fallstar thought Ash March was beneath him. And the only time that changed, or *seemed* to change, was during their lovemaking in the tent.

Perhaps things were changing for him. Perhaps his request revealed a growing, but reluctant, regard. The Far Rider's gaze was level, his eyes inhumanly bright as they refracted light from the snow.

Ash drew the mercy blade from her belt. Lan watched her intently as she separated a lock of hair from the damp sections surrounding her face. Drawing the blade close to her scalp she cut it off. The lock was two feet in length and about as wide as her little finger, and she wondered how many separate silver-blond hairs were within it. She knotted it, not gently, and handed it to him.

He took it with a deeply formal bow, and for a moment she was reminded of the time when Ark Veinsplitter and Mal Naysayer had greeted her outside the Ice Trapper village. They had lain facedown in the snow, prostrating themselves before the Reach. Uneasy, she awaited the Far Rider's response.

Lan Fallstar touched the knot of hair to his lips. "A toll must be paid on such a gift." The words seemed genuine, and Ash found herself relieved. Carefully he wound the hair around itself and tucked it into his weapon pouch. She was surprised when he unsheathed his letting knife; she had thought the words a gallantry.

The knife was plain but beautifully made, as all Sull letting knives were. Handle and blade were formed from a single bar of alloy. The blade had been case-hardened with carbon and was darker than the handle. It had a single edge, and inky green and blue rings shimmered beneath its surface. Lan used the same arm that he had burned the first night they met, making a cut an inch below the black and crusted scar. Blood welled in a short line, and the Far Rider pumped his fist until the redness rolled down his arm and dripped into the snow. This was the first time she had watched him let blood, and Ash wondered why he hadn't done the same that night by the Flow. Why burn himself so badly that even now, over ten days later, the skin still split open and wept watery blood? Did the birch way require that high a toll?

Ash lifted her great lynx-fur cloak from the lakeshore and shook it free of snow. The temperature was dropping and her wet bits were getting cold. She could not watch Lan's bare arm anymore; the sight of it was too confusing. Just visualizing his hand between her legs made her skin flush with heat. She had never imagined that a single finger sliding against wet skin could bring such pleasure. Every night as they made camp she felt filled with reckless need. Part of her knew that it wasn't a wise thing to do, that she did not know Lan Fallstar and was not even sure that she trusted him, but her body ignored her doubts. She became intensely self-aware whenever he drew close to her to perform small tasks like help her mount or dismount her horse, or offer a hand as she jumped over logs and streams. Her body tensed, in anticipation of the slightest and most casual touch. She found herself disappointed if the imagined contact did not come, and fired up and dissatisfied if it did. Lan had to be aware of her heightened and confused state, yet he treated her coolly, and did not acknowledge in any way what they might have done the night before. Was he ashamed of their lovemaking? Should she be?

It was all incredibly bewildering. And just when she thought she at least understood that he meant to keep their travels by day separate from their nights in the wolfskin tent, he went and asked her for a lock of hair. In daylight, with still an hour or two to go before sunset.

Ash frowned with force, pushing her lips against her teeth and driving her eyebrows together. On impulse she decided to leave the Far Rider there with the horses and take a walk around the lake. As she walked she became aware of a pleasant soreness between her legs. She frowned harder.

Rafts of transparent ice floated across the lake's surface in no discernible pattern. Some spun slowly, turning on their axes like wheels, while others sailed right by. One triangular-shaped raft floated blithely in the opposite direction. On the other side of the lake she could see a great blue heron holding itself very still, and somewhere deep within the woods a hawk owl was screeching. The trees surrounding the shoreline looked as if they'd been thinned, for the spruces and cedars were well spaced and animal paths and thin rills of snowmelt led between them. Ash didn't think she had ever been in a more unearthly place. The spruces were so big they looked as if they belonged in a different, larger world. Did they mean she was close to the Heart of Sull?

They had left the birch way two days after Lan had taken her virginity. It was snowing and the forest was very quiet. The fine black stallion, who always walked unleashed beside its master, had suddenly broken into a canter and raced ahead. Lan made no move to stop or chase it and after a moment Ash felt the gelding tug at its lead reins.

"Let him go," the Far Rider said to her. So she had.

The gelding's tail and ears went up in excitement and it bolted through the trees after the stallion. Ash watched the horse disappear and then said, "Will you tell me what you and the horses know and I do not?" She had meant to pitch the comment lightly, but she could hear the hurt in her voice.

Lan replied, "Horses are always first to know when the birch way ends."

Mollified, Ash had fallen into silence. After a while she thought she heard the sound of running water. A few minutes later she picked out the *shishing* of evergreens moving on the breeze. Ahead she could see nothing but birches and whirling snow. Glancing at Lan Fallstar's remote and golden face, she wished he would speak to her; explain how the horses knew the forest was changing, confide that he too was relieved the birches were coming to an end, dare her to a race to see who could escape first. *Something.* Instead he just faced forward, gaze ahead, and kept up the same pace he had maintained all day.

When she couldn't take it anymore she had burst into a run. She could see the hoofprints of both horses filling up with new snow and she followed them exactly, planting her heels into the holes. She thought that Lan might follow her and for a while was disappointed when she didn't hear the sound of his footfalls. The breathless and crazy joy of running soon took over, though, and it began to seem like a much better idea simply to run away. And not come back.

The birches ended with such abruptness you could have snapped a chalk line on them. Stands of blue spruce faced off against the birches like an armed camp. A no-man's-land of gray weeds, perhaps fifteen feet across, separated the two colonies of trees. Despite the unsavory look of the weeds both horses were tugging them from the snow. Ash's gelding was so excited it didn't actually swallow any, just let the stalks hang from its mouth as it trotted about looking for more. Even the snooty stallion was in high spirits, coming over to head-butt Ash before galloping down the strip of no-man's-land as if it were a racecourse.

Ash grinned, delighted. She was out of breath and so hot in her lynx cloak she thought she might faint. Shucking it off, she ran into the middle of the no-man's-land and collapsed into the snow. Her heat quickly melted the new snow and she could feel the back of her dress getting wet. She intended to get up but then the gelding wandered over and began lipping her face and the whole thing was so funny and . . . *good* . . . that she just lay there, kicked up her feet and laughed.

Footsteps crunched in the snow and then Lan Fallstar appeared in her line of view. He was carrying her cloak. "Take it," he said, thrusting it toward her. "We must go."

That had been four days ago. Traveling had been harder

since then—the birch way was flat and had no hills, rocks, fallen logs or water to circumvent—but Ash had liked it a whole lot better. She loathed birches—and all trees that looked like them. She couldn't think of any offhand but birches couldn't be the only trees that grew as straight and slender as bars.

It had been good to see the purple, blue and silver of the pines. On the first day out she'd been driven giddy by their resinous scents. If she had been with Ark Veinsplitter and Mal Naysayer she doubted whether she could have stopped talking. There were so many questions to ask, so many unusual things to comment on. Why were the trees so big? What made the strange sideways tracks in the snow? Why were there halos around the sun and moon? What were those ruins in the distance?

As they'd ridden east, the sounds of snowmelt running and dripping had chimed through the forest. Day owls growled, and sometimes Ash would hear the low moans of big snow cats. So far they had not crossed paths with any other Sull, but Ash had seen signs of them: horse tracks, blazes, clearings, blood-streaked snow. When she spotted these things she felt a tightening in her gut. Here was where Sull lived and hunted. Yesterday she had seen a line of blue smoke on the southern horizon and she thought they might head toward it, but Lan had altered their course northeast.

Ash wished she had paid more attention to her foster father's maps. She had only the most shadowy ideas about how the Racklands were laid out. Rumor had it that no outsiders knew the location of the Heart Fires, but her foster father's maps had contained some details of coastlines, rivers and watchtowers. The deepwater gulf of the Innerway, where the Easterly Flow and the Great Shadow River emptied into the Night Sea, might not be far away, but she could not be sure. Once she and Lan had emerged from the birch way she imagined they would head south, if only for the reason that on her foster father's onionskin maps the legend *Here be where Sull are most fierce* was always writ across the stretch of land that bordered the Stonefields of Trance Vor. The Stonefields were a long way south of the Flow; she knew that much.

Spying something ahead in the water, Ash worked her way

closer to the shore. As she hiked along the bank, thin panes of ice underlain by gravel cracked beneath her boots. The air temperature was dropping and the lake had begun to steam. A few flakes of snow drifted in the air as she leaned over the water and looked within its depths. The ledge was deeply undercut here and some stray current had dragged piles of animal bones into the bowl-like depression. Skulls, mandibles, rib cages, pelvic girdles, scapulas and chunks of spine formed a boneyard beneath the water. Every one of them was a bright, livid green. Ash blinked. One of the skulls looked human.

Cutting away from the shore, she headed back to Lan Fallstar and the horses. The sense that she was no longer in territory claimed by Man created strange tensions in her chest. She had a feeling that if she were to look at anything closely here—animal tracks, snow, fallen logs—secrets would be revealed. This land was old. Its trees were old, and its lakes could turn bones green. Again she noticed the sideways tracks in the snow, odd disjointed curves that headed from the lake to the trees.

"What are those tracks over there?" she asked Lan Fallstar with some force as she returned. It was stupid to be here and not be able to ask basic questions.

The Far Rider had been sitting on the folded tent skins carrying out maintenance work on his arrows. He slid them into his hard-sided horn case as she approached. Although he could not see the tracks she meant, he said, "Moonsnakes feed here. They move in ways that minimize contact with the snow."

His reply took wind from her. She had been spoiling for a fight, she realized, yet hardly knew why. Fine snow had begun to fall and she hugged her cloak to her chest and asked in a softer voice, "How big are they?"

"The females grow to thirty feet." The Far Rider stood. "On full moons they form covens to hunt and feed."

She was surprised by how easily Lan answered her questions. This was not normal, but she would use it. "And the lake? Why are the bones green?"

He shrugged. "This Sull does not know."

"How far are we from the Heart Fires?"

Muscles in the Far Rider's jaw contracted and the golden

skin tightened across his cheeks. With a sharp tug he pulled up the tent canvas. "We ride on. The Heart Fires will burn until we come."

Ash looked at the flattened rectangle of snow left behind by the canvas. She did not move as Lan packed the stallion and slung his glassy longbow across his shoulder.

"It is unsafe to travel this land alone," he said, mounting. "You will not find other defenses as passive as the birch way."

He never used her name. Not even when he slid his man sex into her at night and accepted her tongue into his mouth. He had done her no harm and had guided her safely through the birch way, but she did not know what to make of him. He changed moods too quickly. Only an hour ago he asked for a lock of her hair. Now he was either scaring or threatening her—she couldn't tell which.

"All Far Riders must return to the Heart Fires."

And there it was again, another change. His voice was stiff, but she realized he had spoken to soften his earlier words. She wished it wasn't so confusing. How could he give her so much pleasure at night yet be so cold to her during the day?

She let the falling snow swirl and sparkle between them. After a while decided she had nothing further to say to him, and went to mount her horse.

It was growing late and the gray sky was slowly darkening to blue. The snow captured and held the light, glowing on the forest floor and along the spruce and cedar boughs. The stallion took the lead at canter and the gelding had to stretch itself to keep up. Lan Fallstar rode effortlessly, his back relaxed, his fingers light upon the reins. As he moved in the saddle, the longsword and bow slung crosswise across his back slapped together, beating time.

Ash was glad to be riding. Bending low against the gelding's neck, she savored the warmth of horseflesh against her chest as she raced after the Far Rider. Her lynx fur flared out over the horse's rump and her hair streamed behind her, heavy with melted snow.

She became aware of movement so gradually that it barely registered at first. In her mind it was something black and distant between the trees. As the snow began to ease it occurred to

her that the blackness was on a path to intercept with her own.
A muscle below her gut loosened. Shortening the reins, she
sent her full awareness toward the thing that was closing in
from the south.

And knew instantly it was *maer dan*. It sucked at her, like air
dragged into a powerful fire. When she turned her eyes toward
it she felt her lenses elongate.

"Lan," she called. The Far Rider had not slowed his pace
and was some distance ahead of her, easily navigating a path
between a giant spruce and a cedar that was growing around a
felled stump like a squid on a rock. He did not hear her, so
called again, louder. "*Lan.*" It felt strange saying his name.

The Far Rider turned and looked at her. Whatever he saw on
her face was enough for him to bring the stallion to a banking
halt. Clods of dirt and snow sprayed the trees. Lan's eyes met
hers and she was surprised to see a question in them. He was
Sull. She had assumed somehow he would have known.

"Something is coming from the south," she murmured, her
wet hair sending icy trickles down her spine. "*Maer dan.*"

Shadowflesh. Lan continued to look at her, his pupils enlarg-
ing. She had a memory of Mal Naysayer drawing his sword at
such a moment, his face hard and terrible, his eyes burning like
the cold blue stars at the farthest edge of the sky. She recalled
feeling . . . not safe exactly, but protected. If anything wanted to
reach her it would have to get past the Naysayer, and his six-foot
longsword, first.

Lan Fallstar reached for his bow. "Point," he demanded, his
voice terse. Light reflecting off the snow illuminated the hollows of his cheeks and the space under his jaw. With a fluid
motion, he drew his first arrow. It had a hole drilled into its steel
head, she noticed, but had no idea why.

Ash drew her own weapon, the sickle knife and weighted
chain. "This way," she cried, kicking the gelding into motion.
She'd be damned if she was going to point.

The creature poured like liquid through the trees. It was
accelerating, and she had the sense of powerful muscles bunch-
ing and unbunching. Something *howled* in a long single note
that made the metal in her hand vibrate. Ash caught sight of a
glistening flash of blackness plunging through shadows cast by

the prehistoric pines. It was massive, and it had never been human. Not even close.

It moved on four limbs and it had thick shoulders and a small, frighteningly sleek head. She was reminded of hyenas and lammergeier—carrion feeders who plunged their entire heads into organ flesh. Its eyes were slits. Its clawed footpads ripped up the snow.

Ash made an uneasy adjustment to the reins, transferring them into one hand so she could be free to swing the chain. The gelding flicked back its ears but held its course. The creature was moving as fast as a big cat, its hip bone springing in a wavelike motion. Its howls hurt Ash's ears. Carefully, as Ark had taught her, she raised the sickle knife above her head. The peridot weight bounced once against her buttocks before she whipped the chain into motion.

The creature was not heading toward her, she realized as the chain built up speed and began to *whumpf*. It was coming straight for Lan Fallstar. The Far Rider had followed her at a slower pace; she could hear the sound of his stallion blowing out air and the jingle of harness metal. Perhaps he was aiming the bow. She did not look round.

Squeezing the gelding with her thighs, she shifted her course. The chain was spinning so fast it had passed into invisibility. The peridots in the weight scribed a green circle in the air. As she judged distance and time, the creature closed in. Its elongated jaws sprang apart, revealing dense layers of inward slanting teeth.

Ash stood in the stirrups and yanked the weight forward. The beast leapt, its muscular hind legs propelling its body like springs. Shocked by its speed, she realized her shot had fallen short. Hot pain coursed along her shoulder as the weight reached the end of its tether with momentum to spare. It snapped with a crack. The chain crumpled in the middle as the weight shot back toward her. Ash flicked her wrist with force, sending tension back into the chain and throwing the weight wide of herself and her horse. As she did this she was aware of a series of soft retorts.

Thuc. Thuc. Thuc.

Three arrows were loosed in quick succession. The creature

dropped as soon as the first one hit, collapsing into the snow with a dull thud. Its flesh began to hiss as the other two arrows struck the big ridge of muscle on its shoulder. The creature rippled. The outline of its body softened, as if it were somehow losing its form. Air crackled like a sheet of breaking ice. Ash breathed it in and wished she hadn't. It was empty of whatever her lungs required for fuel.

A soft hiss escaped from the creature's gut. All was still for a moment, and then shadow discharged from its carcass in an explosive rolling ring. The shock wave blasted Ash's face and riffled through the fur on her cloak. It was cold in different ways than the snow, coating her skin with the substance of another world. Even as she struggled to make sense of it, the substance smoked away to nothing, tingling as it ceased to exist. It smelled like the thin air-starved atmosphere at the top of mountains.

Shivering, she turned her horse. Lan Fallstar stood on his stallion's stirrups, resting his eared longbow. His chest was pumping rapidly. He had a fourth arrow ready and unused in his hand. He sat back in the saddle as Ash looked on and scooped up the reins from his horse's neck. Slinging the bow over his shoulder, he said to her, "It was foolish to get so close." His voice was low and loose, and she was glad to hear the fear in it. It made her like him better.

"It was a good shot. The first one. Must have been a heart-kill."

His eyes went blank for the briefest moment before he nodded. "This Sull had a good arrow."

Ash smiled at his modesty. She had traveled with Raif Sevrance: she knew all about the cost and difficulty of heart kills. "Come," she said, drawing abreast of him. "Let's make camp away from this place."

Lan Fallstar returned the unused arrow to its case, and actually allowed Ash to take the lead. The gelding was panting and a bit scuddy around the neck so she spoke soft words to him and set an easy pace. She did not look back at the blasted remains of the creature in the snow.

As soon as they found a place away from the carcass, they set up camp. Ash picked a clearing between the cedars—the towering spruces made her feel too small. She brushed down both horses while Lan built a fire and prepared food. The stallion held itself perfectly still as she combed through its long silky tail. When she was done it delighted her by presenting its right foreleg for inspection. She checked and discovered part of a pine cone wedged under its nail. Using her letting knife, she winkled it out.

When she raised her head, she found Lan Fallstar staring at her through the flames. She smiled, and although he did not smile back she imagined she saw a softening in his face. His skin was deeply golden in the firelight.

He had pitched the wolfskin tent. The sight of it made heat come to Ash's face. Water spilled from her cup as she drank. Fear had left her muscles and tendons humming. As she ate her simple meal of cured horse meat and wafers, she tried to calm herself. She'd felt better with the horses, she realized. Less jumpy.

Lan had heart-killed a creature that had forced its way out of the Blind, and somehow that meant she had misjudged him. It seemed more believable now that he was what he claimed: a Far Rider. Why had she doubted him when he drew the bow? What did she know about Sull and all the ways they had of fighting the Unmade? Mal Naysayer was a giant, solid as a block of granite and terrifying in battle, but she doubted that even he could have disposed of the carrion feeder more efficiently than Lan Fallstar. One arrow, shot at distance. She would not have been able to bring down the creature herself. It was too fast and strong to be held by a chain. It would have dragged her from the back of her horse. A Reach did not have physical power, it seemed. She could track the creatures of the Blind, but not much else.

Briefly she looked north and wondered where the Naysayer rested this night. She would have liked to talk to him just then.

Ash held her hands over the fire, letting its heat warm her palms. The cedar logs were riddled with pitch holes and the flames turned ameythst as they burned. Snow had stopped falling but ice crystals moved through the air like pollen. Lan Fallstar reached out and took Ash's hands in his. "Come."

He led her to the wolfskin tent where he had already laid out blankets and furs in a single pile. Light came from the fire;

muted reds and golds that flickered on Ash's skin. She stepped out of her cloak, unbuckled her belt, and pulled her dress over her head. She could smell her sweat, salty and darkly sweet. Her stomach felt hollow and when Lan touched it muscles quivered. His hand pushed under her breast, forcing it out so he could close his mouth around the small hard nipple. His other hand slid between her legs. Ash gasped. Losing her footing she stumbled backward and Lan grabbed her hips and guided her down to the floor. As she lay on the furs he pulled off her boots. He was naked and his sex stood out from his body. When he had removed both her boots he lowered his head between her thighs and kissed her sex. Ash tensed, surprised. Slowly she relaxed as warm liquid heat rolled over belly and thighs. His tongue slid back and forth, wet and soft. Soon the gentle pressure was no longer enough and she pushed herself against Lan's face. His tongue stiffened in response. She could hardly believing anything could feel this good.

She wondered why she kept seeing the shadow beast tearing between the trees. Lan's tongue was moving along folds of tender skin and she stopped breathing as its rhythm grew more insistent. A single arrow to the heart. Such a small, compact head and it had stopped something larger and more densely muscled than a horse.

Ash grabbed at the furs as his tongue entered her. Urgent pressure built in her belly. She did not want him to stop.

Do not wake, the voice called from the darkness.

As muscles contracted in her thighs and stomach, she realized she had not seen the first arrow go in.

THIRTY-THREE

The Field of Graves and Swords

Vaylo Bludd rode his borrowed horse north to the Field of Graves and Swords. Mogo Salt, second son of Cawdo, and Hammie Faa were behind him. The wind was up and ragging, pushing high and low clouds across the sky. An overnight frost had crisped the receding snow and it cracked pleasingly when punctured. Vaylo's horse was a fiery stallion, jet black, with a long, sculpted head. When he dug in his heels and loosened the reins, the animal raced up the valley slope at full gallop.

Gods, but it was good not to think. Just ride and be damned as your ears chilled to freezing and your tailbone took a hammering against the cantle. He'd been shut up for too long in the furry black walls of the hillfort. Too much damp, too many whisperings, too much fear of what was to come. A hundred and seventy Bluddsmen were garrisoned there. When had they turned into frightened girls? We are Bludd, Vaylo wanted to shout out at the morning. We are not built to sit and wait.

Arriving at the headland that topped the valley, Vaylo reined in his horse. The Field of Graves and Swords lay directly ahead of him and he felt the pressure that had been building in his chest ease. Dead clansmen lay here. Respect was due. He walked the horse forward through the dried out heather stalks, rye grass and snow. The stallion's neck steamed. Vaylo smelled horse sweat and frozen mud. When he drew enough to see the canker on the nearest blade, he dismounted. His feet punched perfect impressions in the snow.

Deciding to trust the stallion, the Dog Lord let the horse stand free. Mayhap it would nose something tasty from the snow. Behind him he was aware of Hammie and Mogo slowing their mounts. Behind them, the wolf dog was high-trotting through the white.

The swords were as Cluff Drybannock said: fallen or falling. Vaylo counted eleven that were wholly upright, and perhaps twice that number that pierced the snow at odd angles. Dozens more must lay beyond sight. You could still make out the barrows, though, the stone mounds that had been raised around the bodies. Vaylo did not know if Dhoone preferred to cover their dead rather than bury them, or if it was a case of men fallen in winter with the earth too hard to be dug. The mounds gave him a chill more than the swords, for he had not been expecting them. Man-shaped but three times as big, they were swollen with new snow. Fox tracks led in toward the middle of the field and Vaylo followed them, his left hand resting on his horn of powdered guidestone.

When he came to the first sword he halted. Drawing his newly-acquired sable cloak around his legs, he knelt in the snow. The sword's point was intact but the blade had been eaten by rust and its edge was gone. It had once been a greatsword, Vaylo reckoned, probably close to six feet long including hilt. Someone strong and able must have wielded it. Leaning forward he touched the cankered edge and was surprised to feel how firmly it was fixed in place. He had thought the lightest pressure might have tilted it, and now he wondered about the men who had formed these mounds and set these swords in place. Had they poured cement into the warrior's chest cavities and plunged the hilts between their ribs? What had they feared? What had happened here to raise these swords?

Slapping a hand on his knee, the Dog Lord rose to standing. Two ovals of snow shed from the fur of his cloak. On the periphery of his vision he saw the wolf dog ghosting along the edge of the mounds. When he heard footsteps approaching he turned.

Hammie Faa and white-haired Mogo Salt stepped forward to pay their respects to the dead. No one spoke. All were warriors here. Mogo was young to have the white hair and Vaylo wondered if he minded it. Not all Salt men had it—Cawdo's hair had been thick and brown—but it was a trait the family was known for.

"Come," Vaylo said to them after some minutes had passed. "Let us away to look at the Rift."

They mounted their horses and rode north until the land ceased rising. Vaylo enjoyed the high-sprung nature of his horse, was glad he had to fight it. He thought about the Dog Horse, his mount for nearly a decade, and wondered what had become of it after it had broken free from the burning stables at Dhoone. He had loved that horse, but doubted anyone else could, and he hoped it hadn't been slaughtered for meat. No Dhoonesman would have been able to master it, that was for sure.

Forcing the stallion into a skidding halt, Vaylo squinted into the far distance. His old, hardened lenses were not what once they were and it took a moment for the Rift to come into focus. You couldn't see the hole itself, just the raised cliffs on the other side of it and the horizon-long shadow that told of something . . . missing.

"It's a sight," he said as Hammie and Mogo rode abreast of him. "But not one to warm a man's heart."

Hammie stood in his stirrups and whistled. He too was kitted with a new cloak and a borrowed horse. The cloak was maroon and trimmed with marten and intended for someone taller. The horse had big nostrils and a powerful neck.

"I was there six days back," Mogo said. "An entire round-house could fall in and you wouldn't be able to find it."

Silence followed as Hammie and the Dog Lord contemplated this fact.

"Where are the Maimed Men?" Hammie asked.

"East of here. Sometimes we see their smoke."

Hammie thought about this. "How do they get across for their raids?"

Mogo brought his white eyebrows together in a frown. "Da told me there was a bridge only no sworn clansman can see it."

Cawdo Salt was dead, killed several months back at Ganmiddich, so Vaylo did not speak up to contradict his wisdom. The Dog Lord did not believe in such things as bridges that could only be seen by select people. He believed in trickiness and subterfuge, and imagined they played some part in the Maimed Men's ability to cross into the clanholds. "You know what I think?" he asked. Both Mogo and Hammie earnestly shook their heads. The Dog Lord put on his most serious chief's face. "Even if I give you a five minute start I'll still beat you back to the fort."

Hammie, who knew how these things worked, took off. Mogo Salt, who was all of twenty-six, and had little experience with his chief just sat there in the saddle and looked confused.

"Go," Vaylo told him, not unkindly. "It's a race."

The boy got the idea soon enough. As Vaylo listened to the drum of horse hoofs he finally felt free to breathe. To the west of him he spied the wolf dog, worrying a piece of fox. Turning the stallion, he looked south at the Copper Hills. He thought he could see the broken turret of the fort's watchtower, but couldn't be sure.

What were Bluddsmen doing here? And why were they staying?

This was Dhoone—and a godforsaken corner of it at that. How long before Robbie Dun Dhoone rode north to reclaim it? How long before whatever monstrosities had slain Derek Blunt and his men stirred for a second feeding? Vaylo could not get the sight of the barrows out of his mind. Men dead and entombed in stone but still fighting.

They had been buried to the north, not to the south to protect against attacks from rival clans. Had the Maimed Men ever warranted such a display of fear and bravado? Vaylo thought not. The Maimed Men were outcasts, left-behinds. Freaks. You could fight off ten of them with a decent crossbow.

Vaylo breathed the icy air through his mouth, punishing his teeth. He did not like it here, and wondered how long he could stay. Kicking the stallion into motion, he raced south.

As he descended the slope into the valley, the sun broke out for a while and its scrawny warmth improved his spirits. He had to remember that here was better than nowhere. Chief of a moldy hillfort was better than no chief at all. Hunkering low against his horse's neck, Vaylo switched paths so he wouldn't have to pass the Field of Swords and Graves. Might even be quicker this way, always supposing he didn't run into rocks and ponds concealed by the snow. The territory was still new to the horse so it didn't have much of an opinion on the route. It didn't like the scent of the wolf dog, that much was certain, and Vaylo thought it a pity that he hadn't trained the hound to chase his horses—he'd get some real speed from them that way.

Hope of catching Hammie and Mogo dwindled as he found himself on the wrong side of a melt creek that had sprung on the valley floor. Of course, Vaylo chided himself, he should have kept an eye to the seasoned man. Mogo Salt had been here the longest; his route would be the best. Irritation made Vaylo force a jump, and the stallion stumbled on the upslope, panicked, and tried to throw him. The Dog Lord hung on grimly, knees clamped to the horse's belly, knuckles white around the reins. It occurred to him that he could end the race—simply trot the horse back and congratulate the winner— but it seemed a petty kind of act. Give up now and he'd deprive either Hammie or Mogo of the satisfaction of beating his chief.

Shaken and with the old pain nagging at his heart, Vaylo galloped back to the hillfort. For a wonder Hammie Faa won. Those big nostrils had meant more air, which made for a faster horse. Both men assailed him with their stories. Hammie's saddle had slid off center, his mount had thrown a shoe. Mogo had taken the lead, hit a pothole, had a near miss with the offending shoe. Vaylo grumbled at them, told them he'd taken time midway to boil himself a cup of tea. Hammie beamed, his cheeks as red as only a Faa man's could be.

"Inside," Vaylo ordered. "And no telling this to the bairns." As he spoke he looked up at the drum-shaped war terrace that extended out from the fort's north ward. Cluff Drybannock stood there speaking to someone Vaylo recognized and knew.

The surprise of it chilled him. He had thought himself at the end of the earth here, yet there was his third son.

It was difficult to keep his mind in the moment. Stirring himself, he frowned skeptically at the hoof that was missing a shoe, told Mogo he'd more than likely ducked horseshit, not iron, and steered his small group onto the path that led to the western door.

The hillfort no longer boasted viable stables and all horses were kept belowground in the western ward. Someone had done a fair job of boxing and partitioning the space, and Vaylo saw that sheets of scrap copper had been molded into troughs. He forced himself to unsaddle and brush down the stallion. Hammie knew something was up and offered to take charge of the feed and watering. Vaylo let him. "For a man with a new horse," he told him, "you didn't do half bad."

Hammie pressed his lips together, nodded, and then said, "Chief."

Vaylo took that word up the stairs with him and into the north ward. The big double doors were open and the air outside blew in. Bluddsmen were sitting on benches and leaning against walls, keeping up the pretense of oiling swords, mending tack, scraping rust from chainmail. One man was actually taking a swipe at the mold on the walls with a cloth soaked in lye; Nan's circle of influence was growing. They were quiet as he walked through the room and onto the war terrace.

Cluff Drybannock and Gangaric HalfBludd were the only men on the balcony. They were standing close to the stone balustrade, off center to avoid the gazes of the Bluddsmen in the ward. Neither man was speaking. The distance between them was a fraction too great to allow relaxed conversation. They turned to him as he stepped outside. Gangaric looked relieved.

"Father," he said. "It has been a long time."

Vaylo clasped his son's arm, and was surprised to feel an equal pressure in return. "Son."

Gangaric HalfBludd had made himself an axman and a HalfBluddsman in memory of his great-grandfather, Thrago, and he wore a fine crimson cloak overmounted with a heavy collar of woodrat skins in the manner of the border clan. His mighty war ax was cradled across his back. The limewood handle rose above his left shoulder for ease of draw. The fierce oyster-shell-shaped blade was protected by a bloodstained mitt. Such was the price of warriorship in HalfBludd, Vaylo recalled: you had to dress in your own drawn blood.

"Have you ridden from the Bluddhouse?"

Gangaric's large head was bare and his scalp featured alarming bands of part-shavings. "I've been on the hoof for thirteen days. The snow slowed me."

Vaylo unpinned his heavy sable warcloak. It would need to

be aired to dispel the stench of panicked horse. Laying it over the balcony he asked, "What news?"

This was the question Gangaric had been waiting for, the one Cluff Drybannock had doubtless asked only to be answered coldly, *I await my father's return.*

Vaylo knew all about his sons.

"Pengo has possession of Ganmiddich," Gangaric said. "He won it from the Spire's army, and is now under fire from Blackhail, Bannen and Scarpe."

Sweet mother of all bastards. This news was so startling it rendered Vaylo speechless. Pengo, his worthless second son, in command of one of the great prizes of the clanholds? How had this happened? How many flukes of fate and pigs escaping from pokes had it taken to bring this piece of good fortune to bear? Ganmiddich taken from city men? Finding his voice he asked, "The Spire routed Blackhail and Ganmiddich?"

"Aye. Pengo rode in at battle's end. Blackhail was beaten, and the city men were set to claim the Crab Gate. Then the city men split their army. Half stayed to shore the gate, and half withdrew."

This just kept getting stranger. "Why would the city men do such a damn fool thing?"

Gangaric shrugged. The skin on his face and neck was deeply ice-tanned and wormed with broken veins. "The half that withdrew crossed the river and headed back to Spire Vanis. The half that Pengo saw off headed west."

Vaylo nodded, thinking. West was good. West was away from Bluddsworn clans. Turning his back on his son, the Dog Lord gazed north across the gray and snow-mounded valley. From here you could not see the Field of Graves and Swords, and he was glad of it. Glad also that the hundreds of Bluddsmen and women Pengo had led from Dhoone all those weeks ago had found a home. And as yet come to no harm.

"Ganmiddich can be held by small numbers as long as the gate remains sealed." It was Cluff Drybannock speaking, the words his first since Vaylo had arrived.

Gangaric challenged them. Pushing his hand against the air that separated him from Drybone, he cried, "Gates sealed!

What sort of Bluddsmen would we be if we hid behind closed doors like frightened maids?"

"Live ones," Vaylo said flatly, spinning about. He was surprised by how closely his third son's words echoed his own thoughts of earlier that day. Hide. Sit and wait. The complaints were almost the same. To distract himself he asked, "What of Withy?"

Gangaric threw a defiant glance at Cluff Drybannock before speaking. "Withy suffers. Hanro took harm when Skinner Dhoone attacked, and has not recovered from his injuries. Thrago holds the house. Dun Dhoone has already mounted one attack."

We are the clan that makes kings. That was the Withy boast, so of course Robbie Dun Dhoone would want to rewin the Withyhouse for Dhoone. You could call yourself a king without Withy, but you couldn't become one until the Withy chief anointed your shoulders and laid some new-made crown on your head. As Vaylo recalled, the old Dhoonish crown had been forged into a Blackhail sword.

Vaylo leant against the stone balcony. His legs and spine were sore after the horse race and he needed the support. Hanro was his sixth son. Thrago his fifth. They had both been at Withy for months, though Hanro had been there the longest and had held the command. Vaylo imagined his sixth son must be ill indeed to secede that command to his older brother. Or worse, Thrago may have seized it. Vaylo glanced at Gangaric. The relationships his sons had with each other was something he did not fully understand. Some were allies. Some not. Gangaric and Thrago had been close as boys, and they had both wed HalfBludd maids.

All wives were dead now, slain by Hailsmen on the Bluddroad, but that was a dark thought for another day.

"You intend to travel south to Withy?" Vaylo asked. It nearly wasn't a question.

"Aye. Thrago needs aid." Gangaric's jaw came up. Pointedly, he looked back at the shambling, crazily roofed hillfort. And then sneered. "We are Bludd. We must fight."

Gods help me not to hit him. Vaylo ground down his seventeen remaining teeth. Directly across from him Cluff

Drybannock stood tall and still, his waist-length braids moving in the breeze, his expression controlled. Watching his fostered son calmed Vaylo and he took a moment to fish inside his belt pouch and pull out a cube of chewing curd. The curd was old and the mold had gotten into it, but he worked it soft in his mouth and swallowed the bitter taste.

What did he need here? Looking at Gangaric's hard, mutinous face, Vaylo decided that what he needed was more information. He spat the chewing curd over the edge. "How does Quarro sit at Bludd?"

Vaylo himself had sent Gangaric to aid his eldest brother, Quarro, after Robbie Dhoone's torching of the Sacred Grove and his tearing down of the outhouse widely believed to have been built from the remains of the last Dhoonestone. If Vaylo remembered rightly Gangaric had not wanted to go, and had insisted on taking a crew of axmen along for comradeship and support. Were those men here today? Probably. Gangaric was not the sort to ride hundreds of leagues across unfriendly territory on his own.

Gangaric kicked a loose chip of masonry with his foot. Uncomfortable. He took a speaking breath, glanced at Drybone, and then exhaled and didn't use it. Finally he blurted, "I would rather we speak alone."

"Speak or I will break your ax arm."

For a long moment no one moved. The holes in the centers of Gangaric's sky blue eyes got bigger and blacker. All of Vaylo's sons had grown up in fear of their father. The question was: had that fear gone? *I am fifty-three*, Vaylo thought. *Am I capable of beating my son?*

It was a question he did not have to answer. Jerking into motion, Gangaric cried, "Here then. If you force me to say it. The Bluddhouse has turned into a stinking well. Quarro grows fat and lazy—drinks ale all day and stays abed with Trench whores. Calls himself chief, though not many call him it back. He and his cronies are holed up in the house. Dun Dhoone's garrisoning men at Wellhouse, spoiling for battle. What does Quarro do? Decides to have a pit dug for bear baiting. A fucking bear pit. With the Sull sneaking on our eastern bounds, the Trenchlanders raiding our farms, and the Thorn King knocking on our door, he digs a bear pit!" Gangaric was shaking so strongly, the limewood ax handle was vibrating above his shoulder like a twanged string. "Something needs to be done before it all goes to hell. I'm not going back there. The place stinks worse than this."

Vaylo breathed in and out, and tried to recall why he'd continued having sons after his first was born. Angarad had had a hard time with the labor, and the mewling purple creature that had been produced after three days did not seem worth the effort and the risk. Quarro, she decided she would name it, after some grandfather's grandfather who might have once worked in a quarry, or possessed only a quarter of something vital—like a ball. Vaylo had not liked him. Straightaway, he knew that. Little Quarro screamed like someone was trying to skin him and shit like a sick dog. What was hard to understand then was why he, Vaylo Bludd, had gone ahead and made six more. For a certainty he should have stopped at two. That way Gangaric HalfBludd, formerly Bludd, would not be standing there, daring to accuse his father of inaction.

"Did Scunner Bone go to Withy?" Questions seemed the best way to deal with his feelings. Firing them off provided some relief.

"The Bone," Gangaric repeated with annoying possessiveness and familiarity. "The old timer's still at Bludd. What of it?"

Scunner Bone was an Otler-trained cowlman, a handful of years older than Vaylo Bludd. Old-timer was an insult to both of them. "Nothing of it. What are your numbers?"

"We're a dozen hatchets in all." Again, there was that snide glance at Drybone, this one specifically aimed at his sword. Hatchetmen—ax and hammer wielders—made no secret of their contempt for narrow blades. Vaylo wondered if Gangaric had ever had the pleasure of watching Drybone take off a man's head. One sweep was all it took. Rather poetically he called it moon upon the water.

Aware that his thoughts were getting muddy, Vaylo took a moment to pace the width of the war terrace. The bit of sun that had sparkled earlier was gone, forced out by a conspiracy of clouds. He imagined it must be cold, but could not feel it. "You say Dun Dhoone's garrisoning men at the Wellhouse? Is he there himself?"

"No. His second-in-command Duglas Oger commands the crews."

That meant Robbie Dhoone himself would move to take Withy . . . and possibly Ganmiddich. "Where are Blackhail's armies?"

"They move southeast from Bannen."

It was, if you thought about it, a pretty steady queue. Nearly everybody in the clanholds—including Drybone and he himself—had possessed the Ganmiddich clanhold at some point in the past seven months. Bludd had it now, Blackhail was aching to retake it, and you could not rule out Dun Dhoone. The three giants of the north, one small but exquisitely placed roundhouse: someone would get crushed.

"There's a new Crab chief. He's housed at Croser."

The politics of the clanholds could be labyrinthian, Vaylo decided. Croser was an eccentric, self-possessed clanhold that usually had the wisdom to avoid other people's fights. "Married to one of the chief's daughters?" Vaylo ventured.

Gangaric actually grinned. "We reckon so."

Vaylo grinned back. Cluff Drybannock's face remained still.

"How long will you stay?" Vaylo asked his third son.

"Today and tomorrow if you'll permit it."

It was probably foolishness to be pleased by the hesitancy in Gangaric's voice. It probably meant he was getting softer as well as older. Just as he was about to give his son leave to stay as long as he and his men saw fit, Cluff Drybannock spoke up.

"You say the Sull are on our borders. What is their business?"

Vaylo felt a chill travel up his spine. He had not thought to ask any questions of the Sull.

Gangaric regarded his fostered brother with some suspicion, his eyes narrowing as he tried to find fault with the question. "They're on the move. They use our paths, cross into our territory at will. Hell's Town is teeming with them, the old Sull. The pure Sull. They're leaving the Heart Fires and heading north."

The wind picked up as Gangaric spoke, blowing hard against their faces and breaking against the walls of the fort. One of the massive copper sheets on the roof began to *whumpf* as air got under it. The sound hammered at Vaylo's thoughts, made him think of the things Drybone had told him in the tower. Terrible, believable things.

"The Sull are not human," Ockish Bull had told Vaylo the night thirty-five years ago after they'd encountered the Sull army in the woods east of Cedarlode. "Remember that and you will know something important." It hadn't seemed like much of a statement at the time and Vaylo had thought Ockish was being Ockish: inscrutable just for the sake of it. He should have known better. The times when Ockish Bull was making the least sense were the times when he spoke the hardest truths.

The silence created by Gangaric's words wore on, gaining meaning. The Dog Lord knew he would have to be the one to break it—Gangaric had the look of a man who'd fallen in a hole and wasn't sure how to get out, and Drybone would not speak a worthless word—yet he found it strangely difficult. Heartiness was beyond him. He kept seeing the Field of Graves and Swords in his mind's eye.

Derek Blunt and his men dead.

Drybone standing at the north-facing window, keeping watch.

Vaylo looked from his flesh-and-blood son to the son he had chosen, and realized he would soon have to make a choice. Gangaric had not ridden hundreds of miles out of his way for a cozy visit with Da.

"Come," Vaylo said to both his sons, "let us go inside and get fed by Nan. We will all be Bluddsmen this night."

Gangaric searched his father's eyes, and then bowed his head with gallantry learned from the HalfBludds. "As you wish." Vaylo imagined he was considering his crew of eleven men.

Drybone observed this, his head level, his nostrils moving as they drew in cool air. "Father," he said quietly, "send Nan my respects. This warrior must keep the watch tonight."

The old pain in Vaylo's heart deepened. Of course Dry could not eat with Gangaric—the man had carelessly mentioned Trench whores. Cluff Drybannock nodded a brief farewell to Gangaric and moved inside the fort.

He took something essential with him. Vaylo felt its loss, but could not put into words what it was.

Gangaric seemed relieved to have him gone. "I forgot to tell you," he said, coming forward to escort his father inside, "you are a grandfather again. Pengo's wife has had the baby."

Shanna. Pengo had gotten her pregnant before his first wife was slain, but Vaylo cared little of that. "Is it healthy?" he asked, allowing his son to guide him through the double doors.

"Aye. She sucks so much they call her Milkweed."

Vaylo laughed, though in truth what he was feeling was fear. Fear for Drybone, fear for his new granddaughter, fear for all of Bludd.

Milkweed. Quite suddenly he remembered the reason for having more children. He had hoped to have a girl.

THIRTY-FOUR
Yiselle No Knife

On the third day the land began to change. The slopes south of the Rift grew greener as the grasses and heathers were replaced with stone pines, blue cedar and hemlock. The hills themselves shifted into rolling valleys, forested hummocks and ridges and rocky bluffs. On the north side of the Rift the Craglands had begun, and spear-shaped hunks of rock towered over dwarfed pines and bushy black spruce. The Rift was perhaps fifty feet across now, and if they had wanted to they could have climbed into it and made the crossing to the clanholds. Boulders as big as barns, and entire dead trees, complete with boughs and root balls, choked the crack. Colonies of ptarmigan nested amid the rocks, and saxifrage and lousewort grew in mats from the Rift's buckled walls. Raif wondered what existed beneath the debris and boulders. Did the Rift still lead to the abyss?

"That's Bludd territory over there," Addie said, wagging his chin south. "See that stand of big red pines on the ridge, that's their marker. Anything east and south from now on is theirs."

Raif had wondered about those trees. In a sea of black, green and blue their rust-colored trunks stood out like a warning. A pair of eagles had made their nest at the top of the tallest pine, building a black ring around the point.

"How far to the Racklands?" Raif asked, working out a sudden twinge of pain in his left shoulder.

The little fair-haired cragsman shrugged. "Depends upon the path."

It was an uncharacteristically vague answer for Addie Gunn,

and Raif wondered if they had reached the edge of his knowledge. The cragsman hailed from a Dhoone-sworn clan, and perhaps he had avoided grazing his sheep in territory claimed by Bludd. Raif glanced over at Addie. The cragsman had tied a band of rabbit fur around his ears; it looked as if he was wearing a bandage. Goat grease on his nose and lips made them shine. "Best keep moving," he said. "It's too cold to stop."

Raif followed him along the deer path that wound between the rocks and shrunken pines. The snow underfoot wasn't deep, but it was all ice and it did not yield to the foot. The temperature had been dropping for the past two days—ever since the new snow—and even though it was midday the air was still several degrees below freezing. The Ice Trapper sealskins helped keep Raif warm. Earlier he'd slathered his ears, nose, and lips with bow wax, and imagined it made for an unlovely sight. Bow wax turned opaque when it cooled.

Overhead the sky was a deep sapphire blue. Lines of high serrated clouds moved from the north. Ice sparkled at groundlevel, coating pine cones and sedge leaves, and the bases of the limestone crags. They had been on the path at dawn and had not stopped except to swig from their water bladders and pee. This was the fourth day of traveling and Raif found he enjoyed the simple hardness of camp life. It was good to go to bed each night bone tired and aching, and satisfying to hike onto a high ledge and see how far you'd come in a day. The cold did not bother him much. Both he and Addie were from northern clans; they were used to the shock of spring frosts.

Addie was a fine traveling companion, able to build fires, skin hares, find running water, sniff out eggs, follow game tracks and cook. He had an eye for the simplest route. Natural stairs leading up cliff faces, dry creekbeds, fallen logs spanning gorges: the cragsman spied things that Raif would have missed. Every evening since they had left the city, Addie had located a sheltered place to camp, and every day he had found something worth bagging for the pot. Last night he had brought down a fat brown rabbit, and today there had been more eggs. Raif was grateful for his presence. There wasn't much talking between them, but silence was different—better—when it was shared.

They had decided to continue east for another day and then

gradually move north from the Rift. Addie said the Craglands appeared to ease to the north and they would need to do less climbing. He did not question Raif's destination, and that seemed no small blessing. In his former life Addie Gunn had kept a herd of sheep on the move in the highlands, only staying in one place during spring lambing. He was a man who didn't need to know where he was going to spend the next night.

Raif did not give much though to the Red Ice. *East*, Thomas Argola had said. That was all, but it was also enough. It made things simple. They would head more or less east, switching directions as the land dictated, and see what they could find. If Tallal of the lamb brothers was right and a great battle had taken place in the Valley of Cold Mists then some evidence somewhere must exist.

Glancing north, Raif wondered where the lamb brothers were this day. Were they in the Want drifting east?

"Some smoke ahead." Addie's voice seemed to come from a great distance. A pause followed while the cragsman figured the ways. "We could turn north now. Rock's looking a mite splintery but if we we keep our feet lively we'll manage."

Raif could neither smell nor see smoke, but he did not doubt Addie's word. The cragsman slowed his pace as he waited for instruction. Breath ice caught in his eyebrows had frozen previously invisible hairs, rendering them white. "It would," he said, "be timely to do a spot of trade for some tea."

Surprised by this, Raif took a moment to sort his thoughts. He had assumed Addie would feel the same way he did, and want to avoid encounters with strangers. Yet how would they learn anything without speaking to people? Was Addie gently pushing him forward, forcing him to hold true to his oath? Raif puffed air through his lips. Maybe he just wanted tea.

"If they are Bluddsmen we cannot stop."

It was Addie's turn to be surprised. The cragsman thought a while, frowning so hard he dislodged ice from his eyebrows. He had to want to know the reason behind Raif's caution. "It'll be tricky," he conceded eventually. "I read animal tracks not woodsmoke. One man's fire smells like the next to me. By the time we get close enough to see who it is it might be too late."

Raif nodded, grateful for not being questioned. He could

not explain to Addie what had happened on the Bluddroad and how he was damned in both Blackhail and Bludd for it. Damned in Blackhail for deserting his clan on the field. Damned in Bludd for slaughtering the Dog Lord's grandchildren. "If it is clansmen do not use my name."

More ice was lost from Addie's eyebrows. "It might be easier to nip north."

Raif grinned maniacally. "Let's go get some tea."

Deer had been on the path recently—there was scat above the snow—and as they made their way east Raif distracted himself by hunting for game. Once he detected movement on the Rift floor itself, a young buck grazing on saxifrage, but decided not to shoot. The time needed to butcher an animal that large was too great. Besides he no longer had the stomach for the blood.

He'd just smelled the smoke.

Let them not be clansmen.

The tents were north of the Rift. There were two of them, raised in tandem, back-to-back. The tent hides were white auroch skins, the color of snow. Raif recognized their form, the point of stiffened fabric on the roof line and the heavy skirting to prevent drafts. Be careful what you wish for, he chided himself. These were not clannish tents. These tents belonged to the Sull.

The camp was situated on a ledge overhanging the ravine, and Raif realized the tent poles must have been driven into rock. Brush had been cleared at the rear for a distance of twenty feet. A horse corral raised from green moose bones contained at least one horse; Raif could see its beautiful sculpted head sticking out from above the windbreaker. As he and Addie drew closer something shrieked in the sky high above them. A glossy gray gyrfalcon circled them once, beat its wings, and then descended toward the tents. Two leather thongs hung with silver disks swung from its legs. Jesses.

"I warned you that by the time we got here it would be too late," Addie remarked. Raif could hear the edge of fear in his voice.

As they hiked on the ledge, one of the tent flaps opened and a man dressed in lynx fur stepped out. For an instant Raif thought it might be the Far Rider Ark Veinsplitter, and his heart leapt. *Ash. Here.* But then the man's head came up revealing different bone structure and facial features, and Raif felt foolish for having allowed himself that hope.

The Sull warrior walked to the center of the ledge and waited. He was tall and lean with long limbs and a long neck. His cheekbones were cut like diamonds and his skin was the color of mercury. He did not draw his sword. He didn't need to. The massive two feet handle rising above his right shoulder was warning enough. He watched Raif with cool gray eyes, barely sparing a glance for the cragsman.

When he was close enough to see the bloodletting scars on the man's neck, Raif spoke. *"Tharo a'zabo."* Greetings, my friend.

Addie Gunn's mouth fell open. The Sull warrior blinked eyelids so narrow they might have belonged to a wolf.

"Tharo, xanani," he replied. Greetings, stranger.

The two stared at each other. Dimly Raif was aware of the shabbiness of his clothes and weapons; the wax on his nose and ears, the foot of limp fabric at the end of his sword sheath, the rawhide strips holding back his hair. Yet the warrior's gaze barely registered them. He looked at only three things: the Orrl cloak, the Sull bow and Raif's eyes.

"Haxi'ma," he said finally.

Hearing the word Raif felt longing. Clansman. Maybe in another life he would be so again.

He shook his head. *"Nij,"* he said, reaching the limit of his Sull. "We are Rift Brothers."

The switch into Common made the Sull warrior easier, as if it somehow lessened the threat, and he relaxed his weight, allowing his heels to make full contact with the rock.

"I'm Addie Gunn," Addie said, stepping abreast of Raif. "And this is my friend Deerhunter. I wish you well this day and hope we may do some trade."

How much does the cragsman know? Raif wondered.

Enough not to use any of Raif Sevrance's many names. Addie waited, chin up, toe tapping, eyebrows like frozen brambles.

The Sull warrior's mouth twitched once, and then he executed a bow with perfect animal grace. "I am Ilya Spinebreaker, and I welcome you to the camp of Yiselle No Knife. Come, let us take shelter. A quarter-moon rises this night." He did not wait on a response, simply turned and headed across the ledge to the farthest tent.

Raif and Addie exchanged a glance. "I'll bet they'll have some fine tea herbs," the cragsman said.

Three horses in the corral, Raif corrected himself as he followed the Sull warrior and Addie at a slower pace. A set of fresh tracks led northeast, the snow around the edges crumbly, not smooth like the other older tracks. One away then. A firewell had been built at the center of the ledge and sharpened staves thrust between the rocks held a bear carcass, skinned and drained of blood. Raif shivered, wished he and Addie had gone north.

The heat of the tent was dizzying and Raif immediately felt the blood rush to his head. His instinct was to strip off his cloak and sealskins and throw cold water over his face and neck, but this was not the place for that. Here he would have to burn.

Yiselle No Knife rose from her position of sitting, cross-legged on a prayer mat woven from indigo silk. She was slender and tall, with long hands and a narrow waist. Her skin was so pale it looked almost blue. Night-black hair was pulled back from her face, revealing the flawless features of a head carved in stone. She could have been sixty years old or less than thirty, so little did the smooth blue surface give away. The gyrfalcon that had inspected them earlier sat on a suede gauntlet at her wrist. Its claws had not been blunted and formed a row of six knives on the glove.

The bird watched Raif with cold black eyes ringed in yellow skin. Its breast feathers were lightly spotted and were plumped out in warning.

The Spinebreaker told Yiselle No Knife their names, and she spoke them back with bites of her teeth. Raif responded to the name "Deerhunter" and bowed.

She regarded him with a glimmer of disbelief. Her dress was formed from the skin of newborn calves that had been whitened with lead. The fabric was so fine he could see the individual outline of each breast. "Break bread with me," she invited, indicating with her free hand they should sit.

Raif and Addie sat on silk mats. Beneath them was bare rock.

To one side, a silver brazier containing rock fuel so pure it burned without smoke gave off light and heat. To the other side lay a thin silk mattress and a shoulder-high perch for the bird. The tent was full with four people. Raif could smell Yiselle No Knife's scent, the faint alien pungency of Sull.

No one spoke while she sat the bird and retrieved a small lacquered box from the shadowy apron of the tent. The Spinebreaker stood in front of the tent flap, in a position almost exactly behind Raif, meaning to make him feel watched. Yiselle pulled off her gauntlet, revealing a right hand subtly different than her left one. The fingernails sat higher and the fingers were leaner and slightly webbed. Raif wondered if this was the reason behind her name.

Kneeling opposite him and Addie she placed the box on the ground, opened it, and took out a tablet of moistureless bread. Placing the tablet in her left palm, she used her strange lean right hand to break it into pieces. She offered it first to Addie, then to Raif, then to the Sull warrior. "May the moon that brings harvest never fail," she said, and placed a crumb beneath her tongue.

Raif tried to swallow. The bread wouldn't go down and he had to let it sit at the back of his throat until it softened. Yiselle No Knife offered no water. Rising, she threw the remaining crumbs on the fire. They crackled like iron filings.

"What brings you east?" she asked Addie.

"Hunting," he said.

"It is not good. Perhaps you should turn back."

The heat of the fire peeled sweat from Raif's skin. Behind him he could hear the Spinebreaker's sword harness creaking.

"Lady," Addie said, "you seemed to have little trouble finding that fine bear draining above your campfire."

The gyrfalcon shrieked, sidling from one end of its perch to the other. Yiselle No Knife closed the lid on the box. "Your friend is injured," she told Addie. "The further you go the further you will have to return alone."

The bread set like cement in Raif's throat. At his side, Addie brushed a drop of moisture from the tip of his nose to give himself time to think. Raif wondered if it was icemelt from his eyebrows or sweat. "I'm keeping an eye on my friend. You need not trouble yourself on his behalf."

"Do you know how to start a stopped heart?"

Addie stood. "Lady, a sheepman can always recognize a wolf. I thank you for the bread, but I'll hear no more. Raif." The moment he spoke the word *Raif* he sucked back air. Yiselle No Knife's eyes glittered. Her gaze jumped to Raif.

"Come on, lad," Addie said hurriedly. Raif stood. The gyrfalcon made a queer chuffing sound.

Yiselle looked straight at Raif, her gaze piercing the shimmers that rose from the amethyst flames, and mouthed the words *Mor Drakka.* His Sull name.

"Escort them to the borders of our camp," she told the Spinebreaker. "They will never find *Mish'al Nij.*"

It was a relief to get out of the heat. The icy cold snapped Raif back to life, and he could not recall speaking a word in the tent. Ilya Spinebreaker marched them north, not east, across the ledge, and into the forest of crags and dwarfed spruce. The Sull warrior did not speak. When he reached whatever limit he found satisfactory he stopped walking. In a single breathtaking motion he drew his sword. Six feet of meteor steel sliced ice crystals forming in the air. The sound produced was like the crackle of the northern lights. Both Addie and Raif drew blades; Addie his thick-bladed hunter, and Raif the Mole's longknife.

If the Sull warrior had meant to kill them at least one of them would have been too late. Instead Ilya Spinebreaker used his deadly, beautiful sword with its crosshilts as wide a child's shoulders and its three-quarter moon pommel to point the way north.

They got the message. Addie led the way, scanning for a path that didn't exist. The spruce formed a continuous waist deep mat, and they waded into it like water, getting scratched by bristles and poked by frozen twigs. Pine needles stuck to Raif's cloak, pants and boots, glued on with sap and ice. Neither he nor Addie spoke. They knew each other well enough to agree on a basic plan: make their way onto the far side of the ridge where they would no longer be in sight or range of the Sull warrior, and then halt and speak.

The small white sun passed into the west as they made their way through the spruce forest. Once they saw the gyrfalcon, gliding high above them before swooping south to ride the thermals channeling along the Rift. Shadows lengthened and the air crisped. Raif swigged from his water bladder. He could hear Addie breathing. The ground had started rising and they were pushing themselves hard. Every step involved avoiding sharp branches likely to tear skin. The stench of pine sap was overpowering, and Raif could feel it working in his skull cavities like a drug.

By the time they crested the ridge the light was failing. Neither man looked back as they clambered over the limestone. The bottom two feet of Raif's Orrl cloak were black with needles. Addie's brown wool cowl looked worse. Muscles aching, breath whitening in explosive bursts, they descended the rocky bluff. It was growing too dark to see exactly what lay north, but Raif got the impression of black forests spreading over humpbacked ridges.

"We should stop," he said quietly, realizing he could no longer make out the way ahead.

"A wee bit further," Addie said, insistent. "There'll be somewhere to camp at the base."

The cragsman used his stick to feel the way. Raif followed, physically exhausted but filled with jittery mental energy. He wanted to grab Addie by the arm and cry, "Here is good."

After some fussing and sidetracking, the cragsman finally decided on a spot. He wasn't happy about it and he kicked several rocks aside and stamped down some low-growing spruce. As they walked Raif had been collecting cones and twigs for a fire, and now he squatted beneath the limestone undercut and built a loose fire. The pine boughs burned yellow, snapping and giving off thick smoke. Addie's heart wasn't in the tea-making and without ceremony he dumped the last of his herbs into the pot. As the water boiled he laid out the snipe eggs he'd found earlier, along with strips of smoked meat. The fat marbling the meat had started to turn green. "Eat," he said, his gray eyes fierce.

They pulled out their blankets and ate in silence with their gloves on. When they had finished, Addie collected the eggshells and dumped them on the fire. He was waiting, Raif realized.

Cupping the hot tin cup under his chin so the steam rolled over his face, Raif said, "I'm sorry, Addie."

Silence. The cragsman pulled a stick from the fire pile and started scraping pine needles from the sole of his boots. He did this for some time. Finally he said, "When a complete stranger knows more about my traveling companion than I do, that makes me look like a fool. I do not like looking like a fool."

Raif nodded, accepting the rebuke. "What do you want to know?"

"No," Addie shot back. "You tell *me* what I need to know. I'm not about to play question and answers. I'm too tired and too mad." Frustrated with the glueyness of the pine needles he threw away the stick.

Raif swallowed a mouthful of watery tea. The Sull bread was no longer stuck in his throat, but he could feel where it had scraped his tissue. "First. She was right—I am injured. Something is lodged in the shoulder muscle at the back of my heart. It's been there for a while, niggling. When the beast attacked me on the ledge I think its talons pushed it further in." *There.* He had said to Addie what he hadn't even been willing to admit to himself. Even as he spoke he could feel the tip of the *Shatan Maer*'s claw. A speck of blackest shadow hovering above his heart.

"Can we cut it out?" Addie asked.

Raif shook his head. "I showed it to the outlander. He said it should only be drawn out by someone with skill, like the Sull."

Addie thought on this statement. "It's a piece of . . . " Words failed him.

"Claw from one of the shadow beasts."

The cragsman's hand hovered above the place where he once kept his portion of powdered guidestone. "Aye. Aye," he said softly. Rousing himself to heartiness, he said, "Well you certainly won't get any help from her ladyship back there. She'd more than likely poke it all the way through."

Raif made himself smile. The tea had gone cold and the metal was now pulling heat from his hands through the gloves. He set it down. "The Sull do not love me. They call me *Mor Drakka*, Watcher of the Dead. It is told in their histories that one day a man bearing that name will bring about their extinction. They fear that man is me. Before I joined the Maimed Men I traveled the Storm Margin with . . . a friend. She was injured and two Sull Far Riders stepped in to save her life. They treated her well, helped her, but they could barely tolerate me. We parted from them, and then met up again later in Ice Trapper Territory. Someone drugged me. When I awoke in the morning my friend was gone. The Sull had taken her."

He let out a long breath. For months he had kept the story of what had happened to Ash to himself and to speak it was a kind of release. *Guard yourself,* she had warned as the drugs pulled him under. Why had she not said more?

On the opposite side of the fire, Addie Gunn nodded slowly and continuously in understanding. "No love lost between you and the Sull." A pinecone jumped from the fire and the cragsman rolled it back with the toe of his boot. Hot flames ignited it instantly. "But they need you, don't they? What you did with that beast on the ledge, the heart-kill, that's what they would have done. Only you do it different. Better."

A cragsman watches his sheep, Raif realized. No small thing must pass him by. Unsure how to reply, Raif just looked at Addie.

Addie looked back. He was still nodding. "They won't help you find what you're looking for."

"Not willingly. I search for a sword once wielded by their kings."

This made Addie stop nodding. "Gods, lad. You're walking a tricky path."

"You walk it with me."

The cragsman snorted. Air left his nostrils, froze, and then sizzled into mist when it hit the flames. "Where is this place we're heading."

We. Raif was glad in his heart to hear it. "It's named the Lake of Red Ice and I do not know where it is save that it lies somewhere to the east."

"That would explain why we were duck-marched north."

"Yes it would."

Both men grinned.

"She knew you by your name?" Addie asked, a question beneath the question.

"I made the mistake of telling the Far Riders my name. They also learned I was a clansman, from Blackhail." Raif tried not to think of the look in Yiselle No Knife's eyes as she had named him *Mor Drakka*. "Word must have spread." Reading the worry on the cragsman's face, he added, "She was close to guessing, Addie. She knew my name wasn't Deerhunter, knew I was clan and heading east."

Addie frowned. "Deerhunter. That was one god-awful name."

Raif laughed and after a moment Addie joined in, and they laughed so hard their bellies ached, rocking back and forth by the fire.

Soon after, huddled in blankets, greased rags over their faces, they slept. Raif roused himself once in the night to feed the fire. The sky was ablaze with stars. When he next awoke they were gone, and gray clouds were heading out from the north. It was past dawn. A lone raven was *kawing* at the top of the ridge.

Addie prepared a breakfast of cold meat and boiled water. "Where to?" he asked as they ate.

Raif looked at the clouds. Without meaning to, Yiselle No Knife had given him information. "Find us a path east," Raif said, standing, "any further north and we could lapse into the Want."

Beating ice and pine needles from their gear, they prepared to break camp and head into land ruled by the Sull.

THIRTY-FIVE

Mistakes

"Has the bruise gone?" Raina Blackhail asked Anwyn Bird, angling her face toward the light. The clan matron folded her arms over the chest and looked critically at all of Raina, not just the bruised section of skin on her cheek. "It's yellow."

Raina put out a hand toward her. "Do not say it, Anny. Who could I go running to?"

"Plenty. You could have started with Orwin Shank."

"His son has just died. How can I put another burden upon him?"

"Corbie Meese then."

"He has lost friends and comrades. His wife has still not risen from her confinement."

Anwyn looked fit to explode. High color flooded her face. "You cannot let Stannig Beade get away with this. You must speak up."

"And say what?" Raina cried. "The clan guide slapped me? He will deny it. He'll bring that sly girl in as a witness and she will confirm his story that I fainted and hit my head against the door." As she was speaking Raina thought she heard a sound coming from behind one of the loom tables, but was too agitated to fully register it. Probably a settling pedal. "I will not be believed. People will pity me. My word will no longer be relied upon. I will be *lessened*."

"Better lessened than dead."

The two women faced each other, shaking. They were standing in the widows' wall alone. Anwyn had chased off everyone earlier and then gone to fetch Raina, pulling her away from the task of packing a war-supply cart alongside other clan wives.

The hearthstone the room was named for was black with creosote and soot. A meager fire burned deep in the grate, and if no one tended it soon it would go out. There were logs enough in the firepile that lay heaped against one side of the chimney wall, but no one had bothered to add any in several hours. Not all of the shutters had been opened either and the light was patchy and gray. Less than twenty days the Scarpes had occupied this hearth—in direct defiance of the widows' wishes—and in that short time they had turned it from the prettiest and brightest chamber in the Hailhouse into a hovel. Handprints and filth on the distemper walls, ring-shaped burns on the floorboards where they'd set their cookstoves, a shutter left open so the snow came in and rotted the plaster, dog shit, food spills, smoke damage: the list went on. Someone had even stolen the big iron candleholder that had been suspended on a chain from the ceiling. Women looming and carding needed good light to work by in the winter months, and Brog Widdie had wrought that candleholder to relieve their eyes. No wonder the widows were reluctant to come back. Beade had ordered the worktables, looms, racks, embroidery hoops, drum carders and benches returned to their original places but he could not order the widows to sit at them and work.

Not yet anyway. Raina pushed her lips together. She knew at some point she would have to arrange the proper cleanup and retempering of the chamber, but right now she didn't have the strength necessary for issuing the dozens of orders needed to carry it out. Right now she wanted to keep her head low and exist in peace.

And she did not want Anwyn accosting her and trying to force her into action. It was easy for the clan matron; the weight she bore was less. She could retire to her kitchen, and have no one inspect, criticize, or challenge her as she carried out her work. Chief's wife was different. Every time she, Raina Blackhail, walked through the roundhouse gazes followed her, judging her every move, storing mistakes for malicious gossip, disapproving, pleading, snooping.

Muscles beneath Anwyn's large round face set into place as

she regarded Raina. "I will give you until supper tonight," she said, "to tell Orwin Shank in person what Stannig Beade did to you. If that hour passes without him knowing, I will visit him myself and tell him what you told me."

Raina inhaled sharply. Anwyn Bird could be hard as stone. Over twenty people worked in her kitchen and she was capable of bullying every one of them. *Now she wants to bully me.* Why did she push so much? What made her so sure she was right? Anwyn had not stood in front of the entire clan and watched as they willingly believed lies. All those months ago in the great-hearth Mace Blackhail had spun the tale of how he and his foster mother had succumbed to mutual lust in the Oldwood. Five hundred warriors had drunk up this outrageous lie.

Truth. Untruth. Didn't Anwyn know that the only thing that mattered in these circumstances was who could sound the most plausible? Stannig Beade was clan guide, practiced in the arts of oratory. He would know how to make his account seem reasonable. *Poor Raina. She was upset and I offered her a cup of malt. She drank it a little too quickly—you know how women are around hard liquor—and when she rose to leave she cried out in grief and fainted right by the door. Her cheek caught the iron bolt on the way down, isn't that so, Jani?*

Raina gazed into Anwyn's dark blue eyes and questioned why she did this. A memory of many moons back came to her, of a package slipped from Angus Lok's hand into Anwyn's belt while neither thought Raina was watching. It had happened in the little dairyshed at midwinter. Raina had known Angus Lok nearly as long as she had lived at Blackhail. Always when he came to visit he stirred things up. *I will be chief*, Raina had declared not long after he had last departed. He had told her things, she remembered. Stories of how Mace was treating his tied clansmen—things that only a Hailsman should have known.

Raina wondered if Anwyn was in cahoots with the ranger. Angus had not hidden his dislike of Mace Blackhail and Clan Scarpe. Perhaps he and Anwyn had grown weary of Raina's inaction. Perhaps they hoped to force conflict and oust Beade.

Or perhaps Anwyn was just worried about a friend. Raina searched her face. "Do not push me, Anny. There's no telling where it could lead."

Anwyn Bird did not soften. Her arms remained clamped to her chest. "Anywhere is better than here. You should have seen yourself the other night—you could barely speak you were so afraid. And yes, it was just a bruise and bruises heal. But what about next time? When a man shows himself capable of violence it is seldom the end of it. He has cowed you, Raina. Frightened you and made you shrink back. If you step out of line he will do it again. Stannig Beade is no clan guide and must be shown as such. We are many. We can send him back to Scarpe."

Almost Anwyn won her over, but the memory of what had happened in the greathearth was too raw. Stannig Beade, Mace Blackhail: Scarpes had sharp tongues. You could not win against them in spoken battle. It was true Hailsmen still outnumbered Scarpes in this house, but for clansmen to back the ousting of Beade they needed to believe Raina's version of events. Raina did not think she had the skills to persuade them. Certainly she had no evidence.

Anwyn saw the answer on her face. "After supper tonight I will go see Orwin Shank."

Raina felt prickles of tears behind her eyes and did not know why. She said, "You will not be rid of Beade so easily."

"Do not be so sure." The words were spoken so fiercely they created their own sense of gravity. Raina felt her heart and mind pull toward them, but stood firm. Having issued them Anwyn herself seemed incapable of further speech. Nodding with satisfaction, she turned on her heels and left.

Raina waited for herself to relax; waited but the sensation did not come. She looked around the widows' wall, at the carelessly placed looms and benches, the Scarpe filth. *I should do something about cleaning this place up. The new widows deserve better.* She did not want to be here though, and followed Anwyn's tracks to the door. Random thoughts were firing in her head. She wondered what use a great big cast iron candleholder was to anyone without a high-ceilinged chamber to hang it. She worried she had parted badly with Anwyn.

As she headed downstairs it occurred to her that the least she could have done was open all the shutters in the widows' hearth and let in some fresh air to drive out the stench of Scarpe. What had Stannig Beade told her? *"Restrict your activities to caring for the bereaved and the sick"*? Raina slowed her descent. He had meant to offend her with small work and she had allowed herself be offended. Since when had caring for the widows of slain warriors become offensive to her? Had she become too proud? Unsure of the answer, she decided to go back and throw open the shutters. Maybe she would move some of the looms to their proper places. They were complicated arrays of harnesses and treadles, but generally more air than wood. A strong woman could push them into motion. Feeling her thoughts begin to settle, she headed up the stairs.

And met Jani Gaylo coming down. Instantly, Raina remembered the noise behind the corner loom. *Little mice with weasels' tails.* Stepping into the center of the stone step, she forced the red-haired maid to walk around her. Raina stared at her, waiting for the girl to meet her eye, but Jani Gaylo kept her pretty head tucked low as she passed.

Oh gods. Was she up there, listening?

Raina continued climbing the stairs, but her sense of purpose had gone. What had she and Anwyn said? Things that did not bear overhearing by anyone in this clan. Uneasy, she let herself into the widows' wall. No sign of any disturbance. But would there be? Quickly she unhooked the closed shutters and pushed them open. The outside air was cold and still, crisp with frost. When she reached the corner loom, she halted. It was one of the large upright frames and a panel of bright blue wool was nearly completed on the harness. That was where Jani Gaylo could have hidden, behind that taut yard of cloth.

Abruptly, Raina turned away. She would not think about it anymore. What was the point? *I'll go and saddle Mercy. Get away from this unsafe house.*

Hurrying down the stairs she pretended to be busy, waving away those who hailed her and frowning in a preoccupied manner as if she were thinking about hop toasting, milk churning or some other household task. Things had changed since news had arrived from Ganmiddich, and the house was subdued. Men got a little drunker at night. Women had trouble applying themselves to everyday work and would sit morosely and chat. Everyone was waiting on more news. Raina had heard a rumor that Stannig Beade had begun to cut hearts from the new Hailstone.

As she crossed the strange gods-charged space of the east hall, she realized that she had abandoned her task of loading the supply wagon. Orwin Shank had arranged for a cart to be sent south with an armed escort, and Merritt Ganlow and Raina had been in charge of filling it with food, ale, blankets and other home comforts for the Hail armies camped north of Ganmiddich. Merritt would not be pleased. As far as the head widow was concerned, Raina could barely do anything right these days.

Raina suspected she had a point. Ever since Stannig Beade had hit her she had not been able to think clearly. Her attention jumped from one thing to another like a bouncing ball, and she did not like to be alone inside in the house. *Jittery* was the word she would use to describe herself. It was the first time she had ever felt such a way in her life.

She did not stop to admire the newly completed arch that led east from the roundhouse. The wall scaffolding was in the process of being reconfigured to support the building of the guidehouse and the east ward. Work crews were taking their afternoon break, and men were sitting on chunks of rock and upturned lime barrels, gnawing on bird bones and drinking foamy brown ale. Longhead was the only one still working. The head keep was squatting on a cracked paving stone, drawing a line in chalk.

"Raina."

She was surprised to hear him call her name, and considered pretending not to hear him. The memory of their last meeting together in the hayloft was not a good one. Longhead had admitted to letting himself be influenced by Stannig Beade. The guide had warned the head keep that Raina might start fussing if she were told about the plans for the new ward. And Longhead had lapped it up. It was a kind of betrayal, that setting aside of all the years they'd spent working together for the good of this house. If anyone should have given her the benefit of the doubt it should have been Longhead.

Halting before him, she was cool. "I have not much time."

The head keep rose to standing. He was dressed in his usual

attire of a leather work apron over burlap pants and a brown wool shirt. Chalk from his fingers was transferred to his forehead as he wiped the hair from his eyes. "Where you off to?"

Raina thought the question impertinent. "I have work in the stables," she lied.

"I'll walk a ways with you."

"Very well," she agreed huffily, realizing she had misjudged the nature of his question. Longhead did not query where she went or what she did. He just wanted to talk to her alone.

If the head keep had noticed her agitation, he made no show of it, and guided her between piles of logs, cut stones and lime barrels with respectful attention, touching her arm lightly to prevent her from stepping into puddles of tar and gray sludge. Snow had been cleared to a distance of thirty feet around the roundhouse, and only when they had reached the end of the clearing did Longhead speak.

"You told me I should inform you when Stannig Beade wants things done in the house," he said, wasting no time on small talk, "and I think perhaps you were right."

Raina's boots punched through the melted then refrozen snow, leaving deep pits. She did not trust herself to say anything—speak and she would make a mistake—so she kept her silence and watched her feet.

Longhead's oversize jaw came up as he squinted at the clouds. "Beade has asked me to prepare your old chambers for the Scarpe chief, Yelma Scarpe. She will visit next month."

Raina's mouth fell open. Of all the things Longhead could have told her she would never have imagined this. The Scarpe chief, here? It was so astonishing she didn't know what to think. Glancing up, she saw the head keep was watching her carefully. She closed her mouth. Had he been looking at the remains of her bruise?

"It's not fitting that she stay in your chambers," he said, shaking his head. "A chief's wife must be allowed superiority in her clan."

I do not care about my chambers, Raina wanted to tell him, not kindly, but didn't. She could see that he was offended as a Hailsman. "When will she come?"

Longhead seemed relieved that she had finally spoken and

jumped to answer her question. "When the weather clears. Beade says she will not travel while snow is on the ground."

Let it freeze hard then. Aware that Longhead was waiting for her opinion, she searched for something comforting to say. And found she had nothing to give. Breaking away from him, she murmured, "You must do as Beade bids."

Raina made her way toward the stables and did not look back. She had no wish to see disappointment on the head keep's face.

The young groom whom she had spoken with during her last visit to the stables helped her saddle Mercy. Raina asked his name and was informed it was Duggin Lye. He was good with the chestnut mare, speaking to her in soft clicks as he tightened her belly cinch. Raina was glad to have him there, for Mercy knew all was not right with her mistress and was restive. Duggin's presence seemed to calm her, and she did not fight the bit. "I took the creek trail myself this morning," Duggin said to Raina, making sure the nose strap was seated properly. "If you're wanting a fair run you couldn't do much better. The Oldwood's sparkly with ice."

Silent, she took the reins from him. The boy had probably spent most of the day alone with the horses and was eager to talk. How would he know that that Oldwood was not a word she loved to hear? She made an effort. "I believe I will go north instead."

Duggin Lye, who had to be all of sixteen and had the black-heads to prove it, looked at her with some wisdom. "North's best when you're needing to clear your mind."

Raina walked Mercy onto the court, mounted her, and trot-ted around the outbuildings. She could smell pigs in their sties, and the loamy sweetness coming from the dairyshed as the cows were being milked. Mercy trod frozen cow pats and clumps of hay into the snow. She was glad to be out and her head was up, but her ears kept flicking back toward her rider.

Deciding she would not think for a while, Raina kicked Mercy into a canter. They were clear of the outbuildings now and free to find a path north. Some old bit of wall stuck up above the snow and Mercy seemed keen to jump it so Raina gave the horse her head. It was then, in midair with her butt no longer in full contact with saddle leather, that Raina began to feel better. The landing was bracing and her spine felt it all the way up to her neck. All the old air ejected from her lungs and she had to fill them with new, outside air instead. This was what she needed. Too much inside, too many whispers, too many calls upon the ragged little bit of herself that was left. When chiefing got too much for Dagro he had simply taken off. A man could do that, go hunting and have everyone agree that it was a worthy thing and that when he got back he would be renewed. During the winter longhunt season Dagro might take off for weeks. He would share a tent with old Meth Ganlow, Merritt's husband, and the two of them would hunt during the day and get drunk as donkeys each night. There'd be dumb tricks—pants would be dipped in the lake and frozen, straight arrows replaced with ones fiendishly steamed into curves— there'd be earnest talk about the best way to make jerky, and someone would always end up getting lost in the woods, initiating the kind of heroic search and rescue that could be bragged about for days.

It was a release, Raina realized now. Dagro had both needed and deserved it. He did not lead the hunt. Even if he had possessed the expertise he wouldn't have wanted to. Let Tem Sevrance or Meth Ganlow do that.

Raina dug her heels into Mercy's belly, whipping her into full gallop. Snow sprayed as high as the saddle and year old saplings were crushed under hoof, releasing the scent of pine. Spying a trapping path running alongside the Leak, Raina guided Mercy northwest. The Leak was running; a thread of crystal clear water overhung by ledges of crackled ice. Tall, desiccated grasses clumped on the bank, and Raina could see peeps of green where the new year's growth had started. Mercy seemed to enjoy flattening them, even going so far as leaving the path to get to them, and this made Raina laugh. Poor plants. First they had to put up with late snows and sudden frosts, and now along comes a horse and squashes them. It was definitely better being Raina Blackhail than a stationary clump of grass.

She laughed even harder at that. And it felt good. Her fine wool cloak and dress were too skimpy for such icy conditions, and she had not thought to bring gloves, but it hardly mattered.

Raina Blackhail had been Raina Kenrick once—and the Kenrick girl rarely dressed for the cold. *"Don't be fussing her,"* Uncle Burdo would tell her mother. *"As long as she keeps moving she'll stay warm."*

Raina kept moving, first along the stream and then north onto one of the trapping paths that led into the forest. Mercy was happy to run. When Dagro had purchased her as a filly from a horse trader at the Dhoone Fair he had been told she was "one-sixteenth Sull." Apparently this number had sealed the deal. Dagro had joked about it later, saying that it meant one of Mercy's ears and half a knee joint were Sullish, but Raina could tell he'd been secretly pleased. It meant that all of Mercy's offspring would be one in thirty-two parts Sull. Yet in the end he'd only let her dam the once. She was Raina's horse by then.

As they approached the first stand of oldgrowth pines, Raina slowed Mercy to a trot. Beyond those trees lay the great northern forest of Blackhail and you had to be in a certain mind and properly equipped to safely enter. An unlined wool cloak would not do. It was one thing to ride carelessly along meadowland. Another thing entirely to take to the woods. Glancing at the sky, she realized it would be dark within the hour and she needed to be heading back. For all she knew Merritt Ganlow was still fuming by the supply cart, wondering what had happened to the goosedowns Raina had promised to deliver four hours earlier.

And then there was Anwyn Bird. As Raina turned Mercy south she wondered what time constituted "supper." It would be after dark certainly. But whose supper exactly? Anwyn's? Orwin's?

Raina thought she should get a move on, and kicked Mercy into a brisk trot. The top layer of snow hardened as the temperature dropped and every hoof fall made an explosive *crack*.

It was easier at first to think about Longhead. Five days back she had asked the head keep to come to her if Beade took any further action concerning the Hailhouse. Today he had done just that. In return she had been short and dismissive, when perhaps she should have been grateful. Longhead was no friend of Beade's. Not informing her about the new ward and guidehouse had been a simple error in judgment. Longhead was

Longhead: he wanted to get things done. He had come to her hoping she would take a problem off his hands so he could keep working and not have to worry about the distressing events happening in the clan. She had been no help to him. Raina blew air from her nostrils, cogitating. He had caught her at a bad moment. Tomorrow she would seek him out and see if there wasn't something they could do. With all the damage to the east wall, the broken well shafts, the disturbed underground springs, it would be regrettable, but hardly surprising, if the chief's wife's chambers were to suddenly and unexpectedly flood.

Smiling softly, Raina patted Mercy's neck. Detecting a subtle shift in her rider's spirits, the mare tossed her head and executed some fancy footwork that took her sideways as well as forward. Raina had always wondered who had taught her that. Maybe it was in her Sull blood.

It was growing dark as they rejoined the path along the Leak. Raina forced herself to think of Anwyn, and found little to like about their conversation in the widows' wall. Anwyn Bird was her oldest and dearest friend. Even if she wanted to rid Blackhail of Stannig Beade it did not change the fact of her concern. That night after Raina had fled the chief's chamber it had been Anwyn who banged on the door of her cell, Anwyn who demanded entry, Anwyn who had looked so murderous upon seeing Raina's inflamed face that Raina thought the clan matron might march through the roundhouse and punch Stannig Beade in the head. It was Anwyn who brought the salves and cool water, and informed people the next morning that Raina had a fever and might be abed for a few days.

It was Anwyn Bird, not Raina Blackhail, who had to watch the bruise turn purple and black.

Raina raised her hand to her cheek, touching the patch of skin that had come in contact with Stannig Beade's fist. A slight tenderness still remained.

He has cowed you, Raina.

It was the truth, she had been cowed. Raina had never told Anwyn what had happened in the Oldwood, but the clan matron must have suspected something. The evening after the wedding had taken place, Anwyn had brought Raina her bride's cup in the greathearth. "What's done is done," she had said, handing Raina the traditional drink of milk, bittersweet and honey. "We'll just have to make the best of it."

Raina thought of those words, trying to remember the exact expression on Anwyn's face. There had been stoicism and . . . disappointment. It was as if Anwyn was disappointed in Raina for not speaking up to defend herself against Mace's claims. Had she known a few words could have stopped all the misery?

Seeing the safelamps being lit outside the stables, Raina picked up Mercy's pace. Orwin Shank had been the one who called her in to account the night after Mace Blackhail had raped her. Orwin had been flustered, upset by what Mace had told him, anxious to get the whole mess over and done with, yet still deeply respectful of Raina. If she had spoken up at that moment, told Orwin the truth, would he have believed her? The answer would not come. It was a different time; Blackhail's chief had just died, Mace was well regarded in the clan and was proving himself capable of taking Dagro's place. The question that mattered now was: would Orwin take her word over Stannig Beade's?

She was surprised by how foolish the answer made her feel. *We are many*, Anwyn had said.

Yes, Raina mouthed. *We are.*

Duggin Lye was lighting the last of the lamps as Raina and Mercy trotted onto the court. Thrusting the burning edge of the torch into the cobbles, he extinguished the flame.

"Take her from me, will you?" Raina asked him, dismounting. "I don't want to be late for supper."

Coming forward to take the reins, he said something Raina did not understand. "Supper's already late."

Assuming it was the grumble of a hungry boy who had gone too long between meals, she ignored it. Dashing across to the east wall, she waved brief acknowledgments to the two men who were spreading burlap sheets over the timber piles and lime barrels. They must be expecting snow in the night. Always when you walked through the east hall there was that jump of metal next to your skin. Raina was expecting it, and had her hand ready on her knife.

It was only when she reached the entrance hall that she began to suspect something was wrong. A roundhouse had an atmosphere, you could read it in the way people sat and stood, the number of torches burning, the doors left open, the smells, the smoke, the noise. It was early evening and it took Raina a few moments to understand and then catalog the absences. The luntman had skimped on his rounds and only a quarter of the torches were burning. Too many doors were open and there was an unfamiliar crosscurrent of drafts. It was too quiet for suppertime when normally the great clangor from the kitchen rang through the house, drowning out the noise of the forge.

And there was no supper smell.

The world spun on that one simple fact, passing from light into darkness as it moved beneath Raina's feet.

Raina broke into a run.

She knew.

People tried to stop her, but she slapped them away and hissed at them. *Don't. Don't. Don't*, she warned, not knowing if she said the words out loud. When she entered the kitchen Corbie Meese came forward to intercept her, but she would not have it. How she stopped him from halting her progress was something she would never know. Down the little steps she went, hesitating only for a moment when she reached the bottom. Two ways led from the stairs: one toward the game-room, and the other to the cells and supply rooms. Orwin Shank stood guard outside Anwyn's chamber. When he saw her he shook his head and told her, "No, my sweet lamb, come no further."

But she could not stop moving and he did not possess the might necessary to halt her and she entered the room where Anwyn Bird lay dead.

THIRTY-SIX

A Bear Trap

Snow fell as they worked their way east. On the first day it fell lightly, a shimmer of crystals in the air in the late afternoon before dark. The day after it did much the same, but the next morning it began more heavily. A persistent wind blew from the east and it was hard to keep warm, but at least it was not bleakly cold. On the fourth day it was warm enough that the ground snow melted . . . but still it managed to snow. The fifth day was different, colder. The snow had come down in hard, glassy pellets; Raif imagined the name for them was "ice." Walking on them was like walking on marbles and they'd headed north into the spruce forest to avoid them. The next day had passed without snow, but Addie said it couldn't reliably be trusted and it was either snowing somewhere very close or would spring upon them while they slept. He was right, for when they woke this morning a steady snow was falling, and half a foot had accumulated overnight.

They were growing accustomed to sleeping through it. Though it had been strange not to be able to *find* the fire let alone relight it. Addie had been stoic. "Next time we'll set it on a stone to keep the heat in." The good thing was the trees were no longer stunted and could be bivouacked for shelter so at least they had some protection from the weather. It meant that camp took longer to set up so they had to stop earlier in the day but they both agreed it was a worthwhile trade. Being snowed on while you slept was an experience not unlike being buried alive. In ice.

Food was growing scarce and the low grade hunting afforded

by being constantly afoot rendered little beyond ptarmigan and molting hares. Snow had driven anything larger into hiding. Given time Addie could prepare a decent bird, but he didn't have any love for plucking and usually assigned feather duty to Raif. Raif seemed to recall that Tem had known a couple of ingenious ways to pluck birds, but couldn't for the life of him remember any of them—one might have had something to do with mud. Oddly enough it was the lack of tea that was felt the most. The ritual of boiling water and steeping the herbs was something they both missed. Addie still insisted on boiling and serving water, and had collected various twigs and leaves along the journey in an attempt to conjure up new kinds of tea. So far saxifrage, goatsbeard, hagberry and dead nettle had delivered various watery, yellowy weed-tasting teas. Addie was still hopeful. Legend had it that a plant existed called trapper's tea that bloomed with white flowers in high summer and could be found growing amidst rocks. The drink produced from crushing and then steeping its leaves was said to be so delicious that Addie could only talk about in a whisper. "Day we find it there'll be some fine drinking," he'd murmured more than once.

Addie had grown chilblains on his nose and hands and was having a spot of bother with his feet. Every night he would dry livermoss on a stick above the fire and every morning he would stuff the springy filaments into the toes of his boots. The cragsman moved no slower for his troubles, but Raif had seen him hesitate a few times before starting a sharp descent, and then lean heavily on his stick. Raif's own feet were holding up. Both he and Addie wore double layers of hareskin socks that kept out all but the worst of the cold, and Raif's ancient hand-me-down boots fitted him so well that there was little chafing. When he touched his face he felt patches of hard and tender skin and he thought there might be some frost damage, but as long as it didn't hurt he didn't spare it much thought.

It was the shoulder that bothered him. Slowly, steadily, over the course of the past seven days Raif had felt it burning a hole in his chest. He'd once watched as Brog Widdie proofed the temperature on a batch of blister steel he had been firing. With his long, crab-craw tongs the master smith had formed a small portion of the red hot metal into a ball, and then pulled it from the fire. Immediately he dropped the ball onto his proofing block and watched how quickly the molten metal burned through the green wood. The ball would blacken and hiss, igniting a ring of flames as it burned a hole through the wood. That's what the *Shatan Maer*'s claw had begun to feel like to Raif; a piece of molten metal incinerating his flesh.

"Do you know how to start a stopped heart?" Yiselle No Knife had asked Addie Gunn in the Sull camp by the Rift. The words haunted Raif, the tone of them, the lightness yet certainty in her voice. She had meant to shock both of them, him and Addie, and she succeeded better than she realized. Until she spoke Raif had managed to squash it into the back of his thoughts. The shoulder hurt. It had grown worse since the creature on the rimrock had smashed him in the back. It ached, sometimes a lot. That was it. Now it loomed constantly in his thoughts, and he couldn't tell if he was *imagining* that it was growing worse, or if it really was growing worse. Either way Yiselle No Knife had won a victory. She hadn't prevented them from heading east as she had intended, but she had intimidated them. The Sull were experts at that.

"Let's head a mite south," Addie mumbled, surprising Raif by speaking for the first time since they'd broken camp earlier that morning. "After those icestones we drifted too far north."

Raif nodded his agreement. They were both wearing face masks roughly shaped from hareskins, and as it was difficult to talk they'd taken to signing basic instructions and requests. It was snowing in big flakes that were as light and airy as dandelion fluff. The clouds were thickly gray and did not appear to be moving. Underfoot the snow formed complicated layers, by turns mushy, grainy, gravelly and plain hard. Some drifts were as deep as Addie's waist, but generally the cover lay between one and one and a half feet. They'd been lucky with the afternoon thaw two days back: it had prevented the snow from becoming too deep.

Neither Addie nor Raif no longer had much idea of where they were. Most mornings they would align themselves with the rising sun, pick a point far in the distance—a stand of big trees, a ridge, a hummock, a frozen pond—and head toward it. If they reached it before dark they'd pick something else, correcting either north or south depending on how Addie felt about the going. This morning Addie had picked a knoll that stuck out above the forest canopy and glinted with blue-green lenses of ice. Now they slowed their pace while the cragsman chose a second target farther south.

Hiking onto a rock, Addie surveyed the land ahead. His brown wool cloak was deeply ringed with pine sap and his boots had been poked so many times by rocks and branches that the leather looked like it had been chewed on by dogs. Never one to waste much time, the cragsman made his decision, and then carefully lowered himself onto the floor of the slope. "Stream. This way," he said, striking a new path that took them down into the trees.

The cedar forests to the south formed a green lake on the valley floor, leaving the slopes and ridges free for other, scrappier trees. Spruce and white pines took the ground the cedars did not want, but even they stayed clear of the higher slopes. Forest fires and bog rot had killed successive generations of trees and there were many fallen logs and standing deadwoods. For the past day and a half Raif and Addie had walked above the northern treeline, following a goat path along the rocks, but now they entered woodland.

Light dimmed and the air grew colder. The snow underfoot was patchy, but you could hear the great weight of it in the trees. Boughs creaked and whirred as they strained to hold their loads. No decent wind in several days meant the trees had been given little relief. Some pines had bent in the middle, forming white humps that looked like bridges. Branches had failed and snapped. Entire trunks had split in two. Raif suggested they pick up their pace. Addie grumbled but agreed.

It was hard to know exactly where they lay in relation to Bludd. At some point in the east, Bludd forests melted into forests claimed and patrolled by the Sull. Bludd was a huge clanhold, and its northeastern reaches were wild and barely populated. Occasionally Raif and Addie saw smoke, but after the encounter with Yiselle No Knife and the Spinebreaker, neither had managed to work up sufficient desire to investigate. Raif assumed they were still above Bludd's borders, but couldn't be sure. Addie had an understandable fear of traveling too far north—the Want lay that way and you might simply blink and find yourself in the middle of it, unable to get out—and tended to steer them due east and southeast.

The Rift no longer existed as an unmissable marker that divided the continent into the clanholds and the lands of the barren north. The great fissure in the earth had narrowed to a canyon filled with debris, then a gulch choked with willow, then a simple gash in the rock. "It's still there," Addie had said, wagging his head at the ground when Raif asked, "but now you have to look for it. With all this snow we could be standing right upon it and wouldn't even know."

Whenever Raif thought of Addie's words he couldn't help looking at his feet. He glanced down now as they made their way through a stand of hundred-year cedar. Nothing underfoot only pine needles and snow.

"Whoa, laddie," Addie said, gripping his arm.

Raif looked at him, startled.

"Nearly lost your footing then." Above the face mask, Addie's gray eyes searched Raif's. "Probably hit a tree root."

A question lay behind the statement. Raif blinked. He felt as if he'd missed something. He'd been looking down at his feet and then . . . then . . . Addie had spoken.

"Rest a minute," Addie said, clenching Raif's elbow like a vise. "Take a mouthful of water."

Considering Addie had him in an arm lock, Raif didn't have much choice. His chest felt strange. Tight. Inside his boarskin glove all five fingers of his left hand were numb. When he held the water bladder above his head to drink, strange tingles passed along his arm to his shoulder.

Addie watched him. Raif knew what the cragsman was thinking. He tried to formulate a reply to the inevitable questions but couldn't think of anything reassuring that wouldn't be a lie.

Snow sifted down to the forest floor as they stood facing each other, silent. Last year's ferns poked through the ground cover like rusted iron bars. Finally Addie said, "Dead men don't fulfill oaths." Angry, he set off along the path on his own.

Raif bit off his glove, swiveled his arm back and rubbed his shoulder with numb fingers. A point deep in his chest felt hollow. Walking back along the course of his and Addie's footsteps, he searched for the exact spot where he'd looked down to check for the Rift. After a minute or two he thought he found it. His footsteps had been steady, evenly paced and all pointing in the same direction, and then one—just one—went awry. The toe of his left boot had made contact at a slightly different angle to the previous steps and the outside edge that led from it formed a wedge shape as if Raif had been in the process of making a sudden turn. There was no heel mark.

That lack of contact turned Raif cold. It was the difference between life and death.

Was that what a heart-kill felt like?

Nothing.

Springing into motion, Raif followed Addie along the path.

They traveled in silence for the rest of the day, stopping once to eat the remains of last night's ptarmigan and search a likely patch of undergrowth for eggs. The cragsman made a point of not watching over Raif, though if it was possible to keep an eye on someone without looking at them that was what Addie was doing. Raif felt odd. Light and not quite sane. He kept seeing the failed footstep and hearing Traggis Mole say, *Swear it.*

They reached the stream about an hour before dark. Snowmelt was running in its middle, skirling over rocks and jammed pine cones. They could have jumped it easily—it wouldn't have even needed a run up—but Addie set about walking upstream. The snow was thicker here and there were more dead trees. Raif thought he caught a whiff of woodsmoke, but when he looked to Addie to confirm it the cragsman's face gave nothing away.

"Here," Addie said, coming to a halt a few minutes later. "It's as good a place as any to set camp."

Three big cedars formed a thick triangle of cover hard along the bank. A root from the largest tree cut right across the stream, forming a spillway where the water widened and slowed before tipping over the root branch and continuing on its way. Addie's gaze dared Raif to find fault. Raif did not. Squatting by the spillway, he stripped off his gloves, scooped up two handfuls of water and threw them over his face. The iciness was startling but it didn't alter the lightness in his head.

That night he did not sleep. He suspected Addie didn't get much rest either, for the cragsman had made himself a bed out of pine boughs that crunched every time he rolled over—and they crunched a lot. They were both short-tempered as they took their morning drink of boiled water. Addie told Raif to fill the waterskins with stream water and when Raif didn't jump to the task quick enough for his liking he found fault. Raif dropped the skins in the snow and went for a piss. How was it his fault that he had ended up with a piece of shadow lodged next to his heart?

Addie's spirits improved as the morning wore on. For once it didn't snow and it looked as if the wind might break up the clouds. After they crossed the stream they decided to head out of the trees. Snow dumps were beginning to happen and the thought of being caught under a tree shedding a half-ton of snow was not comforting. Occasionally Addie would dart from the path, checking ground cover, snowbanks and rock piles for nests.

"Raif. Take a look at this."

Raif had gone on ahead while Addie investigated the area surrounding a recently fallen cedar, and Raif had to backtrack to join him. He found the cragsman staring at one of the grounded cedar bows, holding his stick above the foliage like a spear. Only when Raif drew abreast of him did he see it: a cast iron tooth-jawed bow trap built to spring a bear.

"Nearly stepped on the paddle. It was hidden in the branches." Addie shook his head at it. "Fetch me a log. I'm going to trigger it."

Raif pried off one of the thick lower branches of the fallen cedar, and then watched as Addie jabbed it against the paddle. *Crack.* The branch was crushed to wood chips as the jaws snapped shut.

"Bastards," Addie said quietly. "Lost two sheep to traps like this." Shaking his head, he picked up his walking stick and turned to Raif. "At least now we know we can head to the smoke."

"It's not Sull?"

"They wouldn't insult big game by trapping it. It's not clannish by the looks of it either, though you never know. Could have been traded. What I can say is that men who set this—and it was recently set, see how there's no snow between the coils— are cowards and varmints. And I'll take them over Sull any day."

Raif opened his mouth to speak, but Addie halted him by raising his stick.

"No. We need some medicine for that . . . that thing in your back. And so help me Gods I'm going to trade for some tea."

Raif didn't have the heart to tell him that he didn't think medicine would work.

It didn't take Addie long to find the trappers' path, and they followed it south and a little west through the trees. A cube of spat chewing curd, an apple core, and a ragged piece of leather fringe were duly noted by the cragsman along the way. After holding the trail for the better part of an hour they knew they were getting close. The smell of woodsmoke was so strong you could taste it in your mouth, and the *chunk* of logs being split with an ax rang through the woods.

Addie wanted to continue down the path, but Raif stopped him. "Let's approach the camp from the back."

"Ain't neighborly," Addie said, by way of agreement.

The trappers' camp consisted of a large A-frame tent over- hung with moose felts, two large wooden stretching frames for big game, a log pile and chopping block, a firepit hung with cookirons and a smoking rack, two cross sections of tree trunk that looked like they were used as seats, various cache bags strung from the nearest cedar and a butchering circle where the snow was trampled with blood. The man who was quartering logs with a small hand ax was tall and rangy. His skin was the color of red clay.

"Trenchlander," Addie murmured. "Poor cousins of the Sull."

They were crouching amidst a small copse of cedar saplings about ninety feet behind the camp. Raif watched the axman carefully, reassuring himself that the man's rhythm hadn't changed and that his focus remained on his work. Raif won- dered about the location of horses and pack animals, but then decided the A-frame was large enough to hold livestock.

"Bear pelts fetch a tidy sum in Hell's Town," Addie whis- pered, "and they sell the gall bladders to traders from the south."

Raif nodded, barely listening. He was fairly sure now that the axman was unaware of their presence. That was good. It meant he lacked the exquisite senses of purebred Sull. "He's probably not alone," Raif said quietly.

"Aye. Maybe his friends're off walking the trap rounds. Shall we?"

Raif felt a sudden twinge in his shoulder, but ignored it. "Lead the way."

To disguise the fact they had sneaked up on the Trenchlanders' camp, they made their way partway to the front and then created a great deal of noise stomping through the remaining trees and snow. Addie began talking in a loud voice, telling some story about the time he'd got drunk in a stove-house and singed off most of his hair. Abruptly, he halted the tale midway and hailed, "Friend! Good day to you!"

The axman had stopped chopping but he still held his ax. He had sunken cheeks and there was slack skin around his jaw. Frostbite had rotted the tips of both his ears. Like Ilya Spinebreaker before him, he inspected Raif's cloak and bow. Addie put up his hands, elbowing Raif along the way to do the same. Raif briefly showed the man his bare palms. "Trade," Addie proclaimed loudly, rubbing his thumbs and fingers together. "Fair exchange of goods."

Finally the man reacted. Thumping the flat of the ax in his free hand, he said, "Tree. Over there." He waited for them to locate it with their gazes. "Tall man. Stick sword. Then talk trade."

His accent was heavy and his command of Common incomplete, but Raif understood him well enough. Leaving Addie's side Raif crossed over to the tree and drew Traggis Mole's longknife. With a light jab he embedded the point in the bark. At eye level. Turning on his heel he locked gazes with the Trenchlander.

"Done," Addie declared.

The Trenchlander did not allow them the fellowship of the tent and indicated they sit by the fire on sawn-off logs. Addie was offended by this lack of hospitality, but Raif preferred it. This way he could keep an eye on his blade. As the Trenchlander unhooked the pot suspended above the flames, Raif heard the sound of braying coming from inside the A-frame. Possibly a donkey or a mule. Once the lidded pot was at the Trenchlander's feet, he deftly tossed three iron thumb cups into the fire. After a few seconds he fished them out one by one with his notched stick. When he poured broth into them it sizzled and spat, shooting out the aroma of meat and peppery herbs. The Trenchlander looked from Addie to Raif as the cups cooled.

Realizing he was expecting some courtesy from them, Raif said, "We are grateful for the hospitality of your hearth."

It was sufficient. The Trenchlander nodded, placed the cups inside larger, leather cups and handed them to Addie and Raif. As was custom in such encounters, the guests drank first. Whatever it was—broth, tea, ale—it was good and spicy. Addie drank his quickly and then studied the dregs.

"Trade," the Trenchlander said.

A moment passed where Raif realized he possessed nothing he would give in trade. The Orrl cloak. The Sull bow. The stormglass. Traggis Mole's longknife. A man would have to kill him to get their hands on any one of them. Addie however seemed prepared for this and slid out one of his spare hareskin socks from his gear belt. A single swinging motion was sufficient to produce the clink of coins.

The Trenchlander waited. He was dressed in cut deerhide that had been sewn together with crude black stitches and an overtunic of black curly-haired sheepskin that was so stiff it hung from his shoulders like a piece of steamed wood. He was not young, and he had several broken veins in his eyes, and his facial hair was showing gray. The Sull blood showed through in the deep cavities beneath his cheekbones and the faint metallic sheen to his red skin.

"Foxglove," Addie said, speaking very precisely. "Lily of the valley. Motherwort. Broom."

He was asking for heart medicines, Raif realized. Before tea herbs. The clanholds had lost a good man when they cast out Addie Gunn.

The Trenchlander immediately nodded at the words *foxglove* and *broom* but the other two did not move him. He tapped his chest, indicating that he knew the herbs' uses, and said, "Flylessi." A nod toward the trees suggested that this might be the name of his trapping companion.

Addie nodded right back. The two were getting along like a house on fire. Raising his cup-within-a-cup, the cragsman said, "Did a fine job with the brewing."

For a wonder the Trenchlander smiled. He had big teeth that showed yellow around the roots. He spoke the name of some herbs in Sull and a few minutes of engaged conversation followed where the two men sorted out their Common equivalents. Raif picked out the words *wintergreen* and *chicory* as he looked around the camp. Something had been skinned recently in the butcher's circle and clumps of fat with the bristles still attached lay amidst the red snow. A piece of steel as thin as a cheesewire was resting atop a nearby stump. A flensing knife, and Raif thought it might have a design of quarter-moons burned into its haft.

Growing up at Blackhail he'd had no contact with Trenchlanders; Blackhail lay far to the west of the Sull Racklands and the two peoples rarely met or traded. Since then he'd learned little. He knew that many Trenchlanders made their livings from the woods—trapping, hunting, logging—but beyond that he had only vague ideas about who they were. They lived in Sull territories and possessed portions of Sull blood, but the pure Sull seemed to tolerate, more than welcome, them.

Feeling some pain in his shoulder, Raif stood. As long as he didn't walk toward the tree holding Traggis Mole's longknife, the Trenchlander shouldn't object to him stretching his muscles around the camp. Best to avoid the flensing knife too. It didn't leave much ground, but he could take a look at the woodpile and inspect the big skins stretched on the racks. Behind him, he heard the conversation waiver as the Trenchlanders' concentration shifted toward the stranger walking between his possessions. Addie's voice soon piped up with a question guaranteed to distract him. "What have your traps been yielding?"

Talk resumed. Raif crossed to the stretching racks. A large silver-backed grizzly pelt with the head still attached was pegged across the frame. Eyes and brain had been picked out of the skull cavity, but Raif saw that pink flesh still moldered in the nostrils.

Swear to me you will fetch the sword that can stop them. Swear you will bring it back and protect my people. Swear it.

Raif shivered. At the last moment Traggis Mole's wooden nose had been gone. A hole in his face sucked in air.

Turning, he asked the Trenchlander, "Have you heard of the Red Ice?"

The two men were enjoying a second drink of broth and they both rested their cups and looked up at him. Addie frowned as if to say, *So much for subtlety, lad.* The Trenchlander was quiet, his eyes taking on the glazed look of a man who was thinking. Calculating.

A noise from the south of the camp distracted everyone, the crunch of tree bark being driven into snow. Raif glanced toward it, and saw an old man walking a white horse toward the camp. A beautiful, thickly maned Sull horse.

And then the world went black.

THIRTY-SEVEN

A Gift Horse

Dalhousie Selco inspected Bram's sword, squinting at the watered-steel blade as if it was a document he was deciphering. He switched the blade over like a man turning a page. "Took some damage here. See?" Dalhousie glanced up at Bram. "Nicely fixed though. Looks like Brog Widdie's work—must have been afore he fell head-over-heels for some Hailsgirl and left Dhoone." Bram had never heard of Brog Widdie, and Dalhousie saw this in his face. "Used to be a smith at Dhoone in your da's time. Youngest master in the clanholds, known for his work with watered steel. Course Blackhail doesn't have any such fancy stuff. Word is that Widdie spends his days making pots."

Flicking the midway point in the blade with his index finger, Dalhousie made the steel ring. "It's a bonnie weapon, no doubt about it. Maybe in a year I'll let you use it." With that, the swordmaster at Castlemilk sheathed the blade in the empty wooden scabbard at his waist.

Bram stared at the scabbard, his mouth slightly open. Dalhousie raised his eyebrows, urging him to spit out any objections so they could both get on to other business. The swordmaster was dressed in a short cloak of glazed nut-brown leather and a pair of heavy-duty wool pants bloused into black boots. The hourglass hanging from its chain around his neck was still. Time had ended.

They were standing in the Churn Hall which was the primary second-floor chamber in the Milkhouse. The fifteen-foot ceilings were hung with ironwork: cranes, cages, hoists, meat hooks and trammels. Emergency supplies such as hay, sacks of grain, quartered logs, barrels of oil and ale and cured sides of ox were suspended high in the vaults for safekeeping. Wooden pickets, loosely held together with leather straps, were piled against two of the four walls. Enoch Odkin said they would be used as makeshift cattle pens if the Milkhouse was ever attacked and cattle had to be brought inside. Crates, rolls of felt, a huge net crowded with caltraps that looked like iron starfish, shelves packed with boxes and scrolls, and an entire fully-assembled ballista lay against the chamber's other walls. The large central space was clear, and used for weapons practice, banquets, warrior parleys and other gatherings. The milkstone floor had been overlaid with packed river sand, and four giant fox-head windows set deep into the hall's external wall let in bleak northern light.

Dalhousie had trained Bram hard for an hour before ordering him to go fetch his personal sword. Up until now Bram had fought with a workmanlike iron chopper that the swordmaster had assigned to him on the first day. When Bram returned to the Churn Hall with Mabb's watered steel sword he had been expecting to use it. Not have it commandeered by Dalhousie Selco.

"What you waiting for, Cormac? We're done here. Tomorrow at dawn on the court."

It was a dismissal. Bram looked at the hare's head pommel of Mabb's sword, now sticking out from Dalhousie's hard-sided scabbard. It had cost him a lot to own that sword. And though he hadn't much wanted it when it had been given to him as a parting gift from his brother Robbie, he couldn't very well give it up without a fight. "That's mine."

"Aye," agreed Dalhousie, kneeling as he wrapped his own sword in a sleeve of felt. "I never said it wasn't."

There seemed to be something in these words that Bram couldn't understand. For a man stealing a weapon in broad daylight Dalhousie looked remarkably bullish. "Go," he said.

Bram considered his options. None seemed good. He was sweating fiercely from the training session, and he'd been bashed so many times around the head that he wasn't certain he was capable of rational thought. He *did* know that you didn't pick a fight with a swordmaster unless you were pretty sure you could beat him. And then there was Millard Flag to consider. The head dairyman was awaiting his presence in the dairy, and after yesterday's bawling-out Bram didn't think it would be a good idea to be late.

As he turned to leave, Dalhousie said to him, "You're getting better on your feet, but you need to work on blocking. Fifty bull rings by tomorrow."

Bram nodded. A bull ring was a training sequence where you moved through a full circle while swinging your sword on its blade axis. Fifty would take some time.

Pol Burmish was entering the Churn Hall as Bram left. The tattooed and gray-haired warrior had drawn his sword in anticipation of a fight. He and Dalhousie often sparred together, keeping one another on their toes, and it was custom for a small crowd to gather and watch as they went through their paces. "Day to you, Cormac," Pol said, as he passed.

Bram nodded an acknowledgment and headed downstairs. Cormac. He was getting used to the name now and it no longer caught him off guard. Bram Cormac, son of Mabb: that was how he was known here. Pretty much everyone in the roundhouse was aware he was Robbie Dun Dhoone's brother, but apart from a few clan maids who teased him about it and Nathaniel Shayrac, the guide's assistant, who seemed to think it gave Bram an unfair advantage, no one ever mentioned it. Mabb Cormac was known and respected as a fine swordsman, and it was he who people named when commenting on Bram's kin. It felt strange but also good. At Dhoone he had been constantly measured against Robbie; his skin judged too dark, his shoulders too narrow, his height insufficient. Every time he had been introduced to someone as Robbie's brother he had seen disappointment in their eyes. At Castlemilk he was just another yearman, expected to work long hours, stay out of trouble, and keep up with his weapons training.

It was something Bram had not expected, this everyday acceptance. After he had spoken First Oath on the banks of the Milk, Wrayan Castlemilk had stood with her skirt hem floating in the water and said to him, "Now you are a Castleman for a year." Bram was only now beginning to realize the power of those words.

Reaching the ground floor, Bram decided not to risk the temptation of the kitchens and headed out the main door instead. Yesterday Millard Flagg had caught him pouring fresh milk into a vat that hadn't been submerged for sufficient time in the boiler. The punishment for this gross violation of dairy law had consisted of something the head dairyman liked to call "pat watch," which involved a lot more forking than watching, and left a man smelling so bad that afterward he had to roll in the snow. Besides, there was usually food in the dairy. Cheese, curds, yogurt: you could scrounge something milky most days.

It had snowed a couple of inches in the night and Enoch Odkin and Beesweese were on shovel duty, clearing the front court of snow. Enoch waved to him, and Bram considered asking the yearman about Dalhousie's strange behavior with the sword, but decided he didn't have time.

Hunching up his shoulders against the cold, he rushed down the Milkhouse steps. Directly ahead, the bargeman was pulling a man and his horse across the river. The horse's dark brown coat was so glossy it looked varnished. Its owner, who was standing talking to the bargeman as he cranked the rope, was dressed in a long wheat-colored saddle coat that was belted at the waist. He was holding something dark in his hand; it might have been a pair of gloves or daypack. As Bram watched, the stranger's gaze turned toward him. It seemed a deliberate thing, as if the man had known Bram was there yet had delayed looking at him until he was good and ready. His eyes were yellow-green.

Bram turned away. A sharp breeze was channeling east along the Milk and it made him shiver. The dairy was situated to the rear of the roundhouse so he broke into a run to keep warm. It was two hours before noon and the sun was as small and pale as a chip of bone.

Last night's snow squeaked under his feet as he neared the first dairyshed. The hard standing would need to be shoveled so the cows who were due to calf could be walked, and Bram thought he might just as well get to it. Popping his head around the door, he called out a greeting. It was between milking times and the dairymaids were standing about eating fancies topped with dried cherries, and supping on watery mead they brewed themselves. They all swore they never drank milk.

"*Bramee*," they cried in chorus, teasing. There were five of them, dressed in stiff white aprons over blue dresses, and dainty caps that were worn in defiance of Millard Flag. The head dairyman would have preferred something bigger. "*Bramee*."

Every morning without fail this greeting accomplished two things: made the girls giggle uncontrollably at their own wit, and caused Bram's face to turn red. He couldn't work out why, after nearly a month, this continued to happen.

As soon as he'd unhooked the snow shovel from its peg behind the door, he went back outside. This morning's training session with Dalhousie had concentrated on the techniques necessary to block blows aimed at the head and chest, and Bram's ribs had taken a beating. He thought he might have blocked one in ten. Dalhousie was fast and he had countless subtle ways of varying an attack. They looked the same, but when they hit you each one felt different. Bram had given up worrying about bruises and now dealt with them the same way as Enoch Odkin, Beesweese and Trotty Pickering did: covered them in pig's lard and boasted about them. It seemed to work.

The new snow was fluffy and only a quarter-foot deep, and it didn't pain his ribs much to shift it. As he was finishing off, Millard Flag came out and informed him he was needed for heavy lifting in the milk room. "Boiler and count to ten a dozen times," he said wagging a finger.

That was the number of seconds that you had to count off before you could remove the churns and steel pails from the hot-water bath and reuse them. Yesterday Bram had stopped count at eighty-four.

The milk room was large and noisy. Worktables lined the space, and both sets of double doors—front and back—were kept open throughout the day. Two dairymaids were skimming the cream from the new pails and a third was pouring milk through a wire strainer. Millard Flag and his apprentice, Little Coll, were tilting one of the big cheese vats to pour off the brine. Bram was told to carry various items—two sealed churns, some trays of newly blocked butter wrapped in cloths, and a stack of cheese in tin molds—down to the cold room which lay

directly beneath the milk room. After that he was to head outside and feed the boiler fire.

Bram was on his third run down the ancient stone steps
when Millard called his name. Hands full with a tray of butter,
Bram called out he would be up in a minute. The cold room
was dark and low-ceilinged, with crumbly stone walls and a
limewashed floor. It smelled like fat and raw earth. None of the
dairymaids liked to come here, and they usually sent for Bram
or Little Coll if they needed something brought aboveground.

As he slid the tray into one of the deep recesses in the walls,
Bram heard a footfall on the stairs.

"I see you are working hard," Wrayan Castlemilk said,
descending the final steps and entering the chill shadows of
the cold room. Fine silver chains at her throat and wrists
gleamed as she moved around the chamber. "I don't believe I
have been down since I was a girl. I imagined it bigger and
more . . . frightful. My brother once told me they slaughtered
cows here. He bolted that door on me one evening. Didn't
come back. The old dairyman Windle Hench found me here
the next morning. Apparently I was sitting right where you stand
now, calmly eating a wedge of cheese."

Bram could believe it. Wiping his hands on his pant legs, he
said, "Lady."

This seemed to amuse her. Her dress was made from smooth
blue wool and she wore a simple matching cloak. A pair of
gloves were tucked into her bodice, and her brown leather boots
had little piles of snow on the toes. Bram seemed to remember
Mabb telling him once that the better the boot the longer the
snow took to melt. "A messenger arrived from Dhoone last
night," she said, apparently in no hurry to head back up the
steps. "Robbie sends his greetings."

Muscles in Bram's chest did strange things. "He knows I am
here?" He heard the hope in his voice and was surprised by it.
He hadn't known it was there.

"Oh yes," Wrayan said, looking at him very carefully. "I
made sure he knew you had arrived safely and taken First
Oath."

Bram understood that she had declared him out of bounds
to his brother. Robbie Dun Dhoone could stake no claim on

Bram Cormac for one year. It was hard not to imagine Robbie's face when he received the news. He must have felt a moment's misgiving. They were brothers. They'd shared breakfast, blankets, head colds, punishments, adventures, secrets, cloaks, boots. It had to mean something. Bram was sure it had to mean something.

"Did he send any message?"

"No." The Milk chief's voice was level. After she had delivered this answer she did Bram the kindness of walking over to the right wall and inspecting the rows of churns that stood there.

He sent his greetings, Bram reminded himself. *Surely that is a good message in itself?* He took a breath, trying to force out the tightness in his chest.

"Someone sent you a message, though," Wrayan said, glancing at Bram over her shoulder. "Apparently Guy Morloch wants his horse back."

Bram hung his head. What could he possibly say to that?

"I told him to go to hell. Formally seized the horse for Castlemilk—I am chief, I do things like that—and now I gift the stallion, without condition, to you." She smiled, and it was such a lovely and unexpected thing it warmed the room. "I believe it's got some godawful name, like Gilderhand or Girdlegloom. Guy Morloch always was a stuck-up little shit."

"Gaberil," Bram said.

They both laughed. Because Wrayan Castlemilk was chief and knew it, she took the lid off one of the vats and poked the setting cheese. If anyone in the dairy had done that they'd be on pat watch for a week.

"So," she said, wiping her finger on one of the cheesecloths. "I believe our swordmaster has taken your sword."

Bram could barely keep up with her. "Yes, lady."

"It's quite a choice you have coming up." Seeing his confusion she explained, "At Castlemilk when a swordmaster takes your sword it means he's claiming you as an apprentice. Dalhousie believes you're quick enough to be a first-rate swordsman."

This was so surprising, Bram had to go over the chief's words one by one in his head. He felt as if he were a piece of cooling metal that she kept plunging into hot and cold water to temper.

Dalhousie wanted him as an apprentice? He'd received only two pieces of praise from the swordmaster in all the weeks he'd trained under him—and one of them was today. *You're getting better on your feet.*

"Of course," Wrayan said, preparing to leave, "training to become a master swordsman is a task that will take up the better part of each day. Just as a guide's training would." Another plunge into hot water. The Milk chief's gaze assessed him shrewdly. "So you must choose which one you will be."

Waving a hand in farewell, Wrayan Castlemilk took the stairs and left.

Bram felt as if he'd lived an entire life in the scant minutes she had been here. He had to stand for a while just to let it all sink in. Bram Cormac now possessed a very fine and slightly needy stallion. Dalhousie wanted him as an apprentice.

And his older brother knew he had taken the Castlemilk oath. Robbie *knew* yet had sent no message of goodwill. *He is busy,* Bram told himself harshly. *He has an entire clanhold to secure.* Suddenly needing to get outside into the light, Bram righted the lid on the cheese vat—Wrayan Castlemilk had not replaced it—and then headed up the steps.

Guide or master swordsman. He knew he was lucky to have such a choice. Yet he didn't feel lucky, just confused. Was it ungrateful to want something more?

The dairymaids were now busy with the churning and the steady *thump* and *slop* of the plungers competed with the sound of Millard Flag and Little Coll stacking vats against the far wall. The head dairyman looked up at Bram as he emerged from the cold room, a question on his small wrinkled face. Bram ignored it. He had to get out of the noise. He knew he was due to feed the boiler, which lay just outside the milk room so the heat from the fire wouldn't spoil the churning, but he passed it right by.

The dairy court was quiet except for a half dozen cows that had been walked onto the newly cleared ground and tossed a bale of hay. The dairymaid watching over them was keeping herself warm by hugging a hot stone wrapped in a blanket to her chest. She regarded Bram with some interest as he passed. Only minutes earlier the chief had visited the milk room and now here was Bram Cormac coming out. That would give the dairymaids something to talk about at second milking.

Bram checked on the sun. It wouldn't be long now before midday. Drouse Ogmore would expect him at the guidehouse at noon and there was no telling how long the guide would keep him—usually till well after dark. Ogmore was currently teaching him how to sift and grade the rock dust that shed from the stone during chiseling. An elaborate succession of hoop-shaped sieves was employed, and once the dust had been separated into particles of similar size, the larger pieces had to be sorted by hand. Stone chips, pieces of chalk, pyrite nuggets, fossils and pellets of hardened shale oil: all had to be separated and judged. It was the judging that was the difficult thing, the developing of an eye for pieces that were extraordinary and needed to be set aside for special use. Bram erred on the side of caution, and had been saving a lot of grit. Trouble was, if you stared at *any* piece of stone for long enough it began to look like it was special. There were always shadings and sparkly bits and veins.

The fine powder that made it to the bottom of the sieving process was easy to deal with. It was packed in small purses and sent out to the farmers to use in the fields. The next level might be employed in the roundhouse—a small percentage of the sand overlaying the Churn Hall floor was guidestone—and it was custom to sprinkle a portion on all hearths that were newly lit. The level up from that was where the grit lay and it was here that things began to get tricky. Tiny pieces of guidestone, no bigger than pumpkin seeds, had to be sorted by hand. Ogmore could do it in a single movement, passing a flat palm over the chips as they lay atop the wire mesh. The action would turn the pieces over and it was this turning, this revelation of a second side, that was enough for Ogmore to pick out anything worthwhile. "The important pieces flash like diamonds," he had said to Bram more than once. "When your eye is trained you will spot them straightaway."

Bram figured his eye needed more training. The day before yesterday he had picked out every shiny piece from the third layer—it had taken him more than two hours—only to have Ogmore come along and dump it all back in the sieve. "No.

No. No," he had cried. "All stones that shine are not precious and not all precious stones shine." Bram had been deeply confused.

Ogmore had picked a chip from the sieve. "This," he had said, holding it between his index finger and thumb so Bram could take a look at it, "is what we look for. See how its lines of cleavage fall counter to its veins?" Bram nodded. It was a tiny thing but if you squinted hard you could just make out where the chip had split off from the guidestone on a plain *counter* to its weak points. Like a piece of meat cut across the grain. "That's where the gods lie. There. They are not bound by the laws of nature. I chip one way, using the lines of cleavage to aid my work, and the gods are content for me to do so and remain passive within the stone. Every so often though they push against the natural order—that is how gods work. This push is what we look for in the stone chips. It gives us evidence the gods are nimble. And reminds us we suffer their tolerance. If they chose to they could sunder the entire stone—look at the Hailstone, blasted to nothing. That is why we must monitor what is shed from the stone. Vigilance is the first and greatest responsibility of all clan guides, and vigilance begins with sifting through the dust."

It had been a lot to take in. It was interesting, but it wasn't enough. Bram wanted to learn about things larger than dust. Where did the Stone Gods come from? Had they existed as long as the Sull gods? What would happen if the Sull decided they wanted the clanholds back? Would the two sets of gods go to war?

There was no fooling Ogmore; he knew when you weren't paying attention. "Go," he had said coldly after Bram had made a series of mistakes. "Perhaps tomorrow you will learn more."

Now, approaching the guidehouse, Bram wasn't sure he had the mind-set necessary to spend the rest of the day sorting tiny pieces of stone. It all seemed very small.

He kept thinking about Robbie, knowing he shouldn't, yet going ahead and doing it anyway. It was like having a sore tooth that you couldn't stop prodding. Why hadn't Robbie sent a message? Did he no longer consider Bram kin?

"Bram Cormac."

Startled Bram looked up. He had been walking through the uncleared snow just west of the guidehouse and had not thought anyone was in sight.

The man with the yellow-green eyes who had taken the ferry crossing earlier stepped out from the shadows of the guidehouse's northern wall. He was older than he looked from a distance, but age rested differently on him than other men. His face had hardened rather than slackened. Bone had grown in to replace fat, and decades of exposure to ice and sunlight had pulled the skin tight across the bridge of his nose and jaw. As he walked toward Bram his floor-length saddle coat left draglines in the snow.

"I am Hew Mallin," he said speaking in the kind of voice that was rarely ignored. "I am a ranger. And friend to Angus Lok."

Bram had a strong memory of Angus Lok's visit to the Dhoonehouse. Yet he would not expect a stranger to know that . . . unless Angus Lok himself had told this man of their meeting.

"Walk with me," Hew Mallin said, assuming many things.

The ranger struck a path northwest toward the woods. Bram saw that he was still carrying the item he'd held during the river crossing. It was a square of black bearskin. A flattened hat.

The guidehouse door-within-a-door was closed and Bram looked at it for a long moment before following the ranger into the cover of the trees.

The woods to the north of the Milkhouse were a dense, snarled cage of choke vines, oaks, elms, hemlocks, basswoods and blackstone pines. Roots, vine runners and thornbushes lurked beneath the snow like traps, ready to trip and stab. Bram thought about stopping for a moment to tuck his pants into his boots but Hew Mallin was walking with purpose and within seconds he would be out of sight. The ranger did not look back to check on Bram's progress.

He had to be armed, Bram reckoned, but any weapons he possessed were concealed beneath his coat. Had he presented himself to Wrayan Castlemilk or the head warrior Harald Mawl? Bram guessed that if the ranger had wanted to arrive in secret he would have come in from the north and not taken the river crossing. How long had he been waiting behind the guide-house? Bram's thoughts raced ahead of him, and he found himself remembering Jackdaw Thundy's words. *Hawk and spider*, that was how the swordmaster had described the ranger Angus Lok.

Reaching a clearing where hardwood saplings were fighting for territory with tiny, perfectly formed pines, Hew Mallin slowed and then stopped. "In Alban's day they used to hold the old ghostwatches here," he said, using the bearskin hat to brush snow from a felled log. "Twice a year, on the longest and short-est days. They'd build a twenty-foot pyramid of timber and light it as the sun set. It's purpose was to ward off ghosts and other evil things. You might say it worked for the ghostwatch hasn't been held since Wrayan took her brother's place, and the ghosts are only now coming back."

Hew Mallin sat on the log. His face was deeply ice-tanned, yet his lips were pale. His brown and graying hair had been needle-braided and pulled back in a warrior's knot. It was the kind of work that took an expert braider an entire day to achieve, yet once done it rendered any sort of care unnecessary for six months.

"What of the forest?" Bram asked, the first words he had spoken. "With a fire that big it could have gone up in flames."

"That is the crux," Mallin replied coolly, fixing Bram with his yellow eyes. "If one is serious about fighting ghosts there is always a cost."

Bram felt the world spinning on him. He had thought it spun earlier, in the cold room, but looking back now he real-ized that was just the first tug necessary to set a jammed wheel in motion. The Castlemilk guidestone had shown him this man: the bearskin hat, the fork in the path.

"You have been marked, Bram Cormac son of Mabb. The rangers have observed you for five years. We have minded you on the practice court and in the scribes' hall at Dhoone. We have asked others about matters concerning you and received answers that satisfied. Your part in Skinner Dhoone's downfall has been noted. Your actions the night Vaylo Bludd was located on a hillside east of Dhoone are known to us. We see much that others do not, and we watch for others like us." A small, weighted pause. "And that watching has brought me to you."

Bram swallowed. Who had told this man about the meeting with Vaylo Bludd? Guy Morloch? Jordie Sarson? The Dog Lord? And how did Mallin know that Bram had visited Skinner Dhoone all those months ago at the Old Round outside of Gnash? Did he know that Bram had looked into Skinner's Dhoone-blue eyes that day and lied? A glance at the ranger's hard, angular face gave Bram his answer. Yes, Hew Mallin knew. He knew and judged it satisfactory.

The strange tightness that had seized Bram's chest in the cold room gripped him again. What was happening here? Why did he feel under threat?

"We are the Brotherhood of the Long Watch, the Phage, and we have stood guard against the Endlords for four thousand years. We watch in this land and many other lands, in the cities and in the clanholds, in the deserts and on the seas. Dark armies are massing and we stand ready at the gate. We are few against many, and while others on this continent fight wars, seize strongholds, kill, breed, *sleep*, we walk in the shadows and patrol against the darkness and the men and women who harbor it." Hew Mallin shifted his position, revealing a lean sword housed in an intricately etched steel scabbard. "Our ways are subtle and the tasks we undertake are seldom pleasant. We know truth but do not always speak it. Enemies forestall us and we must act to wipe them out. We do not serve one man or one people, and our home is on the horse paths, animal tracks, dirt roads and riverways. As darkness moves so must we.

"We are the Phage and we know the names of the creatures in the Blind and are afraid. The world lies on the brink, and the first question I bring you, Bram Cormac, is this: how long can it stay there unsupported?"

Snapping his gaze away from Bram, the ranger began to walk the rough circle of the clearing.

Bram looked at the sky. He was about an hour late for Drouse Ogmore. Every day since the guide had asked him to consider becoming his apprentice Bram had gone to the guide-house thinking, *Today will be the day Ogmore asks for my decision.* So far that day had not come. Now Dalhousie Selco wanted to make a master swordsman from him—and for a son of a swordsman that meant something. Bram had lost count of the times he had been told he was too small to wield the hammer, the ax and the big two-handed longswords that were favored by Dhoonesmen. Here at Castlemilk they preferred a smaller, fighting sword. And Dalhousie believed that given time Bram could wield such a weapon with skill.

Already it was a wealth of choices. He had come here with nothing and now owned a horse. At Dhoone he possessed no worth save his kinship to Robbie. Now he had two trades to choose from, two ways to gain merit in this clan.

Bram listened to the sound of the trees moving, the hemlocks *shushing* and the old oaks creaking like swinging doors. Leaves had budded on the elms too early and the frost was rotting them off.

Not thinking any answer was required from him, Bram kept his silence. It seemed as if the world had sharpened. He could see the light *in* the snow as well as upon it, see the blues and greens that waited there like memories of water. The shadows were darker and more menacing, biding behind trees like coiled springs. When he saw his footprints had exposed earth as well as pine needles, he graded the stones. Nothing shiny or unusual. Nothing that went against the grain.

When Hew Mallin's circuit turned him back toward Bram, he spoke. "You have guessed what the second question is but I will ask it anyway. Formalities serve their purpose." The ranger halted three feet from Bram and pinned him with a gaze so sharp Bram felt it cut like a wire through his head. "I, Hew Mallin of the Brotherhood of the Long Watch, ask you, Bram Cormac son of Mabb, to leave the clanholds with me this night and beginning training as a ranger for the Phage."

I cannot. Yet he was stirred beyond all sense. Hew Mallin was shaking. So was Bram. "Do you teach the histories?"

"Knowledge is power."

It was a yes. Bram swallowed. "I have spoken an oath to Castlemilk."

"Break it. The gods are dead, and what remains is here to destroy, not judge us."

But the stones. Ogmore said the gods' presence could be read in the stones. Close to panic now, Bram thought about Ogmore waiting in the guidehouse, of Dalhousie training in the Churn Hall with Mabb's sword, of Wrayan Castlemilk standing in the water and saying, *Now you are a Castleman for a year.*

"My sword?"

"Swords kill. As long as a blade is sharp one will do as well as another."

Bram breathed in great gouts of air. The snow was dazzling him it was so full of light. He should not have come, that was his mistake. Should have walked right past Hew Mallin and taken the door-within-the-door.

Wrayan Castlemilk knew, Bram realized quite suddenly. She had only come to deliver Robbie's greetings and gift him with Guy Morloch's horse *after* the ranger had made the crossing.

But Dalhousie had not known. Nor had Drouse Ogmore.

And what of Robbie?

Did he send any message?

No.

A muscle pulled deep within Bram's chest. Hawk and spider, knowledge and sword: here was everything he wanted . . . and more. Meeting Hew Mallin's yellow-green gaze he gave the ranger his answer and broke First Oath.

By nightfall Bram Cormac had started a new life.

THIRTY-EIGHT

A Pox Upon the Heart

Raif Sevrance was awoken by a mule lipping his ear. Through sleepy, focusing eyes he saw many big teeth and a ridge of pink gums. Wet lips tickled him, and a little push of air revealed stupendously bad breath. Raif thought it would be a good idea to move, tried to move, but somehow could not roll off his stomach onto his back. Islands of pain—that's what they felt like, lumps of hurt sticking out above water level—emerged from the fog of sleep. His left shoulder was throbbing. The midsection of his left arm, but not the top, was so tender that the weight of the blanket resting upon it was excruciating.

He was in a tent and blotches of light were coming through the uneven canvas overhead. The mule walked a few feet and began crunching on quartered onions that had been placed on a wooden board. A second animal stood some distance behind the mule; a white horse with a long, fountainlike tail. Its brown-blue eye watched Raif with both interest and caution.

Voices were coming from outside the tent and Raif was relieved to hear Addie Gunn say quite clearly, "I think we've seen the end of the snow."

Raif croaked Addie's name. Even the mule didn't look up.

The blanket that was pulled up to his chin felt like sandpaper, and he tried to push it down with a motion of his right shoulder. Something wasn't right with his back. Something was there. Like a growth.

"Addie," he cried. "*Addie.*"

"Whoa, laddie," the cragsman responded from outside the tent. "I hear you. I'm coming."

Footfalls followed. Onion wedges dropped from the mule's mouth as it turned to look at the person entering the tent. Addie came into view. His eyes were very gray and bright. Quickly squatting by Raif's pillow, the cragsman said, "It's good . . . good to see you awake."

"It's good to be awake."

Addie Gunn seemed to find some wisdom in this. "Aye," he agreed softly. "It usually is."

The cragsman left him briefly to fetch water from a tin canteen insulated with mouse fur. "D'you think you can get up to drink it?" he said frowning from the canteen to Raif and back again.

Raif tried to roll onto his back.

"No," Addie said in a dither, setting down the canteen and rushing forward. "You can't put weight on your back. The thing's there."

"What thing?" Raif heard the panic in his voice, and forced some movement from his spine.

"The pox—on your heart." Kneeling, Addie helped Raif to execute a half roll onto his side, and then clamped him around the head and heaved him into a sitting position.

"I hope you were gentler with your sheep," Raif said, dizzy with pain and seeing red splotches before his eyes. He could feel it now, something sticking out from his back, sucked hard against his skin. Rotating his neck as far as it would go, he saw something moving in a place where there should have been fresh air. Raif's right hand came up to swat it away, but the cragsman's hand was faster.

Gripping Raif's wrist so hard it shook, the cragsman said, "It's a poultice of leeches and right now it's the only thing keeping you alive. That piece of shadow is pushing against your heart and those leeches—gods bless their black little souls—are sucking the other way."

Oh gods. Raif relaxed the tension in his wrist and Addie released his grip. He thought he might be sick. "What's keeping them back there?"

Addie shrugged. "They gorge, they drop off. Old Flawless sticks another one right in place. He's built up plaster around the wound so they can't crawl away and find a better spot. Had to cut into your skin to give the plaster something to bind on to, so I'm telling you now I ain't fetching no mirror." Addie paused to let the full meaning of this sink in. His gaze was frank and unflinching. "Here. Drink water. Be glad you're alive."

Raif took the canteen with his left hand, testing. The muscles were sore in the same way they would be if he'd chopped wood all day. And all night. Aware that Addie was waiting for some response from him, some sign that everything was all right with Raif Sevrance, he said, "Water's good."

It was enough to satisfy Addie Gunn, and Raif could see something physically easing in the cragsman, a softening around the shoulders.

"Old Flawless adds a pinch of soda to it. Who'd a thought to do such a thing?" He appeared genuinely impressed. "That Trenchlander's full o' tricks."

Addie's accent got thicker when he was distressed or relieved, Raif realized for the first time. "How long have I been out?"

"Three days."

Raif understood then the worry he had caused his friend. "I'm sorry, Addie."

Throwing a hand out, the cragsman rose to standing. "A man can hardly go apologizing for dropping clean dead. And even if he did it'd take a hard sort of nutgall to accept it." Again, the eyes were bright.

From the back of the tent, the Sull horse made a wicking noise and threw back its beautiful elongated head.

"Easy, lady," Addie said, using his sheep voice. He walked over and gently knuckled her nose. The animal pushed against him, calmed.

"What happened?" Raif asked.

Addie sighed. "You fell. Just crumpled clean at the knees right by the drying rack. Me and Gordo upped and ran straight for you. Neither of us knew what the hell to do. I set my ear to your chest—you were gone. Clean gone. That's when old Flawless gets there. Didn't run—he's not the sort—but he gets to it soon enough, starts pumping your ribs like they were bellows. All the while he's speaking in Sull, ordering Gordo to fetch this and that, telling me in Common to stop casting my shadow in his way. *Sit*, he tells me. *I see to the boy.* Next thing

I know your legs start jerking, a noise comes from your throat like you're being strangled. Gordo's bringing all kind of medicines—leaves and tiny bottles and potions. Flawless pulls out his hunting knife, slices off your tunic as if it's a deerhide he fancies mounting for a trophy, and tells me to boil some water for the herbs. It all happened so fast I could barely track it. A minute later you're half naked on a horseblanket, being rolled onto your stomach so Flawless can have a look at the puncture wound."

Addie patted the horse's head. Noticing her nose band had ridden up, he automatically pulled it back in place. "Flawless asked what was up with you and I couldn't see a way around it so I told him everything: the piece of shadow that was lodged in your shoulder, the thing Yiselle No Knife said about it stopping your heart. Too damned shaken to lie. Too afraid that if I didn't speak the truth you just might die there in front of that bloody skinned bear."

Recalling the hollowed out eyes of the bear skull, Raif shivered. He could feel the leeches sucking on his back, feel hundreds of tiny teeth clamped to his flesh. "Who is this Flawless?"

"Some old trapper coot. Been around awhile, knows some stuff. Flawless isn't his real name, but it's as close as these old gums can get to it. He doesna seem to mind—specially after I explained to him what it meant. *That will be my new name*, he says. He's quite a one. He'll be in soon to check on your, you know . . . *back*."

Raif tried to control his revulsion. They were moving, that was the thing, their slimy bellies contracting as they pumped in blood. Motioning to the Sull horse, he asked, "Is that his?"

Addie understood this question. "Aye. Flawless has some Sull in him, more than Gordo that's for sure. Don't think he has much love for them though. I get the feeling the Sull aren't too happy about him trapping bears." Lowering his voice, the cragsman returned to Raif's side. "Know that trap I sprung the other day by the fallen cedar?" Raif nodded. "Gordo finds it yesterday, tells Flawless, who's convinced it was the Sull that did it."

Raif thought about this. "We're in Sull territory?"

"Just about. Apparently the borders are a little hazy around the top of Bludd."

"Help me up," Raif said, planting his palms on the tent floor.

"You can't get up," Addie protested, stepping back. "You need to lie there and rest."

"I *need*," Raif said, gritting his teeth as he leveraged his weight forward, "to find the Red Ice."

"Traggis Mole is dead. What does it matter when you find the damn sword?"

Pain shot along Raif's left arm as he pushed himself to standing. The tent spun and he stumbled as he tried to orientate himself. Light floated sideways and blurred. Addie's hand clamped on to his right arm. "Steady now."

Braced against Addie's weight, Raif waited for the tent to stop spinning. He felt a small loosening on his back. Something moved. A leech dropped to the floor. Addie kicked it away with the side of his boot, but not before Raif had seen something brown and bloody, like a piece of liver.

"Addie, I have to go. I need to find the sword." *Swear to me you will fetch the sword that can stop them. Swear it.* "I spoke an oath. I intend to keep it."

He had meant to say more, to tell Addie that he had broken his word so many times that there was now nothing solid beneath anything he said, that his fate was to wield the sword named Loss and slay the creatures that could be destroyed only with such a blade, and that every day he spent in territory claimed by the Sull he risked both his own life and Addie's. Yet he stopped himself. At the end of everything it was the oath to Traggis Mole that counted.

Addie had trained to be a Wellhouse warrior and then deserted his clan in favor of a life herding sheep. When Raif had asked him about it all those months ago in the Rift, the cragsman had said only one thing in his defense. *I never took the oath.* Those words defined Addie Gunn's life.

The cragsman guided Raif to one of the tent's vertical support poles. "Set here," he said, handing him off to the unstripped birch log. "I'll fetch Flawless."

Raif held on to the pole as he watched the little fair-haired cragsman slip between the tent flaps. He didn't think he had ever met a better man.

The mule wandered over to inspect the blankets Raif had

been lying on. A piece of onion was stuck against its nose. The Sull horse moved forward a few steps and then stopped. Raif wondered if she had watched him while he slept.

"Sick man go back to bed," came a voice from the far side of the tent wall. A moment later two small brown hands parted the canvas and the man named Flawless stepped through.

It looked as if he had been hammered from bronze. He was tiny and his skin was darkly burnished. His cheekbones were high and angular and the rest of his face seemed to hang from them. His eyes were startlingly blue. "Bed now," he said jabbing his finger accusingly at Raif. "A pox upon the heart."

Shaking his head, Raif hung on grimly to the pole. "How long will it work for, the poultice?"

The little man put his hands on his hips. He was dressed in hunter's greens with many belts and pouches strapped and slung around his waist and chest. A silver bar as thick as a child's finger pierced the cartilage of his right upper ear. "No leeches. No work. *Bed*."

Raif realized he didn't even know what time of day it was. The light seeping in through the canvas had been diffused by thick cloud. Stubbornly he said, "I'm leaving today. So do whatever you need to"—he jerked his head backward—"with that to keep me going awhile."

Flawless hissed a few soft words in Sull. It sounded like he was cursing. Pulling a glass jar from the large rawhide pouch at his waist, he said, "Need another leech. Need at least twelve a day." As he unwrapped the twine holding the cloth lid in place, Raif saw the jaw was full of black squirming worms. Leeches. "Have thirty left."

Raif made the calculation.

"Turn," Flawless commanded, plucking a long wet leech from the jar. The creature's three-lobed mouth was open and it wriggled in the old man's grip, trying to attach itself to his thumb.

Raif turned. Forehead pressing against the tent canvas he waited. Flawless started whistling. Raif felt a light touch close to the center of his back, and then the suckers bit into his skin.

"Bad back there," the Trenchlander said. "Keep clean."

Raif unclenched his jaw. Deciding it was time he got

dressed, he released his grip on the pole. His legs felt like wet sticks, and he willed his knees to firmness as he stepped toward the blankets.

Flawless folded his arms and watched him. He was still holding the open jar in his fist.

"Need go Hell's Town," he said in his sharp, biting voice. "See healers in Maggot Quarter. Cut it out."

Raif nodded. He could not see his clothes, and remembered that Addie had said his tunic was cut into strips. *The stormglass.*

"Friend has belongings," the Trenchlander said, batting the mule away as it came to investigate the jar. "You know where you go?"

"Maggot Quarter."

"No. Red Ice. Friend tell you where?"

Raif kept his face calm. He did not blink. "You tell me."

"Red Ice not far north. Many bears. *Maygi* hide it. Do not know where going, won't find it. Bluddsmen ride past, never see. On border. Half Sull. Half Bludd. *North.*"

The man's ice blue eyes burned intensely as he spoke and Raif realized there were things here he did not fully understand. Histories and betrayals, hurts and resentments. Trenchlander versus Sull; and all that went along with being second best. Raif thought about Yiselle No Knife and the Spinebreaker and before them Ark Veinsplitter and Mal Naysayer: prideful people not easy to like.

Something cold in Raif thought, *My gain.* And he switched his thoughts elsewhere. "What is the Sull word for cloud?"

The little man did not appear surprised by the question. "*Mish.*"

Raif had thought it was. The two stood facing each other as the leeches tried to squirm their way out of the jar, wriggling on top of each other and arching their bellies into hoops.

"Take," Flawless said eventually, holding the jar out to Raif. "Friend knows what to do."

Raif did not thank him. They were beyond such things now. A jar of leeches. A betrayal of one's people. A pox upon the heart.

The little man left, the skin on the back of his neck flashing like sheet metal as he ducked between the tent flaps. Flawless the Bear Trapper was nearly pure Sull. And he had spilled Sull secrets to a man who could destroy his people.

Raif set down the jar of leeches, dragged a blanket from the tent floor, and covered his bare chest. The woolen fabric dragged against the thing on his back and he realized he would have to be careful with clothing from now on. Holes would need to be cut. That made him smile. Grimly.

For some reason then he thought of Mallia Argola. Perhaps it was something to do with the careful way she had mended his Orrl cloak. He imagined the curve between her waist and hips, and the way the fabric of both her dresses had strained across her breasts. Shaking himself, he took a drink from the canteen and then went over to take a look at the Sull horse.

No partition separated the animal space from the human space, though the ground here had been spread with pine boughs. Raif imagined that when the animals soiled, the trappers merely brushed out the branches and spread new ones. A makeshift trough had been dug out of a halved log. The Sull horse kept her head level as he approached but her tail was high and twitching. Raif raised a hand so she could smell it and watched as her delicate black-and-pink nostrils twitched. "Easy, girl." She did not make any move toward him, and he did not force it. After a moment he let his hand drop.

It was time to go.

Addie came a few minutes later, bringing several folded items and two small sacks. Raif found his boots and Orrl cloak in good order, but his tunic, pants and undershirt were not there.

"Weren't worth the mending," Addie said smartly, about to take no fuss. "Here. These were Gordo's. Good skins. Just a bit stiff, is all."

Raif barely looked at them. "Where's the small brown pouch that was in my tunic?"

"You mean this?" Addie said, fishing into his underarm pack. He pulled out the sleeve containing the stormglass and handed it to Raif. "I didna look to see what was inside."

Raif had not thought for one moment he would. An odd silence followed and Raif tried to understand what, if anything, was happening. The cragsman left the sacks on the ground and went to look at something on the other side of the tent. He might have been checking on blankets.

Suddenly it dawned on Raif. "What do I owe you, Addie?" All the medicines and attention, the shelter, leeches, clothes. The price of Flawless' betrayal of the Sull.

The cragsman stared hard at the blankets piled against the support pole. "You owe me nothing, lad."

"I don't believe that." Raif was surprised by the emotion in his voice. Surprised by how quickly this had become serious between them. Addie had thought Raif had nothing of value, but now he knew the object in the pouch was worth something. And it upset him. Raif remembered back to the negotiation by the campfire, the meager clink of coins in Addie's sock. "How did you pay for all this?"

Finally the cragsman turned and looked at him. "A gold bar. It was my cut for the raid on Black Hole."

Of course. Any meaningful kind of betrayal was always paid for in gold.

Raif slid the stormglass from the sleeve and watched as it sucked in the light. The tent actually grew darker. Holding it out toward Addie, he said, "Take it."

Addie's head was already shaking. "Nay, lad. What's done is done. It's a pretty bauble. Keep it."

You knew when there was no arguing with Addie Gunn. Raif closed his fist around the icy piece of glass. A gold bar was enough for a man to buy himself a piece of land with a building upon it and a half-dozen sheep. The cragsman had given that up.

Raif swallowed; there was a soreness in his throat. "I will pay you back, Addie. I swear it."

"I do not accept your oath," he said softly. "Save your word. Do not waste it on a cragsman like me."

His gray eyes met Raif's, and Raif knew something had forever changed between him and Addie Gunn.

Watcher of the Dead. He had nearly forgotten all the things that meant. If the stormglass had been given to Raif Sevrance, son of Tem, Raif knew he would have given it up three days ago when Addie brought out his sock. But the stormglass had been given to *Mor Drakka*, Watcher of the Dead. And it was not a gift. It was a marker.

Raif slid the piece of glass back into its sleeve and dressed himself in new skins. In one of the sacks he found his daypack, arrows, gear belt, weapon pouch and Traggis Mole's longknife. In the other he found the simple items Addie had first traded for: the medicine herbs, food and tea. He could barely look at them. Locating the scrap of fabric and length of twine that formed the lid of the leech jar, Raif sealed in the black worms. Leaving the jar on the floor for Addie to pick up, he headed outside.

Flawless was sitting on an upturned log by the fire, rubbing some kind of clear fluid into the Sull bow. Raif immediately saw the bow was brighter, bluer. The silver markings beneath the surface rippled like liquid mercury. "Nice work," Flawless said when he saw Raif. "Shoot arrows long way."

Raif wanted to snatch it away from him. Instead he said, "The Red Ice. How far?"

The Trenchlander shrugged. "Couple days. Trade for bow?"

He did take the bow then, yanking it from the old man's clawlike hands. Inches above Raif's heart, the coven of leeches stirred.

Flawless whistled as Raif walked away from the camp.

As he waited for Addie by the first stand of big trees, he tried to work out what time of day it was. The sun was hidden from view by banks of slow-moving clouds, but the light still had some force to it. Not long after noon then. Good. It was above freezing, and the ground snow was full of holes. The air smelled of cedar and damp earth. Raif itched to be gone.

The second bear trapper, the one whom Addie had called Gordo, emerged from the woods not far from where Raif was pacing. He was walking a thick-legged stallion that was carrying something dead on its back. When the trapper saw Raif he raised a hand in greeting, and Raif remembered that the man had been friendly in his own way, eager to talk to Addie about herbs. Raif looked at him but did not wave back.

The carcass slung over the horse's rump was a fine, white-throated doe. Fresh blood oozed from an arrow wound high on her back, just below her neck. One of her rear legs was crushed and older, blacker blood stained the dun-colored fur. The tale told by the two wounds disgusted Raif. The man hadn't even allowed the trapped animal the dignity of a swift death with a well-placed blade. He had shot her from distance with his bow.

Quite suddenly Raif could not bear it and headed off into the woods. Addie Gunn would have to catch up with him.

Watcher of the Dead was on the move.

And he wanted to kill something before he reached the Red Ice.

THIRTY-NINE

Spire Vanis

Marafice Eye squinted at the horseman riding at full gallop from his slowly advancing army and thought, *If I had any sense I would kill him.* Order a mercenary or a one-in-seven to loose a nice thick quarrel at the back of his leather-capped head. Whoever had said "Don't kill the messenger" was a fool of the highest order. Kill all messengers and stop all messages: that was wisdom to live by.

"Should I?" Tat Mackelroy asked, tapping the small and wicked-looking crossbow that he had taken to wearing in a sling at his waist.

Marafice grunted the word "No." At this point they were so damn close to the city that if they set out to kill everyone who intended to dash ahead of them with news and details of their arrival it would take a considerable toll on the population. Not to mention be a waste of good crossbolts.

News had to have arrived by now. An army with foot soldiers, carts and walking wounded moved at a snail's pace. Any codger with a cane could outrun it. Word had probably arrived days back, passing from village to village, tavern to tavern, relayed by teams of professional messengers who'd likely have fresh horses ready at each post. Information like this could earn good money in the Spire. Off the top of his head Marafice could think of at least six people who would pay gold for it. Exact position, numbers, makeup, condition: every detail was worth its own separate purse.

Marafice had ordered the killing of dozens of suspicious-looking men on horses, but the closer they got to the city the more suspicious everyone looked and the more futile the whole endeavor became. Even doing it for sport had become boring.

Runners were another thing entirely. Anyone who slunk away from his army meaning to trade inside information for personal gain was a dead man. Marafice killed them himself. It was a phenomenon which had genuinely surprised him. No one from Rive Company had attempted it yet, but these past few nights they'd had their hands full with deserting mercenaries. Steffan Grimes, who led the mercenary contingent, had told Marafice that such derelictions were not uncommon when an army was this close to home and that a good portion of these men wanted nothing more than to get back to wives and children. Marafice had listened politely—he was getting good at that—and then killed the deserters anyway. In his experience reasons just clouded things. What you did, not *why* you did it, was what counted.

It had caused some dissension, but no one, including Steffan Grimes, had said anything to his face. Andrew Perish, the former master-at-arms of the Rive Watch, had backed him up like a rock. "We've been abandoned on the field, won a round-house then lost it to a fresh army, been stranded on the wrong side of the Wolf, and sat through one of the worst storms God in his Garden ever created. If a mercenary can't wait a few more days to get home then I don't see why we should wait to discover his motives." Disloyalty of any kind was intolerable to Perish. He was a man of God, but also a man of fighting men.

Marafice didn't know what he himself was anymore. Protector General of the Rive Watch? Surlord-in-waiting? Commander of a ragtag army of mercenaries, old-timers, religious fanatics, machinists without machines and walking—*and* lying—wounded? One thing was certain though. He was a man finished with the clanholds. It was a dog-eat-dog world full of wild-eyed warriors and cunning chiefs, and the day he'd crossed the Wolf and left it was the day he vowed to himself he'd never go back.

"Will you call a halt?" Tat asked, breaking through his thoughts.

It was a good question and one Marafice had minded all day. Did he stop north of the city and approach Spire Vanis in the morning, refreshed, or march on and arrive by night? They were approaching the town of Oxbow in the Vale of Spires and it was growing late. Men who had been on their feet since dawn were weary. Marafice was weary, but it was not the kind of weariness that would let him sleep. The nearer they drew to the city the more tense he became. He did not know what he would meet at the gate, couldn't even be sure if they would let him in.

The journey south from the Wolf had been hard and slow. Ille Glaive had to be avoided, which had meant a detour through the Bitter Hills. Hill country was cold and barren, policed by sharp winds and thick snowfalls. Food had been hard to come by and they'd had to mount raids. Sheep were not afield, and farms had to be struck. It had not been pretty. There might have been rapings; Marafice did not get involved in what went on. He had three thousand men, a thousand horses, and two hundred pack mules to feed: pretty was seldom possible.

The hardest thing to bear had been the weather. Storms had hit in succession; great whiteouts where they had been forced to overtake barns and farm buildings and bed down in the manure and hay. The worst storm had hit after they'd left hill country and entered the great floodplains of the Black Spill. It had acted strangely, that storm, everyone had agreed so later; the way it had seemed to pass overhead and then thought better of it, and turned right back for a second swipe. Its length and ferocity had caught them off-guard, and when the whiteout came it was so sudden and complete that it had left them stranded. These were grasslands and there were no woods to look to for protection. No farms either, at least none that could be found in a hurry. The winds were so high they couldn't erect the tents, and they'd had to dig themselves into snowbanks, an experience so miserable and backbreaking that men had died with shovels in their hands.

Perish had made a killing that night. Men scared that if they fell asleep in the snow they would not wake up, were ripe for religious conversion. He had them chanting the pieties like ten-year-old boys. Marafice would have none of it—his balls might be freezing to hailstones but he wasn't crazy. Yet he could see that in this instance it had worth. Men were comforted in a place where there had been no comfort. It was something to be grateful for, Perish's makeshift church in the snow.

Two days had been lost. The greatest number of deaths were amongst the horses. Marafice had detected some relation between the fanciness of a horse—the length and skinniness of its legs and the shininess of its coat—to its ability to withstand cold. Fancy died faster. Men and mules fared better, though pretty much everyone and everything had ended up with chilblains, frostbite, dead skin, shed hair and snow blindness. Marafice's left foot, which had been badly frostbitten once before, had been paining him ever since. He would not put weight on it and spent all his days in the saddle, atop his decidedly unfancy stallion.

His eye socket had had to be stuffed with balled horse mane and sword grease. After the first few hours in the snowbank it had begun to smell. Men would not look at him, he'd noticed. Marafice One Eye, at the best of times, was rarely an appealing sight. Strange how you could forget all about how you looked. Spend months on end imagining that your appearance did not matter and that you were being judged solely on your actions, only to be reminded with a shock that it wasn't true. A man with an ugly face was set apart. A man with only one eye in that ugly face was judged a monster.

Marafice told himself it was of no consequence, and mostly it was not, yet there were times, such as in the snowbank, where he felt filled with layers of hard-to-place resentment. Those men chanting their crazy pieties with Andrew Perish could all go to hell.

"We'll call a halt when we reach the rocks," Marafice said to Tat Mackelroy, guiding his horse around a pothole filled with frozen mud. "There's open ground. We'll make camp there."

Tat nodded slowly, thoughtful. They were riding eight abreast along a wide, unpaved road that led through closely spaced goose and pig farms. It was late afternoon, and the air was cool and clear and reeked of animal foulness. "Some in the company won't like it."

Marafice grinned unpleasantly. "Anyone with objections, send 'em to me."

The rocks were the strange circle of freestanding granite spires that gave both the Vale of Spires and Spire Vanis its name. Some superstition surrounded their nature, and various legends, both sacred and profane, claimed to explain their existence. Marafice didn't give two bird farts about that. The things that counted to him were the facts that the rocks were set on open ground well away from the roads, farms, towns and villages that crowded the region northeast of the city. And that the land they stood upon had long been claimed by Mask Fortress on behalf of the people of Spire Vanis. And did not fall within any grange. This was Whitehog territory they walked through now, land held and protected by House Hews. The granite spires not only were no-man's-land, but also marked the southern boundary of the vast Eastern and Long Grass Granges. Once Marafice and his army were there they'd be off Garric Hews' land for good.

Well it was Lisereth Hews' land to be exact, but mother and son were much the same beast. The Lady of the Eastern Granges and her son the Whitehog were united in a single ambition: to place Garric Hews as the one hundred and forty-second Surlord of Spire Vanis.

And that put them in direct opposition to Marafice Eye.

It was a risk, albeit a small one, to march on the western border of their lands, using a Hews-patrolled road to head south into the city. An attack could be mounted, though judging from the latest intelligence Marafice had received from the dark-cloaks this seemed unlikely.

Apparently the surlordship of Spire Vanis was still open to contention. Roland Stornoway, his own father-in-law, held Mask Fortress. This fact so amazed Marafice that when he'd first heard it six days back he had laughed in Greenslade's face. "Who have you been talking to? The blind drunk or the insane?"

Greenslade was a small foxlike man, outfitted to look like a trapper. He had the red and flaky skin of someone who was out in the woods all day skinning weasels and foxes, but his eyes were city-cold and sharp. "I pass along nothing that has not been confirmed by two sources. Three days after Iss went missing, whilst workers were still digging through the rubble for his remains, Roland Stornoway entered the fortress with a small force of hideclads and seized control of it."

"Are you sure it was not his son?" Roland Stornoway was an old dry stick of a man who walked with the aid of two canes.

Marafice had marked his father-in-law as both shrewd and greedy. He had not marked him as a man capable of such a bold and surprising move.

"Roland Stornoway's son, also named Roland, stands within the fortress with him. But it was the father, not the son, who entered first."

Marafice thought a long while on this information, and could not for the life of him decide if it was good or bad. "Is my wife within the fortress?" he asked finally. The phrase "my wife" did not come easy from his lips; it made him spit.

Greenslade pretended not to notice. "She is with her father and brother, and has delivered a healthy boy."

Dear God of Mercy it just got stranger. Married under three months and the happy couple now had a baby. Tactfully, the darkcloak had avoided using the word *son*. Marafice reckoned he'd be hard-pressed to find a single soul in the north who believed the boy to be his. It had been a marriage of convenience. She was a rich slut who had bedded some starving scholar—a bookbinder's son if he wasn't mistaken—and he, Marafice Eye, was the man who had agreed to wed her once she'd reached the point where she could no longer conceal her pregnancy from prying eyes.

Liona, her name was. Marafice feared she wasn't right in the head. The one night they'd spent together as man and wife had been challenging to say the least. Legally he had to fuck her. So legally he did. The hair she'd ripped off his legs still hadn't grown back. Now she was standing by in Mask Fortress with her newborn son, who was lawfully and in the eyes of God an Eye. Marafice could not begin to comprehend what it meant.

He and Greenslade had been standing at the back of the supply tent, the usual place for such assignations. It was long after midnight and the darkcloak's breath smelled of cheap, overhopped beer. He had been in the alehouse of a village the army would pass tomorrow at noon; a lone trapper looking for company and some free warmth from the stove. Marafice could imagine what the man did, how cleverly he engaged local farmers and road-weary travelers in conversation. Armed with silver pieces from Marafice's own purse he could afford to grease throats and buy goodwill.

Marafice had not intended to use the darkcloaks again, but the nearer he drew to the city the more pressing his need for information. At first he had thought he could just enter such a tavern himself and demand people tell him things. He was Marafice Eye, Protector General, the Knife. He had not counted on the very real fear his motley army and his motley self generated in such places. Entire villages would board themselves up as he passed. When he and Tat Mackelroy had ridden ahead of the front line at Natural Bridge and entered the town a good two hours before the army, they had found the people who lived there in a state of panic. A cattle auction had been due to take place in the market square, and drovers and farmers were beating bony steers with sticks to get them to move along the streets in haste. The smith was barricading his shop with metal bars and an alekeep was burying two wooden barrels in the snow outside his alehouse. Marafice had ordered Tat to rough up the man and slash both barrels with his sword. The alekeep's behavior was an insult to men who had gone to war.

On their way out they had taken a steer. It was an odd thing, but Marafice could not recall such ill regard on the journey north. They had pursued a more direct route, one that took them predominately over fields and pasture, but even so the farmers had not trembled to see them. Had the presence of the grand and shiny grangelords been such a reassuring sight? Or was it just that everyone was leaner and hungrier after two additional months of winter?

One thing was certain: no one in these places was going to talk to him. Town and village folk assumed, correctly, that Marafice Eye and his army were going to rob them.

That was where Greenslade and his fellows came in. They had swift horses, and little problem with riding through the night to gain a crucial half-day advantage on the army. Sometimes they fell back. Other times they spotted the smoke of farms or cabins in the distance and simply took off over fields. They were good at their work and discovered information to the army's advantage. It was Greenslade's advice that had led to Marafice's decision to pursue a more easterly route. The roads were better and there had been few reports of trouble upon them.

It also seemed the Whitehog had taken a succession of blows, God bless his small and porcine heart. According to Greenslade the army that had deserted the Crab Gate had quickly fragmented. Various grangelords including Alistair Sperling and Tranter Lennix had split from the main body of the army, believing they could steal a march on Garric Hews and reach Spire Vanis before him. A dog-and-pony race had ensued with a whole fistful of grangelords racing to take the prize. Alistair Sperling had arrived first only to find all gates dropped and barred. Lisereth Hews was outside Almsgate with an army of two thousand, trying to ram her way in. When the good lady spotted Sperling she ordered her hideclads to attack.

"Attacked him herself, by all accounts," Greenslade had told Marafice, "ahorse and armed with her late husband's sword."

That one fact had genuinely frightened Marafice Eye. He found it surprisingly easy to picture Lisereth Hews armed and worked up into a tooth-and-nail frenzy. She had been daughter and granddaughter to surlords; she knew what it took to seize power.

"Lisereth Hews' hideclads trounced Sperling," Greenslade had continued easily, confident in his facts. "His men were exhausted; saddle sores burning holes in their arses, horses falling beneath them. Sperling could barely raise a defense. Took a spear to the gut and fell. Lisereth wasted no time and used her momentum to make another strike on the gate. That's when the storm hit. Twice."

The smallest upward lilt in Greenslade's voice had suggested unnatural events. His green eyes had glittered knowingly as he awaited the next question. He was a darkcloak, master of tricks and illusions. The cloak he wore could conceal him from dusk to dawn. He could compel a man to look at him in a crowd, draw smoke away from a fire, and project his voice into the bustling spaces of public halls and squares whilst concealing its origin. Marafice did not wish to know how he did these things. He had learned his lesson at Ganmiddich, and would not involve himself in anything that had the taint of sorcery about it. His name was Eye. Not Iss.

Pointedly he had directed the conversation away from the strangeness of the storm. "What happened to Lisereth Hews?"

"As her hideclads rammed the gate, word came that her son was just to the north. The storm was raging by then, temperature dropping, wind whipping up the snow, but she waited for him. Meantime Garric Hews has called a halt. He knows what's been happening five leagues to the south at Almsgate but he imagines his mother will have withdrawn. She imagines he will force his way through, and refuses to abandon the gate. Hideclads start deserting her and she orders them shot. Large-scale mutiny breaks out and Hews is fighting Hews in the whiteout. The temperature falls so low that timbers in the gate roof start exploding and tiles begin flying like axes. When it's all over and done four hundred hideclads lay dead. Most were wounded then frozen alive. Lisereth Hews survived the fighting but not the cold. Garric had to dig his mother's body out of the snow two days later. It was said her husband's sword was frozen in her fist."

Marafice had shuddered. "What of the Whitehog?"

"He retired to his grange. Some believe he should have pushed that last five leagues to meet his mother and he's lost some support over it. His momentum's gone, his remaining hideclads are disheartened, the ground's still too hard to bury the dead. Word is that he'll rally but it'll take time." Again the green eyes had glittered. "All due to a storm."

Marafice had dismissed the man, and resolved then and there to never use him again.

It was three days later and he knew he would break that resolve and call Greenslade into his presence tonight. Information was his lifeblood. If he intended to approach Hoargate tomorrow he needed to know what to expect.

His father-in-law held Mask Fortress, yet as of three days ago Roland Stornoway had not declared himself surlord. Marafice could not imagine a stranger turn of events. Spire Vanis without a surlord for a month? He did not know the histories and perhaps such a thing had happened before. But he doubted it. He had lived in Spire Vanis all his life, spent twenty-two years close to surlords—first Borhis Horgo and then Penthero Iss. This was not a city that could tolerate a vacuum. Something was happening, but he was not a scholar or a politician; he needed Greenslade and his brethren to help him figure it out.

"All halt!" Tat Mackelroy cried, standing in his stirrups and bellowing down the ranks. "Make camp. All halt!"

Marafice was surprised to see they had arrived at the Vale of Spires. Hours had passed where he had left his progress in the hoofs of his big black warhorse. The sun was failing, dipping into bands of red and silver clouds at the edge of the sky. All farm stench had gone and the air was crisp and gusting. They had approached the granite spires from the east and Marafice wondered how long he had ridden in their long, needle-like shadows and not known it.

Most people believed the spires had been formed by God, given as both gift and warning to the people of Spire Vanis. *See my power*. A few claimed they had been raised by ancient sorcerer kings who had died in the War of Blood and Shadow, long before the city at the foot of Mount Slain existed. Marafice could not understand the need to explain such things. They were there, you could see them, why invent fancies to turn them into things they were not? What they were was a rough circle of granite fangs that thrust straight out of the bedrock at the center of a grassy plain. Some were as tall as a hundred and twenty feet and others less than thirty. The granite was a dirty off-white color, streaked and potholed with black. To Marafice's mind they looked like rotting shark's teeth. He supposed they might be an alarming sight to those who had never seen them before, especially the taller ones that had edges like serrated knives, but he had always found them oddly pleasing.

And it pleased him to make camp here this night. He dismounted and started issuing orders. Anyone who looked even remotely afraid or doubtful was given latrine duty. Marafice had found it worked as well as anything when it came to refocusing a man's mind. Feeling full of energy, he hammered posts with the mercenaries and raised tents. Cook fires were a problem as they had run out of timber two days back and had not been able to forage or strip much since. All trees had long since gone from this part of the country, felled to make way for pasture and farms. Marafice thought a fire would be good thing for the men. "Chop down the small cart," he commanded Tat Mackelroy on impulse. "There's no reason why the captives can't walk to the city tomorrow. The wounded can be jammed into the remaining two."

This turned out to be a spectacularly popular order. Mercenaries and men of Rive Company came together to hack the wooden cart into sticks. One of the old Rive men fetched his stringboard and started plucking out a tune, some outrageously lewd song about a woman who went up a mountain and ended up getting fucked by a bear. Pretty much everyone joined in the chorus. Ale kegs were tapped. The cartbed was reduced to chips. Work began on the wheels. Perish frowned at all the ungodly activity, but had the sense to let it be. He knew the value of such releases to men who had been away from home for too long.

"What should we do with the captives?" Jon Burden was the one sober presence in the camp. As commander of Rive Company, the four clansmen who remained alive were his responsibility.

"Lash them to one of the fangs," Marafice said. "Take off their boots and razor the souls of their feet. Lightly, but enough to keep them from running. Those men aren't fools. They would have figured out by now that tonight's their last chance to escape before we enter the city."

"Aye," Jon Burden said, glancing south toward the mountains and Spire Vanis. From here you could just see the haze of gray smoke the city created billowing above the ice fields of Mount Slain. "Always supposing we are allowed entry."

Marafice had known Jon Burden for as long as he had been in the Rive Watch. They had trained together under Perish; pulled themselves up from lowly brothers to captains, learned how to eat in the grand banquet halls of Mask Fortress without causing grange ladies to faint in disgust, and discovered hard truths about the city they guarded. Marafice would not lie to him. "We'll see what we see."

Jon Burden pulled air into his thick powerful chest. The rubies in the killhound brooch at his throat fired in the setting sun. "A pity we had to trade the ram."

Marafice barked out a laugh. Clapping Burden hard on the shoulder, he said, "Count yourself lucky you never had the pleasure of meeting the Weasel chief firsthand. She's been figuring in my dreams ever since—and God help me, sometimes she's naked."

Burden snorted. "I'll see to the clansmen."

Carefully avoiding favoring his left foot, Marafice left the campsite and walked amongst the granite spires. It was colder here, the air still. Odd bits of debris littered the ground surrounding the stones: incense burners, lamb-gut sheaths, glass vials, ale cups, moldering lumps of food. Something that looked a lot like blood had been sprayed against the base of the tallest spire. Marafice frowned at it, deeply disgusted.

"Protector General." It was Greenslade, slipping between the fangs. Always it was difficult to keep your gaze on his cloak. Somehow it kept sliding off. "You wanted to see me?"

Marafice glanced back at the camp. Walking deep into the thick of stone spires, he said, "What is the latest news from the city?"

Greenslade was not a man to waste time. "Roland Stornoway still controls the fortress. As he's yet to make a formal announcement about the surlordship. Word is that he's holding it for his son-in-law."

"The watch?"

"They've been with him right from the start. It's my guess he's been telling the captains that by supporting him they're supporting you."

It would certainly explain how easy it had been for Roland Stornoway to control Mask Fortress and the city gates. You needed the watch on your side for that. Marafice reached out and touched the closest stone spire. The edges were sharp enough to open skin. "What's the status of the gates?"

"Hoargate and Almsgate are still closed. Wrathgate remains open for limited hours each day. Stornoway has forbidden the breaks to be put on the gear shanks, so the gate can be dropped at a moment's notice."

It made sense. "Who polices them?"

"The watch, though I've heard rumors that Stornoway has hideclads garrisoned in all the gate towers."

Marafice took his hand from the stone. Skin along his index finger had split but not bled. He did not find much comfort in these facts. What was Roland Stornoway up to? The old nutgall was no friend of his. Yet how better to gain access to power than to have a son-in-law as surlord? Stornoway could never have managed such a coup without the Rive Watch. He *must* have taken power in Marafice's name.

"My lord. It may be possible to rig the gate."

"*No*," Marafice blasted at him. He would have no tricks and sorceries. He'd had his fill of such foulness at Ganmiddich. The weird green lights, the bad-eggs smell. He would not use unnatural forces ever again.

Greenslade appraised his Protector General and seemed to find him wanting. "As you wish. Tonight my brethren and I go on ahead. We will await you in the city."

Before Marafice Eye could even begin to frame a reply Greenslade took his leave, the fabric of his cloak swirling around him like dark water. It was dusk now and his figure was lost to the eye within the space of five seconds.

Marafice cursed softly and with feeling. His foot was throbbing and the coldness in his eye socket seemed to freeze half his brain. The good half, the one he needed to make sense of what was happening in the city. Stornoway in Mask Fortress. It was a puzzle he could not solve.

As he made his way back to the camp he passed the granite fang the clansmen had been roped against. They formed a rough circle, one on each compass point. Their feet were bare and bleeding, though not badly. They would survive. Burden had a clean blade. The young one with the brown eyes marked Marafice in silence. He had a couple of fresh bruises on his face and a nasty gash across the bridge of his nose. Jon Burden and Tat Mackelroy had interrogated all four men some days back, and the brown-eyed one had fought back like a demon.

Marafice reminded himself to ask Burden what, if anything, he had discovered. For now, though, he wanted nothing but the peace of his tent. It seemed Greenslade had performed an unwitting service. The darkcloak had succeeded in tiring him out sufficiently to the point where he believed it was possible to sleep.

Small cookfires dotted the camp, and the smell of charring pork fat and onions wetted his mouth. He was pleased to see a large central bonfire had been built as a gathering point. A wrestling match was under way—a member of Rive Company against one of Steffan Grimes' professional mercenaries—and the cheering and booing was raucous. Marafice watched the match for a while—Rive was looking like dead meat—and then found himself a plate of food and retired to his tent.

He ate methodically in the darkness. He couldn't be bothered lighting a lamp. Before he slept it occurred to him that the day he'd spent fighting at the Crab Gate had not left him as mentally exhausted as he felt right now. How had Iss managed it, all the intrigue and uncertainty?

An hour before dawn he awoke and gave the order for camp to be struck. Tat Mackelroy helped him into full war armor, snapping latches, strapping buckles and shoving down great wads of linen padding. Marafice looked south toward Spire Vanis and spied the suggestion of light on the edge of mountains and sky. He had been moving toward this moment for years, decades even, yet he had never thought it would come in circumstances such as these. What did Iss used to say? *"You cannot plan for the strangeness of being surlord."* Much wisdom seemed to exist in those words.

Mist washed through the granite fangs as Jon Burden, Andrew Perish and Steffan Grimes formed up ranks. The spires towered above them, stone sentinels thousands of years older than the city the army went to claim. Men were quiet. Formally armed and armored, most needed mounting stools to bestride their horses. The foot soldiers—there were a hundred and fifty extra thanks to Yelma Scarpe—stamped their feet restlessly as the cavalry took its own good time to close ranks.

Marafice waited. He found himself not impatient. The stars were fading in a clear sky. Crows were calling in the fields, gathering in readiness to pick through the remains of the camp. When the carts were loaded and the ranks evenly formed, Marafice gave the order to the drummers to sound the slow march. As the booms of the kettledrums synchronized, he trotted his horse to the center of the front line.

"To Wrathgate," he bellowed. "South!"

An army of three thousand moved out on his order.

Progress was slow for the first hour. Marafice kept both hands on the reins and did not think. Keeping his head forward to avoid his neck piece chafing, he watched the sun rise. When they rejoined the road he caught his first glimpse of the city walls in the distance. A small shock of remembrance charged the sheet of muscle beneath his lungs. The Splinter had gone. The pale limestone tower that had risen six hundred feet above the earth no longer existed. He had been told that it had fallen, but Iss' death had seized his attention and he had not spared a thought for the city's tallest tower. Its absence was shocking, the unobstructed view of Mount Slain's northern face.

Every man in the party felt it. Andrew Perish, who was riding two lines back, cried out the third piety. *"God brings destruction so that we as men can restore His order to the world."*

Marafice did not believe in God, but the ancient words pulled at him all the same. Restore order: that would not be a bad thing. Calling out to the drummers he commanded a quick march. They were on the road now; the mules and footsoldiers could keep pace.

The villages they passed through were deserted, and all healthy animals were gone from the fields. When they reached the fork in the road that led east to Wrathgate Marafice took it without hesitation. He could see the great iron edifice of Almsgate, flanked by its twin towers. Tat said the double portcullises were down and they looked like they'd taken a few bashes. A chunk of the gate roof had collapsed and there was a big bald patch without tiles. All was as Greenslade had said.

Marafice's heart began to pound as they neared the city's eastern gate. The kettledrums were booming, combining with the clatter of hooves and armor to create a wall of sound. Red and silver pennants flying from Spire Vanis' limestone walls ripped and darted in the mountain winds. Men were patrolling the ramparts; you could see their heads and the top three feet of their spears. No one was at the gate. No merchants, farmers, tradesmen, scholars. No one. Everyone within the city and without must know that Marafice Eye had come home.

"Is it open?" he asked Tat, his voice wild.

Tat squinted. Wrathgate was built from granite blocks as big as horse stalls. It was a square and bulky gate, the least elegant of the city's four gates, and it was guarded by two four-sided towers and a stone hood. The gate itself was deeply overhung.

"Portcullis is down," Tat said quietly.

Marafice felt the state of his body change. Things that had been slack tightened, and others that had been tight loosened in unpleasant ways. "We keep going," he said, his voice suddenly calm.

When the front line drew within two hundred feet of the gate, the sound of horns blasted forth from the eastern wall. Hundreds of red cloaks stepped into view. Rive Watch. His men. As he looked on they drew their swords in salute. Red steel flashed in the sunlight. The cast-iron portcullis juddered into motion with a great rattling of chains. Clods of snow and turf fell from its spikes.

And there, waiting in the courtyard on the other side, was his father-in-law Roland Stornoway, dressed in fantastically gilded armor that was too big for his small and bony frame, and flanked by a double guard. Hideclads and red cloaks. Marafice had not realized until now that the old goat was still capable of sitting a horse. Seeing Stornoway's cold and rheumy eyes, Marafice suddenly understood several things.

Of course the old man would welcome him back. If he didn't the red cloaks would turn on him. Today, right at this moment, they would turn. Marafice Eye had been their leader for seventeen years, and hard fighting men like the red cloaks did not easily set aside such loyalties. Stornoway's plan would be to support his son-in-law until the poor soul died a sudden but natural-seeming death. Poison, if Marafice wasn't mistaken. Then Stornoway could simply step into place as Surlord and the red cloaks would stand by him.

With his scrawny neck and baldy head sticking out from the carapace of dress armor, Stornoway looked like a vulture. He was putting on a fine show, Marafice had to give him that. He had to be nervous. This was the tricky bit; waiting to see how his son-in-law and his son-in-law's army would react. Yet Stornoway didn't look nervous. Stornoway looked sour and bloody-minded. Marafice blew air through his lips in frustration. His brain wasn't large enough to cope with all this double-dealing.

Yet if he wanted to be lord of this city he didn't really have a choice. A show was called for. Stornoway had set the stage, betting heavily that his son-in-law would play his assigned part.

Spire Vanis was watching and Marafice knew it would not serve his cause to look confused. He must be seen to be in control and armed with foreknowledge; pretend that he and the old goat had hatched this plan together. The Surlord and his father-in-law. Stornoway and his new son.

They both knew it. They both needed it. It was a perfectly executed deadlock.

Iss would have figured it out a lot sooner, Marafice reckoned, raising a fist in greeting to the man who almost certainly intended to kill him.

To keep himself calm he addressed Tat Mackelroy, making a necessary show of nonchalance. Reveal surprise and he also revealed weakness. "What did you learn from the hostages?" he asked, saying the first thing that sprang into his head.

Tat, God love him, went right along with the game, squaring his shoulders and keeping eyes front as he said, "The young one, the ringleader, is called Drey Sevrance. Wouldn't give me the name himself, but I beat it from one of the others."

"Good, good," Marafice replied, barely listening. His father-in-law was riding forth to meet him. Marafice had thought Stornoway to be greedy but harmless, and he wondered how he could have been so thoroughly wrong. The man was a cold and calculating opportunist.

"Welcome," Stornoway hailed as Marafice Eye rode through the gate, "Lord Commander, Surlord. And son."

Marafice entered Spire Vanis as its one hundred and forty-second Surlord, with the man who intended to be its one hundred and forty-third raising his dry and wrinkly cheek to be kissed by him.

FORTY

The Cursed Clan

T he river smelled different at night, older and deeper, black with tar. Insects hunted its surfaces, black flies and phantom crane flies, mosquitoes and biting midges. Effie wondered if they hatched from the snow. Mist slid along the sides of the boat, keeping close to its breeding ground, the water. The alders and water willows were quiet, unmoved by wind, and the only sounds beyond the splash of poles breaking the surface were the hollow cry of the night heron and the shriek of wild dogs far to the north.

It was a bleak and uncertain landscape filled with traps for the boat. The Curseway, Waker had called it. The watery path that led to Clan Gray. Effie swallowed and tried not to think about what Eggtooth the pirate had said about the Cursed Clan. She tried, but did not succeed. *"Know what they do to young uns there? Tie stones to their chest and sink 'em."* Effie began shivering and could not stop. She really should have learned how to swim.

Waker Stone and his father had taken to poling after sunset and often struck camp during the bright hours of the day. Until today this had suited Effie Sevrance well enough, for in all her eight-almost-nine-year life she could never recall being afraid of the dark. Tonight was different, though. Cold and strange-smelling. And she couldn't get Eggtooth's words out of her head.

"Pull 'em up a week later and eat what the fish didn't want."

A water rat launching itself into the river nearby made a soft sloshing noise as it carved a trough in the water. Overhead the quarter-moon seemed to keep pace with the boat. Directly ahead of her Chedd Limehouse had faked his way into sleep. It had started out with a bout of pretend head-nodding and some truly stupendous wet-sounding snores—he had definitely taken notes from Eggtooth's pig. The next thing you knew the snoring had gotten softer, the head had tipped forward and he was really, properly asleep. That boy had some undeniable talents, Effie reckoned. Until she'd met him she'd never realized that a space *existed* between fake and real, let alone that it could be exploited.

Thinking about Chedd helped Effie feel better. Not that she was afraid, of course. Just . . . anxious.

Chedd was interesting to Effie. He knew things in the way she knew things. Different knowledge, but got the same way. Take that water rat. All she'd need to do was poke Chedd's chubby shoulder and ask "Girl or boy?" and Chedd would tell her its sex. Might tell her a few other things too. Like whether or not the rat was hunting or fleeing or simply out to have a cooling swim. He was good at finding hibernating turtles and salamanders under rocks, though for some reason he had less luck with fish. Always he saw things on the shore before she did; the beaver amidst the sticks, the fawn in the trees, the heron standing still in the rushes. "There's a bear cub over there," he would say casually, flicking his hand toward one of the banks. Effie had given up trying to prove him wrong, for even when the animal never emerged from hiding they both knew it was there. "How do you know?" Effie had asked him more than once.

Chedd had a way of shrugging that made his neck disappear into his chest. "Dunno," he'd told her just this morning as they stood ankle-deep in the snowmelt pool searching for fairy shrimp. "Until I was your age I thought everyone knew when animals were around."

Your age. She'd feigned some disgust over that particular comment but in a way Chedd's answer was oddly reassuring. You knew what you knew. That's how Effie had always felt about her lore: when it was there, hanging around her neck, she just knew things. Nothing fancy about it. No hocus-pocus or song-and-dance. Knowledge was there and if she chose to she could draw it in. It was like spotting something blurry in the distance: you could stop and look and concentrate upon the object, or pass it right by.

Effie extended her arm over the gunwale and let her hand touch the greasy black water. She hoped it wasn't bog. Eggtooth had been most particular about that: it was bog she and Chedd would be fed to, not river water.

Annoyed with herself for still shivering, she set her mind on something else. She tried to sort out who and what she was without her lore. Effie Sevrance, daughter to Tem and Megg, sister to Drey and Raif, bearer of the stone lore, Hailsman: those were her names and titles. Tem and Megg were dead. Drey might be too. She doubted if she'd see Blackhail in a very long time—Clan Gray was the direct diagonal opposite of Blackhail, and maybe a thousand leagues away—and to top it all off a fish had eaten her lore. Now she was simply Effie, sister to Raif, bearer of no lore, not even the twine that had held it. Did that mean her knowledge had gone? She didn't know. Some days it felt as if it had.

And then there were days like today when something tingled in the center of her breastbone, right in the place where her lore used to lie.

It had happened while she and Chedd were eating the fairy shrimp. They were tiny things, floating upside down in the icy water. Chedd said you ate them whole and raw, so that's what they did. They'd tasted like fish fins, which, as far as Effie knew, were the one part of the fish you weren't supposed to eat. Chedd had disagreed and said quite seriously they tasted like fish eyes. *Bony fish eyes.* That had them both laughing. And that was when she'd felt the queerness in her chest. It was like a thumb jabbing against her chest. No laughing matter. Not today.

After that she didn't eat any more shrimp and went to sit alone by the boat. Some of the shrimp shell had stuck in her throat. Now Eggtooth's words were stuck back there too. *Tie stones to their chests and sink 'em.*

The ghost of her lore, that's what she decided to name the sensation in her chest. The ghost of her lore had spoken and given her a warning about today.

And tonight. Effie swatted a black fly who fancied a piece of her wrist. The horn-covered lamp clipped to the bow of the boat created an eerie circle of light. She wished she could paddle. To do something would be good, to get tired and a bit sore, and have something else beside her thoughts to think about—if that made any sense. Waker and Waker's father were poling though, standing in the boat and using long sticks to punt through the water. The river was too shallow for paddling, barely a river at all anymore.

The Mouseweed. Only a few days earlier Effie had thought it an undeserving sort of name. She and Chedd had spotted beaver dams and big barnacly trout, and the river was at least thirty feet across. Now the only things to spot were flies. And its width had grown decidedly uncertain. Black water wept beyond the banks and into fields of sedge and rushes. The hills had ended and the land had sunk. The tallest things around were the alders and silky willows, trees clinging grimly to last summer's crisped leaves.

The river was too shallow for paddling. And too full of weeds. The water meandered around great islands of bulrushes and cattails, and then widened into wet fields. Channels were no longer obvious and Waker and his father needed to be able to turn the boat on a point.

Four days back they had passed Clan Otler's roundhouse in the night. Waker had snuffed the prow lamp and his father had propelled the boat while he himself did something strange. Waker had sat forward in the prow seat and made sweeping motions with the pole. Chedd had whispered that Waker was checking for trip wires above the water. Effie had frowned at this at first, thinking it a highly unlikely figment of Chedd's overly dramatic imagination. Trip wires above the water indeed. What was next, attack fish? This odd behavior had gone on for nearly an hour—Waker pivoting the butt of the pole against his chest as he swung the tip in a half-circle—and during that time Effie couldn't come up with a single explanation that sounded better. And Waker had never repeated the action any night since then. It certainly made her think.

Otler's roundhouse had been lit with fiery red torches that doubled their light by reflecting in the water. It was strange to see a roundhouse built from wood and raised on stilts. The

Otlerhouse was huge and beautifully made. Entire stripped logs had been carved into curves to form the roundwall. The cedar gleamed in the firelight, thickly oiled against mist and river damp. Three turrets rose from its domed roof. Lamps burned in the top galleries of each tower and the windows were guarded by meshed wire stretched over X-shaped frames. Both the towers and the roundhouse were roofed in white lead; probably to reduce the risk of fire, Effie guessed. Lead had also been added to the chinking between the logs, endowing the roundhouse with a series of pale horizontal stripes that reflected in the dark water as glowing rings.

As far as Effie could tell normal kinds of trees—oaks and cedars and elms—grew at the rear of the roundhouse, so solid ground must lie back there. At the front of the roundhouse a series of landings and jetties projected out across the water and many small boats were tied up there. Guards were watching from both the turrets and the highest landing, but they never spotted Waker's boat. Waker's father was poling through the reeds on the southern shore and you couldn't even hear his paddle enter the water.

Effie had wondered about the passing. Beforehand both Waker and his father had been nervous, shifting in their seats, making adjustments to the load, communicating in the terse hand signals they seemed to prefer over language. Clouds had snuffed the moon and there was no mist. Good and bad. Just as they spied the first lights, Effie felt a little creepy sensation crawl along her skin. She thought it might be a cloud of midges, only how had the midges managed to fly into the bodice of her dress? Then she thought about the day Eggtooth had stopped the boat by chucking a big stone into the water. She remembered the prickly sensation in her mouth when Waker's father had removed her tongue and teeth; either winking them out of existence entirely or concealing them behind shadows so deep that no normal glance could find them. Whatever had gone on, Effie had been mightily glad to get them back.

The night they'd floated past Otler she suspected Waker's father had been up to his tricks. Nothing as drastic as with her teeth but something—a blurring or shadowing or some subtle misdirection—had taken place. How else could you explain the fact Otlermen armed with crossbows and looking out across the water had not seen a shallow boat containing four people moving along the opposite shore?

The creepiness Effie had felt subsided quickly once they'd passed the roundhouse. Waker's father had rested in the back while Waker returned to poling. The whole episode struck Effie as odd. Otler and Gray were neighbors, they shared borders and vulnerability to Trance Vor. You'd think they'd be friendly out of necessity if nothing else, seeing as they were both stranded in the far southeastern reaches of the clanholds. *And* they both held war oaths to Bludd. So why then couldn't a Grayman paddle past Otler at midday?

Because Clan Gray is different, stupid. It's cursed.

Effie frowned. Needing some distraction she did the crawly hands on the back of Chedd's neck. Chedd's head jerked back and his hand came up to slap away the fly. Effie pressed her lips together to stop laughing and ended up making a snorting noise instead. The beauty of the crawly hands was that she could do it easily to Chedd but Chedd couldn't do it easily back. It was a masterstroke of gaming and it very nearly made up for the now-legendary disaster that had become bear: *naked!*

"Eff," Chedd said, using the kind of voice she had not expected, quiet and puzzled. "There's half-things around."

"Ssh," Waker warned from the bow of the boat.

Effie looked at the back of Chedd's head. Her feet and legs suddenly felt cold, and the chains around her ankles chinked as she shivered.

"The way to Gray is lined with prey," Waker's father whispered softly in her ear. *"Nothing worse than being cursed."*

She hoped Chedd hadn't heard him.

The moon was setting now, slipping behind the low alders. Something rustled on the near shore, hopefully a muskrat or river rat—or weird nocturnal duck. Waker's father thrust his pole deep into the river mud and held it there for a moment, allowing Waker to swiftly turn the boat. As the butt of the poll came out of the water Effie saw it was glistening with tar.

Old peat and tar beds lay here, Chedd had told her earlier back at the camp, that was why the water was so black. You could dig up the mud, light it, and watch it burn. He was all for giving it a try, but then they'd found the pool with the fairy shrimp and got distracted. The water had been clear in the pool, she remembered. Snowmelt, not river water. It was difficult to imagine fairy shrimp—or much else for that matter—living within this murky, acidic water.

She really, *really* hoped it wasn't bog.

Things had started to change pretty quickly the day after the encounter with Eggtooth. The river cliffs north of the Mouseweed had sunk into the river, forming huge mounds of boulders and gravel. The hills to the south had begun to fail, and soon there were no uplands at all, just rolling forested plains. After that the entire landmass had seemed to sink. They'd passed a flooded forest and a series of big muddy river pools that smelled bad. East of Otler the water had begun to darken, and it wasn't always easy to tell when the river ended and the land began. Waker and his father appeared to know the area well and the campsites they chose were always firm ground above the water.

People lived here, for sometimes Effie would spot lights on the shore. Occasionally they passed other rivercraft, shallow skiffs and one-seat longboats pulled by gaunt-looking men and women wrapped in boiled skins and beaver furs. Waker and his father offered no greeting to their fellow boatmen. Effie guessed they were in the Graylands by then.

She and Chedd didn't talk much about Clan Gray anymore. Eggtooth's words had thrown a large damp blanket on the subject. She could no longer argue against Chedd's crazy notions of human sacrifices and bog baiting. She'd even started thinking that she and Chedd would have been better off if they'd been pirated by Eggtooth. You could stab a pig.

She wasn't so sure about half-things. Leaning forward, she touched Chedd lightly on the cheek. "What's wrong?" she murmured as quietly as she could.

Chedd shook his head. They were both aware that Waker's father was behind them, watching their every move. It was so dark now that you could see only the few feet of water beyond the boat that were illuminated by the bow lamp. Chedd made a small motion with his right arm, flexing it as if he was warding off a cramp. Something plonked into the water nearby and as it did so Chedd murmured over his shoulder to Effie, "It's like ghosts."

For her own sake just as much as Chedd's Effie Sevrance decided she was going to stay calm. She decided this very firmly, nodding her head. Whatever Chedd perceived—and she believed he perceived something—was probably not unknown to Waker and his father. They knew these waters. This was their clanhold. And unless it happened to be one of those special nights that came around once or twice a year when all sorts of spirits and dead things were permitted to walk the earth for reasons that were unclear to Effie—then this was a normal occurrence. It didn't mean it was good—Waker was paddling like a fiddler playing a particularly fast and difficult tune—but it didn't mean there was any reason to panic.

No reason at all.

We are Gray and Stone Gods fear us and leave us be. Repeating part of the Gray boast didn't help. So she tried the Blackhail one instead. *We are Blackhail, first amongst clans. And we do not cower and we do not hide. And we will have our revenge.* That was more like it.

Waker and his father executed a series of sharp turns that zigzagged the boat around an island of woody rushes and steered them away from the main channel. Soon the rushes began closing in. They formed fences on either side of the boat, rising as tall as ten feet, bristling and pale, flattened in places and crushed in others. They stank like meat broth turned bad. Effie scrunched up her shoulders and brought her elbows to meet across her chest. She did not want them scratching her. *Festerers*, that's what Drey would have called them.

Both Waker and his father sat. Waker ceased poling completely, but his father began a tilling motion with the paddle, gently keeping the boat in motion. The channel narrowed and the rushes created a tunnel around the hull. Rush heads scraped against the gunwales, rustling and scratching, bending and snapping off. A sting of pain on her cheek told Effie she had been stabbed, and as she raised her hand to bat the offending stem away she spotted the dim glow of lights reflecting in the water. The sight of them made her gulp. They were a deep, unearthly green.

Waker grunted something to his father, and the old man

took his paddle from the water. Effie turned to look at him and she watched as he cupped his hands around his lips and issued a deep whooping noise, like a crane. A second passed and then the call was returned from two separate locations. Waker's father grinned at Effie as she turned to track them.

"Feed the dog a bone. Girlie's coming home."

Suddenly the reed stands cleared and water opened up ahead. Effie saw rings of green lights burning just above the surface. Waker stood again, but before he resumed poling he glanced over his shoulder at Effie and Chedd. *A man checking on his cargo,* Effie thought. She hoped Chedd had stopped feeling the ghosts. Behind her, Waker's father began rummaging noisily through a sack. Effie tried to resist thinking about what he was up to but in the end she could not bear it, and looked round.

It took her a moment to understand what she was seeing. Waker's father was combing his near baldy head with a pickax, dragging the scant and greasy hairs back one by one. He had a mean and victorious look in his eye. Effie began work on her best, most withering glare—the man truly was insane—and then the missing piece of the puzzle fell into place. The memory of Waker's words from a month earlier burned through her brain like drops of acid. *"Tomorrow I put leg irons on you. Once they are on there is nothing in my possession that can remove them. I carry no ax strong enough to cut the chains or no pick with the correct bore to punch out the pins."*

She had believed him. She and Chedd had believed them.

She had lost her lore and nearly died because of those chains. *And he had still kept them on her.* Foolishly she had thought there was some honor between them and that after Waker had pulled her from the water she owed it to him to be a good passenger. She had owed him nothing. He and his father were kidnappers, and if she and Chedd had thought there was a possibility of freeing themselves from the chains they would have tried an escape. Chedd Limehouse and Effie Sevrance would have given it a go. The master faker and master gamer could have cooked something up.

Effie felt betrayed. And stupid. And suddenly very afraid. She and Chedd were going to be fed to the bog.

Waker's father waited for full comprehension to dawn's on Effie's face and then carelessly tossed the pickax in the water.

Facing front, Effie tried to breathe away the tightness in her chest. She should have snatched the pickax from him and put it through his eye. More soberly she wondered if she would ever tell Chedd. Was there any point? *Only if the fish decide not to eat us.*

A fortress of bulrushes encircled the open water that contained Clan Gray's roundhouse. Dark paths led through the tangle of hard canes like mouse cracks in a wall. Waker completed punting the boat through one such crack and they floated into the shallow lake. Giant rings of green light burned just above the water. Effie could hear the hiss of marsh gases and smell the methane. The Gray roundhouse was a black hump in the center of the lake. Massive torches circled it, their stands twenty feet high, their heads shaped like giant beehives. The same eerie green flames that flickered above the water burned at the top of each torch.

The roundhouse sat on an island of oozing mud shored with stones, bird skeletons, muskrat bones and a basketwork of canes. Wooden landings and causeways extended out from the main structure, supported by pilings for the first few feet and then left to float upon the lake. Ladders woven from canes and rushes led below the black water. Rafts and other shallow craft were tied to mooring poles. Some poles sticking out from the lake had iron baskets lashed to them; Effie could not see what was inside them.

Gray's roundhouse was not round; it was an octagon made from rotting cedar planks and marsh mud baked into clinker. Part of it looked to be sinking. Bands of square windows ran along its upper stories but all of the shutters were closed. Some had been boarded up. A few had been sealed with metal bars. Weeds were growing from softened sections of roof timber and a snarl of chokevines was threatening to overgrow the clan door.

"Buckets of mother-mud!" Chedd whispered with feeling. Effie had never heard that particular curse before but it seemed to sum things up.

A man and a woman floating on a basic raft of lashed logs moved to intercept the boat. The woman had a scrawny coon hat perched on her head like a bird's nest—she was the one doing the poling. The man was sitting cross-legged. He was wearing muskrat furs dyed green, and his skin was mottled like a newt's.

"*Way-Ker*," he said, turning the name into two separate words and seeming somehow to disparage it. "What birdies have you brought us today?"

Waker set down the pole and let the boat drift toward the raft. "Boy and a girl. Real nice. The boy has the old animal skills and the girl . . ." Waker turned to look at Effie with his oversize bulging eyes. "She's a smart one. There's no telling all she can do."

Effie spat at him.

Waker's expression didn't change as the spittle landed on his cheek and in his eye. He blinked, and as he did so he seemed to be dismissing Effie Sevrance as someone who no longer held his interest. Raising his fist he wiped his face clean and returned his attention to the green-fur man.

"She's from Blackhail," Waker told him, "and the boy's a Bannerman."

The man's gaze settled on Effie. His eyes were the same black tar as the water. "Haul 'em up. Come see me tomorrow—I'll mind you get paid."

Waker's father steered the boat so it pulled alongside the raft. The woman with the coon hat set down her pole and gripped the boat's gunwales to dock the boat against raft. Waker turned to Chedd and said, "Up." He meant both of them, but he never looked at Effie Sevrance again.

Chedd and Effie stood, their leg chains rattling in unison. Understanding that they had limited movement, the green-fur man slid over to the edge of the raft and helped them alight. Chedd first. Effie next. The man's hands dug deep into Effie's armpits as she stumbled against him. "*Good shot,*" he whispered, as he guided her down onto her backside. He might have winked at her, but she couldn't be sure.

As soon as she and Chedd were safely on board and sitting down, the coon hat woman pushed off from the boat.

"*Girlie, girlie, girlie, girlie. Never assume you'll be treated fairly.*"

It was the old man's idea of a farewell. Effie ignored it. She did not look at him or his son as the woman turned the raft and poled toward the Grayhouse.

"I reckon you'll both be hungry," said the green-fur man, tossing Effie and Chedd an apple each. "That Waker is a tight one with his stores."

Chedd and Effie looked at each other and then the apples. Was the green-fur man trying to fatten them up?

Suspicious, Effie dropped her apple in the water. Chedd looked regretfully at his own apple but eventually did the same.

The green-fur man shrugged. The coon-hat woman shot out a hand and plucked Chedd's apple from the water.

"We won't go willingly to the bog," Effie said loudly and firmly. "We're prepared to fight."

The green-fur man chuckled knowingly. "Believe me, girl. If I intended to feed you to the bog, the pike would be eating your eyeballs by now."

Chedd Limehouse and Effie Sevrance exchanged a long and surprised glance as they floated across the black-water lake toward the Grayhouse on a raft made entirely of relief.

FORTY-ONE

Raina Blackhail

Anwyn Bird was laid to rest in the manner of honored clansmen. Laida Moon, the clan healer, and Merritt Ganlow, the head widow, prepared the body over several days. Anwyn's brain was scraped out with a bladed spoon, and her torso was split open and the organ tree removed. Her skin was washed with milk of mercury and left overnight to dry. A soft putty of gray clay, silver filings, powdered guidestone and mercury salts was packed into her body cavity and skull. Her eyelids and mouth were drawn closed and sealed with clear resin. Laida fastened the torso with sutures of silver wire. Merritt brushed and braided the three-foot-long hair, securing it with a silver-and-jet clasp given by Raina Blackhail. The body was covered in a winding sheet of black linen and rested on a stone-and-timber plinth in the destroyed eastern hall.

As the women prepared the body the men rode out to the Oldwood to select and fell a basswood. A hundred-and-twenty-year tree was chosen and a loose line of over three hundred men formed, each waiting to take his turn with the ax. The felled log was limbed and dragged back to Blackhail by a team of horses. As the weather was judged uncertain it was brought into the house. Longhead hollowed it out with a carpenter's chisel, and the roughly finished log was left to cure for two days.

It had not been long enough, for the sap was still oozing and the sulfur wash that had been brushed on the inside walls now dripped on Anwyn's naked body. The clan matron had been entombed in the hollow of the tree. Raina shivered as she saw the yellow splotches on the mottled blue skin of the corpse. She stood on the greatcourt and watched the men lift the basswood onto a flat-bedded cart, their movements synchronized by terse orders from Orwin Shank. The great weight of the twelve-foot log made some of the older clansmen shake, but pride kept them shouldering their share of the burden.

Hundreds of clansmen and clanswomen stood in silence as Orwin Shank clicked the team of horses into motion and drove Anwyn Bird's body east toward the Wedge. It had been a small victory for Raina, that insistence that Anwyn not be laid to rest in the Oldwood as was planned and considered proper. She had won it not by reasonable argument or by wielding whatever small power she had left as chief's wife. She had won it by a near-hysterical fit thrown in the presence of many people in the greathearth. "No," she had cried when she learned where Stannig Beade intended to place the body. "No. No. NO!"

After the outburst Stannig Beade had seemed pleased to let Raina have her way. It had been dark days for her then and she looked back now and realized she had lost some essential portion of control. And she was not sure she had it back.

Certainly she knew enough to play her role as grieving friend and chief's wife on the greatcourt this gray and cloudy morning. She kept her silence and nodded acknowledgments at people, her bearing grave. But beyond that she felt wild and not-properly-hinged; an insane person playing at being sane.

People were treating her as if she were a damaged piece of pottery likely to break. They were careful with her, watchful, attempting to buffer her from shocks. Raina despised such treatment and would not normally have stood for it, but she could not rally the will to bring it to an end. It had its comforts, the buffering, the cautious care. She was fed and clucked over, shielded from the messages that arrived nearly daily from Ganmiddich and Bannen, and relieved of the duty of running this vast and creaking house.

Merritt had stepped into her place, emerging from the widows' hearth like an ancient warrior called by a sacred horn. Raina did not mind it much. At least Merritt was a Hailsman.

"Are you not coming?" Merritt said to her now as the cart

lurched from the solid stone of the court onto the softer, lower surface of the road. "I'll walk with you."

The head widow's hand fluttered toward Raina's arm but Raina stepped away from it. She wanted no one touching her. "I am not going."

Merritt opened her mouth to protest this latest strangeness, but then thought better of it. Lips pressed into a tense line, she nodded curtly, and left to join the procession that was forming behind the cart.

Raina stood still against the flow of people. Corbie Meese, holding his delicate wife Sarolyn firmly by the waist, nodded to her as he passed. No man or woman would ride a horse to the laying-down of Anwyn Bird. They would walk the league and a half to the Wedge, where Stannig Beade would be waiting for them by a site he had deemed suitable to one of such high status. It would be a wooded glade cleared of snow or a stone bank above a stream, or perhaps she would be laid close to one of the paths so all that used the Wedge in the coming months would see her slowly blackening corpse and pay the respects that were its due.

Blackhail never buried its dead. They were left to rot on open ground, often in full view of hunting tracks, roads, rivers and lakes. Children who played in the woods and fields might stumble upon the hollowed-out basswoods and receive a lesson in death. No matter how beautifully a corpse was prepared, how it was rubbed with poisons and packed with precious metals, the flesh always corrupted in the end.

Raina recalled a nasty trick played on her the first summer she was here. She had befriended a handful of clan maids, Ellie Horn was one of them, and it had been decided they would go to the Oldwood to collect the wood violets that were in bloom and could be brought home and pressed into oil to make unctions. The girls were high-spirited that day, their voices sharp, their whispers theatrical and broken off by sudden gales of laugher. Raina recalled Ellie Horn complimenting her most particularly on her dove gray wool dress. "So pretty," she had said. "What would you call the color? Mouse? Mud?" The rest of the girls had giggled wildly while Ellie just looked at Raina with big fake-innocent eyes. Raina remembered the skin on her face pulling tight. She had been unsure of herself in such new company and had said nothing in her own defense. They had reached the first stand of trees by then and it seemed easier to go along and pick violets.

After they had spent an hour or so in the woods Ellie Horn had sought her out. "I'm sorry for what I said about your dress. It was mean of me." There was such candor in Ellie's voice, such appeal in her bright blue eyes, that Raina had immediately believed her. "Look," Ellie had continued, moving closer. "I just found the best, most purply violets growing out of that downed log over there. I was going to take them myself, but then I started feeling bad about what happened and I thought to myself, I'll let Raina pick them." Raina had hesitated. Ellie nodded vigorously toward the old felled log. "Go on. You'll be surprised by how fine they smell."

That was the first time in her life Raina had seen a dead body. She had approached the log hopeful, not about the violets as much as about the prospect of friendship with Ellie Horn. Ellie was the important girl in the clan. The prettiest, the most smartly dressed, the ringleader. Raina recalled seeing something black and burned-looking and not understanding what it was. She had moved closer, smelled the sickly foulness of rank meat, and then recognized the contours of a face. The blackened skin was floating above the skull, suspended on a sea of maggots.

She had not screamed. That must have disappointed Ellie Horn and the other three girls who were hiding in the shadows behind the yews. The girls had broken into nervous, excited laughter and it was only then that Raina fled.

It had been one of the many hard lessons she'd had to learn at Blackhail. This was not an easy clan. Its roundhouse lay the farthest north of any in the clanholds, and had not been designed to keep out the cold or take advantage of the bright northern sun. It had been built solely for defense. The main structure had so few windows that there was only one chamber in the entire building where you could be sure to feel sunlight on a cloudless day. The winters were long here, and springs came late. Raina had learned to set aside the light and airy pleasures of Dregg—the dancing, the hotwall gardening, the embroidering with city-bought silks—and had replaced them with more earthly ones instead. There was the pleasure of a sprung trap with a mink in it, the delight of being recognized by a herd of milk cows and the satisfaction of building a hot blazing fire against the cold.

She had learned to love Blackhail, and its proud, grim ways. She had even become proud and grim herself, and when friends or kin visited from Dregg she would feel superior to them. *We are the first amongst clans*, she would remind herself as she tolerated their frivolities. That claim was Blackhail's alone. Dregg might be brighter and better situated, but it would never be first.

Raina stared at the cart rolling across the graze and the crowd of people walking behind it and tried to hold on to some of that old and deeply held pride. She had the sense that if she could it might anchor her. She feared that she, Raina Blackhail, was drifting free of this clan.

How much could a person lose and remain whole? A husband, peace of mind, a dear friend? What was left? Dagro was gone. Effie was gone. Now Anwyn. She lived in a house full of strangers, some of whom wished her harm. Since Dagro had died her life had been this clan. But this clan had changed. The Hailstone had shattered and the gods had fled. Stannig Beade had wheeled in half of the Scarpestone to lure them back, but no god would enter such an ill-begot stone. Blackhail was cursed. Its chief had murdered its chief, its guide was a man who would stop at nothing to gain power, and the guidestone at its heart was as dead and useless as Anwyn Bird's corpse.

Breathing hard, Raina turned her back on the procession. She found herself staring directly at the Scarpestone that stood on its tarnished silver plinth at the center of the greatcourt. Work had just been completed on a wooden canopy that would be hung with skins to protect the narrow hunk of granite from rain and snow. Raina's lip twitched as she looked at it. At first she had wondered why the gods didn't simply destroy it as they had the first Hailstone. It would be an easy thing for a god—an exhalation. Now she realized the gods didn't care.

So why should I?

Tugging her shawl across her shoulders, Raina crossed the short distance to the roundhouse. People walking in the opposite direction minded her then looked away. Some elbowed their companions and whispers were exchanged. She could guess what they were saying: "Why is she not attending Anwyn Bird's death march and laying?"

Because the man who murdered her will lead the ceremony. And if I were forced to watch it there would be no telling what I would do.

Perhaps some of this answer was showing in her face, for clan maids and children seemed afraid of her and were quick to step out of her way. Raina felt an odd and bitter smile come to her face and she let it stay there as she made her way through the roundhouse.

Anwyn Bird's throat had been slit so deeply that the bone at the back of her neck had been exposed. Laida Moon had told Raina that the clan matron would have died instantly. Was that statement supposed to bring comfort? Sheela Cobbin, one of the bakers, had found her. Anwyn's absence had been noted for several hours but no one was too concerned—the clan matron had other responsibilities beside running the kitchens—and it wasn't until it was time to prepare the pork legs for supper that people began to wonder where she was. Anwyn was known to be fussy about pork and she had left no instructions regarding its preparation. One of the cooks thought they should parboil the legs to speed cooking. Another said you shouldn't parboil a leg that had been brined—it'd boil out all the taste. A heated argument erupted and Sheela Cobbin, who had been listening with growing impatience by the bread ovens, said they could both stop their hollering as she was off to fetch Anwyn Bird.

Everyone in the kitchen heard her scream two minutes later. Anwyn was found slumped by the little box pallet she used as a bed in her cell beneath the kitchen. There was so much blood it had seeped through the blanket, sheets and mattress and onto the rush matting that covered the stone floor. The last anyone had seen or heard of her was when she was seen heading down the stairs from the widows' wall and stopped to tell Gat Murdock that she'd meet him in the stillroom in a quarter to discuss the latest malt they were aiming to distill. Apparently Gat Murdock had gone to the stillroom, grown impatient with being kept waiting, taken more than a few tipples of the low wines, and then wandered off to dice with the old-timers in the greathearth. In fairness he was in a terrible state about it later, telling anyone who listened that Anwyn was the finest girl in the clan and that he'd give up his one remaining arm to have her back.

Raina had expected to feel sorry for him. But didn't.

Something had happened to her when she caught sight of the body and now she was something *other* instead. She could look back and recall the old Raina and know exactly how she would feel and act in any given situation, but she could no longer feel and act that way herself. The old Raina had gone the way of the gods. And the new one didn't even know if she was sane.

Orwin Shank had been the first to perceive the change in her. He had held her in a mighty bear hug and rocked her back and forth as they stood in Anwyn's cell. "It's all right, my sweet lamb," he kept repeating softly. Quite suddenly she could not stand the raw-beef smell of blood.

"Unhand me," she had said.

Orwin had paused, surprised. Deciding that her tone was a symptom of grief he had continued rocking her. She had raised a hand and slammed him hard in the ribs.

"I said *unhand* me."

He had released her immediately and she left the room.

It was the strangest night she could ever recall spending in Blackhail's roundhouse. Dagro's death had not caused the disruption that Anwyn's did. The shattering of the Hailstone had not left the clan as purposeless and bereft. She had always been the rallying point, the one who marched into the middle of a crisis, issued orders, served beer, put a lid on unnecessary fussing, made sure everyone was well fed. They had needed an Anwyn Bird or someone like her to cope with Anwyn's death. Instead they had a chief's wife who left them to their misery, a kitchen staff who would have roused themselves to make hot food and bring cool beer if anyone had thought to direct them, a chief who was afield at war, and a clan guide who had spent much of the evening locked up in the greathearth with the elder warriors.

Raina had seen the great oaken doors barred by yearmen

with crossed spears and had not cared enough to force entry. She understood that some manipulation was happening behind them and that she would learn soon enough its nature.

Cowlmen was the word that came out of the greathearth later in that long night. Hailsmen were tense, their hands returning often to the hilts of their swords as they descended their stairs, their gazes flickering around the groups of people who had gathered in the entrance hall below them.

Robbie Dun Dhoone had sent an assassin into the Hailhouse to spread terror and strike at the heart of clan. The Thorn King had surveyed the strength of the Hailish armies camped on Bannen Field and had judged them too great a threat to Dhoone's reclaiming of Ganmiddich. He was a chief known to have no scruples—look how he had dealt with his rival and uncle Skinner Dhoone—and now he had employed the kind of vicious tactics you would expect from such a man. His plan was to cause sufficient terror to force Mace Blackhail into ordering half of his army home.

"We should expect more strikes," Stannig Beade had warned the sworn clansmen. "The death of our beloved Anwyn is just the start."

He had not addressed these words to the clan, and Raina had only heard them repeated secondhand later. Corbie Meese had given her a brief account of what had happened behind closed doors. "Raina," he had said, his voice low and filled with strong emotion, "Stannig believes there may be a cowlman concealed in this house."

Raina had simply stared at him. How could it be possible that a good man like Corbie could believe such lies? *Cowlmen?* Did he not recall the last time there were rumors of cowlmen in the Hailhold, how they supposedly killed Shor Gormalin and then left never to be heard of again? How was it possible that both she and the hammerman had lived through that time and come out with two separate experiences of the truth?

She had said one thing to him, because it was the only solid truth she possessed. "Skinner Dhoone was not Robbie's uncle. Robbie was a Cormac who named himself Dhoone after he'd decided that if he looked far enough back into his mother's lineage he would find her related to the Dhoone kings."

Corbie had looked at her strangely. "Stannig said it only as a figure of speech."

She bet he did. She damn well bet he did.

Sworn clansmen had mounted a torch party that night, riding out from the Hailhouse with long flaming firebrands housed in their spear horns. Raina could not discern its purpose, beyond the need of decent men to take action against evil. Stannig Beade had ridden at the party's head, and it appeared that no one else beside herself questioned whether this was fitting behavior for a guide.

The woman with the greatest respect in the clan was dead. He was guide. Didn't he have to grind some bones?

Two days later, whilst Laida Moon and Merritt Ganlow were preparing Anwyn's body with milk of mercury, two Scarpemen had found Jani Gaylo dead. Her throat had been slit from ear to ear and her body had been dumped down the old wellshaft in the kaleyard. It was frozen solid.

If there had been any doubt in Raina's mind, that cleared it up. Stannig Beade had murdered both women. Anwyn Bird had been a threat to him. Her status in the clan was high and she wielded her influence with subtlety, and the day she had decided to take overt action against him was the day she'd ended up dead. *"Stannig Beade is no clan guide and must be shown as such. We are many. We can send him back to Scarpe."* Those were close to Anwyn's last words, doubtless repeated imperfectly by pretty little Jani Gaylo not much longer after they were originally spoken.

Poor, silly girl. She had probably not been much older than seventeen. Too young to be killed for telling tales.

As there were only two people in the roundhouse who understood the relationship between Anwyn and Jani, the maid's death was taken as further evidence of cowlmen. The girl had been tilling the onion beds in the kaleyard, the story went, when she had been jumped from behind by her assassin. He was growing bolder now, people whispered. It was the closest thing to the truth that had been said.

Stannig Beade was growing bold. So where did that leave Raina Blackhail? Three people had been in the widows' wall that day. Two were dead. Sworn clansmen were distracted and tense: a whisper could make them draw a sword. For the first time Raina could remember, the clandoor was shut to tied clansmen. Those who were already within the house were permitted to remain under its protection, but those farmers, miners, loggers, trappers, dairymen, tradesmen, cotters, charcoal-burners, weavers, tanners and millers who applied at the door for safekeeping—as was their right as men and women making their living within the Hailhold—were turned away.

Dagro Blackhail would no longer have recognized his clan. Or his wife.

Raina stood for a moment at the foot of the great stone staircase and wondered what to do with herself. The Hailhouse was half empty now. Anwyn Bird's funeral rites had pulled hundreds away. Her absence could be felt in dozens of large and small ways. Smoke-blackened cobwebs were collecting in the corners of the hall. The scant torches that were lit had been improperly dried and dipped and were giving off more smolder than light. A sour and greasy smell was wafting from the kitchen; the hearths had not been raked in days. The list could go on, but Raina no longer saw the point of cataloguing the decline in Blackhail's house. Who was left to mind it? Anwyn was no longer here to stand stubbornly against the chaos. Merritt Ganlow might have a go, but she was all sharp edges and would rub people the wrong way. Anwyn Bird had been a block.

Oh gods, Anny. Raina breathed in the smoky air and felt the tar settle in her lungs. A Scarpeman sitting above her on one of the steps was taking a breakfast of headcheese and rye bread. He had a chunk of brain-and-tongue loaf and was chipping off pieces with his handknife and popping them in his mouth. His eyes had the yellowish tint of many Scarpes. Chewing and swallowing he watched Raina, daring her to move him. Six days ago when Anwyn was alive he would not have been allowed to block the way to the greathearth, let alone eat on the stairs. The old Raina would have been incensed, but would not have risked the potential humiliation that might occur if she made an aggressive move toward a man. The new Raina didn't care either way. If she'd had the will to stop him she would have marched up the stairs and snatched the headcheese right from his hand and slapped it into his face.

The old Raina had worried too much about what people thought of her. She had wanted to be liked as well as respected. Her mistake was in believing that if she worked hard enough at being a good chief's wife she would eventually make a good chief.

Chief's wife was not the same as chief. That fact was so clear to the new Raina she wondered how it was possible she could ever have believed anything else. The evidence was there— look at Mace Blackhail, Robbie Dun Dhoone, and the Dog Lord. You didn't rule a roundhouse by being nice. The Stone Gods were gods of war. Not gods of hearth and home.

The old Raina had *supported* the clan, but never once thought to lead it. *I will be chief.* The words could have been spoken by a child, so little understanding lay behind them. Anwyn had tried to push her; once that day on the balcony as they'd watched the Scarpestone roll in from Scarpe, and once in the widows' wall on the day that Anwyn had died. And she, Raina Blackhail, had not allowed herself to be pushed.

Always cautious. Always wary of her standing in the clan.

Her caution had killed Anwyn Bird. I will be *lessened*, she had cried when Anwyn had tried to force her into speaking up against Stannig Beade. She must have had a hole in her head.

There were no holes there now, but she was not sure what she was left with. She remembered going to see Laida Moon in the sickroom while the healer was preparing Anwyn's corpse. Laida had been holding a glass tube full of mercury in her fist. The metal pooled and roiled as they spoke, forming shiny beads that rolled from one end of the flask to the other. When Laida set it down to fetch a jug of water, it had taken less than ten seconds for the metal to harden into a dull lump. The room had to be cold, Laida had explained to Raina later, so the body would not soften and corrupt. The mercury existed in an uncertain state between liquid and solid, and the difference in temperature between her hand and the cold air was sufficient to flash between them.

That was how Raina felt, standing by the foot of the staircase: in an uncertain form between two states. Liable to soften into hysterics one moment and harden into anger and contempt the next.

She had not slept through the night in six days. How could she? Every floorboard creaking in the night might be Stannig Beade come to kill her. She was the only one left who knew what he was. The only one in the clan who understood how very little Blackhail's guide cared about the gods.

For six nights she had slept in the widows' wall with Merritt Ganlow, Hatty Hare, Biddie Byce and a half-dozen other widows who had come together to reestablish the hearth after the Scarpes had left. Safety in numbers, Raina supposed. Yet she did not feel safe. And she barely slept.

When you do not sleep eventually you do not eat. Appetite had left her and she could not recall the last time she had eaten a proper meal. Yesterday morning she had taken a little milk in honey offered to her by young Biddie Byce. Biddie was a quiet and gentle girl, yet quite capable of perceiving the changes in the chief's wife. She was afraid of what it meant to herself and her clan, Raina realized as their fingertips had touched over the milk cup.

She had reason to be.

Uncertain what to do, Raina left the entry hall and headed for the kitchens. As she passed the doorway leading to the east hall, her maiden's helper stirred against her hip. Ignoring it she entered the cavernous space of the main kitchen. Not much was being done. Two Scarpewomen were skinning a freshly trapped rabbit on the kneading table. The older woman had pinned its skull to the wood with her knife while the younger one flensed the legs. Blood was soaking into the highly polished hickory surface. Poor Anwyn. Six days dead and Scarpes were not only using her kitchen, they were bloodying her bread table.

Borrie Sweed, the broom boy, was sweeping spilled flour halfheartedly across the floor. He looked up when Raina entered, his expression hopeful, but she passed him by without greeting. She had an idea that she might simply sleep. Stannig Beade would be gone for several hours. Anwyn's laying would take time and he would not dare dishonor her memory by returning from the Wedge ahorse. No. He would have to walk with the rest of them. Anything less would be unseemly. That would give her two or three hours where she could be sure she was safe. But where to go?

The widows' wall would be too empty and exposed. The greathearth was open to sworn Scarpemen. Anywhere above-ground seemed unsafe. She would go to the underlevels, rest in the peace and darkness beneath the Hailhouse, and see if she could regain her mind. It wasn't much, but at least it was a decision. And it would stop her having to think about what was happening to Anwyn's corpse.

Carefully avoiding the area where Anwyn's cell had been located, Raina grabbed a safelamp and worked her way down-stairs. She smelled dead mice and ripe mud. The air was thick with gases that were not easy to breathe. The lower she went the wetter the stone underfoot became, and the deeper the silence. It was soothing to be in a place so quiet and dark, where she could be sure to meet nothing except mice and cellar rats. She felt the weight of her exhaustion pressing against her shoulders and kneecaps. She could tell from the trembling of the light that she must be shaking. Perhaps she should have brought a blanket, for it was icily cold, and she had nothing except her mohair shawl to keep out the chill. Longhead had once told her that the farther you went underground the warmer it became. She would go deep then, perhaps even as far as the secret room where she had hidden the last remaining chunk of Hailstone.

Yes, she would go there. It would be still and safe, and the few belongings of Dagro's that she had kept for her own were there as well. To touch them would be good.

The journey was much easier this time as she had no sixty-pound weight on her back. Within hardly any time at all she found herself crouching in the low-ceilinged foundation space. It was a short journey then, past support columns, drain walls, sealed wellheads and ancient dungeons to the T-junction where she needed to turn.

The standing water was a foot deep here and Raina hiked up her skirts and grimaced as cool, gelid liquid flooded over the tops of her boots. Luckily, Yarro Blackhail's strongroom had been built a half-level higher than the corridor, and when she slid back the stone tile that concealed the entrance she was pleased to see dry ground below her. Feeling a spike of girlish energy, she vaulted through the opening.

The Hailstone stood here. She could feel its presence

straightaway. The gods no longer lived there and the small chunk of granite retained no power, but some residue remained. It charged the space in the strongroom, lightly, almost imperceptibly pulsing the air. Raina looked, but did not approach it. It stood in the corner, a dull stone placed against a wall of dull stone. No dust had settled upon it and no spider had dared use it to anchor a web. The old Raina had had some jaw, she realized. To steal the stone: that took balls.

Quite suddenly she was too tired to think. Pulling off her boots, she glanced about for a place to sleep. Yarro Blackhail had built his small square strongroom to house treasure, not people, and beside the single market crate which she had brought here herself many months earlier there was nothing to interrupt the hardness of the stone floor. At least it was dry.

Raina lay down, bundled her shawl into a pillow, and fell into an exhausted asleep.

She dreamed of the gods. With the empty shell they had lived in less than ten feet away from her head, how could she not?

When she awoke she knew what she must do.

The flame in the safelamp was guttering, and she worried about the time. How long had she been asleep? How much oil had the lamp reservoir contained when she first picked it up from the shelf by the kitchen stair? Had it been full? Or half empty? Stiff and muddy-headed, she found she could not be sure. All was quiet. Quickly she rose and stepped into her boots. The leather felt like pulp. Her dress was soggy around the hem and didn't smell good. She crossed to the tile entrance, placed an open hand on the indents in the stone and drew it back. Just as she swung a foot up to climb out, she thought about Dagro's belongings on the crate. Planting the foot back on the ground, she hesitated.

The light in the lamp could go out any moment. The oil in the reservoir was gone. A tremor of panic passed along her spine, and in defiance of it, or perhaps because of it, she turned back in to the room. The few items she had secreted after her husband's death lay on the top of the balsa-wood crate, gathering dust. Raina brushed her fingers over the tops of them, touching them one by one. She took what she needed and left.

She was going to have to kill Stannig Beade.

The price of regaining her peace of mind was his death.

The price of avenging Anwyn's murder was his death.

The price of becoming Hail chief was his death.

This time she did not bother to hike up her skirts. She had no idea what time it was and uncertainty made her hurry. Water sloshed at her feet, rippling ahead of her every step. *Light do not go out*, she told the lamp. The flame had shrunk to a small tooth of red. It illuminated a weak circle around her body, barely touching the walls and the surface of the water. She could smell decay now. The rot at the heart of the Hailhouse.

Tht.

Raina's head shot sideways to track the noise. She had just emerged from the foundation space and had climbed the half-stair to the lower cellar level. The sound had come from a corridor off to her right. Her gaze could not penetrate the blackness. She extended the lamp, but its light just created a red corona around the dark. *Rat*, she told herself, and moved on.

The second flight of steps seemed steeper than she remembered them and the weight of water in her dress dragged against her. Sections of the second, middle, level of the cellars were open to the space above and Raina realized she was missing the faint pools of diffused light that would filter down in daylight. It was after dark. She had slept in the strongroom all day.

Well and good. He would be back by now, and it did not take a scholar to guess where he would head once the business of settling the clan was done. Stannig Beade was growing bold in his use of this house. Raina turned from her usual path, entering a section of the underworld she had never entered before this night. *Then I will have to grow bolder.*

And this is my house. Not his.

Strange, but the air was different here beneath the western quadrangle. Not fresher exactly, but moving. It skimmed over the surface of the standing water, raising ripples and creating a scum of foam. The corridors narrowed, and Raina hunched her shoulders and drew her free arm close to her body. According to Effie this section had been dug at a later date than the others. Raina guessed the girl was right. The edges of the stone blocks were sharp and still square, and the mortar between them was visible as a network of pale lines. Which chief had ordered this excavation? she wondered. Which one had been worried about his head?

Raina climbed a short flight of stairs, took a right turn, and then ascended a ramp. She was moving quickly now. The standing water was gone, and the drenched hem of her skirt slapped against the ramp. For a wonder, the lamp was still burning. Raina thought about that as she reached the top of the ramp, recalling something Effie had said many months ago, when asked how she made her way through the underlevels. *Don't know. Never seem to need a light. You just see after a while. And no one can sneak up on you.*

But you could sneak up on them.

Raina turned the lamp key. Her steps grew more certain . . . and more hushed. The passageways appeared to her as a series of shadowy frames, and after a while she could walk without brushing against the walls. Effie had told her about the route to the chief's chamber while Dagro was still alive, but a sense of propriety had forbade Raina from taking it in until now. It had been Dagro's domain, and she'd had no wish to violate his privacy. Later, when Mace had become chief, her overwhelming desire had been to avoid any place where she might encounter her second husband. With Stannig Beade it was different. The Scarpe guide could—and *would*—go to hell.

On impulse, Raina set down the lamp. She had no need of it now. She had remembered something that old, turkey-necked Gat Murdock had said the morning of the Sundering while dust from the Hailstone still blew in the air. *"The Hail Wolf has returned."* She had paid no attention to it at the time. Gat was Gat; known for his good riddances, not his good sense. Now she realized she had missed an essential truth. The badge of Blackhail wasn't two swords crossed in parley. It wasn't a she-bear suckling her cubs. It was a lone wolf, scribed in silver on a black field. She, Raina Blackhail, had to become that wolf.

The darkness was her black field. She moved through it toward the chief's chamber. When she passed beneath the entrance hall she heard footsteps and voices. A strong, rumbling vibration shook the walls. It took her a moment to realize it was the great clan door being drawn closed for the night.

Good. It meant sworn clansmen would retire to the greathearth to game and sup. Clanwives would retire to their chambers with their bairns, and Scarpers would lie low and await opportunities to do whatever mischief weasels did.

It must be getting colder, Raina decided. She was shivering, and her feet were growing numb. Halting for a moment, she pulled off her boots. A cup of water swilled out from each of them. Leaving the boots in the center of the passageway, she moved on.

She padded as quietly as a wolf after that.

Effie had told her little about the passageway leading to the chief's chamber, save that it passed beneath the entrance hall and then led down. Raina took the turn she needed and descended a series of steep, low-ceilinged ramps. Now that she'd heard the clan door being drawn on its track, she had a sense of where she stood in relation to the aboveground spaces. The knowledge that she was approaching the chief's chamber worked upon muscles in her throat. Her airways tightened. An artery in her neck beat a pulse.

When she saw a band of light ahead, she slowed. Crouching, she touched her maiden's helper, made sure it was there.

The light was coming from an opening at the top of the ramp. The opening was a quarter of a foot high and over twice that in length. As Raina crept toward it she saw that a slim brass grille was fixed over the aperture. The light coming through the opening was faint and softly orange. Smoke snaked between the bars of the grille. Glancing around, Raina tried to make sense of it. The ramp had come to an end by a corner where two walls met. At first she thought the passageway had ended also, but as her eyes grew accustomed to the light she spied a narrow ledge winding around the corner.

The ramp's angle meant that she approached the opening from below. Rocking forward she switched from a crouch to a kneel. Her damp skirt hem sucked against her calves. Raising her face so that it was parallel to the opening, Raina peered through the grille.

And saw four wood poles and a pair of feet. The feet were sandaled and pointed away from her. They were a man's feet; there was no doubt about that. They were large and covered with coarse black hairs. The right little toenail was crusty with fungus. Realizing she would see more if she altered her perspective, Raina lowered her head. The singed and ragged hem of Stannig Beade's ceremonial robe slid into view. It was hiked up to shin height. He was sitting, she decided. That explained the four wooden poles: chair legs. And now that she could see further, she understood that he was sitting behind the Chief's Cairn, the big chunk of iron gray granite that Hail chiefs used as a worktable. As she watched, tendons in his ankles relaxed and his heels rose up from the soles of his sandals. Scratching sounds followed, and Raina guessed Stannig was leaning forward to write.

Raina used the opportunity to breathe. The opening was probably a drainage conduit, cut to prevent flooding in the chief's chamber. Excess water would drain down the ramp. Had Effie crouched here, she wondered, watching Dagro's feet as they moved back and forth across the chamber? It was a bewildering thought. Raina remembered herself as an eight-year-old girl: men's feet had not figured in her interests.

Suddenly tendons in Beade's ankles sprung to life. His heels came down and his robe hem dropped to his ankles. He was standing. Swiftly, he moved across the chamber. The farther away he walked, the more Raina could see of him. Soon she could see as high as his waist. His hands were at his sides. Big, scarred, and covered in the same coarse hairs as his feet, they twitched as he moved. Abruptly he passed out of sight, screened off by a corner of the Chief's Cairn. Sounds followed; rustling and soft thuds. Two slaps were followed by a ripe-sounding fart.

And then the lamp was snuffed. *Of course, he sleeps here now.*

Raina's nostrils flared as she drew breath down constricted airways. She waited and did not move. Time passed. Dust settled. Little tingles of pain racked her knees. Mice scurried on the ramps below her; busy, aware. The roundhouse groaned as it cooled, shifting and shrinking through the night. All was quiet in the chief's chamber. Beade slept as soundly as a man with no one to fear.

When a mouse streaked across her legs, Raina didn't make a sound. Instead, she began to rise. The mice no longer knew she was here. It was time.

The transition from kneeling to standing took minutes as she allowed her body the opportunity to adjust to its change in state. Once upright, she padded across the ramp to the ledge. This was her darkness now. She could smell it and taste it. Her pupils felt as large as wells.

The ledge was two and a half feet wide. A drop of varying depth lay below it. Raina had some fear of it—it was not as harmless as mice, after all—but she did not let it slow her. She had found a way of moving, a rhythm, that propelled her forward without sound.

The ledge turned a perfectly square corner and ended twelve feet later. No openings here, nothing that could be peered through and used to gather intelligence. Raina did not need it. She knew the chief's chamber well, knew exactly where the end of the ledge stood in relation to the interior space. Close to the door, and opposite Beade's sleeping mat. Raising both palms to the wall, she searched for a mechanism that would allow entry to the chamber. She did not know what to expect. There was nothing on the interior of this wall that gave anything away— certainly not a panel of tile that slid on a track.

Tiny pills of mortar crumbled as she touched them. She had started the search at chest height and now moved higher. Fingertips ghosting across stone, she walked the length of the ledge. Nothing. She searched higher, raising her hands over her head. More nothing. Why hadn't she thought to ask Effie for details? Because she had been appalled at the thought of spying on her husband; that was why. Virtuous Raina scuttling herself yet again.

Raina continued searching. Effie, Effie, Effie. Such a strange and endearing girl. What mischief had brought her here and kept her coming back? It was not slyness—Effie Sevrance was not that sort of girl—so it must have been curiosity. She was a child who liked to know things.

Lifting her hands away from the wall, Raina stopped in her tracks. A child. Effie had been five when she'd found this secret entrance. A wee little thing, barely three feet high. She probably hadn't been looking for anything—just trailing her hand across the wall. Raina crouched, approximating a height of three feet. Bending her arm to shorten its length and letting her fingers idly bounce over the stone, she walked along the ledge once more. No luck. Raina deepened her crouch, and let her hand drop all the way to the base of the wall.

A foot from the end of the ledge she found it. Four finger-holes. One large hole on the bottom, three smaller ones above it. Raina inserted her thumb into the large hole and her three middle fingers into the smaller ones. Her fingertips quickly passed from stone to wood to air. This part of the wall was nothing more than a veneer; stone facing fixed to wood. A hollow core lay in its center. Raina hooked her fingertips around the lip of the wood and tugged gently. A section of wall, two feet long and a foot high, began to slide back onto the ledge. If it had been solid sandstone it would have weighed twenty stone. Yet as a hollow wooden block faced with sandstone on two sides it had to weigh under twenty pounds. And it moved freely. Something—perhaps a thin pad of felt or suede—had been fixed to the base of the block to allow ease of movement.

Raina drew it back slowly. The edges of the hollow section chinked softly against the solid wall. When the block was free she slid it along the ledge. Stale smoke wafted through the opening. All was dark and still on the other side. Hearing the faint piping of Stannig's breath, she waited. Listened. Once she was sure the breaths were evenly paced, she drew her maiden's helper.

A wolf, she told herself as she bellied through the hole.

Raina knew this space. An old Hailish banner depicting a silver hammer smashing the Dhoonehouse was suspended above the opening. Raina's head brushed against its base as she passed into the chamber. Some chief's wife famous for her constancy had embroidered the damn thing over a period of five years. All the details of the Dhoonehouse were said to be technically correct and rendered in perfect scale. It was a clan treasure now, albeit a lesser one. Raina wondered about its placement. It seemed convenient that its base covered the join where the fake wall and real wall met. Good for her, though. It meant there had been one less discrepancy capable of catching Beade's eye.

Raina stood. The chamber was a fraction brighter than the passageway. A torch burning in the adjacent stairwell sent a ghostly plane of light under the door. After hours of near total darkness, Raina found it easy to see through the gloom. The chamber was sparsely furnished: a single chair, the chief's cairn, various weaponry suspended from the ceiling and walls. Beade's sleeping mat.

The clan guide of Scarpe and Blackhail lay asleep and naked on his back. A light-colored blanket was twisted around his legs. His head had lolled to the side and his mouth was open. Drool rolling toward his left ear shone faintly in the borrowed light. Raina took in all the details: the hands resting on the belly, the eyelids twitching as he dreamed, the dense, graying mat of pubic hair, the water jug standing close to his shoulder. It was power she felt, not fear or bravery. A cold and joyless satisfaction that spoke to her and said, *He's mine.*

Was this how chiefs felt when they rode to war with superior numbers and weapons? No pleasure, just an emotion that lived between pride and contempt? Was this how Beade felt as he waited to murder Anwyn?

No. Raina shook her head as she glided toward him. *Because I feel fury as well.*

Anwyn Bird was the single best clansman in Blackhail; its solid, dependable heart. A protector to a thirteen-year-old newly arrived from Dregg. *Girl, you will stay in the kitchen with me and I'll hear no fussing about it.* Those had been Anwyn's first words to her; the beginning of a twenty-year friendship that had been the most complicated and long-lived relationship of Raina's life.

I failed you, Anny. My dear one. My love.

Do wolves weep as they kill? Raina did not think so. Forcing herself not to blink, she kept her eyes dry. She had a job to do and moved into position to accomplish it.

Claiming power.

Becoming the Hail Wolf.

Leaving the old Raina behind.

When she was ready, she picked up the water jug in her free hand and emptied its contents over Beade's face. His eyes snapped opened and his head jerked upright. Several things happened quickly one after another then. He recognized the person kneeling over him, instantly understood her intent, felt the blade of the maiden's helper enter his throat, reared up his shoulders in an instinct he was powerless to stop—the desire to be upright when facing danger—felt the blade go deeper, coughed in panic and swung his big right hammerman's fist up toward Raina. She took an angled blow to the underside of her jaw. Her teeth were firmly clamped together and the force was transferred to her skull. Vertebrae in her neck crunched together as her head traveled sideways and back. Her vision rippled like a stone dropped into water. But her grip on the knife's handle held firm.

Beade watched as she murdered him.

There were hard sinews and thickly walled tubing in a man's throat and Raina had to saw with the knife to sever them. Blood pumped from the ragged hole, coating her hand. It was as warm as bathwater. Beade was losing strength. His hands and lower arms flailed, yet he could no longer lift his upper arms from the sleeping mat. His teeth were bared. Surprise and panic had left his eyes. The eyelids fluttered, preparing to close.

Rising higher, Raina applied more force. "Look at me," she whispered. "You waited too long, Scarpeman. Should have killed me the same day you murdered Anwyn. Should have watched your back. The Hail Wolf returned and you didn't even know it."

She spoke other things then, dark words that spilled out of her like poison, words that had been trapped inside her body ever since the day in the Oldwood when she had been raped by her foster son, Mace Blackhail. She spoke and sawed as blood rolled across the floor and pooled around her knees and the lamplight beyond the door flickered and waned. *Mace*, she named the dying man. *Mace. Mace. Mace.*

When his heart began seizing she reached behind her back and pulled Dagro's silver ceremonial knife from her belt. Probably she was damned forever for what happened next, for she took the knife in both hands and stabbed him through the heart. She was smiling.

Rising, she left him there: a corpse in the chief's chamber, a chief's knife sticking out from its chest. She felt wild and filled with power.

Released.

One more job to do and she was done. Hieronymus Buck, a tied miner, had once told her what they did to open seams in the mine. "Light fires we do. Heat up the rock face so it nearly glows. Then we pumps the water from the Bluey. Water hits the rock and it's the mother of all explosions. I've seen thirty feet shatter in a single go."

Raina Blackhail wiped the blood from her hands as she made her way through the roundhouse. She'd be lighting a fire under the Scarpestone this night.

FORTY-TWO

The Dark of the Moon

"**K**hal Gora," Lan Fallstar said as they crossed the last stretch of causeway leading over the sunken fields of brown and black sedge, dwarf pine, and hackled ice. "Fort Defeat. Its ruins stand here. There is good water. We will spend the night."

Ash looked ahead to where the headland rose from the saturated tundra. Charcoal gray limestone bluffs, deeply fissured by running water and pulverized by tree roots, led up to a tableland that on first glance seemed overrun by cedar and silver pine. As her gaze followed the ridgeline she spied a blank rampart of stone partially concealed by the crowns of the trees. The fort wall appeared to be slightly domed, and it was smooth, without windows, arrow slits or battlements of any kind on its southwestern face. Three towers, all broken and fallen in, rose to heights not much higher than the fort itself. The tallest was open-walled and Ash could see the square-shaped shadows of its inner chambers. Frozen blue snow glowed in the corners.

She shivered. The air was raw here in the lowlands. "Why is it named Fort Defeat?"

They were riding in single file on a narrow path of piled stone and Lan did not look around as he replied. "In the Time of *Maygi* it was called *Khal Hark'rial*, the Fortress of the Hard Gate. A battle was fought and we were defeated at great cost. A thousand years later we remanned the fortress, believing our ancestors' previous defense to be at fault. It was a mistake. We were overrun and tens of thousands of lives were lost. The fortress is flawed. No one who holds it is safe. After the defeat

He Who Leads decreed that its name should be changed so that future generations would never forget."

Ash gathered her loose hair in her fist and tucked it beneath the collar of her cloak. Winds cutting through the open fields had been making it blow in her face. She would have liked to ask Lan more questions about the fortress, but knew better than to push her luck. Ask something else and she risked him turning cold; this way they could ride in amiable silence and she wouldn't have to endure being belittled or ignored.

Stupidly she had thought that after the night Lan heart-killed the unmade creature in the woods, things would change between them, become easier. That night he had seemed almost tender when he held and entered her, and later when he ran his fine golden fingers through her hair. Yet since then he had been colder than ever. She supposed it was just his character, and decided she did not like it very much.

The attack had taken place seven days ago and they'd been traveling hard ever since. East and then south, through ancient forests overgrown with moss and ghostvines, along worn stone roads that ran alongside icy green rivers and blackwater lakes, through hills milky with pale winter grasses, and past the valley of blasted trees. That had been the only day when they had seen other people, when they had ridden along the valley's rim and looked down upon square leagues of flattened and blackened pines. The valley was a perfectly shaped bowl and the trees had fallen in a radial pattern as if blasted from a central point. Their trunks were black and greasy and some had crumbled into sections like fallen pillars. An open mine was being worked in the valley's center, and Ash saw the distant figures of men and women digging with picks and working machines. The chink and rumble of their labors was amplified by the valley's steep walls.

She could smell the stale char of the trees. "What's happening down there?" she had asked Lan.

Lan had been maintaining a brisk pace along the ridgeline and did not slow to answer her. "It is *Scara'il Ixa*. A Hole Made By God." He would say no more.

Ash had the sense that he wanted to be gone as quickly as possible. He did not acknowledge the faces that turned upward to look at them, or the two horsemen armed with longbows who patrolled the head of the valley. She wondered if he had been nervous. He held the reins more closely than normal and his gaze continually scanned the spaces between the trees.

"Where are we going?" she had asked him later that day as he crouched by a stream of snowmelt to fill his waterskin. "The Heart Fires are to the south." She didn't know this for a fact but she stated it like one anyway. "And we are heading east."

"Tomorrow we turn south," he had said.

She had decided she would leave him if they did not head south in the morning.

That night she did not sleep in the tent and had bundled in her blankets by the fire. The sky had been diamond clear and crushed with stars. As she watched the constellations turn, the horses wandered over to check on her. The stallion held itself at a companionable distance and began nosing the snow for grass, while the gelding stood right over her and blew on her face. She'd had to push him away in the end, but it had felt good to know that both horses had offered their company.

As she settled down to sleep, she glanced over at the wolfhide tent. The entrance flap was moving back and forth. Ash watched it come to rest, and then waited to see if a stray gust of wind might set it into motion. It did not. Had Lan been watching her? Or had he simply heard the horses stirring and put out his head to check on them? Uneasy, she had fallen asleep.

Her dreams were of the gray, unsettled place, and the armies of creatures that suffered within it. They roiled with the smoke, hissing, arching their spines, jerking back their heads and clawing at each other and themselves. To be there was a torture. And they wanted out. Something dark and infinitely evil moved along the edge of her perception. It was the calm in the rage, the master of the chaos. *Mistresssss*, it warned. *Do not come here in the flesh.*

Ash snapped awake. Cold sweat had pooled in the hollow of her throat and it rolled down her dress as she sat upright. Dawn was a silver line on the horizon, and woodcocks were performing their strange slow mating flights above the trees. The horses were asleep; their elbows and stifles locked in place, their eyelids fluttering but not completely closed. Ash knew that if she were to stand she would wake them.

Smoky red coals were all that was left of the fire. Reaching for a stick to poke some air in them, she glanced over at the tent. The hide was still. Footsteps led from the flap into the trees. Was he gone? She tried to remember their movements last night. The stream was behind the tent. They had come in from the north. The footsteps led south.

She stood. The horses' ears tracked the movement and their heads came up. Cutting toward the trees, she felt for her sickle knife. She was still sweating, and when she blinked she saw images from the dream. Claws uncurling. Limbs writhing. Eye sockets filled with the cold black substance of space. It occurred to her that she should call Lan's name and look inside the tent, but she did neither. She had some knowledge of path lores and once she saw the footprints close up she decided they were fresh. The surrounding snow was icy, but the little lumps kicked up by the boot heels were soft. They would have hardened if they'd been left overnight.

Camp had been made in a small depression in a sloped woodland of mixed hardwood and pine. Old and swollen oaks lay dormant beside ladders of purple hemlock. Ash headed into the trees, following the path created by the footsteps. It never occurred to her that Lan might be in danger; later she would think about that.

As she waded her way through a tangle of burdock and cloudberries, the Far Rider appeared on the path ahead. His bow was braced and he was carrying a lean and bloody coati by its ringed tail. When he saw her he blinked in surprise. Ash felt heat rush to her face. It looked as if she was spying on him. Silently, he held up the coati for her to see. There was a smear of blood on his forearm, but it was probably from the animal. She backed out of the bushes, feeling ashamed.

Later that morning they'd headed south.

Ash watched Lan Fallstar as he rode ahead of her on the causeway. She suspected she did not know enough about the Sull to accurately judge him. Ark Veinsplitter and Mal Naysayer might have appeared more forthcoming, but they had kept their silence on many things. Neither one would tell her what it meant to be Reach. She recalled Ark warning her once that she was in danger unless she became Sull. He had not told her why. Perhaps this was the way it would be with all of them. She was an outsider, not to be trusted with their deepest secrets. The color of her eyes might have darkened from gray to midnight blue that night in the mountain pool, but nothing else on the outside had changed. She did not look Sull, so how could she expect Lan Fallstar to treat her as an equal? She had known all along the Sull believed themselves to be superior to men.

Reaching the end of the raised path, Lan slowed his stallion to a walk. Without any signal from Ash, the gelding followed his lead. Wind moaned in her ears as the horses climbed up a narrow and crumbling stair cut into the bluff. Pale weeds grew in the cracks in the steps, and icy streams trickling along their edges had deposited streaks of green algae and calcium salts. The horses moved slowly, placing their hoofs with care. Ash spotted a footprint stamped half in the snow and half in the algae. Did Sull still come here?

Light faded as they passed into a tunnel mined deep into the crenellations of the cliff. Water dripped and plonked in the darkness. Ash smelled tree roots and the faint tinge of sulfur. Quite suddenly she realized she had never opened a vein and paid a toll for passage; she did not possess that Sull instinct. Yet as she moved through the tunnel something within her thought, *Now would be a good time to let blood.* When light from the exit came sliding along the walls, she saw marks tattooed into the rock. Star maps, tailed comets, meteor showers, eclipsed suns and the moon in all its phases had been carved into limestone and filled with a cloudy white substance that was slowly moldering to green. Seeing the markings Ash had a sense that finally she was drawing close to the heart of Sull. They had fought and lost major battles here. *Khal Hark'rial.* The Fortress of the Hard Gate.

They emerged on a circular stairwell whose ancient stone floor was speckled with calcium deposits and lichen. The patches looked like bird droppings. A spring gurgled over the raw rockwall before passing into an underground channel. Lan headed up more steps and Ash followed him. She could see the sky again now. Clouds were fleeing west with the sun.

Finally they reached the plateau, climbing onto land that was flat and green with trees. Fort Defeat was a massive and featureless curtainwall built from dressed ashlar that was paler than the limestone bluffs. It was larger than she had imagined, its ramparts rising fifty feet. The walls were curved outward like barrels and nothing had been done to add grace or bring relief to its primitive form. Earthworks mounded at its base were overgrown with burdock, nettles and white thorns. A full-grown cedar grew straight out from a crack in the wall, its pale roots grasping the stone like claws.

Lan spoke a word in Sull she did not know and dismounted. A stone path led through the woods and around to the northern face of the fortress. Ash remained in the saddle as they took it. The wind was high here and it blew the fur on her cloak flat, revealing the pin-holed pink skin of the lynx.

As they rounded the northern facade Ash spied the first of the towers and the arched gate. The tower was the tallest of the three, and had no exterior walls on its remaining top floors. The gate was a gaping and undefended hole in the curtainwall. Some of the capstones had gone, and others were smashed and crumbling. A relief carving of a raven in flight that surmounted the gate had been broken into shards. Its wingtips and feet were missing, and its head and bill were a spiderweb of cracks. Ash felt some slight hesitation from the gelding as she guided the horse underneath it.

The fortress was doubled-walled, and as she passed through the gate she could clearly see the dark passageway that led between the exterior wall and the jacket wall. The temperature dropped as they moved into the fort's collapsed outer ward. All ceilings and interior walls had fallen and giant heaps of debris had been claimed by ivy, burdock, moss and scrub pine. Mature cedars grew in the center of the open space. Ahead a second, smaller gate led to the inner ward, but Lan came to a halt by a waist-high section of standing wall.

"We will set camp here," he said.

Ash slid from her horse. She felt as if she were standing in a crater. Sounds echoed across the hollowed-out fort. As she lifted the saddle from the gelding, Lan cleared an area of snow. He seemed distracted and did not unpack his saddlebags in his normal sequence. Nor did he set about building a fire. It was early for camp, she realized. Still an hour or so of daylight left. There was little need to rush the preparations. The stallion had found something to its liking growing on one of the stone heaps and was busy munching on yellow stalks. Once it was free of its saddle, the gelding trotted over to investigate.

"Does anyone ever come here?" Ash asked Lan, thinking of the footstep on the stair.

"No," he replied. "This is *Glor Yatanga*. The Saturated Lands."

She waited, listening to his words bounce off the walls and break up into pieces, but he said nothing more. She considered mentioning the footprint, but decided against it. A small hum of wariness was sounding in her gut.

"Come," Lan said, standing upright. "I will show you the Thirteen Wells."

She followed him through the second gate to the inner ward. The roof had caved in here but some interior walls were still standing. Lan led her along a narrow corridor and down a short flight of stone steps.

"The fortress was built around the wells," he explained to her as they entered a dim cavernous space, lit by sky holes. "Their water has not run dry in five thousand years."

The chamber was damp and smelled of bats and their droppings. Odd pieces of glazed tile still clung to upper portions of the wall, and the sky holes were glazed with thick lenses of rock crystal. Wisps of mist rising from the wells scudded across the natural rock floor. The wells were laid out in a honeycomb pattern, with only thin strips of rock between them. Some steamed more than others, and their colors varied from milky blue and green, to rusty yellow and pink, to crystal clear sapphire and inky black.

"No two share the same temperature or taste," Lan said, pulling two horn cups from the pack around his waist. "It is custom to sample twelve of the thirteen."

He had thought ahead, she realized, for the cups were normally in one of his saddlebags. Realizing he was making an effort to be amiable, she took one of the cups from his hand. "You go first."

He crossed to one of the wells at the back of the chamber, easily balancing on the narrow stone gangways. "This Sull will try the water that looks the worst."

Ash laughed, surprised by his humor. Following his path along the lips of the wells, she went to join him. Crouching, Lan scooped up a cup of gray water and drank. She watched him swallow and then did the same. The water smelled of sulfur and bubbled in her mouth. It was lukewarm.

"You must choose the next one," he told her.

She picked the largest well. Steam peeled off the surface, and its water was hot and clear and salty. Lan chose one of the rust-colored wells next and Ash was impressed by its coldness. They moved between the wells in silence, crouching, sniffing, tasting. Lan kept count, and when they had sampled eleven of the thirteen wells he said, "It is custom to bathe in the twelfth well."

She looked at him carefully. His sharply angled face was still. Mist had coated his skin in a fine film.

"We have been lucky in our choices. The two wells that remain are both warm." He shrugged off his buckskin cloak. "Make a choice."

Ash followed the motion of his hand. One of the wells was clear and black and barely steamed. The other lay at the center of the honeycomb and was milky green with a circle of cloud above it. "That one," she said. "As long as it is not too hot."

Lan undressed and left his clothes and gear in a neat pile on the rock floor. Naked, he stepped into the pool. His body was lean and muscular, covered by a fine down of golden hair that darkened around his pubis. Ash looked at him and found she had no desire. Outside the sun was setting and the sky holes let in rings of amber light. The mist and dimness were making her drowsy and she yawned as she pulled off her clothes. Once she'd removed her boots she carried her clothes to Lan's pile and dumped them on top. The boots knocked against his horn arrowcase, making the arrows slide out. A few of them came out all the way, revealing their steel heads with the holes drilled through them. The heads were socketed into the wooden shafts and bound with wire. One of the three was bound with something else.

"Come," Lan called. "This Sull does not wish to boil alone."

Ash turned quickly and went to join him. Tiptoeing around the wells, she thought about the arrow. It did not seem such a bad thing. With a high squeal she jumped into the pool.

Water splashed up, soaking Lan and sloshing into the other pools. It was shockingly hot and Ash's skin reddened immediately. Dipping her head under, she wetted her hair and face. Lan was leaning against the bowl of the well, his arms stretched wide. The lead clasps that bound his braids had reacted to something in the water and turned silver-black. Ash floated away from him, coming to rest on the opposite side of the bowl. A ledge cut below the surface provided a place to rest and Ash sat and luxuriated in the steaming water.

"Drink," Lan said after a while.

Of course, this was the twelfth well and she hadn't sampled its water yet. Leaning forward she opened her mouth and let it fill with sweet-tasting liquid. Lan watched as she swallowed.

Ash closed her eyes. "It's getting dark," she said. "We may have to wait for the moon to rise to get back."

"It is the dark of moon tonight."

The Far Rider's voice rippled toward her across the delicious warmth of the water. She tilted her head back and let her arms and legs float to the surface. Heat enveloped her, wrapping around her belly and thighs, and cupping her neck. She drifted free, slowly turning in the water. Sleep came as a gentle relaxing of thought and muscle.

At first the nightmares did not come. She floated in darkness, insulated. Something *sissed* softly. Laughter tinkled then faded away.

Mistressss.

The word roused her and she swung away from it. Far in the distance water lapped against rock.

A massive and unknowable presence turned in the darkness, watchful, cunning, *waiting*. It had bided in the shadows for hundreds of years, and its time was drawing close.

Wake.

Ash inhaled deeply, opened her eyes. All was dark and still. Memories slid into place and she realized she was in water. The sun had set and the sky holes let in no light. "Lan?" she called, not expecting an answer. Kicking, she propelled herself to the edge of the bowl. The stone felt cool against her palm. Cool and good. She waited a moment, gathering her strength, and then pulled herself out of the pool.

Water streamed down her body. Her legs felt like wet sticks, barely able to take her weight. Tentatively, she took a step across the stone in the direction of the entrance, seeking a flat surface with the pad of her toe. She knew the direction of the stairs, but she and Lan had been bathing in one of the middle wells and that meant that other wells stood between her and a way out. Crouching, she felt her way along the rim. The pressure on her knees made them shake in spasms, and she doubted if she could hold her weight this way for long. The hot water had robbed her strength.

Slowly, she edged between the pools. Mist purled under her chin. Water bubbled. The blackness was absolute, but she found she wasn't afraid of it. She just wanted to be gone from the wells. An enchantment had been practiced here. Twelve of the thirteen wells: Lan had tricked her with a spell to make her sleep.

Finally her toes and fingers detected a broad shelf of rock. Collapsing onto her butt she just sat for a while to think. She decided she had been very stupid. After seeing what was wrapped around the tang of Lan's arrowhead she should not have entered the water. She should have been afraid, not flattered.

The thick lock of hair she had given to the Far Rider had been divided in two, and half of it had been bound to the arrow. And she thought she knew what had happened to the other half.

It had made a creature of the Blind explode. There had been no heart-kill. Lan's second and third arrows had penetrated shoulder flesh. She had made the mistake of assuming that his first shot, the one she had not seen, had hit the creature's heart. She had been dead wrong. Lan Fallstar was no Raif Sevrance.

He had been experimenting that night in the woods, testing to see if the girl he had stumbled upon on the south bank of the Flow could really be what he suspected: the Reach. He had never been interested in her safe passage to the Heart Fires. The only thing he cared about was whether or not she was useful. And he had wanted to keep her isolated until he knew for sure.

Now what?

Ash rose to standing. Her body was cooling and she felt some of her physical strength returning. She would not think about their lovemaking, the betrayal of her flesh. *I initiated it*, she reminded herself sharply. *The fault was mine.*

Casting around in the darkness, she attempted to locate her clothes and weapons. Nothing was there. Not even her boots or dress. This had been carefully planned, she realized. Right down to the dark of moon. He might have been planning it from that very first night, when he had paid a terrible toll in burned flesh. Ark Veinsplitter and Mal Naysayer had never put red-hot knives to their arms—and they'd had many costly tolls to pay.

The burned flesh was the price of killing a Reach. The hair on her head alone had to be worth five hundred Unmade deaths.

Do not come here in the flesh. The creatures themselves had warned her. She was *rakhar dan*, Reachflesh, and they loved and feared her above all things. Ark Veinsplitter had predicted that Sull would come after her. Now she understood why. Her flesh destroyed *maer dan*. It was the other side of the double-edged sword. She brought them into the world by creating a breach in the Blindwall. She could send them back.

They had never attacked her directly. Not the unmade wolves on the bridge, nor the carrion feeder in the woods. Why had she not realized that until now? Perhaps their swords of voided steel could harm her, but she no longer believed their flesh could.

Was she worth more dead then alive? How many Unmade could her blood, teeth, hair, and nails destroy? She did not know the answer. Ark Veinsplitter and Mal Naysayer could have slain her, yet they had chosen to protect her instead. *Daughter*, Ark had called her. It was not the word of a man who wanted her dead.

Ash crossed toward the stairs. Hands and feet probing the darkness, she searched for edges, walls, the risers of steps. A leathery shuffling sound came from above; the bats were taking flight. They did not touch her as they flew up the stairs, though she felt the air they displaced riffle against her naked body. Their silent calls pricked the membranes in her ears.

As she reached the top step, she became aware of a slight increase in light. She was on the ground floor of the fortress now and her eyes could make out the dim and blocky forms of walls. No moon may have risen but the stars provided a thin blue veil of light. When she looked up she could see streaks of cloud and constellations, and the strange, leaflike forms of the bats.

Her nipples hardened in the raw air and every hair on her body rose upright. The snow beneath her feet did not seem cold and she walked easily upon it, barely making a sound. She was moving along a corridor framed by tall walls. When the side of her foot hit a fallen stone, she crouched and pried the square piece of rock out of the snow. Her thoughts were oddly calm and disconnected. *He will try to slay me. He is probably watching as I walk along this corridor. All the advantages are his.*

Yet she was a Reach and she was just beginning to understand that was something to be feared. She, Ash March, was something to be feared.

Could she call them forth, the creatures of the Blind? What could she do that would make the Sull fear her?

Weighing the rock in her fist, she stepped into the open space of Fort Defeat's inner ward. Nothing moved in the blue-black darkness. No wind penetrated the double walls. No mist snaked across the ground. The snow glowed dully as it froze. Ash cut toward the gate that led to the outer ward. Nothing within her wanted to stand still.

The gate was a black hole in the wall. As she passed through it her gaze searched for the place where Lan had made camp. He had cleared the snow earlier and the patch of dark ground caught her eye. The horses were gone. The packs were gone. Lan Fallstar was nowhere to be seen.

Her body was growing cold now. Water in her hair was stiffening to ice, and she could feel the gooseflesh tightening her skin. Slowly she walked toward the circle of cleared ground. Something was happening in her stomach; muscles

were contracting and relaxing in strange ways. Her left arm
began to feel light, as if it were still in water. The right one was
weighed down by the rock.

Two men stepped from the shadows to meet her. Metal slith-
ered against leather as they drew longswords. They were
silhouettes in the darkness. She could not see their faces or
details of their weapons and dress. Two men. Two swords. This
was a ceremonial slaying.

Neither warrior was Lan Fallstar; she knew it for a certainty.
He had summoned others to do what he would not do himself.
Had he invoked them that first night? Or the other morning
when he returned to camp with the coati?

No matter, Ash said to herself, feeling her left hand begin to
float from her body. *I will destroy them all.*

They stepped to meet her: black shadows armed with two-
handed swords. Starlight ran along the edges of their blades.
Breath fogged. Ash felt a muscle high in her right arm spasm as
it fought the weight of the rock.

Grayness merged with darkness, and as she moved forward
she crossed into *Glor Rhakis*. No-Man's-Land.

All was the same. The swordsmen came toward her, stepping
apart as they prepared to take her from both sides. The stars
burned blue. The fortress still stood. It was the edges that were
different, the margins, the shadows, the cracks in the walls.
They became charged with the energy of another world.

The ancient and evil presence was here, sliding along the
deeply black shadows cast by Fort Defeat's double walls.
Turning the huge millwheel of its awareness toward her, it murmured an instruction.

Reach.

Ash dropped the rock. Swords came for her. Weightless, her
right hand drifted up. A breach existed in the Blindwall, but it
had never been big enough. They had always wanted more.

Aid me, she commanded them.

As her right hand drew parallel with her left she heard a
word spoken in a dread and terrible voice.

"Daughter."

Mal Naysayer, Son of the Sull and chosen Far Rider, rode
through the fortress's main gate. His six-foot longsword with

the raven pommel was drawn and in motion. Galloping forward, he swung it in a great arc and severed the first man's head. Hot blood sprayed across Ash's belly and breasts. The head came bouncing toward her and hit her shin. The eyes were blinking.

The Naysayer spun his huge blue stallion and kicked it into motion. His teeth were bared and his eyes burned colder than ice. Dropping the reins, he wrapped both hands around the grip of his sword as he charged. The second man hesitated, torn between standing his ground and defending himself, and running. The hesitation cost him more than his head. Mal Naysayer's fearful blade ripped through the muscle and organs in his stomach, cleaving his body in two. The pieces thudded dully as they fell into the snow.

Ash heard a noise beyond the wall; the drum of hooves on stone. Lan was riding away. The Naysayer heard it too, for his head tilted for a moment as he listened.

There was never any question that Mal would go after him. She had a sense that it would not be the last either of them saw of Lan Fallstar. For now, though, the coward could wait. The Naysayer slid from his horse and unhooked his wolverine greatcloak. He was breathing hard and she thought she saw tears sparkling in his eyes. His sword was streaked with blood and stomach chyme and he laid it on the ground before he approached.

"Daughter," he said, his voice rough as he slipped the cloak around her naked and bloody body. "I have come."

Ash fell against him. She was shivering intensely, and her arms were burning with pain. The world of shadows had gone now, dissolved like salt in water. What had happened just then, she wondered. Had she reached?

Mal Naysayer picked her up with great gentleness and carried her through the gate.

FORTY-THREE

A Place of No Cloud

The night after they left the trappers' camp the sky cleared and the temperature began to drop. The thaw had reversed while Raif and Addie slept, and when they woke in the morning oozing snow had been frozen into glasslike mounds. Addie took one look at the sky and deemed it a "nosebleeder." All clouds had gone and there were none on the horizon. Suddenly the north had turned to ice.

"Pray the clouds don't come back," Addie said, warming his hands around a steaming cup of tea. "If warm air hits this freezing ground we'll be in for the devil of a storm."

"It's spring," Raif replied, knowing his voice sounded strained yet forcing himself to speak anyway. It had not been easy for him to talk to Addie last night and this morning. "You'd think we'd be due some mild weather."

The cragsman frowned at him thoughtfully. "I'm not sure spring's going to come, lad. Not this year."

They were quiet after that. Sitting on opposite sides of the crackling and fragrant cedar fire, blankets pulled tight across their shoulders, they supped on hot, spicy tea.

The remains of the young deer Raif had brought down at sunset had frozen into pink chunks. He'd done a hasty job of the butchering and had not skinned the carcass. Addie had helped, but there was only so much you could do after dark. Neither of them had expected the hard frost, and now most of the meat would have to be either cached or discarded. The pieces were too large to carry and could no longer be divided into smaller parts. They had the liver, which Addie had sliced into squares before he went to sleep, and the remains of the hind leg had been roasted with some of the Trenchlanders' sharp and soapy-tasting herbs. Looking at the frozen hunks of meat with the deer hide still attached Raif wondered if he was any better than the bear trappers. Even the ravens wouldn't be able to feed on it until it thawed.

"I'll put some of it in a wee bag and haul it up the tree," Addie said, showing that he had been following Raif's gaze. "But first we'd better check on those little suckers on your back."

It was not a pleasant few minutes for either of them. Addie had slept with the jar of leeches and had to travel with them close to his body all day. The risk of freezing was too great. Maybe a frozen leech could be revived, maybe it couldn't, but neither of them were taking any chances. They were already down to twenty-one and counting. Twenty after Addie rolled his fingers in the snow to cool them, spoke the three-worded prayer *Gods help me* and stuck his hand in the jar of black worms. He did not have Flawless' knack for it and gripped the leech mid-belly, rather than below either of its sucking heads, and that meant he had to move fast. Two sets of mouth parts wanted a go at him. Raif could do nothing but pull his new rawhide tunic around his shoulders and present his back to Addie Gunn.

The cragsman's breaths were telling: short and wet with disgust. "Keep still," he cautioned, though in truth Raif had not been moving. "Sweet mother of gods."

When it was done the skin on Addie's face was tinged green. "You're gonna need to get that whole mess seen to," he said. "There's half a dozen wounds back there leaking blood, skin's peeling, something's turned black." He shuddered. "We'd better get a move on."

While Addie cached the meat—for no purpose, it seemed, other than treating the slain deer with some respect; neither of them expected to be back here again—Raif broke up the camp.

They had made good time yesterday and were now deep into the rolling cedar forests northwest of the Trenchlanders' camp. Once Raif had brought down the deer, Addie had attempted to locate some kind of meaningful clearing for setting camp, but had been forced instead to call a halt in a fallen timber gap between the trees. The ancient cedar that had toppled had provided partially seasoned wood for the fire and they'd had good, hot flames for roasting and tea-making. The embers were still firing as Raif covered them with snow.

He wished Addie had kept his opinions to himself about his back. With every movement he made he could feel the wrongness; the tight skin where the plaster had been attached, the bloating, the wounds. The teeth. Last night he'd slept on his back and when he'd risen two bloated leeches had dropped onto the blankets. They were slimy with his blood.

"Here," Addie said, startling Raif. "Eat."

Raif took the frozen cube of liver and popped it in his mouth. He sucked on it as they struck a path north through cedars the size of watch towers. It didn't please him very much, but he appreciated Addie's care. Blood for blood.

The rising sun was piercingly bright, illuminating individual ice crystals floating in the air and bringing out the red and purple tones that lay beneath the dark greens of the cedars. The trees had shed their snow and now had frozen moats around the bases of the trunks. If the temperature held trees would be lost. Sudden frosts after thaws could split pines clean in two.

Raif and Addie did not speak as they hiked up the rise, and this suited Raif well enough. He had some thinking to do. Woodpeckers were the only birds making noise in the forest and the sound of them drilling tree bark sharpened and clipped his thoughts.

The Red Ice. The Valley of Cold Mists. *Mish'al Nij.* The place where he was headed had many names. *North*, the Trenchlander had said, seeming to think that was instruction enough. Thomas Argola had been even less helpful. *"The Lake of Red Ice exists at the border of four worlds and to break it you must stand in all four worlds at once."* Raif had found the words so vague and self-important that he had barely thought of them since. To him they were just another of Argola's games.

Yet now he went over them again. Both the outlander and the Trenchlander had mentioned borders. Flawless had said the Red Ice lay on the border of Sull land and Bludd land. The clanholds and the Sull: they were two separate worlds.

Could the Want be the third?

Raif ducked his head to avoid a low slung cedar bow. Out of habit he glanced over at Addie, reassuring himself that all was well with the little cragsman. Addie's gaze was focused on the way ahead, reading the paths between the trees, searching out all potential routes.

Perhaps there was a point where Bludd, the Racklands and the Want met? Addie had said the Bludd borders were uncertain this far northeast, and Raif himself had firsthand knowledge of how intangible the margins of the Great Want could be. Perhaps here it dipped south? That might explain why the lake was difficult to find. If any part of it lay within the Want then it was no wonder Bluddsmen could ride right past it. If they didn't there was a chance they would never be seen again.

Feeling one of the leeches stir against his back, Raif shivered and spat out the grizzly remains of the liver. He was wearing two layers of trenchlander skins beneath the Orrl cloak, and he had tucked neither of them beneath his gear belt. That way when the gorged leeches disengaged they'd end up falling onto the ground, and not hanging around his waist. Like yesterday. It was possibly the strangest piece of wisdom he'd ever learned.

Knowing he had a short tolerance for leech thoughts, Raif turned his mind back to the Red Ice. If there was a possibility that Thomas Argola's words were right, then there should be a fourth border. Sull. Bludd. Want. What was the fourth? Was there something he was missing? The Racklands stretched from the Breaking Grounds to the Sea of Souls; the Trenchlands were contained within them. Did that mean something? Did the Trenchland border come into play?

"Addie," he said. "Where does the Trenchlander border lie?"

The cragsman shrugged. He was in the process of subtly adjusting their route, turning them due north into a mixed stand of spruce and white pine. "Trenchland's just a name. The lowlands around Hell's Town have been carved by the Flow— that's where it gets its name. There's no border as such."

Raif nodded, disappointed. "Is there any way we can tell when we're on the border between Sull and Bludd?"

Addie looked at him. Flawless had given the cragsman the same directions as he had given Raif, and Addie had probably already considered this problem himself. "In this part of the world the only way to know for sure whose land we're standing on is if someone steps out from the trees and attacks us. If that happens we should be sure to take a real good look at them."

Raif fell silent. He felt stung by Addie's tone. Had he insulted the cragsman by asking the question? It was hard to judge things with Addie now.

They stopped three times before noon for leech duty. One of the creatures wouldn't attach itself to Raif's back; it looked as sick as a leech could look. Addie returned it to the jar, but they were both thinking the same thing: spoilage had not been factored into the equation.

At noon they had a good meal of roasted venison and salted hardbread that had been traded from the Trenchlanders. The cold was numbing so they ate with their gloves on. Afterward they greased their skin and slid on face masks. As they headed out, the first of the cedars exploded in the valley below them. The woodpeckers fell silent and the only sound was Raif's and Addie's boots crunching frozen snow.

After a few hours the land began to rise and warp, and bare rock broke through the forest duff. The cedars were not as tall here, and enough light penetrated the canopy to support groundcover; hagberries, bearberries, and balsam. Raif perceived animals denning beneath rotting logs and between cracks in the rocks. Their heartbeats were faint and winter-slow.

Raif tried not to think about his own heart, tried not to recall how easily it had failed him. One moment beating, the next stopped. A blink of an eye, a failure of muscle to contract: that's all it took to kill a man.

He forced his mind elsewhere, and ended up considering the name Yiselle No Knife had given to the Red Ice. *Mish'al Nij.* A place of no cloud, yet the lamb brothers had named it the Valley of Cold Mists.

More trees exploded as the sun moved into the west. One cracked right on the path, its trunk fracturing from the crown to the base as if it had been hit with a giant ax. The sudden release of pitch and gases made the air smell like a primed firestack.

As the sky grew dark Addie began to rest more heavily on his stick, and Raif thought about calling an early halt. Progress had not been good; nearly every hour they'd had to stop to apply leeches and Addie was getting no quicker with practice. His hands froze, Raif's back froze, the leeches were starting to get sluggish. Just as Raif opened his mouth to speak, Addie raised his stick.

"Stand of red pines beyond the rocks."

The sign of the Bludd border. They headed west toward it, their spirits lifting. Here was a marker that could help them. The trees were planted along a north-south axis in single file along a south-facing slope. It was dark by the time they reached them, and you could no longer tell they were red pines.

"Let's set camp," Addie said, smiling for the first time in two days. "I think this calls for a spot of tea."

They set camp hard against the pines, both fearing that if they didn't the trees might disappear in the night. A new leech was applied, a fire built. Roasted meat was set to warm on rocks.

As they sat, bending their heads toward the searing heat of the fire and enjoying the dregs of the tea, Raif's raven lore stirred. It had been so long since the hard, black piece of bird ivory had moved he had not spared it a thought in weeks. Some disturbance in his heart or blood triggered the leeches, and the two that were attached to him dropped off. Raif stood, his hand feeling for Traggis Mole's longknife.

Addie rose a moment later, and both men pulled their bows and arrowcases from the gear pile that had been lazily heaped on broken-off cedar boughs. Swiftly they pulled off gloves. Neither spoke. Things had changed between them. But not this.

With his gaze facing out from the fire, the cragsman tugged at the cedar boughs, tumbling packs and blankets into the snow. Without looking at the flames he fed them. Raif faced north, toward a slope he could barely see. The stars were out in cold lightless force. There was no moon.

Crack.

Both men swung to face the sound of an exploding tree. In Sull territory: they could say that with conviction now as the noise came from east of the red pines. Addie Gunn and Raif Sevrance trained drawn bows into the darkness. Addie's sturdy self-made yew ticked with a reassuring sound as it held tension. The Sull longbow made no sound.

When a soft crackling noise came from the west neither one was expecting it. Addie swung around and immediately loosed his bow through the pines. Raif perceived the damning suction of an unmade heart.

And then felt its small and deadly echo a hair breadth away from his own. The *Shatan Maer*'s claw was trying to home.

Leeches are my friends, he thought inanely, his gaze searching for forms in the blackness. Addie raised a second arrow to the plate, and as he pulled back the twine Raif became aware of a second heart. Back in Sull territory, moving forward from a position not far from where the tree had exploded. Quickly he made a calculation. Swinging his attention fully east he left the creature on the other side of the red pines for Addie Gunn.

East was where the greatest threat lay. He could feel it in his lore and his plagued and punctured heart.

A shape rippled into existence, then disappeared. It was big and man-shaped and Raif did not want it near him. Ever since the night on the rimrock he'd had no trust in hand-to-hand combat with blades. Let the Sull bow and the case-hardened arrowheads do the work.

Keep away, he murmured under his breath. *Keep away*.

Suddenly there was a series of crunches to the west. Addie loosed a second arrow, fumbled, replated. The footfalls accelerated, smashing the frozen snow with their force. Raif could no longer stand it and swung to second his friend.

Both men loosed their arrows in perfect time. A single *thuc* sounded with the depth and richness of a musical chord. The arrowheads converged . . . and slammed together in the unmade heart. Sparks shot out of shadowflesh. Something not human jerked upward and then collapsed. A sound on the edge of hearing sizzled through the forest air.

Pivoting east on the balls of his feet, Raif reloaded and drew his bow. The cragsman was a half-second behind him. Flames shivered at their backs, casting fans of jittery shadows at their feet. Clouds of bitter-smelling smoke pumped outward from the fire stack; items from their gear pile were going up in flames.

Raif scanned the darkness for the man-shaped thing's heart. His own heart was fluttering queerly, and he could feel the shadowflesh burning through it like a hot ember set upon wax.

All was still. Addie's breaths were ragged, but his grip on the bow was rock-firm. The moon began to rise above the treeline, its light beaming in their faces and moving between the trees. Without realizing it both men edged away from the camp. Addie was taking Raif's lead, and Raif was moving in the direction he'd last seen the Unmade.

The fire went out. Darkness was sudden and complete. Flattened coals popped and spat. Something hot landed by Raif's heel. He and Addie swung back to face the killed fire. Addie let an arrow fly into the swirling blackness of night and smoke. Raif understood the impulse but held. He knew exactly how long it took him to reload and draw a bow. It was too long. An eyeblink, that was the difference between life and death.

The man-shaped thing rushed them. It pushed its own shape before it in smoke. Moonlight bent toward its thick diamond-shaped blade. Raif loosed his arrow. Even before the twine recoiled he had thrown down the bow. The arrowhead had penetrated heart muscle but it had not gone deep enough into the gristle and the thing still came at them.

"*Addie. Get back,*" he heard himself scream as Traggis Mole's longknife scribed the quarter-circle from his hip to a position at right-angle to his chest. Raif saw the creature's hollow, craving eyes. Heard the explosive *crack* of its weight coming down upon pine needles suspended in ice. Its blade had to be four feet long. Raif's was two.

Raif leaped forward, feinted right. The man-shaped thing swung his sword at him like a club. It was screeching like a seagull. Raif stepped behind it, made the thing turn. Voided steel came at him: its edge the glistening razor where chaos and destruction met. It stunk like the absence of all things. Raif rolled ahead of it, felt it touch his lower rib. Life heat sucked from the hole. Springing up Raif braced the Mole's longknife against the hard plate where muscle met bone in the exact center of his ribcage. The man-thing was yanking back its blade for another strike. There was air around its chest.

Traggis Mole's longknife was inhumanly sharp, sharper than any sword Raif had ever wielded in his entire eighteen-year life. It seemed to take no pressure at all to puncture shadowflesh, no effort at all to slide between the dark ventricles of the grossly inhuman heart. Voided steel came up, touched real steel with a queer vibrating tone. That carried no force.

Raif yanked out the blade, rolled clear onto the snow. Embers and pine needles crackled as his spine crushed them. The man-thing rocked like a wedge-cut tree about to topple, and then went crashing to the ground.

Deep and perfect silence followed. Neither Raif nor Addie moved. The cragsman was standing upslope from the camp by the tallest of the red pines. Moonlight made his face blue. A great gray owl calling out across the forest broke the silence. *Hoo. Hoo. Hoo.* Addie was the first to move, rushing toward Raif. Raif thought he'd like to stay awhile lying down in the snow and did just that.

"C'mon, lad." Addie's voice was hard, angry. His finger poked at Raif's ribs like sticks. "Get up now. Get up."

Raif blinked at him and thought, *Leave me be, old man. I'm tired.*

Addie Gunn would not let Raif Sevrance be. He was a cragsman and he knew how to leverage his weight to haul sheep, and that's what he did to Raif. He hauled Raif up over his shoulders and carried him clear of the camp. When he found a bed of tender yearling spruce he deposited Raif upon it. Two layers of rawhide were yanked up. The leech jar was opened. Curses were sworn, and then Raif felt the circle-bite of a fresh leech on his back.

"Wait here," Addie said, unclasping his cloak and laying it over him. "I'm going back to get the gear."

Raif waited and then slept.

Two times in the night he was roused by Addie, yet Raif managed to submit to the cragsman's ministrations while not fully waking. His dreams were all of death, of that moment that divided this world from the next. The eyeblink. The thin line. The failure of the heart.

When he awoke fully and properly it was light. He was still lying on the spruce, curled up on his side. A new pain in his lowest rib just above his spleen throbbed with dull persistence. He supposed he should be grateful the voided steel had touched bone.

Addie was sitting by a fire the size of a horse, toasting a piece of liver on a stick. He had a wild, disheveled look about him. His hair was sticking up and some of it was frozen. A pine needle was embedded in his cheek. The corner of one of the blankets that hung across his shoulders had been scorched. When he heard Raif move he looked over and said, "Ain't getting no easier."

It was the closest Addie Gunn had ever come to complaining.

Raif stood. It took a moment for all the various hurts and bruises to settle themselves into place. Some kind of order was being established, a hierarchy of pain. A snap of dizziness hit as he crossed to the fire, but he forced himself to walk through it. "Breakfast?" he asked, coming to a halt by the wall of yellow flames.

"Aye. Tea's gone. Liver's dry. There's hardbread on the rock."

Raif took a drink of hot water and forced himself to eat the liver. The hardbread had been placed on a rock in the embers and was slowly turning black.

The heat from the fire was intense. After a while Raif had to step away. The cragsman must have been up all night building and tending it. As he walked around the hastily set camp that lay about a hundred feet above the old one, Raif wondered what to say to Addie. *Sleep, I'll stand watch. Sorry about worrying you sick. Sorry I didn't offer the stormglass for trade that day by the campfire.* All apologies were too late, he comprehended, running a gloved hand along an icicle that hung from one of the red pines. And Raif Sevrance did not have the time to watch Addie Gunn while he slept.

Returning to the fire, he asked, "How many leeches?"

Addie rose to his feet. He understood what the question meant—time to get moving—and by making himself suddenly busy he could duck the need for an answer. They had to be down to the last ten by now: not enough to outlast the day.

The sack containing the tea had been lost to last night's fire, along with one of Addie's mitts and some spare clothing. Addie cut the toe off one of his socks and declared it a glove. Raif threw snow on the flames and watched it turn to steam. It took ten precious minutes to kill the fire. The sun was already visible above the forest canopy; a slender disk circled by mirages.

They'd already lost an hour and a half of daylight. What was Addie thinking, leaving him to sleep?

Raif set the pace north. Even when the stand of red pines was hidden behind the crest of the slope the path was clear. They had to keep heading along the same axis. If the red pines marked the true border between the Racklands and Bludd then all they had to do was maintain their bearings and eventually they'd cross the Red Ice. If what the Trenchlander said was true. It had to be true. Raif didn't have time for it not to be.

One border. Four worlds. If they went far enough north would they enter the Want? And if they did would they know it? Raif looked down at the forested valley that lay below them, the spires of cedar, the knuckles of red rock, the frozen streams, the kitty hawk circling for prey. It looked too full of life to be named the Great Want.

"Clouds are coming in."

Raif saw that Addie was right. A dark crack had opened up on the edge of the horizon. A blackness in the silver of the sky.

They spent the morning crossing the valley, eating on foot and stopping only to apply new leeches. The air was raw and changing, and the wind started to show its teeth. Raif walked huddled in the Orrl cloak, slightly bent at the waist to relieve the pressure of the wound. Addie had cleaned and bandaged it in the night; he said it was shaped like an X.

Raif found his thoughts kept returning to the moment the fire had gone out. If the Unmade had extinguished it then that meant they were capable of cunning. And *that* was something new and dangerous. Creatures that could plan as well as fight.

By the time they reached the valley's northern slope the clouds were moving with force. Sharp gusts broke icicles and brittle branches from the pines. Addie and Raif walked against the headwind, shoulders hunched. When they came across two big trees with boughs interlaced they stopped to shelter from the weather and apply another leech. They were down to one at a time now. As Addie took the jar from his gear pouch, Raif saw how few were left. And not all of them were moving.

The cragsman had trouble getting the leech to bite and prodded Raif's back several times. When he took his hand away his fingers were red with blood. "It's hanging," he said grimly. "Gods help it to stay in place."

To change the subject, Raif told Addie about Thomas Argola's words. "Four worlds?" Addie pondered, wiping his hand on his cloak. "Clanholds. Sull." He frowned. "The Want?"

Raif shrugged. "What could be the fourth?"

Addie tugged on the sock with force, quickly losing his patience with puzzling. "How the hell would I know that, lad? I'm a sheepman not a scholar. If it's land I know it. If it's fancy worlds dreamed up by Argola then I can't see that either of us has much of a chance of figuring it out."

Raif considered this. "I think you just insulted me."

Addie harrumphed. "Well I insulted myself as well."

The day darkened quickly as the thunderheads charged the sky. Raif felt wire-drawn and full of energy. His thoughts thrived in the gray stormlight, rippled along with the trees. He saw Traggis Mole take his final breath, sucking air through his nose hole, heard Yiselle No Knife ask quite clearly *Do you know how to start a stopped heart?* And smelled the emptiness of the space between the stars, the stench of voided steel.

Soon, something promised within him.

Soon.

"Well would you look here." Addie's voice seemed to come from a great distance, and Raif had to force himself from the dreamworld to understand it.

The cragsman had stopped. They had reached the lip of the valley and a landscape of crags, rocky hills, and swaths of evergreen forest lay before them.

But Addie Gunn wasn't looking ahead. He was looking at a shrubby dried-up plant by his feet. "Trapper's tea, I swear it." His voice was filled with quiet awe. He plucked off a leaf, chewed on it, and then nodded with satisfaction. Squatting he pinched the stem of the plant close to the base and plucked the entire thing, roots and all, from the snow. "I'm a happy man," he said as if he meant it.

Raif murmured something. As Addie was chewing he had been looking east. Far in the east a break in the stormheads allowed sunlight to pour down onto a circle of heavily wooded hills.

Mish'al Nij.

A place of no cloud.

It had been a mistake to imagine the border between Bludd and Sull would run straight south to west.

Addie tucked the shrub inside his game pouch, and applied the last of the moving leeches to Raif's back. As he led the way due east, the first bolt of lightning split the air.

FORTY-FOUR

Chosen by the Stone Gods

I t was a Bludd sunset, firing the entire breadth of the sky from north to south, the cloud banks glowing like rubies, the sun shimmering like a bronze disk. Vaylo wasn't given much to fancy, but he was sure he could feel the sun's brilliance on his face. You couldn't call it warmth, as it was cold enough to freeze the spit on your teeth if you smiled, yet he had the sensation that he could feel individual waves of light bouncing off his skin.

Vaylo frowned at Hammie across the ramparts of the hillfort, suspicious that this bout of poeticism might be his fault. The Faa man *had* just said the sunset reminded him of Burning River.

That legend was sacred to Bludd; it struck something close to its heart. Touched fear and pride, gave children images to bring to their nightmares, and grown clansmen a sense of what it meant to belong to Bludd. Ockish Bull had been the one who first told him the tale in full. Vaylo must have been about nine; Ockish about twenty-one. Ockish had led a two-day hunt into the Bluddwilds north of the roundhouse and they'd bivouacked in a chest-high snowdrift. Ockish was the eldest so he had them doing all the grunt work. Vaylo remembered one of his half-brothers had come along. Arno. It had been a good two days. There'd been the wonder of digging a shelter from the snow, followed by the second wonder of it not melting when they lit a fire. Deer had been caught, gods bless their overstruck, overkilled souls—no one except Ockish had exercised any restraint. Even Arno hadn't been too bad, and there'd been a point when they'd mounted a water-bladder fight when he and Arno had been working together as a team, laughing, soaking and perfectly synchronizing the filling and the throwing of the missiles. For that one fine hour it had been "us" against "them." Both of his half-brothers were easier to get along with when they weren't together, Vaylo had realized later.

That second night Ockish had ordered the construction of a parley fire. No one but him knew what this was meant, yet seven boys all under the age of fifteen had moved sharp to his orders, building a six-feet-wide hollow sphere of logs. "It's for light, not warmth," he had told them once it was done. "That way we'll be sure to see each other's faces when we talk."

Vaylo and Arno had agreed that it was a fine thing. Ockish had lit the primed sphere with ceremonial flourish, and then handed Vaylo a flask to pass around the circle. "One swig per man." Whatever it was it had tasted like wood varnish and made everything Vaylo looked at that night seem sharp in the middle and blurred around the edges.

In his own good time, Ockish Bull had then told them about the legend of Burning River. "It was the time of the great Vor lord, Wardwir Crane, a thousand years deep in the past. Wardwir was a fearsome general and rode to battle wearing the black and winged cranehelm and wielding the sword named Beheader. His enemies shivered to see it. He wanted land and fancied HalfBludd and he took it on the Night of Wralls. It is told that Wardwir beheaded one hundred and thirty-one Halfmen in battle before he ordered his war scribes to cease the count. Wardwir judged that if a higher number was recorded his enemies might disbelieve the tale. And cease to fear him." A pause had followed where Ockish Bull's gaze had traveled around the parley fire, waiting for everyone present to register their agreement. Vaylo had nodded vigorously. A hundred and thirty-one *was* a good number.

Satisfied, Ockish had continued. Even at that young age he'd had a way with spinning tales. "The new Bludd chief Mannangler Bludd had no choice but to ride his armies south to meet Wardwir. *When a Bluddsworn clan is invaded,* he told his men, *so is Bludd.* Wardwir assembled his host on a field south of the Wolf and waited for Mannangler to make the crossing.

Mannangler had been camped south of Broddic and arrived with many rafts and boats. The crossing was made in the dead of night. Five hundred Bluddsmen were on the river when it ignited. Wardwir had been waiting for him and had ordered naphtha floated on the water. When he gave the signal his cross-bowmen loosed a thousand arrows primed with bone phosphor. The fire of hells erupted. Flames as tall as towers lit up the night as if it were day. Bluddsmen burned on the river. When they threw themselves in the water to douse the flames they still burned. Some made it to the other side and cooked within their armor as they fought. Mannangler himself boiled so intensely in his full plate he exploded. The Bluddsmen who were still await-ing crossing heard the terrible cries of the clansmen and many took to the water, knowing they too would be burned but unable to stand by and watch their brothers die. Hundreds of Bluddsmen lost their lives that night, their weapons and armor melted to their skin, their bodies crisped to husks."

Even now, forty-five years later, Vaylo could remember the silence that had followed Ockish's tale. It had weight and mean-ing. *Many took to the water,* those were the words Vaylo had cherished the most. That was what it meant to be Bludd.

Or so he had thought back then.

Now he wondered about other things in the tale. How could Wardwir have taken HalfBludd so easily? Both the Wolf and the Lonewater guarded its clanhold, and the HalfBludd round-house was not known for nothing as "the Siegebreaker." And what was the Night of Wralls anyway? At first Vaylo had assumed Ockish meant to say "Walls" but he had heard varia-tions on the tale many times since then and although several details changed from telling to telling that word remained the same. Wralls.

Vaylo shivered. "Hammie," he said, "why did you have to go and get me thinking about Burning River?"

Hammie knew when an apology was called for even when he wasn't exactly sure about the nature of his trespass. "Sorry, Chief."

Vaylo wagged his head. "You should be. Keep watch."

"Aye." Hammie Faa stood to attention. He was dressed in his new maroon cloak, and Vaylo could see that at some point in the past few days it had been tailored to fit him more precisely. Nan Culldayis had been busy with a needle. That woman had a giant soft spot for anyone whose named ended in Faa.

Thinking about Nan made him want to see her, and he took the short walk along the western rampart that led to the stairs. The sunset was fading to purples and dried-blood reds and black. Thicker, more serious clouds were heading in from the northeast. Old compacted snow that had been around for several weeks felt like stone underfoot. Part of the rampart wall had collapsed decades earlier leaving an exposed gap where a man could simply walk off into thin air. Vaylo considered why he had been here for nearly thirty days and not given the order to have it timbered. Nan was busy fixing things. Why wasn't he?

Waving a hand in farewell to Hammie, Vaylo took the stairs. Someone had thought to salt here and the steps were less treacherous than the rampart. The wind was beginning to pick up and he could hear it warping the sheet copper on the roof.

The blond swordsman Big Borro was heading up as Vaylo was heading down. "Snow?" Vaylo asked as Borro backed against the stairwell to make room for his chief to pass.

Borro had an apple pinned between his teeth and it made a sucking noise as he dislodged it. "Aye. Storm's brewing to the east."

Over Bludd. The Dog Lord nodded. He noticed Borro had a basic shortbow clipped to a brain hook on his shoulder belt. "Taking the watch from Hammie?"

"Joining him. Drybone says on the nights when the clouds cover the moon we need to mount a double guard."

It was the first Vaylo had ever heard of such an order. But he did not let Barro know it. "Don't stand still. You might freeze."

"I know it," Big Borro said, nodding toward the cloak, face mask, and overmitts he had rolled in a loose pile and tucked under his left arm. "Got some spare for Hammie. Some of . . . Der's old stuff."

Vaylo met Marcus Borro's dark blue eyes. Der was Derek Blunt. And Derek Blunt was dead, attacked by only the gods knew what. If the Dog Lord remembered rightly Big Borro and Derek had married sisters. Pretty dark-haired girls who were waiting back at the Bluddhouse. "Derek was a fine warrior. One of the best men I ever saw wield a sword from the saddle."

Muscles in Borro's large fleshy face tightened. He was a big man, wide as well as tall, with some hard fat at his gut and the beginnings of a third chin. "Makes it harder to figure how he could have been taken while mounted."

Few replies possible to that and Vaylo did not attempt any. The two parted in silence, exchanging blunt and knowing nods.

Vaylo found himself little warmed when he entered the hill-fort. Fires were burning somewhere, but not here in the west ward, in the hall above the temporary stables. There *was* a fire-place—a vast black cavity the size of a beer cellar topped with a stone mantle carved with thistles and fisher heads—but the cook irons had gone, and an ominous split in the flue wall, running from the mantel all the way to the roof, perhaps pro-vided the reason why. At least the cold had killed off some of the molds. The green ones, if Vaylo wasn't mistaken. The black ones could probably live on the moon.

Even without the warmth of the fire some men still bar-racked here, and untidy rows of makeshift stretcher-beds, rush mats, burlap sacking and weapons gear lined three of the five walls. A few men were sleeping. Some were engaged in a tense game of knucklebones. Little Aaron was sitting beside Mogo Salt, watching with keen interest as Mogo rubbed yellow tung oil into Cawdo's peel-bladed Morning Star hammerhead. Aaron looked up as his grandfather passed, but the lure of such an exotic piece of weaponry was too great and he bared his bottom teeth in a hopeful grimace that meant something like, *Sorry, Granda, don't be mad, but this is better than spending time with you.*

Vaylo glared at him. Keep the boy on his toes.

It had been sobering to see how quickly his grandson had been won over by Gangaric. The boy's uncle had stayed at the hillfort for only three days, but by the second day Aaron was fol-lowing Gangaric around like a puppy. *"What's it like at HalfBludd? Do they eat slugs? Is Quarro Bludd chief now? Which hammer did Da wield at the Crab Gate? If we hold Withy why can't Granda be king? Where are you going? Can I come?"* The questions had been relentless, and in fairness to Gangaric he had dealt with them with patience and some tact. He'd had twin boys himself, Ferrin and Yago, and he knew something about how to deal with bairns. He also knew, Vaylo was sure, what an impression he was making upon the boy. Aaron was seven, and easily swayed. Gangaric had wooed him with tales of the Bluddhouse, of Pengo's brilliance on Ganmiddich Field, of the importance of wielding a hammer, not a sword.

"Why don't you have a hammer, Granda?" the boy had actually asked yesterday.

"Because I lost it in a Dhoonesman's chest," he had replied, surprised by how sharply the question touched him. "And I never it got it back." *And it happened because your father, the supposed hero of Ganmiddich Pengo Bludd, deserted the Dhoonehouse leaving behind a crew of forty men. Forty. And you, my grandson, are one of the handful of people inside the house that night who escaped alive.* He had come so close to saying those words that if Aaron had been older he could have read them on his granda's face. As it was the boy had left him, his shoulders drooping, his skinny arms hugging his skinny chest.

Gangaric and his crew were well gone now. They had ridden south to Withy eight days back, but damage had been done. Little Aaron's head was filled with tales of his father's and his uncles' bravery, and he had begun asking Nan when they were going back. Even Nan wasn't sure where he meant by this. It could be Dhoone, Ganmiddich or Bludd. Certainly in the past year Aaron had seen more of Dhoone than any other clanhold. He'd been barely six when they left Bludd, and could hardly be expected to remember it.

Vaylo exited the west hall, plucked a rushlight from a wall sconce, and took the stair up to the highest floor in the hillfort. Nan had made herself a solar there, and it was the time of night when she'd be done with her kitchen chores, and hopefully would have left the cleanup to the men. With Nan you could never be sure. She might stay and talk with the young ones. She had a way with them, a calmness that settled them and made them want to do things for her. Just this morning she'd had them stuffing mattresses with dried sedge and straw. Vaylo had caught them all in the stables, laughing as they'd stuffed one particular mattress with scratchy burrs. "For Hammie," young Midge Pool had declared, beaming. "We're taking bets on how long it'll take him to notice."

Poor Hammie, Vaylo had thought, waving them on. It was good to see them doing something lighthearted, good to know also that his own lady, Nan Culldayis, had set them on the path toward it.

One of these days he was going to have to marry her. He was no fool. He knew that of the two of them she was the one with all the admirers. And the teeth.

The upper level of the hillfort was an oddly disjointed place, filled with tiny slant-ceilinged rooms that led from one another like jammed-in boxes. Corridors as such ceased to exist. To get to a room you had to walk through a room. The only spaces that were remotely private where those that abutted exterior walls— and most of them were running with damp. Vaylo sincerely hoped that the man who had designed this place had been forced to live in it. Between the deeply flawed roof and this dungeon-like maze it was about the most ill-planned, ill-formed lump of stone he'd ever had the misfortune to stay in. Made the Bluddhouse look like a palace.

Made it look very good indeed.

The Dog Lord made his way across the floor, walking from room to room. Most of them were empty, but if you weren't careful you might surprise some poor sod on a chamber pot, or give someone who'd just fallen asleep the fright of his life. Vaylo made a lot of noise.

Trouble with Gangaric's visit was that it hadn't just unsettled the boy. It had unsettled him as well. Bludd was being run into the ground, its defenses neglected. Gangaric had said that Quarro had grown lazy and distracted—claims Vaylo found easy to believe. Out of the seven of them Quarro had always been the one with the greatest sense of entitlement. First born, first sworn, first to get his own roundhouse—none of it through any effort of his own. The only reason why he'd ended up with the Bluddhouse was because his fool of a father had decided to head west and conquer Dhoone. Quarro had never had to fight or struggle for anything in his entire life. And what was beginning to make less and less sense was why he, Vaylo Bludd, was stuck in this godforsaken mold heap in the middle of nowhere while Quarro was sleeping with whores and digging bear pits at Bludd.

It had been different when he thought all was well there. The Bluddhouse secure in the hands of his eldest son was something he could live with. For a certainty he would not set Bluddsmen against Bluddsmen for the sake of claiming a house. Yet what if he was needed? What if all Gangaric's words were true and Bludd was vulnerable and *known* to be vulnerable? Quarro Bludd was not the Bludd chief.

The Dog Lord was.

Big Borro's wife was there. Mogo Salt's mother and his two sisters. All sorts of Faas and HalfFaas, Nan's older sister with the beautiful name, Irilana, Scunner Bone, Odwin Two Bears' large and sprawling family, who always made a point of having two of something in their names, the fine and ancient family of Bulls . . . the list went on. Clan was there, in the Bluddhouse, and if Quarro was not watching over it then something had to be done.

So what was keeping him here?

Vaylo took the door to Nan's solar, and as he passed into the light and the warmth he knew the answer was his fostered son.

"Granda, where's the wolf dog? You said you were going to bring him." Pasha Bludd, nine years old and bossy as a general, scrambled from the sheepskin rug by the hearth to accost him, arms folded. "The others are waiting."

It was true enough. He did remember telling his grand-daughter a few hours ago that he was going to fetch the wolf dog, but then he'd had men to see and Hammie to check on, and between the sun setting and Hammie's remark about Burning River he'd clean forgot about the dog. "He'll be with Dry, in the tower." The wolf dog and Cluff Drybannock had always been close.

Pasha marched toward him. "I'll go and fetch him then."

"No you won't."

People remarked that Pasha Bludd looked like her granda when she frowned. He certainly hoped it wasn't true. He didn't think it would be becoming for a chief to look so delightful. "Sit. Play with the other dogs. Rub my feet."

She tried to hold the frown, but it crumpled on her at the mention of his feet and she barked out a laugh. "Rather rub pickled eggs."

This statement left him speechless. The three dogs lying by the fire did not bestir themselves. The big black-and-orange bitch was on her back, all four legs splayed like sticks in a jar. The other two were more decently arranged, but one of them was smelling bad. "Where's Nan?"

Pasha shrugged. "She came and went."

Vaylo unhooked his cloak and headed toward the fire. Somehow Nan had managed to turn this damp room with its single south-facing window, its hole-in-the-wall fireplace and its uneven floor into the brightest place in the hillfort. As the room was small the fire had some real effect; green mold had been banished entirely and the black mold, while not gone, was at least dry. Nan had scattered the floor with hay and laid sheep-skins on top. A simple but graceful table made from sheet copper hammered over fox pine had been set beneath the window. When it turned up out of the blue ten days back, Vaylo had asked Nan about it and received a surprising reply. "Cluff made it for me. He remembered me telling him how I didn't like to leave things on the floor overnight." Nan was the only person who ever called Drybone "Cluff."

Vaylo pushed one of the dogs out of the way and squatted close to the hearth. Heat made blood rush to his face. Pasha brought him a cup of water and a thumb cup of malt. The liquor had been a gift from Gangaric, carried all the way from Bludd. It was such a treasure that Vaylo thought he'd be quite happy never to drink it; just uncork the flask once a day and inhale.

"Why you being so good to me?" he said, his eyes narrowing at his granddaughter. "You think I'm going to forget about the foot rub?"

It was then as he rolled onto the rug and made a great show of pulling off his left boot that all three dogs stood. Ears moving, they tracked a noise the Dog Lord could not hear. Immediately Vaylo pulled himself to his feet. Fear jumped so quickly in his heart it must have been there all along.

The bitch began to growl, a terrible low whirring that sounded like the moving of gears on a war machine.

"With me," he told her. To the other two he said, "Guard my granddaughter." His voice was so fearsome they shrank away from it.

Pasha's black eyes were bright. Her features moved through several uncertain states as she stepped toward him. "Granda?"

"*Stay here!*" he roared, his voice harder than it had been with the dogs. "Draw the bolt when I have gone and let only those you know in."

The girl's bladder gave way and urine shot down her dress, splashing at her feet. She stood still, and pressed her lips together very tightly. Her jaw and teeth started doing something behind them, like gnawing, but he did not have the time to comfort her.

The black-and-orange bitch pushed her head into his thigh as she followed him from the solar. The last thing he saw as he closed the door was the remaining two dogs moving to flank his granddaughter. He waited until he heard the charge of the bolt before he and the hound made their way downstairs.

It was full dark now and few torches were burning. Vaylo had left his rushlight in the solar and had to step carefully through the shadows. Below him he was aware of noises, of sharp calls and urgent footsteps and chiming metal. The first person he spotted coming down the stairs was red-haired Midge Pool. The young swordsman was running between the east ward and the west. Vaylo hailed him.

Midge had a lot of freckles, some of them on his lips. "Drybone spotted mounted men to the north. He's raising a party to meet them."

North? The fear ticked softly in Vaylo's chest, seemed almost to turn over and reveal itself for what it really was: recognition. Nothing but the Rift lay to the north. No Dhoonesmen or Hailsmen were out there about to knock down the door. A Bluddsman's true fate lay beyond the simple taking and defending of land and houses. A Bluddsman's true fate lay on the borders.

We are chosen by the Stone Gods to guard them.

"Wait for me," Vaylo commanded Midge Pool.

On their way to the stables, Vaylo arranged the securing of the fort. Aaron was located and sent up to Nan's solar in the company of Mogo Salt. Just as Mogo and Aaron were about to leave the ward, Vaylo stopped them.

"Your father's hammer."

Mogo nodded with understanding and returned to his bedroll, where his gear lay. Like all the men in the fort this day Mogo was a swordsman, but his father Cawdo had been handy with a hammer and he had taught Mogo a thing or two about hatchet-wielding. He had also left him his hammer. Vaylo ill-liked commandeering a man's weapon, but in this case it was not Mogo's primary armament. The five-foot longsword holstered at his back was the weapon Mogo Salt would draw in a melee.

"I don't have the cradle or chains," Mogo said handing the wedge-shaped hammer to his chief.

"Less to rattle," Vaylo said, winking at his grandson. "I thank you, Mogo Salt, son of Cawdo. Fetch Nan. Watch my grandchildren."

Mogo bowed formally at the neck. "Chief."

Vaylo left them, and hurried down the stairs to the stables. He'd lost Midge Pool somewhere along the way but the bitch was still at his heels.

Through a throng of men saddling horses, checking cinches, and harnessing swords, Vaylo Bludd met gazes with Cluff Drybannock. The flame blue eyes were always a shock. The intenseness of them, the fuel that burned there.

"What do we face?" Vaylo asked his fostered son as he came toward him. Drybone was wearing the red wool cloak with the owl-feather collar and the lead weights sewn in to the hem. The opal bands that bound his waist-length hair glowed like coronas around the moon. "Nine mounted. They head from the direction of the Field of Graves and Swords."

Nine. Vaylo looked into the holes at the center of Dry's eyes and saw his worst fears confirmed. He said, "We ride with thirty. I will not leave this fort undefended." His name was Vaylo, not *Pengo*, Bludd.

"Aye." Cluff Drybannock nodded tersely, went off to make the cull. The wolf dog trotted after him.

Vaylo saddled the black stallion. The beast was skittish and eager; it nipped his hand as he fastened the nose piece. Behind him, he was aware of men disappointed, of grumblings, and hay-kicking. A slammed door.

Do not rush to your own destruction, Vaylo wanted to tell them. If Angus Lok was right they stood at the sunset of the long night. There'd be time enough to get killed in the years of darkness to come.

"Bludd!" Vaylo hollered as he swung himself atop the horse. "We are chosen by the Stone Gods to guard their borders. Death is our companion. A life long-lived is our reward." Raising his hammer high in the air, Vaylo led the charge from the west ward.

Hooves clattered behind him. Men shouted, "Bludd! Bludd! Bludd!" Harness leather creaked and sawed. The cold night air snapped at Vaylo's skin, bringing hair upright and raising hard white mounds of gooseflesh. Cawdo's hammer felt a couple of pounds too light and about half a foot too short. Its balance was off-center and the head swung like a seesaw. Vaylo wondered if it hadn't been designed for throwing.

Gods, but it was raw. The snow underfoot crackled as if it held a charge. Pressure was dropping and the air had that loose changeable feeling that meant something was coming in. Big Borro had probably been right about snow.

Vaylo headed north into the valley, the bitch at his horse's hoofs. The land was open here, without trees or tall shrubs to break the view. All was blue. Overhead clouds held streaks of light. Dry rode close to his back, his lean and sinewy stallion effortlessly keeping pace. He had not drawn his sword yet, though others in the line had. When Vaylo turned his neck to get a better look at his fostered son he saw someone who looked wholly Sull.

"West of the Field of Graves and Swords," he said, seeing movements in the dark blueness that Vaylo did not.

Tightening his left rein, Vaylo made the shift in course. The snow hit as they rode out of the north wall of the valley and up to the headland. Flakes the size and shape of fish lures began to fall.

Vaylo spotted the horsemen as he topped the ride. Nine, as Dry had said. They rode horses of black oil whose bodies rippled on the edge between solid and liquid like something seen through thickly distorted glass. The men, if you could call them men, were armed with blades that killed air. Snowflakes were sucked in, and nothing came out. The men's calls were high and terrible birdlike screeches that raked the nerves like knives. Their bodies existed on a plain where shadow could support weight. Their faces were no longer recognizable as human. Skin and features were black and sucked inward, distorted by dark hungers.

Vaylo set his hammer in motion. Drybone pulled his horse abreast of his chief's, reached over his left shoulder and in a single breathtaking motion drew his sword. Vaylo imagined that if the horsemen were capable of fear they would have felt it then. Cluff Drybannock wielded a longsword: any enemy with sense should take flight.

The two lines met in a sickening clash. Vaylo's stallion reared at the last moment, its eye whites huge with fear. These creatures that looked like horses smelled like empty pits filled with frozen air. It was too late to stop the momentum, and both Vaylo and the horse were propelled forward into space held by creatures of another world. The Dog Lord's instinct as a hammerman was to use the force created, whiplash it into a blow. Cawdo's hammer moved a fraction ahead of Vaylo himself, arcing through the swirling snow. Steel slammed into shadowflesh. There was an instant of unnatural give, where Vaylo truly realized that he fought something other than flesh-and-blood men, and then the hammerhead found purchase in the thing's torso. A strange, wet noise sounded. The being that had once been Derek Blunt was thrown sideways in the saddle.

Vaylo's horse screamed. He did not understand why, but yanked its head back to control it. His hammer popped as it came free of shadowflesh. The metal smoked, blackened as if it had been thrust into acid.

Cluff Drybannock's longsword cracked like lightning into the space Vaylo had just vacated, entering what was left of Derek Blunt's heart. Something hissed. Vaylo felt air move on the back of his neck, sucked toward the hole. Blunt fell. His beast horse continued to charge. Its mouth was open and Vaylo saw a bit of razor spikes between its teeth. More spikes were mounted onto the breast straps and nosepiece, and the Dog

Lord realized why the stallion had screamed. It had been stabbed.

Glancing down at the horse's head he saw blood pumping from a puncture wound on its nostril. It would hurt, but it would live. Digging heels into horseflesh Vaylo drew back his hammer for another blow.

The screeches of the mounted shadows were deafening. Snow whipped in sheets into the faces of the Bluddsmen. Men screamed, charged, placed swords. Vaylo felt blood spray against his face as he fought, saw men delimbed and split open at the shoulders. Horse after horse reared. He had imagined thirty against nine to be a good number. He was wrong.

Wrong about the hammer too. For he could bash the shadow men with it but could not stop them. One fell from its horse and continued fighting afoot, its blade of voided steel mercilessly hacking horseflesh. Vaylo dropped the hammer. "Dry," he called out to the man who had never left his side during the battle. "Fetch me that sword."

It was a sword dropped by a young Bluddsmen who would never again use it. A good plain weapon that had not once found shadowflesh; the blade was perfectly silver.

"My lord and father," Dry said, presenting his mighty six feet longsword to Vaylo Bludd.

"No," Vaylo said softly. Cluff Drybannock was holding the blunt of the blade in his fist, offering the crosshilts. As a beast horse charged them, Dry thrust the sword into his father's hand.

Vaylo took it and wrested it into jerking motion. He had forgotten all it took—the balance, the space, the wrist and arm coordination—to wield such a blade. Gamely, he drove his horse forward. Dry must be shielded while he found himself a weapon.

It was hell. The oily black forms of the horses. The screeches. The snarling of the wolf dog and the bitch as they danced around the only two people they cared about in the melee, tearing shadowflesh, launching themselves at throats, shaking their heads like the insane. Snow was everywhere, in Vaylo's eyes, on his sword blade, jammed in the cavities between his bared teeth.

When one of the dark riders made a lunge for Drybone,

Vaylo punched his sword forward and twisted it into shadowflesh. It was possibly the ugliest move ever made with a longsword, more suited to knife brawls than swordcraft, but somehow the tip entered at exactly the right angle to slide the blade into the heart.

"Chosen!" Vaylo screamed, suddenly filled with mad joy. "We are Bludd."

Dry came to his side, now armed with a sword a foot and a half shorter than his old one, and the two men swapped glances through the chaos and the snow. Cluff Drybannock rarely smiled, and he did not smile now, but later when Vaylo recalled this moment he believed he saw something close to contentment on his fostered son's face. This was what he wanted most in life. Not just to fight shadows, but to fight them at his father's side.

The old soft pain sounded in Vaylo's heart. He loved Dry so much and so completely he thought it might break. Already his decision was made.

Vaylo never knew how long the battle lasted. Time ceased to pass at normal rate, rhythms were found, a longsword mastered, men died, hearts imploded, voided steel burned sword-shapes in the ground snow. Finally there was a time when the dark riders were dead and Drybone was the only man still fighting. Chasing down the last of the beast horses, he slew it in the Field of Graves and Swords.

Vaylo dismounted. His legs were shaking like leaves. The bitch came over and pushed against him, mewling and anxious, her tail down. The wolf dog was with Dry in the field. Unclasping his sable cloak, the Dog Lord went to aid the Bluddsman who had fallen. Others helped him in this, but it fell to the Bludd chief to take those whose injuries were fatal. He kissed the men on the foreheads, brushed snow from their cheeks, named them Bluddsmen and sons. Cluff Drybannock's sword was a blessing, its perfect sharpness. Vaylo's eyes were dry, his chest tight.

When he was done he cleaned his sword in the snow and waited for Drybone to join him. When he drew close, Cluff Drybannock dismounted. He would never sit a horse while his chief stood. Snowflakes whirled between them. The wolf dog began to howl.

It knew.

And then Drybone knew. Nothing changed in his stance or face, but Vaylo knew his son.

"Dry," he said. "I leave for Bludd tomorrow. Come with me."

A moment passed where Vaylo was filled with reckless hope, and then Cluff Drybannock shook his head. "I cannot, my father. I am Bludd and I am Sull. This is where I choose to make my stand."

The wolf dog keened in the darkness. Its sound broke Vaylo's heart.

FORTY-FIVE

The Red Ice

I t was the eye of the storm and they were heading toward it, the peace at the center of a vast and unsettled underworld of clouds. Hail blasted their faces, coming at them head-on. Wind howled, ripping off tree limbs weakened by days of frost and sending them flying through the air. They walked bent forward against the onslaught, face masks pulled up to their eyes, mitted hands snatching their cloaks taut across their bodies. If the wind got under them it could tear the cloth off their backs. The flap of Raif's daypack made a sound like a whumpfing of a large bird taking flight.

Lightning shot though the darkness in massive gridlike forks. The entire north smelled like something just ignited. The membranes in Raif's ears began popping as air pressure switched back and forth and thunder rumbled.

He wondered if one of the definitions of insanity could be "anyone who talks to leeches." That was what he was doing, muttering words that were not intended for either Addie or himself. *Give me another hour, another hour, another night.* The leech was with him, a good strong biter on his back. A parasite feeding on his blood.

The attack by the Unmade at the stand of red pines had altered the position of the claw next to his heart. Shadow homed to shadow. Something felt different; there was the smallest possible delay in the completion of a beat of his heart. It was muscle, he knew that. He of all people knew that. And it contracted in rhythm and that rhythm had been changed.

You did not know when you died. Perhaps that was a blessing, that short but untrackable distance between life and death. If he fell dead on this hillside all oaths would be null and void. Yet he did not want to die. He did not want to leave the world where Drey Sevrance, Effie Sevrance and Ash March existed. Drey, who had taken his swearstone that morning on the greatcourt, was the center of all things. Raif could still remember his brother's last touch on the rivershore west of Ganmiddich. *We part here. For always. Take my portion of guidestone . . . I would not see you unprotected.*

Raif Sevrance would not see Drey unprotected either. If he found the sword. If he lived. Any unmade man or beast he slew with it would be one less evil in the world, one less threat to his family, and his clan.

The circle of clear sky was close now. *Mish'al Nij.* The hillside leading toward it was steep. Long spines of red rock pushed through the ground and snow. White pines and cedars crowded the spaces in between them. The wind was bending the trees, revealing the silvery underside of their boughs. Addie had given up on a path. A ditchlike springbed cut deep into the slope was the best he could manage. The spring was dry of water, but scree and pinecones bounced downstream. When they reached the springhead—a lens of thick blue ice that was leaking rust— they were forced back into the trees.

Raif lost sight of the sky. Cedar branches swiped his cloak and face mask and all he could see were green terraces of pine. Addie had the lead and Raif followed his small and lightly stamped footprints in the frozen snow. Lightning struck. Hailstones sizzled into puffs of steam.

"I see the ridge ahead," Addie shouted.

Raif concentrated on his feet. The sandstone was cracked and loose here and days of thaws followed by frost had left every surface slick. He wouldn't think about the Red Ice until he saw it with his own two eyes.

The cragsman disappeared into the green. Raif found himself remembering the night on the rimrock when the Forsworn sword had given way. Was that the moment his future had been lost, the instant the blade had bent? If the sword had stayed true would he be here today? Traggis Mole would not have been torn open by the Unmade serpent, and a new oath would not have been spoken. A dying man's request. Behind his hareskin face mask, Raif cracked a dark smile. Request was hardly the word for it. Traggis Mole had *demanded*.

Swear it.

Noticing the trees had begun to clear, Raif picked up his pace. The wound he'd taken back at the camp pulled at the skin on his gut as he straightened upright. He'd been bent against the wind for so long it had begun to heal. Ahead, Raif saw Addie standing on the ridgeline. The cragsman had released his hold on his cloak and the brown wool billowed out like a boat. Five minutes earlier it would have been ripped from his throat. Yet the wind wasn't dying; Raif could hear it below him in the trees. It was as if the storm could not reach beyond Addie Gunn. He stood on a barrier it could not pass.

The cragsman did not turn as Raif drew abreast of him. He had removed his face mask and gray stormlight lit the side of his face. His jaw was moving. He was naming the Stone Gods.

"Ganolith, Hammada, Ione, Loss, Uthred, Oban, Larannyde, Malweg, Behathmus."

Loss.

The fourth Stone God. And the name of the sword.

Raif looked down into a valley framed by steep and wooded hills on three sides and by a dam of mist on the fourth. The mist wall spanned the space between hills to the north, a towering rampart of white and shifting haze that plumed and curled, switching between states. The mist rivers of the Want lay behind there, Raif realized. This was the border between worlds.

Raif thought of the lamb brothers, and touched the piece of stormglass tucked between the trapper skins at his chest. They had not been as far from their goal as he, and possibly they, had imagined. If he was right and the Want lay beyond that dam they could be just a short walk away on the other side.

Or so far they would never reach it in a million years.

Lightning lit up the sky to the east as Raif Sevrance looked down upon the Red Ice. Hills rose steeply from the lake, denying it shoreline on all sides. It was roughly circular and perhaps a league across, and he could not tell exactly where it ended in the north and the wall of mist began. Its surface was covered in a fine crystalline powder of snow, but you could still see the true color of the ice. It was as the lamb brothers had said: a lake of frozen blood.

Seeing it Raif understood Addie Gunn's impulse to name the old gods. The cragsman had broken no oath and perhaps he had a claim to that comfort. Raif knew he had no such claim himself.

Pushing aside his face mask, he set off down the slope. The woods were not as dense on this side of the valley and it was easy to make a path. The groundsnow was lighter, crisper. If you looked directly overhead you could view the night's first stars. They seemed familiar, but Raif was on guard against the Want and no longer wholly believed what he saw. Flawless had told him that Bluddsmen rode right past this valley and did not see it. He had been doubtful of that claim. Now he was not.

The nearer he drew to the ice the deeper its color became. Light was failing strangely, staying close to the ground as it drained. Around him he was aware of the storm waging a war upon the north, but here in its eye all was calm.

"Night falls and the shadows gather, and to watch you must grow accustomed to the dark. Bide where I stand, Raif Twelve Kill—alone and armed in the darkness—and ask yourself is this a prize worth winning, or a hole without end that will suck away your life?"

Traggis Mole's words seemed to steal out of the mist, snaking toward him like the Want. They contained truth without hope. The sword's name promised more of the same. Loss.

Raif steeled himself against the bleakness of his thoughts. He had come this far. Ahead, somewhere in that dark expanse of Red Ice, lay the chance to fulfill his oath to Traggis Mole. And arm himself against the Endlords.

Grow wide shoulders, Clansman. You'll need them for all of your burdens.

About a hundred feet above the ice he stopped and pulled off his pack. Addie was closing distance through the cedars and Raif waited for him. The air was well below freezing here and his breath crackled into clouds. How long had this lake been frozen? How many thousands of years?

When the cragsman reached him, he said, "You have been a good friend to me, Addie Gunn."

Addie knew all that this meant. As he went to stand by Raif's pack there was sadness in his eyes, but no surprise. "Think I'll try some of that tea. Good luck to you, lad."

Their gazes locked. *You seconded my oath,* Raif wanted to tell him. *Like Drey.* He remained silent though, and left the cragsman alone on the hill as he headed down to the Red Ice.

All trees stopped thirty feet above the lake and nothing grew on the bare rock. Raif was careful as he descended. Things were happening to his body. Old wounds and new wounds were stretching his skin tight like nails hammered into a canvas. His fingertips were tingling.

He realized the ice was groaning when he neared the shore. When he had first heard the sound he had mistaken it for thunder. Now he could tell it was the low moan of a substance under pressure. Cautiously he slid down the rocks toward it.

The instant he slid his toe upon the Red Ice, the leech dropped from his back. Its slimy, rubbery body landed with a squelch on the surface of the lake. It was the same color as the ice.

Oh gods. Raif moved past it and took his first steps upon the lake. Ice whitened in starbursts where it took his weight. He looked down and could see nothing beyond the iron-dark surface. Stilling himself, he waited for lightning to strike close by. When three bolts hit in quick succession over the eastern hills, he used the flashes of brightness to search the lake's depths. The ice was opaque, blacky red and partly frosted. Nothing could be seen beneath the surface. Raif let his gaze circle the lake. He reckoned it would take him a quarter hour to cross from one side to the other.

And there was no telling how deep the ice ran. He would never find the sword unless he knew exactly where it lay.

Although he didn't much want to, he forced himself to consider the vast dam of mist. If he walked toward it at what point would the Want grab him and not let go? He had entered the Want before and the one thing he knew for certain was that you were never aware when you passed the point of no return. It was like death that way. That same short but untrackable distance.

Feeling the soft give of pain in his shoulder, Raif set out cross the Red Ice. He scanned west and then east and wondered if it might be as simple as locating the lake's exact center. Four worlds meeting in the middle. It wasn't a bad idea, but instinct told him it wasn't right. The Want was in play here. Even if half the lake lay in Bludd territory and the other half in Sull lands there would still be something else.

What was he missing? What was the fourth world?

The moon rose in the clearing above the valley, a lean sickle of silver surrounded by a blue corona. It had grown too dark to make out the details of the clouds, and it was strange to see the stars restricted to the space above his head. Lightning and the distant rumble of thunder were his only indications that the storm was still playing itself out across the northern forests.

Raif went over everything anyone had ever told him about the sword named Loss and the Red Ice. There wasn't much. Sadaluk of the Ice Trappers had been the first one to mention Loss, though not by name. *Did you really think this will be the sword that makes you?* Those had been his words as he'd handed Raif the Forsworn blade. He had not mentioned where this better, second sword might be found. Tallal of the lamb brothers had known about the sword also. The Red Ice was sacred to them: a flooded battlefield where thousands of their dead lay frozen.

Raif shivered. Squatting, he placed his gloved hands upon the ice and scrubbed away at the surface. He thought perhaps that if he generated enough friction it might melt the top layer of ice and help to clear it. The lake was too cold though and as he scratched its surface it refroze in pale streaks. What had kept it frozen for so long? Even this far north there were summers. *Maygi hide it*, that was what Flawless had claimed. Perhaps he was right and some ancient sorcery held it in place.

Or perhaps it had something to do with the Want. For there it was, curling out its mist limbs toward him, beckoning him back.

Step too far and I am lost. Step back and I will never fulfill my oath.

Maybe he could just stay here, squatting on the ice.

Lightning bolted across the sky in a thick, muscular fork. Raif stood. As his legs took his weight he experienced a brief instant of disorientation. Not dizziness, he told himself quickly. Just the normal thing that happens when you rise quickly to your feet.

He could no longer feel the fingers on his left hand.

Ignoring them, he forced his mind elsewhere. What held the Want in place, he wondered. Why didn't the wall of mist just come tumbling across the lake? One thing he had always assumed about the shifting uncertainty that topped the continent was that it was unbounded, able to stretch and shrink at will. Yet it only stretched partway across the Red Ice. Why?

The tone of his footsteps changed as he neared the center of the lake. There was a hollowness to them now. They rang. On impulse he drove the heel of his boot deep into the ice. It was like kicking a wall.

"To break it you must stand in all four worlds at once." Argola's words sounded like a taunt.

Clanholds. Sull. Want. *What else?*

Raif Sevrance's heart failed a beat. He perceived it as a moment of prolonged suction, a hardness, followed by softness, followed by the release of another beat. He carried on walking . . . because there was nothing else to do.

Shadow homes to shadow.

Four worlds.

The Want held in place.

Raif looked down at his feet. He thought for a moment he saw something pale and head-shaped lying beneath the ice. Perhaps it was one of the lamb brothers' lost souls. Perhaps it was his own reflection. It did not matter. Either way the ice would not break.

He needed to find its weak point.

Raif suddenly remembered what Addie had told him, that morning after the first camp out of the city. A small charge of possibility fired along his nerves. Quickening his pace he headed toward the dam of mist. He could feel it now, the freezing fog, switching back and forth between ice and superfine droplets of water, moving between worlds.

The Red Ice spread out before him like an eye full of blood. How many men had died here? How many bodies waited beneath the surface to be released? He believed he saw them now, pale legs and torsos, severed heads and smashed feet, sections of gut with gray and pipelike intestines spilled out, bow-curved hips with the sexual organs frozen into forms that looked like split fruit. All mouths and eyes were open and gaping; black holes in the ice where the terror still lived. The demon hordes of the Unmade had slaughtered thousands. It was easy to close his eyes and see the violent fury, the cracking of spines, the fountaining of blood, the blades that sucked in light hacking limbs. Was it possible that such a battle would need to be fought again?

Raid Sevrance could not say *No*.

The mist dam spread before him, soaring hundreds of feet into the air. Lobes of cloud broke off and floated south across the lake. They peeled and divided, rotating into ever-thinning veils before vanishing. Sucked dry. Raif had assumed that if he walked close enough to the mist he would be lost, but now he was not so sure. Something held the Want back. And he was beginning to think he knew what that was.

He was far into the ice now and the hills were nothing but dark mounds in the distance. When lightning flashed, he judged the distance between the east and west shore and and altered his course to center himself between the two. Sull and clanholds. Satisfied, he concentrated upon the ice beneath his feet as he walked toward the Great Want.

His left hand was numb to the wrist now and tingles jumped along his arm toward his heart. *Stay*, he told something. He wasn't sure what.

The crack in the ice was as fine as a drawn wire, a line of perfect blackness cutting through the Red Ice. The Want's mists would not, could not, pass it. It was the great flaw in the continent.

The Rift.

It never closes, not wholly. North of Bludd it narrows so that men can cross it, but it's always there, a black crack running through the forests between here and the Night Sea.

Raif fell to his knees before it. Stupid tears were coming to his eyes. Relief and longing welled up in his failing heart. This was the fourth world, the darkness that lay in wait beneath the earth. The passageway to the Blind.

Ice fog coated his face and clothing as he drew Traggis Mole's longknife. The Want existed less than a foot away, on the north side of the Rift, and Raif breathed it in as he stripped off his gloves and molded his left hand around the haft. Using his right hand to fasten the numb fingers in place, he raised the knife above his head.

For Drey. Always and everything for Drey.

For the oath he had seconded. And Raif had failed.

A tower of lightning lit up the north as Raif Sevrance drove his blade into the Red Ice. A *whoosh* of air shot across the lake. The ice groaned as steel went deep into the hairline fissure of the Rift, down into the frozen blood. Cracks ran along the ice like burning fuses. Explosive charges followed them, firing up fist-size bursts of frozen matter and shattering the lake's surface like glass. As destruction fled outward from the blade, the surrounding clouds closed in. Whatever sorcery had held them at bay had snapped the instant the ice was breached, and the storm now rolled in.

The knife went deep. When the crosshilts slammed into the ice the knife continued sinking. Raif's fists slid down after them, and he leaned forward driving the steel as far as it could go. Around him the lake was fracturing and whitening, riding up in great plates and splintering into fragments. Corpses encased in ice were flung into the air. He could smell the battle now, the blood and fear, the horse shit and unmade flesh.

Thunder concussed the valley as Traggis Mole's knife ground to a halt. Freezing dust shimmered like falling snow. Raif looked at the shattered plates in front of his knees and saw the shadow of a man lying beneath the debris. As he dislodged the knife he was aware of a tightness in his chest. It seemed important that he did not die before he found the sword so he moved quickly, using his hands as shovels to dig and push aside the broken ice.

He saw the hand first, the flesh so bloated that each finger had exploded, leaving peels of skin around the bones. The ghostly remains of the hand still grasped something. The black and cankered haft of a sword. Raif picked at the ice with his knife, wedged his fingers under the plates and pried them out. He could see the blade now, its edge shining as dimly as an old coin, its crosshilts overgrown with rusticles. It lay upon a torso that was twisted sideways and had no head. Dark metallic armor ridged in spines still protected what little was left of the man who had worn it. Raven lord, Tallal had called him. Raif had never seen such thick and brutal plate before; it looked like an armored sarcophagus.

Who was he, this warrior who had ridden into a battle and single-handedly changed its course? The lamb brothers had not known his name.

Raif thought about that. He owned many names now, but fewer and fewer people knew his real name, the one he shared with Effie and Drey. Was that how it had happened for the raven lord? Had he started out as a young man with a normal name and normal prospects, and as his life altered and darkened had people called him by other names? And had those new names created him?

Mor Drakka. Watcher of the Dead. Twelve Kill.

Raif thrust his hand through chunks of crumbling ice and grasped the hilt of the sword. The raven lord's frozen fingers cleaved to his and for a moment they were joined. In that instant Raif knew things. He saw the Endlords, massive forces compressed into forms that could be comprehended by man. He felt their perfect and unearthly coldness, and the absolute singularity of their purpose. They were coming to destroy the world.

Soon. They promised, their bleak and glittering gazes meeting Raif's through the dead man's flesh.

Soon.

Raif Sevrance drew the sword named Loss from the Red Ice. It was heavier than he imagined, long and ugly. Black. As he brought his left arm up to support the weight, a spasm shot up his shoulder to his heart.

Shadowflesh moved.

Homed.

Raif's heart stopped beating. An eyeblink. An untrackable journey. A flash of lightning. And he was gone.

FORTY-SIX

Aftermath

Raif let Addie Gunn help him out of the tent. "Go," he said to the cragsman once they were a short distance from the camp. "I need to piss."

Addie frowned like he didn't much believe this. Given the subject matter he could hardly object. "Here," he said, holding out the simple oak staff he used for walking. "Take the stick."

Raif took the stick.

"Don't piss too long," Addie warned before leaving.

Pushing the butt of the stick into the snow and pine needles of the forest floor, Raif waited for him to be gone. It was warm again today and the snow was loose and full of holes. You could smell the earth, the minerals and tannins and rotting leaves. Black flies and mosquitoes were hatching. Something buzzed close to his ear, but he couldn't trust himself to swat it away. He needed the stick more than he had realized. Half of his weight had sunk upon it. It was a good piece of wood, smoothly sanded and sturdy. It vibrated only because the person who held it was shaking; it had been designed to transfer force.

When he saw Addie return to the tent he felt free to breathe and slump further into the stick. Addie was a good man and a good friend, but Raif needed a break from his watching. He needed to think.

Spying a rock in the shade of the cedars he decided it looked like a fine place to sit and rest. The hardest part of getting there was yanking the stick out of the ground. He moved slowly, aware of the heaviness of his body and his legs' inability to bear it. The pain in his chest, the depth of it, was something he would not think about. Enough worry had been spent there. No more today.

It took him a long time to reach the rock. The sun moved while he was shambling from foot to foot, rising high in the pale and clear sky and stealing away the shade. Raif found the rock's appeal undiminished. It was a big spur of sandstone, flaking and chalky, and so deeply undercut it looked like a boulder. Maybe it was a boulder. Raif wondered what was happening to his mind.

Sitting down was a more challenging discipline than walking and he found himself awkward at it. Several tiring moments followed where he attempted to lever his weight with the stick. That didn't work, and the best he could manage was a barely controlled drop.

Won't be getting up any time soon, he realized, settling down on the cool and slightly damp stone. His heart was beating swiftly, accelerated and under strain, and his legs were shaking in fierce jumps. He could not make them stop.

Below he saw the camp and counted all five clarified hide tents and the animal corral. It was strange to see them in this place, this hillside of giant cedars and white pines. They must have cleared some timber to make the campsite; saplings and yearlings from the looks of things. Addie carried a hand adze, but its small rounded head was insufficient for logging. That meant one of the lamb brothers possessed a decent ax. It was disconcerting to think of them chopping up timber. They were strong men, he understood that, but they were Sand People. None of Tallal's stories had ever mentioned trees.

It looked as if none of the brothers were around. With Addie standing watch over the fire and the camp, they were free to do their work. Raif would be forever grateful to the cragsman for insisting that the camp be raised out of sight of the lake.

"Told 'em, I did," Addie had explained to him last night. "Said if you ever did wake up the last thing you'd want to see is that damned Red Ice. *But here there is a natural clearing*, says the tall one, pointing at some fool place above the shore. *Let's go unnatural*, I says back."

Raif smiled at the thought of Addie's conversation with the

lamb brothers. Both parties had acted well. The camp was on the far side of one of the western hills bordering the lake. If he wanted to, if either Addie or one of the mules would carry him, he could travel the short distance to the wooded ridge and look down upon the Red Ice.

He never would. Addie, who was wise about many things, had been wisest about this. The ice was slowly melting, and the lamb brothers were out upon it, doing whatever they needed to do to release the souls of their dead. Things were being burned, he knew that much. Even when he had been unconscious he smelled the meaty smoke.

He had lost nine days of his life. The time was gone and he had nothing but the memories of nightmares to show for it. The first time he could recall waking was yesterday morning. He'd heard blue jays calling. *Ornery, mad-dog birds*, that's what Tem always called. Raif seemed to recall some incident involving Da, some strips of cured elk, and a pair of jays. It was the pleasure of reconstructing the event—Was Da actually curing the meat himself? Had the first bird distracted him while the other sneaked up to the fire rack? And had the fire really been burning?—that had finally awakened him. He had mistaken his thoughts for a real world.

Addie and then Tallal had attended him. They treated him with a kind of concerned awe, as if they were equally amazed and worried by his recovery. Raif supposed he might feel the same way himself if he were in their shoes. Addie had fussed himself into a state and then left. The lamb brother had been more composed. And efficient. Washing and doctoring had been done. Tallal's long brown fingers had been careful as they touched Raif's back and the livid purple burn on his chest.

Raif looked at the burn and realized he knew its shape. "The stormglass."

Tallal had nodded once, a movement close to a bow. He was wearing his hood and veil so that only his dark eyes with their bluish eye whites showed. "It drew the lightning. This lamb brother believes that when the lightning touched the stormglass it started a stalled heart."

Raif had lain there, remembering things he had no desire to remember. Dead fingers clutching a sword. Armor raised into brutal ridges. The inhuman forms of the Endlords. What he could not recall was what had happened after he pulled the sword from the ice.

"You wore the glass against your heart."

Had he? If it was so it was not by design. He'd been hanging on by sheer luck there.

"The glass called us." Tallal's expression seemed gentle. "We came."

Raif thought of the dam of mist, of all that lay behind it. "How long?"

Tallal touched each black dot on the bridge of his nose. "The Want is a desert of many mysteries. The lamb brothers know few of them. The stormglass called as we lay down our mats for *Alash*, the evening prayer. One of our brothers noted that a sickle moon appeared in the sky at the same moment. That moon stayed with us through the journey, and before it set we found you and the One Who Knows Sheep on the ice."

Addie. The thought of the cragsman coming to find him, having to walk across the landscape of raised and frozen corpses and shattered ice, stirred Raif deeply. He would never know what the cragsman had found, never understand what it cost him to approach the burned and lifeless body that belonged to his friend.

Raif knew he owed Addie Gunn. There didn't seem much chance of paying back a debt like that. You just had to live with it.

He was less sure what he owed to the lamb brothers. They had opened up his shoulder and drawn out the *Shatan Maer*'s claw. It had been the elder brother, not Tallal, who had done the work. Raif was glad he had been asleep. Addie had told him that he had lain on his stomach for three days while the strange and unstable remains of shadowflesh were placed on the oozing wound. Shadow drew shadow. The Unmade had been frozen in the lake too. Their flesh corrupted quickly as it thawed, smoking to nothing like a pure form of fuel. Addie said the brothers had farmed a single corpse for the poultice, moderating its temperature by exposing the carcass to sunlight or covering it with lake ice and skins. New strips were cut and laid every hour. The cragsman had been eager to tell more, but

Raif did not want to hear it. At some point in the story the leeches had started to look good.

"Popped out like a piece of gristle," Addie had said, unable to resist revealing the final detail. "Little black thing, it was. Shiny as a dead fly."

Raif had told Addie to go. He could only take knowledge like that in small doses. And he had not liked word *farmed*.

Easing himself further back against the rock, Raif braced the weight of his upper body with his right arm. He knew better than to use his left. It was still weak and spasms passed along at unexpected moments, making it impossible to use with any confidence. Tallal said it would heal, given time.

A cool breeze channeled up the hillside, stirring the dark sea of trees. A lone heron was heading north, its scrawny yellow feet swaying from side to side as it beat its powerful wings. To the west the clanholds spread out in a series of hills and rolling valleys. Clansmen must have taken to the woods, for Raif could see several lines of smoke rising above the canopy. The warmer weather had brought out hunters. Elk would be moving north, like the heron, and moose would be calving. Boars would be out from their dens, snuffling for bulbs in the damp earth beneath the trees. Raif thought perhaps Tallal was right: he *would* heal. Already he wanted down there. He wanted to be deep in the woods, hunting with a good heavy spear and the Sull bow.

If he had no obligations that was what he would choose to do with his life, he realized, idly scanning the valley for game. If he could not be a clansman he would be a woodsman. Build himself a cabin for the winters, take to the trails in spring and summer, hunt, fish, learn some things about animals and nature. Swim in black-water pools, eat rosehips warmed by the sun and berries frozen by sudden frosts. Hopefully not die from cooking the wrong kind of mushrooms. It would be a life not without struggle and hardship. And it would be a life alone.

Raif thought of Ash then, her silver hair and fine hands and long legs . . . and he could not imagine her into that life. The dreams had no traction.

None of them did.

Back at the camp, Addie had walked the ewe from the corral

and was grooming it with something that looked like a raccoon's ribcage. "Curly-haired," he'd said to Raif this morning. "Solid little milker. Wouldn't have expected it from a fancy." Between the sheep, the trapper's tea, and the lamb brothers' herbs, Addie Gunn was a happy man. Still, his attention wasn't fully on the ewe. Every now and then he'd sneak a look at Raif whilst pretending to pull hairs from his newfangled comb. He was very bad at pretending.

Raif angled his face to get some sun. It felt good. Renewing. He now existed in a world where he had given his word and kept it. Traggis Mole's bidding—half of it—had been done, and Raif now possessed the sword named Loss. It was waiting for him in the tent. He had not laid eyes on it since the day on the ice. According to Addie it would need some work. "Never seen anything like it," was the only comment he had offered on its form. Raif felt a stirring of curiosity about the blade, and wondered if he would ever learn the raven lord's name and history.

He also wondered, but would never ask, whether the lamb brothers had released the man's soul. The raven lord's fate was important to Raif Sevrance. He feared it would become his own.

Soon, the Endlords had promised him.

The warmth of the sun could not stop the chill from entering the damaged spaces in Raif's heart. They had touched him through the frozen fingers of the raven lord. He'd seen them . . . and been seen.

They knew him now, knew his name and his purpose.

And where to find him.

Pushing himself up with his fist, Raif muscled himself to standing. He was Watcher of the Dead and he had a sword to grind and sand. And here was Addie coming toward him to help him down the slope.

Soon.

EPILOGUE

A Stranger at Drover Jack's

Liddie Lott was spilling the ale again. It was bad enough that she had kept the ewemen waiting five minutes while she swapped labor-pains stories with Bronwyn Quince, but now that she had actually managed to fill the tankards, a quarter of their contents was splashing onto the floor. What was wrong with the woman, that she couldn't even walk straight? Was one leg shorter than the other?

Gull Moler, owner and sole proprietor of Drover Jack's, dabbed the sweat from his forehead with a yellow shammy. It wouldn't do. It just wouldn't do. Those tankards were intended for his three best customers: Burdale Ruff, Clyve Wheat and Silus Craw. They were hard-talking ewemen and thrifty with their pennies and any moment now the complaining would begin.

Silus Craw, who had arrived earlier than the others and already had one ale inside him, was the first to notice the short measures. Sitting behind an upended beer keg with his chair against the wall, the little rat-faced drover made a show of peering deep into the newly delivered tankard. "There's something missing here if you ask me, Clyve."

Blond-eyebrowed Clyve Wheat leaned forward and squinted into his own ale cup. After a moment of deep thought he declared, "We should call her Liddie Spill-A-Lott."

Burdale Ruff and Silus Craw exploded into laughter, stamping their feet against the floor and banging their cups against the table. Liddie was only a few feet away, tending the stew kettle, and she had to hear it when Silus cried, "Either that or Liddie Talk-A-Lott."

As a second round of laughter erupted, Gull grabbed the nearest ale jug from the counter and moved in to calm everyone down. "Gentlemen," he said, greeting the drovers. "Allow me to top up your cups." The ale in the jug happened to be his best barley stout, and although all of the men were drinking yellow wheat none of them complained. Burdale Ruff had actually downed most of his original drink, but Gull topped his cup to the rim regardless. There were times to split hairs, and this wasn't one of them. Business had been bad all week.

Just look at the place now. Early evening like this and one of the god's days no less: every bench in the room should be straining under the weight of fat traders, ewemen, day laborers, and dairy girls. Talk should be loud and getting louder, and someone somewhere should be singing about his sheep. Instead there was a low and dreary hum, and sometimes even silence. *Silence.* Only a third of the chairs were spoken for—and that was counting Will Snug, who was passed out across two of them—and there was not one single patron singing, gaming, or attempting to impress the ladies with some puffed-up story about a small rod and a very big fish.

It was not a sight to warm a tavernkeep's heart. Oh, Drover Jack's itself was glowing. Those little pewter safelamps he'd bought from the thane's stablemaster last spring burned cozily from the oak-panelled walls, and every bench back, floorboard, and tabletop was freshly waxed and gleaming. Smells of yeast, cured leather, and woodsmoke combined to create a manly, welcoming scent. It was a trim tavern, low-ceilinged, dim and inviting, and Gull liked to imagine that there were some in these parts who'd count themselves lucky to sup here. He just wished a few more of them had gotten off their backsides and come here this night, is all.

A storm was passing through Ewe Country. As Gull adjusted the stove's air vent, he could hear the wind howling outside, blowing south from the Bitter Hills. The tavern creaked and shuddered, and when Bronwyn Quince opened the door to leave, the entire building wrestled with the wind.

Gull shivered. He was trying to decide whether he should burn fresh coal or take his chances with more wood. The cord of bog willow sent over by Will Snug in lieu of payment for an outstanding debt burned like cow pats, and was probably worth about as much. Still, there was a lot of it, and unlike coal it cost Gull nothing to burn. Gull thought and frowned, reached for the wood, stopped himself, and loaded his shovel with coal instead. Tonight marked the beginning of Grass Watch and was therefore the holiest night of spring, and if a man couldn't breathe clean air now then it didn't bode well for the rest of the year.

Besides, you never knew when business might pick up. As if on cue, the door swung open and a column of air rushed in the room. The flames in the stove leapt up as wooden beams shifted in their cuppings and a dozen patrons looked toward the door.

Freezing rain sprayed through the entranceway, glowing orange where the stovelight touched it. A figure, thickly cloaked against the cold, stood in the doorway and surveyed the room. After a moment, Silus Craw piped up "Close the door!" but the figure did not heed him. A deep hood concealed the stranger's face. Gull marked bulges at the stranger's waist and hip that had the look of serious weaponry. Beginning to get worried, Gull set down his shovel. He was going to have to do something about this. The action drew the stranger's gaze his way, and Gull found himself looking into a pair of copper eyes.

With a movement that wasted nothing, the stranger closed the door. At that exact moment Liddie Lott came down the stairs carrying a tray of beer taps that had been soaking all night in lye. Liddie's mind was on her feet and her head was down, and all you could see of her at first was her long chestnut hair. Like a whip-crack the stranger's gaze came down upon her. Gull felt real fear then. He had seen something he recognized in the stranger's copper eyes, and his experience of dealing with men and women over the past fifty years warned him it was the worst of all possible states of mind. Desperation.

Aware that something queer was going on around her, Liddie Lott looked up. The instant her ruddy well-fed face caught the light, the stranger's gaze swept away. Whatever it was he searched for, Liddie Lott did not possess.

"Welcome, stranger," Gull said, aiming for good cheer yet falling a little short. "Have you come to mark the Grass Watch with us?"

Again the stranger's gaze fell on Gull. Slowly, he grasped the center point of his hood and pulled it back. Ice-tanned and deeply lined, his face told of a lifetime spent outside. Not for one moment did Gull make the mistake of imagining the stranger to be a farmer or eweman. No. The man had a way of standing and looking—a particular type of confidence that only those with martial skills possessed—that told Gull he had to be an adventurer or mercenary or grangelord.

Every patron in Drover Jack's was held rapt by his presence. Looking around, seeing Lottie standing, mouth agape by the beer kegs, Burdale Ruff sitting in the corner with his meaty hand ready on his sword hilt, and the two Mundy boys shifting their position to align themselves more truly with the door, Gull suddenly wished for a little peace. His business was to serve food and ale, not tackle dangerous strangers. Trouble was, people *expected* him to take charge. Whatever drama happened in this tavern, be it a patron sick with the spurting vomits, a drunken brawl over a comely girl, or a lightning strike on the stove—Gull Moler was supposed to take care of it.

So that's what he did. To Liddie he said, "Fill everyone's cups with yellow wheat—on the house." To Clyve Wheat: "I see you have your stringboard with you. How about picking out a tune? It'd be a poor Grass Watch if we didn't have a song." Then, without waiting for a reply, Gull moved forward to greet the stranger.

"On a night as cold as this a man needs two things. A warm stove and a fine malt. I'd be honored if you'd share them both with me." Gull spoke quietly, and although he couldn't quite bring himself to touch the stranger, he did his best to usher the man toward the back of the room where it was quiet and dim.

The stranger let himself be led away. His cloak was steaming, giving off a sharp wild-animal scent.

Out of the corner of his eye, Gull noted that the free beer was going down well: Jon Mundy was laughing with Liddie Lott, holding out his tankard for more. As yet Clyve Wheat hadn't turned out a song, but Gull could hear him picking the strings as he tuned the board.

"Sit," Gull said to the stranger, indicating the chair and tables in the corner. "I'll be back in a blink with the malt."

As Gull slipped behind the tavern's small wooden counter, Burdale Ruff moved to speak with him. "Do you know who he is?" asked the big eweman, wagging his head toward the stranger.

Gull stepped on a crate to reach for his best malt, tucked high out of reach on the top shelf. "No. Never see him before in my life."

"I have."

That made Gull spin around. "Where?"

Burdale raised his considerable eyebrows. "Here, in the Three Villages. Saw him talking to some men-at-arms last Spring Faire."

"Do you know anything about him?"

"You mean apart from what's sodden obvious—he's as dangerous as a half-skinned polecat?"

Unsure if that was actually a question, Gull tucked the malt under his arm and said, "I can't keep him waiting."

Burdale didn't argue with this. "I'll be keeping an eye on you."

Strangely enough that didn't make Gull feel one bit better as he walked to the back of his one room tavern. The stranger had pulled off his cloak, and there was no mistaking the hardware of war. Three knives arranged by blade-length hung from a wide belt slung across his hips, and a five foot longsword, unsheathed, rested within arm's reach, against the wall.

The stranger watched Gull assessing the sword. "You have nothing to fear from me," he said quietly.

Gull could think of no reply. The stranger's voice was deep and weary, and it had a familiar lilt. Bear was right: this man came from around here. Setting down two wooden thumb cups, Gull said, "My name is Gwillem Moler and I own this tavern. How can I help you this night?"

The man's face remained unchanged as Gull spoke, and Gull realized he had told the stranger nothing he did not already know. Silence followed. Gull made himself useful by pouring the malt. Behind him, the stove was still sending out black smoke that smelled faintly of damp. Liddie must have fed it more wood.

During Grass Watch it was custom to sprinkle rye seeds on

the first meal and drink of the night. Padric the Proselyte had spent thirty days sitting in a rye field in late winter waiting for the first shoots of grass to poke through the thawing earth. Every morning when he awoke to find nothing but bare soil he denied God. Finally, on the thirtieth day, tiny, pale-green points emerged at sunset. That was the day Padric received God. Gull was generally disinterested in the stories of the First Followers, but Padric's tale always moved him. Something about the man's quiet dignity as he sat and waited struck a chord with Gull. Not many men would ask for proof of God and then sit in the cold for a month to get it. It had always seemed to Gull that Padric had proved himself by waiting, and that God probably wouldn't have revealed himself to a man who had waited one day less.

In any event, Gull liked to honor the custom of the seeds. Just this evening he had stocked his apron pouch with long, stripy rye seeds—the best they had in the market. Now he found himself hesitating to use them.

"Go ahead. You will not offend me."

Taken aback, Gull stared at the stranger's face. The copper eyes glinted for a moment, sharp as tacks, before he veiled them.

How could he know what I'm thinking? Gull wondered if perhaps the stranger had seen him reach briefly for his apron pouch. But no, that couldn't be. No one watched anyone that closely.

Anyway, he had to do it now. As he scooped up a dozen seeds and sprinkled them over the two thumb cups, the first strains of Clyve Wheat's song filled the tavern. Clyve was not a great thinker and couldn't hold his drink, yet no one could deny he had a talent for music. Nothing fussy or complicated, mind, that wasn't his style. He knew the simple shepherd songs and played them well. This one, Gull recognized, was an old cradlesong.

Sleep and in the morning all will be well, my daughter.
Sleep and all will be well.

Abruptly, the stranger reached forward and grabbed his cup. Without waiting for the customary toast, he threw the malt down his throat. He did not breathe for a moment, Gull realized, simply tipped his head back and waited. When whatever relief he was waiting upon failed to arrive he returned the empty cup to the table.

"My name is Angus Lok. And I am looking for my daughter."

What was it Burdale Ruff had called him? *Half-skinned*, that was it. Gull had seen many men in many states during the thirty years he'd spent running Drover Jack's, but this man was different. He lived but he was also dead.

Gull took a mouthful of the malt. It was warm, peaty and golden, and it made him very sad. For a moment he thought of saying many things to this stranger before him, telling him that he too had lost a daughter; that not four weeks ago his Desmi had run off with some freebooter from the Glaive. Silly, headstrong girl. Barely seventeen. Also Gull thought of showing the stranger to the door and telling him, *I have enough problems. Do not bring me any more.*

Instead, he said, "How can I help?"

Angus Lok searched Gull's face with such force that Gull felt as if his skin were being pulled across the table. "What do you know of a man named Thurlo Pike?"

Gull was surprised at the question. "Thurlo? He used to roof around here last winter. Haven't seen him in a couple of months."

"What sort of man is he?"

Although he did not normally speak ill of former patrons, Gull told the stranger the truth. "He was a dishonest roofer and a short-tempered man. Caused trouble here last time I saw him. Insulting the good name of my tavern, asking all sorts of questions, spilling ale."

Angus Lok leaned forward in his chair. "What sort of questions?"

Gull shrugged. "About some women, I think. Women living alone or something. You'd really have to ask Maggy that. She's the one who spoke with him."

Something happened to the stranger's face as Gull spoke. His mouth tightened and a muscle in his cheek began to pump. "Where is this Maggy?"

"Gone. Went missing a couple of days after Thurlo. No one's seen hide nor hair of her since."

"What was her full name?

"Maggy Sea. The best tavern maid ever to set down a tankard in Ille Glaive." Gull couldn't seem to stop himself from lauding her, and would have continued singing her praises if it hadn't been for the strange, dangerous look in Angus Lok's eyes.

"What do you know of this woman?"

Gull opened his mouth to speak and then closed it as he realized he knew absolutely nothing about Maggy Sea.

Angus Lok rested for a moment, as if Gull's lack of words were a blow he had to absorb. Gull took the opportunity to refill his cup.

"How long did she work here?"

For a reason he could not understand, Gull was reluctant to give the answer. "Thirteen days."

Angus Lok sucked in breath. He had not shaven in a month and his beard was growing in. The hair on his head was lighter than the beard stubble. "Tell me what she looks like."

Now, here was a question Gull could answer. Maggy Sea had simply appeared one day in the tavern and set about cleaning his copper bath. As he remembered it he had need of help and she was willing, and he hired her on the spot. Best thing he ever did. Maggy Sea had been a treasure, a fine woman who knew the value of hard work. She'd cleaned his pumps, mended his roof and cooked a lamb stew so fine and dense that it just about ate itself. "Well Maggy's tall, but not really tall. More medium height, now that I think of it. But she's definitely slender—except for her shoulders and hips which are round." Gull couldn't understand why he was fumbling. The picture he had in his head of Maggy Sea was crystal clear. It just wasn't easy to describe it, that was all. Gamely, he tried again. "She was certainly comely, but more often than not she looked plain, if you understand what I mean. And her eyes—"

"It does not matter." The finality with which the stranger spoke made Gull jump.

"Gull. I need your help. I can't get the tap in the keg." Liddie Lott drew abreast of the table. Sweat was beading above her upper lip and she looked a little frayed around the edges. She had never been left to work alone for so long.

"He will help you later."

Both Liddie and Gull turned to look at the stranger. Liddie raised an eyebrow and then turned to Gull.

"Go on, Liddie. If anyone complains that they can't have their preferred beer give them a free pint of something else."

"But—"

"Go." Gull shooed her away.

Angus Lok waited until she was out of earshot before he said, "The woman's voice, was it unusual?"

At last. Here was something Gull Moler could get his teeth into. "Yes. Yes. Golden, like maple syrup. Made you start nodding your head before she'd even asked a question."

Angus Lok reached for his sword. It was a beautiful weapon; the blade forged from patterned steel that scattered light, the single, central fuller cut so unusually deep that it looked as if it might bisect the blade. Resting it across his lap, Angus ran a finger along the trench. "What do you know of the people who died in the farmhouse fire a day east of here?"

Here it was, Gull realized. The reason why this man had come. The reason he smelled like a wild animal and the normal sense of time and place was missing from his eyes. He could be sitting anywhere at any point in the day, Gull realized, and would mark it solely by what he learned about his family. He was a clock who kept striking the same time.

Gull glanced back at the tavern, checking. Clyve Wheat had finished playing his song and Liddie was bringing him the traditional payment: a measure of malt and a wedge of blue cheese. Gull was glad to see she had remembered the old custom. Burdale Ruff was sitting with his chair swung back against the wall so it rested on its back two legs. Still watching. He was an imposing sight, Gull reckoned, dark and big and armed, but Gull didn't think he had a pat of butter in hell's chance of defending himself against this man.

Angus Lok waited. Gull spoke.

"Happened about two months back now. Was a bad business. Family of girls, as I heard it, working the farm while their father was away. By all accounts the chimney had been causing them trouble—that's why Thurlo Pike was called in. Those bad storms last winter had cracked the flue and smoke was coming back down into the house. Of course, no one will ever know for sure what happened that night, but the magistrate from Keen rode over the day after. Said it looked as if the family was trapped inside the house while it burned and by the time they figured a way out it was too late." Unable to help himself, Gull made the sign of the Three Tears against this chest. *God help them.*

"The bodies were in no state to identify. Blackened bones, the magistrate said. He ordered them to be buried twenty-five feet from the house and posted a warning that no one was to enter the farm until further notice."

Gull could have said more, gone on to mention current speculation about the deaths, or the fact that the magistrate was anxious to locate the owner of the farmhouse, but he stopped himself. Something had caught his eye whilst he was speaking and the thought that formed after it set him spinning.

This man had dug up the graves. The dirt was there to see, under his fingertips. The truth was in his copper eyes.

Of course. How else could he know that one of his daughters might still be alive? He would have had to view the remains.

Gull's throat began to ache. *What a life this is. What a terrible, terrible life.*

Angus Lok regarded Gull with a steady gaze. He had seen Gull glance at his fingernails, watched as the revelation took place behind his eyes. "My daughter's name is Casilyn Lok. We call her Cassie. She's eighteen, tall for her age, with hair . . ." he took a breath to steady himself, "hair the same color as your tavern maid, and hazel eyes."

"I have not seen her." Gull spoke quickly, to kill false hope. "Nor have I heard of a young girl traveling alone."

Angus Lok accepted this, unsurprised. He stood. "One day you may hear of something. If that happens send word to Heritas Cant in Ille Glaive."

"Heritas Cant in Ille Glaive," Gull repeated, anxious to show this man that he did not take the task lightly.

Sheathing the sword in a soft buckskin scabbard, the stranger gave Gull no thanks. Gull had not expected it. He was struck with the idea that this man was on a journey into hell.

And few ever made it back.

"The farmhouse," Gull said, speaking to delay him. "If the

magistrate is unable to locate the owner within a year he'll claim it as revenue for the Glaive."

Angus Lok threw on his cloak and made his way toward the door, his last words to Gull Moler, "Let them keep it."

Wind howled across the tavern as he left.

EXTRAS

www.orbitbooks.net

About the Author

J. V. Jones was born in Liverpool in 1963. When she was twenty, she began working for a record label and was part of the Liverpool music scene of the early eighties. She later moved to San Diego, California, where she ran an export business for several years and was the marketing director for an interactive software company. Her interests include cooking, gardening, reading, playing RPGs, watching old black-and-white movies, and pottering around the house.

A Sword from Red Ice is J. V. Jones' seventh novel. Her first three, making up the Book of Words trilogy, were *The Baker's Boy*, *A Man Betrayed* and *Master and Fool*. These were followed by a stand-alone novel, *The Barbed Coil*. *A Cavern of Black Ice* and *A Fortress of Grey Ice* are the first two volumes in her latest Sword of Shadows series. For more information on J. V. Jones and her books, please visit www.jvj.com

You can also find out more about J. V. Jones, and other Orbit authors, by registering for the free monthly newsletter at www.orbitbooks.net

If you enjoyed
A SWORD FROM RED ICE,
look out for

FEAST OF SOULS

The Magister trilogy: Book One

by

Celia Friedman

PROLOGUE

IMNEA KNEW when she awoke that Death was waiting for her.

She had been seeing the signs of his presence for some time now. A chill breeze in the corners of the house that wouldn't go away. Shadows that seeped in through the windows, that didn't move with the light. The icy touch of a presence upon her skin when she healed the Hardings' little girl, that left her shuddering for hours afterward.

The mirror revealed little. Of course. It wasn't the way of witching folk to age and die like normal people. The fuel within them was consumed too quickly, like a fire into which all the winter's wood had been placed at once. What a blaze it made! Yet quickly gone, all of it, until it smothered in its own ash.

How long ago had the dying begun? Did it start in her youth, when she first discovered she could do odd things— tiny little miracles, hardly worth noting—or not until later? Did Death first notice her when she made tiny points of fire dance on the windowsill, with a child's unconscious delight (and how her mother had punished her for that!), or not until she reached deep within herself with conscious intent to draw strength from her very soul—from that central font of spiritual power that mystics called the *athra*—and to bend it to her purpose? When and where was the contract with Death sealed, and what act marked its closing? The healing of Atkin's boy? The calling of rain after the Great Drought of '92? The day she had cleansed Dirum's leg of its gangrene, so that they wouldn't have to cut it off?

She was thirty-five. She looked much older.

She felt eighty.

Soon, Death whispered, his voice disguised as the whisper of falling snow. *Soon . . .*

With a sigh she fed some more wood into the stove and tried to stoke its dying embers to more radiant heat. It had been more than a year now since she'd last used the power. She'd hoped that if she stopped, some of her strength would return. Surely whatever internal energies created the athra in the first place could restore it to strength, if it was no longer used for witchery. But even if that were true, how much of her life was gone already? Each time she had used the magic to heal a child, cast out a demon, or bless a field against the onslaught of locusts, she had drawn upon her own life force for power. The supply wasn't endless. All the witching folk knew that. Just as the flesh became exhausted in time, so did the fires of the spirit bank low, smolder, and finally extinguish. Use the fuel for things other than staying alive and the fire would be extinguished that much sooner.

Yet how could you have the power to heal, and not use it? How could you watch a child turn blue before you and not clear out its lungs and give it life again, even if the cost was a few precious minutes of your own life?

Minutes had seemed like nothing in the beginning. What do young people know of time, especially when the power is pounding in their veins, demanding expression? By the time you became aware that minutes combine to make hours, and hours add up to days, and days to years . . . by then Death was already knocking on your door.

No more witchery, she had promised herself a year ago. Whatever time she had left, it would be her own. She had let the village know she wouldn't be able to do healing for them anymore, and that was the end of it. Let them hate her for it if they wished. It would be a poor answer to her years of service if they did, but she wouldn't be surprised. Human nature was remarkably ungrateful when it came to expecting sacrifice of others.

And already it had begun. She had heard the whispers. Every child that died of the pox now died because of her inaction. Every injury that led to death now was due to her callousness. Never mind that illness and injury were a natural part of life that only costly miracles could defy. Never mind that for two decades she had expended her own life-energy to provide those miracles. Never mind that Death was breathing down her neck now because of those very acts. This year she had turned them all away, and that was all that anyone seemed to care about.

Human nature.

She leaned forward over the fire, trying not to ask herself the question that all the witching folk did, in the end. *Was it worth it?* Too much danger in that internal dialogue. Answer no, and your last days would be filled with regret. Answer yes, and then your dying was your own damned fault.

Suddenly a knock on the door drew her from her reverie.

Who on earth was visiting her in these final days, when all the town was treating her like a pariah?

She walked to the heavy oaken door and pulled it open. By the dying light of the winter day she could see two figures standing outside. No need to ask what they'd come for. One of the figures held a small bundle in her arms, and from its size and drape she guessed it to be a child, swathed in blankets. A pang of emotion stabbed her in the heart, guilt and anger hotly combined.

Isn't it enough that I refuse you in the marketplace, in the temple, in the very streets? Must you bring your sick ones to my very door, to be turned away?

For a moment she almost shut the door in their faces, but a lifetime's habit of hospitality proved too strong to overcome. Grunting, she stepped aside for the two to come in. By the stove's dim light she could see them better: a tall, gaunt woman, peasant-born, who had clearly seen better days, and a young girl by her side, hardly looking better. The kind you healed and sent home knowing that Death might claim them the next year anyway, from starvation or abuse or any one of the thousand things no witching power could heal. The girl had a hard edge about her, as if she had already seen the rotting underbelly of the world and become inured to its stink; it was a frightening look, in one so young. The woman . . . looked merely desperate.

"Mother," the woman began respectfully. "I'm sorry to bother you. . . ."

"I don't do healing anymore," Imnea said curtly. "If you want a cup of tea to warm you before you set on your way again I'll give you that. I might have a scrap of bread. But that's all."

She expected the woman to argue with her and she was braced for it. Gods knew she'd been through this before, a hundred times over, it seemed. But instead the woman said nothing, merely lowered a corner of the blanket wrapped around her child. The glimmering green pustules on his fevered face spoke volumes in that moment, before she covered them up again.

Green Plague. Imnea had seen it only once, years ago. That was after it had claimed half a town. The witching folk had banded together then—an event as rare as the Red Moon that had shone down upon the effort—trying to burn away the infection not only from a handful of bodies, but from the village itself. It was said there were times in the old days when the Green Plague, sweeping through the land, had killed two out of every three people. That time it didn't. Maybe their efforts had helped stop it. Maybe the gods had seen so many witching folk offering up years of their own lives to heal others that they decided it was time for a single act of divine mercy to be granted. Or maybe Death was just too busy gathering up all the new contracts the witching folk had offered him that night to worry about spreading the convulsive disease further.

She didn't need to feel the boy's skin to know he had fever. Or to read his future to know the terrible suffering that awaited him if the disease went unchecked. It was a horrible way to die.

"I don't do healing anymore." The words lacked the conviction she wanted them to have. Damn these people, why did they have to bring the boy here, into her home?

"You have the power. They say you've healed this sickness before."

"And I don't anymore. I'm sorry. That's the way it is." Each word scored her throat like a hot knife as she forced it out. Didn't the woman understand what such a healing would cost her?

What gives you the right to demand my life?

The Plague would force the boy into seizures soon, terrible seizures in which he would scream out for water, but vomit up anything that was given to him. It would go on for days, if his family didn't put him out of his misery. And they wouldn't. They'd pray and they'd make offerings and they'd ask the gods to please, please make this boy one of the few who were strong enough to survive the Plague. And so he would suffer, endless days of agony, until all that was left was a desiccated husk from which the human soul had long since departed, begging unheard for the final mercy to be granted.

And then others would follow. The whole town, sooner or later. Maybe even Gansang itself, if the infection spread far enough. Very little could check the Green Plague once it had taken hold in a place.

He was still in the early stages. If she healed him now, if there were no others infected yet, the town might be spared.

Imnea turned away to stoke the fire. The new log wasn't catching. The embers were growing dim.

"Please," the mother whispered.

No bribes. No threats. No promises. Imnea was prepared to counter all those. But the simple heartfelt plea was none of those things, and all of them combined. Guilt stabbed like a hot blade into her heart.

I should give her a knife and tell her to end it. For the child's sake. If she doesn't handle the body fluids when she kills him there's a chance it won't spread.

With a sigh she turned back to face the pair. They deserved

that much, these villagers, that at least she would meet their eyes while she shattered their hopes. But it was the girl's eyes that caught her own this time, not the woman's. Clear eyes, remarkably so given the hollows of hunger and hardship that hung beneath them like dark moons. Green eyes, flecked with gold as if with fairy dust. Yet it wasn't color or clarity that made the girl's gaze so arresting as much as an indefinable *something* . . . as much out of place in these dim surroundings as a gleaming star would be.

Such depth, in that gaze. Remarkable in one so young. Imnea wondered briefly if she had the Power . . . but only briefly. She had no time to worry about matters of Power, least of all to appraise the potential of some fledgling witch who would probably die of hunger and cold in the gutters of Gansang long before she ever found a suitable teacher.

Perhaps it was that thought which plucked at her heart like a harp string. Perhaps it was the memories of the ones she had taught, and the children she had borne, and all those people who had turned to her for healing or counsel or simply comfort, in her thirty-five years of life. Maybe it was something about the Power that made her hear their voices now, begging her to help this woman . . . or maybe it was Death playing tricks on her. Trying to hurry her along, so that he wouldn't be late for his appointment with the next witch on his list.

Damn you to hell, she thought. *My life you can have, that was mine give up, but not this boy's. Not yet.*

In a voice as harsh as winter ice she said, "Give him to me."

The bundle was given to her wordlessly. It was lighter than it should be, she noted; mostly blankets. The child hadn't been big to start with, and the early stages of the Plague had probably stripped his bones of what little meat they'd had. Her own bones ached as she shifted his weight in her arms. *Poor child, poor child, at least if you live through this you can tend to any others who get sick. There's comfort in that.*

For a moment she shut her eyes. Just resting, gathering her spirit, letting the aches and pains of her premature aging settle into the background so that her rational mind was foremost. The gods hadn't taken that away from her yet.

I wouldn't want to live through another Plague year anyway, she told herself. *One horror like that is enough for anyone.*

She began to hum softly, a focus for her witchery. She could sense the woman and the girl watching, fascinated, as she prepared herself. If only she could show them what it felt like! If only she could share with another person—any person— the pain and joy and fear and exultation of such an act! For one of them to understand what the Power was like, how terribly it cost her to use it, that would be worth everything. Because then her sacrifice would be understood. Then she would be loved for what she had given up, not hated for all the times she had failed.

At last, when the music was ready, when the room was ready—when the child and the mother and the time and the night outside and all the world were ready—she reached inside her soul to where the heart of all power lay. It was faint these days, so very faint, not the resplendent beacon of power she had discovered in her youth, but a much older soul, nearly exhausted now. It wouldn't have lasted another year, she told herself. And it would have been a cold and lonely year to live through, with all the villagers hating her.

Are you sure? Death whispered in her ear. *Very sure, Imnea? This time there is no turning back.*

"Go to hell," she whispered to him.

The warmth of her living soul filled her flesh, driving out the chill of the winter night. Then outward it flowed, into the boy. Clean, pure, a gift of healing. She shut her eyes, trusting to other senses to observe as it bolstered his own failing spirit, feeding strength into his athra, giving it focus. Fire burned along his veins and the boy cried out, but neither the mother nor the girl flinched.

The disease was strong in his flesh, rooted in a thousand places; she burned them all, drawing upon her athra for fuel and the boy's own soul for focus. Some witches said that a disease was like a living thing, that fought back when you tried to kill it; she thought of it more as a thousand living things, or tens of thousands, that might fight or hide or burrow deep into the flesh for protection from such an assault. You had to find them all or the disease would come back later with renewed strength. How much of her life force had she wasted in her early years, learning that lesson?

The log in the stove hadn't caught; the fire was dying. Winter's chill seeped into the cabin and into her bones, and she let it. There wasn't enough power left within her to keep her flesh warm and heal the boy as well. Not that any witch with a brain would waste power on the former task anyway . . . not when there was wood to be burned. The Power was too precious to waste on simple things. If only she'd understood that, in the youth of her witchery! A tear coursed down her cheek as she remembered the hundred and one little magics she could have done without, the tricks performed for pleasure or show or physical comfort. If she could undo them all now, how much time would they add up to? Would they buy her another week, another year of life?

Too late now, Death whispered.

Dying. She was dying. This is what it felt like, when the embers of the soul expired at last. She could feel the last tiny sparks of her athra flickering weakly inside her. So little power left. How much time? Merely minutes, or did she have all of an hour left to wonder if she had done the right thing?

"It is done," she said quietly.

The mother leaned down to take the boy, but hesitated when she saw his face. "He looks the same."

"His soul is clean. The pustules will drain within a day or two. He will be safe after that."

And you, his mother . . . if you have caught this thing too, I am sorry, there will be no one to beg for favors when the first signs show . . .

She tried to rise, to see them out. Hospitality. But her legs had no strength, and her heart . . . her heart labored in her chest with an odd, unsteady beat, as if the drummer which had guided it for thirty-five years had stopped his music and left it to flounder.

She was cold. So cold.

"Mother?"

The eyes of the girl were fixed upon her. So deep, so hungry, so very determined. Drinking in knowledge as if it was the fuel her soul required. *See, child, what the Power can do. See what happens to you when you use it.* There was no wonder in the child's eyes, or even fear . . . only hunger.

Heed this lesson well, my child. Remember it, when the Power beckons. Remember the price.

"Come, child." It was the mother's voice, nearly inaudible. Imnea's hearing was growing dim; the world was an insubstantial thing, all murmurings, windsong and shadow. "Come away now."

Are you ready? Death whispered to her.

Imnea clung to life for a moment more. A single moment, to savor those dreams which had guided her . . . and to mourn those which had gone unfulfilled.

Then: *Yes,* she whispered. Voice without sound. *Yes, I am ready.*

In the stove the last embers of the fire sputtered and died, leaving the room in darkness.